Little Women

Little Women

OR MEG, JO, BETH AND AMY

PARTS I AND II

LOUISA MAY ALCOTT

ILLUSTRATED BY KEVIN MCINTYRE

COLLIER BOOKS

Macmillan Publishing Company

NEW YORK

COLLIER MACMILLAN PUBLISHERS

LONDON

© 1962 by Macmillan Publishing Company, a division of Macmillan, Inc. All rights reserved. No part of this book may be reproduced or transmitted in any form or by any means, electronic or mechanical, including photocopying, recording or by any information storage and retrieval system, without permission in writing from the Publisher Library of Congress Catalog Card Number: 62-20197 First Collier Books Edition 1962.

ISBN: 0-02-041240-1

34 33 32 31 30

Macmillan Publishing Company, 866 Third Avenue, New York, N.Y 10022. Collier Macmillan Canada, Inc. Printed in the United States of America.

Preface

"Go then, my little Book, and show to all
That entertain and bid thee welcome shall,
What thou dost keep close shut up in thy breast;
And wish what thou dost show them may be blest
To them for good, may make them choose to be
Pilgrims better, by far, than thee or me.
Tell them of Mercy; she is one
Who early hath her pilgrimage begun.
Yea, let young damsels learn of her to prize
The world which is to come, and so be wise;
For little tripping maids may follow God
Along the ways which saintly feet have trod."

Adapted from JOHN BUNYAN

Contents

Part I

Part II

Chapter 1

Playing Pilgrims

"CHRISTMAS won't be Christmas without any presents," grumbled Jo, lying on the rug.

"It's so dreadful to be poor!" sighed Meg, looking down at her old dress.

"I don't think it's fair for some girls to have plenty of pretty things, and other girls nothing at all," added little Amy, with an injured sniff.

"We've got Father and Mother and each other," said Beth contentedly from her corner.

The four young faces on which the firelight shone brightened at the cheerful words, but darkened again as Jo said sadly, "We haven't got Father, and shall not have him for a long time." She didn't say "perhaps never," but each silently added it, thinking of Father far away, where the fighting was.

Nobody spoke for a minute; then Meg said in an altered tone, "You know the reason Mother proposed not having any presents this Christmas was because it is going to be a hard winter for everyone; and she thinks we ought not to spend money for pleasure, when our men are suffering so in the army. We can't do much, but we can make our little sacrifices, and ought to do it gladly. But I am afraid I don't." And Meg shook her head, as she thought regretfully of all the pretty things she wanted.

"But I don't think the little we should spend would do any good. We've each got a dollar, and the army wouldn't be much helped by our giving that. I agree not to expect anything from Mother or you, but I do want to buy *Undine and Sintram* for myself. I've wanted it *so* long," said Jo, who was a bookworm.

"I planned to spend mine in new music," said Beth, with a little sigh, which no one heard but the hearth brush and kettle holder.

"I shall get a nice box of Faber's drawing pencils. I really need them," said Amy decidedly.

"Mother didn't say anything about our money, and she won't wish us to give up everything. Let's each buy what we want, and have a little fun. I'm sure we work hard enough to earn it," cried Jo, examining the heels of her shoes in a gentlemanly manner.

"I know *I* do—teaching those tiresome children nearly all day, when I'm longing to enjoy myself at home," began Meg, in the complaining tone again.

"You don't have half such a hard time as I do," said Jo. "How would you like to be shut up for hours with a nervous, fussy old lady, who keeps you trotting, is never satisfied, and worries you till you're ready to fly out of the window or cry?"

"It's naughty to fret, but I do think washing dishes and keeping things tidy is the worst work in the world. It makes me cross, and my hands get so stiff, I can't practice well at all." And Beth looked at her rough hands with a sigh that any one could hear that time.

"I don't believe any of you suffer as I do," cried Amy, "for you don't have to go to school with impertinent girls, who plague you if you don't know your lessons, and laugh at your dresses, and label your father if he isn't rich, and insult you when your nose isn't nice."

"If you mean *libel*, I'd say so, and not talk about *labels*, as if Papa was a pickle bottle," advised Jo, laughing.

"I know what I mean, and you needn't be *statirical* about it. It's proper to use good words, and improve your *vocabilary*," returned Amy, with dignity.

"Don't peck at one another, children. Don't you wish we had the money Papa lost when we were little, Jo? Dear me! how happy and good we'd be, if we had no worries!" said Meg, who could remember better times.

"You said the other day you thought we were a deal happier than the King children, for they were fighting and fretting all the time, in spite of their money."

"So I did, Beth. Well, I think we are; for, though we do

have to work, we make fun for ourselves, and are a pretty jolly set, as Jo would say."

"Jo does use such slang words!" observed Amy, with a reproving look at the long figure stretched on the rug. Jo immediately sat up, put her hands in her pockets, and began to whistle.

"Don't, Jo, it's so boyish!"

"That's why I do it."

"I detest rude, unladylike girls!"

"I hate affected, niminy-piminy chits!"

" 'Birds in their little nests agree,' " sang Beth, the peacemaker, with such a funny face that both sharp voices softened to a laugh, and the "pecking" ended for that time.

"Really, girls, you are both to be blamed," said Meg, beginning to lecture in her elder-sisterly fashion. "You are old enough to leave off boyish tricks, and to behave better, Josephine. It didn't matter so much when you were a little girl; but now you are so tall, and turn up your hair, you should remember that you are a young lady."

"I'm not! And if turning up my hair makes me one, I'll wear it in two tails till I'm twenty," cried Jo, pulling off her net, and shaking down a chestnut mane. "I hate to think I've got to grow up, and be Miss March, and wear long gowns, and look as prim as a China aster! It's bad enough to be a girl, anyway, when I like boys' games and work and manners! I can't get over my disappointment in not being a boy; and it's worse than ever now, for I'm dying to go and fight with Papa, and I can only stay at home and knit, like a poky old woman!" And Jo shook the blue army sock till the needles rattled like castanets, and her ball bounded across the room.

"Poor Jo! It's too bad, but it can't be helped. So you must try to be contented with making your name boyish, and playing brother to us girls," said Beth, stroking the rough head at her knee with a hand that all the dishwashing and dusting in the world could not make ungentle in its touch.

"As for you, Amy," continued Meg, "you are altogether too particular and prim. Your airs are funny now, but you'll grow up an affected little goose, if you don't take care. I like your nice manners and refined ways of speaking, when you don't try to be elegant. But your absurd words are as bad as Jo's slang."

"If Jo is a tomboy and Amy a goose, what am I, please?" asked Beth, ready to share the lecture.

"You're a dear, and nothing else," answered Meg warmly; and no one contradicted her, for the "Mouse" was the pet of the family.

As young readers like to know "how people look," we will take this moment to give them a little sketch of the four sisters, who sat knitting away in the twilight, while the December snow fell quietly without, and the fire crackled cheerfully within. It was a comfortable old room, though the carpet was faded and the furniture very plain; for a good picture or two hung on the walls, books filled the recesses, chrysanthemums and Christmas roses bloomed in the windows, and a pleasant atmosphere of home peace pervaded it.

Margaret, the eldest of the four, was sixteen, and very pretty, being plump and fair, with large eyes, plenty of soft, brown hair, a sweet mouth, and white hands, of which she was rather vain. Fifteen-year-old Jo was very tall, thin, and brown, and reminded one of a colt, for she never seemed to know what to do with her long limbs, which were very much in her way. She had a decided mouth, a comical nose, and sharp, gray eyes, which appeared to see everything, and were by turns fierce, funny, or thoughtful. Her long, thick hair was her one beauty, but it was usually bundled into a net, to be out of her way. Round shoulders had Jo, big hands and feet, a flyaway look to her clothes, and the uncomfortable appearance of a girl who was rapidly shooting up into a woman and didn't like it. Elizabeth—or Beth, as everyone called her—was a rosy, smooth-haired, bright-eyed girl of thirteen, with a shy manner, a timid voice, and a peaceful expression which was seldom disturbed. Her father called her "Little Tranquillity," and the name suited her excellently, for she seemed to live in a happy world of her own, only venturing out to meet the few whom she trusted and loved. Amy, though the youngest, was a most important person—in her own opinion at least. A regular snow maiden, with blue eyes, and yellow hair curling on her shoulders, pale and slender, and always carrying herself like a young lady mindful of her manners. What the characters of the four sisters were we will leave to be found out.

The clock struck six and, having swept up the hearth, Beth put a pair of slippers down to warm. Somehow the sight of the old shoes had a good effect upon the girls, for Mother was coming, and everyone brightened to welcome her. Meg stopped lecturing, and lighted the lamp, Amy got out of the easy chair without being asked, and Jo forgot how tired she was as she sat up to hold the slippers nearer to the blaze.

"They are quite worn out. Marmee must have a new pair."

"I thought I'd get her some with my dollar," said Beth.

"No, I shall!" cried Amy.

"I'm the oldest," began Meg, but Jo cut in with a decided—

"I'm the man of the family now Papa is away, and *I* shall provide the slippers, for he told me to take special care of Mother while he was gone."

"I'll tell you what we'll do," said Beth, "let's each get her something for Christmas, and not get anything for ourselves."

"That's like you, dear! What will we get?" exclaimed Jo.

Everyone thought soberly for a minute, then Meg announced, as if the idea was suggested by the sight of her own pretty hands, "I shall give her a nice pair of gloves."

"Army shoes, best to be had," cried Jo.

"Some handkerchiefs, all hemmed," said Beth.

"I'll get a little bottle of cologne. She likes it, and it won't cost much, so I'll have some left to buy my pencils," added Amy.

"How will we give the things?" asked Meg.

"Put them on the table, and bring her in and see her open the bundles. Don't you remember how we used to do on our birthdays?" answered Jo.

"I used to be *so* frightened when it was my turn to sit in the big chair with the crown on, and see you all come marching round to give the presents, with a kiss. I liked the things and the kisses, but it was dreadful to have you sit looking at me while I opened the bundles," said Beth, who was toasting her face and the bread for tea at the same time.

"Let Marmee think we are getting things for ourselves, and then surprise her. We must go shopping tomorrow afternoon, Meg. There is so much to do about the play for Christmas night," said Jo, marching up and down, with her hands behind her back and her nose in the air.

"I don't mean to act any more after this time. I'm getting too old for such things," observed Meg, who was as much a child as ever about "dressing-up" frolics.

"You won't stop, I know, as long as you can trail round in a white gown with your hair down, and wear gold-paper jewelry. You are the best actress we've got, and there'll be an end of everything if you quit the boards," said Jo. "We ought to rehearse tonight. Come here, Amy, and do the fainting scene, for you are as stiff as a poker in that."

"I can't help it; I never saw anyone faint, and I don't choose to make myself all black and blue, tumbling flat as you do. If I can go down easily, I'll drop; if I can't, I shall fall into a chair and be graceful. I don't care if Hugo does come at me with a pistol," returned Amy, who was not gifted with dramatic power, but was chosen because she was small enough to be borne out shrieking by the villain of the piece.

"Do it this way: clasp your hands so, and stagger across the room, crying frantically, 'Roderigo! save me! save me!'" and away went Jo, with a melodramatic scream which was truly thrilling.

Amy followed, but she poked her hands out stiffly before her, and jerked herself along as if she went by machinery, and her "Ow!" was more suggestive of pins being run into her than of fear and anguish. Jo gave a despairing groan, and Meg laughed outright, while Beth let her bread burn as she watched the fun with interest.

"It's no use! Do the best you can when the time comes, and if the audience laughs, don't blame me. Come on, Meg."

Then things went smoothly, for Don Pedro defied the world in a speech of two pages without a single break; Hagar, the witch, chanted an awful incantation over her kettleful of simmering toads, with weird effect; Roderigo rent his chains asunder manfully, and Hugo died in agonies of remorse and arsenic, with a wild "Ha! ha!"

"It's the best we've had yet," said Meg, as the dead villain sat up and rubbed his elbows.

"I don't see how you can write and act such splendid things, Jo. You're a regular Shakespeare!" exclaimed Beth, who firmly believed that her sisters were gifted with wonderful genius in all things.

"Not quite," replied Jo modestly. "I do think *The Witch's Curse, an Operatic Tragedy* is rather a nice thing, but I'd like to try *Macbeth,* if we only had a trapdoor for Banquo. I always wanted to do the killing part. 'Is that a dagger that I see before me?'" muttered Jo, rolling her eyes and clutching at the air, as she had seen a famous tragedian do.

"No, it's the toasting fork, with mother's shoe on it instead of the bread. Beth's stage-struck!" cried Meg, and the rehearsal ended in a general burst of laughter.

"Glad to find you so merry, my girls," said a cheery voice at the door, and actors and audience turned to welcome a tall, motherly lady with a "can-I-help-you" look about her which was truly delightful. She was not elegantly dressed, but a noble-looking woman, and the girls thought the gray cloak and unfashionable bonnet covered the most splendid mother in the world.

"Well, dearies, how have you got on today? There was so much to do, getting the boxes ready to go tomorrow, that I didn't come home to dinner. Has anyone called, Beth? How is your cold, Meg? Jo, you look tired to death. Come and kiss me, baby."

While making these maternal inquiries Mrs. March got her wet things off, her warm slippers on, and sitting down in the easy chair, drew Amy to her lap, preparing to enjoy the happiest hour of her busy day. The girls flew about, trying to make things comfortable, each in her own way. Meg arranged the tea table, Jo brought wood and set chairs, dropping, overturning, and clattering everything she touched, Beth trotted to and fro between parlor and kitchen, quiet and busy, while

Amy gave directions to everyone, as she sat with her hands folded.

As they gathered about the table, Mrs. March said, with a particularly happy face, "I've got a treat for you after supper."

A quick, bright smile went round like a streak of sunshine. Beth clapped her hands, regardless of the biscuit she held, and Jo tossed up her napkin, crying, "A letter! a letter! Three cheers for Father!"

"Yes, a nice long letter. He is well, and thinks he shall get through the cold season better than we feared. He sends all sorts of loving wishes for Christmas, and an especial message to you girls," said Mrs. March, patting her pocket as if she had got a treasure there.

"Hurry and get done! Don't stop to quirk your little finger and simper over your plate, Amy," cried Jo, choking in her tea and dropping her bread, butter side down, on the carpet in her haste to get at the treat.

Beth ate no more, but crept away to sit in her shadowy corner and brood over the delight to come, till the others were ready.

"I think it was so splendid in Father to go as a chaplain when he was too old to be drafted, and not strong enough for a soldier," said Meg warmly.

"Don't I wish I could go as a drummer, a *vivan*—what's its name? or a nurse, so I could be near him and help him," exclaimed Jo, with a groan.

"It must be very disagreeable to sleep in a tent, and eat all sorts of bad-tasting things, and drink out of a tin mug," sighed Amy.

"When will he come home, Marmee?" asked Beth, with a little quiver in her voice.

"Not for many months, dear, unless he is sick. He will stay and do his work faithfully as long as he can, and we won't ask for him back a minute sooner than he can be spared. Now come and hear the letter."

They all drew to the fire, Mother in the big chair with Beth at her feet, Meg and Amy perched on either arm of the chair, and Jo leaning on the back, where no one would see any sign of emotion if the letter should happen to be touching. Very few letters were written in those hard times that were not touching, especially those which fathers sent home. In this one little was said of the hardships endured, the dangers faced, or the homesickness conquered. It was a cheerful, hopeful letter, full of lively descriptions of camp life, marches, and military news, and only at the end did the writer's heart overflow with fatherly love and longing for the little girls at home.

"Give them all my dear love and a kiss. Tell them I think of them by day, pray for them by night, and find my best comfort in their affection at all times. A year seems very long to wait before I see them, but remind them that while we wait we may all work, so that these hard days need not be wasted. I know they will remember all I said to them, that they will be loving children to you, will do their duty faithfully, fight their bosom enemies bravely, and conquer themselves so beautifully that when I come back to them I may be fonder and prouder than ever of my little women."

Everybody sniffed when they came to that part; Jo wasn't ashamed of the great tear that dropped off the end of her nose, and Amy never minded the rumpling of her curls as she hid her face on her mother's shoulder and sobbed out, "I *am* a selfish girl! but I'll truly try to be better, so he mayn't be disappointed in me by-and-by."

"We all will!" cried Meg. "I think too much of my looks and hate to work, but won't any more, if I can help it."

"I'll try and be what he loves to call me, 'a little woman,' and not be rough and wild, but do my duty here instead of wanting to be somewhere else," said Jo, thinking that keeping her temper at home was a much harder task than facing a rebel or two down South.

Beth said nothing, but wiped away her tears with the blue army sock and began to knit with all her might, losing no time in doing the duty that lay nearest her, while she resolved in her quiet little soul to be all that Father hoped to find her when the year brought round the happy coming home.

Mrs. March broke the silence that followed Jo's words, by saying in her cheery voice, "Do you remember how you used to play Pilgrim's Progress when you were little things? Nothing delighted you more than to have me tie my piece bags on your backs for burdens, give you hats and sticks and rolls of paper, and let you travel through the house from the cellar, which was the City of Destruction, up, up, to the housetop, where you had all the lovely things you could collect to make a Celestial City."

"What fun it was, especially going by the lions, fighting Apollyon, and passing through the Valley where the hob-goblins were!" said Jo.

"I liked the place where the bundles fell off and tumbled downstairs," said Meg.

"My favorite part was when we came out on the flat roof where our flowers and arbors and pretty things were, and all stood and sung for joy up there in the sunshine," said Beth, smiling, as if that pleasant moment had come back to her.

"I don't remember much about it, except that I was afraid of the cellar and the dark entry, and always liked the cake and milk we had up at the top. If I wasn't too old for such things, I'd rather like to play it over again," said Amy, who began to talk of renouncing childish things at the mature age of twelve.

"We never are too old for this, my dear, because it is a play we are playing all the time in one way or another. Our burdens are here, our road is before us, and the longing for goodness and happiness is the guide that leads us through many troubles and mistakes to the peace which is a true Celestial City. Now, my little pilgrims, suppose you begin again, not in play, but in earnest, and see how far on you can get before Father comes home."

"Really, Mother? Where are our bundles?" asked Amy, who was a very literal young lady.

"Each of you told what your burden was just now, except Beth. I rather think she hasn't got any," said her mother.

"Yes, I have. Mine is dishes and dusters, and envying girls with nice pianos, and being afraid of people."

Beth's bundle was such a funny one that everybody wanted to laugh, but nobody did, for it would have hurt her feelings very much.

"Let us do it," said Meg thoughtfully. "It is only another

name for trying to be good, and the story may help us; for though we do want to be good, it's hard work and we forget, and don't do our best."

"We were in the Slough of Despond tonight, and Mother came and pulled us out as Help did in the book. We ought to have our roll of directions, like Christian. What shall we do about that?" asked Jo, delighted with the fancy which lent a little romance to the very dull task of doing her duty.

"Look under your pillows Christmas morning, and you will find your guidebook," replied Mrs. March.

They talked over the new plan while old Hannah cleared the table, then out came the four little workbaskets, and the needles flew as the girls made sheets for Aunt March. It was uninteresting sewing, but tonight no one grumbled. They adopted Jo's plan of dividing the long seams into four parts, and calling the quarters Europe, Asia, Africa, and America, and in that way got on capitally, especially when they talked about the different countries as they stitched their way through them.

At nine they stopped work, and sang, as usual, before they went to bed. No one but Beth could get much music out of the old piano, but she had a way of softly touching the yellow keys and making a pleasant accompaniment to the simple songs they sang. Meg had a voice like a flute, and she and her mother led the little choir. Amy chirped like a cricket, and Jo wandered through the airs at her own sweet will, always coming out at the wrong place with a croak or a quaver that spoiled the most pensive tune. They had always done this from the time they could lisp

Crinkle, crinkle, 'ittle 'tar,

and it had become a household custom, for the mother was a born singer. The first sound in the morning was her voice as she went about the house singing like a lark, and the last sound at night was the same cheery sound, for the girls never grew too old for that familiar lullaby.

Chapter 2

A Merry Christmas

Jo WAS the first to wake in the gray dawn of Christmas morning. No stockings hung at the fireplace, and for a moment she felt as much disappointed as she did long ago, when her little sock fell down because it was so crammed with goodies. Then she remembered her mother's promise and, slipping her hand under her pillow, drew out a little crimson-covered book. She knew it very well, for it was that beautiful old story of the best life ever lived, and Jo felt that it was a true guidebook for any pilgrim going the long journey. She woke Meg with a "Merry Christmas," and bade her see what was under her pillow. A green-covered book appeared, with the same picture inside, and a few words written by their mother, which made their one present very precious in their eyes. Presently Beth and Amy woke to rummage and find their little books also— one dove-colored, the other blue—and all sat looking at and talking about them, while the east grew rosy with the coming day.

In spite of her small vanities, Margaret had a sweet and pious nature, which unconsciously influenced her sisters, especially Jo, who loved her very tenderly, and obeyed her because her advice was so gently given.

"Girls," said Meg seriously, looking from the tumbled head beside her to the two little nightcapped ones in the room beyond, "Mother wants us to read and love and mind these books, and we must begin at once. We used to be faithful about it, but since Father went away and all this war trouble unsettled us, we have neglected many things. You can do as you please, but *I* shall keep my book on the table here and read a little every morning as soon as I wake, for I know it will do me good and help me through the day."

Then she opened her new book and began to read. Jo put

Jo put her arm round her and, leaning cheek to cheek,
read also . . .

her arm round her and, leaning cheek to cheek, read also, with the quiet expression so seldom seen on her restless face.

"How good Meg is! Come, Amy, let's do as they do. I'll help you with the hard words, and they'll explain things if we don't understand," whispered Beth, very much impressed by the pretty books and her sisters' example.

"I'm glad mine is blue," said Amy. And then the rooms were very still while the pages were softly turned, and the winter sunshine crept in to touch the bright heads and serious faces with a Christmas greeting.

"Where is Mother?" asked Meg, as she and Jo ran down to thank her for their gifts, half an hour later.

"Goodness only knows. Some poor creeter come a-beggin', and your ma went straight off to see what was needed. There never *was* such a woman for givin' away vittles and drink, clothes and firin'," replied Hannah, who had lived with the family since Meg was born, and was considered by them all more as a friend than a servant.

"She will be back soon, I think, so fry your cakes, and have everything ready," said Meg, looking over the presents which were collected in a basket and kept under the sofa, ready to be produced at the proper time. "Why, where is Amy's bottle of cologne?" she added, as the little flask did not appear.

"She took it out a minute ago, and went off with it to put a ribbon on it, or some such notion," replied Jo, dancing about the room to take the first stiffness off the new army slippers.

"How nice my handkerchiefs look, don't they? Hannah washed and ironed them for me, and I marked them all myself," said Beth, looking proudly at the somewhat uneven letters which had cost her such labor.

"Bless the child! She's gone and put 'Mother' on them instead of 'M. March.' How funny!" cried Jo, taking up one.

"Isn't it right? I thought it was better to do it so, because Meg's initials are M. M., and I don't want anyone to use these but Marmee," said Beth, looking troubled.

"It's all right, dear, and a very pretty idea—quite sensible, too, for no one can ever mistake now. It will please her very much, I know," said Meg, with a frown for Jo and a smile for Beth.

"There's Mother. Hide the basket, quick!" cried Jo, as a door slammed and steps sounded in the hall.

Amy came in hastily, and looked rather abashed when she saw her sisters all waiting for her.

"Where have you been, and what are you hiding behind you?" asked Meg, surprised to see, by her hood and cloak, that lazy Amy had been out so early.

"Don't laugh at me, Jo! I didn't mean anyone should know till the time came. I only meant to change the little bottle for a big one, and I gave *all* my money to get it, and I'm truly trying not to be selfish any more."

As she spoke, Amy showed the handsome flask which replaced the cheap one, and looked so earnest and humble in her little effort to forget herself that Meg hugged her on the spot, and Jo pronounced her "a trump," while Beth ran to the window, and picked her finest rose to ornament the stately bottle.

"You see I felt ashamed of my present, after reading and talking about being good this morning, so I ran round the corner and changed it the minute I was up: and I'm *so* glad, for mine is the handsomest now."

Another bang of the street door sent the basket under the sofa, and the girls to the table, eager for breakfast.

"Merry Christmas, Marmee! Many of them! Thank you for our books; we read some, and mean to every day," they cried, in chorus.

"Merry Christmas, little daughters! I'm glad you began at once, and hope you will keep on. But I want to say one word before we sit down. Not far away from here lies a poor woman with a little newborn baby. Six children are huddled into one bed to keep from freezing, for they have no fire. There is nothing to eat over there, and the oldest boy came to tell me they were suffering hunger and cold. My girls, will you give them your breakfast as a Christmas present?"

They were all unusually hungry, having waited nearly an

hour, and for a minute no one spoke—only a minute, for Jo exclaimed impetuously, "I'm so glad you came before we began!"

"May I go and help carry the things to the poor little children?" asked Beth eagerly.

"*I* shall take the cream and the muffins," added Amy, heroically giving up the articles she most liked.

Meg was already covering the buckwheats, and piling the bread into one big plate.

"I thought you'd do it," said Mrs. March, smiling as if satisfied. "You shall all go and help me, and when we come back we will have bread and milk for breakfast, and make it up at dinnertime."

They were soon ready, and the procession set out. Fortunately it was early, and they went through back streets, so few people saw them, and no one laughed at the queer party.

A poor, bare, miserable room it was, with broken windows, no fire, ragged bedclothes, a sick mother, wailing baby, and a group of pale, hungry children cuddled under one old quilt, trying to keep warm.

How the big eyes stared and the blue lips smiled as the girls went in!

"*Ach, mein Gott!* It is good angels come to us!" said the poor woman, crying for joy.

"Funny angels in hoods and mittens," said Jo, and set them laughing.

In a few minutes it really did seem as if kind spirits had been at work there. Hannah, who had carried wood, made a fire, and stopped up the broken panes with old hats and her own cloak. Mrs. March gave the mother tea and gruel, and comforted her with promises of help, while she dressed the little baby as tenderly as if it had been her own. The girls meantime spread the table, set the children round the fire, and fed them like so many hungry birds—laughing, talking, and trying to understand the funny broken English.

"*Das ist gut!*" "*Die Engel-kinder!*" cried the poor things as they ate and warmed their purple hands at the comfortable blaze.

The girls had never been called angel children before, and thought it very agreeable, especially Jo, who had been considered a "Sancho" ever since she was born. That was a very happy breakfast, though they didn't get any of it; and when they went away, leaving comfort behind, I think there were not in all the city four merrier people than the hungry little girls who gave away their breakfasts and contented themselves with bread and milk on Christmas morning.

"That's loving our neighbor better than ourselves, and I like it," said Meg, as they set out their presents while their mother was upstairs collecting clothes for the poor Hummels.

Not a very splendid show, but there was a great deal of love done up in the few little bundles, and the tall vase of red roses, white chrysanthemums, and trailing vines, which stood in the middle, gave quite an elegant air to the table.

"She's coming! Strike up, Beth! Open the door, Amy! Three cheers for Marmee!" cried Jo, prancing about while Meg went to conduct Mother to the seat of honor.

Beth played her gayest march, Amy threw open the door, and Meg enacted escort with great dignity. Mrs. March was both surprised and touched, and smiled with her eyes full as she examined her presents and read the little notes which accompanied them. The slippers went on at once, a new handkerchief was slipped into her pocket, well scented with Amy's cologne, the rose was fastened in her bosom, and the nice gloves were pronounced a "perfect fit."

There was a good deal of laughing and kissing and explaining, in the simple, loving fashion which makes these home festivals so pleasant at the time, so sweet to remember long afterward, and then all fell to work.

The morning charities and ceremonies took so much time that the rest of the day was devoted to preparations for the evening festivities. Being still too young to go often to the theater, and not rich enough to afford any great outlay for private performances, the girls put their wits to work, and— necessity being the mother of invention—made whatever they needed. Very clever were some of their productions—pasteboard guitars, antique lamps made of old-fashioned butter boats covered with silver paper, gorgeous robes of old cotton, glittering with tin spangles from a pickle factory, and armor covered with the same useful diamond-shaped bits left in sheets when the lids of tin preserve pots were cut out. The furniture was used to being turned topsy-turvy, and the big chamber was the scene of many innocent revels.

No gentlemen were admitted, so Jo played male parts to her heart's content and took immense satisfaction in a pair of russet-leather boots given her by a friend, who knew a lady who knew an actor. These boots, an old foil, and a slashed doublet once used by an artist for some picture, were Jo's chief treasures and appeared on all occasions. The smallness of the company made it necessary for the two principal actors to take several parts apiece, and they certainly deserved some credit for the hard work they did in learning three or four different parts, whisking in and out of various costumes, and managing the stage besides. It was excellent drill for their memories, a harmless amusement, and employed many hours which otherwise would have been idle, lonely, or spent in less profitable society.

On Christmas night, a dozen girls piled onto the bed which was the dress circle, and sat before the blue and yellow chintz curtains in a most flattering state of expectancy. There was a good deal of rustling and whispering behind the curtain, a trifle of lamp smoke, and an occasional giggle from Amy, who was apt to get hysterical in the excitement of the moment. Presently a bell sounded, the curtains flew apart, and the *Operatic Tragedy* began.

"A gloomy wood," according to the one playbill, was represented by a few shrubs in pots, green baize on the floor, and a cave in the distance. This cave was made with a clotheshorse for a roof, bureaus for walls, and in it was a small furnace in full blast, with a black pot on it and an old witch bending over it. The stage was dark and the glow of the furnace had a fine effect, especially as real steam issued from the kettle when the witch took off the cover. A moment was allowed for the first thrill to subside, then Hugo, the villain, stalked in with a clanking sword at his side, a slouched hat, black beard, mysterious cloak, and the boots. After pacing to and fro in much agitation, he struck his forehead, and burst out in a wild strain, singing of his hatred to Roderigo, his love for Zara, and his pleasing resolution to kill the one and win the other. The gruff tones of Hugo's voice, with an occasional shout when his feelings overcame him, were very impressive, and the audience applauded the moment he paused for breath. Bowing with the air of one accustomed to public praise, he stole to the cavern and ordered Hagar to come forth with a commanding, "What ho, minion! I need thee!"

Out came Meg, with gray horsehair hanging about her face, a red and black robe, a staff, and cabalistic signs upon her cloak. Hugo demanded a potion to make Zara adore him, and one to destroy Roderigo. Hagar, in a fine dramatic melody, promised both, and proceeded to call up the spirit who would bring the love philter:

> Hither, hither, from thy home,
> Airy sprite, I bid thee come!
> Born of roses, fed on dew,
> Charms and potions canst thou brew?
> Bring me here, with elfin speed,
> The fragrant philter which I need;
> Make it sweet and swift and strong,
> Spirit, answer now my song!

A soft strain of music sounded, and then at the back of the cave appeared a little figure in cloudy white, with glittering wings, golden hair, and a garland of roses on its head. Waving a wand, it sang,

> Hither I come,
> From my airy home,
> Afar in the silver moon.
> Take the magic spell,
> And use it well,
> Or its power will vanish soon!

And dropping a small, gilded bottle at the witch's feet, the spirit vanished. Another chant from Hagar produced another apparition—not a lovely one, for with a bang an ugly black imp appeared and, having croaked a reply, tossed a dark bottle at Hugo and disappeared with a mocking laugh. Having warbled his thanks and put the potions in his boots, Hugo departed, and Hagar informed the audience that, as he had killed a few of her friends in times past, she has cursed him, and intends to thwart his plans, and be revenged on him. Then the curtain fell, and the audience reposed and ate candy while discussing the merits of the play.

A good deal of hammering went on before the curtain rose again, but when it became evident what a masterpiece of stage carpentering had been got up, no one murmured at the delay. It was truly superb! A tower rose to the ceiling; halfway up appeared a window with a lamp burning at it, and behind the white curtain appeared Zara in a lovely blue and silver dress, waiting for Roderigo. He came in gorgeous array, with plumed cap, red cloak, chestnut lovelocks, a guitar, and the boots, of course. Kneeling at the foot of the tower, he sang a serenade in melting tones. Zara replied and, after a musical dialogue, consented to fly. Then came the grand effect of the play. Roderigo produced a rope ladder, with five steps to it, threw up one end, and invited Zara to descend. Timidly she crept from her lattice, put her hand on Roderigo's shoulder, and was about to leap gracefully down when "Alas! alas for Zara!" she forgot her train—it caught in the window, the tower tottered, leaned forward, fell with a crash, and buried the unhappy lovers in the ruins!

A universal shriek arose as the russet boots waved wildly from the wreck and a golden head emerged, exclaiming, "I told you so! I told you so!" With wonderful presence of mind, Don Pedro, the cruel sire, rushed in, dragged out his daughter, with a hasty aside—

"Don't laugh! Act as if it was all right!"—and, ordering Roderigo up, banished him from the kingdom with wrath and scorn. Though decidedly shaken by the fall of the tower upon him, Roderigo defied the old gentleman and refused to stir. This dauntless example fired Zara: she also defied her sire, and he ordered them both to the deepest dungeons of the castle. A stout little retainer came in with chains and led them away, looking very much frightened and evidently forgetting the speech he ought to have made.

Act third was the castle hall, and here Hagar appeared, having come to free the lovers and finish Hugo. She hears him coming and hides, sees him put the potions into two cups of wine and bid the timid little servant, "Bear them to the captives in their cells, and tell them I shall come anon." The servant takes Hugo aside to tell him something, and Hagar changes the cups for two others which are harmless. Ferdinando, the "minion," carries them away, and Hagar puts back the cup which holds the poison meant for Roderigo. Hugo, getting thirsty after a long warble, drinks it, loses his wits, and after a good deal of clutching and stamping, falls flat and dies, while Hagar informs him what she has done in a song of exquisite power and melody.

This was a truly thrilling scene, though some persons might have thought that the sudden tumbling down of a quantity of long hair rather marred the effect of the villain's death. He was called before the curtain, and with great propriety appeared, leading Hagar, whose singing was considered more wonderful than all the rest of the performance put together.

Act fourth displayed the despairing Roderigo on the point of stabbing himself because he has been told that Zara has deserted him. Just as the dagger is at his heart, a lovely song is sung under his window, informing him that Zara is true but in danger, and he can save her if he will. A key is thrown in, which unlocks the door, and in a spasm of rapture he tears off his chains and rushes away to find and rescue his ladylove.

Act fifth opened with a stormy scene between Zara and Don Pedro. He wishes her to go into a convent, but she won't hear of it and, after a touching appeal, is about to faint when Roderigo dashes in and demands her hand. Don Pedro refuses, because he is not rich. They shout and gesticulate tremendously but cannot agree, and Roderigo is about to bear away the exhausted Zara, when the timid servant enters with a letter and a bag from Hagar, who has mysteriously disappeared. The latter informs the party that she bequeaths untold wealth to the young pair and an awful doom to Don Pedro, if he doesn't make them happy. The bag is opened, and several quarts of tin money shower down upon the stage till it is quite glorified with the glitter. This entirely softens the "stern sire." He consents without a murmur, all join in a joyful chorus, and the curtain falls upon the lovers kneeling to receive Don Pedro's blessing in attitudes of the most romantic grace.

Tumultuous applause followed but received an unexpected check, for the cot bed, on which the "dress circle" was built, suddenly shut up and extinguished the enthusiastic audience. Roderigo and Don Pedro flew to the rescue, and all were taken out unhurt, though many were speechless with laughter. The excitement had hardly subsided when Hannah appeared, with "Mrs. March's compliments, and would the ladies walk down to supper."

This was a surprise even to the actors, and when they saw the table, they looked at one another in rapturous amazement. It was like Marmee to get up a little treat for them, but anything so fine as this was unheard of since the departed days of plenty. There was ice cream—actually two dishes of it, pink and white—and cake and fruit and distracting French bonbons and, in the middle of the table, four great bouquets of hothouse flowers!

It quite took their breath away; and they stared first at the table and then at their mother, who looked as if she enjoyed it immensely.

"Is it fairies?" asked Amy.

"It's Santa Claus," said Beth.

"Mother did it." And Meg smiled her sweetest, in spite of her gray beard and white eyebrows.

"Aunt March had a good fit and sent the supper," cried Jo, with a sudden inspiration.

"All wrong. Old Mr. Laurence sent it," replied Mrs. March.

"The Laurence boy's grandfather! What in the world put such a thing into his head? We don't know him!" exclaimed Meg.

"Hannah told one of his servants about your breakfast party. He is an odd old gentleman, but that pleased him. He knew my father years ago, and he sent me a polite note this afternoon, saying he hoped I would allow him to express his friendly feeling toward my children by sending them a few trifles in honor of the day. I could not refuse, and so you have a little feast at night to make up for the bread-and-milk breakfast."

"That boy put it into his head, I know he did! He's a capital fellow, and I wish we could get acquainted. He looks as if he'd like to know us but he's bashful, and Meg is so prim she won't let me speak to him when we pass," said Jo, as the plates went round, and the ice began to melt out of sight, with ohs and ahs of satisfaction.

"You mean the people who live in the big house next door, don't you?" asked one of the girls. "My mother knows old Mr. Laurence, but says he's very proud and doesn't like to mix with his neighbors. He keeps his grandson shut up, when he isn't riding or walking with his tutor, and makes him study very hard. We invited him to our party, but he didn't come. Mother says he's very nice, though he never speaks to us girls."

"Our cat ran away once, and he brought her back, and we talked over the fence, and were getting on capitally—all about cricket, and so on—when he saw Meg coming, and walked off. I mean to know him some day, for he needs fun, I'm sure he does," said Jo decidedly.

"I like his manners, and he looks like a little gentleman; so I've no objection to your knowing him, if a proper opportunity comes. He brought the flowers himself, and I should have asked him in, if I had been sure what was going on upstairs. He looked so wistful as he went away, hearing the frolic and evidently having none of his own."

"It's a mercy you didn't, Mother!" laughed Jo, looking at

her boots. "But we'll have another play sometime that he *can* see. Perhaps he'll help act. Wouldn't that be jolly?"

"I never had such a fine bouquet before! How pretty it is!" And Meg examined her flowers with great interest.

"They *are* lovely! But Beth's roses are sweeter to me," said Mrs. March, smelling the half-dead posy in her belt.

Beth nestled up to her, and whispered softly, "I wish I could send my bunch to Father. I'm afraid he isn't having such a merry Christmas as we are."

Chapter 3

The Laurence Boy

"Jo! Jo! where are you?" cried Meg at the foot of the garret stairs.

"Here!" answered a husky voice from above, and, running up, Meg found her sister eating apples and crying over the *Heir of Redclyffe*, wrapped up in a comforter on an old three-legged sofa by the sunny window. This was Jo's favorite refuge; and here she loved to retire with half a dozen russets and a nice book, to enjoy the quiet and the society of a pet rat who lived near by and didn't mind her a particle. As Meg appeared, Scrabble whisked into his hole. Jo shook the tears off her cheeks and waited to hear the news.

"Such fun! Only see! A regular note of invitation from Mrs. Gardiner for tomorrow night!" cried Meg, waving the precious paper and then proceeding to read it with girlish delight.

"'Mrs. Gardiner would be happy to see Miss March and Miss Josephine at a little dance on New Year's Eve.' Marmee is willing we should go, now what *shall* we wear?"

"What's the use of asking that, when you know we shall wear our poplins, because we haven't got anything else?" answered Jo with her mouth full.

"If I only had a silk!" sighed Meg. "Mother says I may when I'm eighteen perhaps, but two years is an everlasting time to wait."

"I'm sure our pops look like silk, and they are nice enough for us. Yours is as good as new, but I forgot the burn and the tear in mine. Whatever shall I do? The burn shows badly, and I can't take any out."

"You must sit still all you can and keep your back out of sight; the front is all right. I shall have a new ribbon for my hair, and Marmee will lend me her little pearl pin, and my new slippers are lovely, and my gloves will do, though they aren't as nice as I'd like."

"Mine are spoiled with lemonade, and I can't get any new ones, so I shall have to go without," said Jo, who never troubled herself much about dress.

"You *must* have gloves, or I won't go," cried Meg decidedly. "Gloves are more important than anything else; you can't dance without them, and if you don't I should be *so* mortified."

"Then I'll stay still. I don't care much for company dancing. It's no fun to go sailing round. I like to fly about and cut capers."

"You can't ask Mother for new ones, they are so expensive, and you are so careless. She said when you spoiled the others that she shouldn't get you any more this winter. Can't you make them do?" asked Meg anxiously.

"I can hold them crumpled up in my hand, so no one will know how stained they are; that's all I can do. No! I'll tell you how we can manage—each wear one good one and carry a bad one. Don't you see?"

"Your hands are bigger than mine, and you will stretch my glove dreadfully," began Meg, whose gloves were a tender point with her.

"Then I'll go without. I don't care what people say!" cried Jo, taking up her book.

"You may have it, you may! Only don't stain it, and do behave nicely. Don't put your hands behind you, or stare, or say 'Christopher Columbus!' will you?"

"Don't worry about me. I'll be as prim as I can and not get into any scrapes, if I can help it. Now go and answer your note, and let me finish this splendid story."

So Meg went away to "accept with thanks," look over her dress, and sing blithely as she did up her one real lace frill, while Jo finished her story, her four apples, and had a game of romps with Scrabble.

On New Year's Eve the parlor was deserted, for the two younger girls played dressing maids and the two elder were absorbed in the all-important business of "getting ready for the party." Simple as the toilets were, there was a great deal of running up and down, laughing and talking, and at one time a strong smell of burned hair pervaded the house. Meg wanted a few curls about her face, and Jo undertook to pinch the papered locks with a pair of hot tongs.

"Ought they to smoke like that?" asked Beth from her perch on the bed.

"It's the dampness drying," replied Jo.

"What a queer smell! It's like burned feathers," observed Amy, smoothing her own pretty curls with a superior air.

"There, now I'll take off the papers and you'll see a cloud of little ringlets," said Jo, putting down the tongs.

She did take off the papers, but no cloud of ringlets appeared, for the hair came with the papers, and the horrified hairdresser laid a row of little scorched bundles on the bureau before her victim.

"Oh, oh, oh! What *have* you done? I'm spoiled! I can't go! My hair, oh, my hair!" wailed Meg, looking with despair at the uneven frizzle on her forehead.

"Just my luck! You shouldn't have asked me to do it. I always spoil everything. I'm so sorry, but the tongs were too hot, and so I've made a mess," groaned poor Jo, regarding the black pancakes with tears of regret.

"It isn't spoiled; just frizzle it, and tie your ribbon so the ends come on your forehead a bit, and it will look like the last fashion. I've seen many girls do it so," said Amy consolingly.

"Serves me right for trying to be fine. I wish I'd let my hair alone," cried Meg petulantly.

"So do I, it was so smooth and pretty. But it will soon grow out again," said Beth, coming to kiss and comfort the shorn sheep.

After various lesser mishaps, Meg was finished at last, and by the united exertions of the family Jo's hair was got up and her dress on. They looked very well in their simple suits— Meg in silvery drab, with a blue velvet snood, lace frills, and the pearl pin; Jo in maroon, with a stiff, gentlemanly linen collar, and a white chrysanthemum or two for her only ornament. Each put on one nice light glove, and carried one soiled one, and all pronounced the effect "quite easy and fine." Meg's high-heeled slippers were very tight and hurt her, though she would not own it, and Jo's nineteen hairpins all seemed stuck straight into her head, which was not exactly comfortable; but, dear me, let us be elegant or die!

"Have a good time, dearies!" said Mrs. March, as the sisters went daintily down the walk. "Don't eat much supper, and come away at eleven when I send Hannah for you." As the gate clashed behind them, a voice cried from a window—

"Girls, girls! *have* you both got nice pocket handkerchiefs?"

"Yes, yes, spandy nice, and Meg has cologne on hers," cried Jo, adding with a laugh as they went on, "I do believe Marmee would ask that if we were all running away from an earthquake."

"It is one of her aristocratic tastes, and quite proper, for a real lady is always known by neat boots, gloves, and handkerchief," replied Meg, who had a good many little "aristocratic tastes" of her own.

"Now don't forget to keep the bad breadth out of sight, Jo. Is my sash right? And does my hair look *very* bad?" said Meg, as she turned from the glass in Mrs. Gardiner's dressing room after a prolonged prink.

"I know I shall forget. If you see me doing anything wrong, just remind me by a wink, will you?" returned Jo, giving her collar a twitch and her head a hasty brush.

"No, winking isn't ladylike. I'll lift my eyebrows if anything is wrong, and nod if you are all right. Now hold your shoulders straight, and take short steps, and don't shake hands if you are introduced to anyone: it isn't the thing."

"How *do* you learn all the proper ways? I never can. Isn't that music gay?"

Down they went, feeling a trifle timid, for they seldom went to parties, and, informal as this little gathering was, it was an event to them. Mrs. Gardiner, a stately old lady, greeted them kindly and handed them over to the eldest of her six daughters. Meg knew Sallie and was at her ease very soon, but Jo, who didn't care much for girls or girlish gossip, stood about, with her back carefully against the wall, and felt as much out of place as a colt in a flower garden. Half a dozen jovial lads were talking about skates in another part of the room, and she longed to go and join them, for skating was one of the joys of her life. She telegraphed her wish to Meg, but the eyebrows went up so alarmingly that she dared not stir. No one came to talk to her, and one by one the group near her dwindled away till she was left alone. She could not roam about and amuse herself, for the burned breadth would show, so she stared at people rather forlornly till the dancing began. Meg was asked at once, and the tight slippers tripped about so briskly that none would have guessed the pain their wearer suffered smilingly. Jo saw a big redheaded youth approaching her corner, and fearing he meant to engage her, she slipped into a curtained recess, intending to peep and enjoy herself in peace. Unfortunately, another bashful person had chosen the same refuge, for, as the curtain fell behind her, she found herself face to face with the "Laurence boy."

"Dear me, I didn't know anyone was here!" stammered Jo, preparing to back out as speedily as she had bounced in.

But the boy laughed and said pleasantly, though he looked a little startled, "Don't mind me, stay if you like."

"Shan't I disturb you?"

"Not a bit. I only came here because I don't know many people and felt rather strange at first, you know."

"So did I. Don't go away, please, unless you'd rather."

The boy sat down again and looked at his pumps, till Jo said, trying to be polite and easy, "I think I've had the pleasure of seeing you before. You live near us, don't you?"

"Next door." And he looked up and laughed outright, for Jo's prim manner was rather funny when he remembered how they had chatted about cricket when he brought the cat home.

That put Jo at her ease and she laughed too, as she said, in her heartiest way, "We did have such a good time over your nice Christmas present."

"Grandpa sent it."

"But you put it into his head, didn't you, now?"

"How is your cat, Miss March?" asked the boy, trying to look sober while his black eyes shone with fun.

"Nicely, thank you, Mr. Laurence; but I am not Miss March, I'm only Jo," returned the young lady.

"I'm not Mr. Laurence, I'm only Laurie."

"Laurie Laurence—what an odd name!"

"My first name is Theodore, but I don't like it, for the fellows called me Dora, so I made them say Laurie instead."

"I hate my name, too—so sentimental! I wish every one would say Jo instead of Josephine. How did you make the boys stop calling you Dora?"

"I thrashed 'em."

"I can't thrash Aunt March, so I suppose I shall have to bear it." And Jo resigned herself with a sigh.

"Don't you like to dance, Miss Jo?" asked Laurie, looking as if he thought the name suited her.

"I like it well enough if there is plenty of room, and everyone is lively. In a place like this I'm sure to upset something, tread on people's toes, or do something dreadful, so I keep out of mischief and let Meg sail about. Don't you dance?"

"Sometimes. You see I've been abroad a good many years, and haven't been into company enough yet to know how you do things here."

"Abroad!" cried Jo. "Oh, tell me about it! I love dearly to hear people describe their travels."

Laurie didn't seem to know where to begin, but Jo's eager questions soon set him going, and he told her how he had been at school in Vevay, where the boys never wore hats and had a fleet of boats on the lake, and for holiday fun went on walking trips about Switzerland with their teachers.

"Don't I wish I'd been there!" cried Jo. "Did you go to Paris?"

"We spent last winter there."

"Can you talk French?"

"We were not allowed to speak anything else at Vevay."

"Do say some! I can read it, but can't pronounce."

"*Quel nom a cette jeune demoiselle en les pantoufles jolis?*" said Laurie good-naturedly.

"How nicely you do it! Let me see—you said, 'Who is the young lady in the pretty slippers,' didn't you?"

"*Oui, mademoiselle.*"

"It's my sister Margaret, and you knew it was! Do you think she is pretty?"

"Yes, she makes me think of the German girls, she looks so fresh and quiet, and dances like a lady."

Jo quite glowed with pleasure at this boyish praise of her sister, and stored it up to repeat to Meg. Both peeped and criticized and chatted till they felt like old acquaintances. Laurie's bashfulness soon wore off, for Jo's gentlemanly demeanor amused and set him at his ease, and Jo was her merry self again, because her dress was forgotten and nobody lifted their eyebrows at her. She liked the "Laurence boy" better than ever and took several good looks at him, so that she might describe him to the girls, for they had no brothers, very few male cousins, and boys were almost unknown creatures to them.

"Curly black hair, brown skin, big black eyes, handsome nose, fine teeth, small hands and feet, taller than I am, very polite, for a boy, and altogether jolly. Wonder how old he is?"

It was on the tip of Jo's tongue to ask, but she checked herself in time and, with unusual tact, tried to find out in a roundabout way.

"I suppose you are going to college soon? I see you pegging away at your books—no, I mean studying hard." And Jo blushed at the dreadful "pegging" which had escaped her.

Laurie smiled but didn't seem shocked, and answered with a shrug, "Not for a year or two; I won't go before seventeen, anyway."

"Aren't you but fifteen?" asked Jo, looking at the tall lad, whom she had imagined seventeen already.

"Sixteen, next month."

"How I wish I was going to college! You don't look as if you liked it."

"I hate it! Nothing but grinding or skylarking. And I don't like the way fellows do either, in this country."

"What do you like?"

"To live in Italy, and to enjoy myself in my own way."

Jo wanted very much to ask what his own way was, but

his black brows looked rather threatening as he knit them, so she changed the subject by saying, as her foot kept time, "That's a splendid polka! Why don't you go and try it?"

"If you will come too," he answered, with a gallant little bow.

"I can't; for I told Meg I wouldn't, because—" There Jo stopped, and looked undecided whether to tell or to laugh.

"Because what?" asked Laurie curiously.

"You won't tell?"

"Never!"

"Well, I have a bad trick of standing before the fire, and so I burn my frocks, and I scorched this one, and though it's nicely mended, it shows, and Meg told me to keep still so no one would see it. You may laugh, if you want to. It is funny, I know."

But Laurie didn't laugh; he only looked down a minute, and the expression of his face puzzled Jo when he said very gently, "Never mind that; I'll tell you how we can manage: there's a long hall out there, and we can dance grandly, and no one will see us. Please come."

Jo thanked him and gladly went, wishing she had two neat gloves, when she saw the nice, pearl-colored ones her partner wore. The hall was empty, and they had a grand polka, for Laurie danced well, and taught her the German step, which delighted Jo, being full of swing and spring. When the music stopped, they sat down on the stairs to get their breath, and Laurie was in the midst of an account of a students' festival at Heidelberg when Meg appeared in search of her sister. She beckoned, and Jo reluctantly followed her into a side room, where she found her on a sofa, holding her foot, and looking pale.

"I've sprained my ankle. That stupid high heel turned and gave me a sad wrench. It aches so, I can hardly stand, and I don't know how I'm ever going to get home," she said, rocking to and fro in pain.

"I knew you'd hurt your feet with those silly shoes. I'm sorry. But I don't see what you can do, except get a carriage, or stay here all night," answered Jo, softly rubbing the poor ankle as she spoke.

"I can't have a carriage without its costing ever so much. I dare say I can't get one at all, for most people come in their own, and it's a long way to the stable, and no one to send."

"I'll go."

"No, indeed! It's past nine, and dark as Egypt. I can't stop here, for the house is full. Sallie has some girls staying with her. I'll rest till Hannah comes, and then do the best I can."

"I'll ask Laurie; he will go," said Jo, looking relieved as the idea occurred to her.

"Mercy, no! Don't ask or tell anyone. Get me my rubbers, and put these slippers with our things. I can't dance any more, but as soon as supper is over, watch for Hannah and tell me the minute she comes."

"They are going out to supper now. I'll stay with you; I'd rather."

"No, dear, run along, and bring me some coffee. I'm so tired, I can't stir!"

So Meg reclined, with rubbers well hidden, and Jo went blundering away to the dining room, which she found after going into a china closet, and opening the door of a room where old Mr. Gardiner was taking a little private refreshment. Making a dart at the table, she secured the coffee, which she immediately spilled, thereby making the front of her dress as bad as the back.

"Oh, dear, what a blunderbuss I am!" exclaimed Jo, finishing Meg's glove by scrubbing her gown with it.

"Can I help you?" said a friendly voice. And there was Laurie, with a full cup in one hand and a plate of ice in the other.

"I was trying to get something for Meg, who is very tired, and someone shook me, and here I am in a nice state," answered Jo, glancing dismally from the stained skirt to the coffee-colored glove.

"Too bad! I was looking for someone to give this to. May I take it to your sister?"

"Oh, thank you! I'll show you where she is. I don't offer to take it myself, for I should only get into another scrape if I did."

Jo led the way, and as if used to waiting on ladies, Laurie drew up a little table, brought a second installment of coffee and ice for Jo, and was so obliging that even particular Meg pronounced him a "nice boy." They had a merry time over the bonbons and mottoes, and were in the midst of a quiet game of "Buzz," with two or three other young people who had strayed in, when Hannah appeared. Meg forgot her foot and rose so quickly that she was forced to catch hold of Jo, with an exclamation of pain.

"Hush! Don't say anything," she whispered, adding aloud, "It's nothing. I turned my foot a little, that's all," and limped upstairs to put her things on.

Hannah scolded, Meg cried, and Jo was at her wits' end, till she decided to take things into her own hands. Slipping out, she ran down and, finding a servant, asked if he could get her a carriage. It happened to be a hired waiter who knew nothing about the neighborhood and Jo was looking round for help when Laurie, who had heard what she said, came up and offered his grandfather's carriage, which had just come for him, he said.

"It's so early! You can't mean to go yet?" began Jo, looking relieved but hesitating to accept the offer.

"I always go early—I do, truly! Please let me take you home. It's all on my way, you know, and it rains, they say."

That settled it; and, telling him of Meg's mishap, Jo gratefully accepted and rushed up to bring down the rest of the party. Hannah hated rain as much as a cat does so she made no trouble, and they rolled away in the luxurious close carriage, feeling very festive and elegant. Laurie went on the box so Meg could keep her foot up, and the girls talked over their party in freedom.

"I had a capital time. Did you?" asked Jo, rumpling up her hair, and making herself comfortable.

"Yes, till I hurt myself. Sallie's friend, Annie Moffat, took a fancy to me, and asked me to come and spend a week with her when Sallie does. She is going in the spring when the opera comes, and it will be perfectly splendid, if Mother only lets me go," answered Meg, cheering up at the thought.

"I saw you dancing with the redheaded man I ran away from. Was he nice?"

"Oh, very! His hair is auburn, not red, and he was very polite, and I had a delicious redowa with him."

"He looked like a grasshopper in a fit when he did the new step. Laurie and I couldn't help laughing. Did you hear us?"

"No, but it was very rude. What *were* you about all that time, hidden away there?"

Jo told her adventures, and by the time she had finished they were at home. With many thanks, they said good night and crept in, hoping to disturb no one, but the instant their door creaked, two little nightcaps bobbed up, and two sleepy but eager voices cried out—

"Tell about the party! tell about the party!"

With what Meg called "a great want of manners," Jo had saved some bonbons for the little girls; and they soon subsided, after hearing the most thrilling events of the evening.

"I declare, it really seems like being a fine young lady, to come home from the party in a carriage and sit in my dressing gown with a maid to wait on me," said Meg, as Jo bound up her foot with arnica and brushed her hair.

"I don't believe fine young ladies enjoy themselves a bit more than we do, in spite of our burned hair, old gowns, one glove apiece, and tight slippers that sprain our ankles when we are silly enough to wear them." And I think Jo was quite right.

Chapter 4

Burdens

"OH, DEAR, how hard it does seem to take up our packs and go on," sighed Meg the morning after the party, for, now the holidays were over, the week of merrymaking did not fit her for going on easily with the task she never liked.

"I wish it was Christmas or New Year's all the time. Wouldn't it be fun?" answered Jo, yawning dismally.

"We shouldn't enjoy ourselves half so much as we do now. But it does seem so nice to have little suppers and bouquets, and go to parties, and drive home, and read and rest, and not work. It's like other people, you know, and I always envy girls who do such things, I'm so fond of luxury," said Meg, trying to decide which of two shabby gowns was the least shabby.

"Well, we can't have it, so don't let us grumble but shoulder our bundles and trudge along as cheerfully as Marmee does. I'm sure Aunt March is a regular Old Man of the Sea to me, but I suppose when I've learned to carry her without complaining, she will tumble off, or get so light that I shan't mind her."

This idea tickled Jo's fancy and put her in good spirits, but Meg didn't brighten, for her burden, consisting of four spoiled children, seemed heavier than ever. She hadn't heart enough even to make herself pretty as usual by putting on a blue neck ribbon and dressing her hair in the most becoming way.

"Where's the use of looking nice, when no one sees me but those cross midgets, and no one cares whether I'm pretty or not?" she muttered, shutting her drawer with a jerk. "I shall have to toil and moil all my days, with only little bits of fun now and then, and get old and ugly and sour, because I'm poor and can't enjoy my life as other girls do. It's a shame!"

So Meg went down, wearing an injured look, and wasn't at all agreeable at breakfast time. Everyone seemed rather out of sorts and inclined to croak. Beth had a headache and lay on the sofa, trying to comfort herself with the cat and three kittens; Amy was fretting because her lessons were not learned, and she couldn't find her rubbers; Jo *would* whistle and make a great racket getting ready; Mrs. March was very busy trying to finish a letter, which must go at once; and Hannah had the grumps, for being up late didn't suit her.

"There never *was* such a cross family!" cried Jo, losing her temper when she had upset an inkstand, broken both boot lacings, and sat down upon her hat.

"You're the crossest person in it!" returned Amy, washing out the sum that was all wrong with the tears that had fallen on her slate.

"Beth, if you don't keep these horrid cats down cellar I'll have them drowned," exclaimed Meg angrily, as she tried to get rid of the kitten which had scrambled up her back and stuck like a burr just out of reach.

Jo laughed, Meg scolded, Beth implored, and Amy wailed because she couldn't remember how much nine times twelve was.

"Girls, girls, do be quiet one minute! I *must* get this off by the early mail, and you drive me distracted with your worry," cried Mrs. March, crossing out the third spoiled sentence in her letter.

There was a momentary lull, broken by Hannah, who stalked in, laid two hot turnovers on the table, and stalked out again. These turnovers were an institution, and the girls called them "muffs," for they had no others and found the hot pies very comforting to their hands on cold mornings. Hannah never forgot to make them, not matter how busy or grumpy she might be, for the walk was long and bleak; the poor things got no other lunch and were seldom home before two.

"Cuddle your cats and get over your headache, Bethy. Good-by, Marmee. We are a set of rascals this morning, but we'll come home regular angels. Now then, Meg!" And Jo tramped away, feeling that the pilgrims were not setting out as they ought to do.

They always looked back before turning the corner, for their mother was always at the window to nod and smile, and wave her hand to them. Somehow it seemed as if they couldn't have got through the day without that, for whatever their mood might be, the last glimpse of that motherly face was sure to affect them like sunshine.

"If Marmee shook her fist instead of kissing her hand to us, it would serve us right, for more ungrateful wretches than we are were never seen," cried Jo, taking a remorseful satisfaction in the snowy walk and bitter wind.

"Don't use such dreadful expressions," said Meg from the depths of the veil in which she had shrouded herself like a nun sick of the world.

"I like good strong words that mean something," replied Jo, catching her hat as it took a leap off her head preparatory to flying away altogether.

"Call yourself any names you like, but *I* am neither a rascal nor a wretch and I don't choose to be called so."

"You're a blighted being, and decidedly cross today because you can't sit in the lap of luxury all the time. Poor dear, just wait till I make my fortune, and you shall revel in carriages and ice cream and high-heeled slippers and posies and red-headed boys to dance with."

"How ridiculous you are, Jo!" But Meg laughed at the nonsense and felt better in spite of herself.

"Lucky for you I am, for if I put on crushed airs and tried to be dismal, as you do, we should be in a nice state. Thank goodness, I can always find something funny to keep me up. Don't croak any more, but come home jolly, there's a dear."

Jo gave her sister an encouraging pat on the shoulder as they parted for the day, each going a different way, each hugging her little warm turnover, and each trying to be cheerful in spite of wintry weather, hard work, and the unsatisfied desires of pleasure-loving youth.

When Mr. March lost his property in trying to help an unfortunate friend, the two oldest girls begged to be allowed to do something toward their own support, at least. Believing that they could not begin too early to cultivate energy, industry, and independence, their parents consented, and both fell to work with the hearty good will which in spite of all obstacles is sure to succeed at last. Margaret found a place as nursery governess and felt rich with her small salary. As she said, she *was* "fond of luxury," and her chief trouble was poverty. She found it harder to bear than the others because she could remember a time when home was beautiful, life full of ease and pleasure, and want of any kind unknown. She tried not to be envious or discontented, but it was very natural that the young girl should long for pretty things, gay friends, accomplishments, and a happy life. At the Kings' she daily saw all she wanted, for the children's older sisters were just out, and Meg caught frequent glimpses of dainty ball dresses and bouquets, heard lively gossip about theaters, concerts, sleighing parties, and merrymakings of all kinds, and saw money lavished on trifles which would have been so precious to her. Poor Meg seldom complained, but a sense of injustice made her feel bitter toward everyone sometimes, for she had not yet learned to know how rich she was in the blessings which alone can make life happy.

Jo happened to suit Aunt March, who was lame and needed an active person to wait upon her. The childless old lady had offered to adopt one of the girls when the troubles came, and was much offended because her offer was declined. Other friends told the Marches that they had lost all chance of being remembered in the rich old lady's will, but the unworldly Marches only said—

"We can't give up our girls for a dozen fortunes. Rich or poor, we will keep together and be happy in one another."

The old lady wouldn't speak to them for a time, but happening to meet Jo at a friend's, something in her comical face and blunt manners struck the old lady's fancy, and she proposed to take her for a companion. This did not suit Jo at all, but she accepted the place since nothing better appeared and, to every one's surprise, got on remarkably well with her irascible relative. There was an occasional tempest, and once Jo had marched home, declaring she couldn't bear it any longer; but Aunt March always cleared up quickly, and sent for her back again with such urgency that she could not refuse, for in her heart she rather liked the peppery old lady.

I suspect that the real attraction was a large library of fine books, which was left to dust and spiders since Uncle March died. Jo remembered the kind old gentleman, who used to let her build railroads and bridges with his big dictionaries, tell her stories about the queer pictures in his Latin books, and buy her cards of gingerbread whenever he met her in the street. The dim, dusty room, with the busts staring down from the tall bookcases, the cozy chairs, the globes, and, best of all, the wilderness of books in which she could wander where she liked, made the library a region of bliss to her. The moment Aunt March took her nap, or was busy with company, Jo hurried to this quiet place, and, curling herself up in the easy chair, devoured poetry, romance, history, travels, and pictures, like a regular bookworm. But, like all happiness, it did not last long; for as sure as she had just reached the heart of the story, the sweetest verse of the song, or the most perilous adventure of her traveler, a shrill voice called, "Josy-phine! Josy-phine!" and she had to leave her paradise to wind yarn, wash the poodle, or read Belsham's *Essays* by the hour together.

Jo's ambition was to do something very splendid; what it was she had no idea as yet, but left it for time to tell her; and, meanwhile, found her greatest affliction in the fact that she couldn't read, run, and ride as much as she liked. A quick temper, sharp tongue, and restless spirit were always getting her into scrapes, and her life was a series of ups and downs, which were both comic and pathetic. But the training she received at Aunt March's was just what she needed, and the thought that she was doing something to support herself made her happy in spite of the perpetual "Josy-phine!"

Beth was too bashful to go to school; it had been tried, but she suffered so much that it was given up, and she did her lessons at home with her father. Even when he went away, and her mother was called to devote her skill and energy to Soldiers' Aid Societies, Beth went faithfully on by herself and did the best she could. She was a housewifely little creature,

and helped Hannah keep home neat and comfortable for the
workers, never thinking of any reward but to be loved. Long,
quiet days she spent, not lonely nor idle, for her little world
was peopled with imaginary friends, and she was by nature a
busy bee. There were six dolls to be taken up and dressed every
morning, for Beth was a child still and loved her pets as well
as ever. Not one whole or handsome one among them, all were
outcasts till Beth took them in; for, when her sisters outgrew
these idols, they passed to her because Amy would have nothing old or ugly. Beth cherished them all the more tenderly
for that very reason, and set up a hospital for infirm dolls. No
pins were ever stuck into their cotton vitals, no harsh words
or blows were ever given them, no neglect ever saddened the
heart of the most repulsive; but all were fed and clothed,
nursed and caressed with an affection which never failed. One
forlorn fragment of *dollanity* had belonged to Jo and, having
led a tempestuous life, was left a wreck in the rag bag, from
which dreary poorhouse it was rescued by Beth and taken
to her refuge. Having no top to its head, she tied on a neat
little cap, and as both arms and legs were gone, she hid these
deficiencies by folding it in a blanket and devoting her best
bed to this chronic invalid. If anyone had known the care
lavished on that dolly, I think it would have touched their
hearts, even while they laughed. She brought it bits of bouquets, she read to it, took it out to breathe the air, hidden
under her coat, she sang it lullabies and never went to bed
without kissing its dirty face and whispering tenderly, "I hope
you'll have a good night, my poor dear."

Beth had her troubles as well as the others, and not being
an angel but a very human little girl, she often "wept a little
weep," as Jo said, because she couldn't take music lessons and
have a fine piano. She loved music so dearly, tried so hard to
learn, and practiced away so patiently at the jingling old instrument, that it did seem as if someone (not to hint Aunt
March) ought to help her. Nobody did, however, and nobody
saw Beth wipe the tears off the yellow keys, that wouldn't keep
in tune, when she was all alone. She sang like a little lark about

her work, never was too tired to play for Marmee and the girls, and day after day said hopefully to herself, "I know I'll get my music some time, if I'm good."

There are many Beths in the world, shy and quiet, sitting in corners till needed, and living for others so cheerfully that no one sees the sacrifices till the little cricket on the hearth stops chirping, and the sweet, sunshiny presence vanishes, leaving silence and shadow behind.

If anybody had asked Amy what the greatest trial of her life was, she would have answered at once, "My nose." When she was a baby, Jo had accidentally dropped her into the coal hod, and Amy insisted that the fall had ruined her nose forever. It was not big nor red, like poor "Petrea's," it was only rather flat, and all the pinching in the world could not give it an aristocratic point. No one minded it but herself, and it was doing its best to grow, but Amy felt deeply the want of a Grecian nose, and drew whole sheets of handsome ones to console herself.

"Little Raphael," as her sisters called her, had a decided talent for drawing, and was never so happy as when copying flowers, designing fairies, or illustrating stories with queer specimens of art. Her teachers complained that instead of doing her sums she covered her slate with animals, the blank pages of her atlas were used to copy maps on, and caricatures of the most ludicrous description came fluttering out of all her books at unlucky moments. She got through her lessons as well as she could, and managed to escape reprimands by being a model of deportment. She was a great favorite with her mates, being good-tempered and possessing the happy art of pleasing without effort. Her little airs and graces were much admired; so were her accomplishments, for beside her drawing, she could play twelve tunes, crochet, and read French without mispronouncing more than two-thirds of the words. She had a plaintive way of saying, "When Papa was rich we did so-and-so," which was very touching, and her long words were considered "perfectly elegant" by the girls.

Amy was in a fair way to be spoiled, for everyone petted her, and her small vanities and selfishnesses were growing nicely. One thing, however, rather quenched the vanities: she had to wear her cousin's clothes. Now Florence's mamma hadn't a particle of taste, and Amy suffered deeply at having to wear a red instead of a blue bonnet, unbecoming gowns, and fussy aprons that did not fit. Everything was good, well made, and little worn, but Amy's artistic eyes were much afflicted, especially this winter, when her school dress was a dull purple with yellow dots and no trimming.

"My only comfort," she said to Meg, with tears in her eyes, "is that Mother doesn't take tucks in my dresses whenever I'm naughty, as Maria Parks' mother does. My dear, it's really dreadful, for sometimes she is so bad her frock is up to her knees, and she can't come to school. When I think of this *deggerredation,* I feel that I can bear even my flat nose and purple gown with yellow skyrockets on it."

Meg was Amy's confidante and monitor, and by some strange attraction of opposites Jo was gentle Beth's. To Jo alone did the shy child tell her thoughts; and over her big, harum-scarum sister Beth unconsciously exercised more influence than anyone in the family. The two older girls were a great deal to one another, but each took one of the younger into her keeping and watched over her in her own way—"playing mother" they called it—and put their sisters in the places of discarded dolls with the maternal instinct of little women.

"Has anybody got anything to tell? It's been such a dismal day I'm really dying for some amusement," said Meg, as they sat sewing together that evening.

"I had a queer time with Aunt today, and, as I got the best of it, I'll tell you about it," began Jo, who dearly loved to tell stories. "I was reading that everlasting Belsham, and droning away as I always do, for Aunt soon drops off, and then I take out some nice book, and read like fury till she wakes up. I actually made myself sleepy, and before she began to nod, I gave such a gape that she asked me what I meant by opening my mouth wide enough to take the whole book in at once.

" 'I wish I could, and be done with it,' " said I, trying not to be saucy.

"Then she gave me a long lecture on my sins, and told me to sit and think them over while she just 'lost' herself for a moment. She never finds herself very soon, so the minute her cap began to bob like a top-heavy dahlia, I whipped the *Vicar of Wakefield* out of my pocket, and read away, with one eye on him and one on Aunt. I'd just got to where they all tumbled into the water when I forgot and laughed out loud. Aunt woke up and, being more good-natured after her nap, told me to read a bit and show what frivolous work I preferred to the worthy and instructive Belsham. I did my very best, and she liked it, though she only said—

" 'I don't understand what it's all about. Go back and begin it, child.'

"Back I went, and made the Primroses as interesting as ever I could. Once I was wicked enough to stop in a thrilling place, and say meekly, 'I'm afraid it tires you, ma'am; shan't I stop now?'

"She caught up her knitting, which had dropped out of her hands, gave me a sharp look through her specs, and said, in her short way, 'Finish the chapter, and don't be impertinent, miss.' "

"Did she own she liked it?" asked Meg.

"Oh, bless you, no! But she let old Belsham rest, and when I ran back after my gloves this afternoon, there she was, so hard at the Vicar that she didn't hear me laugh as I danced a jig in the hall because of the good time coming. What a pleasant life she might have if she only chose! I don't envy her much, in spite of her money, for after all rich people have about as many worries as poor ones, I think," added Jo.

"That reminds me," said Meg, "that I've got something to tell. It isn't funny, like Jo's story, but I thought about it a good deal as I came home. At the Kings' today I found everybody in a flurry, and one of the children said that her oldest brother had done something dreadful, and Papa had sent him away. I heard Mrs. King crying and Mr. King talking very loud, and Grace and Ellen turned away their faces when they passed me, so I shouldn't see how red their eyes were. I didn't ask any questions, of course, but I felt so sorry for them and was rather glad I hadn't any wild brothers to do wicked things and disgrace the family."

"I think being disgraced in school is a great deal try*inger* than anything bad boys can do," said Amy, shaking her head, as if her experience of life had been a deep one. "Susie Perkins came to school today with a lovely red carnelian ring. I wanted it dreadfully, and wished I was her with all my might. Well, she drew a picture of Mr. Davis, with a monstrous nose and a hump, and the words, 'Young ladies, my eye is upon you!' coming out of his mouth in a balloon thing. We were laughing over it when all of a sudden his eye *was* on us, and he ordered Susie to bring up her slate. She was *parry*lized with fright, but she went, and oh, what *do* you think he did? He took her by the ear—the ear! just fancy how horrid!—and led her to the recitation platform, and made her stand there half an hour, holding that slate so everyone could see."

"Didn't the girls laugh at the picture?" asked Jo, who relished the scrape.

"Laugh? Not one! They sat as still as mice, and Susie cried quarts, I know she did. I didn't envy her then, for I felt that millions of carnelian rings wouldn't have made me happy after that. I never, never should have got over such a agonizing mortification." And Amy went on with her work, in the proud consciousness of virtue and the successful utterance of two long words in a breath.

"I saw something that I liked this morning, and I meant to tell it at dinner, but I forgot," said Beth, putting Jo's topsy-turvy basket in order as she talked. "When I went to get some oysters for Hannah, Mr. Laurence was in the fishshop; but he didn't see me, for I kept behind a barrel, and he was busy with Mr. Cutter the fishman. A poor woman came in with a pail and a mop, and asked Mr. Cutter if he would let her do some scrubbing for a bit of fish, because she hadn't any dinner for her children, and had been disappointed of a day's work. Mr. Cutter was in a hurry, and said 'No,' rather crossly; so she was going away, looking hungry and sorry, when Mr.

Laurence hooked up a big fish with the crooked end of his cane and held it out to her. She was so glad and surprised she took it right in her arms, and thanked him over and over. He told her to 'go along and cook it,' and she hurried off, so happy! Wasn't it good of him? Oh, she did look so funny, hugging the big, slippery fish, and hoping Mr. Laurence's bed in heaven would be 'aisy.' "

When they had laughed at Beth's story, they asked their mother for one, and, after a moment's thought, she said soberly, "As I sat cutting out blue flannel jackets today at the rooms, I felt very anxious about Father, and thought how lonely and helpless we should be, if anything happened to him. It was not a wise thing to do, but I kept on worrying till an old man came in with an order for some clothes. He sat down near me, and I began to talk to him, for he looked poor and tired and anxious.

" 'Have you sons in the army?' I asked, for the note he brought was not to me.

" 'Yes, ma'am. I had four, but two were killed, one is a prisoner, and I'm going to the other, who is very sick in a Washington hospital,' he answered quietly.

" 'You have done a great deal for your country, sir,' I said, feeling respect now, instead of pity.

" 'Not a mite more than I ought, ma'am. I'd go myself, if I was any use; as I ain't, I give my boys, and give 'em free.'

"He spoke so cheerfully, looked so sincere, and seemed so glad to give his all, that I was ashamed of myself. I'd given one man and thought it too much, while he gave four without grudging them. I had all my girls to comfort me at home, and his last son was waiting, miles away, to say good-by to him, perhaps! I felt so rich, so happy, thinking of my blessings, that I made him a nice bundle, gave him some money, and thanked him heartily for the lesson he had taught me."

"Tell another story, Mother—one with a moral to it, like this. I like to think about them afterward, if they are real and not too preachy," said Jo, after a minute's silence.

Mrs. March smiled and began at once, for she had told

stories to this little audience for many years, and knew how to please them.

"Once upon a time, there were four girls, who had enough to eat and drink and wear, a good many comforts and pleasures, kind friends and parents who loved them dearly, and yet they were not contented." (Here the listeners stole sly looks at one another, and began to sew diligently.) "These girls were anxious to be good and made many excellent resolutions, but they did not keep them very well, and were constantly saying, 'If we only had this,' or 'If we could only do that,' quite forgetting how much they already had, and how many pleasant things they actually could do. So they asked an old woman what spell they could use to make them happy, and she said, 'When you feel discontented, think over your blessings, and be grateful.'" (Here Jo looked up quickly, as if about to speak, but changed her mind, seeing that the story was not done yet.)

"Being sensible girls, they decided to try her advice, and soon were surprised to see how well off they were. One discovered that money couldn't keep shame and sorrow out of rich people's houses; another that, though she was poor, she was a great deal happier, with her youth, health, and good spirits, than a certain fretful, feeble old lady who couldn't enjoy her comforts; a third that, disagreeable as it was to help get dinner, it was harder still to have to go begging for it; and the fourth, that even carnelian rings were not so valuable as good behavior. So they agreed to stop complaining, to enjoy the blessings already possessed, and try to deserve them, lest they should be taken away entirely, instead of increased; and I believe they were never disappointed or sorry that they took the old woman's advice."

"Now, Marmee, that is very cunning of you to turn our own stories against us, and give us a sermon instead of a romance!" cried Meg.

"I like that kind of sermon. It's the sort Father used to tell us," said Beth thoughtfully, putting the needles straight on Jo's cushion.

"I don't complain near as much as the others do, and I

shall be more careful than ever now, for I've had warning from Susie's downfall," said Amy morally.

"We needed that lesson, and we won't forget it. If we do, you just say to us, as old Chloe did in *Uncle Tom*, 'Tink ob yer marcies, chillen! tink ob yer marcies!'" added Jo, who could not, for the life of her, help getting a morsel of fun out of the little sermon, though she took it to heart as much as any of them.

Chapter 5

Being Neighborly

"WHAT IN the world are you going to do now, Jo?" asked Meg one snowy afternoon, as her sister came tramping through the hall, in rubber boots, old sack, and hood, with a broom in one hand and a shovel in the other.

"Going out for exercise," answered Jo with a mischievous twinkle in her eyes.

"I should think two long walks this morning would have been enough! It's cold and dull out, and I advise you to stay warm and dry by the fire, as I do," said Meg with a shiver.

"Never take advice! Can't keep still all day, and not being a pussycat, I don't like to doze by the fire. I like adventures, and I'm going to find some."

Meg went back to toast her feet and read *Ivanhoe*, and Jo began to dig paths with great energy. The snow was light, and with her broom she soon swept a path all round the garden, for Beth to walk in when the sun came out and the invalid dolls needed air. Now, the garden separated the Marches' house from that of Mr. Laurence. Both stood in a suburb of the city, which was still countrylike, with groves and lawns, large gardens, and quiet streets. A low hedge parted the two estates. On one side was an old, brown house, looking rather bare and shabby, robbed of the vines that in summer covered its walls and the flowers which then surrounded it. On the other side was a stately stone mansion, plainly betokening every sort of comfort and luxury, from the big coach house and well-kept grounds to the conservatory and the glimpses of lovely things one caught between the rich curtains. Yet it seemed a lonely, lifeless sort of house, for no children frolicked on the lawn, no motherly face ever smiled at the windows, and few people went in and out, except the old gentleman and his grandson.

To Jo's lively fancy, this fine house seemed a kind of enchanted palace, full of splendors and delights which no one enjoyed. She had long wanted to behold these hidden glories, and to know the "Laurence boy," who looked as if he would like to be known, if he only knew how to begin. Since the party, she had been more eager than ever, and had planned many ways of making friends with him; but he had not been seen lately, and Jo began to think he had gone away, when she one day spied a brown face at an upper window, looking wistfully down into their garden, where Beth and Amy were snowballing one another.

"That boy is suffering for society and fun," she said to herself. "His grandpa does not know what's good for him, and keeps him shut up all alone. He needs a party of jolly boys to play with, or somebody young and lively. I've a great mind to go over and tell the old gentleman so!"

The idea amused Jo, who liked to do daring things and was always scandalizing Meg by her queer performances. The plan of "going over" was not forgotten; and when the snowy afternoon came, Jo resolved to try what could be done. She saw Mr. Laurence drive off, and then sallied out to dig her way down to the hedge, where she paused and took a survey. All quiet—curtains down at the lower windows, servants out of sight, and nothing human visible but a curly black head leaning on a thin hand at the upper window.

"There he is," thought Jo, "poor boy! All alone and sick this dismal day. It's a shame! I'll toss up a snowball and make him look out, and then say a kind word to him."

Up went a handful of soft snow, and the head turned at once, showing a face which lost its listless look in a minute, as the big eyes brightened and the mouth began to smile. Jo nodded and laughed, and flourished her broom as she called out—

"How do you do? Are you sick?"

Laurie opened the window, and croaked out as hoarsely as a raven—

"Better, thank you. I've had a bad cold, and been shut up a week."

"I'm sorry. What do you amuse yourself with?"

"Nothing. It's as dull as tombs up here."

"Don't you read?"

"Not much. They won't let me."

"Can't somebody read to you?"

"Grandpa does sometimes, but my books don't interest him, and I hate to ask Brooke all the time."

"Have someone come and see you, then."

"There isn't anyone I'd like to see. Boys make such a row, and my head is weak."

"Isn't there some nice girl who'd read and amuse you? Girls are quiet and like to play nurse."

"Don't know any."

"You know us," began Jo, then laughed, and stopped.

"So I do! Will you come, please?" cried Laurie.

"I'm not quiet and nice, but I'll come, if Mother will let me. I'll go ask her. Shut that window, like a good boy, and wait till I come."

With that, Jo shouldered her broom and marched into the house, wondering what they would all say to her. Laurie was in a flutter of excitement at the idea of having company, and flew about to get ready; for, as Mrs. March said, he was "a little gentleman," and did honor to the coming guest by brushing his curly pate, putting on a fresh collar, and trying to tidy up the room, which, in spite of half a dozen servants, was anything but neat. Presently there came a loud ring, then a decided voice, asking for "Mr. Laurie," and a surprised-looking servant came running up to announce a young lady.

"All right, show her up, it's Miss Jo," said Laurie, going to the door of his little parlor to meet Jo, who appeared, looking rosy and kind and quite at her ease, with a covered dish in one hand and Beth's three kittens in the other.

"Here I am, bag and baggage," she said briskly. "Mother sent her love, and was glad if I could do anything for you. Meg wanted me to bring some of her blancmange, she makes it very nicely; and Beth thought her cats would be comforting. I knew you'd laugh at them, but I couldn't refuse, she was so anxious to do something."

It so happened that Beth's funny loan was just the thing, for in laughing over the kits, Laurie forgot his bashfulness, and grew sociable at once.

"That looks too pretty to eat," he said, smiling with pleasure, as Jo uncovered the dish, and showed the blancmange, surrounded by a garland of green leaves, and the scarlet flowers of Amy's pet geranium.

"It isn't anything, only they all felt kindly and wanted to show it. Tell the girl to put it away for your tea: it's so simple, you can eat it, and, being soft, it will slip down without hurting your sore throat. What a cozy room this is!"

"It might be if it was kept nice; but the maids are lazy, and I don't know how to make them mind. It worries me, though."

"I'll right it up in two minutes, for it only needs to have the hearth brushed, so—and the things made straight on the mantelpiece, so—and the books put here, and the bottles there, and your sofa turned from the light, and the pillows plumped up a bit. Now, then, you're fixed."

And so he was; for, as she laughed and talked, Jo had whisked things into place and given quite a different air to the room. Laurie watched her in respectful silence, and when she beckoned him to his sofa, he sat down with a sigh of satisfaction, saying gratefully—

"How kind you are! Yes, that's what it wanted. Now please take the big chair and let me do something to amuse my company."

"No, I came to amuse you. Shall I read aloud?" and Jo looked affectionately toward some inviting books near by.

"Thank you! I've read all those, and if you don't mind, I'd rather talk," answered Laurie.

"Not a bit. I'll talk all day if you'll only set me going. Beth says I never know when to stop."

"Is Beth the rosy one, who stays at home a good deal and sometimes goes out with a little basket?" asked Laurie with interest.

"Yes, that's Beth. She's my girl, and a regular good one she is, too."

"The pretty one is Meg, and the curly-haired one is Amy, I believe?"

"How did you find that out?"

Laurie colored up, but answered frankly, "Why, you see, I often hear you calling to one another, and when I'm alone up here, I can't help looking over at your house, you always seem to be having such good times. I beg your pardon for being so rude, but sometimes you forget to put down the curtain at the window where the flowers are; and when the lamps are lighted, it's like looking at a picture to see the fire, and you all round the table with your mother; her face is right opposite, and it looks so sweet behind the flowers, I can't help watching it. I haven't got any mother, you know." And Laurie poked the fire to hide a little twitching of the lips that he could not control.

The solitary, hungry look in his eyes went straight to Jo's warm heart. She had been so simply taught that there was no nonsense in her head, and at fifteen she was as innocent and frank as any child. Laurie was sick and lonely, and feeling how rich she was in home love and happiness, she gladly tried to share it with him. Her face was very friendly and her sharp voice unusually gentle as she said—

"We'll never draw that curtain any more, and I give you leave to look as much as you like. I just wish, though, instead of peeping, you'd come over and see us. Mother is so splendid, she'd do you heaps of good, and Beth would sing to you if *I* begged her to, and Amy would dance; Meg and I would make you laugh over our funny stage properties, and we'd have jolly times. Wouldn't your grandpa let you?"

"I think he would, if your mother asked him. He's very kind, though he does not look so; and he lets me do what I like, pretty much, only he's afraid I might be a bother to strangers," began Laurie, brightening more and more.

"We are not strangers, we are neighbors, and you needn't think you'd be a bother. We *want* to know you, and I've been trying to do it this ever so long. We haven't been here a great while, you know, but we have got acquainted with all our neighbors but you."

"You see Grandpa lives among his books, and doesn't mind much what happens outside. Mr. Brooke, my tutor, doesn't stay here, you know, and I have no one to go about with me, so I just stop at home and get on as I can."

"That's bad. You ought to make an effort and go visiting everywhere you are asked; then you'll have plenty of friends, and pleasant places to go to. Never mind being bashful; it won't last long if you keep going."

Laurie turned red again, but wasn't offended at being accused of bashfulness, for there was so much good will in Jo it was impossible not to take her blunt speeches as kindly as they were meant.

"Do you like your school?" asked the boy, changing the subject, after a little pause, during which he stared at the fire and Jo looked about her, well pleased.

"Don't go to school; I'm a businessman—girl, I mean. I go to wait on my great-aunt, and a dear, cross old soul she is, too," answered Jo.

Laurie opened his mouth to ask another question, but remembering just in time that it wasn't manners to make too many inquiries into people's affairs, he shut it again, and looked uncomfortable. Jo liked his good breeding, and didn't mind having a laugh at Aunt March, so she gave him a lively description of the fidgety old lady, her fat poodle, the parrot that talked Spanish, and the library where she reveled. Laurie enjoyed that immensely; and when she told about the prim old gentleman who came once to woo Aunt March, and, in the middle of a fine speech, how Poll had tweaked his wig off to his great dismay, the boy lay back and laughed till the tears ran down his cheeks, and a maid popped her head in to see what was the matter.

"Oh! That does me no end of good. Tell on, please," he said, taking his face out of the sofa cushion, red and shining with merriment.

Much elated with her success, Jo did "tell on," all about their plays and plans, their hopes and fears for Father, and the most interesting events of the little world in which the sisters lived. Then they got to talking about books, and to Jo's delight, she found that Laurie loved them as well as she did, and had read even more than herself.

"If you like them so much, come down and see ours. Grandpa is out, so you needn't be afraid," said Laurie, getting up.

"I'm not afraid of anything," returned Jo, with a toss of the head.

"I don't believe you are!" exclaimed the boy, looking at her with much admiration, though he privately thought she would have good reason to be a trifle afraid of the old gentleman, if she met him in some of his moods.

The atmosphere of the whole house being summerlike, Laurie led the way from room to room, letting Jo stop to examine whatever struck her fancy; and so at last they came to the library, where she clapped her hands and pranced, as she always did when especially delighted. It was lined with books, and there were pictures and statues, and distracting little cabinets full of coins and curiosities, and Sleepy Hollow chairs, and queer tables, and bronzes, and, best of all, a great open fireplace with quaint tiles all round it.

"What richness!" sighed Jo, sinking into the depth of a velvet chair and gazing about her with an air of intense satisfaction. "Theodore Laurence, you ought to be the happiest boy in the world," she added impressively.

"A fellow can't live on books," said Laurie, shaking his head as he perched on a table opposite.

Before he could say more, a bell rang, and Jo flew up, exclaiming with alarm, "Mercy me! It's your grandpa!"

"Well, what if it is? You are not afraid of anything, you know," returned the boy, looking wicked.

"I think I am a little bit afraid of him, but I don't know why I should be. Marmee said I might come, and I don't think you're any the worse for it," said Jo, composing herself, though she kept her eyes on the door.

"I'm a great deal better for it, and ever so much obliged. I'm only afraid you are very tired talking to me; it was *so* pleasant, I couldn't bear to stop," said Laurie gratefully.

"The doctor to see you, sir," and the maid beckoned as she spoke.

"Would you mind if I left you for a minute? I suppose I must see him," said Laurie.

"Don't mind me. I'm as happy as a cricket here," answered Jo.

Laurie went away, and his guest amused herself in her own way. She was standing before a fine portrait of the old gentleman when the door opened again, and, without turning, she said decidedly, "I'm sure now that I shouldn't be afraid of him, for he's got kind eyes, though his mouth is grim, and he looks as if he had a tremendous will of his own. He isn't as handsome as *my* grandfather, but I like him."

"Thank you, ma'am," said a gruff voice behind her, and there, to her great dismay, stood old Mr. Laurence.

Poor Jo blushed till she couldn't blush any redder, and her heart began to beat uncomfortably fast as she thought what she had said. For a minute a wild desire to run away possessed her, but that was cowardly, and the girls would laugh at her; so she resolved to stay and get out of the scrape as she could. A second look showed her that the living eyes, under the bushy gray eyebrows, were kinder even than the painted ones; and there was a sly twinkle in them, which lessened her fear a good deal. The gruff voice was gruffer than ever, as the old gentleman said abruptly, after the dreadful pause, "So you're not afraid of me, hey?"

"Not much, sir."

"And you don't think me as handsome as your grandfather?"

"Not quite, sir."

"And I've got a tremendous will, have I?"

"I only said I thought so."

"But you like me in spite of it?"

"Yes, I do, sir."

That answer pleased the old gentleman; he gave a short laugh, shook hands with her, and, putting his finger under her chin, turned up her face, examined it gravely, and let it go, saying with a nod, "You've got your grandfather's spirit, if you haven't his face. He *was* a fine man, my dear; but, what is better, he was a brave and an honest one, and I was proud to be his friend."

"Thank you, sir." And Jo was quite comfortable after that, for it suited her exactly.

"What have you been doing to this boy of mine, hey?" was the next question, sharply put.

"Only trying to be neighborly, sir." And Jo told how her visit came about.

"You think he needs cheering up a bit, do you?"

"Yes, sir, he seems a little lonely, and young folks would do him good perhaps. We are only girls, but we should be glad to help if we could, for we don't forget the splendid Christmas present you sent us," said Jo eagerly.

"Tut, tut, tut! That was the boy's affair. How is the poor woman?"

"Doing nicely, sir." And off went Jo, talking very fast, as she told all about the Hummels, in whom her mother had interested richer friends than they were.

"Just her father's way of doing good. I shall come and see your mother some fine day. Tell her so. There's the tea bell, we have it early on the boy's account. Come down and go on being neighborly."

"If you'd like to have me, sir."

"Shouldn't ask you, if I didn't." And Mr. Laurence offered her his arm with old-fashioned courtesy.

"What *would* Meg say to this?" thought Jo, as she was marched away, while her eyes danced with fun as she imagined herself telling the story at home.

"Hey! Why, what the dickens has come to the fellow?" said the old gentleman, as Laurie came running downstairs and brought up with a start of surprise at the astonishing sight of Jo arm in arm with his redoubtable grandfather.

"I didn't know you'd come, sir," he began, as Jo gave him a triumphant little glance.

"That's evident, by the way you racket downstairs. Come to your tea, sir, and behave like a gentleman." And having pulled the boy's hair by way of a caress, Mr. Laurence walked on, while Laurie went through a series of comic evolutions behind their backs, which nearly produced an explosion of laughter from Jo.

The old gentleman did not say much as he drank his four cups of tea, but he watched the young people, who soon chatted away like old friends, and the change in his grandson did not escape him. There was color, light, and life in the boy's face now, vivacity in his manner, and genuine merriment in his laugh.

"She's right, the lad *is* lonely. I'll see what these little girls can do for him," thought Mr. Laurence, as he looked and listened. He liked Jo, for her odd, blunt ways suited him, and she seemed to understand the boy almost as well as if she had been one herself.

If the Laurences had been what Jo called "prim and poky," she would not have got on at all, for such people always made her shy and awkward; but finding them free and easy, she was so herself, and made a good impression. When they rose she proposed to go, but Laurie said he had something more to show her, and took her away to the conservatory, which had been lighted for her benefit. It seemed quite fairylike to Jo, as she went up and down the walks, enjoying the blooming walls on either side, the soft light, the damp sweet air, and the wonderful vines and trees that hung about her, while her new friend cut the finest flowers till his hands were full; then he tied them up, saying, with the happy look Jo liked to see, "Please give these to your mother, and tell her I like the medicine she sent me very much."

They found Mr. Laurence standing before the fire in the great drawing room, but Jo's attention was entirely absorbed by a grand piano, which stood open.

"Do you play?" she asked, turning to Laurie with a respectful expression.

"Sometimes," he answered modestly.

"Please do now. I want to hear it, so I can tell Beth."

"Won't you first?"

"Don't know how. Too stupid to learn, but I love music dearly."

So Laurie played and Jo listened, with her nose luxuriously buried in heliotrope and tea roses. Her respect and regard for the "Laurence boy" increased very much, for he played remarkably well and didn't put on any airs. She wished Beth could hear him, but she did not say so, only praised him till he was quite abashed, and his grandfather came to the rescue. "That will do, that will do, young lady. Too many sugarplums are not good for him. His music isn't bad, but I hope he will do as well in more important things. Going? Well, I'm much obliged to you, and I hope you'll come again. My respects to your mother. Good night, Doctor Jo."

He shook hands kindly, but looked as if something did not please him. When they got into the hall, Jo asked Laurie if she had said anything amiss. He shook his head.

"No, it was me; he doesn't like to hear me play."

"Why not?"

"I'll tell you some day. John is going home with you, as I can't."

"No need of that. I am not a young lady, and it's only a step. Take care of yourself, won't you?"

"Yes, but you will come again, I hope?"

"If you promise to come and see us after you are well."

"I will."

"Good night, Laurie!"

"Good night, Jo, good night!"

When all the afternoon's adventures had been told, the family felt inclined to go visiting in a body, for each found something very attractive in the big house on the other side of the hedge. Mrs. March wanted to talk of her father with the old man who had not forgotten him, Meg longed to walk in the conservatory, Beth sighed for the grand piano, and Amy was eager to see the fine pictures and statues.

"Mother, why didn't Mr. Laurence like to have Laurie play?" asked Jo, who was of an inquiring disposition.

"I am not sure, but I think it was because his son, Laurie's father, married an Italian lady, a musician, which displeased the old man, who is very proud. The lady was good and lovely and accomplished, but he did not like her, and never saw his son after he married. They both died when Laurie was a little child, and then his grandfather took him home. I fancy the boy, who was born in Italy, is not very strong, and the old man is afraid of losing him, which makes him so careful. Laurie comes naturally by his love of music, for he is like his mother, and I dare say his grandfather fears that he may want to be a musician. At any rate, his skill reminds him of the woman he did not like, and so he 'glowered,' as Jo said."

"Dear me, how romantic!" exclaimed Meg.

"How silly!" said Jo. "Let him be a musician if he wants to, and not plague his life out sending him to college, when he hates to go."

"That's why he has such handsome black eyes and pretty manners, I suppose. Italians are always nice," said Meg, who was a little sentimental.

"What do you know about his eyes and his manners? You never spoke to him, hardly," cried Jo, who was *not* sentimental.

"I saw him at the party, and what you tell shows that he knows how to behave. That was a nice little speech about the medicine Mother sent him."

"He meant the blancmange, I suppose."

"How stupid you are, child! He meant you, of course."

"Did he?" And Jo opened her eyes as if it had never occurred to her before.

"I never saw such a girl! You don't know a compliment when you get it," said Meg, with the air of a young lady who knew all about the matter.

"I think they are great nonsense, and I'll thank you not to be silly and spoil my fun. Laurie's a nice boy and I like him, and I won't have any sentimental stuff about compliments and such rubbish. We'll all be good to him because he hasn't got any mother, and he *may* come over and see us, mayn't he, Marmee?"

"Yes, Jo, your little friend is very welcome, and I hope Meg will remember that children should be children as long as they can."

"I don't call myself a child, and I'm not in my teens yet," observed Amy. "What do you say, Beth?"

"I was thinking about our 'Pilgrim's Progress,' " answered Beth, who had not heard a word. "How we got out of the Slough and through the Wicket Gate by resolving to be good, and up the steep hill by trying; and that maybe the house over there, full of splendid things, is going to be our Palace Beautiful."

"We have got to get by the lions first," said Jo, as if she rather liked the prospect.

Chapter 6

Beth Finds the Palace Beautiful

THE BIG HOUSE did prove a Palace Beautiful, though it took some time for all to get in, and Beth found it very hard to pass the lions. Old Mr. Laurence was the biggest one, but after he had called, said something funny or kind to each one of the girls, and talked over old times with their mother, nobody felt much afraid of him, except timid Beth. The other lion was the fact that they were poor and Laurie rich, for this made them shy of accepting favors which they could not return. But, after a while, they found that he considered them the benefactors, and could not do enough to show how grateful he was for Mrs. March's motherly welcome, their cheerful society, and the comfort he took in that humble home of theirs. So they soon forgot their pride and interchanged kindnesses without stopping to think which was the greater.

All sorts of pleasant things happened about that time, for the new friendship flourished like grass in spring. Every one liked Laurie, and he privately informed his tutor that "the Marches were regularly splendid girls." With the delightful enthusiasm of youth, they took the solitary boy into their midst and made much of him, and he found something very charming in the innocent companionship of these simple-hearted girls. Never having known mother or sisters, he was quick to feel the influences they brought about him, and their busy, lively ways made him ashamed of the indolent life he led. He was tired of books, and found people so interesting now that Mr. Brooke was obliged to make very unsatisfactory reports, for Laurie was always playing truant and running over to the Marches'.

"Never mind, let him take a holiday, and make it up afterward," said the old gentleman. "The good lady next door says he is studying too hard and needs young society, amusement, and exercise. I suspect she is right, and that I've been coddling the fellow as if I'd been his grandmother. Let him do what he likes, as long as he is happy. He can't get into mischief in that little nunnery over there, and Mrs. March is doing more for him than we can."

What good times they had, to be sure! Such plays and tableaux, such sleigh rides and skating frolics, such pleasant evenings in the old parlor, and now and then such gay little parties at the great house. Meg could walk in the conservatory whenever she liked and revel in bouquets, Jo browsed over the new library voraciously, and convulsed the old gentleman with her criticisms, Amy copied pictures and enjoyed beauty to her heart's content, and Laurie played "lord of the manor" in the most delightful style.

But Beth, though yearning for the grand piano, could not pluck up courage to go to the "Mansion of Bliss," as Meg called it. She went once with Jo, but the old gentleman, not being aware of her infirmity, stared at her so hard from under his heavy eyebrows, and said "Hey!" so loud, that he frightened her so much her "feet chattered on the floor," she told her mother; and she ran away, declaring she would never go there any more, not even for the dear piano. No persuasions or enticements could overcome her fear, till, the fact coming to Mr. Laurence's ear in some mysterious way, he set about mending matters. During one of the brief calls he made, he artfully led the conversation to music, and talked away about great singers whom he had seen, fine organs he had heard, and told such charming anecdotes that Beth found it impossible to stay in her distant corner, but crept nearer and nearer, as if fascinated. At the back of his chair she stopped and stood listening, with her great eyes wide open and her cheeks red with the excitement of this unusual performance. Taking no more notice of her than if she had been a fly, Mr. Laurence talked on about Laurie's lessons and teachers; and presently, as if the idea had just occurred to him, he said to Mrs. March—

"The boy neglects his music now, and I'm glad of it, for he was getting too fond of it. But the piano suffers for want of use. Wouldn't some of your girls like to run over, and practice on it now and then, just to keep it in tune, you know, ma'am?"

Beth took a step forward, and pressed her hands tightly together to keep from clapping them, for this was an irresistible temptation, and the thought of practicing on that splendid instrument quite took her breath away. Before Mrs. March could reply, Mr. Laurence went on with an odd little nod and smile—

"They needn't see or speak to anyone, but run in at any time; for I'm shut up in my study at the other end of the house, Laurie is out a great deal, and the servants are never near the drawing room after nine o'clock."

Here he rose, as if going, and Beth made up her mind to speak, for that last arrangement left nothing to be desired. "Please tell the young ladies what I say, and if they don't care to come, why, never mind." Here a little hand slipped into his, and Beth looked up at him with a face full of gratitude, as she said, in her earnest yet timid way—

"O sir, they do care, very, very much!"

"Are you the musical girl?" he asked, without any startling "Hey!" as he looked down at her very kindly.

"I'm Beth. I love it dearly, and I'll come, if you are quite sure nobody will hear me—and be disturbed," she added, fearing to be rude, and trembling at her own boldness as she spoke.

"Not a soul, my dear. The house is empty half the day; so come and drum away as much as you like, and I shall be obliged to you."

"How kind you are, sir!"

Beth blushed like a rose under the friendly look he wore; but she was not frightened now, and gave the big hand a grateful squeeze because she had no words to thank him for the precious gift he had given her. The old gentleman softly stroked the hair off her forehead, and, stooping down, he kissed her, saying, in a tone few people ever heard—

"I had a little girl once, with eyes like these. God bless you, my dear! Good day, madam." And away he went, in a great hurry.

Beth had a rapture with her mother, and then rushed up to impart the glorious news to her family of invalids, as the girls were not at home. How blithely she sang that evening, and how they all laughed at her because she woke Amy in the night by playing the piano on her face in her sleep. Next day, having seen both the old and young gentleman out of the house, Beth, after two or three retreats, fairly got in at the side door, and made her way as noiselessly as any mouse to the drawing room where her idol stood. Quite by accident, of course, some pretty, easy music lay on the piano, and with trembling fingers and frequent stops to listen and look about, Beth at last touched the great instrument, and straightway forgot her fear, herself, and everything else but the unspeakable delight which the music gave her, for it was like the voice of a beloved friend.

She stayed till Hannah came to take her home to dinner; but she had no appetite, and could only sit and smile upon everyone in a general state of beatitude.

After that, the little brown hood slipped through the hedge nearly every day, and the great drawing room was haunted by a tuneful spirit that came and went unseen. She never knew that Mr. Laurence often opened his study door to hear the old-fashioned airs he liked; she never saw Laurie mount guard in the hall to warn the servants away; she never suspected that the exercise books and new songs which she found in the rack were put there for her especial benefit; and when he talked to her about music at home, she only thought how kind he was to tell things that helped her so much. So she enjoyed herself heartily, and found, what isn't always the case, that her granted wish was all she had hoped. Perhaps it was because she was so grateful for this blessing that a greater was given her; at any rate, she deserved both.

"Mother, I'm going to work Mr. Laurence a pair of slippers. He is so kind to me, I must thank him, and I don't know any other way. Can I do it?" asked Beth, a few weeks after that eventful call of his.

"Yes, dear. It will please him very much, and be a nice way of thanking him. The girls will help you about them, and I will pay for the making up," replied Mrs. March, who took peculiar pleasure in granting Beth's requests because she so seldom asked anything for herself.

After many serious discussions with Meg and Jo, the pattern was chosen, the materials bought, and the slippers begun. A cluster of grave yet cheerful pansies on a deeper purple ground was pronounced very appropriate and pretty, and Beth worked away early and late, with occasional lifts over hard parts. She was a nimble little needlewoman, and they were finished before anyone got tired of them. Then she wrote a very short, simple note, and, with Laurie's help, got them smuggled onto the study table one morning before the old gentleman was up.

When this excitement was over, Beth waited to see what would happen. All that day passed and a part of the next before any acknowledgment arrived, and she was beginning to fear she had offended her crotchety friend. On the afternoon of the second day, she went out to do an errand and give poor Joanna, the invalid doll, her daily exercise. As she came up the street, on her return, she saw three, yes, four heads popping in and out of the parlor windows, and the moment they saw her, several hands were waved, and several joyful voices screamed—

"Here's a letter from the old gentleman! Come quick, and read it!"

"O Beth, he's sent you—" began Amy, gesticulating with unseemly energy, but she got no further, for Jo quenched her by slamming down the window.

Beth hurried on in a flutter of suspense. At the door her sisters seized and bore her to the parlor in a triumphal procession, all pointing and all saying at once, "Look there! look there!" Beth did look, and turned pale with delight and surprise, for there stood a little cabinet piano, with a letter lying on the glossy lid, directed like a sign board to "Miss Elizabeth March."

"For me?" gasped Beth, holding onto Jo and feeling as if

she should tumble down, it was such an overwhelming thing altogether.

"Yes, all for you, my precious! Isn't it splendid of him? Don't you think he's the dearest old man in the world? Here's the key in the letter. We didn't open it, but we are dying to know what he says," cried Jo, hugging her sister and offering the note.

"You read it! I can't, I feel so queer! Oh, it is too lovely!" And Beth hid her face in Jo's apron, quite upset by her present.

Jo opened the paper and began to laugh, for the first words she saw were—

"MISS MARCH:
    Dear Madam—"

"How nice it sounds! I wish someone would write to me so!" said Amy, who thought the old-fashioned address very elegant.

" 'I have had many pairs of slippers in my life, but I never had any that suited me so well as yours,' " continued Jo. " 'Heartsease is my favorite flower, and these will always remind me of the gentle giver. I like to pay my debts, so I know you will allow "the old gentleman" to send you something which once belonged to the little granddaughter he lost. With hearty thanks and best wishes, I remain

" 'Your grateful friend and humble servant,
                                        " 'JAMES LAURENCE.'

"There, Beth, that's an honor to be proud of, I'm sure! Laurie told me how fond Mr. Laurence used to be of the child who died, and how he kept all her little things carefully. Just think, he's given you her piano. That comes of having big blue eyes and loving music," said Jo, trying to soothe Beth, who trembled and looked more excited than she had ever been before.

"See the cunning brackets to hold candles, and the nice green silk, puckered up, with a gold rose in the middle, and the pretty rack and stool, all complete," added Meg, opening the instrument and displaying its beauties.

" 'Your humble servant, James Laurence.' Only think of his writing that to you. I'll tell the girls. They'll think it's splendid," said Amy, much impressed by the note.

"Try it, honey. Let's hear the sound of the baby pianny," said Hannah, who always took a share in the family joys and sorrows.

So Beth tried it, and everyone pronounced it the most remarkable piano ever heard. It had evidently been newly tuned and put in apple-pie order, but, perfect as it was, I think the real charm of it lay in the happiest of all happy faces which leaned over it, as Beth lovingly touched the beautiful black and white keys and pressed the bright pedals.

"You'll have to go and thank him," said Jo, by way of a joke, for the idea of the child's really going never entered her head.

"Yes, I mean to. I guess I'll go now, before I get frightened thinking about it." And, to the utter amazement of the assembled family, Beth walked deliberately down the garden, through the hedge, and in at the Laurences' door.

"Well, I wish I may die if it ain't the queerest thing I ever see! The pianny has turned her head! She'd never have gone in her right mind," cried Hannah, staring after her, while the girls were rendered quite speechless by the miracle.

They would have been still more amazed if they had seen what Beth did afterward. If you will believe me, she went and knocked at the study door before she gave herself time to think, and when a gruff voice called out, "Come in!" she did go in, right up to Mr. Laurence, who looked quite taken aback, and held out her hand, saying, with only a small quaver in her voice, "I came to thank you, sir, for——" But she didn't finish, for he looked so friendly that she forgot her speech and, only remembering that he had lost the little girl he loved, she put both arms round his neck and kissed him.

If the roof of the house had suddenly flown off, the old gentleman wouldn't have been more astonished; but he liked it —oh, dear, yes, he liked it amazingly!—and was so touched and pleased by that confiding little kiss that all his crustiness vanished; and he just set her on his knee, and laid his wrinkled cheek against her rosy one, feeling as if he had got his own little granddaughter back again. Beth ceased to fear him from that moment, and sat there talking to him as cozily as if she had known him all her life, for love casts out fear, and gratitude can conquer pride. When she went home, he walked with her to her own gate, shook hands cordially, and touched his hat as he marched back again, looking very stately and erect, like a handsome, soldierly old gentleman, as he was.

When the girls saw that performance, Jo began to dance a jig, by way of expressing her satisfaction, Amy nearly fell out of the window in her surprise, and Meg exclaimed, with uplifted hands, "Well, I do believe the world is coming to an end!"

Chapter 7

Amy's Valley of Humiliation

"THAT BOY is a perfect Cyclops, isn't he?" said Amy, one day, as Laurie clattered by on horseback, with a flourish of his whip as he passed.

"How dare you say so, when he's got both his eyes? And very handsome ones they are, too," cried Jo, who resented any slighting remarks about her friend.

"I didn't say anything about his eyes, and I don't see why you need fire up when I admire his riding."

"Oh, my goodness! That little goose means a centaur, and she called him a Cyclops," exclaimed Jo, with a burst of laughter.

"You needn't be so rude, it's only a 'lapse of lingy,' as Mr. Davis says," retorted Amy, finishing Jo with her Latin. "I just wish I had a little of the money Laurie spends on that horse," she added, as if to herself, yet hoping her sisters would hear.

"Why?" asked Meg kindly, for Jo had gone off in another laugh at Amy's second blunder.

"I need it so much. I'm dreadfully in debt, and it won't be my turn to have the rag money for a month."

"In debt, Amy? What do you mean?" And Meg looked sober.

"Why, I owe at least a dozen pickled limes, and I can't pay them, you know, till I have money, for Marmee forbade my having anything charged at the shop."

"Tell me all about it. Are limes the fashion now? It used to be pricking bits of rubber to make balls." And Meg tried to keep her countenance, Amy looked so grave and important.

"Why, you see, the girls are always buying them, and unless you want to be thought mean, you must do it, too. It's nothing but limes now, for everyone is sucking them in their desks in schooltime, and trading them off for pencils, bead rings, paper dolls, or something else, at recess. If one girl likes another, she gives her a lime; if she's mad with her, she eats one before her face, and doesn't offer even a suck. They treat by turns, and I've had ever so many but haven't returned them, and I ought, for they are debts of honor, you know."

"How much will pay them off, and restore your credit?" asked Meg, taking out her purse.

"A quarter would more than do it, and leave a few cents over for a treat for you. Don't you like limes?"

"Not much; you may have my share. Here's the money. Make it last as long as you can, for it isn't very plenty, you know."

"Oh, thank you! It must be so nice to have pocket money! I'll have a grand feast, for I haven't tasted a lime this week. I felt delicate about taking any, as I couldn't return them, and I'm actually suffering for one."

Next day Amy was rather late at school; but could not resist the temptation of displaying, with pardonable pride, a moist brown-paper parcel, before she consigned it to the inmost recesses of her desk. During the next few minutes the rumor that Amy March had got twenty-four delicious limes (she ate one on the way) and was going to treat circulated through her "set," and the attentions of her friends became quite overwhelming. Katy Brown invited her to her next party on the spot; Mary Kingsley insisted on lending her her watch till recess; and Jenny Snow, a satirical young lady, who had basely twitted Amy upon her limeless state, promptly buried the hatchet and offered to furnish answers to certain appalling sums. But Amy had not forgotten Miss Snow's cutting remarks about "some persons whose noses were not too flat to smell other people's limes, and stuck-up people who were not too proud to ask for them"; and she instantly crushed "that Snow girl's" hopes by the withering telegram, "You needn't be so polite all of a sudden, for you won't get any."

A distinguished personage happened to visit the school that morning, and Amy's beautifully drawn maps received praise, which honor to her foe rankled in the soul of Miss Snow, and caused Miss March to assume the airs of a studious young peacock. But, alas, alas! Pride goes before a fall, and the revengeful Snow turned the tables with disastrous success. No sooner had the guest paid the usual stale compliments and bowed himself out, than Jenny, under pretense of asking an important question, informed Mr. Davis, the teacher, that Amy March had pickled limes in her desk.

Now Mr. Davis had declared limes a contraband article, and solemnly vowed to publicly ferrule the first person who was found breaking the law. This much-enduring man had succeeded in banishing chewing gum after a long and stormy war, had made a bonfire of the confiscated novels and newspapers, had suppressed a private post office, had forbidden distortions of the face, nicknames, and caricatures, and done all that one man could do to keep half a hundred rebellious girls in order. Boys are trying enough to human patience, goodness knows, but girls are infinitely more so, especially to nervous gentlemen with tyrannical tempers and no more talent for teaching than Dr. Blimber. Mr. Davis knew any quantity of Greek, Latin, algebra, and ologies of all sorts so he was called a fine teacher, and manners, morals, feelings, and examples were not considered of any particular importance. It was a most unfortunate moment for denouncing Amy, and Jenny knew it. Mr. Davis had evidently taken his coffee too strong that morning, there was an east wind, which always affected his neuralgia, and his pupils had not done him the credit which he felt he deserved: therefore, to use the expressive, if not elegant, language of a schoolgirl, "he was as nervous as a witch and as cross as a bear." The word "limes" was like fire to powder, his yellow face flushed, and he rapped on his desk with an energy which made Jenny skip to her seat with unusual rapidity.

"Young ladies, attention, if you please!"

At the stern order the buzz ceased, and fifty pairs of blue, black, gray, and brown eyes were obediently fixed upon his awful countenance.

"Miss March, come to the desk."

Amy rose to comply with outward composure, but a secret

fear oppressed her, for the limes weighed upon her conscience.

"Bring with you the limes you have in your desk" was the unexpected command which arrested her before she got out of her seat.

"Don't take all," whispered her neighbor, a young lady of great presence of mind.

Amy hastily shook out half a dozen and laid the rest down before Mr. Davis, feeling that any man possessing a human heart would relent when that delicious perfume met his nose. Unfortunately, Mr. Davis particularly detested the odor of the fashionable pickle, and disgust added to his wrath.

"Is that all?"

"Not quite," stammered Amy.

"Bring the rest immediately."

With a despairing glance at her set, she obeyed.

"You are sure there are no more?"

"I never lie, sir."

"So I see. Now take these disgusting things two by two, and throw them out of the window."

There was a simultaneous sigh, which created quite a little gust, as the last hope fled, and the treat was ravished from their longing lips. Scarlet with shame and anger, Amy went to and fro six dreadful times, and as each doomed couple—looking oh! so plump and juicy—fell from her reluctant hands, a shout from the street completed the anguish of the girls, for it told them that their feast was being exulted over by the little Irish children, who were their sworn foes. This—this was too much; all flashed indignant or appealing glances at the inexorable Davis, and one passionate lime-lover burst into tears.

As Amy returned from her last trip, Mr. Davis gave a portentous "Hem!" and said, in his most impressive manner—

"Young ladies, you remember what I said to you a week ago. I am sorry this has happened, but I never allow my rules to be infringed, and I *never* break my word. Miss March, hold out your hand."

Amy started, and put both hands behind her, turning on him an imploring look which pleaded for her better than the words she could not utter. She was rather a favorite with "old

Davis," as, of course, he was called, and it's my private belief that he *would* have broken his word if the indignation of one irrepressible young lady had not found vent in a hiss. That hiss, faint as it was, irritated the irascible gentleman, and sealed the culprit's fate.

"Your hand, Miss March!" was the only answer her mute appeal received; and, too proud to cry or beseech, Amy set her teeth, threw back her head defiantly, and bore without flinching several tingling blows on her little palm. They were neither many nor heavy, but that made no difference to her. For the first time in her life she had been struck, and the disgrace, in her eyes, was as deep as if he had knocked her down.

"You will now stand on the platform till recess," said Mr. Davis, resolved to do the thing thoroughly, since he had begun.

That was dreadful. It would have been bad enough to go to her seat, and see the pitying faces of her friends, or the satisfied ones of her few enemies; but to face the whole school, with that shame fresh upon her, seemed impossible, and for a second she felt as if she could only drop down where she stood, and break her heart with crying. A bitter sense of wrong and the thought of Jenny Snow helped her to bear it, and, taking the ignominious place, she fixed her eyes on the stove funnel above what now seemed a sea of faces, and stood there, so motionless and white that the girls found it very hard to study with that pathetic figure before them.

During the fifteen minutes that followed, the proud and sensitive little girl suffered a shame and pain which she never forgot. To others it might seem a ludicrous or trivial affair, but to her it was a hard experience, for during the twelve years of her life she had been governed by love alone, and a blow of that sort had never touched her before. The smart of her hand and the ache of her heart were forgotten in the sting of the thought, "I shall have to tell at home, and they will be so disappointed in me!"

The fifteen minutes seemed an hour, but they came to an end at last, and the word "Recess!" had never seemed so welcome to her before.

"You can go, Miss March," said Mr. Davis, looking, as he felt, uncomfortable.

He did not soon forget the reproachful glance Amy gave him, as she went, without a word to anyone, straight into the anteroom, snatched her things, and left the place "forever," as she passionately declared to herself. She was in a sad state when she got home, and when the older girls arrived, some time later, an indignation meeting was held at once. Mrs. March did not say much but looked disturbed, and comforted her afflicted little daughter in her tenderest manner. Meg bathed the insulted hand with glycerine and tears, Beth felt that even her beloved kittens would fail as a balm for griefs like this, Jo wrathfully proposed that Mr. Davis be arrested without delay, and Hannah shook her fist at the "villain" and pounded potatoes for dinner as if she had him under her pestle.

No notice was taken of Amy's flight, except by her mates; but the sharp-eyed demoiselles discovered that Mr. Davis was quite benignant in the afternoon, also unusually nervous. Just before school closed, Jo appeared, wearing a grim expression as she stalked up to the desk, and delivered a letter from her mother, then collected Amy's property, and departed, carefully scraping the mud from her boots on the door mat, as if she shook the dust of the place off her feet.

"Yes, you can have a vacation from school, but I want you to study a little every day with Beth," said Mrs. March that evening. "I don't approve of corporal punishment, especially for girls. I dislike Mr. Davis's manner of teaching and don't think the girls you associate with are doing you any good, so I shall ask your father's advice before I send you anywhere else."

"That's good! I wish all the girls would leave, and spoil his old school. It's perfectly maddening to think of those lovely limes," sighed Amy, with the air of a martyr.

"I am not sorry you lost them, for you broke the rules, and deserved some punishment for disobedience" was the severe reply, which rather disappointed the young lady, who expected nothing but sympathy.

"Do you mean you are glad I was disgraced before the whole school?" cried Amy.

"I should not have chosen that way of mending a fault," replied her mother, "but I'm not sure that it won't do you more good than a milder method. You are getting to be rather conceited, my dear, and it is quite time you set about correcting it. You have a good many little gifts and virtues, but there is no need of parading them, for conceit spoils the finest genius. There is not much danger that real talent or goodness will be overlooked long; even if it is, the consciousness of possessing and using it well should satisfy one, and the great charm of all power is modesty."

"So it is!" cried Laurie, who was playing chess in a corner with Jo. "I knew a girl once, who had a really remarkable talent for music, and she didn't know it, never guessed what sweet little things she composed when she was alone, and wouldn't have believed it if anyone had told her."

"I wish I'd known that nice girl; maybe she would have helped me, I'm so stupid," said Beth, who stood beside him, listening eagerly.

"You do know her, and she helps you better than anyone else could," answered Laurie, looking at her with such mischievous meaning in his merry black eyes that Beth suddenly turned very red, and hid her face in the sofa cushion, quite overcome by such an unexpected discovery.

Jo let Laurie win the game to pay for that praise of her Beth, who could not be prevailed upon to play for them after her compliment. So Laurie did his best, and sang delightfully, being in a particularly lively humor, for to the Marches he seldom showed the moody side of his character. When he was gone, Amy, who had been pensive all the evening, said suddenly, as if busy over some new idea, "Is Laurie an accomplished boy?"

"Yes, he has had an excellent education, and has much talent; he will make a fine man, if not spoiled by petting," replied her mother.

"And he isn't conceited, is he?" asked Amy.

"Not in the least. That is why he is so charming and we all like him so much."

"I see. It's nice to have accomplishments and be elegant, but not to show off or get perked up," said Amy thoughtfully.

"These things are always seen and felt in a person's manner and conversation, if modestly used, but it is not necessary to display them," said Mrs. March.

"Any more than it's proper to wear all your bonnets and gowns and ribbons at once, that folks may know you've got them," added Jo; and the lecture ended in a laugh.

Chapter 8

Jo Meets Apollyon

"GIRLS, WHERE are you going?" asked Amy, coming into their room one Saturday afternoon, and finding them getting ready to go out with an air of secrecy which excited her curiosity.

"Never mind. Little girls shouldn't ask questions," returned Jo sharply.

Now if there *is* anything mortifying to our feelings when we are young, it is to be told that; and to be bidden to "run away, dear" is still more trying to us. Amy bridled up at this insult, and determined to find out the secret, if she teased for an hour. Turning to Meg, who never refused her anything very long, she said coaxingly, "Do tell me! I should think you might let me go, too, for Beth is fussing over her piano, and I haven't got anything to do, and am *so* lonely."

"I can't, dear, because you aren't invited," began Meg, but Jo broke in impatiently, "Now, Meg, be quiet or you will spoil it all. You can't go, Amy, so don't be a baby, and whine about it."

"You are going somewhere with Laurie, I know you are; you were whispering and laughing together on the sofa last night, and you stopped when I came in. Aren't you going with him?"

"Yes, we are; now do be still, and stop bothering."

Amy held her tongue, but used her eyes, and saw Meg slip a fan into her pocket.

"I know! I know! You're going to the theater to see the *Seven Castles*!" she cried, adding resolutely, "and I *shall* go, for Mother said I might see it; and I've got my rag money, and it was mean not to tell me in time."

"Just listen to me a minute, and be a good child," said Meg soothingly. "Mother doesn't wish you to go this week, because your eyes are not well enough yet to bear the light of this fairy piece. Next week you can go with Beth and Hannah, and have a nice time."

"I don't like that half as well as going with you and Laurie. Please let me. I've been sick with this cold so long, and shut up, I'm dying for some fun. Do, Meg! I'll be ever so good," pleaded Amy, looking as pathetic as she could.

"Suppose we take her. I don't believe Mother would mind, if we bundle her up well," began Meg.

"If *she* goes *I* shan't; and if I don't, Laurie won't like it; and it will be very rude, after he invited only us, to go and drag in Amy. I should think she'd hate to poke herself where she isn't wanted," said Jo crossly, for she disliked the trouble of overseeing a fidgety child when she wanted to enjoy herself.

Her tone and manner angered Amy, who began to put her boots on, saying, in her most aggravating way, "I *shall* go; Meg says I may; and if I pay for myself, Laurie hasn't anything to do with it."

"You can't sit with us, for our seats are reserved, and you mustn't sit alone; so Laurie will give you his place, and that will spoil our pleasure; or he'll get another seat for you, and that isn't proper when you weren't asked. You shan't stir a step, so you may just stay where you are," scolded Jo, crosser than ever, having just pricked her finger in her hurry.

Sitting on the floor with one boot on, Amy began to cry and Meg to reason with her, when Laurie called from below, and the two girls hurried down, leaving their sister wailing; for now and then she forgot her grown-up ways and acted like a spoiled child. Just as the party was setting out, Amy called over the banisters in a threatening tone, "You'll be sorry for this, Jo March, see if you ain't."

"Fiddlesticks!" returned Jo, slamming the door.

They had a charming time, for *The Seven Castles of the Diamond Lake* was as brilliant and wonderful as heart could wish. But, in spite of the comical red imps, sparkling elves, and gorgeous princes and princesses, Jo's pleasure had a drop of bitterness in it: the fairy queen's yellow curls reminded her of Amy, and between the acts she amused herself with wondering what her sister would do to make her "sorry for it." She and Amy had had many lively skirmishes in the course of their lives, for both had quick tempers and were apt to be violent when fairly roused. Amy teased Jo, and Jo irritated Amy, and semioccasional explosions occurred, of which both were much ashamed afterward. Although the oldest, Jo had the least self-control, and had hard times trying to curb the fiery spirit which was continually getting her into trouble, her anger never lasted long, and having humbly confessed her fault, she sincerely repented and tried to do better. Her sisters used to say that they rather liked to get Jo into a fury because she was such an angel afterward. Poor Jo tried desperately to be good, but her bosom enemy was always ready to flame up and defeat her, and it took years of patient effort to subdue it.

When they got home, they found Amy reading in the parlor. She assumed an injured air as they came in, never lifted her eyes from her book, or asked a single question. Perhaps curiosity might have conquered resentment, if Beth had not been there to inquire and receive a glowing description of the play. On going up to put away her best hat, Jo's first look was toward the bureau, for in their last quarrel Amy had soothed her feelings by turning Jo's top drawer upside down on the floor. Everything was in its place, however, and after a hasty glance into her various closets, bags, and boxes, Jo decided that Amy had forgiven and forgotten her wrongs.

There Jo was mistaken, for next day she made a discovery which produced a tempest. Meg, Beth, and Amy were sitting together, late in the afternoon, when Jo burst into the room, looking excited and demanding breathlessly, "Has anyone taken my book?"

Meg and Beth said, "No," at once, and looked surprised. Amy poked the fire and said nothing. Jo saw her color rise and was down upon her in a minute.

"Amy, you've got it!"

"No, I haven't."

"You know where it is, then!"

"No, I don't."

"That's a fib!" cried Jo, taking her by the shoulders, and looking fierce enough to frighten a much braver child than Amy.

"It isn't. I haven't got it, don't know where it is now, and don't care."

"You know something about it, and you'd better tell at once, or I'll make you." And Jo gave her a slight shake.

"Scold as much as you like, you'll never see your silly old book again," cried Amy, getting excited in her turn.

"Why not?"

"I burned it up."

"What! My little book I was so fond of, and worked over, and meant to finish before Father got home? Have you really burned it?" said Jo, turning very pale, while her eyes kindled and her hands clutched Amy nervously.

"Yes, I did! I told you I'd make you pay for being so cross yesterday, and I have, so—"

Amy got no farther, for Jo's hot temper mastered her, and she shook Amy till her teeth chattered in her head, crying, in a passion of grief and anger—

"You wicked, wicked girl! I never can write it again, and I'll never forgive you as long as I live."

Meg flew to rescue Amy, and Beth to pacify Jo, but Jo was quite beside herself; and, with a parting box on her sister's ear, she rushed out of the room up to the old sofa in the garret, and finished her fight alone.

The storm cleared up below, for Mrs. March came home, and, having heard the story, soon brought Amy to a sense of the wrong she had done her sister. Jo's book was the pride of her heart, and was regarded by her family as a literary sprout of great promise. It was only half a dozen little fairy tales, but Jo had worked over them patiently, putting her whole heart into her work, hoping to make something good enough to print. She had just copied them with great care, and had destroyed the old manuscript, so that Amy's bonfire had consumed the loving work of several years. It seemed a small loss to others, but to Jo it was a dreadful calamity, and she felt that it never could be made up to her. Beth mourned as for a departed kitten, and Meg refused to defend her pet; Mrs. March looked grave and grieved, and Amy felt that no one would love her till she had asked pardon for the act which she now regretted more than any of them.

When the tea bell rang, Jo appeared, looking so grim and unapproachable that it took all Amy's courage to say meekly—

"Please forgive me, Jo, I'm very, very sorry."

"I never shall forgive you" was Jo's stern answer, and from that moment she ignored Amy entirely.

No one spoke of the great trouble—not even Mrs. March —for all had learned by experience that when Jo was in that mood words were wasted, and the wisest course was to wait till some little accident, or her own generous nature, softened Jo's resentment and healed the breach. It was not a happy evening, for, though they sewed as usual, while their mother read aloud from Bremer, Scott, or Edgeworth, something was wanting, and the sweet home peace was disturbed. They felt this most when singing time came, for Beth could only play, Jo stood dumb as a stone, and Amy broke down, so Meg and Mother sang alone. But, in spite of their efforts to be as cheery as larks, the flutelike voices did not seem to chord as well as usual, and all felt out of tune.

As Jo received her good-night kiss, Mrs. March whispered gently, "My dear, don't let the sun go down upon your anger; forgive each other, help each other, and begin again tomorrow."

Jo wanted to lay her head down on that motherly bosom, and cry her grief and anger all away; but tears were an unmanly weakness, and she felt so deeply injured that she really *couldn't* quite forgive yet. So she winked hard, shook her head, and said gruffly because Amy was listening, "It was an abominable thing, and she doesn't deserve to be forgiven."

With that she marched off to bed, and there was no merry or confidential gossip that night.

Amy was much offended that her overtures of peace had been repulsed, and began to wish she had not humbled herself, to feel more injured than ever, and to plume herself on her superior virtue in a way which was particularly exasperating. Jo still looked like a thundercloud, and nothing went well all day. It was bitter cold in the morning; she dropped her precious turnover in the gutter, Aunt March had an attack of fidgets, Meg was pensive, Beth *would* look grieved and wistful when she got home, and Amy kept making remarks about people who were always talking about being good and yet wouldn't try when other people set them a virtuous example.

"Everybody is so hateful, I'll ask Laurie to go skating. He is always kind and jolly, and will put me to rights, I know," said Jo to herself, and off she went.

Amy heard the clash of skates, and looked out with an impatient exclamation.

"There! she promised I should go next time, for this is the last ice we shall have. But it's no use to ask such a crosspatch to take me."

"Don't say that. You *were* very naughty, and it *is* hard to forgive the loss of her precious little book; but I think she might do it now, and I guess she will, if you try her at the right minute," said Meg. "Go after them; don't say anything till Jo has got good-natured with Laurie, then take a quiet minute and just kiss her, or do some kind thing, and I'm sure she'll be friends again with all her heart."

"I'll try," said Amy, for the advice suited her, and after a flurry to get ready, she ran after the friends, who were just disappearing over the hill.

It was not far to the river, but both were ready before Amy reached them. Jo saw her coming, and turned her back. Laurie did not see, for he was carefully skating along the shore, sounding the ice, for a warm spell had preceded the cold snap.

"I'll go on to the first bend, and see if it's all right before we begin to race," Amy heard him say, as he shot away, looking like a young Russian in his fur-trimmed coat and cap.

Jo heard Amy panting after her run, stamping her feet and blowing her fingers as she tried to put her skates on, but Jo never turned and went slowly zigzagging down the river, taking a bitter, unhappy sort of satisfaction in her sister's troubles. She had cherished her anger till it grew strong and took possession of her, as evil thoughts and feelings always do unless cast out at once. As Laurie turned the bend, he shouted back—

"Keep near the shore; it isn't safe in the middle."

Jo heard, but Amy was just struggling to her feet and did not catch a word. Jo glanced over her shoulder, and the little demon she was harboring said in her ear—

"No matter whether she heard or not, let her take care of herself."

Laurie had vanished round the bend, Jo was just at the turn, and Amy, far behind, striking out toward the smoother ice in the middle of the river. For a minute Jo stood still with a strange feeling at her heart; then she resolved to go on, but something held and turned her round, just in time to see Amy throw up her hands and go down, with the sudden crash of rotten ice, the splash of water, and a cry that made Jo's heart stand still with fear. She tried to call Laurie, but her voice was gone; she tried to rush forward, but her feet seemed to have no strength in them; and, for a second, she could only stand motionless, staring with a terror-stricken face at the little blue hood above the black water. Something rushed swiftly by her, and Laurie's voice cried out—

"Bring a rail. Quick, quick!"

How she did it, she never knew; but for the next few minutes she worked as if possessed, blindly obeying Laurie, who was quite self-possessed, and, lying flat, held Amy up by his arm and hockey till Jo dragged a rail from the fence, and together they got the child out, more frightened than hurt.

"Now then, we must walk her home as fast as we can; pile our things on her, while I get off these confounded skates," cried Laurie, wrapping his coat round Amy, and tugging away at the straps, which never seemed so intricate before.

Shivering, dripping, and crying, they got Amy home, and after an exciting time of it, she fell asleep, rolled in blankets before a hot fire. During the bustle Jo had scarcely spoken but flown about, looking pale and wild, with her things half off, her dress torn, and her hands cut and bruised by ice and rails and refractory buckles. When Amy was comfortably asleep, the house quiet, and Mrs. March sitting by the bed, she called Jo to her and began to bind up the hurt hands.

"Are you sure she is safe?" whispered Jo, looking remorse-fully at the golden head, which might have been swept away from her sight forever under the treacherous ice.

"Quite safe, dear. She is not hurt, and won't even take cold, I think, you were so sensible in covering and getting her home quickly," replied her mother cheerfully.

"Laurie did it all. I only let her go. Mother, if she *should* die, it would be my fault." And Jo dropped down beside the bed in a passion of penitent tears, telling all that had happened, bitterly condemning her hardness of heart, and sobbing out her gratitude for being spared the heavy punishment which might have come upon her.

"It's my dreadful temper! I try to cure it; I think I have, and then it breaks out worse than ever. Oh, Mother, what shall I do? What shall I do?" cried poor Jo, in despair.

"Watch and pray, dear, never get tired of trying, and never think it is impossible to conquer your fault," said Mrs. March, drawing the blowzy head to her shoulder and kissing the wet cheek so tenderly that Jo cried harder than ever.

"You don't know, you can't guess how bad it is! It seems as if I could do anything when I'm in a passion; I get so savage, I could hurt anyone and enjoy it. I'm afraid I *shall* do something dreadful some day, and spoil my life, and make everybody hate me. Oh, Mother, help me, do help me!"

"I will, my child, I will. Don't cry so bitterly, but remember this day, and resolve with all your soul that you will never know another like it. Jo, dear, we all have our temptations, some far greater than yours, and it often takes us all our lives to conquer them. You think your temper is the worst in the world, but mine used to be just like it."

"Yours, Mother? Why, you are never angry!" And for the moment Jo forgot remorse in surprise.

"I've been trying to cure it for forty years, and have only succeeded in controlling it. I am angry nearly every day of my life, Jo, but I have learned not to show it; and I still hope to learn not to feel it, though it may take me another forty years to do so."

The patience and the humility of the face she loved so well was a better lesson to Jo than the wisest lecture, the sharpest reproof. She felt comforted at once by the sympathy and confidence given her; the knowledge that her mother had a fault like hers, and tried to mend it, made her own easier to bear and strengthened her resolution to cure it, though forty years seemed rather a long time to watch and pray to a girl of fifteen.

"Mother, are you angry when you fold your lips tight together and go out of the room sometimes, when Aunt March scolds or people worry you?" asked Jo, feeling nearer and dearer to her mother than ever before.

"Yes, I've learned to check the hasty words that rise to my lips, and when I feel that they mean to break out against my will, I just go away a minute, and give myself a little shake for being so weak and wicked," answered Mrs. March with a sigh and a smile, as she smoothed and fastened up Jo's disheveled hair.

"How did you learn to keep still? That is what troubles me —for the sharp words fly out before I know what I'm about, and the more I say the worse I get, till it's a pleasure to hurt people's feelings and say dreadful things. Tell me how you do it, Marmee dear."

"My good mother used to help me—"

"As you do us—" interrupted Jo, with a grateful kiss.

"But I lost her when I was a little older than you are, and for years had to struggle on alone, for I was too proud to confess my weakness to anyone else. I had a hard time, Jo, and shed a good many bitter tears over my failures, for in spite of my efforts I never seemed to get on. Then your father came, and I was so happy that I found it easy to be good. But by-and-by, when I had four little daughters round me and we were poor, then the old trouble began again, for I am not patient by nature, and it tried me very much to see my children wanting anything."

"Poor Mother! What helped you then?"

"Your father, Jo. He never loses patience—never doubts or complains—but always hopes, and works and waits so cheerfully that one is ashamed to do otherwise before him. He helped and comforted me, and showed me that I must try to practice all the virtues I would have my little girls possess, for I was their example. It was easier to try for your sakes than for my own; a startled or surprised look from one of you when I spoke sharply rebuked me more than any words could have done; and the love, respect, and confidence of my children was the sweetest reward I could receive for my efforts to be the woman I would have them copy."

"Oh, Mother, if I'm ever half as good as you, I shall be satisfied," cried Jo, much touched.

"I hope you will be a great deal better, dear, but you must keep watch over your 'bosom enemy,' as father calls it, or it may sadden, if not spoil your life. You have had a warning; remember it, and try with heart and soul to master this quick temper, before it brings you greater sorrow and regret than you have known today."

"I will try, Mother, I truly will. But you must help me, remind me, and keep me from flying out. I used to see Father sometimes put his finger on his lips, and look at you with a very kind but sober face, and you always folded your lips tight or went away: was he reminding you then?" asked Jo softly.

"Yes. I asked him to help me so, and he never forgot it, but saved me from many a sharp word by that little gesture and kind look."

Jo saw that her mother's eyes filled and her lips trembled as she spoke, and fearing that she had said too much, she whispered anxiously, "Was it wrong to watch you and to speak of it? I didn't mean to be rude, but it's so comfortable to say all I think to you, and feel so safe and happy here."

"My Jo, you may say anything to your mother, for it is my greatest happiness and pride to feel that my girls confide in me and know how much I love them."

"I thought I'd grieved you."

"No, dear; but speaking of Father reminded me how much I miss him, how much I owe him, and how faithfully I should watch and work to keep his little daughters safe and good for him."

"Yet you told him to go, Mother, and didn't cry when he went, and never complain now, or seem as if you needed any help," said Jo, wondering.

"I gave my best to the country I love, and kept my tears till he was gone. Why should I complain, when we both have merely done our duty and will surely be the happier for it in the end? If I don't seem to need help, it is because I have a better friend, even than Father, to comfort and sustain me. My child, the troubles and temptations of your life are beginning and may be many, but you can overcome and outlive them all if you learn to feel the strength and tenderness of your Heavenly Father as you do that of your earthly one. The more you love and trust Him, the nearer you will feel to Him, and the less you will depend on human power and wisdom. His love and care never tire or change, can never be taken from you, but may become the source of lifelong peace, happiness, and strength. Believe this heartily, and go to God with all your little cares, and hopes, and sins, and sorrows, as freely and confidingly as you come to your mother."

Jo's only answer was to hold her mother close, and in the silence which followed the sincerest prayer she had ever prayed left her heart without words; for in that sad yet happy hour, she had learned not only the bitterness of remorse and despair, but the sweetness of self-denial and self-control; and, led by her mother's hand, she had drawn nearer to the Friend who welcomes every child with a love stronger than that of any father, tenderer than that of any mother.

Amy stirred and sighed in her sleep, and, as if eager to begin at once to mend her fault, Jo looked up with an expression on her face which it had never worn before.

"I let the sun go down on my anger; I wouldn't forgive her, and today, if it hadn't been for Laurie, it might have been too late! How could I be so wicked?" said Jo, half aloud, as she leaned over her sister softly stroking the wet hair scattered on the pillow.

As if she heard, Amy opened her eyes, and held out her arms, with a smile that went straight to Jo's heart. Neither said a word, but they hugged one another close, in spite of the blankets, and everything was forgiven and forgotten in one hearty kiss.

Chapter 9

Meg Goes to Vanity Fair

"I DO THINK it was the most fortunate thing in the world that those children should have the measles just now," said Meg, one April day, as she stood packing the "go abroady" trunk in her room, surrounded by her sisters.

"And so nice of Annie Moffat not to forget her promise. A whole fortnight of fun will be regularly splendid," replied Jo, looking like a windmill as she folded skirts with her long arms.

"And such lovely weather, I'm so glad of that," added Beth, tidily sorting neck and hair ribbons in her best box, lent for the great occasion.

"I wish I was going to have a fine time and wear all these nice things," said Amy with her mouth full of pins, as she artistically replenished her sister's cushion.

"I wish you were all going, but as you can't, I shall keep my adventures to tell you when I come back. I'm sure it's the least I can do when you have been so kind, lending me things and helping me get ready," said Meg, glancing round the room at the very simple outfit, which seemed nearly perfect in their eyes.

"What did Mother give you out of the treasure box?" asked Amy, who had not been present at the opening of a certain cedar chest in which Mrs. March kept a few relics of past splendor, as gifts for her girls when the proper time came.

"A pair of silk stockings, that pretty carved fan, and a lovely blue sash. I wanted the violet silk, but there isn't time to make it over, so I must be contented with my old tarlatan."

"It will look nice over my new muslin skirt, and the sash will set it off beautifully. I wish I hadn't smashed my coral bracelet, for you might have had it," said Jo, who loved to give and lend, but whose possessions were usually too dilapidated to be of much use.

"There is a lovely old-fashioned pearl set in the treasure box, but Mother said real flowers were the prettiest ornament for a young girl, and Laurie promised to send me all I want," replied Meg. "Now, let me see, there's my new gray walking suit—just curl up the feather in my hat, Beth—then my poplin for Sunday and the small party—it looks heavy for spring, doesn't it? The violet silk would be so nice; oh, dear!"

"Never mind, you've got the tarlatan for the big party, and you always look like an angel in white," said Amy, brooding over the little store of finery in which her soul delighted.

"It isn't low-necked, and it doesn't sweep enough, but it will have to do. My blue housedress looks so well, turned and freshly trimmed, that I feel as if I'd got a new one. My silk sacque isn't a bit the fashion, and my bonnet doesn't look like Sallie's; I didn't like to say anything, but I was sadly disappointed in my umbrella. I told Mother black with a white handle, but she forgot and bought a green one with a yellowish handle. It's strong and neat, so I ought not to complain, but I know I shall feel ashamed of it beside Annie's silk one with a gold top," sighed Meg, surveying the little umbrella with great disfavor.

"Change it," advised Jo.

"I won't be so silly, or hurt Marmee's feelings, when she took so much pains to get my things. It's a nonsensical notion of mine, and I'm not going to give up to it. My silk stockings and two pairs of new gloves are my comfort. You are a dear to lend me yours, Jo. I feel so rich and sort of elegant, with two new pairs, and the old ones cleaned up for common." And Meg took a refreshing peep at her glove box.

"Annie Moffat has blue and pink bows on her nightcaps; would you put some on mine?" she asked, as Beth brought up a pile of snowy muslins, fresh from Hannah's hands.

"No, I wouldn't, for the smart caps won't match the plain gowns without any trimming on them. Poor folks shouldn't rig," said Jo decidedly.

"I wonder if I shall *ever* be happy enough to have real lace on my clothes and bows on my caps?" said Meg impatiently.

"You said the other day that you'd be perfectly happy if

you could only go to Annie Moffat's," observed Beth in her quiet way.

"So I did! Well, I *am* happy, and I *won't* fret, but it does seem as if the more one gets the more one wants, doesn't it? There, now, the trays are ready, and everything in but my ball dress, which I shall leave for mother to pack," said Meg, cheering up, as she glanced from the half-filled trunk to the many-times-pressed-and-mended white tarlatan, which she called her "ball dress" with an important air.

The next day was fine, and Meg departed in style for a fortnight of novelty and pleasure. Mrs. March had consented to the visit rather reluctantly, fearing that Margaret would come back more discontented than she went. But she had begged so hard, and Sallie had promised to take good care of her, and a little pleasure seemed so delightful after a winter of irksome work that the mother yielded, and the daughter went to take her first taste of fashionable life.

The Moffats *were* very fashionable, and simple Meg was rather daunted, at first, by the splendor of the house and the elegance of its occupants. But they were kindly people, in spite of the frivolous life they led, and soon put their guest at her ease. Perhaps Meg felt, without understanding why, that they were not particularly cultivated or intelligent people, and that all their gilding could not quite conceal the ordinary material of which they were made. It certainly was agreeable to fare sumptuously, drive in a fine carriage, wear her best frock every day, and do nothing but enjoy herself. It suited her exactly, and soon she began to imitate the manners and conversation of those about her, to put on little airs and graces, use French phrases, crimp her hair, take in her dresses, and talk about the fashions as well as she could. The more she saw of Annie Moffat's pretty things, the more she envied her and sighed to be rich. Home now looked bare and dismal as she thought of it, work grew harder than ever, and she felt that she was a very destitute and much-injured girl, in spite of the new gloves and silk stockings.

She had not much time for repining, however, for the three young girls were busily employed in "having a good time."

They shopped, walked, rode, and called all day, went to theaters and operas or frolicked at home in the evening, for Annie had many friends and knew how to entertain them. Her older sisters were very fine young ladies, and one was engaged, which was extremely interesting and romantic, Meg thought. Mr. Moffat was a fat, jolly old gentleman, who knew her father, and Mrs. Moffat, a fat, jolly old lady, who took as great a fancy to Meg as her daughter had done. Everyone petted her, and "Daisy," as they called her, was in a fair way to have her head turned.

When the evening for the "small party" came, she found that the poplin wouldn't do at all, for the other girls were putting on thin dresses and making themselves very fine indeed; so out came the tarlatan, looking older, limper, and shabbier than ever beside Sallie's crisp new one. Meg saw the girls glance at it and then at one another, and her cheeks began to burn, for with all her gentleness she was very proud. No one said a word about it, but Sallie offered to dress her hair, and Annie to tie her sash, and Belle, the engaged sister, praised her white arms; but in their kindness Meg saw only pity for her poverty, and her heart felt very heavy as she stood by herself, while the others laughed, chattered, and flew about like gauzy butterflies. The hard, bitter feeling was getting pretty bad, when the maid brought in a box of flowers. Before she could speak, Annie had the cover off, and all were exclaiming at the lovely roses, heath, and fern within.

"It's for Belle, of course, George always sends her some, but these are altogether ravishing," cried Annie, with a great sniff.

"They are for Miss March, the man said. And here's a note," put in the maid, holding it to Meg.

"What fun! Who are they from? Didn't know you had a lover," cried the girls, fluttering about Meg in a high state of curiosity and surprise.

"The note is from Mother, and the flowers from Laurie," said Meg simply, yet much gratified that he had not forgotten her.

"Oh, indeed!" said Annie with a funny look, as Meg slipped

the note into her pocket as a sort of talisman against envy, vanity, and false pride, for the few loving words had done her good, and the flowers cheered her up by their beauty.

Feeling almost happy again, she laid by a few ferns and roses for herself, and quickly made up the rest in dainty bouquets for the breasts, hair, or skirts of her friends, offering them so prettily that Clara, the elder sister, told her she was "the sweetest little thing she ever saw," and they looked quite charmed with her small attention. Somehow the kind act finished her despondency; and when all the rest went to show themselves to Mrs. Moffat, she saw a happy, bright-eyed face in the mirror, as she laid her ferns against her rippling hair and fastened the roses in the dress that didn't strike her as so *very* shabby now.

She enjoyed herself very much that evening, for she danced to her heart's content; everyone was very kind, and she had three compliments. Annie made her sing, and some one said she had a remarkably fine voice. Major Lincoln asked who "the fresh little girl with the beautiful eyes" was, and Mr. Moffat insisted on dancing with her because she "didn't dawdle, but had some spring in her," as he gracefully expressed it. So altogether she had a very nice time, till she overheard a bit of a conversation, which disturbed her extremely. She was sitting just inside the conservatory, waiting for her partner to bring her an ice, when she heard a voice ask on the other side of the flowery wall—

"How old is he?"

"Sixteen or seventeen, I should say," replied another voice.

"It would be a grand thing for one of those girls, wouldn't it? Sallie says they are very intimate now, and the old man quite dotes on them."

"Mrs. M. has made her plans, I dare say, and will play her cards well, early as it is. The girl evidently doesn't think of it yet," said Mrs. Moffat.

"She told that fib about her mamma, as if she did know, and colored up when the flowers came quite prettily. Poor thing! She'd be so nice if she was only got up in style. Do you think she'd be offended if we offered to lend her a dress for Thursday?" asked another voice.

"She's proud, but I don't believe she'd mind, for that dowdy tarlatan is all she has got. She may tear it tonight, and that will be a good excuse for offering a decent one."

"We'll see. I shall ask young Laurence, as a compliment to her, and we'll have fun about it afterward."

Here Meg's partner appeared, to find her looking much flushed and rather agitated. She *was* proud, and her pride was useful just then, for it helped her hide her mortification, anger, and disgust at what she had just heard; for, innocent and unsuspicious as she was, she could not help understanding the gossip of her friends. She tried to forget it, but could not, and kept repeating to herself, "Mrs. M. has made her plans," "that fib about her mamma," and "dowdy tarlatan," till she was ready to cry and rush home to tell her troubles and ask for advice. As that was impossible, she did her best to seem gay, and being rather excited, she succeeded so well that no one dreamed what an effort she was making. She was very glad when it was all over and she was quiet in her bed, where she could think and wonder and fume till her head ached and her hot cheeks were cooled by a few natural tears. Those foolish, yet well-meant words, had opened a new world to Meg, and much disturbed the peace of the old one in which till now she had lived as happily as a child. Her innocent friendship with Laurie was spoiled by the silly speeches she had overheard; her faith in her mother was a little shaken by the worldly plans attributed to her by Mrs. Moffat, who judged others by herself; and the sensible resolution to be contented with the simple wardrobe which suited a poor man's daughter was weakened by the unnecessary pity of girls who thought a shabby dress one of the greatest calamities under heaven.

Poor Meg had a restless night, and got up heavy-eyed, unhappy, half resentful toward her friends, and half ashamed of herself for not speaking out frankly and setting everything right. Everybody dawdled that morning, and it was noon before the girls found energy enough even to take up their worsted work. Something in the manner of her friends struck

Meg at once: they treated her with more respect, she thought, took quite a tender interest in what she said, and looked at her with eyes that plainly betrayed curiosity. All this surprised and flattered her, though she did not understand it till Miss Belle looked up from her writing, and said, with a sentimental air—

"Daisy, dear, I've sent an invitation to your friend, Mr. Laurence, for Thursday. We should like to know him, and it's only a proper compliment to you."

Meg colored, but a mischievous fancy to tease the girls made her reply demurely, "You are very kind, but I'm afraid he won't come."

"Why not, *cherie?*" asked Miss Belle.

"He's too old."

"My child, what do you mean? What is his age, I beg to know!" cried Miss Clara.

"Nearly seventy, I believe," answered Meg, counting stitches to hide the merriment in her eyes.

"You sly creature! Of course we meant the young man," exclaimed Miss Belle, laughing.

"There isn't any, Laurie is only a little boy." And Meg laughed also at the queer look which the sisters exchanged as she thus described her supposed lover.

"About your age," Nan said.

"Nearer my sister Jo's, *I* am seventeen in August," returned Meg, tossing her head.

"It's very nice of him to send you flowers, isn't it?" said Annie, looking wise about nothing.

"Yes, he often does, to all of us, for their house is full, and we are so fond of them. My mother and old Mr. Laurence are friends, you know, so it is quite natural that we children should play together." And Meg hoped they would say no more.

"It's evident Daisy isn't out yet," said Miss Clara to Belle with a nod.

"Quite a pastoral state of innocence all round," returned Miss Belle with a shrug.

"I'm going out to get some little matters for my girls; can

I do anything for you, young ladies?" asked Mrs. Moffat, lumbering in like an elephant in silk and lace.

"No, thank you, ma'am," replied Sallie. "I've got my new pink silk for Thursday and don't want a thing."

"Nor I—" began Meg, but stopped because it occurred to her that she *did* want several things and could not have them.

"What shall you wear?" asked Sallie.

"My old white one again, if I can mend it fit to be seen; it got sadly torn last night," said Meg, trying to speak quite easily, but feeling very uncomfortable.

"Why don't you send home for another?" said Sallie, who was not an observing young lady.

"I haven't got any other." It cost Meg an effort to say that, but Sallie did not see it and exclaimed in amiable surprise, "Only that? How funny—" She did not finish her speech, for Belle shook her head at her and broke in, saying kindly—

"Not at all; where is the use of having a lot of dresses when she isn't out? There's no need of sending home, Daisy, even if you had a dozen, for I've got a sweet blue silk laid away, which I've outgrown, and you shall wear it to please me, won't you, dear?"

"You are very kind, but I don't mind my old dress if you don't, it does well enough for a little girl like me," said Meg.

"Now do let me please myself by dressing you up in style. I admire to do it, and you'd be a regular little beauty with a touch here and there. I shan't let anyone see you till you are done, and then we'll burst upon them like Cinderella and her godmother going to the ball," said Bell in her persuasive tone.

Meg couldn't refuse the offer so kindly made, for a desire to see if she would be "a little beauty" after touching up caused her to accept and forget all her former uncomfortable feelings toward the Moffats.

On the Thursday evening, Belle shut herself up with her maid, and between them they turned Meg into a fine lady. They crimped and curled her hair, they polished her neck and arms with some fragrant powder, touched her lips with coral-line salve to make them redder, and Hortense would have added "a *soupçon* of rouge," if Meg had not rebelled. They laced her into a sky-blue dress, which was so tight she could hardly breathe and so low in the neck that modest Meg blushed at herself in the mirror. A set of silver filagree was added, bracelets, necklace, brooch, and even earrings, for Hortense tied them on with a bit of pink silk which did not show. A cluster of tea-rose buds at the bosom and a ruche, reconciled Meg to the display of her pretty white shoulders, and a pair of high-heeled blue silk boots satisfied the last wish of her heart. A lace handkerchief, a plumy fan, and a bouquet in a silver holder finished her off, and Miss Belle surveyed her with the satisfaction of a little girl with a newly dressed doll.

"Mademoiselle is *charmante, très jolie*, is she not?" cried Hortense, clasping her hands in an affected rapture.

"Come and show yourself," said Miss Belle, leading the way to the room where the others were waiting.

As Meg went rustling after, with her long skirts trailing, her earrings tinkling, her curls waving, and her heart beating, she felt as if her "fun" had really begun at last, for the mirror had plainly told her that she *was* "a little beauty." Her friends repeated the pleasing phrase enthusiastically, and for several minutes she stood, like the jackdaw in the fable, enjoying her borrowed plumes, while the rest chattered like a party of magpies.

"While I dress, do you drill her, Nan, in the management of her skirt and those French heels, or she will trip herself up. Take your silver butterfly, and catch up that long curl on the left side of her head, Clara, and don't any of you disturb the charming work of my hands," said Belle, as she hurried away, looking well pleased with her success.

"I'm afraid to go down, I feel so queer and stiff and half-dressed," said Meg to Sallie, as the bell rang, and Mrs. Moffat sent to ask the young ladies to appear at once.

"You don't look a bit like yourself, but you are very nice. I'm nowhere beside you, for Belle has heaps of taste, and you're quite French, I assure you. Let your flowers hang, don't be so careful of them, and be sure you don't trip," returned Sallie, trying not to care that Meg was prettier than herself.

Keeping that warning carefully in mind, Margaret got

safely downstairs and sailed into the drawing rooms where the Moffats and a few early guests were assembled. She very soon discovered that there is a charm about fine clothes which attracts a certain class of people and secures their respect. Several young ladies, who had taken no notice of her before, were very affectionate all of a sudden; several young gentlemen, who had only stared at her at the other party, now not only stared, but asked to be introduced, and said all manner of foolish but agreeable things to her; and several old ladies, who sat on sofas, and criticized the rest of the party, inquired who she was with an air of interest. She heard Mrs. Moffat reply to one of them.

"Daisy March—father a colonel in the army—one of our first families, but reverses of fortune, you know; intimate friends of the Laurences; sweet creature, I assure you; my Ned is quite wild about her."

"Dear me!" said the old lady, putting up her glass for another observation of Meg, who tried to look as if she had not heard and been rather shocked at Mrs. Moffat's fibs.

The "queer feeling" did not pass away, but she imagined herself acting the new part of fine lady and so got on pretty well, though the tight dress gave her a side-ache, the train kept getting under her feet, and she was in constant fear lest her earrings should fly off and get lost or broken. She was flirting her fan and laughing at the feeble jokes of a young gentleman who tried to be witty, when she suddenly stopped laughing and looked confused, for, just opposite, she saw Laurie. He was staring at her with undisguised surprise, and disapproval also, she thought, for, though he bowed and smiled, yet something in his honest eyes made her blush and wish she had her old dress on. To complete her confusion, she saw Belle nudge Annie, and both glance from her to Laurie, who, she was happy to see, looked unusually boyish and shy.

"Silly creatures, to put such thoughts into my head. I won't care for it, or let it change me a bit," thought Meg, and rustled across the room to shake hands with her friend.

"I'm glad you came, I was afraid you wouldn't," she said, with her most grown-up air.

"Jo wanted me to come, and tell her how you looked, so I did," answered Laurie, without turning his eyes upon her, though he half smiled at her maternal tone.

"What shall you tell her?" asked Meg, full of curiosity to know his opinion of her, yet feeling ill at ease with him for the first time.

"I shall say I didn't know you, for you look so grown-up and unlike yourself, I'm quite afraid of you," he said, fumbling at his glove button.

"How absurd of you! The girls dressed me up for fun, and I rather like it. Wouldn't Jo stare if she saw me?" said Meg, bent on making him say whether he thought her improved or not.

"Yes, I think she would," returned Laurie gravely.

"Don't you like me so?" asked Meg.

"No, I don't" was the blunt reply.

"Why not?" in an anxious tone.

He glanced at her frizzled head, bare shoulders, and fantastically trimmed dress with an expression that abashed her more than his answer, which had not a particle of his usual politeness about it.

"I don't like fuss and feathers."

That was altogether too much from a lad younger than herself, and Meg walked away, saying petulantly, "You are the rudest boy I ever saw."

Feeling very much ruffled, she went and stood at a quiet window to cool her cheeks, for the tight dress gave her an uncomfortably brilliant color. As she stood there, Major Lincoln passed by, and a minute after she heard him saying to his mother—

"They are making a fool of that little girl; I wanted you to see her, but they have spoiled her entirely; she's nothing but a doll tonight."

"Oh, dear!" sighed Meg. "I wish I'd been sensible and worn my own things, then I should not have disgusted other people, or felt so uncomfortable and ashamed myself."

She leaned her forehead on the cool pane, and stood half hidden by the curtains, never minding that her favorite waltz

"Don't you like me so? asked Meg. No, I don't was the blunt reply."

had begun, till some one touched her; and, turning, she saw Laurie, looking penitent, as he said, with his very best bow and his hand out—

"Please forgive my rudeness, and come and dance with me."

"I'm afraid it will be too disagreeable to you," said Meg, trying to look offended and failing entirely.

"Not a bit of it, I'm dying to do it. Come, I'll be good. I don't like your gown, but I do think you are—just splendid." And he waved his hands, as if words failed to express his admiration.

Meg smiled and relented, and whispered as they stood waiting to catch the time, "Take care my skirt doesn't trip you up; it's the plague of my life and I was a goose to wear it."

"Pin it round your neck, and then it will be useful," said Laurie, looking down at the little blue boots, which he evidently approved of.

Away they went fleetly and gracefully, for, having practiced at home, they were well matched, and the blithe young couple were a pleasant sight to see, as they twirled merrily round and round, feeling more friendly than ever after their small tiff.

"Laurie, I want you to do me a favor, will you?" said Meg, as he stood fanning her when her breath gave out, which it did very soon though she would not own why.

"Won't I!" said Laurie, with alacrity.

"Please don't tell them at home about my dress tonight. They won't understand the joke, and it will worry Mother."

"Then why did you do it?" said Laurie's eyes, so plainly that Meg hastily added—

"I shall tell them myself all about it, and 'fess' to Mother how silly I've been. But I'd rather do it myself; so you'll not tell, will you?"

"I give you my word I won't, only what shall I say when they ask me?"

"Just say I looked pretty well and was having a good time."

"I'll say the first with all my heart, but how about the

other? You don't look as if you were having a good time. Are you?" And Laurie looked at her with an expression which made her answer in a whisper—

"No, not just now. Don't think I'm horrid. I only wanted a little fun, but this sort doesn't pay, I find, and I'm getting tired of it."

"Here comes Ned Moffat; what does he want?" said Laurie, knitting his black brows as if he did not regard his young host in the light of a pleasant addition to the party.

"He put his name down for three dances, and I suppose he's coming for them. What a bore!" said Meg, assuming a languid air which amused Laurie immensely.

He did not speak to her again till suppertime, when he saw her drinking champagne with Ned and his friend Fisher, who were behaving "like a pair of fools," as Laurie said to himself, for he felt a brotherly sort of right to watch over the Marches and fight their battles whenever a defender was needed.

"You'll have a splitting headache tomorrow, if you drink much of that. I wouldn't, Meg, your mother doesn't like it, you know," he whispered, leaning over her chair, as Ned turned to refill her glass and Fisher stooped to pick up her fan.

"I'm not Meg tonight, I'm 'a doll' who does all sorts of crazy things. Tomorrow I shall put away my 'fuss and feathers' and be desperately good again," she answered with an affected little laugh.

"Wish tomorrow was here, then," muttered Laurie, walking off, ill-pleased at the change he saw in her.

Meg danced and flirted, chattered and giggled, as the other girls did; after supper she undertook the German, and blundered through it, nearly upsetting her partner with her long skirt, and romping in a way that scandalized Laurie, who looked on and meditated a lecture. But he got no chance to deliver it, for Meg kept away from him till he came to say good night.

"Remember!" she said, trying to smile, for the splitting headache had already begun.

"*Silence à la mort,*" replied Laurie, with a melodramatic flourish, as he went away.

This little bit of byplay excited Annie's curiosity, but Meg was too tired for gossip and went to bed, feeling as if she had been to a masquerade and hadn't enjoyed herself as much as she expected. She was sick all the next day, and on Saturday went home, quite used up with her fortnight's fun and feeling that she had "sat in the lap of luxury" long enough.

"It does seem pleasant to be quiet, and not have company manners on all the time. Home *is* a nice place, though it isn't splendid," said Meg, looking about her with a restful expression, as she sat with her mother and Jo on the Sunday evening.

"I'm glad to hear you say so, dear, for I was afraid home would seem dull and poor to you after your fine quarters," replied her mother, who had given her many anxious looks that day; for motherly eyes are quick to see any change in children's faces.

Meg had told her adventures gayly and said over and over what a charming time she had had, but something still seemed to weigh upon her spirits, and when the younger girls were gone to bed, she sat thoughtfully staring at the fire, saying little and looking worried. As the clock struck nine and Jo proposed bed, Meg suddenly left her chair and, taking Beth's stool, leaned her elbows on her mother's knee, saying bravely—

"Marmee, I want to 'fess.'"

"I thought so; what is it, dear?"

"Shall I go away?" asked Jo discreetly.

"Of course not. Don't I always tell you everything? I was ashamed to speak of it before the children, but I want you to know all the dreadful things I did at the Moffats'."

"We are prepared," said Mrs. March, smiling but looking a little anxious.

"I told you they dressed me up, but I didn't tell you that they powdered and squeezed and frizzled, and made me look like a fashion plate. Laurie thought I wasn't proper. I know he did, though he didn't say so, and one man called me 'a doll.' I knew it was silly, but they flattered me and said I was a beauty, and quantities of nonsense, so I let them make a fool of me."

"Is that all?" asked Jo, as Mrs. March looked silently at the downcast face of her pretty daughter, and could not find it in her heart to blame her little follies.

"No, I drank champagne and romped and tried to flirt, and was altogether abominable," said Meg self-reproachfully.

"There is something more, I think." And Mrs. March smoothed the soft cheek, which suddenly grew rosy as Meg answered slowly—

"Yes. It's very silly, but I want to tell it, because I hate to have people say and think such things about us and Laurie."

Then she told the various bits of gossip she had heard at the Moffats', and as she spoke, Jo saw her mother fold her lips tightly, as if ill pleased that such ideas should be put into Meg's innocent mind.

"Well, if that isn't the greatest rubbish I ever heard," cried Jo indignantly. "Why didn't you pop out and tell them so on the spot?"

"I couldn't, it was so embarrassing for me. I couldn't help hearing at first, and then I was so angry and ashamed, I didn't remember that I ought to go away."

"Just wait till *I* see Annie Moffat, and I'll show you how to settle such ridiculous stuff. The idea of having 'plans,' and being kind to Laurie because he's rich and may marry us by-and-by! Won't he shout when I tell him what those silly things say about us poor children?" And Jo laughed, as if on second thoughts the thing struck her as a good joke.

"If you tell Laurie, I'll never forgive you! She mustn't, must she, Mother?" said Meg, looking distressed.

"No, never repeat that foolish gossip, and forget it as soon as you can," said Mrs. March gravely. "I was very unwise to let you go among people of whom I know so little—kind, I dare say, but worldly, ill-bred, and full of these vulgar ideas about young people. I am more sorry than I can express for the mischief this visit may have done you, Meg."

"Don't be sorry, I won't let it hurt me. I'll forget all the bad and remember only the good, for I did enjoy a great deal, and thank you very much for letting me go. I'll not be sentimental or dissatisfied, Mother. I know I'm a silly little girl, and I'll stay with you till I'm fit to take care of myself. But it *is* nice to be praised and admired, and I can't help saying I like it," said Meg, looking half ashamed of the confession.

"That is perfectly natural, and quite harmless, if the liking does not become a passion and lead one to do foolish or unmaidenly things. Learn to know and value the praise which is worth having, and to excite the admiration of excellent people by being modest as well as pretty, Meg."

Margaret sat thinking a moment, while Jo stood with her hands behind her, looking both interested and a little perplexed, for it was a new thing to see Meg blushing and talking about admiration, lovers, and things of that sort; and Jo felt as if during that fortnight her sister had grown up amazingly, and was drifting away from her into a world where she could not follow.

"Mother, do you have 'plans,' as Mrs. Moffat said?" asked Meg bashfully.

"Yes, my dear, I have a great many; all mothers do, but mine differ somewhat from Mrs. Moffat's, I suspect. I will tell you some of them, for the time has come when a word may set this romantic little head and heart of yours right, on a very serious subject. You are young, Meg, but not too young to understand me, and mothers' lips are the fittest to speak of such things to girls like you. Jo, your turn will come in time, perhaps, so listen to my 'plans,' and help me carry them out, if they are good."

Jo went and sat on one arm of the chair, looking as if she thought they were about to join in some very solemn affair. Holding a hand of each, and watching the two young faces wistfully, Mrs. March said, in her serious yet cheery way—

"I want my daughters to be beautiful, accomplished, and

good; to be admired, loved, and respected; to have a happy youth, to be well and wisely married, and to lead useful, pleasant lives, with as little care and sorrow to try them as God sees fit to send. To be loved and chosen by a good man is the best and sweetest thing which can happen to a woman, and I sincerely hope my girls may know this beautiful experience. It is natural to think of it, Meg, right to hope and wait for it, and wise to prepare for it, so that when the happy time comes, you may feel ready for the duties and worthy of the joy. My dear girls, I *am* ambitious for you, but not to have you make a dash in the world—marry rich men merely because they are rich, or have splendid houses, which are not homes because love is wanting. Money is a needful and precious thing—and, when well used, a noble thing—but I never want you to think it is the first or only prize to strive for. I'd rather see you poor men's wives, if you were happy, beloved, contented, than queens on thrones, without self-respect and peace."

"Poor girls don't stand any chance, Belle says, unless they put themselves forward," sighed Meg.

"Then we'll be old maids," said Jo stoutly.

"Right, Jo; better be happy old maids than unhappy wives, or unmaidenly girls, running about to find husbands," said Mrs. March decidedly. "Don't be troubled, Meg, poverty seldom daunts a sincere lover. Some of the best and most honored women I know were poor girls, but so love-worthy that they were not allowed to be old maids. Leave these things to time; make this home happy, so that you may be fit for homes of your own, if they are offered you, and contented here if they are not. One thing remember, my girls: Mother is always ready to be your confidante, Father to be your friend; and both of us trust and hope that our daughters, whether married or single, will be the pride and comfort of our lives."

"We will, Marmee, we will!" cried both, with all their hearts, as she bade them good night.

Chapter 10

The P. C. and P. O.

As SPRING CAME on, a new set of amusements became the fashion, and the lengthening days gave long afternoons for work and play of all sorts. The garden had to be put in order, and each sister had a quarter of the little plot to do what she liked with. Hannah used to say, "I'd know which each of them gardings belonged to, ef I see 'em in Chiny;" and so she might, for the girls' tastes differed as much as their characters. Meg's had roses and heliotrope, myrtle, and a little orange tree in it. Jo's bed was never alike two seasons, for she was always trying experiments; this year it was to be a plantation of sun-flowers, the seeds of which cheerful and aspiring plant were to feed Aunt Cockle-top and her family of chicks. Beth had old-fashioned, fragrant flowers in her garden—sweet peas and mignonette, larkspur, pinks, pansies, and southernwood, with chickweed for the bird and catnip for the pussies. Amy had a bower in hers—rather small and earwiggy, but very pretty to look at—with honeysuckles and morning-glories hanging their colored horns and bells in graceful wreaths all over it, tall white lilies, delicate ferns, and as many brilliant, picturesque plants as would consent to blossom there.

Gardening, walks, rows on the river, and flower hunts employed the fine days, and for rainy ones, they had house diversions—some old, some new—all more or less original. One of these was the "P. C.," for as secret societies were the fashion, it was thought proper to have one; and as all of the girls admired Dickens, they called themselves the Pickwick Club. With a few interruptions, they had kept this up for a year, and met every Saturday evening in the big garret, on which occasions the ceremonies were as follows: Three chairs were arranged in a row before a table on which was a lamp, also four white badges, with a big "P. C." in different colors on each, and the weekly newspaper called, *The Pickwick Portfolio,* to which all contributed something, while Jo, who reveled in pens and ink, was the editor. At seven o'clock, the four members ascended to the clubroom, tied their badges round their heads, and took their seats with great solemnity. Meg, as the eldest, was Samuel Pickwick; Jo, being of a literary turn, Augustus Snodgrass; Beth, because she was round and rosy, Tracy Tupman; and Amy, who was always trying to do what she couldn't, was Nathaniel Winkle. Pickwick, the president, read the paper, which was filled with original tales, poetry, local news, funny advertisements, and hints, in which they good-naturedly reminded each other of their faults and shortcomings. On one occasion, Mr. Pickwick put on a pair of spectacles without any glasses, rapped upon the table, hemmed, and, having stared hard at Mr. Snodgrass, who was tilting back in his chair, till he arranged himself properly, began to read:

"The Pickwick Portfolio"

MAY 20, 18——

Poet's Corner

ANNIVERSARY ODE

Again we meet to celebrate
  With badge and solemn rite,
Our fifty-second anniversary,
  In Pickwick Hall, tonight.

We all are here in perfect health,
  None gone from our small band;
Again we see each well-known face,
  And press each friendly hand.

Our Pickwick, always at his post,
  With reverence we greet,
As, spectacles on nose, he reads
  Our well-filled weekly sheet.

Although he suffers from a cold,
  We joy to hear him speak,
For words of wisdom from him fall,
  In spite of croak or squeak.

Old six-foot Snodgrass looms on high,
  With elephantine grace,
And beams upon the company,
  With brown and jovial face.

Poetic fire lights up his eye,
  He struggles 'gainst his lot.
Behold ambition on his brow,
  And on his nose a blot!

Next our peaceful Tupman comes,
  So rosy, plump, and sweet,
Who chokes with laughter at the puns,
  And tumbles off his seat.

Prim little Winkle too is here,
  With every hair in place,
A model of propriety,
  Though he hates to wash his face.

The year is gone, we still unite
  To joke and laugh and read,
And tread the path of literature
  That doth to glory lead.

Long may our paper prosper well,
  Our club unbroken be,
And coming years their blessings pour
  On the useful, gay "P. C."
                              A. SNODGRASS.

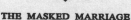

THE MASKED MARRIAGE

A TALE OF VENICE

Gondola after gondola swept up to the marble steps, and left its lovely load to swell the brilliant throng that filled the stately halls of Count de Adelon. Knights and ladies, elves and pages, monks and flower girls, all mingled gaily in the dance Sweet voices and rich melody filled the air, and so with mirth and music the masquerade went on.

"Has your Highness seen the Lady Viola tonight?" asked a gallant troubadour of the fairy queen who floated down the hall upon his arm.

"Yes, is she not lovely, though so sad! Her dress is well chosen, too, for in a week she weds Count Antonio, whom she passionately hates."

"By my faith, I envy him. Yonder he comes, arrayed like a bridegroom, except the black mask. When that is off we shall see how he regards the fair maid whose heart he cannot win, though her stern father bestows her hand," returned the troubadour.

" 'Tis whispered that she loves the young English artist who haunts her steps, and is spurned by the old count," said the lady, as they joined the dance.

The revel was at its height when a priest appeared, and, withdrawing the young pair to an alcove hung with purple velvet, he motioned them to kneel. Instant silence fell upon the gay throng; and not a sound, but the dash of fountains or the rustle of orange groves sleeping in the moonlight, broke the hush, as Count de Adelon spoke thus:

"My lords and ladies, pardon the ruse by which I have gathered you here to witness the marriage of my daughter. Father, we wait your services."

All eyes turned toward the bridal party, and a low murmur of amazement went through the throng, for neither bride nor groom removed their masks. Curiosity and wonder possessed all hearts, but respect restrained all tongues till the holy rite was over. Then the eager spectators gathered round the count, demanding an explanation.

"Gladly would I give it if I could, but I only know that it was the whim of my timid Viola, and I yielded to it. Now, my children, let the play end. Unmask and receive my blessing."

But neither bent the knee, for the young bridegroom replied in a tone that startled all listeners as the mask fell, disclosing the noble face of Ferdinand Devereux, the artist lover, and leaning on the breast where now flashed the star of an English earl was the lovely Viola, radiant with joy and beauty.

"My lord, you scornfully bade me claim your daughter when I could boast as high a name and vast a fortune as the Count Antonio. I can do more, for even your ambitious soul cannot refuse the Earl of Devereux and De Vere, when he gives his ancient name and boundless wealth in return for the beloved hand of this fair lady, now my wife."

The count stood like one changed to stone, and turning to the bewildered crowd, Ferdinand added, with a gay smile of triumph, "To you, my gallant friends, I can only wish that your wooing may prosper as mine has done, and that you may all win as fair a bride as I have by this masked marriage."

S. PICKWICK.

Why is the P. C. like the Tower of Babel? It is full of unruly members.

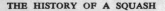

THE HISTORY OF A SQUASH

Once upon a time a farmer planted a little seed in his garden, and after a while it sprouted and became a vine and bore many squashes. One day in October, when they were ripe, he picked one and took it to market. A grocerman bought and put it in his shop. That same morning, a little girl in a brown hat and blue dress, with a round face and snub nose, went and bought it for her mother. She lugged it home, cut it up, and boiled it in the big pot; mashed some of it, with salt and butter, for dinner; and to the rest she added a pint of milk, two eggs, four spoons of sugar, nutmeg, and some crackers; put it in a deep dish, and baked it till it was brown and nice; and next day it was eaten by a family named March.

T. TUPMAN.

MR. PICKWICK, *Sir:*—

I address you upon the subject of sin the sinner I mean is a man named Winkle who makes trouble in his club by laughing and sometimes won't write his piece in this fine paper I hope you will pardon his badness and let him send a French fable because he can't write out of his head as he has so many lessons to do and no brains in future I will try to take time by the fetlock and prepare some work which will be all *commy la fo* that means all right I am in haste as it is nearly school time

Yours respectably, N. WINKLE.

[The above is a manly and handsome acknowledgment of past misdemeanors. If our young friend studied punctuation, it would be well.]

A SAD ACCIDENT

On Friday last, we were startled by a violent shock in our basement, followed by cries of distress. On rushing in a body to the cellar, we discovered our beloved President prostrate upon the floor, having tripped and fallen while getting wood for domestic purposes. A perfect scene of ruin met our eyes; for in his fall Mr. Pickwick had plunged his head and shoulders into a tub of water, upset a keg of soft soap upon his manly form, and torn his garments badly. On being removed from this perilous situation, it was discovered that he had suffered no injury but several bruises; and, we are happy to add, is now doing well.

ED.

THE PUBLIC BEREAVEMENT

It is our painful duty to record the sudden and mysterious disappearance of our cherished friend, Mrs. Snowball Pat Paw. This lovely and beloved cat was the pet of a large circle of warm and admiring friends; for her beauty attracted all eyes, her graces and virtues endeared her to all hearts, and her loss is deeply felt by the whole community.

When last seen, she was sitting at the gate, watching the butcher's cart; and it is feared that some villain, tempted by her charms, basely stole her. Weeks have passed, but no trace of her has been discovered; and we relinquish all hope, tie a black ribbon to her basket, set aside her dish, and weep for her as one lost to us forever.

---◆---

A sympathizing friend sends the following gem:

A LAMENT

FOR S. B. PAT PAW

We mourn the loss of our little pet,
  And sigh o'er her hapless fate,
For never more by the fire she'll sit,
  Nor play by the old green gate.

The little grave where her infant sleeps
  Is 'neath the chestnut tree;
But o'er *her* grave we may not weep,
  We know not where it may be.

Her empty bed, her idle ball,
  Will never see her more;
No gentle tap, no loving purr
  Is heard at the parlor door.

Another cat comes after her mice,
  A cat with a dirty face;
But she does not hunt as our darling did,
  Nor play with her airy grace.

Her stealthy paws tread the very hall
  Where Snowball used to play.
But she only spits at the dogs our pet
  So gallantly drove away.

She is useful and mild, and does her best,
  But she is not fair to see;
And we cannot give her your place, dear,
  Nor worship her as we worship thee.

A. S.

ADVERTISEMENTS

A NEW PLAY will appear at the Barnville Theatre, in the course of a few weeks, which will surpass anything ever seen on the American stage. "THE GREEK SLAVE, or Constantine the Avenger," is the name of this thrilling drama! ! !

HINTS

If S. P. didn't use so much soap on his hands, he wouldn't always be late at breakfast. A. S. is requested not to whistle in the street. T. T., please don't forget Amy's napkin. N. W. must not fret because his dress has not nine tucks.

WEEKLY REPORT

Meg—Good.
Jo—Bad.
Beth—Very good.
Amy—Middling.

As the President finished reading the paper (which I beg leave to assure my readers is a *bona fide* copy of one written by *bona fide* girls once upon a time), a round of applause followed, and then Mr. Snodgrass rose to make a proposition.

"Mr. President and gentlemen," he began, assuming a parliamentary attitude and tone, "I wish to propose the admission of a new member—one who highly deserves the honor, would be deeply grateful for it, and would add immensely to the spirit of the club, the literary value of the paper, and be no end jolly and nice. I propose Mr. Theodore Laurence as an honorary member of the P. C. Come now, do have him."

Jo's sudden change of tone made the girls laugh, but all looked rather anxious, and no one said a word as Snodgrass took his seat.

"We'll put it to vote," said the President. "All in favor of this motion please to manifest it by saying, 'Aye.'"

A loud response from Snodgrass, followed, to everybody's surprise, by a timid one from Beth.

"Contrary-minded say, 'No.'"

Meg and Amy were contrary-minded, and Mr. Winkle rose to say with great elegance, "We don't wish any boys, they only joke and bounce about. This is a ladies' club, and we wish to be private and proper."

"I'm afraid he'll laugh at our paper, and make fun of us afterward," observed Pickwick, pulling the little curl on her forehead, as she always did when doubtful.

Up rose Snodgrass, very much in earnest. "Sir, I give you my word as a gentleman, Laurie won't do anything of the sort. He likes to write, and he'll give a tone to our contributions and keep us from being sentimental, don't you see? We can do so little for him, and he does so much for us, I think the least we can do is to offer him a place here, and make him welcome if he comes."

This artful allusion to benefits conferred brought Tupman to his feet, looking as if he had quite made up his mind.

"Yes, we ought to do it, even if we *are* afraid. I say he *may* come, and his grandpa, too, if he likes."

This spirited burst from Beth electrified the club, and Jo left her seat to shake hands approvingly. "Now then, vote again. Everybody remember it's our Laurie, and say, 'Aye!' " cried Snodgrass excitedly.

"Aye! aye! aye!" replied three voices at once.

"Good! Bless you! Now, as there's nothing like 'taking time by the *fetlock*,' as Winkle characteristically observes, allow me to present the new member." And, to the dismay of the rest of the club, Jo threw open the door of the closet, and displayed Laurie sitting on a rag bag, flushed and twinkling with suppressed laughter.

"You rogue! You traitor! Jo, how could you?" cried the three girls, as Snodgrass led her friend triumphantly forth, and producing both a chair and a badge, installed him in a jiffy.

"The coolness of you two rascals is amazing," began Mr. Pickwick, trying to get up an awful frown and only succeeding in producing an amiable smile. But the new member was equal to the occasion, and rising, with a grateful salutation to the Chair, said in the most engaging manner, "Mr. President and ladies—I beg pardon, gentlemen—allow me to introduce myself as Sam Weller, the very humble servant of the club."

"Good! Good!" cried Jo, pounding with the handle of the old warming pan on which she leaned.

"My faithful friend and noble patron," continued Laurie

with a wave of the hand, "who has so flatteringly presented me, is not to be blamed for the base stratagem of tonight. I planned it, and she only gave in after lots of teasing."

"Come now, don't lay it all on yourself; you know I proposed the cupboard," broke in Snodgrass, who was enjoying the joke amazingly.

"Never you mind what she says. I'm the wretch that did it, sir," said the new member, with a Welleresque nod to Mr. Pickwick. "But on my honor, I never will do so again, and henceforth *dewote* myself to the interest of this immortal club."

"Hear! Hear!" cried Jo, clashing the lid of the warming pan like a cymbal.

"Go on, go on!" added Winkle and Tupman, while the President bowed benignly.

"I merely wish to say, that as a slight token of my gratitude for the honor done me, and as a means of promoting friendly relations between adjoining nations, I have set up a post office in the hedge in the lower corner of the garden, a fine, spacious building with padlocks on the doors and every convenience for the mails—also the females, if I may be allowed the expression. It's the old martin house, but I've stopped up the door and made the roof open, so it will hold all sorts of things, and save our valuable time. Letters, manuscripts, books, and bundles can be passed in there, and as each nation has a key, it will be uncommonly nice, I fancy. Allow me to present the club key, and with many thanks for your favor, take my seat."

Great applause as Mr. Weller deposited a little key on the table and subsided, the warming pan clashed and waved wildly, and it was some time before order could be restored. A long discussion followed, and everyone came out surprising, for everyone did her best; so it was an unusually lively meeting, and did not adjourn till a late hour, when it broke up with three shrill cheers for the new member. No one ever regretted the admittance of Sam Weller, for a more devoted, well-behaved, and jovial member no club could have. He certainly did add "spirit" to the meetings, and "a tone" to the paper, for his orations convulsed his hearers and his contributions were excellent, being patriotic, classical, comical, or dramatic, but never sentimental. Jo regarded them as worthy of Bacon, Milton, or Shakespeare, and remodeled her own works with good effect, she thought.

The P. O. was a capital little institution, and flourished wonderfully, for nearly as many queer things passed through it as through the real office. Tragedies and cravats, poetry and pickles, garden seeds and long letters, music and gingerbread, rubbers, invitations, scoldings, and puppies. The old gentleman liked the fun, and amused himself by sending odd bundles, mysterious messages, and funny telegrams; and his gardener, who was smitten with Hannah's charms, actually sent a love letter to Jo's care. How they laughed when the secret came out, never dreaming how many love letters that little post office would hold in the years to come!

Chapter 11

Experiments

"THE FIRST OF June! The Kings are off to the seashore to-morrow, and I'm free. Three months' vacation—how I shall enjoy it!" exclaimed Meg, coming home one warm day to find Jo laid upon the sofa in an unusual state of exhaustion, while Beth took off her dusty boots, and Amy made lemonade for the refreshment of the whole party.

"Aunt March went today, for which, oh, be joyful!" said Jo. "I was mortally afraid she'd ask me to go with her; if she had, I should have felt as if I ought to do it, but Plumfield is about as gay as a churchyard, you know, and I'd rather be excused. We had a flurry getting the old lady off, and I had a fright every time she spoke to me, for I was in such a hurry to be through that I was uncommonly helpful and sweet, and feared she'd find it impossible to part from me. I quaked till she was fairly in the carriage, and had a final fright, for as it drove off, she popped out her head, saying, 'Josyphine, won't you—?' I didn't hear any more, for I basely turned and fled. I did actually run, and whisked round the corner where I felt safe."

"Poor old Jo! She came in looking as if bears were after her," said Beth, as she cuddled her sister's feet with a motherly air.

"Aunt March is a regular samphire, is she not?" observed Amy, tasting her mixture critically.

"She means *vampire*, not seaweed, but it doesn't matter; it's too warm to be particular about one's parts of speech," murmured Jo.

"What shall you do all your vacation?" asked Amy, changing the subject with tact.

"I shall lie abed late, and do nothing," replied Meg, from the depths of the rocking chair. "I've been routed up early all winter and had to spend my days working for other people, so now I'm going to rest and revel to my heart's content."

"No," said Jo, "that dozy way wouldn't suit me. I've laid in a heap of books, and I'm going to improve my shining hours reading on my perch in the old apple tree, when I'm not having l—"

"Don't say 'larks!'" implored Amy, as a return snub for the "samphire" correction.

"I'll say 'nightingales,' then, with Laurie; that's proper and appropriate, since he's a warbler."

"Don't let us do any lessons, Beth, for a while, but play all the time and rest, as the girls mean to," proposed Amy.

"Well, I will, if Mother doesn't mind. I want to learn some new songs, and my children need fitting up for the summer; they are dreadfully out of order and really suffering for clothes."

"May we, Mother?" asked Meg, turning to Mrs. March, who sat sewing in what they called "Marmee's corner."

"You may try your experiment for a week and see how you like it. I think by Saturday night you will find that all play and no work is as bad as all work and no play."

"Oh, dear, no! It will be delicious, I'm sure," said Meg complacently.

"I now propose a toast, as my 'friend and pardner, Sairy Gamp,' says. Fun forever, and no grubbing!" cried Jo, rising, glass in hand, as the lemonade went round.

They all drank it merrily, and began the experiment by lounging for the rest of the day. Next morning, Meg did not appear till ten o'clock; her solitary breakfast did not taste nice, and the room seemed lonely and untidy, for Jo had not filled the vases, Beth had not dusted, and Amy's books lay scattered about. Nothing was neat and pleasant but "Marmee's corner," which looked as usual; and there Meg sat, to "rest and read," which meant yawn and imagine what pretty summer dresses she would get with her salary. Jo spent the morning on the river with Laurie and the afternoon reading and crying over *The Wide, Wide World*, up in the apple tree. Beth began by rummaging everything out of the big closet where her family resided, but getting tired before half 'done, she left her establishment topsy-turvy and went to her music, rejoicing that she had no dishes to wash. Amy arranged her bower, put on her best white frock, smoothed her curls, and sat down to draw under the honeysuckles, hoping someone would see and inquire who the young artist was. As no one appeared but an inquisitive daddy-longlegs, who examined her work with interest, she went to walk, got caught in a shower, and came home dripping.

At teatime they compared notes, and all agreed that it had been a delightful, though unusually long day. Meg, who went shopping in the afternoon and got a "sweet blue muslin," had discovered, after she had cut the breadths off, that it wouldn't wash, which mishap made her slightly cross. Jo had burned the skin off her nose boating, and got a raging headache by reading too long. Beth was worried by the confusion of her closet and the difficulty of learning three or four songs at once, and Amy deeply regretted the damage done her frock, for Katy Brown's party was to be the next day and now, like Flora McFlimsey, she had "nothing to wear." But these were mere trifles, and they assured their mother that the experiment was working finely. She smiled, said nothing, and with Hannah's help did their neglected work, keeping home pleasant and the domestic machinery running smoothly. It was astonishing what a peculiar and uncomfortable state of things was produced by the "resting and reveling" process. The days kept getting longer and longer, the weather was unusually variable and so were tempers, an unsettled feeling possessed everyone, and Satan found plenty of mischief for the idle hands to do. As the height of luxury, Meg put out some of her sewing, and then found time hang so heavily that she fell to snipping and spoiling her clothes in her attempts to furbish them up à la Moffat. Jo read till her eyes gave out and she was sick of books, got so fidgety that even good-natured Laurie had a quarrel with her, and so reduced in spirits that she desperately wished she had gone with Aunt March. Beth got on pretty well, for she was constantly forgetting that it was to be *all play and no work*, and fell back into her old ways now and then; but something in the air affected her, and more than once her tranquillity was much disturbed—so much so that on one occasion she actually shook poor dear Joanna and told her she was "a fright." Amy fared worst of all, for her resources were small, and when her sisters left her to amuse and care for herself, she soon found that accomplished and important little self a great burden. She didn't like dolls, fairy tales were childish, and one couldn't draw all the time; tea parties didn't amount to much, neither did picnics unless very well conducted. "If one could have a fine house, full of nice girls, or go traveling, the summer would be delightful, but to stay at home with three selfish sisters and a grown-up boy was enough to try the patience of a Boaz," complained Miss Malaprop, after several days devoted to pleasure, fretting, and ennui.

No one would own that they were tired of the experiment, but by Friday night each acknowledged to herself that she was glad the week was nearly done. Hoping to impress the lesson more deeply, Mrs. March, who had a good deal of humor, resolved to finish off the trial in an appropriate manner, so she gave Hannah a holiday and let the girls enjoy the full effect of the play system.

When they got up on Saturday morning, there was no fire in the kitchen, no breakfast in the dinning room, and no mother anywhere to be seen.

"Mercy on us! What *has* happened?" cried Jo, staring about her in dismay.

Meg ran upstairs and soon came back again, looking relieved but rather bewildered, and a little ashamed.

"Mother isn't sick, only very tired, and she says she is going to stay quietly in her room all day and let us do the best we can. It's a very queer thing for her to do, she doesn't act a bit like herself; but she says it has been a hard week for her, so we mustn't grumble but take care of ourselves."

"That's easy enough, and I like the idea, I'm aching for something to do—that is, some new amusement, you know," added Jo quickly.

In fact it *was* an immense relief to them all to have a little work, and they took hold with a will, but soon realized the truth of Hannah's saying, "Housekeeping ain't no joke." There was plenty of food in the larder, and while Beth and Amy set the table, Meg and Jo got breakfast, wondering as they did so why servants ever talked about hard work.

"I shall take some up to Mother, though she said we were not to think of her, for she'd take care of herself," said Meg, who presided and felt quite matronly behind the teapot.

So a tray was fitted out before anyone began, and taken up with the cook's compliments. The boiled tea was very bitter, the omelet scorched, and the biscuits speckled with saleratus, but Mrs. March received her repast with thanks and laughed heartily over it after Jo was gone.

"Poor little souls, they will have a hard time, I'm afraid, but they won't suffer, and it will do them good," she said, producing the more palatable viands with which she had provided herself, and disposing of the bad breakfast, so that their feelings might not be hurt—a motherly little deception for which they were grateful.

Many were the complaints below, and great the chagrin of the head cook at her failures. "Never mind, I'll get the dinner and be servant, you be mistress, keep your hands nice, see company, and give orders," said Jo, who knew still less than Meg about culinary affairs.

This obliging offer was gladly accepted, and Margaret retired to the parlor, which she hastily put in order by whisking the litter under the sofa and shutting the blinds to save the trouble of dusting. Jo, with perfect faith in her own powers and a friendly desire to make up the quarrel, immediately put a note in the office, inviting Laurie to dinner.

"You'd better see what you have got before you think of having company," said Meg, when informed of the hospitable but rash act.

"Oh, there's corned beef and plenty of potatoes, and I

shall get some asparagus and a lobster, 'for a relish,' as Hannah says. We'll have lettuce and make a salad. I don't know how, but the book tells. I'll have blancmange and strawberries for dessert, and coffee, too, if you want to be elegant."

"Don't try too many messes, Jo, for you can't make anything but gingerbread and molasses candy fit to eat. I wash my hands of the dinner party, and since you have asked Laurie on your own responsibility, you may just take care of him."

"I don't want you to do anything but be civil to him and help to the pudding. You'll give me your advice if I get in a muddle, won't you?" asked Jo, rather hurt.

"Yes, but I don't know much, except about bread and a few trifles. You had better ask Mother's leave before you order anything," returned Meg prudently.

"Of course I shall. I'm not a fool." And Jo went off in a huff at the doubts expressed of her powers.

"Get what you like, and don't disturb me. I'm going out to dinner and can't worry about things at home," said Mrs. March, when Jo spoke to her. "I never enjoyed housekeeping, and I'm going to take a vacation today, and read, write, go visiting, and amuse myself."

The unusual spectacle of her busy mother rocking comfortably and reading early in the morning made Jo feel as if some natural phenomenon had occurred, for an eclipse, an earthquake, or a volcanic eruption would hardly have seemed stranger.

"Everything is out of sorts, somehow," she said to herself, going downstairs. "There's Beth crying, that's a sure sign that something is wrong with this family. If Amy is bothering, I'll shake her."

Feeling very much out of sorts herself, Jo hurried into the parlor to find Beth sobbing over Pip, the canary, who lay dead in the cage with his little claws pathetically extended, as if imploring the food for want of which he had died.

"It's all my fault—I forgot him—there isn't a seed or a

drop left. Oh, Pip! Oh, Pip! How could I be so cruel to you?" cried Beth, taking the poor thing in her hands and trying to restore him.

Jo peeped into his half-open eye, felt his little heart, and finding him stiff and cold, shook her head, and offered her domino box for a coffin.

"Put him in the oven, and maybe he will get warm and revive," said Amy hopefully.

"He's been starved, and he shan't be baked now he's dead. I'll make him a shroud, and he shall be buried in the garden, and I'll never have another bird, never, my Pip! For I am too bad to own one," murmured Beth, sitting on the floor with her pet folded in her hands.

"The funeral shall be this afternoon, and we will all go. Now, don't cry, Bethy; it's a pity, but nothing goes right this week, and Pip has had the worst of the experiment. Make the shroud and lay him in my box, and after the dinner party, we'll have a nice little funeral," said Jo, beginning to feel as if she had undertaken a good deal.

Leaving the others to console Beth, she departed to the kitchen, which was in a most discouraging state of confusion. Putting on a big apron, she fell to work and got the dishes piled up ready for washing, when she discovered that the fire was out.

"Here's a sweet prospect!" muttered Jo, slamming the stove door open, and poking vigorously among the cinders.

Having rekindled the fire, she thought she would go to market while the water heated. The walk revived her spirits, and flattering herself that she had made good bargains, she trudged home again, after buying a very young lobster, some very old asparagus, and two boxes of acid strawberries. By the time she got cleared up, the dinner arrived, and the stove was red-hot. Hannah had left a pan of bread to rise, Meg had worked it up early, set it on the hearth for a second rising, and forgotten it. Meg was entertaining Sallie Gardiner in the parlor, when the door flew open and a floury, crocky, flushed, and disheveled figure appeared, demanding tartly—

"I say, isn't bread 'riz' enough when it runs over the pans?"

Sallie began to laugh, but Meg nodded and lifted her eyebrows as high as they would go, which caused the apparition to vanish and put the sour bread into the oven without further delay. Mrs. March went out, after peeping here and there to see how matters went, also saying a word of comfort to Beth, who sat making a winding sheet, while the dear departed lay in state in the domino box. A strange sense of helplessness fell upon the girls as the gray bonnet vanished round the corner, and despair seized them when a few minutes later Miss Crocker appeared, and said she'd come to dinner. Now, this lady was a thin, yellow spinster, with a sharp nose and inquisitive eyes, who saw everything and gossiped about all she saw. They disliked her, but had been taught to be kind to her, simply because she was old and poor and had few friends. So Meg gave her the easy chair and tried to entertain her, while she asked questions, criticized everything, and told stories of the people whom she knew.

Language cannot describe the anxieties, experiences, and exertions which Jo underwent that morning, and the dinner she served up became a standing joke. Fearing to ask any more advice, she did her best alone, and discovered that something more than energy and good will is necessary to make a cook. She boiled the asparagus for an hour and was grieved to find the heads cooked off and the stalks harder than ever. The bread burned black, for the salad dressing so aggravated her that she let everything else go till she had convinced herself that she could not make it fit to eat. The lobster was a scarlet mystery to her, but she hammered and poked till it was unshelled and its meager proportions concealed in a grove of lettuce leaves. The potatoes had to be hurried, not to keep the asparagus waiting, and were not done at last. The blancmange was lumpy, and the strawberries not as ripe as they looked, having been skilfully "deaconed."

"Well, they can eat beef and bread and butter, if they are hungry, only it's mortifying to have to spend your whole morning for nothing," thought Jo, as she rang the bell half an hour later than usual, and stood, hot, tired, and dispirited, surveying the feast spread for Laurie, accustomed to all sorts of elegance, and Miss Crocker, whose curious eyes would mark all failures and whose tattling tongue would report them far and wide.

Poor Jo would gladly have gone under the table, as one thing after another was tasted and left, while Amy giggled, Meg looked distressed, Miss Crocker pursed up her lips, and Laurie talked and laughed with all his might to give a cheerful tone to the festive scene. Jo's one strong point was the fruit, for she had sugared it well, and had a pitcher of rich cream to eat with it. Her hot cheeks cooled a trifle, and she drew a long breath as the pretty glass plates went round, and everyone looked graciously at the little rosy islands floating in a sea of cream. Miss Crocker tasted first, made a wry face, and drank some water hastily. Jo, who refused, thinking there might not be enough, for they dwindled sadly after the picking over, glanced at Laurie, but he was eating away manfully, though there was a slight pucker about his mouth and he kept his eye fixed on his plate. Amy, who was fond of delicate fare, took a heaping spoonful, choked, hid her face in her napkin, and left the table precipitately.

"Oh, what is it?" exclaimed Jo, trembling.

"Salt instead of sugar, and the cream is sour," replied Meg with a tragic gesture.

Jo uttered a groan and fell back in her chair, remembering that she had given a last hasty powdering to the berries out of one of the two boxes on the kitchen table, and had neglected to put the milk in the refrigerator. She turned scarlet and was on the verge of crying, when she met Laurie's eyes, which *would* look merry in spite of his heroic efforts; the comical side of the affair suddenly struck her, and she laughed till the tears ran down her cheeks. So did everyone else, even "Croaker," as the girls called the old lady, and the unfortunate dinner ended gaily, with bread and butter, olives and fun.

"I haven't strength of mind enough to clear up now, so we will sober ourselves with a funeral," said Jo, as they rose; and Miss Crocker made ready to go, being eager to tell the new story at another friend's dinner table.

They did sober themselves for Beth's sake; Laurie dug a grave under the ferns in the grove, little Pip was laid in, with many tears by his tenderhearted mistress, and covered with moss, while a wreath of violets and chickweed was hung on the stone which bore his epitaph, composed by Jo while she struggled with the dinner:

> Here lies Pip March,
> Who died the 7th of June;
> Loved and lamented sore,
> And not forgotten soon.

At the conclusion of the ceremonies, Beth retired to her room, overcome with emotion and lobster; but there was no place of repose, for the beds were not made, and she found her grief much assuaged by beating up pillows and putting things in order. Meg helped Jo clear away the remains of the feast, which took half the afternoon and left them so tired that they agreed to be contented with tea and toast for supper. Laurie took Amy to drive, which was a deed of charity, for the sour cream seemed to have had a bad effect upon her temper. Mrs. March came home to find the three older girls hard at work in the middle of the afternoon, and a glance at the closet gave her an idea of the success of one part of the experiment.

Before the housewives could rest, several people called, and there was a scramble to get ready to see them; then tea must be got, errands done, and one or two necessary bits of sewing neglected till the last minute. As twilight fell, dewy and still, one by one they gathered on the porch where the June roses were budding beautifully, and each groaned or sighed as she sat down, as if tired or troubled.

"What a dreadful day this has been!" began Jo, usually the first to speak.

"It has seemed shorter than usual, but *so* uncomfortable," said Meg.

"Not a bit like home," added Amy.

"It can't seem so without Marmee and little Pip," sighed Beth, glancing with full eyes at the empty cage above her head.

"Here's Mother, dear, and you shall have another bird tomorrow, if you want it."

As she spoke, Mrs. March came and took her place among them, looking as if her holiday had not been much pleasanter than theirs.

"Are you satisfied with your experiment, girls, or do you want another week of it?" she asked, as Beth nestled up to her and the rest turned toward her with brightening faces, as flowers turn toward the sun.

"I don't!" cried Jo decidedly.

"Nor I," echoed the others.

"You think, then, that it is better to have a few duties and live a little for others, do you?"

"Lounging and larking doesn't pay," observed Jo, shaking her head. "I'm tired of it and mean to go to work at something right off."

"Suppose you learn plain cooking; that's a useful accomplishment, which no woman should be without," said Mrs. March, laughing inaudibly at the recollection of Jo's dinner party, for she had met Miss Crocker and heard her account of it.

"Mother, did you go away and let everything be, just to see how we'd get on?" cried Meg, who had had suspicions all day.

"Yes, I wanted you to see how the comfort of all depends on each doing her share faithfully. While Hannah and I did your work, you got on pretty well, though I don't think you were very happy or amiable; so I thought, as a little lesson, I would show you what happens when everyone thinks only of herself. Don't you feel that it is pleasanter to help one another, to have daily duties which make leisure sweet when it comes, and to bear and forbear, that home may be comfortable and lovely to us all?"

"We do, Mother, we do!" cried the girls.

"Then let me advise you to take up your little burdens again, for though they seem heavy sometimes, they are good for us, and lighten as we learn to carry them. Work is wholesome, and there is plenty for everyone; it keeps us from ennui and mischief, is good for health and spirits, and gives us a sense of power and independence better than money or fashion."

"We'll work like bees, and love it too, see if we don't!" said Jo. "I'll learn plain cooking for my holiday task, and the next dinner party I have shall be a success."

"I'll make the set of shirts for Father, instead of letting you do it, Marmee. I can and I will, though I'm not fond of sewing; that will be better than fussing over my own things, which are plenty nice enough as they are," said Meg.

"I'll do my lessons every day, and not spend so much time with my music and dolls. I am a stupid thing, and ought to be studying, not playing," was Beth's resolution, while Amy followed their example by heroically declaring, "I shall learn to make buttonholes, and attend to my parts of speech."

"Very good! Then I am quite satisfied with the experiment, and fancy that we shall not have to repeat it, only don't go to the other extreme and delve like slaves. Have regular hours for work and play, make each day both useful and pleasant, and prove that you understand the worth of time by employing it well. Then youth will be delightful, old age will bring few regrets, and life became a beautiful success, in spite of poverty."

"We'll remember, Mother!" And they did.

Chapter 12

Camp Laurence

BETH WAS postmistress, for, being most at home, she could attend to it regularly, and dearly liked the daily task of unlocking the little door and distributing the mail. One July day she came in with her hands full, and went about the house leaving letters and parcels like the penny post.

"Here's your posy, Mother! Laurie never forgets that," she said, putting the fresh nosegay in the vase that stood in "Marmee's corner" and was kept supplied by the affectionate boy.

"Miss Meg March, one letter and a glove," continued Beth, delivering the articles to her sister, who sat near her mother, stitching wristbands.

"Why, I left a pair over there, and here is only one," said Meg, looking at the gray cotton glove. "Didn't you drop the other in the garden?"

"No, I'm sure I didn't, for there was only one in the office."

"I hate to have odd gloves! Never mind, the other may be found. My letter is only a translation of the German song I wanted. I think Mr. Brooke did it, for this isn't Laurie's writing."

Mrs. March glanced at Meg, who was looking very pretty in her gingham morning gown, with the little curls blowing about her forehead, and very womanly, as she sat sewing at her little worktable, full of tidy white rolls, so unconscious of the thought in her mother's mind as she sewed and sang, while her fingers flew and her thoughts were busied with girlish fancies as innocent and fresh as the pansies in her belt, that Mrs. March smiled and was satisfied.

"Two letters for Doctor Jo, a book, and a funny old hat, which covered the whole post office, stuck outside," said Beth, laughing as she went into the study where Jo sat writing.

"What a sly fellow Laurie is! I said I wished bigger hats

were the fashion, because I burn my face every hot day. He said, 'Why mind the fashion? Wear a big hat, and be comfortable!' I said I would if I had one, and he has sent me this to try me. I'll wear it for fun, and show him I *don't* care for the fashion." And hanging the antique broadbrim on a bust of Plato, Jo read her letters.

One from her mother made her cheeks glow and her eyes fill, for it said to her—

MY DEAR:

I write a little word to tell you with how much satisfaction I watch your efforts to control your temper. You say nothing about your trials, failures, or successes, and think, perhaps, that no one sees them but the Friend whose help you daily ask, if I may trust the well-worn cover of your guidebook. *I,* too, have seen them all, and heartily believe in the sincerity of your resolution, since it begins to bear fruit. Go on, dear, patiently and bravely, and always believe that no one sympathizes more tenderly with you than your loving

MOTHER.

"That does me good! That's worth millions of money and pecks of praise. Oh, Marmee, I do try! I will keep on trying, and not get tired, since I have you to help me."

Laying her head on her arms, Jo wet her little romance with a few happy tears, for she *had* thought that no one saw and appreciated her efforts to be good, and this assurance was doubly precious, doubly encouraging, because unexpected and from the person whose commendation she most valued. Feeling stronger than ever to meet and subdue her Apollyon, she pinned the note inside her frock, as a shield and a reminder, lest she be taken unaware, and proceeded to open her other letter, quite ready for either good or bad news. In a big, dashing hand, Laurie wrote—

DEAR JO,
What ho!

Some English girls and boys are coming to see me tomorrow and I want to have a jolly time. If it's fine, I'm going to pitch my tent in Longmeadow, and row up the whole crew to lunch and croquet—have a fire, make messes, gypsy fashion, and all sorts of larks. They are nice people, and like such things. Brooke will go, to keep us boys steady, and Kate Vaughn will play propriety for the girls. I want you all to come, can't let Beth off at any price, and nobody shall worry her. Don't bother about rations—I'll see to that and everything else— only do come, there's a good fellow!

In a tearing hurry,
Yours ever, LAURIE.

"Here's richness!" cried Jo, flying in to tell the news to Meg.

"Of course we can go, Mother? It will be such a help to Laurie, for I can row, and Meg see to the lunch, and the children be useful in some way."

"I hope the Vaughns are not fine, grown-up people. Do you know anything about them, Jo?" asked Meg.

"Only that there are four of them. Kate is older than you, Fred and Frank (twins) about my age, and a little girl (Grace), who is nine or ten. Laurie knew them abroad, and liked the boys; I fancied, from the way he primmed up his mouth in speaking of her, that he didn't admire Kate much."

"I'm so glad my French print is clean, it's just the thing and so becoming!" observed Meg complacently. "Have you anything decent, Jo?"

"Scarlet and gray boating suit, good enough for me. I shall row and tramp about, so I don't want any starch to think of. You'll come, Betty?"

"If you won't let any of the boys talk to me."

"Not a boy!"

"I like to please Laurie, and I'm not afraid of Mr. Brooke, he is so kind; but I don't want to play, or sing, or say anything. I'll work hard and not trouble anyone, and you'll take care of me, Jo, so I'll go."

"That's my good girl; you do try to fight off your shyness, and I love you for it. Fighting faults isn't easy, as I know, and a cheery word kind of gives a lift. Thank you, Mother," And

Jo gave the thin cheek a grateful kiss, more precious to Mrs. March than if it had given back the rosy roundness of her youth.

"I had a box of chocolate drops, and the picture I wanted to copy," said Amy, showing her mail.

"And I got a note from Mr. Laurence, asking me to come over and play to him tonight, before the lamps are lighted, and I shall go," added Beth, whose friendship with the old gentleman prospered finely.

"Now let's fly round, and do double duty today, so that we can play tomorrow with free minds," said Jo, preparing to replace her pen with a broom.

When the sun peeped into the girls' room early next morning to promise them a fine day, he saw a comical sight. Each had made such preparation for the fete as seemed necessary and proper. Meg had an extra row of little curlpapers across her forehead, Jo had copiously anointed her afflicted face with cold cream, Beth had taken Joanna to bed with her to atone for the approaching separation, and Amy had capped the climax by putting a clothespin on her nose to uplift the offending feature. It was one of the kind artists use to hold the paper on their drawing boards, therefore quite appropriate and effective for the purpose to which it was now put. This funny spectacle appeared to amuse the sun, for he burst out with such radiance that Jo woke up and roused all her sisters by a hearty laugh at Amy's ornament.

Sunshine and laughter were good omens for a pleasure party, and soon a lively bustle began in both houses. Beth, who was ready first, kept reporting what went on next door, and enlivened her sisters' toilets by frequent telegrams from the window.

"There goes the man with the tent! I see Mrs. Barker doing up the lunch in a hamper and a great basket. Now Mr. Laurence is looking up at the sky and the weathercock; I wish he would go, too. There's Laurie, looking like a sailor—nice boy! Oh, mercy me! Here's a carriage full of people—a tall lady, a little girl, and two dreadful boys. One is lame; poor thing, he's got a crutch. Laurie didn't tell us that. Be quick, girls! It's getting late. Why, there is Ned Moffat, I do declare. Look, Meg, isn't that the man who bowed to you one day when we were shopping?"

"So it is. How queer that he should come. I thought he was at the mountains. There is Sallie; I'm glad she got back in time. Am I all right, Jo?" cried Meg in a flutter.

"A regular daisy. Hold up your dress and put your hat straight, it looks sentimental tipped that way and will fly off at the first puff. Now, then, come on!"

"Oh, Jo, you are not going to wear that awful hat? It's too absurd! You shall *not* make a guy of yourself," remonstrated Meg, as Jo tied down with a red ribbon the broad-brimmed, old-fashioned leghorn Laurie had sent for a joke.

"I just will, though, for it's capital—so shady, light, and big. It will make fun, and I don't mind being a guy if I'm comfortable." With that Jo marched straight away and the rest followed—a bright little band of sisters, all looking their best in summer suits, with happy faces under the jaunty hatbrims.

Laurie ran to meet and present them to his friends in the most cordial manner. The lawn was the reception room, and for several minutes a lively scene was enacted there. Meg was grateful to see that Miss Kate, though twenty, was dressed with a simplicity which American girls would do well to imitate, and she was much flattered by Mr. Ned's assurances that he came especially to see her. Jo understood why Laurie "primmed up his mouth" when speaking of Kate, for that young lady had a stand-off-don't-touch-me air, which contrasted strongly with the free and easy demeanor of the other girls. Beth took an observation of the new boys and decided that the lame one was not "dreadful," but gentle and feeble, and she would be kind to him on that account. Amy found Grace a well-mannered, merry little person, and after staring dumbly at one another for a few minutes, they suddenly became very good friends.

Tents, lunch, and croquet utensils having been sent on beforehand, the party was soon embarked, and the two boats pushed off together, leaving Mr. Laurence waving his hat on the shore. Laurie and Jo rowed one boat, Mr. Brooke and Ned the other, while Fred Vaughn, the riotous twin, did his best to upset both by paddling about in a wherry like a disturbed water bug. Jo's funny hat deserved a vote of thanks, for it was of general utility: it broke the ice in the beginning by producing a laugh, it created quite a refreshing breeze, flapping to and fro as she rowed, and would make an excellent umbrella for the whole party, if a shower came up, she said. Kate looked rather amazed at Jo's proceedings, especially as she exclaimed "Christopher Columbus!" when she lost her oar; and Laurie said, "My dear fellow, did I hurt you?" when he tripped over her feet in taking his place. But after putting up her glass to examine the queer girl several times, Miss Kate decided that she was "odd, but rather clever," and smiled upon her from afar.

Meg, in the other boat, was delightfully situated, face to face with the rowers, who both admired the prospect and feathered their oars with uncommon "skill and dexterity." Mr. Brooke was a grave, silent young man, with handsome brown eyes and a pleasant voice. Meg liked his quiet manners and considered him a walking encyclopedia of useful knowledge. He never talked to her much, but he looked at her a good deal, and she felt sure that he did not regard her with aversion. Ned, being in college, of course put on all the airs which freshmen think it their bounden duty to assume; he was not very wise, but very good-natured, and altogether an excellent person to carry on a picnic. Sallie Gardiner was absorbed in keeping her white piqué dress clean and chattering with the ubiquitous Fred, who kept Beth in constant terror by his pranks.

It was not far to Longmeadow, but the tent was pitched and the wickets down by the time they arrived. A pleasant green field, with three wide-spreading oaks in the middle and a smooth strip of turf for croquet.

"Welcome to Camp Laurence!" said the young host, as they landed with exclamations of delight.

"Brooke is commander in chief, I am commissary general, the other fellows are staff officers, and you, ladies, are company. The tent is for your especial benefit and that oak is your drawing room, this is the messroom and the third is the camp kitchen. Now, let's have a game before it gets hot, and then we'll see about dinner."

Frank, Beth, Amy, and Grace sat down to watch the game played by the other eight. Mr. Brooke chose Meg, Kate, and Fred; Laurie took Sallie, Jo, and Ned. The English played well, but the Americans played better, and contested every inch of the ground as strongly as if the spirit of '76 inspired them. Jo and Fred had several skirmishes and once narrowly escaped high words. Jo was through the last wicket and had missed the stroke, which failure ruffled her a good deal. Fred was close behind her and his turn came before hers, he gave a stroke, his ball hit the wicket, and stopped an inch on the wrong side. No one was very near, and running up to examine, he gave it a sly nudge with his toe, which put it just an inch on the right side.

"I'm through! Now, Miss Jo, I'll settle you, and get in first," cried the young gentleman, swinging his mallet for another blow.

"You pushed it; I saw you; it's my turn now," said Jo sharply.

"Upon my word, I didn't move it; it rolled a bit, perhaps, but that is allowed; so stand off, please, and let me have a go at the stake."

"We don't cheat in America, but you can, if you choose," said Jo angrily.

"Yankees are a deal the most tricky, everybody knows. There you go!" returned Fred, croqueting her ball far away.

Jo opened her lips to say something rude, but checked herself in time, colored up to her forehead and stood a minute, hammering down a wicket with all her might, while Fred hit the stake and declared himself out with much exultation. She went off to get her ball, and was a long time finding it among the bushes, but she came back, looking cool and quiet, and waited her turn patiently. It took several strokes to regain the place she had lost, and when she got there, the other side had nearly won, for Kate's ball was the last but one and lay near the stake.

"By George, it's all up with us! Good-by, Kate. Miss Jo owes me one, so you are finished," cried Fred excitedly, as they all drew near to see the finish.

"Yankees have a trick of being generous to their enemies," said Jo, with a look that made the lad redden, "especially when they beat them," she added, as, leaving Kate's ball untouched, she won the game by a clever stroke.

Laurie threw up his hat, then remembered that it wouldn't do to exult over the defeat of his guests, and stopped in the middle of a cheer to whisper to his friend, "Good for you, Jo! He did cheat, I saw him; we can't tell him so, but he won't do it again, take my word for it."

Meg drew her aside, under pretense of pinning up a loose braid, and said approvingly, "It was dreadfully provoking, but you kept your temper, and I'm so glad, Jo."

"Don't praise me, Meg, for I could box his ears this minute. I should certainly have boiled over if I hadn't stayed among the nettles till I got my rage under enough to hold my tongue. It's simmering now, so I hope he'll keep out of my way," returned Jo, biting her lips as she glowered at Fred from under her big hat.

"Time for lunch," said Mr. Brooke, looking at his watch. "Commissary general, will you make the fire and get water, while Miss March, Miss Sallie, and I spread the table? Who can make good coffee?"

"Jo can," said Meg, glad to recommend her sister. So Jo, feeling that her late lessons in cookery were to do her honor, went to preside over the coffeepot, while the children collected dry sticks, and the boys made a fire and got water from a spring near by. Miss Kate sketched and Frank talked to Beth, who was making little mats of braided rushes to serve as plates.

The commander in chief and his aides soon spread the tablecloth with an inviting array of eatables and drinkables, prettily decorated with green leaves. Jo announced that the coffee was ready, and everyone settled themselves to a hearty meal, for youth is seldom dyspeptic, and exercise develops wholesome appetites. A very merry lunch it was, for everything seemed fresh and funny, and frequent peals of laughter startled a venerable horse who fed near by. There was a pleasing inequality in the table, which produced many mishaps to cups and plates, acorns dropped into the milk, little black ants partook of the refreshments without being invited, and fuzzy caterpillars swung down from the tree to see what was going on. Three white-headed children peeped over the fence, and an objectionable dog barked at them from the other side of the river with all his might and main.

"There's salt here, if you prefer it," said Laurie, as he handed Jo a saucer of berries.

"Thank you, I prefer spiders," she replied, fishing up two unwary little ones who had gone to a creamy death. "How dare you remind me of that horrid dinner party, when yours is so nice in every way?" added Jo, as they both laughed and ate out of one plate, the china having run short.

"I had an uncommonly good time that day, and haven't got over it yet. This is no credit to me, you know, I don't do anything; it's you and Meg and Brooke who make it go, and I'm no end obliged to you. What shall we do when we can't eat any more?" asked Laurie, feeling that his trump card had been played when lunch was over.

"Have games till it's cooler. I brought Authors, and I dare say Miss Kate knows something new and nice. Go and ask her; she's company, and you ought to stay with her more."

"Aren't you company too? I thought she'd suit Brooke, but he keeps talking to Meg, and Kate just stares at them through that ridiculous glass of hers. I'm going, so you needn't try to preach propriety, for you can't do it, Jo."

Miss Kate did know several new games, and as the girls would not, and the boys could not, eat any more, they all adjourned to the drawing room to play Rig-marole.

"One person begins a story, any nonsense you like, and tells as long as he pleases, only taking care to stop short at some exciting point, when the next takes it up and does the same. It's very funny when well done, and makes a perfect jumble of tragical comical stuff to laugh over. Please start it, Mr. Brooke," said Kate, with a commanding air, which surprised Meg, who treated the tutor with as much respect as any other gentleman.

Lying on the grass at the feet of the two young ladies, Mr. Brooke obediently began the story, with the handsome brown eyes steadily fixed upon the sunshiny river.

"Once on a time, a knight went out into the world to seek his fortune, for he had nothing but his sword and his shield. He traveled a long while, nearly eight-and-twenty years, and had a hard time of it, till he came to the palace of a good old king, who had offered a reward to anyone who would tame and train a fine but unbroken colt, of which he was very fond. The knight agreed to try, and got on slowly but surely, for the colt was a gallant fellow, and soon learned to love his new master, though he was freakish and wild. Every day, when he gave his lessons to this pet of the king's, the knight rode him through the city; and, as he rode, he looked everywhere for a certain beautiful face, which he had seen many times in his dreams, but never found. One day, as he went prancing down a quiet street, he saw at the window of a ruinous castle the lovely face. He was delighted, inquired who lived in this old castle, and was told that several captive princesses were kept there by a spell, and spun all day to lay up money to buy their liberty. The knight wished intensely that he could free them, but he was poor and could only go by each day, watching for the sweet face and longing to see it out in the sunshine. At last he resolved to get into the castle and ask how he could help them. He went and knocked; the great door flew open, and he beheld—"

"A ravishingly lovely lady, who exclaimed, with a cry of rapture, 'At last! At last!' " continued Kate, who had read French novels, and admired the style. " ' 'Tis she!' cried Count Gustave, and fell at her feet in an ecstasy of joy. 'Oh, rise!' she said, extending a hand of marble fairness. 'Never! till you tell me how I may rescue you,' swore the knight, still kneeling. 'Alas, my cruel fate condemns me to remain here till my tyrant is destroyed.' 'Where is the villain?' 'In the mauve salon. Go, brave heart, and save me from despair.' 'I obey, and return victorious or dead!' With these thrilling words he rushed away, and flinging open the door of the mauve salon, was about to enter, when he received—"

"A stunning blow from the big Greek lexicon, which an

old fellow in a black gown fired at him," said Ned. "Instantly Sir What's-his-name recovered himself, pitched the tyrant out of the window, and turned to join the lady, victorious, but with a bump on his brow; found the door locked, tore up the curtains, made a rope ladder, got halfway down when the ladder broke, and he went head first into the moat, sixty feet below. Could swim like a duck, paddled round the castle till he came to a little door guarded by two stout fellows, knocked their heads together till they cracked like a couple of nuts, then, by a trifling exertion of his prodigious strength, he smashed in the door, went up a pair of stone steps covered with dust a foot thick, toads as big as your fist, and spiders that would frighten you into hysterics, Miss March. At the top of these steps he came plump upon a sight that took his breath away and chilled his blood——"

"A tall figure, all in white with a veil over its face and a lamp in its wasted hand," went on Meg. "It beckoned, gliding noiselessly before him down a corridor as dark and cold as any tomb. Shadowy effigies in armor stood on either side, a dead silence reigned, the lamp burned blue, and the ghostly figure ever and anon turned its face toward him, showing the glitter of awful eyes through its white veil. They reached a curtained door, behind which sounded lovely music; he sprang forward to enter, but the specter plucked him back, and waved threateningly before him a——"

"Snuffbox," said Jo, in a sepulchral tone, which convulsed the audience. " 'Thankee,' said the knight politely, as he took a pinch and sneezed seven times so violently that his head fell off. 'Ha! ha!' laughed the ghost, and having peeped through the keyhole at the princesses spinning away for dear life, the evil spirit picked up her victim and put him in a large tin box, where there were eleven other knights packed together without their heads, like sardines, who all rose and began to——"

"Dance a hornpipe," cut in Fred, as Jo paused for breath, "and, as they danced, the rubbishy old castle turned to a man-of-war in full sail. 'Up with the jib, reef the tops'l halliards, helm hard alee, and man the guns!' roared the captain, as a Portuguese pirate hove in sight, with a flag black as ink flying from her foremast. 'Go in and win, my hearties!' says the captain, and a tremendous fight began. Of course the British beat, they always do."

"No, they don't!" cried Jo, aside.

"Having taken the pirate captain prisoner, sailed slap over the schooner, whose decks were piled with dead and whose lee scuppers ran blood, for the order had been 'Cutlasses, and die hard!' 'Bosun's mate, take a bight of the flying-jib sheet, and start this villain if he doesn't confess his sins double quick,' said the British captain. The Portuguese held his tongue like a brick, and walked the plank, while the jolly tars cheered like mad. But the sly dog dived, came up under the man-of-war, scuttled her, and down she went, with all sail set, 'To the bottom of the sea, sea, sea,' where—"

"Oh gracious! what *shall* I say?" cried Sallie, as Fred ended his rigmarole, in which he had jumbled together pell-mell nautical phrases and facts out of one of his favorite books. "Well, they went to the bottom, and a nice mermaid welcomed them, but was much grieved on finding the box of headless knights, and kindly pickled them in brine, hoping to discover the mystery about them, for, being a woman, she was curious. By-and-by a diver came down, and the mermaid said, 'I'll give you this box of pearls if you can take it up,' for she wanted to restore the poor things to life, and couldn't raise the heavy load herself. So the diver hoisted it up, and was much disappointed on opening it to find no pearls. He left it in a great lonely field, where it was found by a—"

"Little goosegirl, who kept a hundred fat geese in the field," said Amy, when Sallie's invention gave out. "The little girl was sorry for them, and asked an old woman what she should do to help them. 'Your geese will tell you, they know everything,' said the old woman. So she asked what she should use for new heads, since the old ones were lost, and all the geese opened their hundred mouths and screamed—"

" 'Cabbages!' " continued Laurie promptly. " 'Just the thing,' said the girl, and ran to get twelve fine ones from her garden. She put them on, the knights revived at once, thanked her, and went on their way rejoicing, never knowing the difference, for there were so many other heads like them in the world that no one thought anything of it. The knight in whom I'm interested went back to find the pretty face, and learned that the princesses had spun themselves free and all gone to be married, but one. He was in a great state of mind at that; and mounting the colt, who stood by him through thick and thin, rushed to the castle to see which was left. Peeping over the hedge, he saw the queen of his affections picking flowers in her garden. 'Will you give me a rose?' said he. 'You must come and get it. I can't come to you, it isn't proper,' said she, as sweet as honey. He tried to climb over the hedge, but it seemed to grow higher and higher; then he tried to push through, but it grew thicker and thicker, and he was in despair. So he patiently broke twig after twig till he had made a little hole through which he peeped, saying imploringly, 'Let me in! Let me in!' But the pretty princess did not seem to understand, for she picked her roses quietly, and left him to fight his way in. Whether he did or not, Frank will tell you."

"I can't; I'm not playing, I never do," said Frank, dismayed at the sentimental predicament out of which he was to rescue the absurd couple. Beth had disappeared behind Jo, and Grace was asleep.

"So the poor knight is to be left sticking in the hedge, is he?" asked Mr. Brooke, still watching the river, and playing ith the wild rose in his buttonhole.

"I guess the princess gave him a posy, and opened the gate fter a while," said Laurie, smiling to himself, as he threw corns at his tutor.

"What a piece of nonsense we have made! With practice ve might do something quite clever. Do you know Truth?" sked Sallie, after they had laughed over their story.

"I hope so," said Meg soberly.

"The game, I mean?"

"What is it?" said Fred.

"Why, you pile up your hands, choose a number, and draw ut in turn, and the person who draws at the number has to answer truly any questions put by the rest. It's great fun."

"Let's try it," said Jo, who liked new experiments.

Miss Kate and Mr. Brooke, Meg, and Ned declined, but Fred, Sallie, Jo, and Laurie piled and drew, and the lot fell to Laurie.

"Who are your heroes?" asked Jo.

"Grandfather and Napoleon."

"Which lady here do you think prettiest?" said Sallie.

"Margaret."

"Which do you like best?" from Fred.

"Jo, of course."

"What silly questions you ask!" And Jo gave a disdainful shrug as the rest laughed at Laurie's matter-of-fact tone.

"Try again; Truth isn't a bad game," said Fred.

"It's a very good one for you," retorted Jo in a low voice. Her turn came next.

"What is your greatest fault?" asked Fred, by way of testing in her the virtue he lacked himself.

"A quick temper."

"What do you most wish for?" said Laurie.

"A pair of boot lacings," returned Jo, guessing and defeating his purpose.

"Not a true answer; you must say what you really do want most."

"Genius; don't you wish you could give it to me, Laurie?" And she slyly smiled in his disappointed face.

"What virtues do you most admire in a man?" asked Sallie.

"Courage and honesty."

"Now my turn," said Fred, as his hand came last.

"Let's give it to him," whispered Laurie to Jo, who nodded and asked at once—

"Didn't you cheat at croquet?"

"Well, yes, a little bit."

"Good! Didn't you take your story out of *The Sea-Lion*?" said Laurie.

"Rather."

"Don't you think the English nation perfect in e' spect?" asked Sallie.

"I should be ashamed of myself if I didn't."

"He's a true John Bull. Now, Miss Sallie, you shall have a chance without waiting to draw. I'll harrow up your feelings first by asking if you don't think you are something of a flirt," said Laurie, as Jo nodded to Fred as a sign that peace was declared.

"You impertinent boy! Of course I'm not," exclaimed Sallie, with an air that proved the contrary.

"What do you hate most?" asked Fred.

"Spiders and rice pudding."

"What do you like best?" asked Jo.

"Dancing and French gloves."

"Well, *I* think Truth is a very silly play; let's have a sensible game of Authors to refresh our minds," proposed Jo.

Ned, Frank, and the little girls joined in this, and while it went on, the three elders sat apart, talking. Miss Kate took out her sketch again, and Margaret watched her, while Mr. Brooke lay on the grass with a book, which he did not read.

"How beautifully you do it! I wish I could draw," said Meg, with mingled admiration and regret in her voice.

"Why don't you learn? I should think you had taste and talent for it," replied Miss Kate graciously.

"I haven't time."

"Your mamma prefers other accomplishments, I fancy. So did mine, but I proved to her that I had talent by taking a fey lessons privately, and then she was quite willing I should go on. Can't you do the same with your governess?"

"I have none."

"I forgot young ladies in America go to school more than with us. Very fine schools they are, too, Papa says. You go to a private one, I suppose?"

"I don't go at all. I am a governess myself."

"Oh, indeed!" said Miss Kate; but she might as well have said, "Dear me, how dreadful!" for her tone implied it, and something in her face made Meg color, and wish she had not been so frank.

Mr. Brooke looked up and said quickly, "Young ladies in America love independence as much as their ancestors did, ʌre admired and respected for supporting themselves."

"Oh, yes, of course it's very nice and proper in them to do so. We have many most respectable and worthy young women who do the same and are employed by the nobility, because, being the daughters of gentlemen, they are both well bred and accomplished, you know," said Miss Kate in a patronizing tone that hurt Meg's pride, and made her work seem not only more distasteful, but degrading.

"Did the German song suit, Miss March?" inquired Mr. Brooke, breaking an awkward pause.

"Oh, yes! It was very sweet, and I'm much obliged to whoever translated it for me." And Meg's downcast face brightened as she spoke.

"Don't you read German?" asked Miss Kate with a look of surprise.

"Not very well. My father, who taught me, is away, and I don't get on very fast alone, for I've no one to correct my pronunciation."

"Try a little now; here is Schiller's *Mary Stuart* and a tutor who loves to teach." And Mr. Brooke laid his book on her lap with an inviting smile.

"It's so hard I'm afraid to try," said Meg, grateful, but bashful in the presence of the accomplished young lady beside her.

"I'll read a bit to encourge you." And Miss Kate read one of the most beautiful passages in a perfectly correct but perfectly expressionless manner.

Mr. Brooke made no comment as she returned the book to Meg, who said innocently, "I thought it was poetry."

"Some of it is. Try this passage."

There was a queer smile about Mr. Brooke's mouth as he opened at poor Mary's lament.

Meg obediently following the long grass-blade which her new tutor used to point with, read slowly and timidly, unconsciously making poetry of the hard words by the soft intonation of her musical voice. Down the page went the green guide, and presently, forgetting her listener in the beau the sad scene, Meg read as if alone, giving a little t tragedy to the words of the unhappy queen. If she ha brown eyes then, she would have stopped short; bu looked up, and the lesson was not spoiled for her.

"Very well indeed!" said Mr. Brooke, as she paused, quite ignoring her many mistakes, and looking as if he did indeed "love to teach."

Miss Kate put up her glass, and, having taken a survey of the little tableau before her, shut her sketchbook, saying with condescension, "You've a nice accent and in time will be a clever reader. I advise you to learn, for German is a valuable accomplishment to teachers. I must look after Grace, she is romping." And Miss Kate strolled away, adding to herself with a shrug, "I didn't come to chaperone a governness, though she *is* young and pretty. What odd people these Yankees are; I'm afraid Laurie will be quite spoiled among them."

"I forgot that English people rather turn up their noses at governesses and don't treat them as we do," said Meg, looking after the retreating figure with an annoyed expression.

"Tutors also have rather a hard time of it there, as I know to my sorrow. There's no place like America for us workers, Miss Margaret." And Mr. Brooke looked so contented and cheerful that Meg was ashamed to lament her hard lot.

"I'm glad I live in it then. I don't like my work, but I get a good deal of satisfaction out of it after all, so I won't complain; I only wish I liked teaching as you do."

"I think you would if you had Laurie for a pupil. I shall be very sorry to lose him next year," said Mr. Brooke, busily punching holes in the turf.

"Going to college, I suppose?" Meg's lips asked that question, but her eyes added, "And what becomes of you?"

"Yes, it's high time he went, for he is ready; and as soon as he is off, I shall turn soldier. I am needed."

"I am glad of that!" exclaimed Meg. "I should think every young man would want to go, though it is hard for the mothers and sisters who stay at home," she added sorrowfully.

"I have neither, and very few friends to care whether I live or die," said Mr. Brooke rather bitterly as he absently put the dead rose in the hole he had made and covered it up, like a little grave.

"Laurie and his grandfather would care a great deal, and

we should all be very sorry to have any harm happen to you," said Meg heartily.

"Thank you, that sounds pleasant," began Mr. Brooke, looking cheerful again; but before he could finish his speech, Ned, mounted on the old horse, came lumbering up to display his equestrian skill before the young ladies, and there was no more quiet that day.

"Don't you love to ride?" asked Grace of Amy, as they stood resting after a race round the field with the others, led by Ned.

"I dote upon it; my sister Meg used to ride when Papa was rich, but we don't keep any horses now, except Ellen Tree," added Amy, laughing.

"Tell me about Ellen Tree. Is it a donkey?" asked Grace curiously.

"Why, you see, Jo is crazy about horses and so am I, but we've only got an old sidesaddle and no horse. Out in our garden is an apple tree that has a nice low branch, so Jo put the saddle on it, fixed some reins on the part that turns up, and we bounce away on Ellen Tree whenever we like."

"How funny!" laughed Grace. "I have a pony at home, and ride nearly every day in the park with Fred and Kate; it's very nice, for my friends go too, and the Row is full of ladies and gentlemen."

"Dear, how charming! I hope I shall go abroad some day, but I'd rather go to Rome than the Row," said Amy, who had not the remotest idea what the Row was and wouldn't have asked for the world.

Frank, sitting just behind the little girls, heard what they were saying, and pushed his crutch away from him with an impatient gesture as he watched the active lads going through all sorts of comical gymnastics. Beth, who was collecting the scattered Author cards, looked up and said, in her shy yet friendly way, "I'm afraid you are tired; can I do anything for you?"

"Talk to me, please; it's dull, sitting by myself," answered Frank, who had evidently been used to being made much of at home.

If he had asked her to deliver a Latin oration, it would not have seemed a more impossible task to bashful Beth; but there was no place to run to, no Jo to hide behind now, and the poor boy looked so wistfully at her that she bravely resolved to try.

"What do you like to talk about?" she asked, fumbling over the cards and dropping half as she tried to tie them up.

"Well, I like to hear about cricket and boating and hunting," said Frank, who had not yet learned to suit his amusements to his strength.

"My heart! What shall I do? I don't know anything about them," thought Beth, and forgetting the boy's misfortune in her flurry, she said, hoping to make him talk, "I never saw any hunting, but I suppose you know all about it."

"I did once; but I can never hunt again, for I got hurt leaping a confounded five-barred gate, so there are no more horses and hounds for me," said Frank with a sigh that made Beth hate herself for her innocent blunder.

"Your deer are much prettier than our ugly buffaloes," she said, turning to the prairies for help and feeling glad that she had read one of the boys' books in which Jo delighted.

Buffaloes proved soothing and satisfactory, and in her eagerness to amuse another, Beth forgot herself, and was quite unconscious of her sisters' surprise and delight at the unusual spectacle of Beth talking away to one of the dreadful boys, against whom she had begged protection.

"Bless her heart! She pities him, so she is good to him," said Jo, beaming at her from the croquet ground.

"I always said she was a little saint," added Meg, as if there could be no further doubt of it.

"I haven't heard Frank laugh so much for ever so long," said Grace to Amy, as they sat discussing dolls and making tea sets out of the acorn cups.

"My sister Beth is a very *fastidious* girl, when she likes to be," said Amy, well pleased at Beth's success. She meant "fascinating," but as Grace didn't know the exact meaning of either word, "fastidious" sounded well and made a good impression.

An impromptu circus, fox and geese, and an amicable game of croquet finished the afternoon. At sunset the tent was struck, hampers packed, wickets pulled up, boats loaded, and the whole party floated down the river, singing at the tops of their voices. Ned, getting sentimental, warbled a serenade with the pensive refrain—

> Alone, alone, ah! woe, alone,

and at the lines—

> We each are young, we each have a heart,
> Oh, why should we stand thus coldly apart?

he looked at Meg with such a lackadaisical expression that she laughed outright and spoiled his song.

"How can you be so cruel to me?" he whispered, under cover of a lively chorus. "You've kept close to that starched-up Englishwoman all day, and now you snub me."

"I didn't mean to, but you looked so funny I really couldn't help it," replied Meg, passing over the first part of his reproach, for it was quite true that she *had* shunned him, remembering the Moffat party and the talk after it.

Ned was offended and turned to Sallie for consolation, saying to her rather pettishly, "There isn't a bit of flirt in that girl, is there?"

"Not a particle, but she's a dear," returned Sallie, defending her friend even while confessing her shortcomings.

"She's not a stricken deer anyway," said Ned, trying to be witty, and succeeding as well as very young gentlemen usually do.

On the lawn where it had gathered, the little party separated with cordial good nights and good-bys, for the Vaughns were going to Canada. As the four sisters went home through the garden, Miss Kate looked after them, saying, without the patronizing tone in her voice, "In spite of their demonstrative manners, American girls are very nice when one knows them."

"I quite agree with you," said Mr. Brooke.

Chapter 13

Castles in the Air

LAURIE LAY luxuriously swinging to and fro in his hammock, one warm September afternoon, wondering what his neighbors were about, but too lazy to go and find out. He was in one of his moods, for the day had been both unprofitable and unsatisfactory, and he was wishing he could live it over again. The hot weather made him indolent, and he had shirked his studies, tried Mr. Brooke's patience to the utmost, displeased his grandfather by practicing half the afternoon, frightened the maidservants half out of their wits by mischievously hinting that one of his dogs was going mad, and, after high words with the stableman about some fancied neglect of his horse, he had flung himself into his hammock to fume over the stupidity of the world in general, till the peace of the lovely day quieted him in spite of himself. Staring up into the green gloom of the horse-chestnut trees above him, he dreamed dreams of all sorts, and was just imagining himself tossing on the ocean in a voyage round the world, when the sound of voices brought him ashore in a flash. Peeping through the meshes of the hammock, he saw the Marches coming out, as if bound on some expedition.

"What in the world are those girls about now?" thought Laurie, opening his sleepy eyes to take a good look, for there was something rather peculiar in the appearance of his neighbors. Each wore a large, flapping hat, a brown linen pouch slung over one shoulder, and carried a long staff. Meg had a cushion, Jo a book, Beth a basket, and Amy a portfolio. All walked quietly through the garden, out at the little back gate, and began to climb the hill that lay between the house and river.

"Well, that's cool," said Laurie to himself, "to have a picnic and never ask me! They can't be going in the boat, for they

. . . the sisters sat together in the shady nook, with sun and shadow flickering over them . . .

haven't got the key. Perhaps they forgot it; I'll take it to them, and see what's going on."

Though possessed of half a dozen hats, it took him some time to find one; then there was a hunt for the key, which was at last discovered in his pocket, so that the girls were quite out of sight when he leaped the fence and ran after them. Taking the shortest way to the boathouse, he waited for them to appear; but no one came, and he went up the hill to take an observation. A grove of pines covered one part of it, and from the heart of this green spot came a clearer sound than the soft sigh of the pines or the drowsy chirp of the crickets.

"Here's a landscape!" thought Laurie, peeping through the bushes, and looking wide-awake and good-natured already.

It *was* rather a pretty little picture, for the sisters sat together in the shady nook, with sun and shadow flickering over them, the aromatic wind lifting their hair and cooling their hot cheeks, and all the little wood people going on with their affairs as if these were no strangers but old friends. Meg sat upon her cushion, sewing daintily with her white hands, and looking as fresh and sweet as a rose in her pink dress among the green. Beth was sorting the cones that lay thick under the hemlock near by, for she made pretty things of them. Amy was sketching a group of ferns, and Jo was knitting as she read aloud. A shadow passed over the boy's face as he watched them, feeling that he ought to go away because uninvited, yet lingering because home seemed very lonely and this quiet party in the woods most attractive to his restless spirit. He stood so still that a squirrel, busy with its harvesting, ran down a pine close beside him, saw him suddenly and skipped back, scolding so shrilly that Beth looked up, espied the wistful face behind the birches, and beckoned with a reassuring smile.

"May I come in, please? Or shall I be a bother?" he asked, advancing slowly.

Meg lifted her eyebrows, but Jo scowled at her defiantly and said at once, "Of course you may. We should have asked you before, only we thought you wouldn't care for such a girl's game as this."

"I always like your games; but if Meg doesn't want me, I'll go away.

"I've no objection, if you do something; it's against the rules to be idle here," replied Meg gravely but graciously.

"Much obliged. I'll do anything if you'll let me stop a bit, for it's as dull as the Desert of Sahara down there. Shall I sew, read, cone, draw, or do all at once? Bring on your bears, I'm ready." And Laurie sat down with a submissive expression delightful to behold.

"Finish this story while I set my heel," said Jo, handing him the book.

"Yes'm" was the meek answer, as he began, doing his best to prove his gratitude for the favor of an admission into the "Busy Bee Society."

The story was not a long one, and when it was finished, he ventured to ask a few questions as a reward of merit.

"Please, ma'am, could I inquire if this highly instructive and charming institution is a new one?"

"Would you tell him?" asked Meg of her sisters.

"He'll laugh," said Amy warningly.

"Who cares?" said Jo.

"I guess he'll like it," added Beth.

"Of course I shall! I give you my word I won't laugh. Tell away, Jo, and don't be afraid."

"The idea of being afraid of you! Well, you see we used to play Pilgrim's Progress, and we have been going on with it in earnest, all winter and summer."

"Yes, I know," said Laurie, nodding wisely.

"Who told you?" demanded Jo.

"Spirits."

"No, I did. I wanted to amuse him one night when you were all away, and he was rather dismal. He did like it, so don't scold, Jo," said Beth meekly.

"You can't keep a secret. Never mind, it saves trouble now."

"Go on, please," said Laurie, as Jo became absorbed in her work, looking a trifle displeased.

"Oh, didn't she tell you about this new plan of ours? Well,

we have tried not to waste our holiday, but each has had a task and worked at it with a will. The vacation is nearly over, the stints are all done, and we are ever so glad that we didn't dawdle."

"Yes, I should think so." And Laurie thought regretfully of his own idle days.

"Mother likes to have us out-of-doors as much as possible, so we bring our work here and have nice times. For the fun of it we bring our things in these bags, wear the old hats, use poles to climb the hill, and play pilgrims, as we used to do years ago. We call this hill the Delectable Mountain, for we can look far away and see the country where we hope to live some time."

Jo pointed, and Laurie sat up to examine, for through an opening in the wood one could look across the wide, blue river, the meadows on the other side, far over the outskirts of the great city, to the green hills that rose to meet the sky. The sun was low, and the heavens glowed with the splendor of an autumn sunset. Gold and purple clouds lay on the hilltops, and rising high into the ruddy light were silvery white peaks that shone like the airy spires of some Celestial City.

"How beautiful that is!" said Laurie softly, for he was quick to see and feel beauty of any kind.

"It's often so, and we like to watch it, for it is never the same, but always splendid," replied Amy, wishing she could paint it.

"Jo talks about the country where we hope to live some time—the real country, she means, with pigs and chickens and haymaking. It would be nice, but I wish the beautiful country up there was real, and we could ever go to it," said Beth musingly.

"There is a lovelier country even than that, where we *shall* go, by-and-by, when we are good enough," answered Meg with her sweet voice.

"It seems so long to wait, so hard to do. I want to fly away at once, as those swallows fly, and go in at that splendid gate."

"You'll get there, Beth, sooner or later, no fear of that,"

said Jo. "I'm the one that will have to fight and work, and climb and wait, and maybe never get in after all."

"You'll have me for company, if that's any comfort. I shall have to do a deal of traveling before I come in sight of your Celestial City. If I arrive late, you'll say a good word for me, won't you, Beth?"

Something in the boy's face troubled his little friend, but she said cheerfully, with her quiet eyes on the changing clouds, "If people really want to go, and really try all their lives, I think they will get in, for I don't believe there are any locks on that door or any guards at the gate. I always imagine it is as it is in the picture, where the shining ones stretch out their hands to welcome poor Christian as he comes up from the river."

"Wouldn't it be fun if all the castles in the air which we make could come true, and we could live in them?" said Jo, after a little pause.

"I've made such quantities it would be hard to choose which I'd have," said Laurie, lying flat and throwing cones at the squirrel who had betrayed him.

"You'd have to take your favorite one. What is it?" asked Meg.

"If I tell mine, will you tell yours?"

"Yes, if the girls will too."

"We will. Now, Laurie."

"After I'd seen as much of the world as I want to, I'd like to settle in Germany and have just as much music as I choose. I'm to be a famous musician myself, and all creation is to rush to hear me; and I'm never to be bothered about money or business, but just enjoy myself and live for what I like. That's my favorite castle. What's yours, Meg?"

Margaret seemed to find it a little hard to tell hers, and waved a brake before her face, as if to disperse imaginary gnats, while she said slowly, "I should like a lovely house, full of all sorts of luxurious things—nice food, pretty clothes, handsome furniture, pleasant people, and heaps of money. I am to be mistress of it, and manage it as I like, with plenty of servants, so I never need work a bit. How I should enjoy it! For I wouldn't be idle, but do good, and make everyone love me dearly."

"Wouldn't you have a master for your castle in the air?" asked Laurie slyly.

"I said 'pleasant people,' you know." And Meg carefully tied up her shoe as she spoke, so that no one saw her face.

"Why don't you say you'd have a splendid, wise, good husband and some angelic little children? You know your castle wouldn't be perfect without," said blunt Jo, who had no tender fancies yet, and rather scorned romance, except in books.

"You'd have nothing but horses, inkstands, and novels in yours," answered Meg petulantly.

"Wouldn't I, though? I'd have a stable full of Arabian steeds, rooms piled with books, and I'd write out of a magic inkstand, so that my works should be as famous as Laurie's music. I want to do something splendid before I go into my castle—something heroic or wonderful that won't be forgotten after I'm dead. I don't know what, but I'm on the watch for it, and mean to astonish you all some day. I think I shall write books, and get rich and famous: that would suit me, so that is *my* favorite dream."

"Mine is to stay at home safe with Father and Mother, and help take care of the family," said Beth contentedly.

"Don't you wish for anything else?" asked Laurie.

"Since I had my little piano, I am perfectly satisfied. I only wish we may all keep well and be together, nothing else."

"I have ever so many wishes, but the pet one is to be an artist, and go to Rome, and do fine pictures, and be the best artist in the whole world" was Amy's modest desire.

"We're an ambitious set, aren't we? Every one of us, but Beth, wants to be rich and famous, and gorgeous in every respect. I do wonder if any of us will ever get our wishes," said Laurie, chewing grass like a meditative calf.

"I've got the key to my castle in the air, but whether I can unlock the door remains to be seen," observed Jo mysteriously.

"I've got the key to mine, but I'm not allowed to try it.

Hang college!" muttered Laurie with an impatient sigh.

"Here's mine!" And Amy waved her pencil.

"I haven't got any," said Meg forlornly.

"Yes, you have," said Laurie at once.

"Where?"

"In your face."

"Nonsense, that's of no use."

"Wait and see if it doesn't bring you something worth having," replied the boy, laughing at the thought of a charming little secret which he fancied he knew.

Meg colored behind the brake, but asked no questions and looked across the river with the same expectant expression which Mr. Brooke had worn when he told the story of the knight.

"If we are all alive ten years hence, let's meet, and see how many of us have got our wishes, or how much nearer we are then than now," said Jo, always ready with a plan.

"Bless me! How old I shall be—twenty-seven!" exclaimed Meg, who felt grown up already, having just reached seventeen.

"You and I will be twenty-six, Teddy, Beth twenty-four, and Amy twenty-two. What a venerable party!" said Jo.

"I hope I shall have done something to be proud of by that time, but I'm such a lazy dog, I'm afraid I shall 'dawdle,' Jo."

"You need a motive, Mother says; and when you get it, she is sure you'll work splendidly."

"Is she? By Jupiter, I will, if I only get the chance!" cried Laurie, sitting up with sudden energy. "I ought to be satisfied to please Grandfather, and I do try, but it's working against the grain, you see, and comes hard. He wants me to be an India merchant, as he was, and I'd rather be shot. I hate tea and silk and spices, and every sort of rubbish his old ships bring, and I don't care how soon they go to the bottom when I own them. Going to college ought to satisfy him, for if I give him four years he ought to let me off from the business; but he's set, and I've got to do just as he did, unless I break away and please myself, as my father did. If there was anyone left to stay with the old gentleman, I'd do it tomorrow."

Laurie spoke excitedly, and looked ready to carry his threat into execution on the slightest provocation, for he was growing up very fast and, in spite of his indolent ways, had a young man's hatred of subjection, a young man's restless longing to try the world for himself.

"I advise you to sail away in one of your ships, and never come home again till you have tried your own way," said Jo, whose imagination was fired by the thought of such a daring exploit, and whose sympathy was excited by what she called "Teddy's wrongs."

"That's not right, Jo; you musn't talk in that way, and Laurie mustn't take your bad advice. You should do just what your grandfather wishes, my dear boy," said Meg in her most maternal tone. "Do your best at college, and when he sees that you try to please him, I'm sure he won't be hard or unjust to you. As you say, there is no one else to stay with and love him, and you'd never forgive yourself if you left him without his permission. Don't be dismal or fret, but do your duty and you'll get your reward, as good Mr. Brooke has, by being respected and loved."

"What do you know about him?" asked Laurie, grateful for the good advice, but objecting to the lecture, and glad to turn the conversation from himself after his unusual outbreak.

"Only what your grandpa told us about him—how he took good care of his own mother till she died, and wouldn't go abroad as tutor to some nice person because he wouldn't leave her; and how he provides now for an old woman who nursed his mother, and never tells anyone, but is just as generous and patient and good as he can be."

"So he is, dear old fellow!" said Laurie heartily, as Meg paused, looking flushed and earnest with her story. "It's like Grandpa to find out all about him without letting him know, and to tell all his goodness to others, so that they might like him. Brooke couldn't understand why your mother was so kind to him, asking him over with me and treating him in her beautiful friendly way. He thought she was just perfect, and talked about it for days and days, and went on about you all in flaming style. If ever I do get my wish, you see what I'll do for Brooke."

"Begin to do something now by not plaguing his life out," said Meg sharply.

"How do you know I do, miss?"

"I can always tell by his face when he goes away. If you have been good, he looks satisfied and walks briskly; if you have plagued him, he's sober and walks slowly, as if he wanted to go back and do his work better."

"Well, I like that! So you keep an account of my good and bad marks in Brooke's face, do you? I see him bow and smile as he passes your window, but I didn't know you'd got up a telegraph."

"We haven't. Don't be angry, and oh, don't tell him I said anything! It was only to show that I cared how you get on, and what is said here is said in confidence, you know," cried Meg, much alarmed at the thought of what might follow from her careless speech.

"*I* don't tell tales," replied Laurie, with his "high and mighty" air, as Jo called a certain expression which he occasionally wore. "Only if Brooke is going to be a thermometer, I must mind and have fair weather for him to report."

"Please don't be offended. I didn't mean to preach or tell tales or be silly. I only thought Jo was encouraging you in a feeling which you'd be sorry for by-and-by. You are so kind to us, we feel as if you were our brother and say just what we think. Forgive me, I meant it kindly." And Meg offered her hand with a gesture both affectionate and timid.

Ashamed of his momentary pique, Laurie squeezed the kind little hand, and said frankly, "I'm the one to be forgiven. I'm cross and have been out of sorts all day. I like to have you tell me my faults and be sisterly, so don't mind if I am grumpy sometimes. I thank you all the same."

Bent on showing that he was not offended, he made himself as agreeable as possible—wound cotton for Meg, recited poetry to please Jo, shook down cones for Beth, and helped Amy with her ferns, proving himself a fit person to belong to the "Busy Bee Society." In the midst of an animated discussion on the domestic habits of turtles (one of those amiable creatures having strolled up from the river), the faint sound of a bell warned them that Hannah had put the tea "to draw," and they would just have time to get home to supper.

"May I come again?" asked Laurie.

"Yes, if you are good, and love your book, as the boys in the primer are told to do," said Meg, smiling.

"I'll try."

"Then you may come, and I'll teach you to knit as the Scotchmen do. There's a demand for socks just now," added Jo, waving hers like a big blue worsted banner as they parted at the gate.

That night, when Beth played to Mr. Laurence in the twilight, Laurie, standing in the shadow of the curtain, listened to the little David, whose simple music always quieted his moody spirit, and watched the old man, who sat with his gray head on his hand, thinking tender thoughts of the dead child he had loved so much. Remembering the conversation of the afternoon, the boy said to himself, with the resolve to make the sacrifice cheerfully, "I'll let my castle go, and stay with the dear old gentleman while he needs me, for I am all he has."

Chapter 14

Secrets

Jo WAS VERY BUSY in the garret, for the October days began to grow chilly, and the afternoons were short. For two or three hours the sun lay warmly in the high window, showing Jo seated on the old sofa, writing busily, with her papers spread out upon a trunk before her, while Scrabble, the pet rat, promenaded the beams overhead, accompanied by his oldest son, a fine young fellow, who was evidently very proud of his whiskers. Quite absorbed in her work, Jo scribbled away till the last page was filled, when she signed her name with a flourish and threw down her pen, exclaming—

"There, I've done my best! If this won't suit I shall have to wait till I can do better."

Lying back on the sofa, she read the manuscript carefully through, making dashes here and there, and putting in many exclamation points, which looked like little balloons; then she tied it up with a smart red ribbon, and sat a minute looking at it with a sober, wistful expression, which plainly showed how earnest her work had been. Jo's desk up here was an old tin kitchen which hung against the wall. In it she kept her papers and a few books, safely shut away from Scrabble, who, being likewise of a literary turn, was fond of making a circulating library of such books as were left in his way by eating the leaves. From this tin receptacle Jo produced another manuscript, and putting both in her pocket, crept quietly downstairs, leaving her friends to nibble her pens and taste her ink.

She put on her hat and jacket as noiselessly as possible, and going to the back entry window, got out upon the roof of a low porch, swung herself down to the grassy bank, and took a roundabout way to the road. Once there, she composed herself, hailed a passing omnibus, and rolled away to town, looking very merry and mysterious.

If anyone had been watching her, he would have thought her movements decidedly peculiar, for on alighting, she went off at a great pace till she reached a certain number in a certain busy street; having found the place with some difficulty, she went into the doorway, looked up the dirty stairs, and after standing stock still a minute, suddenly dived into the street and walked away as rapidly as she came. This maneuver she repeated several times, to the great amusement of a black-eyed young gentleman lounging in the window of a building opposite. On returning for the third time, Jo gave herself a shake, pulled her hat over her eyes, and walked up the stairs, looking as if she were going to have all her teeth out.

There was a dentist's sign, among others, which adorned the entrance, and after staring a moment at the pair of artificial jaws which slowly opened and shut to draw attention to a fine set of teeth, the young gentleman put on his coat, took his hat, and went down to post himself in the opposite doorway, saying with a smile and a shiver, "It's like her to come alone, but if she has a bad time she'll need someone to help her home."

In ten minutes Jo came running downstairs with a very red face and the general appearance of a person who had just passed through a trying ordeal of some sort. When she saw the young gentleman she looked anything but pleased, and passed him with a nod; but he followed, asking with an air of sympathy, "Did you have a bad time?"

"Not very."

"You got through quickly."

"Yes, thank goodness!"

"Why did you go alone?"

"Didn't want anyone to know."

"You're the oddest fellow I ever saw. How many did you have out?"

Jo looked at her friend as if she did not understand him, then began to laugh as if mightily amused at something.

"There are two which I want to have come out, but I must wait a week."

"What are you laughing at? You are up to some mischief, Jo," said Laurie, looking mystified.

"So are you. What were you doing, sir, up in that billiard saloon?"

"Begging your pardon, ma'am, it wasn't a billiard saloon, but a gymnasium, and I was taking a lesson in fencing."

"I'm glad of that."

"Why?"

"You can teach me, and then when we play *Hamlet*, you can be Laertes, and we'll make a fine thing of the fencing scene."

Laurie burst out with a hearty boy's laugh, which made several passers-by smile in spite of themselves.

"I'll teach you whether we play *Hamlet* or not; it's grand fun and will straighten you up capitally. But I don't believe that was your only reason for saying 'I'm glad' in that decided way; was it, now?"

"No, I was glad that you were not in the saloon, because I hope you never go to such places. Do you?"

"Not often."

"I wish you wouldn't."

"It's no harm, Jo. I have billiards at home, but it's no fun unless you have good players; so, as I'm fond of it, I come sometimes and have a game with Ned Moffat or some of the other fellows."

"Oh dear, I'm so sorry, for you'll get to liking it better and better, and will waste time and money, and grow like those dreadful boys. I did hope you'd stay respectable and be a satisfaction to your friends," said Jo, shaking her head.

"Can't a fellow take a little innocent amusement now and then without losing his respectability?" asked Laurie, looking nettled.

"That depends upon how and where he takes it. I don't like Ned and his set, and wish you'd keep out of it. Mother won't let us have him at our house, though he wants to come; and if you grow like him she won't be willing to have us frolic together as we do now."

"Won't she?" asked Laurie anxiously.

"No, she can't bear fashionable young men, and she'd shut us all up in bandboxes rather than have us associate with them."

"Well, she needn't get out her bandboxes yet. I'm not a fashionable party and don't mean to be, but I do like harmless larks now and then, don't you?"

"Yes, nobody minds them, so lark away, but don't get wild, will you? Or there will be an end of all our good times."

"I'll be a double-distilled saint."

"I can't bear saints: just be a simple, honest, respectable boy, and we'll never desert you. I don't know what I *should* do if you acted like Mr. King's son; he had plenty of money, but didn't know how to spend it, and got tipsy and gambled, and ran away, and forged his father's name, I believe, and was altogether horrid."

"You think I'm likely to do the same? Much obliged."

"No, I don't—oh, *dear*, no!—but I hear people talking about money being such a temptation, and I sometimes wish you were poor; I shouldn't worry then."

"Do you worry about me, Jo?"

"A little, when you look moody or discontented, as you sometimes do; for you've got such a strong will, if you once get started wrong, I'm afraid it would be hard to stop you."

Laurie walked in silence a few minutes, and Jo watched him, wishing she had held her tongue, for his eyes looked angry, though his lips still smiled as if at her warnings.

"Are you going to deliver lectures all the way home?" he asked presently.

"Of course not. Why?"

"Because if you are, I'll take a bus; if you are not, I'd like to walk with you and tell you something very interesting."

"I won't preach any more, and I'd like to hear the news immensely."

"Very well, then, come on. It's a secret, and if I tell you, you must tell me yours."

"I haven't got any," began Jo, but stopped suddenly, remembering that she had.

"You know you have—you can't hide anything, so up and fess, or I won't tell," cried Laurie.

"Is your secret a nice one?"

"Oh, isn't it! All about people you know, and such fun! You ought to hear it, and I've been aching to tell it this long time. Come, you begin."

"You'll not say anything about it at home, will you?"

"Not a word."

"And you won't tease me in private?"

"I never tease."

"Yes, you do. You get everything you want out of people. I don't know how you do it, but you are a born wheedler."

"Thank you. Fire away."

"Well, I've left two stories with a newspaperman, and he's to give his answer next week," whispered Jo, in her confidant's ear.

"Hurrah for Miss March, the celebrated American authoress!" cried Laurie, throwing up his hat and catching it again, to the great delight of two ducks, four cats, five hens, and half a dozen Irish children, for they were out of the city now.

"Hush! It won't come to anything, I dare say, but I couldn't rest till I had tried, and I said nothing about it because I didn't want anyone else to be disappointed."

"It won't fail. Why, Jo, your stories are works of Shakespeare compared to half the rubbish that is published every day. Won't it be fun to see them in print, and shan't we feel proud of our authoress?"

Jo's eyes sparkled, for it is always pleasant to be believed in, and a friend's praise is always sweeter than a dozen newspaper puffs.

"Where's *your* secret? Play fair, Teddy, or I'll never believe you again," she said, trying to extinguish the brilliant hopes that blazed up at a word of encouragement.

"I may get into a scrape for telling, but I didn't promise not to, so I will, for I never feel easy in my mind till I've told you any plummy bit of news I get. I know where Meg's glove is."

"Is that all?" said Jo, looking disappointed, as Laurie nodded and twinkled with a face full of mysterious intelligence.

"It's quite enough for the present, as you'll agree when I tell you where it is."

"Tell, then."

Laurie bent, and whispered three words in Jo's ear, which produced a comical change. She stood and stared at him for a minute, looking both surprised and displeased, then walked on, saying sharply, "How do you know?"

"Saw it."

"Where?"

"Pocket."

"All this time?"

"Yes, isn't that romantic?"

"No, it's horrid."

"Don't you like it?"

"Of course I don't. It's ridiculous, it won't be allowed. My patience! What would Meg say?"

"You are not to tell anyone. Mind that."

"I didn't promise."

"That was understood, and I trusted you."

"Well, I won't for the present, anyway, but I'm disgusted, and wish you hadn't told me."

"I thought you'd be pleased."

"At the idea of anybody coming to take Meg away? No, thank you."

"You'll feel better about it when somebody comes to take you away."

"I'd like to see anyone try it," cried Jo fiercely.

"So should I!" And Laurie chuckled at the idea.

"I don't think secrets agree with me, I feel rumpled up in my mind since you told me that," said Jo rather ungratefully.

"Race down this hill with me, and you'll be all right," suggested Laurie.

No one was in sight, the smooth road sloped invitingly before her, and finding the temptation irresistible, Jo darted away, soon leaving hat and comb behind her and scattering hairpins as she ran. Laurie reached the goal first and was quite satisfied with the success of his treatment, for his Atalanta came panting up with flying hair, bright eyes, ruddy cheeks, and no signs of dissatisfaction in her face.

"I wish I was a horse, then I could run for miles in this splendid air, and not lose my breath. It was capital, but see what a guy it's made me. Go, pick up my things, like a cherub as you are," said Jo, dropping down under a maple tree, which was carpeting the bank with crimson leaves.

Laurie leisurely departed to recover the lost property, and Jo bundled up her braids, hoping no one would pass by till she was tidy again. But someone did pass, and who should it be but Meg, looking particularly ladylike in her state and festival suit, for she had been making calls.

"What in the world are you doing here?" she asked, regarding her disheveled sister with well-bred surprise.

"Getting leaves," meekly answered Jo, sorting the rosy handful she had just swept up.

"And hairpins," added Laurie, throwing half a dozen into Jo's lap. "They grow on this road, Meg; so do combs and brown straw hats."

"You have been running, Jo. How could you? When *will* you stop such romping ways?" said Meg reprovingly, as she settled her cuffs and smoothed her hair, with which the wind had taken liberties.

"Never till I'm stiff and old and have to use a crutch. Don't try to make me grow up before my time, Meg: it's hard enough to have you change all of a sudden; let me be a little girl as long as I can."

As she spoke, Jo bent over the leaves to hide the trembling of her lips, for lately she had felt that Margaret was fast getting to be a woman, and Laurie's secret made her dread the separation which must surely come some time and now seemed very near. He saw the trouble in her face and drew Meg's attention from it by asking quickly, "Where have you been calling, all so fine?"

"At the Gardiners', and Sallie has been telling me all about

Belle Moffat's wedding. It was very splendid, and they have gone to spend the winter in Paris. Just think how delightful that must be!"

"Do you envy her, Meg?" said Laurie.

"I'm afraid I do."

"I'm glad of it!" muttered Jo, tying on her hat with a jerk.

"Why?" asked Meg, looking surprised.

"Because if you care much about riches, you will never go and marry a poor man," said Jo, frowning at Laurie, who was mutely warning her to mind what she said.

"I shall never 'go and marry' anyone," observed Meg, walking on with great dignity while the others followed, laughing, whispering, skipping stones, and "behaving like children," as Meg said to herself, though she might have been tempted to join them if she had not had her best dress on.

For a week or two, Jo behaved so queerly that her sisters were quite bewildered. She rushed to the door when the postman rang, was rude to Mr. Brooke whenever they met, would sit looking at Meg with a woe-begone face, occasionally jumping up to shake and then to kiss her in a very mysterious manner; Laurie and she were always making signs to one another, and talking about "Spread Eagles" till the girls declared they had both lost their wits. On the second Saturday after Jo got out of the window, Meg, as she sat sewing at her window, was scandalized by the sight of Laurie chasing Jo all over the garden and finally capturing her in Amy's bower. What went on there, Meg could not see, but shrieks of laughter were heard, followed by the murmur of voices and a great flapping of newspapers.

"What shall we do with that girl? She never *will* behave like a young lady," sighed Meg, as she watched the race with a disapproving face.

"I hope she won't; she is so funny and dear as she is," said Beth, who had never betrayed that she was a little hurt at Jo's having secrets with anyone but her.

"It's very trying, but we never can make her *commy la fo*," added Amy, who sat making some new frills for herself, with her curls tied up in a very becoming way—two agreeable things which made her feel unusually elegant and ladylike.

In a few minutes Jo bounced in, laid herself on the sofa, and affected to read.

"Have you anything interesting there?" asked Meg with condescension.

"Nothing but a story; won't amount to much, I guess," returned Jo, carefully keeping the name of the paper out of sight.

"You'd better read it aloud; that will amuse us and keep you out of mischief," said Amy in her most grown-up tone.

"What's the name?" asked Beth, wondering why Jo kept her face behind the sheet.

"The Rival Painters."

"That sounds well; read it," said Meg.

With a loud "Hem!" and a long breath, Jo began to read very fast. The girls listened with interest, for the tale was romantic, and somewhat pathetic, as most of the characters died in the end.

"I like that about the splendid picture" was Amy's approving remark, as Jo paused.

"I prefer the lovering part. Viola and Angelo are two of our favorite names, isn't that queer?" said Meg, wiping her eyes, for the "lovering part" was tragical.

"Who wrote it?" asked Beth, who had caught a glimpse of Jo's face.

The reader suddenly sat up, cast away the paper, displaying a flushed countenance, and with a funny mixture of solemnity and excitement replied in a loud voice, "Your sister."

"You?" cried Meg, dropping her work.

"It's very good," said Amy critically.

"I knew it! I knew it! Oh, my Jo, I am so proud!" And Beth ran to hug her sister and exult over this splendid success.

Dear me, how delighted they all were, to be sure! How Meg wouldn't believe it till she saw the words, "Miss Josephine March," actually printed in the paper; how graciously Amy criticized the artistic parts of the story, and offered hints for a sequel, which unfortunately couldn't be carried out, as the hero and heroine were dead; how Beth got excited, and skipped and sang with joy; how Hannah came in to exclaim "Sakes alive, well I never!" in great astonishment at "that Jo's doin's"; how proud Mrs. March was when she knew it; how Jo laughed, with tears in her eyes, as she declared she might as well be a peacock and done with it; and how the "Spread Eagle" might be said to flap his wings triumphantly over the House of March, as the paper passed from hand to hand.

"Tell us all about it." "When did it come?" "How much did you get for it?" "What *will* Father say?" "Won't Laurie laugh?" cried the family, all in one breath as they clustered about Jo, for these foolish, affectionate people made a jubilee of every little household joy.

"Stop jabbering, girls, and I'll tell you everything," said Jo, wondering if Miss Burney felt any grander over her *Evelina* than she did over her "Rival Painters." Having told how she disposed of her tales, Jo added, "And when I went to get my answer, the man said he liked them both, but didn't pay beginners, only let them print in his paper, and noticed the stories. It was good practice, he said, and when the beginners improved, anyone would pay. So I let him have the two stories, and today this was sent to me, and Laurie caught me with it and insisted on seeing it, so I let him; and he said it was good, and I shall write more, and he's going to get the next paid for, and I *am* so happy, for in time I may be able to support myself and help the girls."

Jo's breath gave out here, and wrapping her head in the paper, she bedewed her little story with a few natural tears; for to be independent and earn the praise of those she loved were the dearest wishes of her heart, and this seemed to be the first step toward that happy end.

Chapter 15

A Telegram

"NOVEMBER IS THE most disagreeable month in the whole year," said Margaret, standing at the window one dull afternoon, looking out at the frostbitten garden.

"That's the reason I was born in it," observed Jo pensively, quite unconscious of the blot on her nose.

"If something very pleasant should happen now, we should think it a delightful month," said Beth, who took a hopeful view of everything, even November.

"I dare say, but nothing pleasant ever *does* happen in this family," said Meg, who was out of sorts. "We go grubbing along day after day, without a bit of change, and very little fun. We might as well be in a treadmill."

"My patience, how blue we are!" cried Jo. "I don't much wonder, poor dear, for you see other girls having splendid times, while you grind, grind, year in and year out. Oh, don't I wish I could manage things for you as I do for my heroines! You're pretty enough and good enough already, so I'd have some rich relation leave you a fortune unexpectedly; then you'd dash out as an heiress, scorn everyone who has slighted you, go abroad, and come home my Lady Something in a blaze of splendor and elegance."

"People don't have fortunes left them in that style nowadays, men have to work and women to marry for money. It's a dreadfully unjust world," said Meg bitterly.

"Jo and I are going to make fortunes for you all; just wait ten years, and see if we don't," said Amy, who sat in a corner making mud pies, as Hannah called her little clay models of birds, fruit, and faces.

"Can't wait, and I'm afraid I haven't much faith in ink and dirt, though I'm grateful for your good intentions."

Meg sighed, and turned to the frostbitten garden again; Jo groaned and leaned both elbows on the table in a despondent attitude, but Amy spatted away energetically, and Beth, who sat at the other window, said, smiling. "Two pleasant things are going to happen right away: Marmee is coming down the street, and Laurie is tramping through the garden as if he had something nice to tell."

In they both came, Mrs. March with her usual question, "Any letter from Father, girls?" and Laurie to say in his persuasive way, "Won't some of you come for a drive? I've been working away at mathematics till my head is in a muddle, and I'm going to freshen my wits by a brisk turn. It's a dull day, but the air isn't bad, and I'm going to take Brooke home, so it will be gay inside, if it isn't out. Come, Jo, you and Beth will go, won't you?"

"Of course we will."

"Much obliged, but I'm busy." And Meg whisked out her workbasket, for she had agreed with her mother that it was best, for her at least, not to drive often with the young gentleman.

"We three will be ready in a minute," cried Amy, running away to wash her hands.

"Can I do anything for you, Madam Mother?" asked Laurie, leaning over Mrs. March's chair with the affectionate look and tone he always gave her.

"No, thank you, except call at the office, if you'll be so kind, dear. It's our day for a letter, and the postman hasn't been. Father is as regular as the sun, but there's some delay on the way, perhaps."

A sharp ring interrupted her, and a minute after Hannah came in with a letter.

"It's one of them horrid telegraph things, mum," she said, handing it as if she was afraid it would explode and do some damage.

At the word "telegraph," Mrs. March snatched it, read the two lines it contained, and dropped back into her chair as white as if the little paper had sent a bullet to her heart. Laurie dashed downstairs for water, while Meg and Hannah supported her, and Jo read aloud, in a frightened voice—

MRS. MARCH:

Your husband is very ill. Come at once.

S. HALE,
Blank Hospital, Washington.

How still the room was as they listened breathlessly, how strangely the day darkened outside, and how suddenly the whole world seemed to change, as the girls gathered about their mother, feeling as if all the happiness and support of the lives was about to be taken from them. Mrs. March was herself again directly, read the message over, and stretched out her arms to her daughters, saying, in a tone they never forgot, "I shall go at once, but it may be too late. Oh, children, children, help me to bear it!"

For several minutes there was nothing but the sound of sobbing in the room, mingled with broken words of comfort, tender assurances of help, and hopeful whispers that died away in tears. Poor Hannah was the first to recover, and with unconscious wisdom she set all the rest a good example, for, with her, work was panacea for most afflictions.

"The Lord keep the dear man! I won't waste no time a-cryin', but git your things ready right away, mum," she said heartily, as she wiped her face on her apron, gave her mistress a warm shake of the hand with her own hard one, and went away to work like three women in one.

"She's right, there's no time for tears now. Be calm, girls, and let me think."

They tried to be calm, poor things, as their mother sat up, looking pale but steady, and put away her grief to think and plan for them.

"Where's Laurie?" she asked presently, when she had collected her thoughts and decided on the first duties to be done.

"Here, ma'am. Oh, let me do something!" cried the boy, hurrying from the next room whither he had withdrawn, feeling that their first sorrow was too sacred for even his friendly eyes to see.

"Send a telegram saying I will come at once. The next train goes early in the morning. I'll take that."

"What else? The horses are ready; I can go anywhere, do anything," he said, looking ready to fly to the ends of the earth.

"Leave a note at Aunt March's. Jo, give me that pen and paper."

Tearing off the blank side of one of her newly copied pages, Jo drew the table before her mother, well knowing that money for the long, sad journey must be borrowed, and feeling as if she could do anything to add a little to the sum for her father.

"Now go, dear, but don't kill yourself driving at a desperate pace; there is no need of that."

Mrs. March's warning was evidently thrown away, for five minutes later Laurie tore by the window on his own fleet horse, riding as if for his life.

"Jo, run to the rooms, and tell Mrs. King that I can't come. On the way get these things. I'll put them down, they'll be needed and I must go prepared for nursing. Hospital stores are not always good. Beth, go and ask Mr. Laurence for a couple of bottles of old wine: I'm not too proud to beg for Father, he shall have the best of everything. Amy, tell Hannah to get down the black trunk; and, Meg, come and help me find my things, for I'm half bewildered."

Writing, thinking, and directing all at once might well bewilder the poor lady, and Meg begged her to sit quietly in her room for a little while, and let them work. Everyone scattered like leaves before a gust of wind, and the quiet, happy household was broken up as suddenly as if the paper had been an evil spell.

Mr. Laurence came hurrying back with Beth, bringing every comfort the kind old gentleman could think of for the invalid, and friendliest promises of protection for the girls during the mother's absence, which comforted her very much. There was nothing he didn't offer, from his own dressing gown to himself as escort. But that last was impossible. Mrs. March would not hear of the old gentleman's undertaking the long journey, yet an expression of relief was visible when he spoke of it, for anxiety ill fits one for traveling. He saw the look, knit his heavy eyebrows, rubbed his hands, and marched abruptly away, saying he'd be back directly. No one had time to think of him again till, as Meg ran through the entry, with a pair of rubbers in one hand and a cup of tea in the other, she came suddenly upon Mr. Brooke.

"I'm very sorry to hear of this, Miss March," he said, in the kind, quiet tone which sounded very pleasantly to her perturbed spirit. "I came to offer myself as escort to your mother. Mr. Laurence has commissions for me in Washington, and it will give me real satisfaction to be of service to her there."

Down dropped the rubbers, and the tea was very near following, as Meg put out her hand, with a face so full of gratitude that Mr. Brooke would have felt repaid for a much greater sacrifice than the trifling one of time and comfort which he was about to make.

"How kind you all are! Mother will accept, I'm sure, and it will be such a relief to know that she has someone to take care of her. Thank you very, very much!"

Meg spoke earnestly, and forgot herself entirely till something in the brown eyes looking down at her made her remember the cooling tea, and lead the way into the parlor, saying she would call her mother.

Everything was arranged by the time Laurie returned with a note from Aunt March, enclosing the desired sum, and a few lines repeating what she had often said before—that she had always told them it was absurd for March to go into the army, always predicted that no good would come of it, and she hoped they would take her advice next time. Mrs. March put the note in the fire, the money in her purse, and went on with her preparations, with her lips folded tightly in a way which Jo would have understood if she had been there.

The short afternoon wore away; all the other errands were done, and Meg and her mother busy at some necessary needlework, while Beth and Amy got tea, and Hannah finished her ironing with what she called a "slap and a bang," but still Jo did not come. They began to get anxious, and Laurie went off to find her, for no one ever knew what freak Jo might take into her head. He missed her, however, and she came walking in with a very queer expression of countenance, for there was a mixture of fun and fear, satisfaction and regret in it, which puzzled the family as much as did the roll of bills she laid before her mother, saying with a little choke in her voice, "That's my contribution toward making Father comfortable and bringing him home!"

"My dear, where did you get it? Twenty-five dollars! Jo, I hope you haven't done anything rash?"

"No, it's mine honestly. I didn't beg, borrow, or steal it. I earned it, and I don't think you'll blame me, for I only sold what was my own."

As she spoke, Jo took off her bonnet, and a general outcry arose, for all her abundant hair was cut short.

"Your hair! Your beautiful hair!" "Oh, Jo, how could you? Your one beauty." "My dear girl, there was no need of this." "She doesn't look like my Jo any more, but I love her dearly for it!"

As everyone exclaimed, and Beth hugged the cropped head tenderly, Jo assumed an indifferent air, which did not deceive anyone a particle, and said, rumpling up the brown bush and trying to look as if she liked it, "It doesn't affect the fate of the nation, so don't wail, Beth. It will be good for my vanity, I was getting too proud of my wig. It will do my brains good to have that mop taken off; my head feels deliciously light and cool, and the barber said I could soon have a curly crop, which will be boyish, becoming, and easy to keep in order. I'm satisfied, so please take the money and let's have supper."

"Tell me all about it, Jo. I am not quite satisfied, but I can't blame you, for I know how willingly you sacrificed your vanity, as you call it, to your love. But, my dear, it was not necessary, and I'm afraid you will regret it one of these days," said Mrs. March.

"No, I won't!" returned Jo stoutly, feeling much relieved that her prank was not entirely condemned.

"What made you do it?" asked Amy, who would as soon have thought of cutting off her head as her pretty hair.

"Well, I was wild to do something for Father," replied Jo, as they gathered about the table, for healthy young people can eat even in the midst of trouble. "I hate to borrow as much as Mother does, and I knew Aunt March would croak; she always does, if you ask for a ninepence. Meg gave all her quarterly salary toward the rent, and I only got some clothes with mine, so I felt wicked, and was bound to have some money, If I sold the nose off my face to get it."

"You needn't feel wicked, my child: you had no winter things and got the simplest with your own hard earnings," said Mrs. March with a look that warmed Jo's heart.

"I hadn't the least idea of selling my hair at first, but as I went along I kept thinking what I could do, and feeling as if I'd like to dive into some of the rich stores and help myself. In a barber's window I saw tails of hair with the prices marked, and one black tail, not so thick as mine, was forty dollars. It came over me all of a sudden that I had one thing to make money out of, and without stopping to think, I walked in, asked if they bought hair, and what they would give for mine."

"I don't see how you dared to do it," said Beth in a tone of awe.

"Oh, he was a little man who looked as if he merely lived to oil his hair. He rather stared at first, as if he wasn't used to having girls bounce into his shop and ask him to buy their hair. He said he didn't care about mine, it wasn't the fashionable color, and he never paid much for it in the first place; the work put into it made it dear, and so on. It was getting late, and I was afraid if it wasn't done right away that I shouldn't have it done at all, and you know when I start to do a thing, I hate to give it up; so I begged him to take it, and told him why I was in such a hurry. It was silly, I dare say, but it changed his mind, for I got rather excited, and told the story in my topsy-turvy way, and his wife heard, and said so kindly, 'Take it, Thomas, and oblige the young lady; I'd do as much for our Jimmy any day if I had a spire of hair worth selling.'"

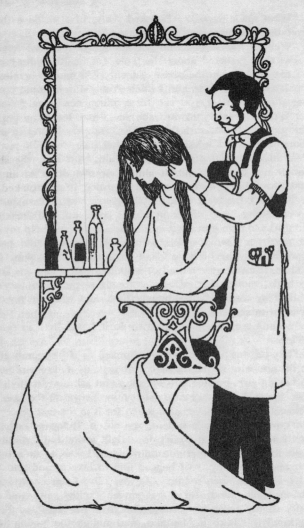

"I took a last look at my hair while the man got his things, and that was the end of it."

"Who was Jimmy?" asked Amy, who liked to have things explained as they went along.

"Her son, she said, who was in the army. How friendly such things make strangers feel, don't they? She talked away all the time the man clipped, and diverted my mind nicely."

"Didn't you feel dreadfully when the first cut came?" asked Meg, with a shiver.

"I took a last look at my hair while the man got his things, and that was the end of it. I never snivel over trifles like that. I will confess, though, I felt queer when I saw the dear old hair laid out on the table, and felt only the short, rough ends of my head. It almost seemed as if I'd an arm or a leg off. The woman saw me look at it, and picked out a long lock for me to keep. I'll give it to you, Marmee, just to remember past glories by, for a crop is so comfortable I don't think I shall ever have a mane again."

Mrs. March folded the wavy chestnut lock, and laid it away with a short gray one in her desk. She only said, "Thank you, deary," but something in her face made the girls change the subject, and talk as cheerfully as they could about Mr. Brooke's kindness, the prospect of a fine day tomorrow, and the happy times they would have when Father came home to be nursed.

No one wanted to go to bed when at ten o'clock Mrs. March put by the last finished job, and said, "Come, girls." Beth went to the piano and played the father's favorite hymn; all began bravely, but broke down one by one till Beth was left alone, singing with all her heart, for to her music was always a sweet consoler.

"Go to bed and don't talk, for we must be up early and shall need all the sleep we can get. Good night, my darlings," said Mrs. March, as the hymn ended, for no one cared to try another.

They kissed her quietly, and went to bed as silently as if the dear invalid lay in the next room. Beth and Amy soon fell asleep in spite of the great trouble, but Meg lay awake, thinking the most serious thoughts she had ever known in her short life. Jo lay motionless, and her sister fancied that she was asleep, till a stifled sob made her exclaim, as she touched a wet cheek—

"Jo, dear, what is it? Are you crying about father?"

"No, not now."

"What then?"

"My—my hair!" burst out poor Jo, trying vainly to smother her emotion in the pillow.

It did not sound at all comical to Meg, who kissed and caressed the afflicted heroine in the tenderest manner.

"I'm not sorry," protested Jo, with a choke. "I'd do it again tomorrow, if I could. It's only the vain, selfish part of me that goes and cries in this silly way. Don't tell anyone, it's all over now. I thought you were asleep, so I just made a little private moan for my one beauty. How came you to be awake?"

"I can't sleep, I'm so anxious," said Meg.

"Think about something pleasant, and you'll soon drop off."

"I tried it, but felt wider awake than ever."

"What did you think of?"

"Handsome faces—eyes particularly," answered Meg, smiling to herself in the dark.

"What color do you like best?"

"Brown—that is, sometimes; blue are lovely."

Jo laughed, and Meg sharply ordered her not to talk, then amiably promised to make her hair curl, and fell asleep to dream of living in her castle in the air.

The clocks were striking midnight and the rooms were very still as a figure glided quietly from bed to bed, smoothing a coverlid here, settling a pillow there, and pausing to look long and tenderly at each unconscious face, to kiss each with lips that mutely blessed, and to pray the fervent prayers which only mothers utter. As she lifted the curtain to look out into the dreary night, the moon broke suddenly from behind the clouds and shone upon her like a bright, benignant face, which seemed to whisper in the silence, "Be comforted, dear soul! There is always light behind the clouds."

Chapter 16

Letters

IN THE COLD gray dawn the sisters lit their lamp and read their chapter with an earnestness never felt before; for now the shadow of a real trouble had come, the little books were full of help and comfort; and as they dressed, they agreed to say good-by cheerfully and hopefully, and send their mother on her anxious journey unsaddened by tears or complaints from them. Everything seemed very strange when they went down—so dim and still outside, so full of light and bustle within. Breakfast at that early hour seemed odd, and even Hannah's familiar face looked unnatural as she flew about her kitchen with her nightcap on. The big trunk stood ready in the hall, Mother's cloak and bonnet lay on the sofa, and Mother herself sat trying to eat, but looking so pale and worn with sleeplessness and anxiety that the girls found it very hard to keep their resolution. Meg's eyes kept filling in spite of herself, Jo was obliged to hide her face in the kitchen roller more than once, and the little girls wore a grave, troubled expression, as if sorrow was a new experience to them.

Nobody talked much, but as the time drew very near and they sat waiting for the carriage, Mrs. March said to the girls, who were all busied about her, one folding her shawl, another smoothing out the strings of her bonnet, a third putting on her overshoes, and a fourth fastening up her travelling bag—

"Children, I leave you to Hannah's care and Mr. Laurence's protection. Hannah is faithfulness itself, and our good neighbor will guard you as if you were his own. I have no fears for you, yet I am anxious that you should take this trouble rightly. Don't grieve and fret when I am gone, or think that you can comfort yourselves by being idle and trying to forget. Go on with your work as usual, for work is a blessed solace. Hope and keep busy, and whatever happens, remember that you never can be fatherless."

"Yes, Mother."

"Meg, dear, be prudent, watch over your sisters, consult Hannah, and, in any perplexity, go to Mr. Laurence. Be patient Jo, don't get despondent or do rash things, write to me often, and be my brave girl, ready to help and cheer us all. Beth, comfort yourself with your music, and be faithful to the little home duties; and you, Amy, help all you can, be obedient, and keep happy safe at home."

"We will, Mother! We will!"

The rattle of an approaching carriage made them all start and listen. That was the hard minute, but the girls stood it well: no one cried, no one ran away or uttered a lamentation, though their hearts were very heavy as they sent loving messages to Father, remembering, as they spoke, that it might be too late to deliver them. They kissed their mother quietly, clung about her tenderly, and tried to wave their hands cheerfully when she drove away.

Laurie and his grandfather came over to see her off, and Mr. Brooke looked so strong and sensible and kind that the girls christened him "Mr. Greatheart" on the spot.

"Good-by, my darlings! God bless and keep us all!" whispered Mrs. March, as she kissed one dear little face after the other, and hurried into the carriage.

As she rolled away, the sun came out, and looking back, she saw it shining on the group at the gate like a good omen. They saw it also, and smiled and waved their hands; and the last thing she beheld as she turned the corner was the four bright faces, and behind them like a bodyguard old Mr. Laurence, faithful Hannah, and devoted Laurie.

"How kind everyone is to us!" she said, turning to find fresh proof of it in the respectful sympathy of the young man's face.

"I don't see how they can help it," returned Mr. Brooke, laughing so infectiously that Mrs. March could not help smiling; and so the long journey began with the good omens of sunshine, smiles, and cheerful words.

"I feel as if there had been an earthquake," said Jo, as their neighbors went home to breakfast, leaving them to rest and refresh themselves.

"It seems as if half the house was gone," added Meg forlornly.

Beth opened her lips to say something, but could only point to the pile of nicely mended hose which lay on Mother's table, showing that even in her last hurried moments she had thought and worked for them. It was a little thing, but it went straight to their hearts; and in spite of their brave resolutions, they all broke down and cried bitterly.

Hannah wisely allowed them to relieve their feelings, and when the shower showed signs of clearing up, she came to the rescue, armed with a coffeepot.

"Now, my dear young ladies, remember what your ma said, and don't fret. Come and have a cup of coffee all round, and then let's fall to work and be a credit to the family."

Coffee was a treat, and Hannah showed great tact in making it that morning. No one could resist her persuasive nods, or the fragrant invitation issuing from the nose of the coffeepot. They drew up to the table, exchanged their handkerchiefs for napkins, and in ten minutes were all right again.

" 'Hope and keep busy,' that's the motto for us, so let's see who will remember it best. I shall go to Aunt March, as usual. Oh, won't she lecture though!" said Jo, as she sipped with returning spirit.

"I shall go to my Kings, though I'd much rather stay at home and attend to things here," said Meg, wishing she hadn't made her eyes so red.

"No need of that. Beth and I can keep house perfectly well," put in Amy, with an important air.

"Hannah will tell us what to do, and we'll have everything nice when you come home," added Beth, getting out her mop and dish tub without delay.

"I think anxiety is very interesting," observed Amy, eating sugar pensively.

The girls couldn't help laughing, and felt better for it, though Meg shook her head at the young lady who could find consolation in a sugar bowl.

The sight of the turnovers made Jo sober again, and when the two went out to their daily tasks, they looked sorrowfully back at the window where they were accustomed to see their mother's face. It was gone, but Beth had remembered the little household ceremony, and there she was, nodding away at them like a rosy-faced mandarin.

"That's so like my Beth!" said Jo, waving her hat, with a grateful face. "Good-by, Meggy, I hope the Kings won't train today. Don't fret about Father, dear," she added, as they parted.

"And I hope Aunt March won't croak. Your hair *is* becoming, and it looks very boyish and nice," returned Meg, trying not to smile at the curly head, which looked comically small on her tall sister's shoulders.

"That's my only comfort." And, touching her hat à la Laurie, away went Jo, feeling like a shorn sheep on a wintry day.

News from their father comforted the girls very much, for, though dangerously ill, the presence of the best and tenderest of nurses had already done him good. Mr. Brooke sent a bulletin every day, and as the head of the family, Meg insisted on reading the dispatches, which grew more and more cheering as the week passed. At first, everyone was eager to write, and plump envelopes were carefully poked into the letter box by one or other of the sisters, who felt rather important with their Washington correspondence. As one of these packets contained characteristic notes from the party, we will rob an imaginary mail, and read them:

MY DEAREST MOTHER,

It is impossible to tell you how happy your last letter made us, for the news was so good we couldn't help laughing and crying over it. How very kind Mr. Brooke is, and how fortunate that Mr. Laurence's business detains him near you so long, since he is so useful to you and Father. The girls are all as good as gold. Jo helps me with the sewing, and insists on doing all sorts of hard jobs. I should be afraid she might overdo, if I didn't know that her 'moral fit' wouldn't last long. Beth is as regular about her tasks as a clock, and never forgets what you told her. She grieves about Father, and looks sober except when she is at her little piano. Amy minds me nicely, and I take great care of her. She does her own hair, and I am teaching her to make buttonholes and mend her stockings. She tries very hard, and I know you will be pleased with her improvement when you come. Mr. Laurence watches over us like a motherly old hen, as Jo says, and Laurie is very kind and neighborly. He and Jo keep us merry, for we get pretty blue sometimes, and feel like orphans, with you so far away. Hannah is a perfect saint; she does not scold at all, and always calls me Miss 'Margaret,' which is quite proper, you know, and treats me with respect. We are all well and busy; but we long, day and night, to have you back. Give my dearest love to Father, and believe me, ever your own

MEG.

This note, prettily written on scented paper, was a great contrast to the next, which was scribbled on a big sheet of thin foreign paper, ornamented with blots and all manner of flourishes and curly-tailed letters:

MY PRECIOUS MARMEE,

Three cheers for dear Father! Brooke was a trump to telegraph right off, and let us know the minute he was better. I rushed up garret when the letter came, and tried to thank God for being so good to us; but I could only cry, and say, "I'm glad! I'm glad!" Didn't that do as well as a regular prayer? For I felt a great many in my heart. We have such funny times; and now I can enjoy them, for everyone is so desperately good, it's like living in a nest of turtledoves. You'd laugh to see Meg head the table and try to be mother-ish. She gets prettier every day, and I'm in love with her sometimes. The children are regular archangels, and I—well, I'm Jo, and never shall be anything else. Oh, I must tell you that I came near having a quarrel with Laurie. I freed my mind about a silly little thing, and he was offended. I was right, but didn't speak as I ought, and he marched home, saying he wouldn't come again till I begged pardon. I declared I wouldn't and got mad. It lasted all day, I felt bad and wanted you very much. Laurie and I are both so proud, it's hard to beg pardon; but I thought he'd come to it, for I *was* in the right. He didn't come; and just at night I remembered what you said when Amy fell into the river. I read my little book, felt better, resolved not to let the sun set on *my* anger, and ran over to tell Laurie I was sorry. I met him at the gate, coming for the same thing. We both laughed, begged each other's pardon, and felt all good and comfortable again.

I made a "pome" yesterday, when I was helping Hannah wash; and, as Father likes my silly little things, I put it in to amuse him. Give him the lovingest hug that ever was, and kiss yourself a dozen times for your

Topsy-Turvy Jo.

A SONG FROM THE SUDS.

Queen of my tub, I merrily sing,
    While the white foam rises high;
And sturdily wash and rinse and wring,
    And fasten the clothes to dry;
Then out in the free fresh air they swing,
    Under the sunny sky.

I wish we could wash from our hearts and souls
    The stains of the week away,
And let water and air by their magic make
    Ourselves as pure as they;
Then on the earth there would be indeed
    A glorious washing-day!

Along the path of a useful life,
    Will heartsease ever bloom;
The busy mind has no time to think
    Of sorrow or care or gloom;
And anxious thoughts may be swept away,
    As we bravely wield a broom.

I am glad a task to me is given,
    To labor at day by day;

For it brings me health and strength and hope,
And I cheerfully learn to say,—
"Head, you may think, Heart, you may feel,
But, Hand, you shall work alway!"

DEAR MOTHER,

There is only room for me to send my love, and some pressed pansies from the root I have been keeping safe in the house for Father to see. I read every morning, try to be good all day, and sing myself to sleep with Father's tune. I can't sing "Land of the Leal" now, it makes me cry. Everyone is very kind, and we are as happy as we can be without you. Amy wants the rest of the page, so I must stop. I didn't forget to cover the holders, and I wind the clock and air the rooms every day.

Kiss dear Father on the cheek he calls mine. Oh, do come soon to your loving

LITTLE BETH.

MA CHERE MAMMA,

We are all well I do my lessons always and never corroberate the girls—Meg says I mean contradick so I put in both words and you can take the properest. Meg is a great comfort to me and lets me have jelly every night at tea its so good for me Jo says because it keeps me sweet tempered. Laurie is not as respeckful as he ought to be now I am almost in my teens, he calls me Chick and hurts my feelings by talking French to me very fast when I say Merci or Bon jour as Hattie King does. The sleeves of my blue dress were all worn out, and Meg put in new ones, but the full front came wrong and they are more blue than the dress. I felt bad but did not fret I bear my troubles well but I do wish Hannah would put more starch in my aprons and have buckwheats every day. Can't she? Didn't I make that interrigation point nice? Meg says my punchtuation and spelling are disgraceful and I am mortyfied but dear me I have so many things to do, I can't stop. Adieu, I send heaps of love to Papa.

Your affectionate daughter,

AMY CURTIS MARCH.

Dear Mis March,

I jes drop a line to say we git on fust rate. The girls is clever and fly round right smart. Miss Meg is going to make a proper good housekeeper; she hes the liking for it, and gits the hang of things surprisin quick. Jo doos beat all for goin ahead, but she don't stop to cal'k'late fust, and you never know where she's like to bring up. She done out a tub of clothes on Monday, but she starched em afore they was wrenched, and blued a pink calico dress till I thought I should a died a laughin. Beth is the best of little creeters, and a sight of help to me, bein so forehanded and dependable. She tries to learn everything, and really goes to market beyond her years; likewise keeps accounts, with my help, quite wonderful. We have got on very economical so fur; I don't let the girls hev coffee only once a week, accordin to your wish, and keep em on plain wholesome vittles. Amy does well about frettin, wearin her best clothes and eatin sweet stuff. Mr. Laurie is as full of didoes as usual, and turns the house upside down frequent; but he heartens up the girls, and so I let em hev full swing. The old gentleman sends heaps of things, and is rather wearin, but means wal, and it aint my place to say nothin. My bread is riz, so no more at this time. I send my duty to Mr. March and hope he's seen the last of his Pewmonia.

Yours Respectful,

Hannah Mullet.

Head Nurse of Ward No. 2,

All serene on the Rappahannock, troops in fine condition, commissary department well conducted, the Home Guard under Colonel Teddy always on duty, Commander in Chief General Laurence reviews the army daily, Quartermaster Mullett keeps order in camp, and Major Lion does picket duty at night. A salute of twenty-four guns was fired on receipt of good news from Washington, and a dress parade took place at headquarters. Commander in chief sends best wishes, in which he is heartily joined by

Colonel Teddy.

DEAR MADAM,

The little girls are all well; Beth and my boy report daily; Hannah is a model servant, and guards pretty Meg like a dragon. Glad the fine weather holds; pray make Brooke useful, and draw on me for funds if expenses exceed your estimate. Don't let your husband want anything. Thank God he is mending.

Your sincere friend and servant,
JAMES LAURENCE.

Chapter 17

Little Faithful

FOR A WEEK the amount of virtue in the old house would have supplied the neighborhood. It was really amazing, for everyone seemed in a heavenly frame of mind, and self-denial was all the fashion. Relieved of their first anxiety about their father, the girls insensibly relaxed their praiseworthy efforts a little, and began to fall back into the old ways. They did not forget their motto, but hoping and keeping busy seemed to grow easier, and after such tremendous exertions, they felt that Endeavor deserved a holiday, and gave it a good many.

Jo caught a bad cold through neglect to cover the shorn head enough, and was ordered to stay at home till she was better, for Aunt March didn't like to hear people read with colds in their heads. Jo liked this, and after an energetic rummage from garret to cellar, subsided on the sofa to nurse her cold with arsenicum and books. Amy found that housework and art did not go well together, and returned to her mud pies. Meg went daily to her pupils, and sewed, or thought she did, at home, but much time was spent in writing long letters to her mother, or reading the Washington dispatches over and over. Beth kept on, with only slight relapses into idleness or grieving.

All the little duties were faithfully done each day, and many of her sisters' also, for they were forgetful, and the house seemed like a clock whose pendulum was gone a-visiting. When her heart got heavy with longings for Mother or fears for Father, she went away into a certain closet, hid her face in the folds of a certain dear old gown, and made her little moan and prayed her little prayer quietly by herself. Nobody knew what cheered her up after a sober fit, but everyone felt how sweet and helpful Beth was, and fell into a way of going to her for comfort or advice in their small affairs.

All were unconscious that this experience was a test of

character, and when the first excitement was over, felt that they had done well and deserved praise. So they did, but their mistake was in ceasing to do well, and they learned this lesson through much anxiety and regret.

"Meg, I wish you'd go and see the Hummels; you know Mother told us not to forget them," said Beth, ten days after Mrs. March's departure.

"I'm too tired to go this afternoon," replied Meg, rocking comfortably as she sewed.

"Can't you, Jo?" asked Beth.

"Too stormy for me with my cold."

"I thought it was almost well."

"It's well enough for me to go out with Laurie, but not well enough to go to the Hummels'," said Jo, laughing, but looking a little ashamed of her inconsistency.

"Why don't you go yourself?" asked Meg.

"I *have* been every day, but the baby is sick, and I don't know what to do for it. Mrs. Hummel goes away to work, and Lottchen takes care of it; but it gets sicker and sicker, and I think you or Hannah ought to go."

Beth spoke earnestly, and Meg promised she would go tomorrow.

"Ask Hannah for some nice little mess, and take it round, Beth, the air will do you good," said Jo, adding apologetically, "I'd go, but I want to finish my writing."

"My head aches and I'm tired, so I thought maybe some of you would go," said Beth.

"Amy will be in presently, and she will run down for us," suggested Meg.

"Well, I'll rest a little and wait for her."

So Beth lay down on the sofa, the others returned to their work, and the Hummels were forgotten. An hour passed: Amy did not come, Meg went to her room to try on a new dress, Jo was absorbed in her story, and Hannah was sound asleep before the kitchen fire, when Beth quietly put on her hood, filled her basket with odds and ends for the poor children, and went out into the chilly air with a heavy head and a grieved look in her patient eyes. It was late when she came back, and no one saw her creep upstairs and shut herself into her mother's room. Half an hour after, Jo went to "Mother's closet" for something, and there found Beth sitting on the medicine chest, looking very grave, with red eyes and a camphor-bottle in her hand.

"Christopher Columbus! What's the matter?" cried Jo, as Beth put out her hand as if to warn her off, and asked quickly, "You've had the scarlet fever, haven't you?"

"Years ago, when Meg did. Why?"

"Then I'll tell you. Oh, Jo, the baby's dead!"

"What baby?"

"Mrs. Hummel's; it died in my lap before she got home," cried Beth with a sob.

"My poor dear, how dreadful for you! I ought to have gone," said Jo, taking her sister in her arms as she sat down in her mother's big chair, with a remorseful face.

"It wasn't dreadful, Jo, only so sad! I saw in a minute that it was sicker, but Lottchen said her mother had gone for a doctor, so I took Baby and let Lotty rest. It seemed asleep, but all of a sudden it gave a little cry and trembled, and then lay very still. I tried to warm its feet, and Lotty gave it some milk, but it didn't stir, and I knew it was dead."

"Don't cry, dear! What did you do?"

"I just sat and held it softly till Mrs. Hummel came with the doctor. He said it was dead, and looked at Heinrich and Minna, who have got sore throats. 'Scarlet fever, ma'am. Ought to have called me before,' he said crossly. Mrs. Hummel told him she was poor, and had tried to cure baby herself, but now it was too late, and she could only ask him to help the others and trust to charity for his pay. He smiled then, and was kinder, but it was very sad, and I cried with them till he turned round all of a sudden, and told me to go home and take belladonna right away, or I'd have the fever."

"No, you won't!" cried Jo, hugging her close, with a frightened look. "Oh, Beth, if you should be sick I never could forgive myself! What *shall* we do?"

"Don't be frightened, I guess I shan't have it badly. I looked in Mother's book, and saw that it begins with headache, sore throat, and queer feelings like mine, so I did take some belladonna, and I feel better," said Beth, laying her cold hands on her hot forehead and trying to look well.

"If Mother was only at home!" exclaimed Jo, seizing the book, and feeling that Washington was an immense way off. She read a page, looked at Beth, felt her head, peeped into her throat, and then said gravely, "You've been over the baby every day for more than a week, and among the others who are going to have it; so I'm afraid *you* are going to have it, Beth. I'll call Hannah, she knows all about sickness."

"Don't let Amy come; she never had it, and I should hate to give it to her. Can't you and Meg have it over again?" asked Beth, anxiously.

"I guess not; don't care if I do; serve me right, selfish pig, to let you go, and stay writing rubbish myself!" muttered Jo, as she went to consult Hannah.

The good soul was wide awake in a minute, and took the lead at once, assuring Jo that there was no need to worry; everyone had scarlet fever, and if rightly treated, nobody died—all of which Jo believed, and felt much relieved as they went up to call Meg.

"Now I'll tell you what we'll do," said Hannah, when she had examined and questioned Beth, "we will have Dr. Bangs, just to take a look at you, dear, and see that we start right; then we'll send Amy off to Aunt March's for a spell, to keep her out of harm's way, and one of you girls can stay at home and amuse Beth for a day or two."

"I shall stay, of course, I'm oldest," began Meg, looking anxious and self-reproachful.

"*I* shall, because it's my fault she is sick; I told Mother I'd do the errands, and I haven't," said Jo decidedly.

"Which will you have, Beth? There ain't no need of but one," said Hannah.

"Jo, please." And Beth leaned her head against her sister with a contented look, which effectually settled that point.

"I'll go and tell Amy," said Meg, feeling a little hurt, yet rather relieved on the whole, for she did not like nursing, and Jo did.

Amy rebelled outright, and passionately declared that she had rather have the fever than go to Aunt March. Meg reasoned, pleaded, and commanded: all in vain. Amy protested that she would *not* go, and Meg left her in despair to ask Hannah what should be done. Before she came back, Laurie walked into the parlor to find Amy sobbing, with her head in the sofa cushions. She told her story, expecting to be consoled, but Laurie only put his hands in his pockets and walked about the room, whistling softly, as he knit his brows in deep thought. Presently he sat down beside her, and said, in his most wheedlesome tone, "Now be a sensible little woman, and do as they say. No, don't cry, but hear what a jolly plan I've got. You go to Aunt March's, and I'll come and take you out every day, driving or walking, and we'll have capital times. Won't that be better than moping here?"

"I don't wish to be sent off as if I was in the way," began Amy in an injured voice.

"Bless your heart, child, it's to keep you well. You don't want to be sick, do you?"

"No, I'm sure I don't; but I dare say I shall be, for I've been with Beth all the time."

"That's the very reason you ought to go away at once, so that you may escape it. Change of air and care will keep you well, I dare say, or if it does not entirely, you will have the fever more lightly. I advise you to be off as soon as you can, for scarlet fever is no joke, miss."

"But it's dull at Aunt March's, and she is so cross," said Amy, looking rather frightened.

"It won't be dull with me popping in every day to tell you how Beth is, and take you out gallivanting. The old lady likes me, and I'll be as sweet as possible to her, so she won't peck at us, whatever we do."

"Will you take me out in the trotting wagon with Puck?"

"On my honor as a gentleman."

"And come every single day?"

"See if I don't."

"And bring me back the minute Beth is well?"

"The identical minute."

"And go to the theater, truly?"

"A dozen theaters, if we may."

"Well—I guess—I will," said Amy slowly.

"Good girl! Call Meg, and tell her you'll give in," said Laurie, with an approving pat, which annoyed Amy more than the "giving in."

Meg and Jo came running down to behold the miracle which had been wrought, and Amy, feeling very precious and self-sacrificing, promised to go, if the doctor said Beth was going to be ill.

"How is the little dear?" asked Laurie, for Beth was his especial pet, and he felt more anxious about her than he liked to show.

"She is lying down on Mother's bed, and feels better. The baby's death troubled her, but I dare say she has only got cold. Hannah *says* she thinks so, but she *looks* worried, and that makes me fidgety," answered Meg.

"What a trying world it is!" said Jo, rumpling up her hair in a fretful sort of way. "No sooner do we get out of one trouble than down comes another. There doesn't seem to be anything to hold on to when Mother's gone, so I'm all at sea."

"Well, don't make a porcupine of yourself, it isn't becoming. Settle your wig, Jo, and tell me if I shall telegraph to your mother, or do anything?" asked Laurie, who never had been reconciled to the loss of his friend's one beauty.

"That is what troubles me," said Meg. "I think we ought to tell her if Beth is really ill, but Hannah says we mustn't, for Mother can't leave Father, and it will only make them anxious. Beth won't be sick long, and Hannah knows just what to do, and Mother said we were to mind her, so I suppose we must, but it doesn't seem quite right to me."

"Hum, well, I can't say. Suppose you ask Grandfather after the doctor has been."

"We will. Jo, go and get Dr. Bangs at once," commanded Meg. "We can't decide anything till he has been."

"Stay where you are, Jo. I'm errand boy to this establishment," said Laurie, taking up his cap.

"I'm afraid you are busy," began Meg.

"No, I've done my lessons for the day."

"Do you study in vacation time?" asked Jo.

"I follow the good example my neighbors set me" was Laurie's answer, as he swung himself out of the room.

"I have great hopes of my boy," observed Jo, watching him fly over the fence with an approving smile.

"He does very well—for a boy" was Meg's somewhat ungracious answer, for the subject did not interest her.

Dr. Bangs came, said Beth had symptoms of the fever, but thought she would have it lightly, though he looked sober over the Hummel story. Amy was ordered off at once, and provided with something to ward off danger, she departed in great state, with Jo and Laurie as escort.

Aunt March received them with her usual hospitality.

"What do you want now?" she asked, looking sharply over her spectacles, while the parrot, sitting on the back of her chair, called out—

"Go away. No boys allowed here."

Laurie retired to the window, and Jo told her story.

"No more than I expected, if you are allowed to go poking about among poor folks. Amy can stay and make herself useful if she isn't sick, which I've no doubt she will be—looks like it now. Don't cry, child, it worries me to hear people sniff."

Amy *was* on the point of crying, but Laurie slyly pulled the parrot's tail, which caused Polly to utter an astonished croak and call out, "Bless my boots!" in such a funny way, that she laughed instead.

"What do you hear from your mother?" asked the old lady gruffly.

"Father is much better," replied Jo, trying to keep sober.

"Oh, is he? Well, that won't last long, I fancy. March never had any stamina" was the cheerful reply.

"Ha, ha! Never say die, take a pinch of snuff, good-by, good-by!" squalled Polly, dancing on her perch, and clawing at the old lady's cap as Laurie tweaked him in the rear.

"Hold your tongue, you disrespectful old bird! And, Jo,

you'd better go at once; it isn't proper to be gadding about so late with a rattlepated boy like—"

"Hold your tongue, you disrespectful old bird!" cried Polly, tumbling off the chair with a bounce, and running to peck the "rattlepated" boy, who was shaking with laughter at the last speech.

"I don't think I *can* bear it, but I'll try," thought Amy, as she was left alone with Aunt March.

"Get along, you fright!" screamed Polly, and at that rude speech Amy could not restrain a sniff.

Chapter 18

Dark Days

BETH DID HAVE the fever, and was much sicker than anyone but Hannah and the doctor suspected. The girls knew nothing about illness, and Mr. Laurence was not allowed to see her, so Hannah had everything all her own way, and busy Dr. Bangs did his best, but left a good deal to the excellent nurse. Meg stayed at home, lest she should infect the Kings, and kept house, feeling very anxious and a little guilty when she wrote letters in which no mention was made of Beth's illness. She could not think it right to deceive her mother, but she had been bidden to mind Hannah, and Hannah wouldn't hear of "Mrs. March bein' told, and worried just for sech a trifle." Jo devoted herself to Beth day and night—not a hard task, for Beth was very patient, and bore her pain uncomplainingly as long as she could control herself. But there came a time when during the fever fits she began to talk in a hoarse, broken voice, to play on the coverlet as if on her beloved little piano, and try to sing with a throat so swollen that there was no music left; a time when she did not know the familiar faces round her, but addressed them by wrong names, and called imploringly for her mother. Then Jo grew frightened, Meg begged to be allowed to write the truth, and even Hannah said she "would think of it, though there was no danger *yet*." A letter from Washington added to their trouble, for Mr. March had had a relapse, and could not think of coming home for a long while.

How dark the days seemed now, how sad and lonely the house, and how heavy were the hearts of the sisters as they worked and waited, while the shadow of death hovered over the once happy home! Then it was that Margaret, sitting alone with tears dropping often on her work, felt how rich she had been in things more precious than any luxuries money could buy—in love, protection, peace, and health, the real blessings of life. Then it was that Jo, living in the darkened room, with that suffering little sister always before her eyes and that pathetic voice sounding in her ears, learned to see the beauty and the sweetness of Beth's nature, to feel how deep and tender a place she filled in all hearts, and to acknowledge the worth of Beth's unselfish ambition to live for others, and make home happy by the exercise of those simple virtues which all may possess, and which all should love and value more than talent, wealth, or beauty. And Amy, in her exile, longed eagerly to be at home, that she might work for Beth, feeling now that no service would be hard or irksome, and remembering, with regretful grief, how many neglected tasks those willing hands had done for her. Laurie haunted the house like a restless ghost, and Mr. Laurence locked the grand piano, because he could not bear to be reminded of the young neighbor who used to make the twilight pleasant for him. Everyone missed Beth. The milkman, baker, grocer, and butcher inquired how she did, poor Mrs. Hummel came to beg pardon for her thoughtlessness and to get a shroud for Minna, the neighbors sent all sorts of comforts and good wishes, and even those who knew her best were surprised to find how many friends shy little Beth had made.

Meanwhile she lay on her bed with old Joanna at her side, for even in her wanderings she did not forget her forlorn protégé. She longed for her cats, but would not have them brought, lest they should get sick, and in her quiet hours she was full of anxiety about Jo. She sent loving messages to Amy, bade them tell her mother that she would write soon, and often begged for pencil and paper to try to say a word, that Father might not think she had neglected him. But soon even these intervals of consciousness ended, and she lay hour after hour, tossing to and fro, with incoherent words on her lips, or sank into a heavy sleep which brought her no refreshment. Dr. Bangs came twice a day, Hannah sat up at night, Meg kept a telegram in her desk all ready to send off at any minute, and Jo never stirred from Beth's side.

The first of December was a wintry day indeed to them,

for a bitter wind blew, snow fell fast, and the year seemed getting ready for its death. When Dr. Bangs came that morning, he looked long at Beth, held the hot hand in both his own a minute, and laid it gently down, saying, in a low tone, to Hannah, "If Mrs. March *can* leave her husband she'd better be sent for."

Hannah nodded without speaking, for her lips twitched nervously, Meg dropped down into a chair as the strength seemed to go out of her limbs at the sound of those words, and Jo, after standing with a pale face for a minute, ran to the parlor, snatched up the telegram, and, throwing on her things, rushed out into the storm. She was soon back, and while noiselessly taking off her cloak, Laurie came in with a letter, saying that Mr. March was mending again. Jo read it thankfully, but the heavy weight did not seem lifted off her heart, and her face was so full of misery that Laurie asked quickly, "What is it? is Beth worse?"

"I've sent for Mother," said Jo, tugging at her rubber boots with a tragic expression.

"Good for you, Jo! Did you do it on your own responsibility?" asked Laurie, as he seated her in the hall chair and took off the rebellious boots, seeing how her hands shook.

"No, the doctor told us to."

"Oh, Jo, it's not so bad as that?" cried Laurie, with a startled face.

"Yes, it is; she doesn't know us, she doesn't even talk about the flocks of green doves, as she calls the vine leaves on the wall; she doesn't look like my Beth, and there's nobody to help us bear it; Mother and Father both gone, and God seems so far away I can't find Him."

As the tears streamed fast down poor Jo's cheeks, she stretched out her hand in a helpless sort of way, as if groping in the dark, and Laurie took it in his, whispering as well as he could with a lump in his throat, "I'm here. Hold onto me, Jo, dear!"

She could not speak, but she did "hold on," and the warm grasp of the friendly human hand comforted her sore heart, and seemed to lead her nearer to the Divine arm which alone could uphold her in her trouble. Laurie longed to say something tender and comfortable, but no fitting words came to him, so he stood silent, gently stroking her bent head as her mother used to do. It was the best thing he could have done, far more soothing than the most eloquent words, for Jo felt the unspoken sympathy, and in the silence learned the sweet solace which affection administers to sorrow. Soon she dried the tears which had relieved her, and looked up with a grateful face.

"Thank you, Teddy, I'm better now. I don't feel so forlorn, and will try to bear it if it comes."

"Keep hoping for the best, that will help you, Jo. Soon your mother will be here, and then everything will be right."

"I'm so glad Father is better; now she won't feel so bad about leaving him. Oh, me! It does seem as if all the troubles came in a heap, and I got the heaviest part on my shoulders," sighed Jo, spreading her wet handkerchief over her knees to dry.

"Doesn't Meg pull fair?" asked Laurie, looking indignant.

"Oh, yes, she tries to, but she can't love Bethy as I do, and she won't miss her as I shall. Beth is my conscience, and I *can't* give her up. I can't! I can't!"

Down went Jo's face into the wet handkerchief, and she cried despairingly, for she had kept up bravely till now and never shed a tear. Laurie drew his hand across his eyes, but could not speak till he had subdued the choky feeling in his throat and steadied his lips. It might be unmanly, but he couldn't help it, and I am glad of it. Presently, as Jo's sobs quieted, he said hopefully, "I don't think she will die; she's so good, and we all love her so much, I don't believe God will take her away yet."

"The good and dear people always do die," groaned Jo, but she stopped crying, for her friend's words cheered her up in spite of her own doubts and fears.

"Poor girl, you're worn out. It isn't like you to be forlorn. Stop a bit. I'll hearten you up in a jiffy."

Laurie went off two stairs at a time, and Jo laid her wearied head down on Beth's little brown hood, which no one had thought of moving from the table where she left it. It must have possessed some magic, for the submissive spirit of its gentle owner seemed to enter into Jo, and when Laurie came running down with a glass of wine, she took it with a smile, and said bravely, "I drink—Health to my Beth! You are a good doctor, Teddy, and *such* a comfortable friend. How can I ever pay you?" she added, as the wine refreshed her body, as the kind words had done her troubled mind.

"I'll send in my bill, by-and-by, and tonight I'll give you something that will warm the cockles of your heart better than quarts of wine," said Laurie, beaming at her with a face of suppressed satisfaction at something.

"What is it?" cried Jo, forgetting her woes for a minute in her wonder.

"I telegraphed to your mother yesterday, and Brooke answered she'd come at once, and she'll be here tonight, and everything will be all right. Aren't you glad I did it?"

Laurie spoke very fast, and turned red and excited all in a minute, for he had kept his plot a secret, for fear of disappointing the girls or harming Beth. Jo grew quite white, flew out of her chair, and the moment he stopped speaking she electrified him by throwing her arms round his neck, and crying out, with a joyful cry, "Oh, Laurie! Oh, Mother! I *am* so glad!" She did not weep again, but laughed hysterically, and trembled and clung to her friend as if she was a little bewildered by the sudden news.

Laurie, though decidedly amazed, behaved with great presence of mind; he patted her back soothingly, and finding that she was recovering, followed it up by a bashful kiss or two, which brought Jo round at once. Holding on to the banisters, she put him gently away, saying breathlessly, "Oh, don't! I didn't mean to, it was dreadful of me, but you were such a dear to go and do it in spite of Hannah that I couldn't help flying at you. Tell me all about it, and don't give me wine again, it makes me act so."

"I don't mind," laughed Laurie, as he settled his tie. "Why, you see I got fidgety, and so did Grandpa. We thought Hannah was overdoing the authority business, and your mother ought to know. She'd never forgive us if Beth—well, if anything happened, you know. So I got Grandpa to say it was high time we did something, and off I pelted to the office yesterday, for the doctor looked sober, and Hannah most took my head off when I proposed a telegram. I never *can* bear to be 'lorded over,' so that settled my mind, and I did it. Your mother will come, I know, and the late train is in at two A.M. I shall go for her, and you've only got to bottle up your rapture, and keep Beth quiet till that blessed lady gets here."

"Laurie, you're an angel! How shall I ever thank you?"

"Fly at me again; I rather like it," said Laurie, looking mischievous—a thing he had not done for a fortnight.

"No, thank you. I'll do it by proxy, when your grandpa comes. Don't tease, but go home and rest, for you'll be up half the night. Bless you, Teddy, bless you!"

Jo had backed into a corner, and as she finished her speech, she vanished precipitately into the kitchen, where she sat down upon a dresser and told the assembled cats that she was "happy, oh, *so* happy!" while Laurie departed, feeling that he had made rather a neat thing of it.

"That's the interferingest chap I ever see, but I forgive him and do hope Mrs. March is coming on right away," said Hannah, with an air of relief, when Jo told the good news.

Meg had a quiet rapture, and then brooded over the letter, while Jo set the sickroom in order, and Hannah "knocked up a couple of pies in case of company unexpected." A breath of fresh air seemed to blow through the house, and something better than sunshine brightened the quiet rooms. Everything appeared to feel the hopeful change; Beth's bird began to chirp again, and a half-blown rose was discovered on Amy's bush in the window; the fires seemed to burn with unusual cheeriness; and every time the girls met, their pale faces broke into smiles as they hugged one another, whispering encouragingly, "Mother's coming, dear! Mother's coming!" Every one rejoiced but Beth; she lay in that heavy stupor, alike unconscious of hope and joy, doubt and danger. It was a piteous sight—the once rosy face so changed and vacant, the once busy hands so weak and wasted, the once smiling lips quite dumb, and the once pretty, well-kept hair scattered rough and tangled on the pillow. All day she lay so, only rousing now and then to mutter, "Water!" with lips so parched they could hardly shape the word; all day Jo and Meg hovered over her, watching, waiting, hoping, and trusting in God and Mother; and all day the snow fell, the bitter wind raged, and the hours dragged slowly by. But night came at last, and every time the clock struck, the sisters, still sitting on either side the bed, looked at each other with brightening eyes, for each hour brought help nearer. The doctor had been in to say that some change, for better or worse, would probably take place about midnight, at which time he would return.

Hannah, quite worn out, lay down on the sofa at the bed's foot and fell fast asleep, Mr. Laurence marched to and fro in the parlor, feeling that he would rather face a rebel battery than Mrs. March's anxious countenance as she entered, Laurie lay on the rug, pretending to rest, but staring into the fire with the thoughtful look which made his black eyes beautifully soft and clear.

The girls never forgot that night, for no sleep came to them as they kept their watch, with that dreadful sense of powerlessness which comes to us in hours like those.

"If God spares Beth, I never will complain again," whispered Meg earnestly.

"If God spares Beth, I'll try to love and serve Him all my life," answered Jo, with equal fervor.

"I wish I had no heart, it aches so," sighed Meg, after a pause.

"If life is often as hard as this, I don't see how we ever shall get through it," added her sister despondently.

Here the clock struck twelve, and both forgot themselves in watching Beth, for they fancied a change passed over her wan face. The house was still as death, and nothing but the wailing of the wind broke the deep hush. Weary Hannah slept on, and no one but the sisters saw the pale shadow which seemed to fall upon the little bed. An hour went by, and nothing happened except Laurie's quiet departure for the station. Another hour—still no one came, and anxious fears of delay in the storm, or accidents by the way, or, worst of all, a great grief at Washington, haunted the poor girls.

It was past two, when Jo, who stood at the window think-ing how dreary the world looked in its winding sheet of snow, heard a movement by the bed, and, turning quickly, saw Meg kneeling before their mother's easy chair with her face hid-den. A dreadful fear passed coldly over Jo, as she thought, "Beth is dead, and Meg is afraid to tell me."

She was back at her post in an instant, and to her excited eyes a great change seemed to have taken place. The fever flush and the look of pain were gone, and the beloved little face looked so pale and peaceful in its utter repose that Jo felt no desire to weep or to lament. Leaning low over this dearest of her sisters, she kissed the damp forehead with her heart on her lips, and softly whispered, "Good-by, my Beth; good-by!"

As if waked by the stir, Hannah started out of her sleep, hurried to the bed, looked at Beth, felt her hands, listened at her lips, and then, throwing her apron over her head, sat down to rock to and fro, exclaiming, under her breath, "The fever's turned, she's sleepin' nat'ral, her skin's damp, and she breathes easy. Praise be given! Oh, my goodness me!"

Before the girls could believe the happy truth, the doctor came to confirm it. He was a homely man, but they thought his face quite heavenly when he smiled and said, with a fatherly look at them, "Yes, my dears, I think the little girl will pull through this time. Keep the house quiet, let her sleep, and when she wakes, give her—"

What they were to give, neither heard, for both crept into the dark hall, and, sitting on the stairs, held each other close, rejoicing with hearts too full for words. When they went back to be kissed and cuddled by faithful Hannah, they found Beth lying, as she used to do, with her cheek pillowed on her hand, the dreadful pallor gone, and breathing quietly, as if just fallen asleep.

"If Mother would only come now!" said Jo, as the winter night began to wane.

"See," said Meg, coming up with a white, half-opened rose, "I thought this would hardly be ready to lay in Beth's hand to-morrow if she—went away from us. But it has blossomed in the night, and now I mean to put it in my vase here, so that when the darling wakes, the first thing she sees will be the little rose, and Mother's face."

Never had the sun risen so beautifully, and never had the world seemed so lovely as it did to the heavy eyes of Meg and Jo, as they looked out in the early morning, when their long, sad vigil was done.

"It looks like a fairy world," said Meg, smiling to herself, as she stood behind the curtain, watching the dazzling sight.

"Hark!" cried Jo, starting to her feet.

Yes, there was a sound of bells at the door below, a cry from Hannah, and then Laurie's voice saying in a joyful whisper, "Girls, she's come! she's come!"

Chapter 19

Amy's Will

WHILE THESE THINGS were happening at home, Amy was having hard times at Aunt March's. She felt her exile deeply, and, for the first time in her life, realized how much she was beloved and petted at home. Aunt March never petted any one; she did not approve of it; but she meant to be kind, for the well-behaved little girl pleased her very much, and Aunt March had a soft place in her old heart for her nephew's children, though she didn't think proper to confess it. She really did her best to make Amy happy, but, dear me, what mistakes she made! Some old people keep young at heart in spite of wrinkles and gray hairs, can sympathize with children's little cares and joys, make them feel at home, and can hide wise lessons under pleasant plays, giving and receiving friendship in the sweetest way. But Aunt March had not this gift, and she worried Amy very much with her rules and orders, her prim ways, and long, prosy talks. Finding the child more docile and amiable than her sister, the old lady felt it her duty to try and counteract, as far as possible, the bad effects of home freedom and indulgence. So she took Amy in hand, and taught her as she herself had been taught sixty years ago—a process which carried dismay to Amy's soul, and made her feel like a fly in the web of a very strict spider.

She had to wash the cups every morning, and polish up the old-fashioned spoons, the fat silver teapot, and the glasses till they shone. Then she must dust the room, and what a trying job that was! Not a speck escaped Aunt March's eye, and all the furniture had claw legs and much carving, which was never dusted to suit. Then Polly must be fed, the lap dog combed, and a dozen trips upstairs and down to get things or deliver orders, for the old lady was very lame and seldom left her big chair. After these tiresome labors, she must do her lessons, which was a daily trial of every virtue she possessed. Then she was allowed one hour for exercise or play, and didn't she enjoy it? Laurie came every day, and wheedled Aunt March till Amy was allowed to go out with him, when they walked and rode and had capital times. After dinner, she had to read aloud, and sit still while the old lady slept, which she usually did for an hour, as she dropped off over the first page. Then patchwork or towels appeared, and Amy sewed with outward meekness and inward rebellion till dusk, when she was allowed to amuse herself as she liked till teatime. The evenings were the worst of all, for Aunt March fell to telling long stories about her youth, which were so un-utterably dull that Amy was always ready to go to bed, in-tending to cry over her hard fate, but usually going to sleep before she had squeezed out more than a tear or two.

If it had not been for Laurie, and old Esther, the maid, she felt that she never could have got through that dreadful time. The parrot alone was enough to drive her distracted, for he soon felt that she did not admire him, and revenged himself by being as mischievous as possible. He pulled her hair whenever she came near him, upset his bread and milk to plague her when she had newly cleaned his cage, made Mop bark by pecking at him while Madam dozed, called her names before company, and behaved in all respects like a repre-hensible old bird. Then she could not endure the dog—a fat, cross beast who snarled and yelped at her when she made his toilet, and who lay on his back with all his legs in the air and a most idiotic expression of countenance when he wanted something to eat, which was about a dozen times a day. The cook was bad-tempered, the old coachman deaf, and Esther the only one who ever took any notice of the young lady.

Esther was a Frenchwoman, who had lived with "Madame," as she called her mistress, for many years, and who rather tyrannized over the old lady, who could not get along without her. Her real name was Estelle, but Aunt March ordered her to change it, and she obeyed, on condition that she was never asked to change her religion. She took a fancy to Mademoiselle, and amused her very much with odd stories of her life in France, when Amy sat with her while she got up Madame's laces. She also allowed her to roam about the great house, and examine the curious and pretty things stored away in the big wardrobes and the ancient chests, for Aunt March hoarded like a magpie. Amy's chief delight was an Indian cabinet, full of queer drawers, little pigeonholes, and secret places, in which were kept all sorts of ornaments, some precious, some merely curious, all more or less antique. To examine and arrange these things gave Amy great satisfaction, especially the jewel cases, in which on velvet cushions reposed the ornaments which had adorned a belle forty years ago. There was the garnet set which Aunt March wore when she came out, the pearls her father gave her on her wedding day, her lover's diamonds, the jet mourning rings and pins, the queer lockets, with portraits of dead friends and weeping willows made of hair inside, the baby bracelets her one little daughter had worn, Uncle March's big watch, with the red seal so many childish hands had played with, and in a box all by itself lay Aunt March's wedding ring, too small now for her fat finger, but put carefully away like the most precious jewel of them all.

"Which would Mademoiselle choose if she had her will?" asked Esther, who always sat near to watch over and lock up the valuables.

"I like the diamonds best, but there is no necklace among them, and I'm fond of necklaces, they are so becoming. I should choose this if I might," replied Amy, looking with great admiration at a string of gold and ebony beads from which hung a heavy cross of the same.

"I, too, covet that, but not as a necklace; ah, no! To me it is a rosary, and as such I should use it like a good Catholic," said Esther, eying the handsome thing wistfully.

"Is it meant to use as you use the string of good-smelling wooden beads hanging over your glass?" asked Amy.

"Truly, yes, to pray with. It would be pleasing to the saints if one used so fine a rosary as this, instead of wearing it as a vain bijou."

"You seem to take a great deal of comfort in your prayers,

Esther, and always come down looking quiet and satisfied. I wish I could."

"If Mademoiselle was a Catholic, she would find true comfort; but as that is not to be, it would be well if you went apart each day to meditate and pray, as did the good mistress whom I served before Madame. She had a little chapel and in it found solacement for much trouble."

"Would it be right for me to do so too?" asked Amy, who in her loneliness felt the need of help of some sort, and found that she was apt to forget her little book, now that Beth was not there to remind her of it.

"It would be excellent and charming, and I shall gladly arrange the litttle dressing room for you if you like it. Say nothing to Madame, but when she sleeps go you and sit alone a while to think good thoughts, and pray the dear God to preserve your sister."

Esther was truly pious, and quite sincere in her advice, for she had an affectionate heart, and felt much for the sisters in their anxiety. Amy liked the idea, and gave her leave to arrange the light closet next her room, hoping it would do her good.

"I wish I knew where all these pretty things would go when Aunt March dies," she said, as she slowly replaced the shining rosary and shut the jewel cases one by one.

"To you and your sisters. I know it, Madame confides in me. I witnessed her will, and it is to be so," whispered Esther, smiling.

"How nice! but I wish she'd let us have them now. Pro-cras-ti-nation is not agreeable," observed Amy, taking a last look at the diamonds.

"It is too soon yet for the young ladies to wear these things. The first one who is affianced will have the pearls—Madame has said it; and I have a fancy that the little turquoise ring will be given to you when you go, for Madame approves your good behavior and charming manners."

"Do you think so? Oh, I'll be a lamb, if I can only have that lovely ring! It's ever so much prettier than Kitty Bryant's. I

do like Aunt March, after all." And Amy tried on the blue
ring with a delighted face and a firm resolve to earn it.

From that day she was a model of obedience, and the old
lady complacently admired the success of her training. Esther
fitted up the closet with a little table, placed a footstool before it, and over it a picture taken from one of the shut-up
rooms. She thought it was of no great value, but, being appropriate, she borrowed it, well knowing that Madame would
never know it, nor care if she did. It was, however, a very
valuable copy of one of the famous pictures of the world, and
Amy's beauty-loving eyes were never tired of looking up at
the sweet face of the divine mother, while tender thoughts of
her own were busy at her heart. On the table she laid her little
Testament and hymnbook, kept a vase always full of the best
flowers Laurie brought her, and came every day to "sit alone,
thinking good thoughts, and praying the dear God to preserve
her sister." Esther had given her a rosary of black beads with
a silver cross, but Amy hung it up and did not use it, feeling
doubtful as to its fitness for Protestant prayers.

The little girl was very sincere in all this, for being left alone
outside the safe home nest, she felt the need of some kind
hand to hold by so sorely that she instinctively turned to the
strong and tender Friend, whose fatherly love most closely
surrounds his little children. She missed her mother's help to
understand and rule herself, but having been taught where to
look, she did her best to find the way and walk in it confidingly. But Amy was a young pilgrim, and just now her
burden seemed very heavy. She tried to forget herself, to keep
cheerful, and be satisfied with doing right, though no one
saw or praised her for it. In her first effort at being very, very
good, she decided to make her will, as Aunt March had done,
so that if she *did* fall ill and die, her possessions might be
justly and generously divided. It cost her a pang even to think
of giving up the little treasures which in her eyes were as
precious as the old lady's jewels.

During one of her play hours she wrote out the important
document as well as she could, with some help from Esther

as to certain legal terms, and when the good-natured French-woman had signed her name, Amy felt relieved and laid it by to show Laurie, whom she wanted as a second witness. As it was a rainy day, she went upstairs to amuse herself in one of the large chambers, and took Polly with her for company. In this room there was a wardrobe full of old-fashioned costumes with which Esther allowed her to play, and it was her favorite amusement to array herself in the faded brocades, and parade up and down before the long mirror, making stately curtsies, and sweeping her train about with a rustle which delighted her ears. So busy was she on this day that she did not hear Laurie's ring nor see his face peeping in at her as she gravely promenaded to and fro, flirting her fan and tossing her head, on which she wore a great pink turban, contrasting oddly with her blue brocade dress and yellow quilted petticoat. She was obliged to walk carefully, for she had on high-heeled shoes, and, as Laurie told Jo afterward, it was a comical sight to see her mince along in her gay suit, with Polly sidling and bridling just behind her, imitating her as well as he could, and occasionally stopping to laugh or exclaim, "Ain't we fine? Get along, you fright! Hold your tongue! Kiss me, dear! Ha! ha!"

Having with difficulty restrained an explosion of merriment, lest it should offend her majesty, Laurie tapped and was graciously received.

"Sit down and rest while I put these things away, then I want to consult you about a very serious matter," said Amy, when she had shown her splendor and driven Polly into a corner. "That bird is the trial of my life," she continued, removing the pink mountain from her head, while Laurie seated himself astride of a chair. "Yesterday, when Aunt was asleep and I was trying to be as still as a mouse, Polly began to squall and flap about in his cage; so I went to let him out, and found a big spider there. I poked it out, and it ran under the bookcase; Polly marched straight after it, stooped down and peeped under the bookcase, saying, in his funny way, with a cock of his eye, 'Come out and take a walk, my dear.' I *couldn't* help laughing, which made Poll swear, and Aunt woke up and scolded us both."

"Did the spider accept the old fellow's invitation?" asked Laurie, yawning.

"Yes, out it came, and away ran Polly, frightened to death, and scrambled up on Aunt's chair, calling out, 'Catch her! Catch her! Catch her!' as I chased the spider."

"That's a lie! Oh lor!" cried the parrot, pecking at Laurie's toes.

"I'd wring your neck if you were mine, you old torment," cried Laurie, shaking his fist at the bird, who put his head on one side and gravely croaked, "Allyluyer! Bless your buttons, dear!"

"Now I'm ready," said Amy, shutting the wardrobe and taking a paper out of her pocket. "I want you to read that, please, and tell me if it is legal and right. I felt that I ought to do it, for life is uncertain and I don't want any ill feeling over my tomb."

Laurie bit his lips, and turning a little from the pensive speaker, read the following document, with praiseworthy gravity, considering the spelling:

MY LAST WILL AND TESTAMENT.

I, Amy Curtis March, being in my sane mind, go give and bequeethe all my earthly property—viz. to wit:—namely

To my father, my best pictures, sketches, maps, and works of art, including frames. Also my $100, to do what he likes with.

To my mother, all my clothes, except the blue apron with pockets—also my likeness, and my medal, with much love.

To my dear sister Margaret, I give my turkquoise ring (if I get it), also my green box with the doves on it, also my piece of real lace for her neck, and my sketch of her as a memorial of her "little girl."

To Jo I leave my breastpin, the one mended with sealing wax, also my bronze inkstand—she lost the cover—and my most precious plaster rabbit, because I am sorry I burned up her story.

To Beth (if she lives after me) I give my dolls and the little bureau, my fan, my linen collars and my new slippers if she can wear them being thin when she gets well. And I herewith also leave her my regret that I ever made fun of old Joanna.

To my friend and neighbor Theodore Laurence I bequeethe my paper mashay portfolio, my clay model of a horse though he did say it hadn't any neck. Also in return for his great kindness in the hour of affliction any one of my artistic works he likes, Noter Dame is the best.

To our venerable benefactor Mr. Laurence I leave my purple box with a looking glass in the cover which will be nice for his pens and remind him of the departed girl who thanks him for his favors to her family, specially Beth.

I wish my favorite playmate Kitty Bryant to have the blue silk apron and my gold-bead ring with a kiss.

To Hannah I give the bandbox she wanted and all the patchwork I leave hoping she "will remember me, when it you see."

And now having disposed of my most valuable property I hope all will be satisfied and not blame the dead. I forgive everyone, and trust we may all meet when the trump shall sound. Amen.

To this will and testiment I set my hand and seal on this 20th day of Nov. Anni Domino 1861.

AMY CURTIS MARCH

Witnesses:

    ESTELLE VALNOR,
    THEODORE LAURENCE.

The last name was written in pencil, and Amy explained that he was to rewrite it in ink and seal it up for her properly.

"What put it into your head? Did anyone tell you about Beth's giving away her things?" asked Laurie soberly, as Amy laid a bit of red tape, with sealing wax, a taper, and a standish before him.

She explained and then asked anxiously, "What about Beth?"

"I'm sorry I spoke, but as I did, I'll tell you. She felt so ill one day that she told Jo she wanted to give her piano to Meg, her cats to you, and the poor old doll to Jo, who would love it for her sake. She was sorry she had so little to give, and left locks of hair to the rest of us, and her best love to Grandpa. *She* never thought of a will."

Laurie was signing and sealing as he spoke, and did not look up till a great tear dropped on the paper. Amy's face was full of trouble; but she only said, "Don't people put sort of postscripts to their wills, sometimes?"

"Yes, 'codicils,' they call them."

"Put one in mine then—that I wish *all* my curls cut off, and given round to my friends. I forgot it, but I want it done, though it will spoil my looks."

Laurie added it, smiling at Amy's last and greatest sacrifice. Then he amused her for an hour, and was much interested in all her trials. But when he came to go, Amy held him back to whisper with trembling lips, "Is there really any danger about Beth?"

"I'm afraid there is, but we must hope for the best, so don't cry, dear." And Laurie put his arm about her with a brotherly gesture which was very comforting.

When he had gone, she went to her little chapel, and sitting in the twilight, prayed for Beth, with streaming tears and an aching heart, feeling that a million turquoise rings would not console her for the loss of her gentle little sister.

Chapter 20

Confidential

I DON'T THINK I have any words in which to tell the meeting of the mother and daughters; such hours are beautiful to live, but very hard to describe, so I will leave it to the imagination of my readers, merely saying that the house was full of genuine happiness, and that Meg's tender hope was realized; for when Beth woke from that long, healing sleep, the first objects on which her eyes fell *were* the little rose and Mother's face. Too weak to wonder at anything, she only smiled and nestled close into the loving arms about her, feeling that the hungry longing was satisfied at last. Then she slept again, and the girls waited upon their mother, for she would not unclasp the thin hand which clung to hers even in sleep.

Hannah had "dished up" an astonishing breakfast for the traveler, finding it impossible to vent her excitement in any other way; and Meg and Jo fed their mother like dutiful young storks, while they listened to her whispered account of Father's state, Mr. Brooke's promise to stay and nurse him, the delays which the storm occasioned on the homeward journey, and the unspeakable comfort Laurie's hopeful face had given her when she arrived, worn out with fatigue, anxiety, and cold.

What a strange yet pleasant day that was! So brilliant and gay without, for all the world seemed abroad to welcome the first snow; so quiet and reposeful within, for everyone slept, spent with watching, and a Sabbath stillness reigned through the house, while nodding Hannah mounted guard at the door. With a blissful sense of burdens lifted off, Meg and Jo closed their weary eyes, and lay at rest, like storm-beaten boats safe at anchor in a quiet harbor. Mrs. March would not leave Beth's side, but rested in the big chair, waking often to look at, touch, and brood over her child, like a miser over some recovered treasure.

Laurie meanwhile posted off to comfort Amy, and told his story so well that Aunt March actually "sniffed" herself, and never once said, "I told you so." Amy came out so strong on this occasion that I think the good thoughts in the little chapel really began to bear fruit. She dried her tears quickly, restrained her impatience to see her mother, and never even thought of the turquoise ring, when the old lady heartily agreed in Laurie's opinion, that she behaved "like a capital little woman." Even Polly seemed impressed, for he called her "good girl," blessed her buttons, and begged her to "come and take a walk, dear," in his most affable tone. She would very gladly have gone out to enjoy the bright wintry weather, but discovering that Laurie was dropping with sleep in spite of manful efforts to conceal the fact, she persuaded him to rest on the sofa, while she wrote a note to her mother. She was a long time about it, and when she returned, he was stretched out with both arms under his head, sound asleep, while Aunt March had pulled down the curtains and sat doing nothing in an unusual fit of benignity.

After a while, they began to think he was not going to wake till night, and I'm not sure that he would, had he not been effectually roused by Amy's cry of joy at sight of her mother. There probably were a good many happy little girls in and about the city that day, but it is my private opinion that Amy was the happiest of all, when she sat in her mother's lap and told her trials, receiving consolation and compensation in the shape of approving smiles and fond caresses. They were alone together in the chapel, to which her mother did not object when its purpose was explained to her.

"On the contrary, I like it very much, dear," looking from the dusty rosary to the well-worn little book, and the lovely picture with its garland of evergreen. "It is an excellent plan to have some place where we can go to be quiet, when things vex or grieve us. There are a good many hard times in this life of ours, but we can always bear them if we ask help in the right way. I think my little girl is learning this."

"Yes, Mother, and when I go home I mean to have a corner in the big closet to put my books and the copy of that picture which I've tried to make. The woman's face is not good—it's too beautiful for me to draw—but the baby is done better, and I love it very much. I like to think He was a little child once, for then I don't seem so far away, and that helps me."

As Amy pointed to the smiling Christ child on his mother's knee, Mrs. March saw something on the lifted hand that made her smile. She said nothing, but Amy understood the look, and after a minute's pause, she added gravely, "I wanted to speak to you about this, but I forgot it. Aunt gave me the ring today; she called me to her and kissed me, and put it on my finger, and said I was a credit to her, and she'd like to keep me always. She gave that funny guard to keep the turquoise on, as it's too big. I'd like to wear them, Mother, can I?"

"They are very pretty, but I think you're rather too young for such ornaments, Amy," said Mrs. March, looking at the plump little hand, with the band of sky-blue stones on the forefinger, and the quaint guard formed of two tiny golden hands clasped together.

"I'll try not to be vain," said Amy. "I don't think I like it only because it's so pretty, but I want to wear it as the girl in the story wore her bracelet, to remind me of something."

"Do you mean Aunt March?" asked her mother, laughing.

"No, to remind me not to be selfish." Amy looked so earnest and sincere about it that her mother stopped laughing, and listened respectfully to the little plan.

"I've thought a great deal lately about my 'bundle of naughties,' and being selfish is the largest one in it; so I'm going to try hard to cure it, if I can. Beth isn't selfish, and that's the reason everyone loves her and feels so bad at the thoughts of losing her. People wouldn't feel half so bad about me if I was sick, and I don't deserve to have them; but I'd like to be loved and missed by a great many friends, so I'm going to try and be like Beth all I can. I'm apt to forget my resolutions, but if I had something always about me to remind me, I guess I should do better. May I try this way?"

"Yes, but I have more faith in the corner of the big closet. Wear your ring, dear, and do your best. I think you will prosper, for the sincere wish to be good is half the battle.

Now I must go back to Beth. Keep up your heart, little daughter, and we will soon have you home again."

That evening, while Meg was writing to her father to report the traveler's safe arrival, Jo slipped upstairs into Beth's room, and finding her mother in her usual place, stood a minute twisting her fingers in her hair, with a worried gesture and an undecided look.

"What is it, deary?" asked Mrs. March, holding out her hand, with a face which invited confidence.

"I want to tell you something, Mother."

"About Meg?"

"How quickly you guessed! Yes, it's about her, and though it's a little thing, it fidgets me."

"Beth is asleep; speak low, and tell me all about it. That Moffat hasn't been here, I hope?" asked Mrs. March rather sharply.

"No, I should have shut the door in his face if he had," said Jo, settling herself on the floor at her mother's feet. "Last summer Meg left a pair of gloves over at the Laurences' and only one was returned. We forgot all about it, till Teddy told me that Mr. Brooke had it. He kept it in his waistcoat pocket, and once it fell out, and Teddy joked him about it, and Mr. Brooke owned that he liked Meg but didn't dare say so, she was so young and he so poor. Now, isn't it a *dread*ful state of things?"

"Do you think Meg cares for him?" asked Mrs. March, with an anxious look.

"Mercy me! I don't know anything about love and such nonsense!" cried Jo, with a funny mixture of interest and contempt. "In novels, the girls show it by starting and blushing, fainting away, growing thin, and acting like fools. Now Meg does not do anything of the sort: she eats and drinks and sleeps like a sensible creature, she looks straight in my face when I talk about that man, and only blushes a little bit when Teddy jokes about lovers. I forbid him to do it, but he doesn't mind me as he ought."

"Then you fancy that Meg is *not* interested in John?"

"Who?" cried Jo, staring.

"Mr. Brooke. I call him 'John' now; we fell into the way of doing so at the hospital, and he likes it."

"Oh, dear! I know you'll take his part: he's been good to Father, and you won't send him away, but let Meg marry him, if she wants to. Mean thing! To go petting Papa and helping you, just to wheedle you into liking him." And Jo pulled her hair again with a wrathful tweak.

"My dear, don't get angry about it, and I will tell you how it happened. John went with me at Mr. Laurence's request, and was so devoted to poor Father that we couldn't help getting fond of him. He was perfectly open and honorable about Meg, for he told us he loved her, but would earn a comfortable home before he asked her to marry him. He only wanted our leave to love her and work for her, and the right to make her love him if he could. He is a truly excellent young man, and we could not refuse to listen to him, but I will not consent to Meg's engaging herself so young."

"Of course not; it would be idiotic! I knew there was mischief brewing, I felt it, and now it's worse than I imagined. I just wish I could marry Meg myself, and keep her safe in the family."

This odd arrangement made Mrs. March smile, but she said gravely, "Jo, I confide in you and don't wish you to say anything to Meg yet. When John comes back and I see them together, I can judge better of her feelings toward him."

"She'll see his in those handsome eyes that she talks about, and then it will be all up with her. She's got such a soft heart, it will melt like butter in the sun if anyone looks sentimentally at her. She read the short reports he sent more than she did your letters, and pinched me when I spoke of it, and likes brown eyes, and doesn't think John an ugly name, and she'll go and fall in love, and there's an end of peace and fun, and cozy times together. I see it all! They'll go lovering around the house, and we shall have to dodge; Meg will be absorbed, and no good to me any more; Brooke will scratch up a fortune somehow, carry her off, and make a hole in the family; and I shall break my heart, and everything will be abominably uncomfortable. Oh, dear me! Why weren't we all boys, then there wouldn't be any bother."

Jo leaned her chin on her knees in a disconsolate attitude and shook her fist at the reprehensible John. Mrs. March sighed, and Jo looked up with an air of relief.

"You don't like it, Mother? I'm glad of it. Let's send him about his business, and not tell Meg a word of it, but all be happy together as we always have been."

"I did wrong to sigh, Jo. It is natural and right you should all go to homes of your own in time, but I do want to keep my girls as long as I can; and I am sorry that this happened so soon, for Meg is only seventeen and it will be some years before John can make a home for her. Your father and I have agreed that she shall not bind herself in any way, nor be married, before twenty. If she and John love one another, they can wait, and test the love by doing so. She is conscientious, and I have no fear of her treating him unkindly. My pretty, tenderhearted girl! I hope things will go happily with her."

"Hadn't you rather have her marry a rich man?" asked Jo, as her mother's voice faltered a little over the last words.

"Money is a good and useful thing, Jo, and I hope my girls will never feel the need of it too bitterly nor be tempted by too much. I should like to know that John was firmly established in some good business, which gave him an income large enough to keep free from debt and make Meg comfortable. I'm not ambitious for a splendid fortune, a fashionable position, or a great name for my girls. If rank and money come with love and virtue, also, I should accept them gratefully, and enjoy your good fortune; but I know, by experience, how much genuine happiness can be had in a plain little house, where the daily bread is earned, and some privations give sweetness to the few pleasures. I am content to see Meg begin humbly, for if I am not mistaken, she will be rich in the possession of a good man's heart, and that is better than a fortune."

"I understand, Mother, and quite agree, but I'm disappointed about Meg, for I'd planned to have her marry Teddy by-and-by and sit in the lap of luxury all her days. Wouldn't it be nice?" asked Jo, looking up with a brighter face.

"He is younger than she, you know," began Mrs. March, but Jo broke in—

"Only a little, he's old for his age, and tall, and can be quite grown-up in his manners if he likes. Then he's rich and generous and good, and loves us all, and *I* say it's a pity my plan is spoiled."

"I'm afraid Laurie is hardly grown-up enough for Meg, and altogether too much of a weathercock just now for anyone to depend on. Don't make plans, Jo, but let time and their own hearts mate your friends. We can't meddle safely in such matters, and had better not get 'romantic rubbish,' as you call it, into our heads, lest it spoil our friendship."

"Well, I won't, but I hate to see things going all crisscross and getting snarled up, when a pull here and a snip there would straighten it out. I wish wearing flatirons on our heads would keep us from growing up. But buds will be roses, and kittens, cats—more's the pity!"

"What's that about flatirons and cats?" asked Meg, as she crept into the room with the finished letter in her hand.

"Only one of my stupid speeches. I'm going to bed; come, Peggy," said Jo, unfolding herself like an animated puzzle.

"Quite right, and beautifully written. Please add that I send my love to John," said Mrs. March, as she glanced over the letter and gave it back.

"Do you call him 'John'?" asked Meg, smiling, with her innocent eyes looking down into her mother's.

"Yes, he has been like a son to us, and we are very fond of him," replied Mrs. March, returning the look with a keen one.

"I'm glad of that, he is so lonely. Good night, Mother, dear. It is so inexpressibly comfortable to have you here," was Meg's answer.

The kiss her mother gave her was a very tender one, and as she went away, Mrs. March said, with a mixture of satisfaction and regret, "She does not love John yet, but will soon learn to."

Chapter 21

Laurie Makes Mischief, and Jo Makes Peace

Jo's FACE was a study next day, for the secret rather weighed upon her, and she found it hard not to look mysterious and important. Meg observed it, but did not trouble herself to make inquiries, for she had learned that the best way to manage Jo was by the law of contraries, so she felt sure of being told everything if she did not ask. She was rather surprised, therefore, when the silence remained unbroken, and Jo assumed a patronizing air, which decidedly aggravated Meg, who in her turn assumed an air of dignified reserve and devoted herself to her mother. This left Jo to her own devices, for Mrs. March had taken her place as nurse, and bade her rest, exercise, and amuse herself after her long confinement. Amy being gone, Laurie was her only refuge; and much as she enjoyed his society, she rather dreaded him just then, for he was an incorrigible tease, and she feared he would coax her secret from her.

She was quite right, for the mischief-loving lad no sooner suspected a mystery than he set himself to find it out, and led Jo a trying life of it. He wheedled, bribed, ridiculed, threatened, and scolded; affected indifference, that he might surprise the truth from her; declared he knew, then that he didn't care; and, at last, by dint of perseverance, he satisfied himself that it concerned Meg and Mr. Brooke. Feeling indignant that he was not taken into his tutor's confidence, he set his wits to work to devise some proper retaliation for the slight.

Meg meanwhile had apparently forgotton the matter and was absorbed in preparations for her father's return, but all of a sudden a change seemed to come over her, and, for a day or two, she was quite unlike herself. She started when spoken to, blushed when looked at, was very quiet, and sat over her sewing, with a timid, troubled look on her face. To her mother's inquiries she answered that she was quite well, and Jo's she silenced by begging to be let alone.

"She feels it in the air—love, I mean—and she's going very fast. She's got most of the symptoms—is twittery and cross, doesn't eat, lies awake, and mopes in corners. I caught her singing that song he gave her, and once she said 'John,' as you do, and then turned as red as a poppy. Whatever shall we do?" said Jo, looking ready for any measures, however violent.

"Nothing but wait. Let her alone, be kind and patient, and Father's coming will settle everything," replied her mother.

"Here's a note to you, Meg, all sealed up. How odd! Teddy never seals mine," said Jo next day, as she distributed the contents of the little post office.

Mrs. March and Jo were deep in their own affairs, when a sound from Meg made them look up to see her staring at her note with a frightened face.

"My child, what is it?" cried her mother, running to her, while Jo tried to take the paper which had done the mischief.

"It's all a mistake—he didn't send it. Oh, Jo, how could you do it?" and Meg hid her face in her hands, crying as if her heart was quite broken.

"Me! I've done nothing! What's she talking about?" cried Jo, bewildered.

Meg's mild eyes kindled with anger as she pulled a crumpled note from her pocket and threw it at Jo, saying reproachfully, "You wrote it, and that bad boy helped you. How could you be so rude, so mean, and cruel to us both?"

Jo hardly heard her, for she and her mother were reading the note, which was written in a peculiar hand.

"MY DEAREST MARGARET—

"I can no longer restrain my passion, and must know my fate before I return. I dare not tell your parents yet, but I think they would consent if they knew that we adored one another. Mr. Laurence will help me to some good place, and then, my sweet girl, you will make me happy. I implore you

to say nothing to your family yet, but to send one word of
hope through Laurie to

"Your devoted JOHN."

"Oh, the little villain! That's the way he meant to pay me
for keeping my word to Mother. I'll give him a hearty scolding and bring him over to beg pardon," cried Jo, burning to
execute immediate justice. But her mother held her back,
saying, with a look she seldom wore—

"Stop, Jo, you must clear yourself first. You have played
so many pranks that I am afraid you have had a hand in
this."

"On my word, Mother, I haven't! I never saw that note
before, and don't know anything about it, as true as I live!"
said Jo, so earnestly that they believed her. "If I *had* taken
a part in it I'd have done it better than this, and have written
a sensible note. I should think you'd have known Mr. Brooke
wouldn't write such stuff as that," she added, scornfully tossing down the paper.

"It's like his writing," faltered Meg, comparing it with the
note in her hand.

"Oh, Meg, you didn't answer it?" cried Mrs. March quickly.

"Yes, I did!" And Meg hid her face again, overcome with
shame.

"Here's a scrape! *Do* let me bring that wicked boy over to
explain and be lectured. I can't rest till I get hold of him."
And Jo made for the door again.

"Hush! Let me manage this, for it is worse than I thought.
Margaret, tell me the whole story," commanded Mrs. March,
sitting down by Meg, yet keeping hold of Jo, lest she should
fly off.

"I received the first letter from Laurie, who didn't look
as if he knew anything about it," began Meg, without looking
up. "I was worried at first and meant to tell you, then I remembered how you liked Mr. Brooke, so I thought you
wouldn't mind if I kept my little secret for a few days. I'm
so silly that I liked to think no one knew, and while I was deciding what to say, I felt like the girls in books, who have

such things to do. Forgive me, Mother, I'm paid for my silliness now; I never can look him in the face again."

"What did you say to him?" asked Mrs. March.

"I only said I was too young to do anything about it yet, that I didn't wish to have secrets from you, and he must speak to Father. I was very grateful for his kindness, and would be his friend, but nothing more, for a long while."

Mrs. March smiled, as if well pleased, and Jo clapped her hands, exclaiming, with a laugh, "You are almost equal to Caroline Percy, who was a pattern of prudence! Tell on, Meg. What did he say to that?"

"He writes in a different way entirely, telling me that he never sent any love letter at all, and is very sorry that my roguish sister, Jo, should take such liberties with our names. It's very kind and respectful, but think how dreadful for me!"

Meg leaned against her mother, looking the image of despair, and Jo tramped about the room, calling Laurie names. All of a sudden she stopped, caught up the two notes, and after looking at them closely, said decidedly, "I don't believe Brooke ever saw either of these letters. Teddy wrote both, and keeps yours to crow over me with because I wouldn't tell him my secret."

"Don't have any secrets, Jo. Tell it to Mother and keep out of trouble, as I should have done," said Meg warningly.

"Bless you, child! Mother told me."

"That will do, Jo. I'll comfort Meg while you go and get Laurie. I shall sift the matter to the bottom, and put a stop to such pranks at once."

Away ran Jo, and Mrs. March gently told Meg Mr. Brooke's real feelings. "Now, dear, what are your own? Do you love him enough to wait till he can make a home for you, or will you keep yourself quite free for the present?"

"I've been so scared and worried, I don't want to have anything to do with lovers for a long while—perhaps never," answered Meg petulantly. "If John doesn't know anything about this nonsense, don't tell him, and make Jo and Laurie hold their tongues. I won't be deceived and plagued and made a fool of—it's a shame!"

Seeing that Meg's usually gentle temper was roused and her pride hurt by this mischievous joke, Mrs. March soothed her by promises of entire silence and great discretion for the future. The instant Laurie's step was heard in the hall, Meg fled into the study, and Mrs. March received the culprit alone. Jo had not told him why he was wanted, fearing he wouldn't come, but he knew the minute he saw Mrs. March's face, and stood twirling his hat with a guilty air which convicted him at once. Jo was dismissed, but chose to march up and down the hall like a sentinel, having some fear that the prisoner might bolt. The sound of voices in the parlor rose and fell for half an hour, but what happened during that interview the girls never knew.

When they were called in, Laurie was standing by their mother with such a penitent face that Jo forgave him on the spot, but did not think it wise to betray the fact. Meg received his humble apology, and was much comforted by the assurance that Brooke knew nothing of the joke.

"I'll never tell him to my dying day—wild horses shan't drag it out of me; so you'll forgive me, Meg, and I'll do anything to show how out-and-out sorry I am," he added, looking very much ashamed of himself.

"I'll try, but it was a very ungentlemanly thing to do. I didn't think you could be so sly and malicious, Laurie," replied Meg, trying to hide her maidenly confusion under a gravely reproachful air.

"It was altogether abominable, and I don't deserve to be spoken to for a month, but you will, though, won't you?" And Laurie folded his hands together with such an imploring gesture, as he spoke in his irresistibly persuasive tone, that it was impossible to frown upon him in spite of his scandalous behavior. Meg pardoned him, and Mrs. March's grave face relaxed, in spite of her efforts to keep sober, when she heard him declare that he would atone for his sins by all sorts of penances, and abase himself like a worm before the injured damsel.

Jo stood aloof, meanwhile, trying to harden her heart against him, and succeeding only in primming up her face into an expression of entire disapprobation. Laurie looked at her once or twice, but as she showed no sign of relenting, he felt injured, and turned his back on her till the others were done with him, when he made her a low bow and walked off without a word.

As soon as he had gone, she wished she had been more forgiving, and when Meg and her mother went upstairs, she felt lonely and longed for Teddy. After resisting for some time, she yielded to the impulse, and armed with a book to return, went over to the big house.

"Is Mr. Laurence in?" asked Jo, of a housemaid, who was coming downstairs.

"Yes, miss, but I don't believe he's seeable just yet."

"Why not? Is he ill?"

"La, no, miss, but he's had a scene with Mr. Laurie, who is in one of his tantrums about something, which vexes the old gentleman, so I dursn't go nigh him."

"Where is Laurie?"

"Shut up in his room, and he won't answer, though I've been a-tapping. I don't know what's to become of the dinner, for it's ready, and there's no one to eat it."

"I'll go and see what the matter is. I'm not afraid of either of them."

Up went Jo, and knocked smartly on the door of Laurie's little study.

"Stop that, or I'll open the door and make you!" called out the young gentleman in a threatening tone.

Jo immediately knocked again; the door flew open, and in she bounced before Laurie could recover from his surprise. Seeing that he really *was* out of temper, Jo, who knew how to manage him, assumed a contrite expression, and going artistically down upon her knees, said meekly, "Please forgive me for being so cross. I came to make it up, and can't go away till I have."

"It's all right. Get up, and don't be a goose, Jo," was the cavalier reply to her petition.

"Thank you, I will. Could I ask what's the matter? You don't look exactly easy in your mind."

"I've been shaken, and I won't bear it!" growled Laurie indignantly.

"Who did it?" demanded Jo.

"Grandfather. If it had been anyone else I'd have——" And the injured youth finished his sentence by an energetic gesture of the right arm.

"That's nothing. I often shake you, and you don't mind," said Jo soothingly.

"Pooh! You're a girl, and it's fun, but I'll allow no man to shake *me*."

"I don't think anyone would care to try it, if you looked as much like a thundercloud as you do now. Why were you treated so?"

"Just because I wouldn't say what your mother wanted me for. I'd promised not to tell, and of course I wasn't going to break my word."

"Couldn't you satisfy your grandpa in any other way?"

"No, he *would* have the truth, the whole truth, and nothing but the truth. I'd have told my part of the scrape, if I could without bringing Meg in. As I couldn't, I held my tongue, and bore the scolding till the old gentleman collared me. Then I got angry and bolted, for fear I should forget myself."

"It wasn't nice, but he's sorry, I know, so go down and make up. I'll help you."

"Hanged if I do! I'm not going to be lectured and pummelled by everyone, just for a bit of a frolic. I *was* sorry about Meg, and begged pardon like a man; but I won't do it again, when I wasn't in the wrong."

"He didn't know that."

"He ought to trust me, and not act as if I was a baby. It's no use, Jo, he's got to learn that I'm able to take care of myself, and don't need anyone's apron string to hold on by."

"What pepper pots you are!" sighed Jo. "How do you mean to settle this affair?"

"Well, he ought to beg pardon, and believe me when I say I can't tell him what the fuss's about."

"Bless you! He won't do that."

"I won't go down till he does."

"Now, Teddy, be sensible. Let it pass, and I'll explain what I can. You can't stay here, so what's the use of being melodramatic?"

"I don't intend to stay here long, anyway. I'll slip off and take a journey somewhere, and when Grandpa misses me he'll come round fast enough."

"I dare say, but you ought not to go and worry him."

"Don't preach. I'll go to Washington and see Brooke; it's gay there, and I'll enjoy myself after the troubles."

"What fun you'd have! I wish I could run off too," said Jo, forgetting her part of mentor in lively visions of martial life at the capital.

"Come on, then! Why not? You go and surprise your father, and I'll stir up old Brooke. It would be a glorious joke; let's do it, Jo. We'll leave a letter saying we are all right, and trot off at once. I've got money enough; it will do you good, and be no harm, as you go to your father."

For a moment Jo looked as if she would agree, for wild as the plan was, it just suited her. She was tired of care and confinement, longed for change, and thoughts of her father blended temptingly with the novel charms of camps and hospitals, liberty and fun. Her eyes kindled as they turned wistfully toward the window, but they fell on the old house opposite, and she shook her head with sorrowful decision.

"If I was a boy, we'd run away together, and have a capital time; but as I'm a miserable girl, I must be proper and stop at home. Don't tempt me, Teddy, it's a crazy plan."

"That's the fun of it," began Laurie, who had got a willful fit on him and was possessed to break out of bounds in some way.

"Hold your tongue!" cried Jo, covering her ears. " 'Prunes and prisms' are my doom, and I may as well make up my mind to it. I came here to moralize, not to hear about things that make me skip to think of."

"I know Meg would wet-blanket such a proposal, but I thought you had more spirit," began Laurie insinuatingly.

"Bad boy, be quiet! Sit down and think of your own sins,

don't go making me add to mine. If I get your grandpa to apologize for the shaking, will you give up running away?" asked Jo seriously.

"Yes, but you won't do it," answered Laurie, who wished to make up, but felt that his outraged dignity must be appeased first.

"If I can manage the young one I can the old one," muttered Jo, as she walked away, leaving Laurie bent over a railroad map with his head propped up on both hands.

"Come in!" And Mr. Laurence's gruff voice sounded gruffer than ever, as Jo tapped at his door.

"It's only me, sir, come to return a book," she said blandly, as she entered.

"Want any more?" asked the old gentleman, looking grim and vexed, but trying not to show it.

"Yes, please. I like old Sam so well, I think I'll try the second volume," returned Jo, hoping to propitiate him by accepting a second dose of Boswell's *Johnson*, as he had recommended that lively work.

The shaggy eyebrows unbent a little as he rolled the steps toward the shelf where the Johnsonian literature was placed. Jo skipped up, and sitting on the top step, affected to be searching for her book, but was really wondering how best to introduce the dangerous object of her visit. Mr. Laurence seemed to suspect that something was brewing in her mind, for after taking several brisk turns about the room, he faced round on her, speaking so abruptly that *Rasselas* tumbled face downward on the floor.

"What has that boy been about? Don't try to shield him. I know he has been in mischief by the way he acted when he came home. I can't get a word from him, and when I threatened to shake the truth out of him he bolted upstairs and locked himself into his room."

"He did do wrong, but we forgave him, and all promised not to say a word to anyone," began Jo reluctantly.

"That won't do; he shall not shelter himself behind a promise from you softhearted girls. If he's done anything amiss, he shall confess, beg pardon, and be punished. Out with it, Jo, I won't be kept in the dark."

Mr. Laurence looked so alarming and spoke so sharply that Jo would have gladly run away, if she could, but she was perched aloft on the steps, and he stood at the foot, a lion in the path, so she had to stay and brave it out.

"Indeed, sir, I cannot tell. Mother forbade it. Laurie has confessed, asked pardon, and been punished quite enough. We don't keep silence to shield him, but someone else, and it will make more trouble if you interfere. Please don't; it was partly my fault, but it's all right now; so let's forget it, and talk about the *Rambler* or something pleasant."

"Hang the *Rambler!* Come down and give me your word that this harum-scarum boy of mine hasn't done anything ungrateful or impertinent. If he has, after all your kindness to him, I'll thrash him with my own hands."

The threat sounded awful, but did not alarm Jo, for she knew the irascible old gentleman would never lift a finger against his grandson, whatever he might say to the contrary. She obediently descended, and made as light of the prank as she could without betraying Meg or forgetting the truth.

"Hum—ha—well, if the boy held his tongue because he promised, and not from obstinacy, I'll forgive him. He's a stubborn fellow and hard to manage," said Mr. Laurence, rubbing up his hair till it looked as if he had been out in a gale, and smoothing the frown from his brow with an air of relief.

"So am I, but a kind word will govern me when all the king's horses and all the king's men couldn't," said Jo, trying to say a kind word for her friend, who seemed to get out of one scrape only to fall into another.

"You think I'm not kind to him, hey?" was the sharp answer.

"Oh, dear, no, sir, you are rather too kind sometimes, and then just a trifle hasty when he tries your patience. Don't you think you are?"

Jo was determined to have it out now, and tried to look

quite placid, though she quaked a little after her bold speech. To her great relief and surprise, the old gentleman only threw his spectacles onto the table with a rattle and exclaimed frankly—

"You're right, girl, I am! I love the boy, but he tries my patience past bearing, and I don't know how it will end, if we go on so."

"I'll tell you, he'll run away." Jo was sorry for that speech the minute it was made; she meant to warn him that Laurie would not bear much restraint, and hoped he would be more forbearing with the lad.

Mr. Laurence's ruddy face changed suddenly, and he sat down, with a troubled glance at the picture of a handsome man, which hung over his table. It was Laurie's father, who *had* run away in his youth, and married against the imperious old man's will. Jo fancied he remembered and regretted the past, and she wished she had held her tongue.

"He won't do it unless he is very much worried, and only threatens it sometimes, when he gets tired of studying. I often think I should like to, especially since my hair was cut, so if you ever miss us, you may advertise for two boys and look among the ships bound for India."

She laughed as she spoke, and Mr. Laurence looked relieved, evidently taking the whole as a joke.

"You hussy, how dare you talk in that way? Where's your respect for me, and your proper bringing up? Bless the boys and girls! What torments they are, yet we can't do without them," he said, pinching her cheeks good-humoredly. "Go and bring that boy down to his dinner, tell him it's all right, and advise him not to put on tragedy airs with his grandfather. I won't bear it."

"He won't come, sir; he feels badly because you didn't believe him when he said he couldn't tell. I think the shaking hurt his feelings very much."

Jo tried to look pathetic but must have failed, for Mr. Laurence began to laugh, and she knew the day was won.

"I'm sorry for that, and ought to thank him for not shaking

me, I suppose. What the dickens does the fellow expect?"
And the old gentleman looked a trifle ashamed of his own
testiness.

"If I were you, I'd write him an apology, sir. He says he
won't come down till he has one, and talks about Washington,
and goes on in an absurd way. A formal apology will make
him see how foolish he is, and bring him down quite amiable.
Try it; he likes fun, and this way is better than talking. I'll
carry it up, and teach him his duty."

Mr. Laurence gave her a sharp look, and put on his spectacles, saying slowly, "You're a sly puss, but I don't mind
being managed by you and Beth. Here, give me a bit of
paper, and let us have done with this nonsense."

The note was written in the terms which one gentleman
would use to another after offering some deep insult. Jo
dropped a kiss on the top of Mr. Laurence's bald head, and
ran up to slip the apology under Laurie's door, advising him
through the keyhole to be submissive, decorous, and a few
other agreeable impossibilities. Finding the door locked again,
she left the note to do its work, and was going quietly away,
when the young gentleman slid down the banisters, and waited
for her at the bottom, saying, with his most virtuous expression of countenance, "What a good fellow you are, Jo! Did
you get blown up?" he added, laughing.

"No, he was pretty mild, on the whole."

"Ah! I got it all round. Even you cast me off over there,
and I felt just ready to go to the deuce," he began apologetically.

"Don't talk in that way, turn over a new leaf and begin
again, Teddy, my son."

"I keep turning over new leaves, and spoiling them, as I
used to spoil my copybooks; and I make so many beginnings
there never will be an end," he said dolefully.

"Go and eat your dinner, you'll feel better after it. Men
always croak when they are hungry," and Jo whisked out at
the front door after that.

"That's a 'label' on my 'sect,'" answered Laurie, quoting
Amy, as he went to partake of humble-pie dutifully with his

grandfather, who was quite saintly in temper and overwhelmingly respectful in manner all the rest of the day.

Everyone thought the matter ended and the little cloud blown over, but the mischief was done, for though others forgot it Meg remembered. She never alluded to a certain person, but she thought of him a good deal, dreamed dreams more than ever, and once Jo, rummaging her sister's desk for stamps, found a bit of paper scribbled over with the words, "Mrs. John Brooke," whereat she groaned tragically and cast it into the fire, feeling that Laurie's prank had hastened the evil day for her.

Chapter 22

Pleasant Meadows

LIKE SUNSHINE AFTER storm were the peaceful weeks which followed. The invalids improved rapidly, and Mr. March began to talk of returning early in the new year. Beth was soon able to lie on the study sofa all day, amusing herself with the well-beloved cats at first, and in time with doll's sewing, which had fallen sadly behindhand. Her once active limbs were so stiff and feeble that Jo took her a daily airing about the house in her strong arms. Meg cheerfully blackened and burned her white hands cooking delicate messes for "the dear," while Amy, a loyal slave of the ring, celebrated her return by giving away as many of her treasures as she could prevail on her sisters to accept.

As Christmas approached, the usual mysteries began to haunt the house, and Jo frequently convulsed the family by proposing utterly impossible or magnificently absurd ceremonies, in honor of this unusually merry Christmas. Laurie was equally impracticable, and would have had bonfires, sky-rockets, and triumphal arches, if he had had his own way. After many skirmishes and snubbings, the ambitious pair were considered effectually quenched and went about with forlorn faces, which were rather belied by explosions of laughter when the two got together.

Several days of unusually mild weather fitly ushered in a splendid Christmas Day. Hannah "felt in her bones" that it was going to be an unusually fine day, and she proved herself a true prophetess, for everybody and everything seemed bound to produce a grand success. To begin with, Mr. March wrote that he should soon be with them, then Beth felt uncommonly well that morning, and, being dressed in her mother's gift—a soft crimson merino wrapper—was borne in triumph to the window to behold the offering of Jo and Laurie. The

244

Out in the garden stood a stately snow maiden, crowned with holly . . .

Unquenchables had done their best to be worthy of the name, for like elves they had worked by night and conjured up a comical surprise. Out in the garden stood a stately snow maiden, crowned with holly, bearing a basket of fruit and flowers in one hand, a great roll of new music in the other, a perfect rainbow of an Afghan round her chilly shoulders, and a Christmas carol issuing from her lips, on a pink paper streamer:

THE JUNGFRAU TO BETH

God bless you, dear Queen Bess!
   May nothing you dismay,
But health and peace and happiness
   Be yours, this Christmas Day.

Here's fruit to feed our busy bee,
   And flowers for her nose;
Here's music for her pianee,
   An Afghan for her toes.

A portrait of Joanna, see,
   By Raphael No. 2,
Who labored with great industry
   To make it fair and true.

Accept a ribbon red, I beg,
   For Madam Purrer's tail;
And ice cream made by lovely Peg,—
   A Mont Blanc in a pail.

Their dearest love my makers laid
   Within my breast of snow:
Accept it, and the Alpine maid,
   From Laurie and from Jo.

How Beth laughed when she saw it, how Laurie ran up and down to bring in the gifts, and what ridiculous speeches Jo made as she presented them!

"I'm so full of happiness, that, if Father was only here, I couldn't hold one drop more," said Beth, quite sighing with contentment as Jo carried her off to the study to rest after the excitement, and to refresh herself with some of the delicious grapes the "Jungfrau" had sent her.

"So am I," added Jo, slapping the pocket wherein reposed the long-desired *Undine and Sintram*.

"I'm sure I am," echoed Amy, poring over the engraved copy of the Madonna and Child, which her mother had given her in a pretty frame.

"Of course I am!" cried Meg, smoothing the silvery folds of her first silk dress, for Mr. Laurence had insisted on giving it.

"How can *I* be otherwise?" said Mrs. March gratefully, as her eyes went from her husband's letter to Beth's smiling face, and her hand caressed the brooch made of gray and golden, chestnut and dark brown hair, which the girls had just fastened on her breast.

Now and then, in this workaday world, things do happen in the delightful storybook fashion, and what a comfort that is. Half an hour after everyone had said they were so happy they could only hold one drop more, the drop came. Laurie opened the parlor door and popped his head in very quietly. He might just as well have turned a somersault and uttered an Indian war whoop, for his face was so full of suppressed excitement and his voice so treacherously joyful that everyone jumped up, though he only said, in a queer, breathless voice, "Here's another Christmas present for the March family."

Before the words were well out of his mouth, he was whisked away somehow, and in his place appeared a tall man, muffled up to the eyes, leaning on the arm of another tall man, who tried to say something and couldn't. Of course there was a general stampede, and for several minutes everybody seemed to lose their wits, for the strangest things were done, and no one said a word. Mr. March became invisible in the embrace of four pairs of loving arms; Jo disgraced herself by nearly fainting away, and had to be doctored by Laurie in the china closet; Mr. Brooke kissed Meg entirely by mistake, as he somewhat incoherently explained; and Amy, the dignified, tumbled over a stool, and, never stopping to get up, hugged and cried over her father's boots in the most touching manner. Mrs. March was the first to recover herself, and held up her hand with a warning, "Hush! Remember Beth!"

But it was too late; the study door flew open, the little red wrapper appeared on the threshold—joy put strength into the feeble limbs—and Beth ran straight into her father's arms. Never mind what happened just after that, for the full hearts overflowed, washing away the bitterness of the past and leaving only the sweetness of the present.

It was not at all romantic, but a hearty laugh set everybody straight again, for Hannah was discovered behind the door, sobbing over the fat turkey, which she had forgotten to put down when she rushed up from the kitchen. As the laugh subsided, Mrs. March began to thank Mr. Brooke for his faithful care of her husband, at which Mr. Brooke suddenly remembered that Mr. March needed rest, and, seizing Laurie, he precipitately retired. Then the two invalids were ordered to repose, which they did, by both sitting in one big chair and talking hard.

Mr. March told how he had longed to surprise them, and how, when the fine weather came, he had been allowed by his doctor to take advantage of it, how devoted Brooke had been, and how he was altogether a most estimable and upright young man. Why Mr. March paused a minute just there, and after a glance at Meg, who was violently poking the fire, looked at his wife with an inquiring lift of the eyebrows, I leave you to imagine; also why Mrs. March gently nodded her head and asked, rather abruptly, if he wouldn't have something to eat. Jo saw and understood the look, and she stalked grimly away to get wine and beef tea, muttering to herself as she slammed the door, "I hate estimable young men with brown eyes!"

There never *was* such a Christmas dinner as they had that day. The fat turkey was a sight to behold, when Hannah sent him up, stuffed, browned, and decorated; so was the plum pudding, which quite melted in one's mouth; likewise the jellies, in which Amy reveled like a fly in a honeypot. Everything turned out well, which was a mercy, Hannah said, "For my mind was that flustered, mum, that it's a merrycle I didn't roast the pudding, and stuff the turkey with raisins, let alone bilin' of it in a cloth."

Mr. Laurence and his grandson dined with them, also Mr. Brooke—at whom Jo glowered darkly, to Laurie's infinite amusement. Two easy chairs stood side by side at the head of the table, in which sat Beth and her father, feasting modestly on chicken and a little fruit. They drank healths, told stories, sang songs, "reminisced," as the old folks say, and had a thoroughly good time. A sleigh ride had been planned, but the girls would not leave their father; so the guests departed early, and as twilight gathered, the happy family sat together round the fire.

"Just a year ago we were groaning over the dismal Christmas we expected to have. Do you remember?" asked Jo, breaking a short pause which had followed a long conversation about many things.

"Rather a pleasant year on the whole!" said Meg, smiling at the fire, and congratulating herself on having treated Mr. Brooke with dignity.

"I think it's been a pretty hard one," observed Amy, watching the light shine on her ring with thoughtful eyes.

"I'm glad it's over, because we've got you back," whispered Beth, who sat on her father's knee.

"Rather a rough road for you to travel, my little pilgrims, especially the latter part of it. But you have got on bravely, and I think the burdens are in a fair way to tumble off very soon," said Mr. March, looking with fatherly satisfaction at the four young faces gathered round him.

"How do you know? Did Mother tell you?" asked Jo.

"Not much. Straws show which way the wind blows, and I've made several discoveries today".

"Oh, tell us what they are!" cried Meg, who sat beside him.

"Here is one." And taking up the hand which lay on the arm of his chair, he pointed to the roughened forefinger, a burn on the back, and two or three little hard spots on the palm. "I remember a time when this hand was white and smooth, and your first care was to keep it so. It was very pretty then, but to me it is much prettier now—for in these seeming blemishes I read a little history. A burnt offering has been made of vanity, this hardened palm has earned something better than blisters; and I'm sure the sewing done by these pricked fingers will last a long time, so much goodwill went into the stitches. Meg, my dear, I value the womanly skill which keeps home happy more than white hands or fashionable accomplishments. I'm proud to shake this good, industrious little hand, and hope I shall not soon be asked to give it away."

If Meg had wanted a reward for hours of patient labor, she received it in the hearty pressure of her father's hand and the approving smile he gave her.

"What about Jo? Please say something nice, for she has tried so hard and been so very, very good to me," said Beth in her father's ear.

He laughed and looked across at the tall girl who sat opposite, with an unusually mild expression in her brown face.

"In spite of the curly crop, I don't see the 'son Jo' whom I left a year ago," said Mr. March. "I see a young lady who pins her collar straight, laces her boots neatly, and neither whistles, talks slang, nor lies on the rug as she used to do. Her face is rather thin and pale just now, with watching and anxiety, but I like to look at it, for it has grown gentler, and her voice is lower; she doesn't bounce, but moves quietly, and takes care of a certain little person in a motherly way which delights me. I rather miss my wild girl, but if I get a strong, helpful, tenderhearted woman in her place, I shall feel quite satisfied. I don't know whether the shearing sobered our black sheep, but I do know that in all Washington I couldn't find anything beautiful enough to be bought with the five-and-twenty dollars which my good girl sent me."

Jo's keen eyes were rather dim for a minute, and her thin face grew rosy in the firelight as she received her father's praise, feeling that she did deserve a portion of it.

"Now Beth," said Amy, longing for her turn, but ready to wait.

"There's so little of her, I'm afraid to say much, for fear she will slip away altogether, though she is not so shy as she used to be," began their father cheerfully; but recollecting how nearly he *had* lost her, he held her close, saying tenderly, with her cheek against his own, "I've got you safe, my Beth, and I'll keep you so, please God."

After a minute's silence, he looked down at Amy, who sat on the cricket at his feet, and said, with a caress of the shining hair—

"I observed that Amy took drumsticks at dinner, ran errands for her mother all the afternoon, gave Meg her place tonight, and has waited on every one with patience and good humor. I also observe that she does not fret much nor look in the glass, and has not even mentioned a very pretty ring which she wears; so I conclude that she has learned to think of other people more and of herself less, and has decided to try and mold her character as carefully as she molds her little clay figures. I am glad of this, for though I should be very proud of a graceful statue made by her, I shall be infinitely prouder of a lovable daughter with a talent for making life beautiful to herself and others."

"What are you thinking of, Beth?" asked Jo, when Amy had thanked her father and told about her ring.

"I read in *Pilgrim's Progress* today how, after many troubles, Christian and Hopeful came to a pleasant green meadow where lilies bloomed all the year round, and there they rested happily, as we do now, before they went on to their journey's end," answered Beth, adding, as she slipped out of her father's arms and went slowly to the instrument, "It's singing time now, and I want to be in my old place. I'll try to sing the song of the shepherd boy which the Pilgrims heard. I made the music for father, because he likes the verses."

So, sitting at the dear little piano, Beth softly touched the keys, and in the sweet voice they had never thought to hear

again, sang to her own accompaniment the quaint hymn,
which was a singularly fitting song for her:

> He that is down need fear no fall,
>   He that is low no pride;
> He that is humble ever shall
>   Have God to be his guide.
>
> I am content with what I have,
>   Little be it or much;
> And, Lord! contentment still I crave,
>   Because Thou savest such.
>
> Fulness to them a burden is,
>   That go on pilgrimage;
> Here little, and hereafter bliss,
>   Is best from age to age!

Chapter 23

Aunt March Settles the Question

LIKE BEES SWARMING after their queen, mother and daughters hovered about Mr. March the next day, neglecting everything to look at, wait upon, and listen to the new invalid, who was in a fair way to be killed by kindness. As he sat propped up in a big chair by Beth's sofa, with the other three close by, and Hannah popping in her head now and then "to peek at the dear man," nothing seemed needed to complete their happiness. But something *was* needed, and the elder ones felt it, though none confessed the fact. Mr. and Mrs. March looked at one another with an anxious expression, as their eyes followed Meg. Jo had sudden fits of sobriety, and was seen to shake her fist at Mr. Brooke's umbrella, which had been left in the hall; Meg was absent-minded, shy, and silent, started when the bell rang, and colored when John's name was mentioned; Amy said, "Everyone seemed waiting for something, and couldn't settle down, which was queer, since Father was safe at home," and Beth innocently wondered why their neighbors didn't run over as usual.

Laurie went by in the afternoon, and seeing Meg at the window, seemed suddenly possessed with a melodramatic fit, for he fell down upon one knee in the snow, beat his breast, tore his hair, and clasped his hands imploringly, as if begging some boon; and when Meg told him to behave himself and go away, he wrung imaginary tears out of his handkerchief, and staggered round the corner as if in utter despair.

"What does the goose mean?" said Meg, laughing and trying to look unconscious.

"He's showing you how your John will go on by-and-by. Touching, isn't it?" answered Jo scornfully.

"Don't say *my John*, it isn't proper or true," but Meg's voice lingered over the words as if they sounded pleasant to her. "Please don't plague me, Jo, I've told you I don't care *much* about him, and there isn't to be anything said, but we are all to be friendly, and go on as before."

"We can't, for something *has* been said, and Laurie's mischief has spoiled you for me. I see it, and so does Mother; you are not like your old self a bit, and seem ever so far away from me. I don't mean to plague you and will bear it like a man, but I do wish it was all settled. I hate to wait, so if you mean ever to do it, make haste and have it over quickly," said Jo pettishly.

"*I* can't say or do anything till he speaks, and he won't, because Father said I was too young," began Meg, bending over her work with a queer little smile, which suggested that she did not quite agree with her father on that point.

"If he did speak, you wouldn't know what to say, but would cry or blush, or let him have his own way, instead of giving a good, decided, No."

"I'm not so silly and weak as you think. I know just what I should say, for I've planned it all, so I needn't be taken unawares; there's no knowing what may happen, and I wished to be prepared."

Jo couldn't help smiling at the important air which Meg had unconsciously assumed and which was as becoming as the pretty color varying in her cheeks.

"Would you mind telling me what you'd say?" asked Jo more respectfully.

"Not at all. You are sixteen now, quite old enough to be my confidante, and my experience will be useful to you by-and-by, perhaps, in your own affairs of this sort."

"Don't mean to have any; it's fun to watch other people philander, but I should feel like a fool doing it myself," said Jo, looking alarmed at the thought.

"I think not, if you liked anyone very much, and he liked you." Meg spoke as if to herself, and glanced out at the lane where she had often seen lovers walking together in the summer twilight.

"I thought you were going to tell your speech to that man," said Jo, rudely shortening her sister's little reverie.

"Oh, I should merely say, quite calmly and decidedly, 'Thank you, Mr. Brooke, you are very kind, but I agree with Father that I am too young to enter into any engagement at present; so please say no more, but let us be friends as we were.'"

"Hum, that's stiff and cool enough! I don't believe you'll ever say it, and I know he won't be satisfied if you do. If he goes on like the rejected lovers in books, you'll give in, rather than hurt his feelings."

"No, I won't. I shall tell him I've made up my mind, and shall walk out of the room with dignity."

Meg rose as she spoke, and was just going to rehearse the dignified exit, when a step in the hall made her fly into her seat and begin to sew as fast as if her life depended on finishing that particular seam in a given time. Jo smothered a laugh at the sudden change, and when someone gave a modest tap, opened the door with a grim aspect which was anything but hospitable.

"Good afternoon. I came to get my umbrella—that is, to see how your father finds himself today," said Mr. Brooke, getting a trifle confused as his eye went from one telltale face to the other.

"It's very well, he's in the rack, I'll get him, and tell it you are here." And having jumbled her father and the umbrella well together in her reply, Jo slipped out of the room to give Meg a chance to make her speech and air her dignity. But the instant she vanished, Meg began to sidle toward the door, murmuring—

"Mother will like to see you. Pray sit down, I'll call her."

"Don't go. Are you afraid of me, Margaret?" And Mr. Brooke looked so hurt that Meg thought she must have done something very rude. She blushed up to the little curls on her forehead, for he had never called her Margaret before, and she was surprised to find how natural and sweet it seemed to hear him say it. Anxious to appear friendly and at her ease, she put out her hand with a confiding gesture, and said gratefully—

"How can I be afraid when you have been so kind to Father? I only wish I could thank you for it."

"Shall I tell you how?" asked Mr. Brooke, holding the small hand fast in both his own, and looking down at Meg with so much love in the brown eyes that her heart began to flutter, and she both longed to run away and to stop and listen.

"Oh no, please don't—I'd rather not," she said, trying to withdraw her hand, and looking frightened in spite of her denial.

"I won't trouble you, I only want to know if you care for me a little, Meg. I love you so much, dear," added Mr. Brooke tenderly.

This was the moment for the calm, proper speech, but Meg didn't make it; she forgot every word of it, hung her head, and answered, "I don't know," so softly that John had to stoop down to catch the foolish little reply.

He seemed to think it was worth the trouble, for he smiled to himself as if quite satisfied, pressed the plump hand gratefully, and said in his most persuasive tone, "Will you try and find out? I want to know *so* much, for I can't go to work with any heart until I learn whether I am to have my reward in the end or not."

"I'm too young," faltered Meg, wondering why she was so fluttered, yet rather enjoying it.

"I'll wait, and in the meantime, you could be learning to like me. Would it be a very hard lesson, dear?"

"Not if I chose to learn it, but—"

"Please choose to learn, Meg. I love to teach, and this is easier than German," broke in John, getting possession of the other hand, so that she had no way of hiding her face as he bent to look into it.

His tone was properly beseeching, but stealing a shy look at him, Meg saw that his eyes were merry as well as tender, and that he wore the satisfied smile of one who had no doubt of his success. This nettled her. Annie Moffat's foolish lessons in coquetry came into her mind, and the love of power, which sleeps in the bosoms of the best of little women, woke up all of a sudden and took possession of her. She felt excited and strange, and not knowing what else to do, followed a capricious impulse, and, withdrawing her hands, said petulantly, "I *don't* choose. Please go away and let me be!"

Poor Mr. Brooke looked as if his lovely castle in the air was tumbling about his ears, for he had never seen Meg in such a mood before, and it rather bewildered him.

"Do you really mean that?" he asked anxiously, following her as she walked away.

"Yes, I do. I don't want to be worried about such things. Father says I needn't, it's too soon and I'd rather not."

"Mayn't I hope you'll change your mind by-and-by? I'll wait and say nothing till you have had more time. Don't play with me, Meg. I didn't think that of you."

"Don't think of me at all. I'd rather you wouldn't," said Meg, taking a naughty satisfaction in trying her lover's patience and her own power.

He was grave and pale now, and looked decidedly more like the novel heroes whom she admired, but he neither slapped his forehead nor tramped about the room as they did; he just stood looking at her so wistfully, so tenderly, that she found her heart relenting in spite of her. What would have happened next I cannot say, if Aunt March had not come hobbling in at this interesting minute.

The old lady couldn't resist her longing to see her nephew, for she had met Laurie as she took her airing, and hearing of Mr. March's arrival, drove straight out to see him. The family were all busy in the back part of the house, and she had made her way quietly in, hoping to surprise them. She did surprise two of them so much that Meg started as if she had seen a ghost, and Mr. Brooke vanished into the study.

"Bless me, what's all this?" cried the old lady with a rap of her cane as she glanced from the pale young gentleman to the scarlet young lady.

"It's Father's friend. I'm *so* surprised to see you!" stammered Meg, feeling that she was in for a lecture now.

"That's evident," returned Aunt March, sitting down. "But what is Father's friend saying to make you look like a peony?

There's mischief going on, and I insist upon knowing what it is," with another rap.

"We were merly talking. Mr. Brooke came for his umbrella," began Meg, wishing that Mr. Brooke and the umbrella were safely out of the house.

"Brooke? That boy's tutor? Ah! I understand now. I know all about it. Jo blundered into a wrong message in one of your Father's letters, and I made her tell me. You haven't gone and accepted him, child?" cried Aunt March, looking scandalized.

"Hush! He'll hear. Shan't I call Mother?" said Meg, much troubled.

"Not yet. I've something to say to you, and I must free my mind at once. Tell me, do you mean to marry this Cook? If you do, not one penny of my money ever goes to you. Remember that, and be a sensible girl," said the old lady impressively.

Now Aunt March possessed in perfection the art of rousing the spirit of opposition in the gentlest people, and enjoyed doing it. The best of us have a spice of perversity in us, especially when we are young and in love. If Aunt March had begged Meg to accept John Brooke, she would probably have declared she couldn't think of it; but as she was peremptorily ordered *not* to like him, she immediately made up her mind that she would. Inclination as well as perversity made the decision easy, and being already much excited, Meg opposed the old lady with unusual spirit.

"I shall marry whom I please, Aunt March, and you can leave your money to anyone you like," she said, nodding her head with a resolute air.

"Highty-tighty! Is that the way you take my advice, miss? You'll be sorry for it by-and-by, when you've tried love in a cottage and found it a failure."

"It can't be a worse one than some people find in big houses," retorted Meg.

Aunt March put on her glasses and took a look at the girl, for she did not know her in this new mood. Meg hardly knew herself, she felt so brave and independent—so glad to defend

John and assert her right to love him, if she liked. Aunt March saw that she had begun wrong, and after a little pause, made a fresh start, saying as mildly as she could, "Now, Meg, my dear, be reasonable and take my advice. I mean it kindly, and don't want you to spoil your whole life by making a mistake at the beginning. You ought to marry well and help your family; it's your duty to make a rich match and it ought to be impressed upon you."

"Father and Mother don't think so, they like John though he *is* poor."

"Your parents, my dear, have no more worldly wisdom than two babies."

"I'm glad of it," cried Meg stoutly.

Aunt March took no notice, but went on with her lecture. "This Rook is poor and hasn't got any rich relations, has he?"

"No, but he has many warm friends."

"You can't live on friends, try it and see how cool they'll grow. He hasn't any business, has he?"

"Not yet. Mr. Laurence is going to help him."

"That won't last long. James Laurence is a crotchety old fellow and not to be depended on. So you intend to marry a man without money, position, or business, and go on working harder than you do now, when you might be comfortable all your days by minding me and doing better? I thought you had more sense, Meg."

"I couldn't do better if I waited half my life! John is good and wise, he's got heaps of talent, he's willing to work and sure to get on, he's so energetic and brave. Everyone likes and respects him, and I'm proud to think he cares for me, though I'm so poor and young and silly," said Meg, looking prettier than ever in her earnestness.

"He knows *you* have got rich relations, child; that's the secret of his liking, I suspect."

"Aunt March, how dare you say such a thing? John is above such meanness, and I won't listen to you a minute if you talk so," cried Meg indignantly, forgetting everything but the injustice of the old lady's suspicions. "My John wouldn't marry for money, any more than I would. We are willing to work, and we mean to wait. I'm not afraid of being poor, for I've been happy so far, and I know I shall be with him because he loves me, and I——"

Meg stopped there, remembering all of a sudden that she hadn't made up her mind, that she had told "her John" to go away, and that he might be overhearing her inconsistent remarks.

Aunt March was very angry, for she had set her heart on having her pretty niece make a fine match, and something in the girl's happy young face made the lonely old woman feel both sad and sour.

"Well, I wash my hands of the whole affair! You are a willful child, and you've lost more than you know by this piece of folly. No, I won't stop. I'm disappointed in you, and haven't spirits to see your father now. Don't expect anything from me when you are married; your Mr. Book's friends must take care of you. I'm done with you forever."

And slamming the door in Meg's face, Aunt March drove off in high dudgeon. She seemed to take all the girl's courage with her, for when left alone, Meg stood a moment, undecided whether to laugh or cry. Before she could make up her mind, she was taken possession of by Mr. Brooke, who said all in one breath, "I couldn't help hearing, Meg. Thank you for defending me, and Aunt March for proving that you *do* care for me a little bit."

"I didn't know how much till she abused you," began Meg.

"And I needn't go away, but may stay and be happy, may I, dear?"

Here was another fine chance to make the crushing speech and the stately exit, but Meg never thought of doing either, and disgraced herself forever in Jo's eyes by meekly whispering, "Yes, John," and hiding her face on Mr. Brooke's waistcoat.

Fifteen minutes after Aunt March's departure, Jo came softly downstairs, paused an instant at the parlor door, and hearing no sound within, nodded and smiled with a satisfied expression, saying to herself, "She has seen him away as we planned, and that affair is settled. I'll go and hear the fun, and have a good laugh over it."

But poor Jo never got her laugh, for she was transfixed upon the threshold by a spectacle which held her there, staring with her mouth nearly as wide open as her eyes. Going in to exult over a fallen enemy and to praise a strong-minded sister for the banishment of an objectionable lover, it certainly *was* a shock to behold the aforesaid enemy serenely sitting on the sofa, with the strong-minded sister enthroned upon his knee and wearing an expression of the most abject submission. Jo gave a sort of gasp, as if a cold shower bath had suddenly fallen upon her—for such an unexpected turning of the tables actually took her breath away. At the odd sound the lovers turned and saw her. Meg jumped up, looking both proud and shy, but "that man," as Jo called him, actually laughed and said coolly, as he kissed the astonished newcomer, "Sister Jo, congratulate us!"

That was adding insult to injury—it was altogether too much—and making some wild demonstration with her hands, Jo vanished without a word. Rushing upstairs, she startled the invalids by exclaiming tragically as she burst into the room, "Oh, *do* somebody go down quick; John Brooke is acting dreadfully, and Meg likes it!"

Mr. and Mrs. March left the room with speed; and casting herself upon the bed, Jo cried and scolded tempestuously as she told the awful news to Beth and Amy. The little girls, however, considered it a most agreeable and interesting event, and Jo got little comfort from them; so she went up to her refuge in the garret, and confided her troubles to the rats.

Nobody ever knew what went on in the parlor that afternoon; but a great deal of talking was done, and quiet Mr. Brooke astonished his friends by the eloquence and spirit with which he pleaded his suit, told his plans, and persuaded them to arrange everything just as he wanted it.

The tea bell rang before he had finished describing the paradise which he meant to earn for Meg, and he proudly took her in to supper, both looking so happy that Jo hadn't the heart to be jealous or dismal. Amy was very much impressed by John's devotion and Meg's dignity, Beth beamed at them from a distance, while Mr. and Mrs. March surveyed the young couple with such tender satisfaction that it was perfectly evident Aunt March was right in calling them as "unworldly as a pair of babies." No one ate much, but everyone looked very happy, and the old room seemed to brighten up amazingly when the first romance of the family began there.

"You can't say nothing pleasant ever happens now, can you, Meg?" said Amy, trying to decide how she would group the lovers in the sketch she was planning to make.

"No, I'm sure I can't. How much has happened since I said that! It seems a year ago," answered Meg, who was in a blissful dream lifted far above such common things as bread and butter.

"The joys come close upon the sorrows this time, and I rather think the changes have begun," said Mrs. March. "In most families there comes, now and then, a year full of events; this has been such a one, but it ends well, after all."

"Hope the next will end better," muttered Jo, who found it very hard to see Meg absorbed in a stranger before her face, for Jo loved a few persons very dearly and dreaded to have their affection lost or lessened in any way.

"I hope the third year from this *will* end better. I mean it shall, if I live to work out my plans,' said Mr. Brooke, smiling at Meg, as if everything had become possible to him now.

"Doesn't it seem very long to wait?" asked Amy, who was in a hurry for the wedding.

"I've got so much to learn before I shall be ready, it seems a short time to me," answered Meg, with a sweet gravity in her face never seen there before.

"You have only to wait, *I* am to do the work," said John, beginning his labors by picking up Meg's napkin, with an expression which caused Jo to shake her head, and then say to herself with an air of relief as the front door banged,

"Here comes Laurie. Now we shall have a little sensible conversation."

But Jo was mistaken, for Laurie came prancing in, over-flowing with spirits, bearing a great bridal-looking bouquet for "Mrs. John Brooke," and evidently laboring under the delusion that the whole affair had been brought about by his excellent management.

"I knew Brooke would have it all his own way, he always does; for when he makes up his mind to accomplish anything, it's done though the sky falls," said Laurie, when he had presented his offering and his congratulations.

"Much obliged for that recommendation. I take it as a good omen for the future and invite you to my wedding on the spot," answered Mr. Brooke, who felt at peace with all mankind, even his mischievous pupil.

"I'll come if I'm at the ends of the earth, for the sight of Jo's face alone on that occasion would be worth a long journey. You don't look festive, ma'am, what's the matter?" asked Laurie, following her into a corner of the parlor, whither all had adjourned to greet Mr. Laurence.

"I don't approve of the match, but I've made up my mind to bear it, and shall not say a word against it," said Jo solemnly. "You can't know how hard it is for me to give up Meg," she continued with a little quiver in her voice.

"You don't give her up. You only go halves," said Laurie consolingly.

"It never can be the same again. I've lost my dearest friend," sighed Jo.

"You've got me, anyhow. I'm not good for much, I know, but I'll stand by you, Jo, all the days of my life. Upon my word I will!" And Laurie meant what he said.

"I know you will, and I'm ever so much obliged. You are always a great comfort to me, Teddy," returned Jo, gratefully shaking hands.

"Well, now, don't be dismal, there's a good fellow. It's all right, you see. Meg is happy, Brooke will fly round and get settled immediately, Grandpa will attend to him, and it will be very jolly to see Meg in her own little house. We'll have capital times after she is gone, for I shall be through college before long, and then we'll go abroad on some nice trip or other. Wouldn't that console you?"

"I rather think it would, but there's no knowing what may happen in three years," said Jo thoughtfully.

"That's true. Don't you wish you could take a look forward and see where we shall all be then? I do," returned Laurie.

"I think not, for I might see something sad, and everyone looks so happy now, I don't believe they could be much improved." And Jo's eyes went slowly round the room, brightening as they looked, for the prospect was a pleasant one.

Father and Mother sat together, quietly reliving the first chapter of the romance which for them began some twenty years ago. Amy was drawing the lovers, who sat apart in a beautiful world of their own, the light of which touched their faces with a grace the little artist could not copy. Beth lay on her sofa, talking cheerily with her old friend, who held her little hand as if he felt that it possessed the power to lead him along the peaceful way she walked. Jo lounged in her favorite low seat, with the grave, quiet look which best became her, and Laurie, leaning on the back of her chair, his chin on a level with her curly head, smiled with his friendliest aspect, and nodded at her in the long glass which reflected them both.

So grouped, the curtain falls upon Meg, Jo, Beth, and Amy. Whether it ever rises again, depends upon the reception given to the first act of the domestic drama called *Little Women*.

PART II

Chapter 24

Gossip

IN ORDER THAT we may start afresh and go to Meg's wedding with free minds, it will be well to begin with a little gossip about the Marches. And here let me premise that if any of the elders think there is too much "lovering" in the story, as I fear they may (I'm not afraid the young folks will make that objection), I can only say with Mrs. March, "What *can* you expect when I have four gay girls in the house, and a dashing young neighbor over the way?"

The three years that have passed have brought but few changes to the quiet family. The war is over, and Mr. March safely at home, busy with his books and the small parish which found in him a minister by nature as by grace—a quiet, studious man, rich in the wisdom that is better than learning, the charity which calls all mankind "brother," the piety that blossoms into character, making it august and lovely.

These attributes, in spite of poverty and the strict integrity which shut him out from the more worldly successes, attracted to him many admirable persons, as naturally as sweet herbs draw bees, and as naturally he gave them the honey into which fifty years of hard experience had distilled no bitter drop. Earnest young men found the gray-headed scholar as young at heart as they, thoughtful or troubled women instinctively brought their doubts to him, sure of finding the gentlest sympathy, the wisest counsel; sinners told their sins to the pure-hearted old man and were both rebuked and saved; gifted men found a companion in him; ambitious men caught glimpses of nobler ambitions than their own; and even worldlings confessed that his beliefs were beautiful and true, although "they wouldn't pay."

To outsiders the five energetic women seemed to rule the house, and so they did in many things; but the quiet scholar, sitting among his books, was still the head of the family, the household conscience, anchor, and comforter, for to him the busy, anxious women always turned in troublous times, finding him, in the truest sense of those sacred words, husband and father.

The girls gave their hearts into their mother's keeping, their souls into their father's; and to both parents, who lived and labored so faithfully for them, they gave a love that grew with their growth and bound them tenderly together by the sweetest tie which blesses life and outlives death.

Mrs. March is as brisk and cheery, though rather grayer, than when we saw her last, and just now so absorbed in Meg's affairs that the hospitals and homes still full of wounded "boys" and soldiers' widows, decidedly miss the motherly missionary's visits.

John Brooke did his duty manfully for a year, got wounded, was sent home, and not allowed to return. He received no stars or bars, but he deserved them, for he cheerfully risked all he had, and life and love are very precious when both are in full bloom. Perfectly resigned to his discharge, he devoted himself to getting well, preparing for business, and earning a home for Meg. With the good sense and sturdy independence that characterized him, he refused Mr. Laurence's more generous offers, and accepted the place of bookkeeper, feeling better satisfied to begin with an honestly earned salary than by running any risks with borrowed money.

Meg had spent the time in working as well as waiting, growing womanly in character, wise in housewifely arts, and prettier than ever, for love is a great beautifier. She had her girlish ambitions and hopes, and felt some disappointment at the humble way in which the new life must begin. Ned Moffat had just married Sallie Gardiner, and Meg couldn't help contrasting their fine house and carriage, many gifts, and splendid outfit with her own, and secretly wishing she could have the same. But somehow envy and discontent soon vanished when she thought of all the patient love and labor John had put into the little home awaiting her, and when they sat together in the twilight, talking over their small plans, the future always grew so beautiful and bright that she forgot Sallie's splendor, and felt herself the richest, happiest girl in Christendom.

Jo never went back to Aunt March, for the old lady took such a fancy to Amy that she bribed her with the offer of drawing lessons from one of the best teachers going; and for the sake of this advantage, Amy would have served a far harder mistress. So she gave her mornings to duty, her afternoons to pleasure, and prospered finely. Jo meantime devoted herself to literature and Beth, who remained delicate long after the fever was a thing of the past. Not an invalid exactly, but never again the rosy, healthy creature she had been, yet always hopeful, happy, and serene, busy with the quiet duties she loved, everyone's friend, and an angel in the house, long before those who loved her most had learned to know it.

As long as *The Spread Eagle* paid her a dollar a column for her "rubbish," as she called it, Jo felt herself a woman of means, and spun her little romances diligently. But great plans fermented in her busy brain and ambitious mind, and the old tin kitchen in the garret held a slowly increasing pile of blotted manuscript, which was one day to place the name of March upon the roll of fame.

Laurie, having dutifully gone to college to please his grandfather, was now getting through it in the easiest possible manner to please himself. A universal favorite, thanks to money, manners, much talent, and the kindest heart that ever got its owner into scrapes by trying to get other people out of them, he stood in great danger of being spoiled, and probably would have been, like many another promising boy, if he had not possessed a talisman against evil in the memory of the kind old man who was bound up in his success, the motherly friend who watched over him as if he were her son, and last, but not least by any means, the knowledge that four innocent girls loved, admired, and believed in him with all their hearts.

Being only "a glorious human boy," of course he frolicked and flirted, grew dandified, aquatic, sentimental, or gymnastic, as college fashions ordained, hazed and was hazed, talked slang, and more than once came perilously near suspension and expulsion. But as high spirits and the love of fun were the causes of these pranks, he always managed to save himself by frank confession, honorable atonement, or the irresistible power of persuasion which he possessed in perfection. In fact, he rather prided himself on his narrow escapes, and liked to thrill the girls with graphic accounts of his triumphs over wrathful tutors, dignified professors, and vanquished enemies. The "men of my class" were heroes in the eyes of the girls, who never wearied of the exploits of "our fellows," and were frequently allowed to bask in the smiles of these great creatures, when Laurie brought them home with him.

Amy especially enjoyed this high honor, and became quite a belle among them, for her ladyship early felt and learned to use the gift of fascination with which she was endowed. Meg was too much absorbed in her private and particular John to care for any other lords of creation, and Beth too shy to do more than peep at them and wonder how Amy dared to order them about so, but Jo felt quite in her element, and found it very difficult to refrain from imitating the gentlemanly attitudes, phrases, and feats, which seemed more natural to her than the decorums prescribed for young ladies. They all liked Jo immensely, but never fell in love with her, though very few escaped without paying the tribute of a sentimental sigh or two at Amy's shrine. And speaking of sentiment brings us very naturally to the "Dovecote."

That was the name of the little brown house which Mr. Brooke had prepared for Meg's first home. Laurie had christened it, saying it was highly appropriate to the gentle lovers who "went on together like a pair of turtledoves, with first a bill and then a coo." It was a tiny house, with a little garden behind and a lawn about as big as a pocket handkerchief in front. Here Meg meant to have a fountain, shrubbery, and a profusion of lovely flowers; though just at present the fountain was represented by a weather-beaten urn, very like a dilapidated slopbowl, the shrubbery consisted of several young larches, undecided whether to live or die, and the profusion of flowers was merely hinted by regiments of sticks to show where seeds were planted. But inside, it was altogether charming, and the happy bride saw no fault from garret to cellar. To be sure, the hall was so narrow it was fortunate that they had no piano, for one never could have been got in whole, the dining room was so small that six people were a tight fit, and the kitchen stairs seemed built for the express purpose of precipitating both servants and china pell-mell into the coalbin. But once get used to these slight blemishes and nothing could be more complete, for good sense and good taste had presided over the furnishing, and the result was highly satisfactory. There were no marble-topped tables, long mirrors, or lace curtains in the little parlor, but simple furniture, plenty of books, a fine picture or two, a stand of flowers in the bay window, and, scattered all about, the pretty gifts which came from friendly hands and were the fairer for the loving messages they brought.

I don't think the Parian Psyche Laurie gave lost any of its beauty because John put up the bracket it stood upon, that any upholsterer could have draped the plain muslin curtains more gracefully than Amy's artistic hand, or that any storeroom was ever better provided with good wishes, merry words, and happy hopes than that in which Jo and her mother put away Meg's few boxes, barrels, and bundles; and I am morally certain that the spandy new kitchen never *could* have looked so cozy and neat if Hannah had not arranged every pot and pan a dozen times over, and laid the fire all ready for lighting, the minute "Mis. Brooke came home." I also doubt if any young matron ever began life with so rich a supply of dusters, holders, and piece bags, for Beth made enough to last till the silver wedding came round, and invented three different kinds of dishcloths for the express service of the bridal china.

People who hire all these things done for them never know what they lose, for the homeliest tasks get beautified if loving hands do them, and Meg found so many proofs of this that everything in her small nest, from the kitchen roller to the silver vase on her parlor table, was eloquent of home love and tender forethought.

What happy times they had planning together, what solemn shopping excursions, what funny mistakes they made, and what shouts of laughter arose over Laurie's ridiculous bargains.

In his love of jokes, this young gentleman, though nearly through college, was as much of a boy as ever. His last whim had been to bring with him on his weekly visits some new, useful, and ingenious article for the young housekeeper. Now a bag of remarkable clothespins, next, a wonderful nutmeg grater which fell to pieces at the first trial, a knife cleaner that spoiled all the knives, or a sweeper that picked the nap neatly off the carpet and left the dirt, labor-saving soap that took the skin off one's hands, infallible cements which stuck firmly to nothing but the fingers of the deluded buyer, and every kind of tinware, from a toy savings bank for odd pennies, to a wonderful boiler which would wash articles in its own steam with every prospect of exploding in the process.

In vain Meg begged him to stop. John laughed at him, and Jo called him "Mr. Toodles." He was possessed with a mania for patronizing Yankee ingenuity, and seeing his friends fitly furnished forth. So each week beheld some fresh absurdity.

Everything was done at last, even to Amy's arranging different colored soaps to match the different colored rooms, and Beth's setting the table for the first meal.

"Are you satisfied? Does it seem like home, and do you feel as if you should be happy here?" asked Mrs. March, as she and her daughter went through the new kingdom arm in arm, for just then they seemed to cling together more tenderly than ever.

"Yes, Mother, perfectly satisfied, thanks to you all, and *so* happy that I can't talk about it," answered Meg, with a look that was better than words.

"If she only had a servant or two it would be all right," said Amy, coming out of the parlor, where she had been trying to decide whether the bronze Mercury looked best on the whatnot or the mantlepiece.

"Mother and I have talked that over, and I have made up my mind to try her way first. There will be so little to do that with Lotty to run my errands and help me here and there, I shall only have enough work to keep me from getting lazy or homesick," answered Meg tranquilly.

"Sallie Moffat has four," began Amy.

"If Meg had four the house wouldn't hold them, and master and missis would have to camp in the garden," broke in Jo, who, enveloped in a big blue pinafore, was giving the last polish to the door handles.

"Sallie isn't a poor man's wife, and many maids are in keeping with her fine establishment. Meg and John begin humbly, but I have a feeling that there will be quite as much happiness in the little house as in the big one. It's a great mistake for young girls like Meg to leave themselves nothing to do but dress, give orders, and gossip. When I was first married, I used to long for my new clothes to wear out or get torn, so that I might have the pleasure of mending them, for I got heartily sick of doing fancywork and tending my pocket handkerchief."

"Why didn't you go into the kitchen and make messes, as Sallie says she does to amuse herself, though they never turn out well and the servants laugh at her," said Meg.

"I did after a while, not to 'mess,' but to learn of Hannah how things should be done, that my servants need *not* laugh at me. It was play then, but there came a time when I was truly grateful that I not only possessed the will but the power to cook wholesome food for my little girls, and help myself when I could no longer afford to hire help. You begin at the other end, Meg, dear, but the lessons you learn now will be of use to you by-and-by when John is a richer man, for the mistress of a house, however, splendid, should know how work ought to be done, if she wishes to be well and honestly served."

"Yes, Mother, I'm sure of that," said Meg, listening respectfully to the little lecture, for the best of women will hold forth upon the all-absorbing subject of house keeping. "Do you know I like this room most of all in my baby house," added Meg, a minute after, as they went upstairs and she looked into her well-stored linen closet.

Beth was there, laying the snowy piles smoothly on the shelves and exulting over the goodly array. All three laughed as Meg spoke, for that linen closet was a joke. You see, having said that if Meg married "that Brooke" she shouldn't have a cent of her money, Aunt March was rather in a quandary when time had appeased her wrath and made her repent her vow. She never broke her word, and was much exercised in her mind how to get round it, and at last devised a plan whereby she could satisfy herself. Mrs. Carrol, Florence's mamma, was ordered to buy, have made, and marked a generous supply of house and table linen, and send it as *her* present, all of which was faithfully done; but the secret leaked out, and was greatly enjoyed by the family, for Aunt March tried to look utterly unconscious, and insisted that she could give nothing but the old-fashioned pearls long promised to the first bride.

"That's a housewifely taste which I am glad to see. I had a young friend who set up housekeeping with six sheets, but she had finger bowls for company and that satisfied her," said Mrs. March, patting the damask tablecloths, with a truly feminine appreciation of their fineness.

"I haven't a single fingerbowl, but this is a setout that will last me all my days, Hannah says." And Meg looked quite contented, as well she might.

"Toodles is coming," cried Jo from below, and they all went down to meet Laurie, whose weekly visit was an important event in their quiet lives.

A tall, broad-shouldered young fellow, with a cropped head, a felt basin of a hat, and a flyaway coat, came tramping down the road at a great pace, walked over the low fence without stopping to open the gate, straight up to Mrs. March, with both hands out and a hearty—

"Here I am, Mother! Yes, it's all right."

The last words were in answer to the look the elder lady gave him, a kindly questioning look which the handsome eyes met so frankly that the little ceremony closed, as usual, with a motherly kiss.

"For Mrs. John Brooke, with the maker's congratulations and compliments. Bless you, Beth! What a refreshing spectacle you are, Jo. Amy, you are getting altogether too handsome for a single lady."

As Laurie spoke, he delivered a brown-paper parcel to Meg, pulled Beth's hair ribbon, stared at Jo's big pinafore, and fell into an attitude of mock rapture before Amy, then shook hands all round, and everyone began to talk.

"Where is John?" asked Meg anxiously.

"Stopped to get the license for tomorrow, ma'am."

"Which side won the last match, Teddy?" inquired Jo, who persisted in feeling an interest in manly sports despite her nineteen years.

"Ours, of course. Wish you'd been there to see."

"How is the lovely Miss Randal?" asked Amy with a significant smile.

"More cruel than ever; don't you see how I'm pining away?" And Laurie gave his broad chest a sounding slap and heaved a melodramatic sigh.

"What's the last joke? Undo the bundle and see, Meg," said Beth, eying the knobby parcel with curiosity.

"It's a useful thing to have in the house in case of fire or thieves," observed Laurie, as a watchman's rattle appeared, amid the laughter of the girls.

"Any time when John is away and you get frightened, Mrs. Meg, just swing that out of the front window, and it will rouse the neighborhood in a jiffy. Nice thing, isn't it?" And Laurie gave them a sample of its powers that made them cover up their ears.

"There's gratitude for you! And speaking of gratitude reminds me to mention that you may thank Hannah for saving your wedding cake from destruction. I saw it going into your house as I came by, and if she hadn't defended it manfully I'd have had a pick at it, for it looked like a remarkably plummy one."

"I wonder if you will ever grow up, Laurie," said Meg in a matronly tone.

"I'm doing my best, ma'am, but can't get much higher, I'm afraid, as six feet is about all men can do in these degenerate days," responded the young gentleman, whose head was about level with the little chandelier.

"I suppose it would be profanation to eat anything in this spick-and-span new bower, so as I'm tremendously hungry, I propose an adjournment," he added presently.

"Mother and I are going to wait for John. There are some last things to settle," said Meg, bustling away.

"Beth and I are going over to Kitty Bryant's to get more flowers for tomorrow," added Amy, tying a picturesque hat over her picturesque curls, and enjoying the effect as much as anybody.

"Come, Jo, don't desert a fellow. I'm in such a state of exhaustion I can't get home without help. Don't take off your apron, whatever you do; it's peculiarly becoming," said Laurie, as Jo bestowed his especial aversion in her capacious pocket and offered him her arm to support his feeble steps.

"Now, Teddy, I want to talk seriously to you about tomorrow," began Jo, as they strolled away together. "You *must* promise to behave well, and not cut up any pranks, and spoil our plans."

"Not a prank."

"And don't say funny things when we ought to be sober."

"I never do. You are the one for that."

"And I implore you not to look at me during the ceremony. I shall certainly laugh if you do."

"You won't see me, you'll be crying so hard that the thick fog round you will obscure the prospect."

"I never cry unless for some great affliction."

"Such as fellows going to college, hey?" cut in Laurie, with a suggestive laugh.

"Don't be a peacock. I only moaned a trifle to keep the girls company."

"Exactly. I say, Jo, how is Grandpa this week? Pretty amiable?"

"Very. Why, have you got into a scrape and want to know how he'll take it?" asked Jo rather sharply.

"Now, Jo, do you think I'd look your mother in the face, and say 'All right,' if it wasn't?" And Laurie stopped short, with an injured air.

"No, I don't."

"Then don't go and be suspicious. I only want some money," said Laurie, walking on again, appeased by her hearty tone.

"You spend a great deal, Teddy."

"Bless you, *I* don't spend it, it spends itself somehow, and is gone before I know it."

"You are so generous and kindhearted that you let people borrow, and can't say 'No' to anyone. We heard about Henshaw and all you did for him. If you always spent money in that way, no one would blame you," said Jo warmly.

"Oh, he made a mountain out of a molehill. You wouldn't have me let that fine fellow work himself to death just for the want of a little help, when he is worth a dozen of us lazy chaps, would you?"

"Of course not, but I don't see the use of your having seventeen waistcoats, endless neckties, and a new hat every time you come home. I thought you'd got over the dandy period, but every now and then it breaks out in a new spot. Just now it's the fashion to be hideous—to make your head look like a scrubbing brush, wear a strait jacket, orange gloves, and clumping square-toed boots. If it was cheap ugliness, I'd say nothing, but it costs as much as the other, and I don't get any satisfaction out of it."

Laurie threw back his head, and laughed so heartily at this attack, that the felt basin fell off, and Jo walked on it, which insult only afforded him an opportunity for expatiating on the advantages of a rough-and-ready costume, as he folded up the maltreated hat, and stuffed it into his pocket.

"Don't lecture any more, there's a good soul! I have enough all through the week, and like to enjoy myself when I come home. I'll get myself up regardless of expense tomorrow and be a satisfaction to my friends."

"I'll leave you in peace if you'll *only* let your hair grow. I'm not aristocratic, but I do object to being seen with a person who looks like a young prize fighter," observed Jo severely.

"This unassuming style promotes study, that's why we adopt it," returned Laurie, who certainly could not be accused of vanity, having voluntarily sacrificed a handsome curly crop to the demand for quarter-of-an-inch-long stubble.

"By the way, Jo, I think that little Parker is really getting desperate about Amy. He talks of her constantly, writes poetry, and moons about in a most suspicious manner. He'd better nip his little passion in the bud, hadn't he?" added Laurie, in a confidential, elder-brotherly tone, after a minute's silence.

"Of course he had. We don't want any more marrying in this family for years to come. Mercy on us, what *are* the children thinking of?" And Jo looked as much scandalized as if Amy and little Parker were not yet in their teens.

"It's a fast age, and I don't know what we are coming to, ma'am. You are a mere infant, but you'll go next, Jo, and we'll be left lamenting," said Laurie, shaking his head over the degeneracy of the times.

"Don't be alarmed. I'm not one of the agreeable sort. Nobody will want me, and it's a mercy, for there should always be one old maid in a family."

"You won't give anyone a chance," said Laurie, with a sidelong glance and a little more color than before in his sunburned face. "You won't show the soft side of your character, and if a fellow gets a peep at it by accident and can't help showing that he likes it, you treat him as Mrs. Gummidge did her sweetheart—throw cold water over him—and get so thorny no one dares touch or look at you."

"I don't like that sort of thing, I'm too busy to be worried with nonsense, and I think it's dreadful to break up families so. Now don't say any more about it. Meg's wedding has turned all our heads, and we talk of nothing but lovers and such absurdities. I don't wish to get cross, so let's change the subject." And Jo looked quite ready to fling cold water on the slightest provocation.

Whatever his feelings might have been, Laurie found a vent for them in a long low whistle and the fearful prediction as they parted at the gate, "Mark my words, Jo, you'll go next."

Chapter 25

The First Wedding

THE JUNE ROSES over the porch were awake bright and early on that morning, rejoicing with all their hearts in the cloudless sunshine, like friendly little neighbors, as they were. Quite flushed with excitement were their ruddy faces, as they swung in the wind, whispering to one another what they had seen, for some peeped in at the dining-room windows where the feast was spread, some climbed up to nod and smile at the sisters as they dressed the bride, others waved a welcome to those who came and went on various errands in garden, porch, and hall, and all, from the rosiest full-blown flower to the palest baby bud, offered their tribute of beauty and fragrance to the gentle mistress who had loved and tended them so long.

Meg looked very like a rose herself, for all that was best and sweetest in heart and soul seemed to bloom into her face that day, making it fair and tender, with a charm more beautiful than beauty. Neither silk, lace, nor orange flowers would she have. "I don't want to look strange or fixed up today," she said. "I don't want a fashionable wedding, but only those about me whom I love, and to them I wish to look and be my familiar self."

So she made her wedding gown herself, sewing into it the tender hopes and innocent romances of a girlish heart. Her sisters braided up her pretty hair, and the only ornaments she wore were the lilies of the valley, which "her John" liked best of all the flowers that grew.

"You *do* look just like our own dear Meg, only so very sweet and lovely that I should hug you if it wouldn't crumple your dress," cried Amy, surveying her with delight when all was done.

"Then I am satisfied. But please hug and kiss me, everyone,

and don't mind my dress, I want a great many crumples of this sort put into it today." And Meg opened her arms to her sisters, who clung about her with April faces for a minute, feeling that the new love had not changed the old.

"Now I'm going to tie John's cravat for him, and then to stay a few minutes with Father quietly in the study." And Meg ran down to perform these little ceremonies, and then to follow her mother wherever she went, conscious that in spite of the smiles on the motherly face, there was a secret sorrow hid in the motherly heart at the flight of the first bird from the nest.

As the younger girls stand together, giving the last touches to their simple toilet, it may be a good time to tell of a few changes which three years have wrought in their appearance, for all are looking their best just now.

Jo's angles are much softened, she has learned to carry herself with ease, if not grace. The curly crop has lengthened into a thick coil, more becoming to the small head atop of the tall figure. There is a fresh color in her brown cheeks, a soft shine in her eyes, and only gentle words fall from her sharp tongue today.

Beth has grown slender, pale, and more quiet than ever; the beautiful, kind eyes are larger, and in them lies an expression that saddens one, although it is not sad itself. It is the shadow of pain which touches the young face with such pathetic patience, but Beth seldom complains and always speaks hopefully of "being better soon."

Amy is with truth considered "the flower of the family," for at sixteen she has the air and bearing of a full-grown woman—not beautiful, but possessed of that indescribable charm called grace. One saw it in the lines of her figure, the make and motion of her hands, the flow of her dress, the droop of her hair—unconscious yet harmonious, and as attractive to many as beauty itself. Amy's nose still afflicted her, for it never *would* grow Grecian, so did her mouth, being too wide, and having a decided chin. These offending features gave character to her whole face, but she never could see it, and consoled herself with her wonderfully fair complexion, keen blue eyes, and curls more golden and abundant than ever.

All three wore suits of thin silver gray (their best gowns for the summer), with blush roses in hair and bosom; and all three looked just what they were—fresh-faced, happy-hearted girls, pausing a moment in their busy lives to read with wistful eyes the sweetest chapter in the romance of womanhood.

There were to be no ceremonious performances, everything was to be as natural and homelike as possible, so when Aunt March arrived, she was scandalized to see the bride come running to welcome and lead her in, to find the bridegroom fastening up a garland that had fallen down, and to catch a glimpse of the paternal minister marching upstairs with a grave countenance and a wine bottle under each arm.

"Upon my word, here's a state of things!" cried the old lady, taking the seat of honor prepared for her, and settling the folds of her lavender *moiré* with a great rustle. "You oughtn't to be seen till the last minute, child."

"I'm not a show, Aunty, and no one is coming to stare at me, to criticize my dress, or count the cost of my luncheon. I'm too happy to care what anyone says or thinks, and I'm going to have my little wedding just as I like it. John, dear, here's your hammer." And away went Meg to help "that man" in his highly improper employment.

Mr. Brooke didn't even say, "Thank you," but as he stooped for the unromantic tool, he kissed his little bride behind the folding door, with a look that made Aunt March whisk out her pocket handkerchief with a sudden dew in her sharp old eyes.

A crash, a cry, and a laugh from Laurie, accompanied by the indecorous exclamation, "Jupiter Ammon! Jo's upset the cake again!" caused a momentary flurry, which was hardly over when a flock of cousins arrived, and "the party came in," as Beth used to say when a child.

"Don't let that young giant come near me, he worries me worse than mosquitoes," whispered the old lady to Amy, as the rooms filled and Laurie's black head towered above the rest.

"He has promised to be very good today, and he *can* be perfectly elegant if he likes," returned Amy, gliding away to warn Hercules to beware of the dragon, which warning caused him to haunt the old lady with a devotion that nearly distracted her.

There was no bridal procession, but a sudden silence fell upon the room as Mr. March and the young pair took their places under the green arch. Mother and sisters gathered close, as if loath to give Meg up; the fatherly voice broke more than once, which only seemed to make the service more beautiful and solemn; the bridegroom's hand trembled visibly, and no one heard his replies; but Meg looked straight up in her husband's eyes, and said, "I will!" with such tender trust in her own face and voice that her mother's heart rejoiced and Aunt March sniffed audibly.

Jo did *not* cry, though she was very near it once, and was only saved from a demonstration by the consciousness that Laurie was staring fixedly at her, with a comical mixture of merriment and emotion in his wicked black eyes. Beth kept her face hidden on her mother's shoulder, but Amy stood like a graceful statue, with a most becoming ray of sunshine touching her white forehead and the flower in her hair.

It wasn't at all the thing, I'm afraid, but the minute she was fairly married, Meg cried, "The first kiss for Marmee!" and, turning, gave it with her heart on her lips. During the next fifteen minutes she looked more like a rose than ever, for everyone availed themselves of their privileges to the fullest extent, from Mr. Laurence to old Hannah, who, adorned with a headdress fearfully and wonderfully made, fell upon her in the hall, crying with a sob and a chuckle, "Bless you, deary, a hundred times! The cake ain't hurt a mite, and everything looks lovely."

Everybody cleared up after that, and said something brilliant, or tried to, which did just as well, for laughter is ready when hearts are light. There was no display of gifts, for they were already in the little house, nor was there an elaborate breakfast, but a plentiful lunch of cake and fruit, dressed with flowers. Mr. Laurence and Aunt March shrugged and

. . . Meg looked straight up in her husband's eyes, and said, "I will!"

smiled at one another when water, lemonade, and coffee were found to be the only sorts of nectar which the three Hebes carried round. No one said anything, however, till Laurie, who insisted on serving the bride, appeared before her, with a loaded salver in his hand and a puzzled expression on his face.

"Has Jo smashed all the bottles by accident?" he whispered, "or am I merely laboring under a delusion that I saw some lying about loose this morning?"

"No, your grandfather kindly offered us his best, and Aunt March actually sent some, but Father put away a little for Beth, and dispatched the rest to the Soldiers' Home. You know he thinks that wine should be used only in illness, and Mother says that neither she nor her daughters will ever offer it to any young man under her roof."

Meg spoke seriously and expected to see Laurie frown or laugh, but he did neither, for after a quick look at her, he said, in his impetuous way, "I like that! For I've seen enough harm done to wish other women would think as you do."

"You are not made wise by experience, I hope?" And there was an anxious accent in Meg's voice.

"No, I give you my word for it. Don't think too well of me, either, this is not one of my temptations. Being brought up where wine is as common as water and almost as harmless, I don't care for it, but when a pretty girl offers it, one doesn't like to refuse, you see."

"But you will, for the sake of others, if not for your own. Come, Laurie, promise, and give me one more reason to call this the happiest day of my life."

A demand so sudden and so serious made the young man hesitate a moment, for ridicule is often harder to bear than self-denial. Meg knew that if he gave the promise he would keep it at all costs, and feeling her power, used it as a woman may for her friend's good. She did not speak, but she looked up at him with a face made very eloquent by happiness, and a smile which said, "No one can refuse me anything today." Laurie certainly could not, and with an answering smile, he gave her his hand, saying heartily, "I promise, Mrs. Brooke!"

"I thank you, very, very much."

"And I drink 'long life to your resolution,' Teddy," cried Jo, baptizing him with a splash of lemonade, as she waved her glass and beamed approvingly upon him.

So the toast was drunk, the pledge made and loyally kept in spite of many temptations, for with instinctive wisdom, the girls had seized a happy moment to do their friend a service, for which he thanked them all his life.

After lunch, people strolled about, by twos and threes, through house and garden, enjoying the sunshine without and within. Meg and John happened to be standing together in the middle of the grassplot, when Laurie was seized with an inspiration which put the finishing touch to this unfashionable wedding.

"All the married people take hands and dance round the new-made husband and wife, as the Germans do, while we bachelors and spinsters prance in couples outside!" cried Laurie, promenading down the path with Amy, with such infectious spirit and skill that everyone else followed their example without a murmur. Mr. and Mrs. March, Aunt and Uncle Carrol began it, others rapidly joined in, even Sallie Moffat, after a moment's hesitation, threw her train over her arm and whisked Ned into the ring. But the crowning joke was Mr. Laurence and Aunt March, for when the stately old gentleman chasséd solemnly up to the old lady, she just tucked her cane under arm, and hopped briskly away to join hands with the rest and dance about the bridal pair, while the young folks pervaded the garden like butterflies on a midsummer day.

Want of breath brought the impromptu ball to a close, and then people began to go.

"I wish you well, my dear, I heartily wish you well; but I think you'll be sorry for it," said Aunt March to Meg, adding to the bridegroom, as he led her to the carriage, "You've got a treasure, young man, see that you deserve it."

"That is the prettiest wedding I've been to for an age, Ned, and I don't see why, for there wasn't a bit of style about it," observed Mrs. Moffat to her husband, as they drove away.

"Laurie, my lad, if you ever want to indulge in this sort of thing, get one of those little girls to help you, and I shall be perfectly satisfied," said Mr. Laurence, settling himself in his easy chair to rest after the excitement of the morning.

"I'll do my best to gratify you, sir," was Laurie's unusually dutiful reply, as he carefully unpinned the posy Jo had put in his buttonhole.

The little house was not far away, and the only bridal journey Meg had was the quiet walk with John from the old home to the new. When she came down, looking like a pretty Quakeress in her dove-colored suit and straw bonnet tied with white, they all gathered about her to say good-by, as tenderly as if she had been going to make the grand tour.

"Don't feel that I am separated from you, Marmee dear, or that I love you any the less for loving John so much," she said, clinging to her mother, with full eyes for a moment. "I shall come every day, Father, and expect to keep my old place in all your hearts, though I *am* married. Beth is going to be with me a great deal, and the other girls will drop in now and then to laugh at my housekeeping struggles. Thank you all for my happy wedding day. Good-by, good-by!"

They stood watching her, with faces full of love and hope and tender pride as she walked away, leaning on her husband's arm, with her hands full of flowers and the June sunshine brightening her happy face—and so Meg's married life began.

Chapter 26

Artistic Attempts

IT TAKES PEOPLE a long time to learn the difference between talent and genius, especially ambitious young men and women. Amy was learning this distinction through much tribulation, for mistaking enthusiasm for inspiration, she attempted every branch of art with youthful audacity. For a long time there was a lull in the "mud-pie" business, and she devoted herself to the finest pen-and-ink drawing, in which she showed such taste and skill that her graceful handiwork proved both pleasant and profitable. But overstrained eyes soon caused pen and ink to be laid aside for a bold attempt at poker sketching.

While this attack lasted, the family lived in constant fear of a conflagration, for the odor of burning wood pervaded the house at all hours, smoke issued from attic and shed with alarming frequency, red-hot pokers lay about promiscuously, and Hannah never went to bed without a pail of water and the dinner bell at her door in case of fire. Raphael's face was found boldly executed on the underside of the moulding board, and Bacchus on the head of a beer barrel; a chanting cherub adorned the cover of the sugar bucket, and attempts to portray Romeo and Juliet supplied kindlings for some time.

From fire to oil was a natural transition for burned fingers, and Amy fell to painting with undiminished ardor. An artist friend fitted her out with his castoff palettes, brushes, and colors, and she daubed away, producing pastoral and marine views such as were never seen on land or sea. Her monstrosities in the way of cattle would have taken prizes at an agricultural fair, and the perilous pitching of her vessels would have produced seasickness in the most nautical observer, if the utter disregard to all known rules of shipbuilding and rigging had not convulsed him with laughter at the first glance.

Swarthy boys and dark-eyed Madonnas, staring at you from one corner of the studio, suggested Murillo; oily-brown shadows of faces with a lurid streak in the wrong place, meant Rembrandt; buxom ladies and dropsical infants, Rubens; and Turner appeared in tempests of blue thunder, orange lightning, brown rain, and purple clouds, with a tomato-colored splash in the middle, which might be the sun or a buoy, a sailor's shirt or a king's robe, as the spectator pleased.

Charcoal portraits came next, and the entire family hung in a row, looking as wild and crocky as if just evoked from a coalbin. Softened into crayon sketches, they did better, for the likenesses were good, and Amy's hair, Jo's nose, Meg's mouth, and Laurie's eyes were pronounced "wonderfully fine." A return to clay and plaster followed, and ghostly casts of her acquaintances haunted corners of the house, or tumbled off closet shelves onto people's heads. Children were enticed in as models, till their incoherent accounts of her mysterious doings caused Miss Amy to be regarded in the light of a young ogress. Her efforts in this line, however, were brought to an abrupt close by an untoward accident, which quenched her ardor. Other models failing her for a time, she undertook to cast her own pretty foot, and the family were one day alarmed by an unearthly bumping and screaming and running to the rescue, found the young enthusiast hopping wildly about the shed with her foot held fast in a pan full of plaster, which had hardened with unexpected rapidity. With much difficulty and some danger she was dug out, for Jo was so overcome with laughter while she excavated that her knife went too far, cut the poor foot, and left a lasting memorial of one artistic attempt, at least.

After this Amy subsided, till a mania for sketching from nature set her to haunting river, field, and wood, for picturesque studies, and sighing for ruins to copy. She caught endless colds sitting on damp grass to book "a delicious bit," composed of a stone, a stump, one mushroom, and a broken mullein stalk, or "a heavenly mass of clouds," that looked like a choice display of featherbeds when done. She sacrificed her complexion floating on the river in the midsummer sun to study light and shade, and got a wrinkle over her nose trying after "points of sight," or whatever the squint-and-string performance is called.

If "genius is eternal patience," as Michelangelo affirms, Amy had some claim to the divine attribute, for she persevered in spite of all obstacles, failures, and discouragements, firmly believing that in time she should do something worthy to be called "high art."

She was learning, doing, and enjoying other things, meanwhile, for she had resolved to be an attractive and accomplished woman, even if she never became a great artist. Here she succeeded better, for she was one of those happily created beings who please without effort, make friends everywhere, and take life so gracefully and easily that less fortunate souls are tempted to believe that such are born under a lucky star. Everybody liked her, for among her good gifts was tact. She had an instinctive sense of what was pleasing and proper, always said the right thing to the right person, did just what suited the time and place, and was so self-possessed that her sisters used to say, "If Amy went to court without any rehearsal beforehand, she'd know exactly what to do."

One of her weaknesses was a desire to move in "our best society," without being quite sure what the *best* really was. Money, position, fashionable accomplishments, and elegant manners were most desirable things in her eyes, and she liked to associate with those who possessed them, often mistaking the false for the true, and admiring what was not admirable. Never forgetting that by birth she was a gentlewoman, she cultivated her aristocratic tastes and feelings, so that when the opportunity came she might be ready to take the place from which poverty now excluded her.

"My lady," as her friends called her, sincerely desired to be a genuine lady, and was so at heart, but had yet to learn that money cannot buy refinement of nature, that rank does not always confer nobility, and that true breeding makes itself felt in spite of external drawbacks.

"I want to ask a favor of you, Mamma," Amy said, coming in with an important air one day.

"Well, little girl, what is it?" replied her mother, in whose eyes the stately young lady still remained "the baby."

"Our drawing class breaks up next week, and before the girls separate for the summer, I want to ask them out here for a day. They are wild to see the river, sketch the broken bridge, and copy some of the things they admire in my book. They have been very kind to me in many ways, and I am grateful, for they are all rich and know I am poor, yet they never made any difference."

"Why should they?" And Mrs. March put the question with what the girls called her "Maria Theresa air."

"You know as well as I that it *does* make a difference with nearly everyone, so don't ruffle up like a dear, motherly hen, when your chickens get pecked by smarter birds; the ugly duckling turned out a swan, you know." And Amy smiled without bitterness, for she possessed a happy temper and hopeful spirit.

Mrs. March laughed, and smoothed down her maternal pride as she asked, "Well, my swan, what is your plan?"

"I should like to ask the girls out to lunch next week, to take them a drive to the places they want to see, a row on the river, perhaps, and make a little artistic fete for them."

"That looks feasible. What do you want for lunch? Cake, sandwiches, fruit, and coffee will be all that is necessary, I suppose?"

"Oh dear, no! We must have cold tongue and chicken, French chocolate and ice cream, besides. The girls are used to such things, and I want my lunch to be proper and elegant, though I *do* work for my living."

"How many young ladies are there?" asked her mother, beginning to look sober.

"Twelve or fourteen in the class, but I dare say they won't all come."

"Bless me, child, you will have to charter an omnibus to carry them about."

"Why, Mother, how can you think of such a thing? Not more than six or eight will probably come, so I shall hire

a beach wagon and borrow Mr. Laurence's cherry-bounce."
(Hannah's pronunciation of charàbanc.)

"All this will be expensive, Amy."

"Not very. I've calculated the cost, and I'll pay for it myself."

"Don't you think, dear, that as these girls are used to such
things, and the best we can do will be nothing new, that some
simpler plan would be pleasanter to them, as a change if
nothing more, and much better for us than buying or bor-
rowing what we don't need, and attempting a style not in
keeping with our circumstances?"

"If I can't have it as I like, I don't care to have it at all.
I know that I can carry it out perfectly well, if you and the
girls will help a little, and I don't see why I can't if I'm willing
to pay for it," said Amy, with the decision which opposition
was apt to change into obstinacy.

Mrs. March knew that experience was an excellent teacher,
and when it was possible she left her children to learn alone
the lessons which she would gladly have made easier, if they
had not objected to taking advice as much as they did salts
and senna.

"Very well, Amy, if your heart is set upon it, and you
see your way through without too great an outlay of money,
time, and temper, I'll say no more. Talk it over with the girls,
and whichever way you decide, I'll do my best to help you."

"Thanks, Mother, you are always *so* kind." And away went
Amy to lay her plan before her sisters.

Meg agreed at once, and promised her aid, gladly offering
anything she possessed, from her little house itself to her very
best saltspoons. But Jo frowned upon the whole project and
would have nothing to do with it at first.

"Why in the world should you spend your money, worry
your family, and turn the house upside down for a parcel
of girls who don't care a sixpence for you? I thought you had
too much pride and sense to truckle to any mortal woman
just because she wears French boots and rides in a coupé,"

said Jo, who, being called from the tragic climax of her novel, was not in the best mood for social enterprises.

"I *don't* truckle, and I hate being patronized as much as you do!" returned Amy indignantly, for the two still jangled when such questions arose. "The girls do care for me, and I for them, and there's a great deal of kindness and sense and talent among them, in spite of what you call fashionable nonsense. You don't care to make people like you, to go into good society, and cultivate your manners and tastes. I do, and I mean to make the most of every chance that comes. *You* can go through the world with your elbows out and your nose in the air, and call it independence, if you like. That's not my way."

When Amy had whetted her tongue and freed her mind she usually got the best of it, for she seldom failed to have common sense on her side, while Jo carried her love of liberty and hate of conventionalities to such an unlimited extent that she naturally found herself worsted in an argument. Amy's definition of Jo's idea of independence was such a good hit that both burst out laughing, and the discussion took a more amiable turn. Much against her will, Jo at length consented to sacrifice a day to Mrs. Grundy, and help her sister through what she regarded as "a nonsensical business."

The invitations were sent, nearly all accepted, and the following Monday was set apart for the grand event. Hannah was out of humor because her week's work was deranged, and prophesied that "ef the washin' and ironin' warn't done reg'lar nothin' would go well anywheres." This hitch in the mainspring of the domestic machinery had a bad effect upon the whole concern, but Amy's motto was *"Nil desperandum,"* and having made up her mind what to do, she proceeded to do it in spite of all obstacles. To begin with, Hannah's cooking didn't turn out well: the chicken was tough, the tongue too salt, and the chocolate wouldn't froth properly. Then the cake and ice cost more than Amy expected, so did the wagon; and various other expenses, which seemed trifling at the outset, counted up rather alarmingly afterward. Beth got cold and took to her bed, Meg had an unusual number of callers to keep her at home, and Jo was in such a divided state of mind that her breakages, accidents, and mistakes were uncommonly numerous, serious, and trying.

"If it hadn't been for Mother I never should have got through," as Amy declared afterward, and gratefully remembered when "the best joke of the season" was entirely forgotten by everybody else.

If it was not fair on Monday, the young ladies were to come on Tuesday—an arrangement which aggravated Jo and Hannah to the last degree. On Monday morning the weather was in that undecided state which is more exasperating than than a steady pour. It drizzled a little, shone a little, blew a little, and didn't make up its mind till it was too late for anyone else to make up theirs. Amy was up at dawn, hustling people out of their beds and through their breakfasts, that the house might be got in order. The parlor struck her as looking uncommonly shabby, but without stopping to sigh for what she had not, she skillfully made the best of what she had, arranging chairs over the worn places in the carpet, covering stains on the walls with pictures framed in ivy, and filling up empty corners with homemade statuary, which gave an artistic air to the room, as did the lovely vases of flowers Jo scattered about.

The lunch looked charming, and as she surveyed it, she sincerely hoped it would taste well, and that the borrowed glass, china, and silver would get safely home again. The carriages were promised, Meg and Mother were all ready to do the honors, Beth was able to help Hannah behind the scenes, Jo had engaged to be as lively and amiable as an absent mind, an aching head, and a very decided disapproval of everybody and everything would allow, and as she wearily dressed, Amy cheered herself with anticipations of the happy moment when, lunch safely over, she should drive away with her friends for an afternoon of artistic delights; for the "cherry-bounce" and the broken bridge were her strong points.

Then came two hours of suspense, during which she vibrated from parlor to porch, while public opinion varied like the weathercock. A smart shower at eleven had evidently quenched the enthusiasm of the young ladies who were to arrive at twelve, for nobody came; and at two the exhausted family sat down in a blaze of sunshine to consume the perishable portions of the feast, that nothing might be lost.

"No doubt about the weather today, they will certainly come, so we must fly round and be ready for them," said Amy, as the sun woke her next morning. She spoke briskly, but in her secret soul she wished she had said nothing about Tuesday, for her interest like her cake was getting a little stale.

"I can't get any lobsters, so you will have to do without salad today," said Mr. March, coming in half an hour later, with an expression of placid despair.

"Use the chicken then, the toughness won't matter in a salad," advised his wife.

"Hannah left it on the kitchen table a minute, and the kittens got at it. I'm very sorry, Amy," added Beth, who was still a patroness of cats.

"Then I *must* have a lobster, for tongue alone won't do," said Amy decidedly.

"Shall I rush into town and demand one?" asked Jo, with the magnanimity of a martyr.

"You'd come bringing it home under your arm without any paper, just to try me. I'll go myself," answered Amy, whose temper was beginning to fail.

Shrouded in a thick veil and armed with a genteel traveling basket, she departed, feeling that a cool drive would soothe her ruffled spirit and fit her for the labors of the day. After some delay, the object of her desire was procured, likewise a bottle of dressing to prevent further loss of time at home, and off she drove again, well pleased with her own forethought.

As the omnibus contained only one other passenger, a sleepy old lady, Amy pocketed her veil and beguiled the tedium of the way by trying to find out where all her money had gone to. So busy was she with her card full of refractory figures that she did not observe a newcomer, who entered without stopping the vehicle, till a masculine voice said,

"Good morning, Miss March," and, looking up, she beheld one of Laurie's most elegant college friends. Fervently hoping that he would get out before she did, Amy utterly ignored the basket at her feet, and congratulating herself that she had on her new traveling dress, returned the young man's greeting with her usual suavity and spirit.

They got on excellently, for Amy's chief care was soon set at rest by learning that the gentleman would leave first, and she was chatting away in a peculiarly lofty strain, when the old lady got out. In stumbling to the door, she upset the basket, and—oh, horror!—the lobster, in all its vulgar size and brilliancy, was revealed to the highborn eyes of a Tudor.

"By Jove, she's forgotten her dinner!" cried the unconscious youth, poking the scarlet monster into its place with his cane, and preparing to hand out the basket after the old lady.

"Please don't—it's—it's mine," murmured Amy, with a face nearly as red as her fish.

"Oh, really, I beg pardon. It's an uncommonly fine one, isn't it?" said Tudor, with great presence of mind, and an air of sober interest that did credit to his breeding.

Amy recovered herself in a breath, set her basket boldly on the seat, and said, laughing, "Don't you wish you were to have some of the salad he's going to make, and to see the charming young ladies who are to eat it?"

Now that was tact, for two of the ruling foibles of the masculine mind were touched: the lobster was instantly surrounded by a halo of pleasing reminiscences, and curiosity about "the charming young ladies" diverted his mind from the comical mishap.

"I suppose he'll laugh and joke over it with Laurie, but I shan't see them, that's a comfort," thought Amy, as Tudor bowed and departed.

She did not mention this meeting at home (though she discovered that, thanks to the upset, her new dress was much damaged by the rivulets of dressing that meandered down the skirt), but went through with the preparations which now seemed more irksome than before, and at twelve o'clock all was ready again. Feeling that the neighbors were interested in her movements, she wished to efface the memory of yesterday's failure by a grand success today; so she ordered the "cherry-bounce," and drove away in state to meet and escort her guests to the banquet.

"There's the rumble, they're coming! I'll go onto the porch to meet them; it looks hospitable, and I want the poor child to have a good time after all her trouble," said Mrs. March, suiting the action to the word. But after one glance, she retired, with an indescribable expression, for, looking quite lost in the big carriage, sat Amy and one young lady.

"Run, Beth, and help Hannah clear half the things off the table; it will be too absurd to put a luncheon for twelve before a single girl," cried Jo, hurrying away to the lower regions, too excited to stop even for a laugh.

In came Amy, quite calm and delightfully cordial to the one guest who had kept her promise; the rest of the family, being of a dramatic turn, played their parts equally well, and Miss Eliott found them a most hilarious set, for it was impossible to control entirely the merriment which possessed them. The remodeled lunch being gaily partaken of, the studio and garden visited, and art discussed with enthusiasm, Amy ordered a buggy (alas for the elegant cherry-bounce!) and drove her friend quietly about the neighborhood till sunset, when "the party went out."

As she came walking in, looking very tired but as composed as ever, she observed that every vestige of the unfortunate fete had disappeared, except a suspicious pucker about the corners of Jo's mouth.

"You've had a lovely afternoon for your drive, dear," said her mother, as respectfully as if the whole twelve had come.

"Miss Eliott is a very sweet girl, and seemed to enjoy herself, I thought," observed Beth, with unusual warmth.

"Could you spare me some of your cake? I really need some, I have so much company, and I can't make such delicious stuff as yours," asked Meg soberly.

"Take it all. I'm the only one here who likes sweet things,

and it will mold before I can dispose of it," answered Amy, thinking with a sigh of the generous store she had laid in for such an end as this.

"It's a pity Laurie isn't here to help us," began Jo, as they sat down to ice cream and salad for the second time in two days.

A warning look from her mother checked any further remarks, and the whole family ate in heroic silence, till Mr. March mildly observed, "Salad was one of the favorite dishes of the ancients, and Evelyn"—here a general explosion of laughter cut short the "history of sallets," to the great surprise of the learned gentleman.

"Bundle everything into a basket and send it to the Hummels: Germans like messes. I'm sick of the sight of this, and there's no reason you should all die of a surfeit because I've been a fool," cried Amy, wiping her eyes.

"I thought I *should* have died when I saw you two girls rattling about in the what-you-call-it, like two little kernels in a very big nutshell, and Mother waiting in state to receive the throng," sighed Jo, quite spent with laughter.

"I'm very sorry you were disappointed, dear, but we all did our best to satisfy you," said Mrs. March, in a tone full of motherly regret.

"I *am* satisfied; I've done what I undertook, and it's not my fault that it failed; I comfort myself with that," said Amy, with a little quiver in her voice. "I thank you all very much for helping me, and I'll thank you still more if you won't allude to it for a month, at least."

No one did for several months; but the word "fete" always produced a general smile, and Laurie's birthday gift to Amy was a tiny coral lobster in the shape of a charm for her watch guard.

Chapter 27

Literary Lessons

FORTUNE SUDDENLY SMILED UPON JO, and dropped a good-luck penny in her path. Not a golden penny, exactly, but I doubt if half a million would have given more real happiness than did the little sum that came to her in this wise.

Every few weeks she would shut herself up in her room, put on her scribbling suit, and "fall into a vortex," as she expressed it, writing away at her novel with all her heart and soul, for till that was finished she could find no peace. Her "scribbling suit" consisted of a black woolen pinafore on which she could wipe her pen at will, and a cap of the same material, adorned with a cheerful red bow, into which she bundled her hair when the decks were cleared for action. This cap was a beacon to the inquiring eyes of her family, who during these periods kept their distance, merely popping in their heads semi-occasionally to ask, with interest, "Does genius burn, Jo?" They did not always venture even to ask this question, but took an observation of the cap, and judged accordingly. If this expressive article of dress was drawn low upon the forehead, it was a sign that hard work was going on, in exciting moments it was pushed rakishly askew, and when despair seized the author it was plucked wholly off, and cast upon the floor. At such times the intruder silently withdrew, and not until the red bow was seen gaily erect upon the gifted brow, did anyone dare address Jo.

She did not think herself a genius by any means; but when the writing fit came on, she gave herself up to it with entire abandon, and led a blissful life, unconscious of want, care, or bad weather, while she sat safe and happy in an imaginary world, full of friends almost as real and dear to her as any in the flesh. Sleep forsook her eyes, meals stood untasted, day and night were all too short to enjoy the happiness which blessed her only at such times, and made these hours worth living, even if they bore no other fruit. The divine afflatus usually lasted a week or two, and then she emerged from her "vortex," hungry, sleepy, cross, or despondent.

She was just recovering from one of these attacks when she was prevailed upon to escort Miss Crocker to a lecture, and in return for her virtue was rewarded with a new idea. It was a People's Course, the lecture on the Pyramids, and Jo rather wondered at the choice of such a subject for such an audience, but took it for granted that some great social evil would be remedied or some great want supplied by unfolding the glories of the Pharaohs to an audience whose thoughts were busy with the price of coal and flour, and whose lives were spent in trying to solve harder riddles than that of the Sphinx.

They were early, and while Miss Crocker set the heel of her stocking, Jo amused herself by examining the faces of the people who occupied the seat with them. On her left were two matrons, with massive foreheads and bonnets to match, discussing Woman's Rights and making tatting. Beyond sat a pair of humble lovers, artlessly holding each other by the hand, a somber spinster eating peppermints out of a paper bag, and an old gentleman taking his preparatory nap behind a yellow bandanna. On her right, her only neighbor was a studious-looking lad absorbed in a newspaper.

It was a pictorial sheet, and Jo examined the work of art nearest her, idly wondering what unfortuitous concatenation of circumstances needed the melodramatic illustration of an Indian in full war costume, tumbling over a precipice with a wolf at his throat, while two infuriated young gentlemen, with unnaturally small feet and big eyes, were stabbing each other close by, and a disheveled female was flying away in the background with her mouth wide open. Pausing to turn a page, the lad saw her looking and, with boyish good nature, offered half his paper, saying bluntly, "Want to read it? That's a first-rate story."

Jo accepted it with a smile, for she had never outgrown her liking for lads, and soon found herself involved in the usual labyrinth of love, mystery, and murder, for the story belonged to that class of light literature in which the passions have a holiday, and when the author's invention fails, a grand catastrophe clears the stage of one half the dramatis personae, leaving the other half to exult over their downfall.

"Prime, isn't it?" asked the boy, as her eye went down the last paragraph of her portion.

"I think you and I could do as well as that if we tried," returned Jo, amused at his admiration of the trash.

"I should think I was a pretty lucky chap if I could. She makes a good living out of such stories, they say." And he pointed to the name of Mrs. S. L. A. N. G. Northbury, under the title of the tale.

"Do you know her?" asked Jo, with sudden interest.

"No, but I read all her pieces, and I know a fellow who works in the office where this paper is printed."

"Do you say she makes a good living out of stories like this?" And Jo looked more respectfully at the agitated group and thickly sprinkled exclamation points that adorned the page.

"Guess she does! She knows just what folks like, and gets paid well for writing it."

Here the lecture began, but Jo heard very little of it, for while Professor Sands was prosing away about Belzoni, Cheops, scarabei, and hieroglyphics, she was covertly taking down the address of the paper, and boldly resolving to try for the hundred-dollar prize offered in its columns for a sensational story. By the time the lecture ended and the audience awoke, she had built up a splendid fortune for herself (not the first founded upon paper), and was already deep in the concoction of her story, being unable to decide whether the duel should come before the elopement or after the murder.

She said nothing of her plan at home, but fell to work next day, much to the disquiet of her mother, who always looked a little anxious when "genius took to burning." Jo had never tried this style before, contenting herself with very mild romances for *The Spread Eagle*. Her theatrical experience and miscellaneous reading were of service now, for they gave her some idea of dramatic effect, and supplied plot, language, and costumes. Her story was as full of desperation and despair as her limited acquaintance with those uncomfortable emotions enabled her to make it, and, having located it in Lisbon, she wound up with an earthquake, as a striking and appropriate denouement. The manuscript was privately dispatched, accompanied by a note, modestly saying that if the tale didn't get the prize, which the writer hardly dared expect, she would be very glad to receive any sum it might be considered worth.

Six weeks is a long time to wait, and a still longer time for a girl to keep a secret, but Jo did both, and was just beginning to give up all hope of ever seeing her manuscript again, when a letter arrived which almost took her breath away, for on opening it, a check for a hundred dollars fell into her lap. For a minute she stared at it as if it had been a snake, then she read her letter and began to cry. If the amiable gentleman who wrote that kindly note could have known what intense happiness he was giving a fellow creature, I think he would devote his leisure hours, if he has any, to that amusement; for Jo valued the letter more than the money, because it was encouraging, and after years of effort it was *so* pleasant to find that she had learned to do something, though it was only to write a sensation story.

A prouder young woman was seldom seen than she, when, having composed herself, she electrified the family by appearing before them with the letter in one hand, the check in the other, announcing that she had won the prize. Of course there was a great jubilee, and when the story came everyone read and praised it; though after her father had told her that the language was good, the romance fresh and hearty, and the tragedy quite thrilling, he shook his head, and said in his unworldly way—

"You can do better than this, Jo. Aim at the highest, and never mind the money."

"*I* think the money is the best part of it. What *will* you do with such a fortune?" asked Amy, regarding the magic slip of paper with a reverential eye.

"Send Beth and Mother to the seaside for a month or two," answered Jo promptly.

"Oh, how splendid! No, I can't do it, dear, it would be so selfish," cried Beth, who had clapped her thin hands and taken a long breath, as if pining for fresh ocean breeze, then stopped herself and motioned away the check which her sister waved before her.

"Ah, but you shall go, I've set my heart on it. That's what I tried for, and that's why I succeeded. I never get on when I think of myself alone, so it will help me to work for you, don't you see? Besides, Marmee needs the change, and she won't leave you, so you *must* go. Won't it be fun to see you come home plump and rosy again? Hurrah for Dr. Jo, who always cures her patients!"

To the seaside they went, after much discussion, and though Beth didn't come home as plump and rosy as could be desired, she was much better, while Mrs. March declared she felt ten years younger; so Jo was satisfied with the investment of her prize money, and fell to work with a cheery spirit, bent on earning more of those delightful checks. She did earn several that year, and began to feel herself a power in the house, for by the magic of a pen, her "rubbish" turned into comforts for them all. *The Duke's Daughter* paid the butcher's bill, *A Phantom Hand* put down a new carpet, and the *Curse of the Coventrys* proved the blessing of the Marches in the way of groceries and gowns.

Wealth is certainly a most desirable thing, but poverty has its sunny side, and one of the sweet uses of adversity is the genuine satisfaction which comes from hearty work of head or hand; and to the inspiration of necessity, we owe half the wise, beautiful, and useful blessings of the world. Jo enjoyed a taste of this satisfaction, and ceased to envy richer girls, taking great comfort in the knowledge that she could supply her own wants, and need ask no one for a penny.

Little notice was taken of her stories, but they found a

market, and encouraged by this fact, she resolved to make a bold stroke for fame and fortune. Having copied her novel for the fourth time, read it to all her confidential friends, and submitted it with fear and trembling to three publishers, she at last disposed of it, on condition that she would cut it down one third, and omit all the parts which she particularly admired.

"Now I must either bundle it back into my tin kitchen to mold, pay for printing it myself, or chop it up to suit purchasers and get what I can for it. Fame is a very good thing to have in the house, but cash is more convenient, so I wish to take the sense of the meeting on this important subject," said Jo, calling a family council.

"Don't spoil your book, my girl, for there is more in it than you know, and the idea is well worked out. Let it wait and ripen," was her father's advice; and he practiced as he preached, having waited patiently thirty years for fruit of his own to ripen, and being in no haste to gather it even now when it was sweet and mellow.

"It seems to me that Jo will profit more by making the trial than by waiting," said Mrs. March. "Criticism is the best test of such work, for it will show her both unsuspected merits and faults, and help her to do better next time. We are too partial, but the praise and blame of outsiders will prove useful, even if she gets but little money."

"Yes," said Jo, knitting her brows, "that's just it. I've been fussing over the thing so long, I really don't know whether it's good, bad, or indifferent. It will be a great help to have cool, impartial persons take a look at it, and tell me what they think of it."

"I wouldn't leave out a word of it; you'll spoil it if you do, for the interest of the story is more in the minds than in the actions of the people, and it will be all a muddle if you don't explain as you go on," said Meg, who firmly believed that this book was the most remarkable novel ever written.

"But Mr. Allen says, 'Leave out the explanations, make it brief and dramatic, and let the characters tell the story,'" interrupted Jo, turning to the publisher's note.

"Do as he tells you, he knows what will sell, and we don't. Make a good, popular book, and get as much money as you can. By-and-by, when you've got a name, you can afford to digress, and have philosophical and metaphysical people in your novels," said Amy, who took a strictly practical view of the subject.

"Well," said Jo, laughing, "if my people *are* 'philosophical and metaphysical,' it isn't my fault, for I know nothing about such things, except what I hear Father say, sometimes. If I've got some of his wise ideas jumbled up with my romance, so much the better for me. Now, Beth, what do you say?"

"I should so like to see it printed *soon*" was all Beth said, and smiled in saying it; but there was an unconscious emphasis on the last word, and a wistful look in the eyes that never lost their childlike candor, which chilled Jo's heart for a minute with a foreboding fear, and decided her to make her little venture "soon."

So, with Spartan firmness, the young authoress laid her first-born on her table, and chopped it up as ruthlessly as any ogre. In the hope of pleasing everyone, she took everyone's advice, and like the old man and his donkey in the fable suited nobody.

Her father liked the metaphysical streak which had unconsciously got into it, so that was allowed to remain though she had her doubts about it. Her mother thought that there *was* a trifle too much description; out, therefore, it nearly all came, and with it many necessary links in the story. Meg admired the tragedy, so Jo piled up the agony to suit her, while Amy objected to the fun, and, with the best intentions in life, Jo quenched the sprightly scenes which relieved the somber character of the story. Then, to complete the ruin, she cut it down one third, and confidingly sent the poor little romance, like a picked robin, out into the big, busy world to try its fate.

Well, it was printed, and she got three hundred dollars for it; likewise plenty of praise and blame, both so much greater than she expected that she was thrown into a state of bewilderment from which it took her some time to recover.

"You said, Mother, that criticism would help me. But how

can it, when it's so contradictory that I don't know whether I've written a promising book or broken all the ten commandments?" cried poor Jo, turning over a heap of notices, the perusal of which filled her with pride and joy one minute, wrath and dire dismay the next. "This man says, 'An exquisite book, full of truth, beauty, and earnestness; all is sweet, pure, and healthy,'" continued the perplexed authoress. "The next, 'The theory of the book is bad, full of morbid fancies, spiritualistic ideas, and unnatural characters.' Now, as I had no theory of any kind, don't believe in Spiritualism, and copied my characters from life, I don't see how this critic *can* be right. Another says, 'It's one of the best American novels which has appeared for years' (I know better than that); and the next asserts that 'though it is original, and written with great force and feeling, it is a dangerous book.' 'Tisn't! Some make fun of it, some overpraise, and nearly all insist that I had a deep theory to expound, when I only wrote it for the pleasure and the money. I wish I'd printed it whole or not at all, for I do hate to be so misjudged."

Her family and friends administered comfort and commendation liberally; yet it was a hard time for sensitive, high-spirited Jo, who meant so well and had apparently done so ill. But it did her good, for those whose opinion had real value gave her the criticism which is an author's best education; and when the first soreness was over, she could laugh at her poor little book, yet believe in it still, and feel herself the wiser and stronger for the buffeting she had received.

"Not being a genius, like Keats, it won't kill me," she said stoutly, "and I've got the joke on my side, after all, for the parts that were taken straight out of real life are denounced as impossible and absurd, and the scenes that I made up out of my own silly head are pronounced 'charmingly natural, tender, and true.' So I'll comfort myself with that, and when I'm ready, I'll up again and take another."

Chapter 28

Domestic Experiences

LIKE MOST other young matrons, Meg began her married life with the determination to be a model housekeeper. John should find home a paradise, he should always see a smiling face, should fare sumptuously every day, and never know the loss of a button. She brought so much love, energy, and cheerfulness to the work that she could not but succeed, in spite of some obstacles. Her paradise was not a tranquil one, for the little woman fussed, was overanxious to please, and bustled about like a true Martha, cumbered with many cares. She was too tired, sometimes, even to smile, John grew dyspeptic after a course of dainty dishes and ungratefully demanded plain fare. As for buttons, she soon learned to wonder where they went, to shake her head over the carelessness of men, and to threaten to make him sew them on himself, and see if *his* work would stand impatient tugs and clumsy fingers any better than hers.

They were very happy, even after they discovered that they couldn't live on love alone. John did not find Meg's beauty diminished, though she beamed at him from behind the familiar coffeepot; nor did Meg miss any of the romance from the daily parting, when her husband followed up his kiss with the tender inquiry, "Shall I send home veal or mutton for dinner, darling?" The little house ceased to be a glorified bower, but it became a home, and the young couple soon felt that it was a change for the better. At first they played keephouse, and frolicked over it like children; then John took steadily to business, feeling the cares of the head of a family upon his shoulders; and Meg laid by her cambric wrappers, put on a big apron, and fell to work, as before said, with more energy than discretion.

While the cooking mania lasted she went through Mrs.

Cornelius's Receipt Book as if it were a mathematical exercise, working out the problems with patience and care. Sometimes her family were invited in to help eat up a too bounteous feast of successes, or Lotty would be privately dispatched with a batch of failures, which were to be concealed from all eyes in the convenient stomachs of the little Hummels. An evening with John over the account books usually produced a temporary lull in the culinary enthusiasm, and a frugal fit would ensue, during which the poor man was put through a course of bread pudding, hash, and warmed-over coffee, which tried his soul, although he bore it with praiseworthy fortitude. Before the golden mean was found, however, Meg added to her domestic possessions what young couples seldom get on long without—a family jar.

Fired with a housewifely wish to see her storeroom stocked with homemade preserves, she undertook to put up her own currant jelly. John was requested to order home a dozen or so of little pots and an extra quantity of sugar, for their own currants were ripe and were to be attended to at once. As John firmly believed that "my wife" was equal to anything, and took a natural pride in her skill, he resolved that she should be gratified, and their only crop of fruit laid by in a most pleasing form for winter use. Home came four dozen delightful little pots, half a barrel of sugar, and a small boy to pick the currants for her. With her pretty hair tucked into a little cap, arms bared to the elbow, and a checked apron which had a coquettish look in spite of the bib, the young housewife fell to work, feeling no doubts about her success, for hadn't she seen Hannah do it hundreds of times? The array of pots rather amazed her at first, but John was so fond of jelly, and the nice little jars would look so well on the top shelf, that Meg resolved to fill them all, and spent a long day picking, boiling, straining, and fussing over her jelly. She did her best, she asked advice of Mrs. Cornelius, she racked her brain to remember what Hannah did that she left undone, she reboiled, resugared, and restrained, but that dreadful stuff wouldn't *"jell."*

She longed to run home, bib and all, and ask Mother to lend

a hand, but John and she had agreed that they would never annoy anyone with their private worries, experiments, or quarrels. They had laughed over that last word as if the idea it suggested was a most preposterous one; but they had held to their resolve, and whenever they could get on without help they did so, and no one interfered, for Mrs. March had advised the plan. So Meg wrestled alone with the refractory sweetmeats all that hot summer day, and at five o'clock sat down in her topsy-turvy kitchen, wrung her bedaubed hands, lifted up her voice and wept.

Now, in the first flush of the new life, she had often said, "My husband shall always feel free to bring a friend home whenever he likes. I shall always be prepared; there shall be no flurry, no scolding, no discomfort, but a neat house, a cheerful wife, and a good dinner. John, dear, never stop to ask my leave, invite whom you please, and be sure of a welcome from me."

How charming that was, to be sure! John quite glowed with pride to hear her say it, and felt what a blessed thing it was to have a superior wife. But, although they had had company from time to time, it never happened to be unexpected, and Meg had never had an opportunity to distinguish herself till now. It always happens so in this vale of tears, there is an inevitability about such things which we can only wonder at, deplore, and bear as we best can.

If John had not forgotten all about the jelly, it really would have been unpardonable in him to choose that day, of all the days in the year, to bring a friend home to dinner unexpectedly. Congratulating himself that a handsome repast had been ordered that morning, feeling sure that it would be ready to the minute, and indulging in pleasant anticipations of the charming effect it would produce, when his pretty wife came running out to meet him, he escorted his friend to his mansion, with the irrepressible satisfaction of a young host and husband.

It is a world of disappointments, as John discovered when he reached the Dovecote. The front door usually stood hospitably open; now it was not only shut, but locked, and yesterday's mud still adorned the steps. The parlor windows were closed and curtained, no picture of the pretty wife sewing on the piazza, in white, with a distracting little bow in her hair, or a bright-eyed hostess, smiling a shy welcome as she greeted her guest. Nothing of the sort, for not a soul appeared but a sanguinary-looking boy asleep under the currant bushes.

"I'm afraid something has happened. Step into the garden, Scott, while I look up Mrs. Brooke," said John, alarmed at the silence and solitude.

Round the house he hurried, led by a pungent smell of burned sugar, and Mr. Scott strolled after him, with a queer look on his face. He paused discreetly at a distance when Brooke disappeared, but he could both see and hear, and being a bachelor, enjoyed the prospect mightily.

In the kitchen reigned confusion and despair; one edition of jelly was trickled from pot to pot, another lay upon the floor, and a third was burning gaily on the stove. Lotty, with Teutonic phlegm, was calmly eating bread and currant wine, for the jelly was still in a hopelessly liquid state, while Mrs. Brooke, with her apron over her head, sat sobbing dismally.

"My dearest girl, what is the matter?" cried John, rushing in, with awful visions of scalded hands, sudden news of affliction, and secret consternation at the thought of the guest in the garden.

"Oh, John, I *am* so tired and hot and cross and worried! I've been at it till I'm all worn out. Do come and help me or I *shall* die!" And the exhausted housewife cast herself upon his breast, giving him a sweet welcome in every sense of the word, for her pinafore had been baptized at the same time as the floor.

"What worries you, dear? Has anything dreadful happened?" asked the anxious John, tenderly kissing the crown of the little cap, which was all askew.

"Yes," sobbed Meg despairingly.

"Tell me quick, then. Don't cry, I can bear anything better than that. Out with it, love."

"The—the jelly won't jell and I don't know what to do!"

John Brooke laughed then as he never dared to laugh afterward, and the derisive Scott smiled involuntarily as he heard the hearty peal, which put the finishing stroke to poor Meg's woe.

"Is that all? Fling it out of window, and don't bother any more about it. I'll buy you quarts if you want it; but for heaven's sake don't have hysterics, for I've brought Jack Scott home to dinner, and—"

John got no further, for Meg cast him off, and clasped her hands with a tragic gesture as she fell into a chair, exclaiming in a tone of mingled indignation, reproach, and dismay—

"A man to dinner, and everything in a mess! John Brooke, how *could* you do such a thing?"

"Hush, he's in the garden! I forgot the confounded jelly, but it can't be helped now," said John, surveying the prospect with an anxious eye.

"You ought to have sent word, or told me this morning, and you ought to have remembered how busy I was," continued Meg petulantly, for even turtledoves will peck when ruffled.

"I didn't know it this morning, and there was no time to send word, for I met him on the way out. I never thought of asking leave, when you have always told me to do as I liked. I never tried it before, and hang me if I ever do again!" added John, with an aggrieved air.

"I should hope not! Take him away at once; I can't see him and there isn't any dinner."

"Well, I like that! Where's the beef and vegetables I sent home, and the pudding you promised?" cried John, rushing to the larder.

"I hadn't time to cook anything; I meant to dine at Mother's. I'm sorry, but I was *so* busy;" and Meg's tears began again.

John was a mild man, but he was human; and after a long day's work to come home tired, hungry, and hopeful, to find a chaotic house, an empty table, and a cross wife was not exactly conducive to repose of mind or manner. He restrained himself, however, and the little squall would have blown over, but for one unlucky word.

"It's a scrape, I acknowledge, but if you will lend a hand,

we'll pull through and have a good time yet. Don't cry, dear, but just exert yourself a bit, and fix us up something to eat. We're both as hungry as hunters, so we shan't mind what it is. Give us the cold meat, and bread and cheese; we won't ask for jelly."

He meant it for a good-natured joke, but that one word sealed his fate. Meg thought it was *too* cruel to hint about her sad failure, and the last atom of patience vanished as he spoke.

"You must get yourself out of the scrape as you can, I'm too used up to 'exert' myself for anyone. It's like a man to propose a bone and vulgar bread and cheese for company. I won't have anything of the sort in my house. Take that Scott up to Mother's, and tell him I'm away, sick, dead— anything. I won't see him, and you two can laugh at me and my jelly as much as you like: you won't have anything else here." And having delivered her defiance all on one breath, Meg cast away her pinafore and precipitately left the field to bemoan herself in her own room.

What those two creatures did in her absence, she never knew; but Mr. Scott was not taken "up to Mother's," and when Meg descended, after they had strolled away together, she found traces of a promiscuous lunch which filled her with horror. Lotty reported that they had eaten "a much, and greatly laughed, and the master bid her throw away all the sweet stuff, and hide the pots."

Meg longed to go and tell Mother, but a sense of shame at her own shortcomings, of loyalty to John, "who might be cruel, but nobody should know it," restrained her, and after a summary clearing up, she dressed herself prettily, and sat down to wait for John to come and be forgiven.

Unfortunately, John didn't come, not seeing the matter in that light. He had carried it off as a good joke with Scott, excused his little wife as well as he could, and played the host so hospitably that his friend enjoyed the impromptu dinner, and promised to come again. But John was angry, though he did not show it; he felt that Meg had got him into a scrape, and then deserted him in his hour of need. "It wasn't fair to tell a man to bring folks home any time, with perfect freedom, and when he took you at your word, to flame up and blame him, and leave him in the lurch, to be laughed at or pitied. No, by George, it wasn't! and Meg must know it." He had fumed inwardly during the feast, but when the flurry was over and he strolled home after seeing Scott off, a milder mood came over him. "Poor little thing! It was hard upon her when she tried so heartily to please me. She was wrong, of course, but then she was young. I must be patient and teach her." He hoped she had not gone home—he hated gossip and interference. For a minute he was ruffled again at the mere thought of it; and then the fear that Meg would cry herself sick softened his heart, and sent him on at a quicker pace, resolving to be calm and kind, but firm, quite firm, and show her where she had failed in her duty to her spouse.

Meg likewise resolved to be "calm and kind, but firm," and show *him* his duty. She longed to run to meet him, and beg pardon, and be kissed and comforted, as she was sure of being; but, of course, she did nothing of the sort, and when she saw John coming, began to hum quite naturally, as she rocked and sewed, like a lady of leisure in her best parlor.

John was a little disappointed not to find a tender Niobe, but feeling that his dignity demanded the first apology, he made none, only came leisurely in and laid himself upon the sofa with the singularly relevant remark, "We are going to have a new moon, my dear."

"I've no objection" was Meg's equally soothing remark. A few other topics of general interest were introduced by Mr. Brooke and wet-blanketed by Mrs. Brooke, and conversation languished. John went to one window, unfolded his paper, and wrapped himself in it, figuratively speaking. Meg went to the other window, and sewed as if new rosettes for her slippers were among the necessaries of life. Neither spoke; both looked quite "calm and firm," and both felt desperately uncomfortable.

"Oh dear," thought Meg, "married life is very trying, and does need infinite patience as well as love, as Mother says." The word "Mother" suggested other maternal counsels given long ago, and received with unbelieving protests.

"John is a good man, but he has his faults, and you must learn to see and bear with them, remembering your own. He is very decided, but never will be obstinate, if you reason kindly, not oppose impatiently. He is very accurate, and particular about the truth—a good trait, though you call him 'fussy.' Never deceive him by look or word, Meg, and he will give you the confidence you deserve, the support you need. He has a temper, not like ours—one flash and then all over—but the white, still anger that is seldom stirred, but once kindled is hard to quench. Be careful, very careful, not to wake his anger against yourself, for peace and happiness depend on keeping his respect. Watch yourself, be the first to ask pardon if you both err, and guard against the little piques, misunderstandings, and hasty words that often pave the way for bitter sorrow and regret."

These words came back to Meg, as she sat sewing in the sunset, especially the last. This was the first serious disagreement; her own hasty speeches sounded both silly and unkind, as she recalled them, her own anger looked childish now, and thoughts of poor John coming home to such a scene quite melted her heart. She glanced at him with tears in her eyes, but he did not see them; she put down her work and got up, thinking, "I *will* be the first to say, 'Forgive me,'" but he did not seem to hear her; she went very slowly across the room, for pride was hard to swallow, and stood by him, but he did not turn his head. For a minute she felt as if she really couldn't do it; then came the thought, "This is the beginning, I'll do my part, and have nothing to reproach myself with," and stooping down, she softly kissed her husband on the forehead. Of course that settled it; the penitent kiss was better than a world of words, and John had her on his knee in a minute, saying tenderly:

"It was too bad to laugh at the poor little jelly pots. Forgive me, dear, I never will again!"

But he did, oh bless you, yes, hundreds of times, and so did Meg, both declaring that it was the sweetest jelly they ever made, for family peace was preserved in that little family jar.

After this, Meg had Mr. Scott to dinner by special invitation, and served him up a pleasant feast without a cooked wife for the first course; on which occasion she was so gay and gracious, and made everything go off so charmingly, that Mr. Scott told John he was a happy fellow, and shook his head over the hardships of bachelorhood all the way home.

In the autumn, new trials and experiences came to Meg. Sallie Moffat renewed her friendship, was always running out for a dish of gossip at the little house, or inviting "that poor dear" to come in and spend the day at the big house. It was pleasant, for in dull weather Meg often felt lonely; all were busy at home, John absent till night, and nothing to do but sew, or read, or potter about. So it naturally fell out that Meg got into the way of gadding and gossiping with her friend. Seeing Sallie's pretty things made her long for such, and pity herself because she had not got them. Sallie was very kind, and often offered her the coveted trifles; but Meg declined them, knowing that John wouldn't like it; and then this foolish little woman went and did what John disliked infinitely worse.

She knew her husband's income, and she loved to feel that he trusted her, not only with his happiness, but what some men seem to value more—his money. She knew where it was, was free to take what she liked, and all he asked was that she should keep account of every penny, pay bills once a month, and remember that she was a poor man's wife. Till now she had done well, been prudent and exact, kept her little account books neatly, and showed them to him monthly without fear. But that autumn the serpent got into Meg's paradise, and tempted her like many a modern Eve, not with apples, but with dress. Meg didn't like to be pitied and made to feel poor; it irritated her, but she was ashamed to confess it, and now and then she tried to console herself by buying something pretty, so that Sallie needn't think she had to economize. She always felt wicked after it, for the pretty things were seldom necessaries; but then they cost so little, it wasn't worth worrying about, so the trifles increased unconsciously, and in the shopping excursions she was no longer a passive looker-on.

But the trifles cost more than one would imagine, and when she cast up her accounts at the end of the month the sum total

rather scared her. John was busy that month and left the bills
to her, the next month he was absent, but the third he had a
grand quarterly settling up, and Meg never forgot it. A few
days before she had done a dreadful thing, and it weighed
upon her conscience. Sallie had been buying silks, and Meg
longed for a new one—just a handsome light one for parties,
her black silk was so common, and thin things for evening
wear were only proper for girls. Aunt March usually gave the
sisters a present of twenty-five dollars apiece at New Year's;
that was only a month to wait, and here was a lovely violet
silk going at a bargain, and she had the money, if she only
dared to take it. John always said what was his was hers, but
would he think it right to spend not only the prospective five-
and-twenty, but another five-and-twenty out of the household
fund? That was the question. Sallie had urged her to do it, had
offered to lend the money, and with the best intentions in
life had tempted Meg beyond her strength. In an evil moment
the shopman held up the lovely, shimmering folds, and said,
"A bargain, I assure you, ma'am." She answered, "I'll take it,"
and it was cut off and paid for, and Sallie had exulted, and she
had laughed as if it were a thing of no consequence, and driven
away, feeling as if she had stolen something, and the police
were after her.

When she got home, she tried to assuage the pangs of remorse by spreading forth the lovely silk; but it looked less
silvery now, didn't become her, after all, and the words "fifty
dollars" seemed stamped like a pattern down each breadth.
She put it away, but it haunted her, not delightfully as a new
dress should, but dreadfully like the ghost of a folly that was
not easily laid. When John got out his books that night, Meg's
heart sank, and for the first time in her married life, she was
afraid of her husband. The kind, brown eyes looked as if they
could be stern, and though he was unusually merry, she fancied
he had found her out, but didn't mean to let her know it.
The house bills were all paid, the books all in order. John
had praised her, and was undoing the old pocketbook which
they called the "bank," when Meg, knowing that it was quite
empty, stopped his hand, saying nervously—

"You haven't seen my private expense book yet."

John never asked to see it; but she always insisted on his doing so, and used to enjoy his masculine amazement at the queer things women wanted, and made him guess what "piping" was, demand fiercely the meaning of a "hug-me-tight," or wonder how a little thing composed of three rosebuds, a bit a velvet, and a pair of strings, could possibly be a bonnet, and cost five or six dollars. That night he looked as if he would like the fun of quizzing her figures and pretending to be horrified at her extravagance, as he often did, being particularly proud of his prudent wife.

The little book was brought slowly out and laid down before him. Meg got behind his chair under pretense of smoothing the wrinkles out of his tired forehead, and standing there, she said, with her panic increasing with every word—

"John, dear, I'm ashamed to show you my book, for I've really been dreadfully extravagant lately. I go about so much I must have things, you know, and Sallie advised my getting it, so I did; and my New Year's money will partly pay for it: but I was sorry after I'd done it, for I knew you'd think it wrong in me."

John laughed, and drew her round beside him, saying goodhumoredly, "Don't go and hide. I won't beat you if you *have* got a pair of killing boots; I'm rather proud of my wife's feet, and don't mind if she does pay eight or nine dollars for her boots, if they are good ones."

That had been one of her last "trifles," and John's eye had fallen on it as he spoke. "Oh, what *will* he say when he comes to that awful fifty dollars!" thought Meg, with a shiver.

"It's worse than boots, it's a silk dress," she said, with the calmness of desperation, for she wanted the worst over.

"Well, dear, what is the 'dem'd total,' as Mr. Mantalini says?"

That didn't sound like John, and she knew he was looking up at her with the straightforward look that she had always been ready to meet and answer with one as frank till now. She turned the page and her head at the same time, pointing to the sum which would have been bad enough without the fifty, but which was appalling to her with that added. For a minute the room was very still, then John said slowly—but she could feel it cost him an effort to express no displeasure—

"Well, I don't know that fifty is much for a dress, with all the furbelows and notions you have to have to finish it off these days."

"It isn't made or trimmed," sighed Meg faintly, for a sudden recollection of the cost still to be incurred quite overwhelmed her.

"Twenty-five yards of silk seems a good deal to cover one small woman, but I've no doubt my wife will look as fine as Ned Moffat's when she gets it on," said John dryly.

"I know you are angry, John, but I can't help it. I don't mean to waste your money, and I didn't think those little things would count up so. I can't resist them when I see Sallie buying all she wants, and pitying me because I don't. I try to be contented, but it is hard, and I'm tired of being poor."

The last words were spoken so low she thought he did not hear them, but he did, and they wounded him deeply, for he had denied himself many pleasures for Meg's sake. She could have bitten her tongue out the minute she had said it, for John pushed the books away and got up, saying with a little quiver in his voice, "I was afraid of this, I do my best, Meg." If he had scolded her, or even shaken her, it would not have broken her heart like those few words. She ran to him and held him close, crying, with repentant tears, "Oh, John, my dear, kind, hard-working boy, I didn't mean it! It was so wicked, so untrue and ungrateful, how could I say it! Oh, how could I say it!"

He was very kind, forgave her readily, and did not utter one reproach; but Meg knew that she had done and said a thing which would not be forgotten soon, although he might never allude to it again. She had promised to love him for better for worse; and then she, his wife, had reproached him with his poverty, after spending his earnings recklessly. It was dreadful, and the worst of it was John went on so quietly afterward, just as if nothing had happened, except that he stayed in town later, and worked at night when she had gone to cry herself to sleep. A week of remorse nearly made Meg sick, and the discovery that John had countermanded the order for his new greatcoat reduced her to a state of despair which was pathetic to behold. He had simply said, in answer to her surprised inquiries as to the change, "I can't afford it, my dear."

Meg said no more, but a few minutes after he found her in the hall with her face buried in the old greatcoat, crying as if her heart would break.

They had a long talk that night, and Meg learned to love her husband better for his poverty, because it seemed to have made a man of him, given him the strength and courage to fight his own way, and taught him a tender patience with which to bear and comfort the natural longings and failures of those he loved.

Next day she put her pride in her pocket, went to Sallie, told the truth, and asked her to buy the silk as a favor. The good-natured Mrs. Moffat willingly did so, and had the delicacy not to make her a present of it immediately afterward. Then Meg ordered home the greatcoat, and, when John arrived, she put it on, and asked him how he liked her new silk gown. One can imagine what answer he made, how he received his present, and what a blissful state of things ensued. John came home early, Meg gadded no more, and that greatcoat was put on in the morning by a very happy husband, and taken off at night by a most devoted little wife. So the year rolled round, and at midsummer there came to Meg a new experience—the deepest and tenderest of a woman's life.

Laurie came sneaking into the kitchen of the Dovecote one Saturday, with an excited face, and was received with the clash of cymbals, for Hannah clapped her hands with a saucepan in one and the cover in the other.

"How's the little mamma? Where is everybody? Why didn't you tell me before I came home?" began Laurie in a loud whisper.

"Happy as a queen, the dear! Every soul of 'em is upstairs a worshipin'; we didn't want no hurrycanes round. Now you go into the parlor, and I'll send 'em down to you," with which somewhat involved reply Hannah vanished, chuckling ecstatically.

Presently Jo appeared, proudly bearing a flannel bundle laid forth upon a large pillow. Jo's face was very sober, but her eyes twinkled, and there was an odd sound in her voice of repressed emotion of some sort.

"Shut your eyes and hold out your arms,' she said invitingly.

Laurie backed precipitately into a corner, and put his hands behind him with an imploring gesture: "No, thank you, I'd rather not. I shall drop it or smash it, as sure as fate."

"Then you shan't see your nevvy," said Jo decidedly, turning as if to go.

"I will, I will! Only you must be responsible for damages." And, obeying orders, Laurie heroically shut his eyes while something was put into his arms. A peal of laughter from Jo, Amy, Mrs. March, Hannah, and John caused him to open them the next minute, to find himself invested with two babies instead of one.

No wonder they laughed, for the expression of his face was droll enough to convulse a Quaker, as he stood and stared wildly from the unconscious innocents to the hilarious spectators with such dismay that Jo sat down on the floor and screamed.

"Twins, by Jupiter!" was all he said for a minute, then turning to the women with an appealing look that was comically piteous, he added, "Take 'em quick, somebody! I'm going to laugh, and I shall drop 'em."

John rescued his babies, and marched up and down, with one on each arm, as if already initiated into the mysteries of baby-tending, while Laurie laughed till the tears ran down his cheeks.

"It's the best joke of the season, isn't it? I wouldn't have you told, for I set my heart on surprising you, and I flatter myself I've done it," said Jo, when she got her breath.

"I never was more staggered in my life. Isn't it fun? Are they boys? What are you going to name them? Let's have another look. Hold me up, Jo, for upon my life it's one too many for me," returned Laurie, regarding the infants with the air of a big, benevolent Newfoundland looking at a pair of infantile kittens.

"Boy and girl. Aren't they beauties?" said the proud papa, beaming upon the little red squirmers as if they were unfledged angels.

"Most remarkable children I ever saw. Which is which?" and Laurie bent like a well-sweep to examine the prodigies.

"Amy put a blue ribbon on the boy and a pink on the girl, French fashion, so you can always tell. Besides, one has blue eyes and one brown. Kiss them, Uncle Teddy," said wicked Jo.

"I'm afraid they mightn't like it," began Laurie, with unusual timidity in such matters.

"Of course they will, they are used to it now. Do it this minute, sir!" commanded Jo, fearing he might propose a proxy.

Laurie screwed up his face and obeyed with a gingerly peck at each little cheek that produced another laugh, and made the babies squeal.

"There, I knew they didn't like it! That's the boy, see him kick, he hits out with his fists like a good one. Now then, young Brooke, pitch into a man of your own size, will you?" cried Laurie, delighted with a poke in the face from a tiny fist, flapping aimlessly about.

"He's to be named John Laurence, and the girl Margaret, after mother and grandmother. We shall call her Daisy, so as not to have two Megs, and I suppose the mannie will be Jack, unless we find a better name," said Amy, with aunt-like interest.

"Name him Demijohn, and call him 'Demi' for short," said Laurie.

"Daisy and Demi—just the thing! I *knew* Teddy would do it," cried Jo, clapping her hands.

Teddy certainly had done it that time, for the babies were "Daisy" and "Demi" to the end of the chapter.

Chapter 29

Calls

"COME Jo, it's time."

"For what?"

"You don't mean to say you have forgotten that you promised to make half a dozen calls with me today?"

"I've done a good many rash and foolish things in my life, but I don't think I ever was mad enough to say I'd make six calls in one day, when a single one upsets me for a week."

"Yes, you did, it was a bargain between us. I was to finish the crayon of Beth for you, and you were to go properly with me, and return our neighbors' visits."

"If it was fair—that was in the bond; and I stand to the letter of my bond, Shylock. There is a pile of clouds in the east, it's *not* fair, and I don't go."

"Now, that's shirking. It's a lovely day, no prospect of rain, and you pride yourself on keeping promises; so be honorable, come and do your duty, and then be at peace for another six months."

At that minute Jo was particularly absorbed in dressmaking; for she was mantua-maker general to the family, and took especial credit to herself because she could use a needle as well as a pen. It was very provoking to be arrested in the act of a first trying-on, and ordered out to make calls in her best array on a warm July day. She hated calls of the formal sort, and never made any till Amy compelled her with a bargain, bribe, or promise. In the present instance there was no escape; and having clashed her scissors rebelliously, while protesting that she smelled thunder, she gave in, put away her work, and taking up her hat and gloves with an air of resignation, told Amy the victim was ready.

"Jo March, you are perverse enough to provoke a saint! You don't intend to make calls in that state, I hope," cried Amy, surveying her with amazement.

"Why not? I'm neat and cool and comfortable, quite proper for a dusty walk on a warm day. If people care more for my clothes than they do for me, I don't wish to see them. You can dress for both, and be as elegant as you please: it pays for you to be fine; it doesn't for me, and furbelows only worry me."

"Oh dear!" sighed Amy, "now she's in a contrary fit, and will drive me distracted before I can get her properly ready. I'm sure it's no pleasure to me to go today, but it's a debt we owe society, and there's no one to pay it but you and me. I'll do anything for you, Jo, if you'll only dress yourself nicely, and come and help me do the civil. You can talk so well, look so aristocratic in your best things, and behave so beautifully, if you try, that I'm proud of you. I'm afraid to go alone, do come and take care of me."

"You're an artful little puss to flatter and wheedle your cross old sister in that way. The idea of my being aristocratic and well-bred, and your being afraid to go anywhere alone! I don't know which is the most absurd. Well, I'll go if I must, and do my best. You shall be commander of the expedition, and I'll obey blindly, will that satisfy you?" said Jo, with a sudden change from perversity to lamblike submission.

"You're a perfect cherub! Now put on all your best things, and I'll tell you how to behave at each place, so that you will make a good impression. I want people to like you, and they would if you'd only try to be a little more agreeable. Do your hair the pretty way, and put the pink rose in your bonnet; it's becoming, and you look too sober in your plain suit. Take your light gloves and the embroidered handkerchief. We'll stop at Meg's, and borrow her white sunshade, and then you can have my dove-colored one."

While Amy dressed, she issued her orders, and Jo obeyed them, not without entering her protest, however, for she sighed as she rustled into her new organdie, frowned darkly at herself as she tied her bonnet strings in an irreproachable bow, wrestled viciously with pins as she put on her collar, wrinkled up her features generally as she shook out the handkerchief, whose embroidery was as irritating to her nose as the

present mission was to her feelings; and when she had squeezed
her hands into tight gloves with three buttons and a tassel, as
the last touch of elegance, she turned to Amy with an imbecile
expression of countenance, saying meekly—

"I'm perfectly miserable; but if you consider me presentable,
I die happy."

"You are highly satisfactory; turn slowly round, and let me
get a careful view." Jo revolved, and Amy gave a touch here
and there, then fell back, with her head on one side, observing
graciously, "Yes, you'll do; your head is all I could ask, for
that white bonnet *with* the rose is quite ravishing. Hold back
your shoulders, and carry your hands easily, no matter if your
gloves do pinch. There's one thing you can do well, Jo, that
is, wear a shawl—I can't; but it's very nice to see you, and I'm
so glad Aunt March gave you that lovely one; it's simple, but
handsome, and those folds over the arm are really artistic. Is
the point of my mantle in the middle, and have I looped my
dress evenly? I like to show my boots, for my feet *are* pretty,
though my nose isn't."

"You are a thing of beauty and a joy forever," said Jo,
looking through her hand with the air of a connoisseur at the
blue feather against the golden hair. "Am I to drag my best
dress through the dust, or loop it up, please, ma'am?"

"Hold it up when you walk, but drop it in the house; the
sweeping style suits you best, and you must learn to trail your
skirts gracefully. You haven't half buttoned one cuff, do it at
once. You'll never look finished if you are not careful about
the little details, for they make up the pleasing whole."

Jo sighed, and proceeded to burst the buttons off her glove,
in doing up her cuff; but at last both were ready, and sailed
away, looking as "pretty as picters," Hannah said, as she
hung out of the upper window to watch them.

"Now, Jo dear, the Chesters consider themselves very elegant people, so I want you to put on your best deportment.
Don't make any of your abrupt remarks, or do anything odd,
will you? Just be calm, cool, and quiet—that's safe and ladylike, and you can easily do it for fifteen minutes," said Amy,
as they approached the first place, having borrowed the white

parasol and been inspected by Meg, with a baby on each arm.

"Let me see. 'Calm, cool, and quiet'—yes, I think I can promise that. I've played the part of a prim young lady on the stage, and I'll try it off. My powers are great, as you shall see, so be easy in your mind, my child."

Amy looked relieved, but naughty Jo took her at her word, for during the first call she sat with every limb gracefully composed, every fold correctly draped, calm as a summer sea, cool as a snowbank, and as silent as a sphinx. In vain Mrs. Chester alluded to her "charming novel," and the Misses Chester introduced parties, picnics, the opera, and the fashions; each and all were answered by a smile, a bow, and a demure "Yes" or "No" with the chill on. In vain Amy telegraphed the word "talk," tried to draw her out, and administered covert pokes with her foot. Jo sat as if blandly unconscious of it all, with deportment like Maud's face, "icily regular, splendidly null."

"What a haughty, uninteresting creature that oldest Miss March is!" was the unfortunately audible remark of one of the ladies, as the door closed upon their guests. Jo laughed noiselessly all through the hall, but Amy looked disgusted at the failure of her instructions, and very naturally laid the blame upon Jo.

"How could you mistake me so? I merely meant you to be properly dignified and composed, and you made yourself a perfect stock and stone. Try to be sociable at the Lambs', gossip as other girls do, and be interested in dress and flirtations and whatever nonsense comes up. They move in the best society, are valuable persons for us to know, and I wouldn't fail to make a good impression there for anything."

"I'll be agreeable, I'll gossip and giggle, and have horrors and raptures over any trifle you like. I rather enjoy this, and now I'll imitate what is called 'a charming girl,' I can do it, for I have May Chester as a model, and I'll improve upon her. See if the Lambs don't say, 'What a lively, nice creature that Jo March is!' "

Amy felt anxious, as well she might, for when Jo turned freakish there was no knowing where she would stop. Amy's face was a study when she saw her sister skim into the next drawing room, kiss all the young ladies with effusion, beam graciously upon the young gentlemen, and join in the chat with a spirit which amazed the beholder. Amy was taken possession of by Mrs. Lamb, with whom she was a favorite, and forced to hear a long account of Lucretia's last attack, while three delightful young gentlemen hovered near, waiting for a pause when they might rush in and rescue her. So situated, she was powerless to check Jo, who seemed possessed by a spirit of mischief, and talked away as volubly as the old lady. A knot of heads gathered about her, and Amy strained her ears to hear what was going on, for broken sentences filled her with alarm, round eyes and uplifted hands tormented her with curiosity, and frequent peals of laughter made her wild to share the fun. One may imagine her suffering on overhearing fragments of this sort of conversation:

"She rides splendidly—who taught her?"

"No one. She used to practice mounting, holding the reins, and sitting straight on an old saddle in a tree. Now she rides anything, for she doesn't know what fear is, and the stableman lets her have horses cheap because she trains them to carry ladies so well. She has such a passion for it, I often tell her if everything else fails she can be a horsebreaker, and get her living so."

At this awful speech Amy contained herself with difficulty, for the impression was being given that she was rather a fast young lady, which was her especial aversion. But what could she do? For the old lady was in the middle of her story, and long before it was done Jo was off again, making more droll revelations and committing still more fearful blunders.

"Yes, Amy was in despair that day, for all the good beasts were gone, and of three left, one was lame, one blind, and the other so balky that you had to put dirt in his mouth before he would start. Nice animal for a pleasure party, wasn't it?"

"Which did she choose?" asked one of the laughing gentlemen, who enjoyed the subject.

"None of them. She heard of a young horse at the farmhouse over the river, and though a lady had never ridden him, she resolved to try, because he was handsome and spirited. Her struggles were really pathetic; there was no one to bring the horse to the saddle, so she took the saddle to the horse. My dear creature, she actually rowed it over the river, put it on her head, and marched up to the barn to the utter amazement of the old man!"

"Did she ride the horse?"

"Of course she did, and had a capital time. I expected to see her brought home in fragments, but she managed him perfectly, and was the life of the party."

"Well, I call that plucky!" And young Mr. Lamb turned an approving glance upon Amy, wondering what his mother could be saying to make the girl look so red and uncomfortable.

She was still redder and more uncomfortable a moment after, when a sudden turn in the conversation introduced the subject of dress. One of the young ladies asked Jo where she got the pretty drab hat she wore to the picnic and stupid Jo, instead of mentioning the place where it was bought two years ago, must needs answer with unnecessary frankness, "Oh, Amy painted it. You can't buy those soft shades, so we paint ours any color we like. It's a great comfort to have an artistic sister."

"Isn't that an original idea?" cried Miss Lamb, who found Jo great fun.

"That's nothing compared to some of her brilliant performances. There's nothing the child can't do. Why, she wanted a pair of blue boots for Sallie's party, so she just painted her soiled white ones the loveliest shade of sky blue you ever saw, and they looked exactly like satin," added Jo, with an air of pride in her sister's accomplishments that exasperated Amy till she felt that it would be a relief to throw her cardcase at her.

"We read a story of yours the other day, and enjoyed it very much," observed the elder Miss Lamb, wishing to compliment the literary lady, who did not look the character just then, it must be confessed.

Any mention of her "works" always had a bad effect upon Jo, who either grew rigid and looked offended, or changed the subject with a brusque remark, as now. "Sorry you could find nothing better to read. I write that rubbish because it sells, and ordinary people like it. Are you going to New York this winter?"

As Miss Lamb had "enjoyed" the story, this speech was not exactly grateful or complimentary. The minute it was made Jo saw her mistake, but fearing to make the matter worse, suddenly remembered that it was for her to make the first move toward departure, and did so with an abruptness that left three people with half-finished sentences in their mouths.

"Amy, we *must* go. *Good*-by, dear, *do* come and see us; we are *pining* for a visit. I don't dare to ask *you,* Mr. Lamb, but if you *should* come, I don't think I shall have the heart to send you away."

Jo said this with such a droll imitation of May Chester's gushing style that Amy got out of the room as rapidly as possible, feeling a strong desire to laugh and cry at the same time.

"Didn't I do that well?" asked Jo, with a satisfied air as they walked away.

"Nothing could have been worse" was Amy's crushing reply. "What possessed you to tell those stories about my saddle, and the hats and boots, and all the rest of it?"

"Why, it's funny, and amuses people. They know we are poor, so it's no use pretending that we have grooms, buy three or four hats a season, and have things as easy and fine as they do."

"You needn't go and tell them all our little shifts, and expose our poverty in that perfectly unnecessary way. You haven't a bit of proper pride, and never will learn when to hold your tongue and when to speak," said Amy despairingly.

Poor Jo looked abashed, and silently chafed the end of her nose with the stiff handkerchief, as if performing a penance for her misdemeanors.

"How shall I behave here?" she asked, as they approached the third mansion.

"Just as you please. I wash my hands of you," was Amy's short answer.

"Then I'll enjoy myself. The boys are at home, and we'll have a comfortable time. Goodness knows I need a little change, for elegance has a bad effect upon my constitution," returned Jo gruffly, being disturbed by her failures to suit.

An enthusiastic welcome from three big boys and several pretty children speedily soothed her ruffled feelings, and leaving Amy to entertain the hostess and Mr. Tudor, who happened to be calling likewise, Jo devoted herself to the young folks and found the change refreshing. She listened to college stories with deep interest, caressed pointers and poodles without a murmur, agreed heartily that "Tom Brown was a brick," regardless of the improper form of praise; and when one lad proposed a visit to his turtle tank, she went with an alacrity which caused Mamma to smile upon her, as that motherly lady settled the cap which was left in a ruinous condition by filial hugs, bearlike but affectionate, and dearer to her than the most faultless coiffure from the hands of an inspired Frenchwoman.

Leaving her sister to her own devices, Amy proceeded to enjoy herself to her heart's content. Mr. Tudor's uncle had married an English lady who was third cousin to a living lord, and Amy regarded the whole family with great respect, for in spite of her American birth and breeding, she possessed that reverence for titles which haunts the best of us—that unacknowledged loyalty to the early faith in kings which set the most democratic nation under the sun in a ferment at the coming of a royal yellow-haired laddie, some years ago, and which still has something to do with the love the young country bears the old, like that of a big son for an imperious little mother, who held him while she could, and let him go with a farewell scolding when he rebelled. But even the satisfaction of talking with a distant connection of the British nobility did not render Amy forgetful of time, and when the proper number of minutes had passed, she reluctantly tore herself from this aristocratic society, and looked about for Jo, fervently hoping that her incorrigible sister would not be found in any position which should bring disgrace upon the name of March.

It might have been worse, but Amy considered it bad; for Jo sat on the grass, with an encampment of boys about her, and a dirty-footed dog reposing on the skirt of her state and festival dress, as she related one of Laurie's pranks to her admiring audience. One small child was poking turtles with Amy's cherished parasol, a second was eating gingerbread over Jo's best bonnet, and a third playing ball with her gloves. But all were enjoying themselves, and when Jo collected her damaged property to go, her escort accompanied her, begging her to come again, "It was such fun to hear about Laurie's larks."

"Capital boys, aren't they? I feel quite young and brisk again after that," said Jo, strolling along with her hands behind her, partly from habit, partly to conceal the bespattered parasol.

"Why do you always avoid Mr. Tudor?" asked Amy, wisely refraining from any comment upon Jo's dilapidated appearance.

"Don't like him, he puts on airs, snubs his sisters, worries his father, and doesn't speak respectfully of his mother. Laurie says he is fast, and *I* don't consider him a desirable acquaintance, so I let him alone."

"You might treat him civilly, at least. You gave him a cool nod, and just now you bowed and smiled in the politest way to Tommy Chamberlain, whose father keeps a grocery store. If you had just reversed the nod and the bow, it would have been right," said Amy reprovingly.

"No, it wouldn't," returned perverse Jo, "I neither like, respect, nor admire Tudor, though his grandfather's uncle's nephew's niece *was* third cousin to a lord. Tommy is poor and bashful and good and very clever. I think well of him, and like to show that I do, for he *is* a gentleman in spite of the brown-paper parcels."

"It's no use trying to argue with you," began Amy.

"Not the least, my dear," interrupted Jo, "so let us look amiable, and drop a card here, as the Kings are evidently out, for which I'm deeply grateful."

The family cardcase having done its duty the girls walked on, and Jo uttered another thanksgiving on reaching the fifth house, and being told that the young ladies were engaged.

"Now let us go home, and never mind Aunt March today. We can run down there any time, and it's really a pity to trail through the dust in our best bibs and tuckers, when we are tired and cross."

"Speak for yourself, if you please. Aunt likes to have us pay her the compliment of coming in style, and making a formal call; it's a little thing to do, but it gives her pleasure, and I don't believe it will hurt your things half so much as letting dirty dogs and clumping boys spoil them. Stoop down, and let me take the crumbs off of your bonnet."

"What a good girl you are, Amy!" said Jo, with a repentant glance from her own damaged costume to that of her sister, which was fresh and spotless still. "I wish it was as easy for me to do little things to please people as it is for you. I think of them, but it takes too much time to do them; so I wait for a chance to confer a great favor, and let the small ones slip; but they tell best in the end, I fancy."

Amy smiled and was mollified at once, saying with a maternal air, "Women should learn to be agreeable, particularly poor ones, for they have no other way of repaying the kindnesses they receive. If you'd remember that, and practice it, you'd be better liked than I am, because there is more of you."

"I'm a crotchety old thing, and always shall be, but I'm willing to own that you are right, only it's easier for me to risk my life for a person than to be pleasant to him when I don't feel like it. It's a great misfortune to have such strong likes and dislikes, isn't it?"

"It's a greater not to be able to hide them. I don't mind saying that I don't approve of Tudor any more than you do, but I'm not called upon to tell him so; neither are you, and there is no use in making yourself disagreeable because he is."

"But I think girls ought to show when they disapprove of young men, and how can they do it except by their manners? Preaching does not do any good, as I know to my sorrow, since I've had Teddy to manage; but there are many little ways in which I can influence him without a word, and I say we *ought* to do it to others if we can."

"Teddy is a remarkable boy, and can't be taken as a sample of other boys," said Amy, in a tone of solemn conviction, which would have convulsed the "remarkable boy," if he had heard it. "If we were belles, or women of wealth and position, we might do something, perhaps, but for us to frown at one set of young gentlemen because we don't approve of them, and smile upon another set because we do, wouldn't have a particle of effect, and we should only be considered odd and puritanical."

"So we are to countenance things and people which we detest, merely because we are not belles and millionaires, are we? That's a nice sort of morality."

"I can't argue about it, I only know that it's the way of the world, and people who set themselves against it only get laughed at for their pains. I don't like reformers, and I hope you will never try to be one."

"I do like them, and I shall be one if I can, for in spite of the laughing the world would never get on without them. We can't agree about that, for you belong to the old set, and I to the new: you will get on the best, but I shall have the liveliest time of it. I should rather enjoy the brickbats and hooting, I think."

"Well, compose yourself now, and don't worry Aunt with your new ideas."

"I'll try not to, but I'm always possessed to burst out with some particularly blunt speech or revolutionary sentiment before her; it's my doom, and I can't help it."

They found Aunt Carrol with the old lady, both absorbed in some very interesting subject, but they dropped it as the girls came in, with a conscious look which betrayed that they had been talking about their nieces. Jo was not in a good humor, and the perverse fit returned, but Amy, who had virtuously done her duty, kept her temper and pleased everybody, was in a most angelic frame of mind. This amiable spirit was felt at once, and both the aunts "my deared" her affectionately, looking what they afterward said emphatically, "That child improves every day."

"Are you going to help about the fair, dear?" asked Mrs.

Carrol, as Amy sat down beside her with the confiding air elderly people like so well in the young.

"Yes, Aunt. Mrs. Chester asked me if I would, and I offered to tend a table, as I have nothing but my time to give."

"I'm not," put in Jo decidedly. "I hate to be patronized, and the Chesters think it's a great favor to allow us to help with their highly connected fair. I wonder you consented, Amy, they only want you to work."

"I am willing to work: it's for the freedmen as well as the Chesters, and I think it very kind of them to let me share the labor and the fun. Patronage does not trouble me when it is well meant."

"Quite right and proper. I like your grateful spirit, my dear; it's a pleasure to help people who appreciate our efforts: some do not, and that is trying," observed Aunt March, looking over her spectacles at Jo, who sat apart, rocking herself, with a somewhat morose expression.

If Jo had only known what a great happiness was wavering in the balance for one of them, she would have turned dove-like in a minute; but, unfortunately, we don't have windows in our breasts, and cannot see what goes on in the minds of our friends; better for us that we cannot as a general thing, but now and then it would be such a comfort, such a saving of time and temper. By her next speech, Jo deprived herself of several years of pleasure, and received a timely lesson in the art of holding her tongue.

"I don't like favors, they oppress and make me feel like a slave. I'd rather do everything for myself, and be perfectly independent."

"Ahem!" coughed Aunt Carrol softly, with a look at Aunt March.

"I told you so," said Aunt March, with a decided nod to Aunt Carrol.

Mercifully unconscious of what she had done, Jo sat with her nose in the air, and a revolutionary aspect which was anything but inviting.

"Do you speak French, dear?" asked Mrs. Carrol, laying her hand on Amy's.

"Pretty well, thanks to Aunt March, who lets Esther talk to me as often as I like," replied Amy, with a grateful look, which caused the old lady to smile affably.

"How are you about languages?" asked Mrs. Carrol of Jo.

"Don't know a word. I'm very stupid about studying anything, can't bear French, it's such a slippery, silly sort of language," was the brusque reply.

Another look passed between the ladies, and Aunt March said to Amy, "You are quite strong and well, now, dear, I believe? Eyes don't trouble you any more, do they?"

"Not at all, thank you, ma'am. I'm very well, and mean to do great things next winter, so that I may be ready for Rome, whenever that joyful time arrives."

"Good girl! You deserve to go, and I'm sure you will some day," said Aunt March, with an approving pat on the head, as Amy picked up her ball for her.

Crosspatch, draw the latch,
Sit by the fire and spin,

squalled Polly, bending down from his perch on the back of her chair to peep into Jo's face, with such a comical air of impertinent inquiry that it was impossible to help laughing.

"Most observing bird," said the old lady.

"Come and take a walk, my dear?" cried Polly, hopping toward the china closet, with a look suggestive of lump sugar.

"Thank you, I will. Come, Amy." And Jo brought the visit to an end, feeling more strongly than ever that calls did have a bad effect upon her constitution. She shook hands in a gentlemanly manner, but Amy kissed both the aunts, and the girls departed, leaving behind them the impression of shadow and sunshine, which impression caused Aunt March to say, as they vanished—

"You'd better do it, Mary, I'll supply the money," and Aunt Carrol to reply decidedly, "I certainly will, if her father and mother consent."

Chapter 30

Consequences

MRS. CHESTER'S fair was so very elegant and select that it was considered a great honor by the young ladies of the neighborhood to be invited to take a table, and everyone was much interested in the matter. Amy was asked, but Jo was not, which was fortunate for all parties, as her elbows were decidedly akimbo at this period of her life, and it took a good many hard knocks to teach her how to get on easily. The "haughty, uninteresting creature" was let severely alone, but Amy's talent and taste were duly complimented by the offer of the art table, and she exerted herself to prepare and secure appropriate and valuable contributions to it.

Everything went on smoothly till the day before the fair opened, then there occurred one of the little skirmishes which it is almost impossible to avoid, when some five-and-twenty women, old and young, with all their private piques and prejudices, try to work together.

May Chester was rather jealous of Amy because the latter was a greater favorite than herself, and just at this time several trifling circumstances occurred to increase the feeling. Amy's dainty pen-and-ink work entirely eclipsed May's painted vases —that was one thorn; then the all-conquering Tudor had danced four times with Amy at a late party and only once with May—that was thorn number two; but the chief grievance that rankled in her soul, and gave her an excuse for her unfriendly conduct, was a rumor which some obliging gossip had whispered to her, that the March girls had made fun of her at the Lambs'. All the blame of this should have fallen upon Jo, for her naughty imitation had been too lifelike to escape detection, and the frolicsome Lambs had permitted the joke to escape. No hint of this had reached the culprits, however, and Amy's dismay can be imagined, when, the very evening before the fair, as she was putting the last touches to her pretty table, Mrs. Chester, who, of course, resented the supposed ridicule of her daughter, said, in a bland tone, but with a cold look—

"I find, dear, that there is some feeling among the young ladies about my giving this table to anyone but my girls. As this is the most prominent, and some say the most attractive table of all, and they are the chief getters-up of the fair, it is thought best for them to take this place. I'm sorry, but I know you are too sincerely interested in the cause to mind a little personal disappointment, and you shall have another table if you like."

Mrs. Chester had fancied beforehand that it would be easy to deliver this little speech, but when the time came, she found it rather difficult to utter it naturally, with Amy's unsuspicious eyes looking straight at her full of surprise and trouble.

Amy felt that there was something behind this, but could not guess what, and said quietly, feeling hurt, and showing that she did, "Perhaps you had rather I took no table at all?"

"Now, my dear, don't have any ill feeling, I beg; it's merely a matter of expediency, you see; my girls will naturally take the lead, and this table is considered their proper place. *I* think it very appropriate to you, and feel very grateful for your efforts to make it so pretty; but we must give up our private wishes, of course, and I will see that you have a good place elsewhere. Wouldn't you like the flower table? The little girls undertook it, but they are discouraged. You could make a charming thing of it, and the flower table is always attractive, you know."

"Especially to gentlemen," added May, with a look which enlightened Amy as to one cause of her sudden fall from favor. She colored angrily, but took no other notice of that girlish sarcasm, and answered with unexpected amiability—

"It shall be as you please, Mrs. Chester. I'll give up my place here at once, and attend to the flowers, if you like."

"You can put your own things on your own table, if you prefer," began May, feeling a little conscience-stricken, as she looked at the pretty racks, the painted shells, and quaint illuminations Amy had so carefully made and so gracefully arranged. She meant it kindly, but Amy mistook her meaning, and said quickly—

"Oh, certainly, if they are in your way"; and sweeping her contributions into her apron, pell-mell, she walked off, feeling that herself and her works of art had been insulted past forgiveness.

"Now she's mad. Oh, dear, I wish I hadn't asked you to speak, Mamma," said May, looking disconsolately at the empty spaces on her table.

"Girls' quarrels are soon over," returned her mother, feeling a trifle ashamed of her own part in this one, as well she might.

The little girls hailed Amy and her treasures with delight, which cordial reception somewhat soothed her perturbed spirit, and she fell to work, determined to succeed florally, if she could not artistically. But everything seemed against her: it was late, and she was tired; everyone was too busy with their own affairs to help her; and the little girls were only hindrances, for the dears fussed and chattered like so many magpies, making a great deal of confusion in their artless efforts to preserve the most perfect order. The evergreen arch wouldn't stay firm after she got it up, but wiggled and threatened to tumble down on her head when the hanging baskets were filled; her best tile got a splash of water, which left a sepia tear on the Cupid's cheek; she bruised her hands with hammering, and got cold working in a draft, which last affliction filled her with apprehensions for the morrow. Any girl reader who has suffered like afflictions will sympathize with poor Amy and wish her well through with her task.

There was great indignation at home when she told her story that evening. Her mother said it was a shame, but told her she had done right, Beth declared she wouldn't go to the fair at all, and Jo demanded why she didn't take all her pretty things and leave those mean people to get on without her.

"Because they are mean is no reason why I should be. I hate such things, and though I think I've a right to be hurt,

I don't intend to show it. They will feel that more than angry speeches or huffy actions, won't they, Marmee?"

"That's the right spirit, my dear; a kiss for a blow is always best, though it's not very easy to give it sometimes," said her mother, with the air of one who had learned the difference between preaching and practicing.

In spite of various very natural temptations to resent and retaliate, Amy adhered to her resolution all the next day, bent on conquering her enemy by kindness. She began well, thanks to a silent reminder that came to her unexpectedly, but most opportunely. As she arranged her table that morning, while the little girls were in an anteroom filling the baskets, she took up her pet production—a little book, the antique cover of which her father had found among his treasures, and in which on leaves of vellum she had beautifully illuminated different texts. As she turned the pages rich in dainty devices with very pardonable pride, her eye fell upon one verse that made her stop and think. Framed in a brilliant scrollwork of scarlet, blue, and gold, with little spirits of good will helping one another up and down among the thorns and flowers, were the words, "Thou shalt love thy neighbor as thyself."

"I ought, but I don't," thought Amy, as her eye went from the bright page to May's discontented face behind the big vases, that could not hide the vacancies her pretty work had once filled. Amy stood a minute, turning the leaves in her hand, reading on each some sweet rebuke for all heartburnings and uncharitableness of spirit. Many wise and true sermons are preached us every day by unconscious ministers in street, school, office, or home; even a fair table may become a pulpit, if it can offer the good and helpful words which are never out of season. Amy's conscience preached her a little sermon from that text, then and there, and she did what many of us do not always do—took the sermon to heart, and straightway put it in practice.

A group of girls were standing about May's table, admiring the pretty things, and talking over the change of saleswomen. They dropped their voices, but Amy knew they were speaking of her, hearing one side of the story and judging accordingly. It was not pleasant, but a better spirit had come over her, and presently a chance offered for proving it. She heard May say sorrowfully—

"It's too bad, for there is no time to make other things, and I don't want to fill up with odds and ends. The table was just complete then: now it's spoiled."

"I dare say she'd put them back if you asked her," suggested someone.

"How could I after all the fuss?" began May, but she did not finish, for Amy's voice came across the hall, saying pleasantly—

"You may have them, and welcome, without asking, if you want them. I was just thinking I'd offer to put them back, for they belong to your table rather than mine. Here they are, please take them, and forgive me if I was hasty in carrying them away last night."

As she spoke, Amy returned her contribution, with a nod and a smile, and hurried away again, feeling that it was easier to do a friendly thing than it was to stay and be thanked for it.

"Now, I call that lovely of her, don't you?" cried one girl.

May's answer was inaudible, but another young lady, whose temper was evidently a little soured by making lemonade, added, with a disagreeable laugh, "Very lovely, for she knew she wouldn't sell them at her own table."

Now, that was hard; when we make little sacrifices we like to have them appreciated, at least; and for a minute Amy was sorry she had done it, feeling that virtue was not always its own reward. But it is—as she presently discovered—for her spirits began to rise, and her table to blossom under her skillful hands, the girls were very kind, and that one little act seemed to have cleared the atmosphere amazingly.

It was a very long day and a hard one to Amy, as she sat behind her table, often quite alone, for the little girls deserted very soon: few cared to buy flowers in summer, and her bouquets began to droop long before night.

The art table *was* the most attractive in the room; there was a crowd about it all day long, and the tenders were constantly flying to and fro with important faces and rattling money boxes. Amy often looked wistfully across, longing to be there, where she felt at home and happy, instead of in a corner with nothing to do. It might seem no hardship to some of us, but to a pretty, blithe young girl, it was not only tedious, but very trying; and the thought of being found there in the evening by her family and Laurie and his friends made it a real martyrdom.

She did not go home till night, and then she looked so pale and quiet that they knew the day had been a hard one, though she made no complaint, and did not even tell what she had done. Her mother gave her an extra cordial cup of tea, Beth helped her dress, and made a charming little wreath for her hair, while Jo astonished her family by getting herself up with unusual care, and hinting darkly that the tables were about to be turned.

"Don't do anything rude, pray, Jo. I won't have any fuss made, so let it all pass and behave yourself," begged Amy, as she departed early, hoping to find a reinforcement of flowers to refresh her poor little table.

"I merely intend to make myself entrancingly agreeable to everyone I know, and to keep them in your corner as long as possible. Teddy and his boys will lend a hand, and we'll have a good time yet," returned Jo, leaning over the gate to watch for Laurie. Presently the familiar tramp was heard in the dusk, and she ran out to meet him.

"Is that my boy?"

"As sure as this is my girl!" And Laurie tucked her hand under his arm with the air of a man whose every wish was gratified.

"Oh, Teddy, such doings!" And Jo told Amy's wrongs with sisterly zeal.

"A flock of our fellows are going to drive over by-and-by, and I'll be hanged if I don't make them buy every flower she's got, and camp down before her table afterward," said Laurie, espousing her cause with warmth.

"The flowers are not at all nice, Amy says, and the fresh

ones may not arrive in time. I don't wish to be unjust or suspicious, but I shouldn't wonder if they never came at all. When people do one mean thing they are very likely to do another," observed Jo in a disgusted tone.

"Didn't Hayes give you the best out of our gardens? I told him to."

"I didn't know that, he forgot, I suppose, and, as your grandpa was poorly, I didn't like to worry him by asking, though I did want some."

"Now, Jo, how could you think there was any need of asking! They are just as much yours as mine. Don't we always go halves in everything?" began Laurie, in the tone that always made Jo turn thorny.

"Gracious, I hope not! Half of some of your things wouldn't suit me at all. But we musn't stand philandering here. I've got to help Amy, so you go and make yourself splendid, and if you'll be so very kind as to let Hayes take a few nice flowers up to the Hall, I'll bless you forever."

"Couldn't you do it now?" asked Laurie, so suggestively that Jo shut the gate in his face with inhospitable haste, and called through the bars, "Go away, Teddy, I'm busy."

Thanks to the conspirators, the tables *were* turned that night, for Hayes sent up a wilderness of flowers, with a lovely basket arranged in his best manner for a centerpiece; then the March family turned out en masse, and Jo exerted herself to some purpose, for people not only came, but stayed, laughing at her nonsense, admiring Amy's taste, and apparently enjoying themselves very much. Laurie and his friends gallantly threw themselves into the breach, bought up the bouquets, encamped before the table, and made that corner the liveliest spot in the room. Amy was in her element now, and, out of gratitude, if nothing more, was as sprightly and gracious as possible—coming to the conclusion, about that time, that virtue *was* its own reward, after all.

Jo behaved herself with exemplary propriety, and when Amy was happily surrounded by her guard of honor, Jo circulated about the hall, picking up various bits of gossip, which enlightened her upon the subject of the Chester change of base. She reproached herself for her share of the ill feeling and resolved to exonerate Amy as soon as possible; she also discovered what Amy had done about the things in the morning, and considered her a model of magnanimity. As she passed the art table, she glanced over it for her sister's things, but saw no signs of them. "Tucked away out of sight, I dare say," thought Jo, who could forgive her own wrongs, but hotly resented any insult offered to her family.

"Good evening, Miss Jo. How does Amy get on?" asked May with a conciliatory air, for she wanted to show that she also could be generous.

"She has sold everything she had that was worth selling, and now she is enjoying herself. The flower table is always attractive, you know, 'especially to gentlemen.'"

Jo *couldn't* resist giving that little slap, but May took it so meekly she regretted it a minute after, and fell to praising the great vases, which still remained unsold.

"Is Amy's illumination anywhere about? I took a fancy to buy that for Father," said Jo, very anxious to learn the fate of her sister's work.

"Everything of Amy's sold long ago; I took care that the right people saw them, and they made a nice little sum of money for us," returned May, who had overcome sundry small temptations, as well as Amy, that day.

Much gratified, Jo rushed back to tell the good news, and Amy looked both touched and surprised by the report of May's words and manner.

"Now, gentlemen, I want you to go and do your duty by the other tables as generously as you have by mine—especially the art table," she said, ordering out "Teddy's Own," as the girls called the college friends.

"'Charge, Chester, charge!' is the motto for that table, but do your duty like men, and you'll get your money's worth of *art* in every sense of the word," said the irrepressible Jo, as the devoted phalanx prepared to take the field.

"To hear is to obey, but March is fairer far than May," said little Parker, making a frantic effort to be both witty and tender, and getting promptly quenched by Laurie, who said,

"Very well, my son, for a small boy!" and walked him off, with a paternal pat on the head.

"Buy the vases," whispered Amy to Laurie, as a final heaping of coals of fire on her enemy's head.

To May's great delight, Mr. Laurence not only bought the vases, but pervaded the hall with one under each arm. The other gentlemen speculated with equal rashness in all sorts of frail trifles, and wandered helplessly about afterward, burdened with wax flowers, painted fans, filigree portfolios, and other useful and appropriate purchases.

Aunt Carrol was there, heard the story, looked pleased, and said something to Mrs. March in a corner, which made the latter lady beam with satisfaction, and watch Amy with a face full of mingled pride and anxiety, though she did not betray the cause of her pleasure till several days later.

The fair was pronounced a success; and when May bade Amy good night, she did not gush as usual, but gave her an affectionate kiss, and a look which said, "Forgive and forget." That satisfied Amy, and when she got home she found the vases paraded on the parlor chimney piece with a great bouquet in each. "The reward of merit for a magnanimous March," as Laurie announced with a flourish.

"You've a deal more principle and generosity and nobleness of character than I ever gave you credit for, Amy. You've behaved sweetly, and I respect you with all my heart," said Jo warmly, as they brushed their hair together late that night.

"Yes, we all do, and love her for being so ready to forgive. It must have been dreadfully hard, after working so long and setting your heart on selling your own pretty things. I don't believe I could have done it as kindly as you did," added Beth from her pillow.

"Why, girls, you needn't praise me so. I only did as I'd be done by. You laugh at me when I say I want to be a lady, but I mean a true gentlewoman in mind and manners, and I try to do it as far as I know how. I can't explain exactly, but I want to be above the little meannesses and follies and faults that spoil so many women. I'm far from it now, but I do my best, and hope in time to be what Mother is."

Amy spoke earnestly, and Jo said, with a cordial hug, "I understand now what you mean, and I'll never laugh at you again. You are getting on faster than you think, and I'll take lessons of you in true politeness, for you've learned the secret, I believe. Try away, deary, you'll get your reward some day, and no one will be more delighted than I shall."

A week later Amy did get her reward, and poor Jo found it hard to be delighted. A letter came from Aunt Carrol, and Mrs. March's face was illuminated to such a degree when she read it that Jo and Beth, who were with her, demanded what the glad tidings were.

"Aunt Carrol is going abroad next month, and wants—"

"Me to go with her!" burst in Jo, flying out of her chair in an uncontrollable rapture.

"No, dear, not you; it's Amy."

"Oh, Mother! She's too young, it's my turn first. I've wanted it so long—it would do me so much good, and be so altogether splendid—I *must* go."

"I'm afraid it's impossible, Jo. Aunt says Amy, decidedly, and it is not for us to dictate when she offers such a favor."

"It's always so. Amy has all the fun and I have all the work. It isn't fair, oh, it isn't fair!" cried Jo passionately.

"I'm afraid it is partly your own fault, dear. When Aunt spoke to me the other day, she regretted your blunt manners and too independent spirit; and here she writes, as if quoting something you had said—'I planned at first to ask Jo, but as "favors burden her," and she "hates French," I think I won't venture to invite her. Amy is more docile, will make a good companion for Flo, and receive gratefully any help the trip may give her.'"

"Oh, my tongue, my abominable tongue! Why can't I learn to keep it quiet?" groaned Jo, remembering words which had been her undoing. When she had heard the explanation of the quoted phrases, Mrs. March said sorrowfully—

"I wish you could have gone, but there is no hope of it this time; so try to bear it cheerfully, and don't sadden Amy's pleasure by reproaches or regrets."

"I'll try," said Jo, winking hard as she knelt down to pick

up the basket she had joyfully upset. "I'll take a leaf out of her book, and try not only to seem glad, but to be so, and not grudge her one minute of happiness; but it won't be easy, for it is a dreadful disappointment." And poor Jo bedewed the little fat pincushion she held with several very bitter tears.

"Jo, dear, I'm very selfish, but I couldn't spare you, and I'm glad you are not going quite yet," whispered Beth, embracing her, basket and all, with such a clinging touch and loving face that Jo felt comforted in spite of the sharp regret that made her want to box her own ears, and humbly beg Aunt Carrol to burden her with this favor, and see how gratefully she would bear it.

By the time Amy came in, Jo was able to take her part in the family jubilation, not quite as heartily as usual, perhaps, but without repinings at Amy's good fortune. The young lady herself received the news as tidings of great joy, went about in a solemn sort of rapture, and began to sort her colors and pack her pencils that evening, leaving such trifles as clothes, money, and passports to those less absorbed in visions of art than herself.

"It isn't a mere pleasure trip to me, girls," she said impressively, as she scraped her best palette. "It will decide my career, for if I have any genius, I shall find it out in Rome, and will do something to prove it."

"Suppose you haven't?" said Jo, sewing away, with red eyes, at the new collars which were to be handed over to Amy.

"Then I shall come home and teach drawing for my living," replied the aspirant for fame, with philosophic composure; but she made a wry face at the prospect, and scratched away at her palette as if bent on vigorous measures before she gave up her hopes.

"No, you won't. You hate hard work, and you'll marry some rich man, and come home to sit in the lap of luxury all your days," said Jo.

"Your predictions sometimes come to pass, but I don't believe that one will. I'm sure I wish it would, for if I can't be an artist myself, I should like to be able to help those who are," said Amy, smiling, as if the part of Lady Bountiful would suit her better than that of a poor drawing teacher.

"Hum!" said Jo, with a sigh. "If you wish it you'll have it, for your wishes are always granted—mine never."

"Would you like to go?" asked Amy, thoughtfully patting her nose with her knife.

"Rather!"

"Well, in a year or two I'll send for you, and we'll dig in the Forum for relics, and carry out all the plans we've made so many times."

"Thank you, I'll remind you of your promise when that joyful day comes, if it ever does," returned Jo, accepting the vague but magnificent offer as gratefully as she could.

There was not much time for preparation, and the house was in a ferment till Amy was off. Jo bore up very well till the last flutter of blue ribbon vanished, when she retired to her refuge, the garret, and cried till she couldn't cry any more. Amy likewise bore up stoutly till the steamer sailed; then, just as the gangway was about to be withdrawn, it suddenly came over her that a whole ocean was soon to roll between her and those who loved her best, and she clung to Laurie, the last lingerer, saying with a sob—

"Oh, take care of them for me, and if anything should happen—"

"I will, dear, I will, and if anything happens, I'll come and comfort you," whispered Laurie, little dreaming that he would be called upon to keep his word.

So Amy sailed away to find the Old World, which is always new and beautiful to young eyes, while her father and friend watched her from the shore, fervently hoping that none but gentle fortunes would befall the happy-hearted girl, who waved her hand to them till they could see nothing but the summer sunshine dazzling on the sea.

Chapter 31

Our Foreign Correspondent

LONDON

DEAREST PEOPLE,

Here I really sit at a front window of the Bath Hotel, Piccadilly. It's not a fashionable place, but Uncle stopped here years ago, and won't go anywhere else; however, we don't mean to stay long, so it's no great matter. Oh, I can't begin to tell you how I enjoy it all! I never can, so I'll only give you bits out of my notebook, for I've done nothing but sketch and scribble since I started.

I sent a line from Halifax, when I felt pretty miserable, but after that I got on delightfully, seldom ill, on deck all day, with plenty of pleasant people to amuse me. Everyone was very kind to me, especially the officers. Don't laugh, Jo, gentlemen really are very necessary aboard ship, to hold on to, or to wait upon one; and as they have nothing to do, it's a mercy to make them useful, otherwise they would smoke themselves to death, I'm afraid.

Aunt and Flo were poorly all the way, and liked to be let alone, so when I had done what I could for them, I went and enjoyed myself. Such walks on deck, such sunsets, such splendid air and waves! It was almost as exciting as riding a fast horse, when we went rushing on so grandly. I wish Beth could have come, it would have done her so much good; as for Jo, she would have gone up and sat on the maintop jib, or whatever the high thing is called, made friends with the engineers, and tooted on the captain's speaking trumpet, she'd have been in such a state of rapture.

It was all heavenly, but I was glad to see the Irish coast, and found it very lovely, so green and sunny, with brown cabins here and there, ruins on some of the hills, and gentlemen's countryseats in the valleys, with deer feeding in the parks. It was early in the morning, but I didn't regret getting up to see it, for the bay was full of little boats, the shore *so* picturesque, and a rosy sky overhead. I never shall forget it.

At Queenstown one of my new acquaintances left us—Mr. Lennox—and when I said something about the Lakes of Killarney, he sighed and sang, with a look at me—

> "Oh, have you e'er heard of Kate Kearney?
> She lives on the banks of Killarney;
> From the glance of her eye,
> Shun danger and fly,
> For fatal's the glance of Kate Kearney."

Wasn't that nonsensical?

We only stopped at Liverpool a few hours. It's a dirty, noisy place, and I was glad to leave it. Uncle rushed out and bought a pair of dogskin gloves, some ugly, thick shoes, and an umbrella, and got shaved à la mutton chop, the first thing. Then he flattered himself that he looked like a true Briton, but the first time he had the mud cleaned off his shoes, the little bootblack knew that an American stood in them, and said, with a grin, "There yer har, sir. I've give 'em the latest Yankee shine." It amused Uncle immensely. Oh, I *must* tell you what that absurd Lennox did! He got his friend Ward, who came on with us, to order a bouquet for me, and the first thing I saw in my room was a lovely one, with "Robert Lennox's compliments," on the card. Wasn't that fun, girls? I like traveling.

I never *shall* get to London if I don't hurry. The trip was like riding through a long picture gallery, full of lovely landscapes. The farmhouses were my delight, with thatched roofs, ivy up to the eaves, latticed windows, and stout women with rosy children at the doors. The very cattle looked more tranquil than ours, as they stood knee-deep in clover, and the hens had a contented cluck, as if they never got nervous like Yankee biddies. Such perfect color I never saw—the grass so green, sky so blue, grain so yellow, woods so dark— I was in a rapture all the way. So was Flo, and we kept bouncing from one side to the other, trying to see everything while we were whisking along at the rate of sixty miles an hour. Aunt was tired and went to sleep, but Uncle read his guidebook, and wouldn't be astonished at anything. This is the way we went on: Amy, flying up—"Oh, that must be Kenilworth, that gray place among the trees!" Flo, darting to my window—"How sweet! We must go there some time, won't we, Papa?" Uncle, calmly admiring his boots—"No, my dear, not unless you want beer; that's a brewery."

A pause—then Flo cried out, "Bless me, there's a gallows and a man going up." "Where, where?" shrieks Amy, staring out at two tall posts with a crossbeam and some dangling chains. "A colliery," remarks Uncle, with a twinkle of the eye. "Here's a lovely flock of lambs all lying down," says Amy. "See, Papa, aren't they pretty!" added Flo sentimentally. "Geese, young ladies," returns Uncle, in a tone that keeps us quiet till Flo settles down to enjoy *The Flirtations of Capt. Cavendish*, and I have the scenery all to myself.

Of course it rained when we got to London, and there was nothing to be seen but fog and umbrellas. We rested, unpacked, and shopped a little between the showers. Aunt Mary got me some new things, for I came off in such a hurry I wasn't half ready. A white hat and blue feather, a muslin dress to match, and the loveliest mantle you ever saw. Shopping in Regent Street is perfectly splendid; things seem so cheap—nice ribbons only sixpence a yard. I laid in a stock, but shall get my gloves in Paris. Doesn't that sound sort of elegant and rich?

Flo and I, for the fun of it, ordered a hansom cab, while Aunt and Uncle were out, and went for a drive, though we learned afterward that it wasn't the thing for young ladies to ride in them alone. It was so droll! for when we were shut in by the wooden apron, the man drove so fast that Flo was frightened, and told me to stop him. But he was up outside behind somewhere, and I couldn't get at him. He didn't hear me call, nor see me flap my parasol in front, and there we were, quite helpless, rattling away, and whirling around corners at a breakneck pace. At last, in my despair,

I saw a little door in the roof, and on poking it open, a red eye appeared, and a beery voice said—

"Now then, mum?"

I gave my order as soberly as I could, and slamming down the door, with an "Aye, aye, mum," the man made his horse walk, as if going to a funeral. I poked again and said, "A little faster," then off he went, helter-skelter as before, and we resigned ourselves to our fate.

Today was fair, and we went to Hyde Park, close by, for we are more aristocratic than we look. The Duke of Devonshire lives near. I often see his footmen lounging at the back gate; and the Duke of Wellington's house is not far off. Such sights as I saw, my dear! It was as good as Punch, for there were fat dowagers rolling about in their red and yellow coaches, with gorgeous Jeameses in silk stockings and velvet coats, up behind, and powdered coachmen in front. Smart maids, with the rosiest children I ever saw, handsome girls, looking half asleep, dandies in queer English hats and lavender kids lounging about, and tall soldiers, in short red jackets and muffin caps stuck on one side, looking so funny I longed to sketch them.

Rotten Row means "*Route de Roi,*" or the king's way, but now it's more like a riding school than anything else. The horses are splendid, and the men, especially the grooms, ride well; but the women are stiff, and bounce, which isn't according to our rules. I longed to show them a tearing American gallop, for they trotted solemnly up and down, in their scant habits and high hats, looking like the women in a toy Noah's Ark. Everyone rides—old men, stout ladies, little children— and the young folks do a deal of flirting here, I saw a pair exchange rose buds, for it's the thing to wear one in the buttonhole, and I thought it rather a nice little idea.

In the P.M. to Westminster Abbey, but don't expect me to describe it, that's impossible—so I'll only say it was sublime! This evening we are going to see Fechter, which will be an appropriate end to the happiest day of my life.

MIDNIGHT

It's very late, but I can't let my letter go in the morning without telling you what happened last evening. Who do you think came in, as we were at tea? Laurie's English friends, Fred and Frank Vaughn! I was *so* surprised, for I shouldn't have known them but for the cards. Both are tall fellows with whiskers, Fred handsome in the English style, and Frank much better, for he only limps slightly, and uses no crutches. They had heard from Laurie where we were to be, and came to ask us to their house; but Uncle won't go, so we shall return the call, and see them as we can. They went to the theater with us, and we did have *such* a good time, for Frank devoted himself to Flo, and Fred and I talked over past, present, and future fun as if we had known each other all our days. Tell Beth Frank asked for her, and was sorry to hear of her ill health. Fred laughed when I spoke of Jo, and sent his "respectful compliments to the big hat." Neither of them had forgotten Camp Laurence, or the fun we had there. What ages ago it seems, doesn't it?

Aunt is tapping on the wall for the third time, so I *must* stop. I really feel like a dissipated London fine lady, writing here so late, with my room full of pretty things, and my head a jumble of parks, theaters, new gowns, and gallant creatures who say "Ah!" and twirl their blond mustaches with the true English lordliness. I long to see you all, and in spite of my nonsense am, as ever, your loving   AMY

PARIS

DEAR GIRLS,

In my last I told you about our London visit—how kind the Vaughns were, and what pleasant parties they made for us. I enjoyed the trips to Hampton Court and the Kensington Museum more than anything else—for at Hampton I saw Raphael's cartoons, and, at the Museum, rooms full of pictures by Turner, Lawrence, Reynolds, Hogarth, and the other great creatures. The day in Richmond Park was charming, for we had a regular English picnic, and I had more splendid oaks and groups of deer than I could copy; also heard a nightingale, and saw larks go up. We "did" London to our hearts' content, thanks to Fred and Frank, and were sorry to go away; for though English people are slow to take you in, when they once make up their minds to do it they cannot be outdone in hospitality, *I* think. The Vaughns hope to meet us in Rome next winter, and I shall be dreadfully disappointed if they don't, for Grace and I are great friends, and the boys very nice fellows—especially Fred.

Well, we were hardly settled here, when he turned up again, saying he had come for a holiday, and was going to Switzerland. Aunt looked sober at first, but he was so cool about it she couldn't say a word; and now we get on nicely, and are very glad he came, for he speaks French like a native, and I don't know what we should do without him. Uncle doesn't know ten words, and insists on talking English very loud, as if that would make people understand him. Aunt's pronunciation is old-fashioned, and Flo and I, though we flattered ourselves that we knew a good deal, find we don't, and are very grateful to have Fred do the "*parley vooing*," as Uncle calls it.

Such delightful times as we are having! Sight-seeing from morning till night, stopping for nice lunches in the gay cafés, and meeting with all sorts of droll adventures. Rainy days I spend in the Louvre, reveling in pictures. Jo would turn up her naughty nose at some of the finest, because she has no soul for art, but *I* have, and I'm cultivating eye and taste as fast as I can. She would like the relics of great people better, for I've seen her Napoleon's cocked hat and gray coat, his baby's cradle and his old toothbrush; also Marie Antoinette's little shoe, the ring of Saint Denis, Charlemagne's sword, and many other interesting things. I'll talk for hours about them when I come, but haven't time to write.

The Palais Royale is a heavenly place—so full of *bijouterie* and lovely things that I'm nearly distracted because I can't buy them. Fred wanted to get me some, but of course I didn't allow it. Then the Bois and the Champs Elysées are *très magnifique*. I've seen the imperial family several times—

the emperor an ugly, hard-looking man, the empress pale and pretty, but dressed in bad taste, *I* thought—purple dress, green hat, and yellow gloves. Little Nap is a handsome boy, who sits chatting to his tutor, and kisses his hand to the people as he passes in his four-horse barouche, with postilions in red satin jackets and a mounted guard before and behind.

We often walk in the Tuileries Gardens, for they are lovely, though the antique Luxembourg Gardens suit me better. Père la Chaise is very curious, for many of the tombs are like small rooms, and looking in, one sees a table, with images or pictures of the dead, and chairs for the mourners to sit in when they come to lament. That is so Frenchy.

Our rooms are on the Rue de Rivoli, and sitting on the balcony, we look up and down the long, brilliant street. It is so pleasant that we spend our evenings talking there when too tired with our day's work to go out. Fred is very entertaining, and is altogether the most agreeable young man I ever knew—except Laurie, whose manners are more charming. I wish Fred was dark, for I don't fancy light men, however, the Vaughns are very rich and come of an excellent family, so I won't find fault with their yellow hair, as my own is yellower.

Next week we are off to Germany and Switzerland, and as we shall travel fast, I shall only be able to give you hasty letters. I keep my diary, and try to "remember correctly and describe clearly all that I see and admire," as Father advised. It is good practice for me, and with my sketchbook will give you a better idea of my tour than these scribbles.

Adieu, I embrace you tenderly.

VOTRE AMIE

HEIDELBERG

MY DEAR MAMMA,

Having a quiet hour before we leave for Berne, I'll try to tell you what has happened, for some of it is very important, as you will see.

The sail up the Rhine was perfect, and I just sat and enjoyed it with all my might. Get Father's old guidebooks and read about it, I haven't words beautiful enough to describe it. At Coblenz we had a lovely time, for some students from Bonn, with whom Fred got acquainted on the boat, gave us a serenade. It was a moonlight night, and about one o'clock Flo and I were waked by the most delicious music under our windows. We flew up, and hid behind the curtains, but sly peeps showed us Fred and the students singing away down below. It was the most romantic thing I ever saw—the river, the bridge of boats, the great fortress opposite, moonlight everywhere, and music fit to melt a heart of stone.

When they were done we threw down some flowers, and saw them scramble for them, kiss their hands to the invisible ladies, and go laughing away—to smoke and drink beer, I suppose. Next morning Fred showed me one of the crumpled flowers in his vest pocket, and looked very sentimental. I laughed at him, and said I didn't throw it, but Flo, which seemed to disgust him, for he tossed it out of the window, and turned sensible again. I'm afraid I'm going to have trouble with that boy, it begins to look like it.

The baths at Nassau were very gay, so was Baden-Baden, where Fred lost some money, and I scolded him. He needs someone to look after him when Frank is not with him. Kate said once she hoped he'd marry soon, and I quite agree with her that it would be well for him. Frankfurt was delightful; I saw Goethe's house, Schiller's statue, and Dannecker's famous *Ariadne*. It was very lovely, but I should have enjoyed it more if I had known the story better. I didn't like to ask, as everyone knew it or pretended they did. I wish Jo would tell me all about it; I ought to have read more, for I find I don't know anything, and it mortifies me.

Now comes the serious part—for it happened here, and Fred is just gone. He has been so kind and jolly that we all got quite fond of him, I never thought of anything but a traveling friendship till the serenade night. Since then I've begun to feel that the moonlight walks, balcony talks, and daily adventures were something more to him than fun. I

haven't flirted, Mother, truly, but remembered what you said
to me, and have done my very best. I can't help it if people
like me; I don't try to make them, and it worries me if I don't
care for them, though Jo says I haven't got any heart. Now
I know Mother will shake her head, and the girls say, "Oh,
the mercenary little wretch!" but I've made up my mind,
and, if Fred asks me, I shall accept him, though I'm not
madly in love. I like him, and we get on comfortably together.
He is handsome, young, clever enough, and very rich—ever
so much richer than the Laurences. I don't think his family
would object, and I should be very happy, for they are all
kind, well-bred, generous people, and they like me. Fred, as
the eldest twin, will have the estate, I suppose, and such a
splendid one as it is! A city house in a fashionable street, not
so showy as our big houses, but twice as comfortable and
full of solid luxury, such as English people believe in. I like
it, for it's genuine. I've seen the plate, the family jewels, the
old servants, and pictures of the country place, with its park,
great house, lovely grounds, and fine horses. Oh, it would be
all I should ask! And I'd rather have it than any title such
as girls snap up so readily, and find nothing behind. I may
be mercenary, but I hate poverty, and don't mean to bear it
a minute longer than I can help. One of us *must* marry well;
Meg didn't, Jo won't, Beth can't yet, so I shall, and make
everything cozy all round. I wouldn't marry a man I hated or
despised. You may be sure of that; and though Fred is not my
model hero, he does very well, and in time I should get fond
enough of him if he was very fond of me, and let me do just
as I liked. So I've been turning the matter over in my mind
the last week, for it was impossible to help seeing that Fred
liked me. He said nothing, but little things showed it; he never
goes with Flo, always gets on my side of the carriage, table,
or promenade, looks sentimental when we are alone, and
frowns at anyone else who ventures to speak to me. Yesterday at dinner, when an Austrian officer stared at us and then
said something to his friend—a rakish-looking baron—about
"ein wonderschönes Blöndchen," Fred looked as fierce as a

lion, and cut his meat so savagely it nearly flew off his plate. He isn't one of the cool, stiff Englishmen, but is rather peppery, for he has Scotch blood in him, as one might guess from his bonnie blue eyes.

Well, last evening we went up to the castle about sunset— at least all of us but Fred, who was to meet us there after going to the Post Restante for letters. We had a charming time poking about the ruins, the vaults where the monster tun is, and the beautiful gardens made by the elector long ago for his English wife. I liked the great terrace best, for the view was divine, so while the rest went to see the rooms inside, I sat there trying to sketch the gray stone lion's head on the wall, with scarlet woodbine sprays hanging round it. I felt as if I'd got into a romance, sitting there, watching the Neckar rolling through the valley, listening to the music of the Austrian band below, and waiting for my lover, like a real storybook girl. I had a feeling that something was going to happen and I was ready for it. I didn't feel blushy or quakey, but quite cool and only a little excited.

By-and-by I heard Fred's voice, and then he came hurrying through the great arch to find me. He looked so troubled that I forgot all about myself, and asked what the matter was. He said he'd just got a letter begging him to come home, for Frank was very ill; so he was going at once on the night train and only had time to say good-by. I was very sorry for him, and disappointed for myself, but only for a minute because he said, as he shook hands—and said it in a way that I could not mistake—"I shall soon come back, you won't forget me, Amy?"

I didn't promise, but I looked at him, and he seemed satisfied, and there was no time for anything but messages and good-bys, for he was off in an hour, and we all miss him very much. I know he wanted to speak, but I think, from something he once hinted, that he had promised his father not to do anything of the sort yet a while, for he is a rash boy, and the old gentleman dreads a foreign daughter-in-law. We shall soon meet in Rome, and then, if I don't change my mind, I'll say "Yes, thank you," when he says "Will you, please?"

Of course this is all *very private*, but I wished you to know what was going on. Don't be anxious about me, remember I am your "prudent Amy," and be sure I will do nothing rashly. Send me as much advice as you like, I'll use it if I can. I wish I could see you for a good talk, Marmee. Love and trust me.

Ever your

AMY

Chapter 32

Tender Troubles

"JO, I'M ANXIOUS ABOUT BETH."

"Why, Mother, she has seemed unusually well since the babies came."

"It's not her health that troubles me now, it's her spirits. I'm sure there is something on her mind, and I want you to discover what it is."

"What makes you think so, Mother?"

"She sits alone a good deal, and doesn't talk to her father as much as she used. I found her crying over the babies the other day. When she sings, the songs are always sad ones, and now and then I see a look in her face that I don't understand. This isn't like Beth, and it worries me."

"Have you asked her about it?"

"I have tried once or twice, but she either evaded my questions or looked so distressed that I stopped. I never force my children's confidence, and I seldom have to wait for it long."

Mrs. March glanced at Jo as she spoke, but the face opposite seemed quite unconscious of any secret disquietude but Beth's, and after sewing thoughtfully for a minute, Jo said, "I think she is growing up, and so begins to dream dreams, and have hopes and fears and fidgets, without knowing why or being able to explain them. Why, mother, Beth's eighteen, but we don't realize it, and treat her like a child, forgetting she's a woman."

"So she is. Dear heart, how fast you do grow up," returned her mother with a sigh and a smile.

"Can't be helped, Marmee, so you must resign yourself to all sorts of worries, and let your birds hop out of the nest, one by one. I promise never to hop very far, if that is any comfort to you."

"It is a great comfort, Jo, I always feel strong when you are at home, now Meg is gone. Beth is too feeble and Amy too young to depend upon, but when the tug comes, you are always ready."

"Why, you know I don't mind hard jobs much, and there must always be one scrub in a family. Amy is splendid in fine works and I'm not, but I feel in my element when all the carpets are to be taken up, or half the family fall sick at once. Amy is distinguishing herself abroad, but if anything is amiss at home, I'm your man."

"I leave Beth to your hands, then, for she will open her tender little heart to her Jo sooner than to anyone else. Be very kind, and don't let her think anyone watches or talks about her. If she only would get quite strong and cheerful again, I shouldn't have a wish in the world."

"Happy woman! I've got heaps."

"My dear, what are they?"

"I'll settle Bethy's troubles, and then I'll tell you mine. They are not very wearing, so they'll keep." And Jo stitched away, with a wise nod which set her mother's heart at rest about her for the present at least.

While apparently absorbed in her own affairs, Jo watched Beth, and after many conflicting conjectures, finally settled upon one which seemed to explain the change in her. A slight incident gave Jo the clue to the mystery, she thought, and lively fancy, loving heart did the rest. She was affecting to write busily one Saturday afternoon, when she and Beth were alone together; yet as she scribbled, she kept her eye on her sister, who seemed unusually quiet. Sitting at the window, Beth's work often dropped into her lap, and she leaned her head upon her hand, in a dejected attitude, while her eyes rested on the dull, autumnal landscape. Suddenly some one passed below, whistling like an operatic blackbird, and a voice called out, "All serene! Coming in tonight."

Beth started, leaned forward, smiled and nodded, watched the passer-by till his quick tramp died away, then said softly as if to herself, "How strong and well and happy that dear boy looks."

"Hum!" said Jo, still intent upon her sister's face, for the bright color faded as quickly as it came, the smile vanished, and presently a tear lay shining on the window ledge. Beth whisked it off and glanced apprehensively at Jo; but she was scratching away at a tremendous rate, apparently engrossed in *Olympia's Oath*. The instant Beth turned, Jo began her watch again, saw Beth's hand go quietly to her eyes more than once, and in her half-averted face read a tender sorrow that made her own eyes fill. Fearing to betray herself, she slipped away, murmuring something about needing more paper.

"Mercy on me, Beth loves Laurie!" she said, sitting down in her own room, pale with the shock of the discovery which she believed she had just made. "I never dreamed of such a thing. What *will* Mother say? I wonder if he—" There Jo stopped and turned scarlet with a sudden thought. "If he shouldn't love back again, how dreadful it would be. He must. I'll make him!" And she shook her head threateningly at the picture of the mischievous-looking boy laughing at her from the wall. "Oh dear, we *are* growing up with a vengeance. Here's Meg married and a mamma, Amy flourishing away at Paris, and Beth in love. I'm the only one that has sense enough to keep out of mischief." Jo thought intently for a minute with her eyes fixed on the picture, then she smoothed out her wrinkled forehead and said, with a decided nod at the face opposite, "No thank you, sir, you're very charming, but you've no more stability than a weathercock; so you needn't write touching notes and smile in that insinuating way, for it won't do a bit of good, and I won't have it."

Then she sighed, and fell into a reverie from which she did not wake till the early twilight sent her down to take new observations, which only confirmed her suspicion. Though Laurie flirted with Amy and joked with Jo, his manner to Beth had always been peculiarly kind and gentle, but so was everybody's; therefore, no one thought of imagining that he cared more for her than for the others. Indeed, a general impression had prevailed in the family of late that "our boy" was getting fonder than ever of Jo, who, however, wouldn't hear a word upon the subject and scolded violently if anyone dared to suggest it. If they had known the various tender passages of the past year, or rather attempts at tender passages which had been nipped in the bud, they would have had the immense satisfaction of saying, "I told you so." But Jo hated "philandering," and wouldn't allow it, always having a joke or a smile ready at the least sign of impending danger.

When Laurie first went to college, he fell in love about once a month; but these small flames were as brief as ardent, did no damage, and much amused Jo, who took great interest in the alternations of hope, despair, and resignation, which were confided to her in their weekly conferences. But there came a time when Laurie ceased to worship at many shrines, hinted darkly at one all-absorbing passion, and indulged occasionally in Byronic fits of gloom. Then he avoided the tender subject altogether, wrote philosophical notes to Jo, turned studious, and gave out that he was going to "dig," intending to graduate in a blaze of glory. This suited the young lady better than twilight confidences, tender pressures of the hand, and eloquent glances of the eye, for with Jo, brain developed earlier than heart, and she preferred imaginary heroes to real ones, because when tired of them, the former could be shut up in the tin kitchen till called for, and the latter were less manageable.

Things were in this state when the grand discovery was made, and Jo watched Laurie that night as she had never done before. If she had not got the new idea into her head, she would have seen nothing unusual in the fact that Beth was very quiet, and Laurie very kind to her. But having given the rein to her lively fancy, it galloped away with her at a great pace, and common sense, being rather weakened by a long course of romance writing, did not come to the rescue. As usual Beth lay on the sofa and Laurie sat in a low chair close by, amusing her with all sorts of gossip, for she depended on her weekly "spin," and he never disappointed her. But that evening Jo fancied that Beth's eyes rested on the lively, dark face beside her with peculiar pleasure, and that she listened with intense interest to an account of some exciting cricket match, though the phrases, "caught off a tice," "stumped off his ground," and "the leg hit for three," were as intelligible to her as Sanskrit. She also fancied, having set her heart upon seeing it, that she saw a certain increase of gentleness in Laurie's manner, that he dropped his voice now and then, laughed less than usual, was a little absent-minded, and settled the afghan over Beth's feet with an assiduity that was really almost tender.

"Who knows? Stranger things have happened," thought Jo, as she fussed about the room. "She will make quite an angel of him, and he will make life delightfully easy and pleasant for the dear, if they only love each other. I don't see how he can help it, and I do believe he would if the rest of us were out of the way."

As everyone *was* out of the way but herself, Jo began to feel that she ought to dispose of herself with all speed. But where should she go? And burning to lay herself upon the shrine of sisterly devotion, she sat down to settle that point.

Now, the old sofa was a regular patriarch of a sofa—long, broad, well-cushioned, and low; a trifle shabby, as well it might be, for the girls had slept and sprawled on it as babies, fished over the back, rode on the arms, and had menageries under it as children, and rested tired heads, dreamed dreams, and listened to tender talk on it as young women. They all loved it, for it was a family refuge, and one corner had always been Jo's favorite lounging place. Among the many pillows that adorned the venerable couch was one, hard, round, covered with prickly horsehair, and furnished with a knobby button at each end; this repulsive pillow was her especial property, being used as a weapon of defense, a barricade, or a stern preventive of too much slumber.

Laurie knew this pillow well, and had cause to regard it with deep aversion, having been unmercifully pummeled with it in former days when romping was allowed, and now frequently debarred by it from taking the seat he most coveted next to Jo in the sofa corner. If "the sausage" as they called it, stood on end, it was a sign that he might approach and repose; but if it lay flat across the sofa, woe to the man, woman, or child who dared disturb it! That evening Jo forgot to barricade her corner, and had not been in her seat five minutes, before a massive form appeared beside her, and, with both arms spread over the sofa back, both long legs stretched out before him, Laurie exclaimed, with a sigh of satisfaction—

"Now, *this* is filling at the price."

"No slang," snapped Jo, slamming down the pillow. But it was too late, there was no room for it, and coasting onto the floor, it disappeared in a most mysterious manner.

"Come, Jo, don't be thorny. After studying himself to a skeleton all the week, a fellow deserves petting and ought to get it."

"Beth will pet you, I'm busy."

"No, she's not to be bothered with me; but you like that sort of thing, unless you've suddenly lost your taste for it. Have you? Do you hate your boy, and want to fire pillows at him?"

Anything more wheedlesome than that touching appeal was seldom heard, but Jo quenched "her boy" by turning on him with the stern query, "How many bouquets have you sent Miss Randal this week?"

"Not one, upon my word. She's engaged. Now then."

"I'm glad of it, that's one of your foolish extravagances—sending flowers and things to girls for whom you don't care two pins," continued Jo reprovingly.

"Sensible girls for whom I do care whole papers of pins won't let me send them 'flowers and things,' so what can I do? My feelings must have a *went*."

"Mother doesn't approve of flirting even in fun, and you do flirt desperately, Teddy."

"I'd give anything if I could answer, 'So do you.' As I can't, I'll merely say that I don't see any harm in that pleasant little game, if all parties understand that it's only play."

"Well, it does look pleasant, but I can't learn how it's done. I've tried, because one feels awkward in company not to do as everybody else is doing, but I don't seem to get on," said Jo, forgetting to play mentor.

"Take lessons of Amy, she has a regular talent for it."

"Yes, she does it very prettily, and never seems to go too far. I suppose it's natural to some people to please without trying, and others to always say and do the wrong thing in the wrong place."

"I'm glad you can't flirt; it's really refreshing to see a sensible, straightforward girl, who can be jolly and kind without making a fool of herself. Between ourselves, Jo, some of the girls I know really do go on at such a rate I'm ashamed of them. They don't mean any harm, I'm sure, but if they knew how we fellows talked about them afterward, they'd mend their ways, I fancy."

"They do the same, and as their tongues are the sharpest, you fellows get the worst of it, for you are as silly as they, every bit. If you behaved properly, they would; but, knowing you like their nonsense, they keep it up, and then you blame them."

"Much you know about it, ma'am," said Laurie in a superior tone. "We don't like romps and flirts, though we may act as if we did sometimes. The pretty, modest girls are never talked about, except respectfully, among gentlemen. Bless your innocent soul! If you could be in my place for a month you'd see things that would astonish you a trifle. Upon my word, when I see one of those harum-scarum girls, I always want to say with our friend Cock Robin—

"Out upon you, fie upon you,
    Bold-faced jig!"

It was impossible to help laughing at the funny conflict between Laurie's chivalrous reluctance to speak ill of womankind, and his very natural dislike of the unfeminine folly of which fashionable society showed him many samples. Jo knew that "young Laurence" was regarded as a most eligible *parti* by worldly mammas, was much smiled upon by their daughters, and flattered enough by ladies of all ages to make a coxcomb of him; so she watched him rather jealously, fearing he would be spoiled, and rejoiced more than she confessed to find that he still believed in modest girls. Returning suddenly to her admonitory tone, she said, dropping her voice, "If you *must* have a 'went,' Teddy, go and devote yourself to one of the 'pretty, modest girls' whom you do respect, and not waste your time with the silly ones."

"You really advise it?" And Laurie looked at her with an odd mixture of anxiety and merriment in his face.

"Yes, I do, but you'd better wait till you are through college, on the whole, and be fitting yourself for the place meantime. You're not half good enough for—well, whoever the modest girl may be." And Jo looked a little queer likewise, for a name had almost escaped her.

"That I'm not!" acquiesced Laurie, with an expression of humility quite new to him, as he dropped his eyes and absently wound Jo's apron tassel round his finger.

"Mercy on us, this will never do," thought Jo, adding aloud, "Go and sing to me. I'm dying for some music, and always like yours."

"I'd rather stay here, thank you."

"Well, you can't, there isn't room. Go and make yourself useful, since you are too big to be ornamental. I thought you hated to be tied to a woman's apron string?" retorted Jo, quoting certain rebellious words of his own.

"Ah, that depends on who wears the apron!" and Laurie gave an audacious tweak at the tassel.

"Are you going?" demanded Jo, diving for the pillow.

He fled at once, and the minute it was well "Up with the bonnets of bonnie Dundee," she slipped away to return no more till the young gentleman had departed in high dudgeon.

Jo lay long awake that night, and was just dropping off when the sound of a stifled sob made her fly to Beth's bedside, with the anxious inquiry, "What is it, dear?"

"I thought you were asleep," sobbed Beth.

"Is it the old pain, my precious?"

"No, it's a new one, but I can bear it." And Beth tried to check her tears.

"Tell me all about it, and let me cure it as I often did the other."

"You can't, there is no cure." There Beth's voice gave way,

and clinging to her sister, she cried so despairingly that Jo was frightened.

"Where is it? Shall I call Mother?"

Beth did not answer the first question, but in the dark one hand went involuntarily to her heart as if the pain were there, with the other she held Jo fast, whispering eagerly, "No, no, don't call her, don't tell her. I shall be better soon. Lie down here and 'poor' my head. I'll be quiet and go to sleep, indeed I will."

Jo obeyed, but as her hand went softly to and fro across Beth's hot forehead and wet eyelids, her heart was very full and she longed to speak. But young as she was, Jo had learned that hearts, like flowers, cannot be rudely handled, but must open naturally; so though she believed she knew the cause of Beth's new pain, she only said, in her tenderest tone, "Does anything trouble you, deary?"

"Yes, Jo," after a long pause.

"Wouldn't it comfort you to tell me what it is?"

"Not now, not yet."

"Then I won't ask, but remember, Bethy, that Mother and Jo are always glad to hear and help you, if they can."

"I know it. I'll tell you by-and-by."

"Is the pain better now?"

"Oh, yes, much better, you are so comfortable, Jo!"

"Go to sleep, dear, I'll stay with you."

So cheek to cheek they fell asleep, and on the morrow Beth seemed quite herself again, for at eighteen neither heads nor hearts ache long, and a loving word can medicine most ills.

But Jo had made up her mind, and after pondering over a project for some days, she confided it to her Mother.

"You asked me the other day what my wishes were. I'll tell you one of them, Marmee," she began, as they sat alone together. "I want to go away somewhere this winter for a change."

"Why, Jo?" And her mother looked up quickly, as if the words suggested a double meaning.

With her eyes on her work Jo answered soberly, "I want

something new. I feel restless and anxious to be seeing, doing, and learning more than I am. I brood too much over my own small affairs, and need stirring up, so as I can be spared this winter, I'd like to hop a little way and try my wings."

"Where will you hop?"

"To New York. I had a bright idea yesterday, and this is it. You know Mrs. Kirke wrote to you for some respectable young person to teach her children and sew. It's rather hard to find just the thing, but I think I should suit if I tried."

"My dear, go out to service in that great boardinghouse!" And Mrs. March looked surprised, but not displeased.

"It's not exactly going out to service, for Mrs. Kirke is your friend—the kindest soul that ever lived—and would make things pleasant for me, I know. Her family is separate from the rest, and no one knows me there. Don't care if they do. It's honest work, and I'm not ashamed of it."

"Nor I. But your writing?"

"All the better for the change. I shall see and hear new things, get new ideas, and, even if I haven't much time there, I shall bring home quantities of material for my rubbish."

"I have no doubt of it, but are these your only reasons for this sudden fancy?"

"No, mother."

"May I know the others?"

Jo looked up and Jo looked down, then said slowly, with sudden color in her cheeks, "It may be vain and wrong to say it, but—I'm afraid—Laurie is getting too fond of me."

"Then you don't care for him in the way it is evident he begins to care for you?" And Mrs. March looked anxious as she put the question.

"Mercy, no! I love the dear boy, as I always have, and am immensely proud of him, but as for anything more, it's out of the question."

"I'm glad of that, Jo."

"Why, please?"

"Because, dear, I don't think you suited to one another. As friends you are very happy, and your frequent quarrels soon

blow over, but I fear you would both rebel if you were mated
for life. You are too much alike and too fond of freedom,
not to mention hot tempers and strong wills, to get on happily
together, in a relation which needs infinite patience and for-
bearance, as well as love."

"That's just the feeling I had, though I couldn't express it.
I'm glad you think he is only beginning to care for me. It
would trouble me sadly to make him unhappy, for I couldn't
fall in love with the dear old fellow merely out of gratitude,
could I?"

"You are sure of his feeling for you?"

The color deepened in Jo's cheeks as she answered, with
the look of mingled pleasure, pride, and pain which young
girls wear when speaking of first lovers, "I'm afraid it is so,
Mother; he hasn't said anything, but he looks a great deal.
I think I had better go away before it comes to anything."

"I agree with you, and if it can be managed you shall go."

Jo looked relieved, and, after a pause, said, smiling, "How
Mrs. Moffat would wonder at your want of management, if
she knew, and how she will rejoice that Annie still may hope."

"Ah, Jo, mothers may differ in their management, but the
hope is the same in all—the desire to see their children happy.
Meg is so, and I am content with her success. You I leave
to enjoy your liberty till you tire of it, for only then will you
find that there is something sweeter. Amy is my chief care
now, but her good sense will help her. For Beth, I indulge
no hopes except that she may be well. By the way, she seems
brighter this last day or two. Have you spoken to her?"

"Yes, she owned she had a trouble, and promised to tell
me by-and-by. I said no more, for I think I know it." And
Jo told her little story.

Mrs. March shook her head, and did not take so romantic
a view of the case, but looked grave, and repeated her opinion
that for Laurie's sake Jo should go away for a time.

"Let us say nothing about it to him till the plan is settled,
then I'll run away before he can collect his wits and be
tragic. Beth must think I'm going to please myself, as I am,
for I can't talk about Laurie to her; but she can pet and

comfort him after I'm gone, and so cure him of this romantic notion. He's been through so many little trials of the sort, he's used to it, and will soon get over his lovelornity."

Jo spoke hopefully, but could not rid herself of the foreboding fear that this "little trial" would be harder than the others, and that Laurie would not get over his "lovelornity" as easily as heretofore.

The plan was talked over in a family council and agreed upon, for Mrs. Kirke gladly accepted Jo, and promised to make a pleasant home for her. The teaching would render her independent, and such leisure as she got might be made profitable by writing, while the new scenes and society would be both useful and agreeable. Jo liked the prospect and was eager to be gone, for the home nest was growing too narrow for her restless nature and adventurous spirit. When all was settled, with fear and trembling she told Laurie, but to her surprise he took it very quietly. He had been graver than usual of late, but very pleasant, and when jokingly accused of turning over a new leaf, he answered soberly, "So I am, and I mean this one shall stay turned."

Jo was very much relieved that one of his virtuous fits should come on just then, and made her preparations with a lightened heart—for Beth seemed more cheerful—and hoped she was doing the best for all.

"One thing I leave to your especial care," she said, the night before she left.

"You mean your papers?" asked Beth.

"No, my boy. Be very good to him, won't you?"

"Of course I will, but I can't fill your place, and he'll miss you sadly."

"It won't hurt him; so remember, I leave him in your charge, to plague, pet, and keep in order."

"I'll do my best, for your sake," promised Beth, wondering why Jo looked at her so queerly.

When Laurie said good-by, he whispered significantly, "It won't do a bit of good, Jo. My eye is on you, so mind what you do, or I'll come and bring you home."

Chapter 33

Jo's Journal

DEAR MARMEE AND BETH,

I'm going to write you a regular volume, for I've got heaps to tell, though I'm not a fine young lady traveling on the continent. When I lost sight of Father's dear old face, I felt a trifle blue, and might have shed a briny drop or two, if an Irish lady with four small children, all crying more or less, hadn't diverted my mind; for I amused myself by dropping gingerbread nuts over the seat every time they opened their mouths to roar.

Soon the sun came out, and taking it as a good omen, I cleared up likewise and enjoyed my journey with all my heart.

Mrs. Kirke welcomed me so kindly I felt at home at once, even in that big house full of strangers. She gave me a funny little sky parlor—all she had, but there is a stove in it, and a nice table in a sunny window, so I can sit here and write whenever I like. A fine view and a church tower opposite atone for the many stairs, and I took a fancy to my den on the spot. The nursery, where I am to teach and sew, is a pleasant room next Mrs. Kirke's private parlor, and the two little girls are pretty children—rather spoiled, I fancy, but they took to me after telling them *The Seven Bad Pigs*, and I've no doubt I shall make a model governess.

I am to have my meals with the children, if I prefer it to the great table, and for the present I do, for I *am* bashful, though no one will believe it.

"Now, my dear, make yourself at home," said Mrs. K. in her motherly way, "I'm on the drive from morning to night, as you may suppose with such a family, but a great anxiety will be off my mind if I know the children are safe with you. My rooms are always open to you, and your own shall be as comfortable as I can make it. There are some pleasant people in the house if you feel sociable, and your evenings are always free. Come to me if anything goes wrong, and be as happy as you can. There's the tea bell, I must run and change my cap." And off she bustled, leaving me to settle myself in my new nest.

As I went downstairs soon after, I saw something I liked. The flights are very long in this tall house, and as I stood waiting at the head of the third one for a little servant girl to lumber up, I saw a gentleman come along behind her, take the heavy hod of coal out of her hand, carry it all the way up, put it down at a door near by, and walk away, saying, with a kind nod and a foreign accent, "It goes better so. The little back is too young to haf such heaviness."

Wasn't it good of him? I like such things, for, as Father says, trifles show character. When I mentioned it to Mrs. K., that evening, she laughed, and said, "That must have been Professor Bhaer, he's always doing things of that sort."

Mrs. K. told me he was from Berlin, very learned and good, but poor as a church mouse, and gives lessons to support himself and two little orphan nephews whom he is educating here, according to the wishes of his sister, who married an American. Not a very romantic story, but it interested me, and I was glad to hear that Mrs. K. lends him her parlor for some of his scholars. There is a glass door between it and the nursery, and I mean to peep at him, and then I'll tell you how he looks. He's almost forty, so it's no harm, Marmee.

After tea and a go-to-bed romp with the little girls, I attacked the big workbasket, and had a quiet evening chatting with my new friend. I shall keep a journal-letter, and send it once a week; so good night, and more tomorrow.

Tuesday Eve

Had a lively time in my seminary this morning, for the children acted like Sancho, and at one time I really thought I should shake them all round. Some good angel inspired me to try gymnastics, and I kept it up till they were glad to sit down and keep still. After luncheon, the girl took them out for a walk, and I went to my needlework like little Mabel "with a willing mind." I was thanking my stars that I'd learned to make nice buttonholes, when the parlor door opened and shut, and someone began to hum,

"Kennst du das Land,"

like a big bumblebee. It was dreadfully improper, I know, but I couldn't resist the temptation, and lifting one end of the curtain before the glass door, I peeped in. Professor Bhaer was there, and while he arranged his books, I took a good look at him. A regular German—rather stout, with brown hair tumbled all over his head, a bushy beard, good nose, the kindest eyes I ever saw, and a splendid big voice that does one's ears good, after our sharp or slipshod American gabble. His clothes were rusty, his hands were large, and he hadn't a really handsome feature in his face, except his beautiful teeth; yet I liked him, for he had a fine head, his linen was very nice, and he looked like a gentleman, though two buttons were off his coat and there was a patch on one shoe. He looked sober in spite of his humming, till he went to the window to turn the hyacinth bulbs toward the sun, and stroke the cat, who received him like an old friend. Then he smiled, and when a tap came at the door, called out in a loud, brisk tone,

"Herein!"

I was just going to run, when I caught sight of a morsel of a child carrying a big book, and stopped to see what was going on.

"Me wants my Bhaer," said the mite, slamming down her book and running to meet him.

"Thou shalt haf thy Bhaer; come, then, and take a goot hug from him, my Tina," said the Professor, catching her up with a laugh, and holding her so high over his head that she had to stoop her little face to kiss him.

"Now me mus tuddy my lessin," went on the funny little thing; so he put her up at the table, opened the great dictionary she had brought, and gave her a paper and pencil, and she scribbled away, turning a leaf now and then, and passing her little fat finger down the page, as if finding a word, so soberly that I nearly betrayed myself by a laugh, while Mr. Bhaer stood stroking her pretty hair with a fatherly look that made me think she must be his own, though she looked more French than German.

Another knock and the appearance of two young ladies sent me back to my work, and there I virtuously remained through all the noise and gabbling that went on next door. One of the girls kept laughing affectedly, and saying "Now Professor," in a coquettish tone, and the other pronounced her German with an accent that must have made it hard for him to keep sober.

Both seemed to try his patience sorely, for more than once I heard him say emphatically, "No, no, it is *not* so, you haf not attend to what I say," and once there was a loud rap, as if he struck the table with his book, followed by the despairing exclamation, "Prut! It all goes bad this day."

Poor man, I pitied him, and when the girls were gone, took just one more peep to see if he survived it. He seemed to have thrown himself back in his chair, tired out, and sat there with his eyes shut till the clock struck two, when he jumped up, put his books in his pocket, as if ready for another lesson, and, taking little Tina who had fallen asleep on the sofa in his arms, he carried her quietly away. I fancy he has a hard life of it. Mrs. Kirke asked me if I wouldn't go down to the five o'clock dinner, and feeling a little bit homesick, I thought I would, just to see what sort of people are under the same roof with me. So I made myself respectable and tried to slip in behind Mrs. Kirke, but as she is short and I'm tall, my efforts at concealment were rather a failure. She gave me a seat by her, and after my face cooled off, I plucked up courage and looked about me. The long table was full, and everyone intent on getting their dinner—the gentlemen especially, who seemed to be eating on time, for they *bolted* in every sense of the word, vanishing as soon as they were done. There was the usual assortment of young men absorbed in themselves, young couples absorbed in each other, married ladies in their babies, and old gentlemen in politics. I don't think I shall care to have much to do with any of them, except one sweet-faced maiden lady, who looks as if she had something in her.

Cast away at the very bottom of the table was the Professor, shouting answers to the questions of a very inquisitive, deaf old gentleman on one side, and talking philosophy with a Frenchman on the other. If Amy had been here, she'd have turned her back on him forever because, sad to relate, he had a great appetite, and shoveled in his dinner in a manner which would have horrified "her ladyship." I didn't mind, for I like "to see folks eat with a relish," as Hannah says, and the poor man must have needed a deal of food after teaching idiots all day.

As I went upstairs after dinner, two of the young men were settling their hats before the hall mirror, and I heard one say low to the other, "Who's the new party?"

"Governess, or something of that sort."

"What the deuce is she at our table for?"

"Friend of the old lady's."

"Handsome head, but no style."

"Not a bit of it. Give us a light and come on."

I felt angry at first, and then I didn't care, for a governess is as good as a clerk, and I've got sense, if I haven't style, which is more than some people have, judging from the remarks of the elegant beings who clattered away, smoking like bad chimneys. I hate ordinary people!

Thursday

Yesterday was a quiet day spent in teaching, sewing, and writing in my little room, which is very cozy, with a light and fire. I picked up a few bits of news and was introduced to the Professor. It seems that Tina is the child of the Frenchwoman who does the fine ironing in the laundry here. The little thing has lost her heart to Mr. Bhaer, and follows him about the house like a dog whenever he is at home, which delights him, as he is very fond of children, though a "bacheldore." Kitty and Minnie Kirke likewise regard him with affection, and tell all sorts of stories about the plays he invents, the presents he brings, and the splendid tales he tells. The young men quiz him, it seems, call him Old Fritz, Lager Beer, Ursa Major, and make all manner of jokes on his name. But he enjoys it like a boy, Mrs. K. says, and takes it so good-naturedly that they all like him in spite of his foreign ways.

The maiden lady is a Miss Norton—rich, cultivated, and kind. She spoke to me at dinner today (for I went to table again, it's such fun to watch people), and asked me to come and see her at her room. She has fine books and pictures, knows interesting persons, and seems friendly, so I shall make myself agreeable, for I *do* want to get into good society, only it isn't the same sort that Amy likes.

I was in our parlor last evening when Mr. Bhaer came in with some newspapers for Mrs. Kirke. She wasn't there, but Minnie, who is a little old woman, introduced me very prettily: "This is Mamma's friend, Miss March."

"Yes, and she's jolly and we like her lots," added Kitty, who is an *enfant terrible*.

We both bowed, and then we laughed, for the prim introduction and the blunt addition were rather a comical contrast.

"Ah, yes, I hear these naughty ones go to vex you, Mees Marsch. If so again, call at me and I come," he said, with a threatening frown that delighted the little wretches.

I promised I would, and he departed; but it seems as if I was doooomed to see a good deal of him, for today as I passed his door on my way out, by accident I knocked against it with my umbrella. It flew open, and there he stood in his dressing gown, with a big blue sock on one hand and a darning needle in the other; he didn't seem at all ashamed of it, for when I explained and hurried on, he waved his hand, sock and all, saying in his loud, cheerful way—

"You haf a fine day to make your walk. *Bon voyage, mademoiselle.*"

I laughed all the way downstairs, but it was a little pathetic, also to think of the poor man having to mend his own clothes. The German gentlemen embroider, I know, but darning hose is another thing and not so pretty.

Saturday

Nothing has happened to write about, except a call on Miss Norton, who has a room full of lovely things, and who was very charming, for she showed me all her treasures, and asked me if I would sometimes go with her to lectures and concerts, as her escort—if I enjoyed them. She put it as a favor, but I'm sure Mrs. Kirke has told her about us, and she does it out of kindness to me. I'm as proud as Lucifer, but such favors from such people don't burden me, and I accepted gratefully.

When I got back to the nursery there was such an uproar in the parlor that I looked in, and there was Mr. Bhaer down on his hands and knees, with Tina on his back, Kitty leading him with a jump rope, and Minnie feeding two small boys with seedcakes, as they roared and ramped in cages built of chairs.

"We are playing *nargerie*," explained Kitty.

"Dis is mine effalunt!" added Tina, holding on by the Professor's hair.

"Mamma always allows us to do what we like Saturday afternoon, when Franz and Emil come, doesn't she, Mr. Bhaer?" said Minnie.

The "effalunt" sat up, looking as much in earnest as any of them, and said soberly to me, "I gif you my wort it is so. If we make too large a noise you shall say Hush! to us, and we go more softly."

I promised to do so, but left the door open and enjoyed the fun as much as they did—for a more glorious frolic I never witnessed. They played tag and soldiers, danced and sang, and when it began to grow dark they all piled onto the sofa about the Professor, while he told charming fairy stories of the storks on the chimney tops, and the little "kobolds," who ride the snowflakes as they fall. I wish Americans were as simple and natural as Germans, don't you?

I'm so fond of writing, I should go spinning on forever if motives of economy didn't stop me; for though I've used thin paper and written fine, I tremble to think of the stamps this long letter will need. Pray forward Amy's as soon as you can spare them. My small news will sound very flat after her splendors, but you will like them, I know. Is Teddy studying so hard that he can't find time to write to his friends? Take good care of him for me, Beth, and tell me all about the babies, and give heaps of love to everyone.

From your faithful   Jo

P.S. On reading over my letter it strikes me as rather Bhaery, but I am always interested in odd people, and I really had nothing else to write about. Bless you!

DECEMBER

My Precious Betsey,

As this is to be a scribble-scrabble letter, I direct it to you, for it may amuse you, and give you some idea of my goings on; for though quiet, they are rather amusing, for which, oh, be joyful! After what Amy would call Herculaneum efforts, in the way of mental and moral agriculture, my young ideas begin to shoot and my little twigs to bend as I could wish. They are not so interesting to me as Tina and the boys, but I do my duty by them, and they are fond of me. Franz and Emil are jolly little lads, quite after my own heart, for the mixture of German and American spirit in them produces a constant state of effervescence. Saturday afternoons are riotous times, whether spent in the house or out, for on pleasant days they all go to walk, like a seminary, with the Professor and myself to keep order, and then such fun!

We are very good friends now, and I've begun to take lessons. I really couldn't help it, and it all came about in such a droll way that I must tell you. To begin at the beginning, Mrs. Kirke called to me one day as I passed Mr. Bhaer's room where she was rummaging.

"Did you ever see such a den, my dear? Just come and help me put these books to rights, for I've turned everything upside down, trying to discover what he has done with the six new handkerchiefs I gave him not long ago."

I went in, and while we worked I looked about me, for it was "a den," to be sure. Books and papers everywhere; a broken meerschaum, and an old flute over the mantelpiece as if done with; a ragged bird without any tail chirped on one window seat, and a box of white mice adorned the other; half-finished boats and bits of string lay among the manuscripts; dirty little boots stood drying before the fire; and traces of the dearly beloved boys, for whom he makes a slave of himself, were to be seen all over the room. After a grand rummage three of the missing articles were found— one over the bird cage, one covered with ink, and a third burned brown, having been used as a holder.

"Such a man!" laughed good-natured Mrs. K., as she put the relics in the rag bag. "I suppose the others are torn up to rig ships, bandage cut fingers, or make kite tails. It's dreadful, but I can't scold him: he's so absent-minded and good-natured, he lets those boys ride over him roughshod. I agreed to do his washing and mending, but he forgets to give out his things and I forget to look them over, so he comes to a sad pass sometimes."

"Let me mend them," said I. "I don't mind it, and he needn't know. I'd like to—he's so kind to me about bringing my letters and lending books."

So I have got his things in order, and knit heels into two pairs of the socks—for they were boggled out of shape with his queer darns. Nothing was said, and I hoped he wouldn't find it out, but one day last week he caught me at it. Hearing the lessons he gives to others has interested and amused me so much that I took a fancy to learn, for Tina runs in and out, leaving the door open, and I can hear. I had been sitting near this door, finishing off the last sock, and trying to understand what he said to a new scholar, who is as stupid as I am. The girl had gone, and I thought he had also, it was so still, and I was busily gabbling over a verb, and rocking to and fro in a most absurd way, when a little crow made me look up, and there was Mr. Bhaer looking and laughing quietly, while he made signs to Tina not to betray him.

"So!" he said, as I stopped and stared like a goose, "you peep at me, I peep at you, and that is not bad; but see, I am not pleasanting when I say, haf you a wish for German?"

"Yes, but you are too busy. I am too stupid to learn," I blundered out, as red as a peony.

"Prut! we will make the time, and we fail not to find the sense. At efening I shall gif a little lesson with much gladness; for, look you, Mees Marsch, I haf this debt to pay." And he pointed to my work. 'Yes,' they say to one another, these so kind ladies, 'he is a stupid old fellow, he will see not what we do, he will never opserve that his sock heels go not in holes any more, he will think his buttons grow out new when they fall, and believe that strings make theirselves.' Ah! But I haf an eye, and I see much. I haf a heart, and I feel the thanks for this. Come, a little lesson then and now, or no more good fairy works for me and mine."

Of course I couldn't say anything after that, and as it really is a splendid opportunity, I made the bargain, and we began. I took four lessons, and then I stuck fast in a grammatical bog. The Professor was very patient with me, but it must have been torment to him, and now and then he'd look at me with such an expression of mild despair that it was a toss-up with me whether to laugh or cry. I tried both ways, and when it came to a sniff of utter mortification and woe, he just threw the grammar on to the floor and marched out of the room. I felt myself disgraced and deserted forever, but didn't blame him a particle, and was scrambling my papers together, meaning to rush upstairs and shake myself hard, when in he came, as brisk and beaming as if I'd covered myself with glory.

"Now we shall try a new way. You and I will read these pleasant little *Märchen* together, and dig no more in that dry book, that goes in the corner for making us trouble."

He spoke so kindly, and opened Hans Andersen's fairy tales so invitingly before me, that I was more ashamed than ever, and went at my lesson in a neck-or-nothing style that seemed to amuse him immensely. I forgot my bashfulness, and pegged away (no other word will express it) with all my might, tumbling over long words, pronouncing according to the inspiration of the minute, and doing my very best. When I finished reading my first page, and stopped for breath, he clapped his hands and cried out, in his hearty way, *"Das ist gut!* Now we go well! My turn. I do him in German, gif me your ear."* And away he went, rumbling out the words with his strong voice and a relish which was good to see as well as hear. Fortunately the story was the *Constant Tin Soldier,* which is droll, you know, so I could laugh—and I did— though I didn't understand half he read, for I couldn't help it, he was so earnest, I so excited, and the whole thing so comical.

After that we got on better, and now I read my lessons pretty well, for this way of studying suits me, and I can see that the grammar gets tucked into the tales and poetry as one gives pills in jelly. I like it very much, and he doesn't seem tired of it yet—which is very good of him, isn't it? I mean to give him something on Christmas, for I dare not offer money. Tell me something nice, Marmee.

I'm glad Laurie seems so happy and busy, that he has given up smoking and lets his hair grow. You see Beth manages him better than I did. I'm not jealous, dear, do your best, only don't make a saint of him. I'm afraid I couldn't like him without a spice of human naughtiness. Read him bits of my letters. I haven't time to write much, and that will do just as well. Thank Heaven Beth continues so comfortable.

JANUARY

A Happy New Year to you all, my dearest family, which of course includes Mr. L. and a young man by the name of Teddy. I can't tell you how much I enjoyed your Christmas bundle, for I didn't get it till night and had given up hoping. Your letter came in the morning, but you said nothing about a parcel, meaning it for a surprise; so I was disappointed, for I'd had a "kind of a feeling" that you wouldn't forget me. I felt a little low in my mind as I sat up in my room after tea, and when the big, muddy, battered-looking bundle was brought to me, I just hugged it and pranced. It was so *homey* and refreshing that I sat down on the floor and read and looked and ate and laughed and cried, in my usual absurd way. The things were just what I wanted, and all the better for being made instead of bought. Beth's new "ink bib" was capital, and Hannah's box of hard gingerbread will be a treasure. I'll be sure and wear the nice flannels you sent, Marmee, and read carefully the books Father has marked. Thank you all, heaps and heaps!

Speaking of books reminds me that I'm getting rich in that line, for on New Year's Day Mr. Bhaer gave me a fine Shakespeare. It is one he values much, and I've often admired it, set up in the place of honor with his German Bible, Plato, Homer, and Milton; so you may imagine how I felt when he brought it down, without its cover, and showed me my name in it, "from my friend Friedrich Bhaer."

"You say often you wish a library: here I gif you one, for between these lids (he meant covers) is many books in one. Read him well, and he will help you much, for the study of character in this book will help you to read it in the world and paint it with your pen."

I thanked him as well as I could, and talk now about "my library," as if I had a hundred books. I never knew how much there was in Shakespeare before, but then I never had a Bhaer to explain it to me. Now *don't* laugh at his horrid name; it isn't pronounced either Bear or Beer, as people *will* say it, but something between the two, as only Germans can give it. I'm glad you both like what I tell you about him, and hope you will know him some day. Mother would admire his warm heart, Father his wise head. I admire both, and feel rich in my new "friend Friedrich Bhaer."

Not having much money, or knowing what he'd like, I got several little things, and put them about the room, where he would find them unexpectedly. They were useful, pretty, or funny—a new standish on his table, a little vase for his flower —he always has one, or a bit of green in a glass, to keep him fresh, he says—and a holder for his blower, so that he needn't burn up what Amy calls "mouchoirs." I made it like those Beth invented—a big butterfly with a fat body, and black and yellow wings, worsted feelers, and bead eyes. It took his fancy immensely, and he put it on his mantelpiece as an article of virtu, so it was rather a failure after all. Poor as he is, he didn't forget a servant or a child in the house, and not a soul here, from the French laundrywoman to Miss Norton, forgot him. I was so glad of that.

They got up a masquerade, and had a gay time New Year's Eve. I didn't mean to go down, having no dress; but at the last minute, Mrs. Kirke remembered some old brocades, and Miss Norton lent me lace and feathers; so I dressed up as Mrs. Malaprop, and sailed in with a mask on. No one knew me, for I disguised my voice, and no one dreamed of the silent, haughty Miss March (for they think I am very stiff and cool, most of them, and so I am to whippersnappers) could dance and dress, and burst out into a "nice derangement of epitaphs, like an allegory on the banks of the Nile." I enjoyed it very much, and when we unmasked it was fun to see them stare at me. I heard one of the young men tell another that he knew I'd been an actress; in fact, he thought he remembered seeing me at one of the minor theaters. Meg will relish that joke. Mr. Bhaer was Nick Bottom, and Tina was Titania—a perfect little fairy in his arms. To see them dance was "quite a landscape," to use a Teddyism.

I had a very happy New Year, after all; and when I thought it over in my room, I felt as if I was getting on a little in spite of my many failures; for I'm cheerful all the time now, work with a will, and take more interest in other people than I used to, which is satisfactory. Bless you all! Ever your loving   Jo

Chapter 34

A Friend

THOUGH VERY HAPPY in the social atmosphere about her, and very busy with the daily work that earned her bread and made it sweeter for the effort, Jo still found time for literary labors. The purpose which now took possession of her was a natural one to a poor and ambitious girl, but the means she took to gain her end were not the best. She saw that money conferred power: money and power, therefore, she resolved to have, not to be used for herself alone, but for those whom she loved more than self.

The dream of filling home with comforts, giving Beth everything she wanted, from strawberries in winter to an organ in her bedroom, going abroad herself, and always having *more* than enough, so that she might indulge in the luxury of charity, had been for years Jo's most cherished castle in the air.

The prize-story experience had seemed to open a way which might, after long traveling and much uphill work, lead to this delightful *château en Espagne*. But the novel disaster quenched her courage for a time, for public opinion is a giant which has frightened stouter-hearted Jacks on bigger beanstalks than hers. Like that immortal hero, she reposed awhile after the first attempt, which resulted in a tumble and the least lovely of the giant's treasures, if I remember rightly. But the "up again and take another" spirit was as strong in Jo as in Jack, so she scrambled up on the shady side this time and got more booty, but nearly left behind her what was far more precious than the moneybags.

She took to writing sensation stories, for in those dark ages, even all-perfect America read rubbish. She told no one, but concocted a "thrilling tale," and boldly carried it herself to Mr. Dashwood, editor of the *Weekly Volcano*. She had never read *Sartor Resartus*, but she had a womanly instinct that clothes possess an influence more powerful over many than the worth of character or the magic of manners. So she dressed herself in her best, and trying to persuade herself that she was neither excited nor nervous, bravely climbed two pairs of dark and dirty stairs to find herself in a disorderly room, a cloud of cigar smoke, and the presence of three gentlemen, sitting with their heels rather higher than their hats, which articles of dress none of them took the trouble to remove on her appearance. Somewhat daunted by this reception, Jo hesitated on the threshold, murmuring in much embarrassment—

"Excuse me, I was looking for the *Weekly Volcano* office. I wished to see Mr. Dashwood."

Down went the highest pair of heels, up rose the smokiest gentleman, and carefully cherishing his cigar between his fingers, he advanced with a nod and a countenance expressive of nothing but sleep. Feeling that she must get through the matter somehow, Jo produced her manuscript and, blushing redder and redder with each sentence, blundered out fragments of the little speech carefully prepared for the occasion.

"A friend of mine desired me to offer—a story—just as an experiment—would like your opinion—be glad to write more if this suits."

While she blushed and blundered, Mr. Dashwood had taken the manuscript, and was turning over the leaves with a pair of rather dirty fingers, and casting critical glances up and down the neat pages.

"Not a first attempt, I take it?" observing that the pages were numbered, covered only on one side, and not tied up with a ribbon—sure sign of a novice.

"No, sir; she has had some experience, and got a prize for a tale in the *Blarneystone Banner*."

"Oh, did she?" And Mr. Dashwood gave Jo a quick look, which seemed to take note of everything she had on, from the bow in her bonnet to the buttons on her boots. "Well, you can leave it, if you like. We've more of this sort of thing on hand than we know what to do with at present, but I'll run my eye over it, and give you an answer next week."

Now, Jo did *not* like to leave it, for Mr. Dashwood didn't suit her at all; but, under the circumstances, there was nothing for her to do but bow and walk away, looking particularly tall and dignified, as she was apt to do when nettled or abashed. Just then she was both, for it was perfectly evident from the knowing glances exchanged among the gentlemen that her little fiction of "my friend" was considered a good joke; and a laugh, produced by some inaudible remark of the editor, as he closed the door, completed her discomfiture. Half resolving never to return, she went home, and worked off her irritation by stitching pinafores vigorously, and in an hour or two was cool enough to laugh over the scene and long for next week.

When she went again, Mr. Dashwood was alone, whereat she rejoiced; Mr. Dashwood was much wider awake than before, which was agreeable; and Mr. Dashwood was not too deeply absorbed in a cigar to remember his manners: so the second interview was much more comfortable than the first.

"We'll take this (editors never say I), if you don't object to a few alterations. It's too long, but omitting the passages I've marked will make it just the right length," he said, in a businesslike tone.

Jo hardly knew her own MS. again, so crumpled and underscored were its pages and paragraphs, but feeling as a tender parent might on being asked to cut off her baby's legs in order that it might fit into a new cradle, she looked at the marked passages and was surprised to find that all the moral reflections—which she had carefully put in as ballast for much romance—had been stricken out.

"But, sir, I thought every story should have some sort of a moral, so I took care to have a few of my sinners repent."

Mr. Dashwood's editorial gravity relaxed into a smile, for Jo had forgotten her "friend," and spoken as only an author could.

"People want to be amused, not preached at, you know. Morals don't sell nowadays"; which was not quite a correct statement, by the way.

"You think it would do with these alterations, then?"

"Yes, it's a new plot, and pretty well worked up—language good, and so on," was Mr. Dashwood's affable reply.

"What do you—that is, what compensation—" began Jo, not exactly knowing how to express herself.

"Oh, yes, well, we give from twenty-five to thirty for things of this sort. Pay when it comes out," returned Mr. Dashwood, as if that point had escaped him; such trifles often do escape the editorial mind, it is said.

"Very well, you can have it," said Jo, handing back the story with a satisfied air, for after the dollar-a-column work, even twenty-five seemed good pay.

"Shall I tell my friend you will take another if she has one better than this?" asked Jo, unconscious of her little slip of the tongue, and emboldened by her success.

"Well, we'll look at it; can't promise to take it. Tell her to make it short and spicy, and never mind the moral. What name would your friend like to put to it?" in a careless tone.

"None at all, if you please, she doesn't wish her name to appear and has no nom de plume," said Jo, blushing in spite of herself.

"Just as she likes, of course. The tale will be out next week. Will you call for the money, or shall I send it?" asked Mr. Dashwood, who felt a natural desire to know who his new contributor might be.

"I'll call. Good morning, sir."

As she departed, Mr. Dashwood put up his feet, with the graceful remark, "Poor and proud, as usual, but she'll do."

Following Mr. Dashwood's directions, and making Mrs. Northbury her model, Jo rashly took a plunge into the frothy sea of sensational literature, but thanks to the life preserver thrown her by a friend, she came up again not much the worse for her ducking.

Like most young scribblers, she went abroad for her characters and scenery; and banditti, counts, gypsies, nuns, and duchesses appeared upon her stage, and played their parts with as much accuracy and spirit as could be expected. Her readers were not particular about such trifles as grammar, punctuation, and probability, and Mr. Dashwood graciously permitted her to fill his columns at the lowest prices, not thinking it necessary to tell her that the real cause of his hospitality was the fact that one of his hacks, on being offered higher wages, had basely left him in the lurch.

She soon became interested in her work, for her emaciated purse grew stout, and the little hoard she was making to take Beth to the mountains next summer grew slowly but surely as the weeks passed. One thing disturbed her satisfaction, and that was that she did not tell them at home. She had a feeling that Father and Mother would not approve, and preferred to have her own way first, and beg pardon afterward. It was easy to keep her secret, for no name appeared with her stories; Mr. Dashwood had of course found it out very soon, but promised to be dumb, and for a wonder kept his word.

She thought it would do her no harm, for she sincerely meant to write nothing of which she should be ashamed, and quieted all pricks of conscience by anticipations of the happy minute when she should show her earnings and laugh over her well-kept secret.

But Mr. Dashwood rejected any but thrilling tales, and as thrills could not be produced except by harrowing up the souls of the readers, history and romance, land and sea, science and art, police records and lunatic asylums, had to be ransacked for the purpose. Jo soon found that her innocent experience had given her but few glimpses of the tragic world which underlies society, so regarding it in a business light, she set about supplying her deficiencies with characteristic energy. Eager to find material for stories, and bent on making them original in plot, if not masterly in execution, she searched newspapers for accidents, incidents, and crimes; she excited the suspicions of public librarians by asking for works on poisons; she studied faces in the street, and characters, good, bad, and indifferent, all about her; she delved in the dust of ancient times for facts or fictions so old that they were as good as new, and introduced herself to folly, sin, and misery, as well as her limited opportunities allowed. She thought she was prospering finely, but unconsciously she was beginning to desecrate some of the womanliest attributes of a woman's character. She was living in bad society, and imaginary though it was, its influence affected her, for she was feeding heart and fancy on dangerous and unsubstantial food, and was fast brushing the innocent bloom from her nature by a premature acquaintance with the darker side of life, which comes soon enough to all of us.

She was beginning to feel rather than see this, for much describing of other people's passions and feelings set her to studying and speculating about her own—a morbid amusement in which healthy young minds do not voluntarily indulge. Wrongdoing always brings its own punishment, and when Jo most needed hers, she got it.

I don't know whether the study of Shakespeare helped her to read character, or the natural instinct of a woman for what was honest, brave, and strong; but while endowing her imaginary heroes with every perfection under the sun, Jo was discovering a live hero, who interested her in spite of many human imperfections. Mr. Bhaer, in one of their conversations, had advised her to study simple, true, and lovely characters, wherever she found them, as good training for a writer. Jo took him at his word, for she coolly turned round and studied him—a proceeding which would have much surprised him, had he known it, for the worthy Professor was very humble in his own conceit.

Why everybody liked him was what puzzled Jo, at first. He was neither rich nor great, young nor handsome; in no respect what is called fascinating, imposing, or brilliant; and yet he was as attractive as a genial fire, and people seemed to gather about him as naturally as about a warm hearth. He was poor, yet always appeared to be giving something away; a stranger, yet everyone was his friend; no longer young, but as happy-hearted as a boy; plain and peculiar, yet his face looked beautiful to many, and his oddities were freely forgiven for his sake. Jo often watched him, trying to discover the charm, and at last decided that it was benevolence which worked the miracle. If he had any sorrow, "it sat with its head under its wing," and he turned only his sunny side to the world. There were lines upon his forehead, but Time seemed to have touched him gently, remembering how kind he was to others. The pleasant curves about his mouth were the memorials of many friendly words and cheery laughs, his eyes were never cold or hard, and his big hand had a warm, strong grasp that was more expressive than words.

His very clothes seemed to partake of the hospitable nature of the wearer. They looked as if they were at ease, and liked to make him comfortable; his capacious waistcoat was suggestive of a large heart underneath; his rusty coat had a social air, and the baggy pockets plainly proved that little hands often went in empty and came out full; his very boots were benevolent, and his collars never stiff and raspy like other people's.

"That's it!" said Jo to herself, when she at length discovered that genuine good will toward one's fellow men could beautify and dignify even a stout German teacher, who shoveled in his dinner, darned his own socks, and was burdened with the name of Bhaer.

Jo valued goodness highly, but she also possessed a most feminine respect for intellect, and a little discovery which she made about the Professor added much to her regard for him. He never spoke of himself, and no one ever knew that in his native city he had been a man much honored and esteemed for learning and integrity, till a countryman came to see him, and in a conversation with Miss Norton divulged the pleasing fact. From her Jo learned it, and liked it all the better because Mr. Bhaer had never told it. She felt proud to know that he was an honored Professor in Berlin, though only a poor language-master in America; and his homely, hard-working life was much beautified by the spice of romance which this discovery gave it.

Another and a better gift than intellect was shown her in a most unexpected manner. Miss Norton had the entree into literary society, which Jo would have had no chance of seeing but for her. The solitary woman felt an interest in the ambitious girl, and kindly conferred many favors of this sort both on Jo and the Professor. She took them with her one night to a select symposium, held in honor of several celebrities.

Jo went prepared to bow down and adore the mighty ones whom she had worshiped with youthful enthusiasm afar off. But her reverence for genius received a severe shock that night, and it took her some time to recover from the discovery that the great creatures were only men and women after all. Imagine her dismay, on stealing a glance of timid admiration at the poet whose lines suggested an ethereal being fed on "spirit, fire, and dew," to behold him devouring his supper with an ardor which flushed his intellectual countenance. Turning as from a fallen idol, she made other discoveries which rapidly dispelled her romantic illusions. The great novelist vibrated between two decanters with the regularity of a pendulum; the famous divine flirted openly with one of the Madame de Staëls of the age, who looked daggers at another Corinne, who was amiably satirizing her, after outmaneuvering her in efforts to absorb the profound philosopher, who imbibed tea Johnsonianly and appeared to slumber, the loquacity of the lady rendering speech impossible. The scientific celebrities, forgetting their mollusks and glacial periods, gossiped about art, while devoting themselves to oysters and ices with characteristic energy; the young musician, who was charming the city like a second Orpheus, talked horses; and the specimen of the British nobility present happened to be the most ordinary man of the party.

Before the evening was half over, Jo felt so completely *désillusionnée*, that she sat down in a corner to recover herself. Mr. Bhaer soon joined her, looking rather out of his element, and presently several of the philosophers, each mounted on his hobby, came ambling up to hold an intellectual tournament in the recess. The conversation was miles beyond Jo's comprehension, but she enjoyed it, though Kant and Hegel were unknown gods, the Subjective and Objective unintelligible terms, and the only thing "evolved from her inner consciousness" was a bad headache after it was all over. It dawned upon her gradually that the world was being picked to pieces, and put together on new and, according to the talkers, on infinitely better principles than before, that religion was in a fair way to be reasoned into nothingness, and intellect was to be the only God. Jo knew nothing about philosophy or metaphysics of any sort, but a curious excitement, half pleasurable, half painful, came over her as she listened with a sense of being turned adrift into time and space, like a young balloon out on a holiday.

She looked round to see how the Professor liked it, and found him looking at her with the grimmest expression she had ever seen him wear. He shook his head and beckoned her to come away, but she was fascinated just then by the freedom of Speculative Philosophy, and kept her seat, trying to find out what the wise gentlemen intended to rely upon after they had annihilated all the old beliefs.

Now, Mr. Bhaer was a diffident man and slow to offer his own opinions, not because they were unsettled, but too sincere and earnest to be lightly spoken. As he glanced from Jo to several other young people, attracted by the brilliancy of the philosophic pyrotechnics, he knit his brows and longed to speak, fearing that some inflammable young soul would be led astray by the rockets, to find when the display was over that they had only an empty stick or a scorched hand.

He bore it as long as he could, but when he was appealed to for an opinion, he blazed up with honest indignation and defended religion with all the eloquence of truth—an eloquence which made his broken English musical and his plain face beautiful. He had a hard fight, for the wise men argued well, but he didn't know when he was beaten and stood to his colors like a man. Somehow, as he talked, the world got right again to Jo; the old beliefs, that had lasted so long, seemed better than the new; God was not a blind force, and immortality was not a pretty fable, but a blessed fact. She felt as if she had solid ground under her feet again; and when Mr. Bhaer paused, outtalked but not one whit convinced, Jo wanted to clap her hands and thank him.

She did neither; but she remembered this scene, and gave the Professor her heartiest respect, for she knew it cost him an effort to speak out then and there, because his conscience would not let him be silent. She began to see that character is a better possession than money, rank, intellect, or beauty, and to feel that if greatness is what a wise man has defined it to be, "truth, reverence, and good will," then her friend Friedrich Bhaer was not only good, but great.

This belief strengthened daily. She valued his esteem, she coveted his respect, she wanted to be worthy of his friendship; and just when the wish was sincerest, she came near losing everything. It all grew out of a cocked hat, for one evening the Professor came in to give Jo her lesson with a paper soldier cap on his head, which Tina had put there and he had forgotten to take off.

"It's evident he doesn't look in his glass before coming down," thought Jo, with a smile, as he said, "Goot efening," and sat soberly down, quite unconscious of the ludicrous contrast between his subject and his headgear, for he was going to read her the *Death of Wallenstein*.

She said nothing at first, for she liked to hear him laugh out his big, hearty laugh when anything funny happened, so she left him to discover it for himself, and presently forgot all about it, for to hear a German read Schiller is rather an absorbing occupation. After the reading came the lesson, which was a lively one, for Jo was in a gay mood that night, and the cocked hat kept her eyes dancing with merriment. The Professor didn't know what to make of her, and stopped at last to ask with an air of mild surprise that was irresistible—

"Mees Marsch, for what do you laugh in your master's face? Haf you no respect for me, that you go on so bad?"

"How can I be respectful, sir, when you forget to take your hat off?" said Jo.

Lifting his hand to his head, the absent-minded Professor gravely felt and removed the little cocked hat, looked at it a minute, and then threw back his head and laughed like a merry bass viol.

"Ah! I see him now, it is that imp Tina who makes me a fool with my cap. Well, it is nothing; but see you, if this lesson goes not well, you too shall wear him."

But the lesson did not go at all for a few minutes because Mr. Bhaer caught sight of a picture on the hat, and unfolding it, said with an air of great disgust, "I wish these papers did not come in the house, they are not for children to see, nor young people to read. It is not well, and I haf no patience with those who make this harm."

Jo glanced at the sheet and saw a pleasing illustration composed of a lunatic, a corpse, a villain, and a viper. She did not like it, but the impulse that made her turn it over was not one of displeasure but fear, because for a minute she fancied the paper was the *Volcano*. It was not, however, and her panic subsided as she remembered that even if it had been and one of her own tales in it, there would have been no name to betray her. She had betrayed herself, however, by a look and a blush, for though an absent man, the Professor saw a good deal more than people fancied. He knew that Jo wrote, and had met her down among the newspaper offices more than once; but as she never spoke of it, he asked no questions in spite of a strong desire to see her work. Now it occurred to him that she was doing what she was ashamed to own, and it troubled him. He did not say to himself, "It is none of my business, I've no right to say anything," as many people would have done; he only remembered that she was young and poor, a girl far away from mother's love and father's care; and he was moved to help her with an impulse as quick and natural as that which would prompt him to put out his hand to save a baby from a puddle. All this flashed through his mind in a minute, but not a trace of it appeared in his face; and by the time the paper was turned, and Jo's needle threaded, he was ready to say quite naturally, but very gravely—

"Yes, you are right to put it from you. I do not like to think that good young girls should see such such things. They are made pleasant to some, but I would more rather give my boys gunpowder to play with than this bad trash."

"All may not be bad, only silly, you know, and if there is a demand for it, I don't see any harm in supplying it. Many very respectable people make an honest living out of what are called sensation stories," said Jo, scratching gathers so energetically that a row of little slits followed her pin.

"There is a demand for whisky, but I think you and I do not care to sell it. If the respectable people knew what harm they did, they would not feel that the living *was* honest. They haf no right to put poison in the sugarplum, and let the small ones eat it. No, they should think a little, and sweep mud in the street before they do this thing."

Mr. Bhaer spoke warmly, and walked to the fire, crumpling the paper in his hands. Jo sat still, looking as if the fire had come to her, for her cheeks burned long after the cocked hat had turned to smoke and gone harmlessly up the chimney.

"I should like much to send all the rest after him," muttered the Professor, coming back with a relieved air.

Jo thought what a blaze her pile of papers upstairs would make, and her hard-earned money lay rather heavily on her conscience at that minute. Then she thought consolingly to herself, "Mine are not like that, they are only silly, never bad, so I won't be worried," and taking up her book, she said, with a studious face, "Shall we go on, sir? I'll be very good and proper now."

"I shall hope so," was all he said, but he meant more than she imagined, and the grave, kind look he gave her made her feel as if the words *Weekly Volcano* were printed in large type on her forehead.

As soon as she went to her room, she got out her papers, and carefully reread every one of her stories. Being a little shortsighted, Mr. Bhaer sometimes used eyeglasess, and Jo had tried them once, smiling to see how they magnified the fine print of her book; now she seemed to have got on the Professor's mental or moral spectacles also, for the faults of these poor stories glared at her dreadfully and filled her with dismay.

"They *are* trash, and will soon be worse than trash if I go on, for each is more sensational than the last. I've gone blindly on, hurting myself and other people, for the sake of money. I know it's so, for I can't read this stuff in sober earnest without being horribly ashamed of it, and what *should*

I do if they were seen at home or Mr. Bhaer got hold of them?"

Jo turned hot at the bare idea, and stuffed the whole bundle into her stove, nearly setting the chimney afire with the blaze.

"Yes, that's the best place for such inflammable nonsense. I'd better burn the house down, I suppose, than let other people blow themselves up with my gunpowder," she thought as she watched the *Demon of the Jura* whisk away, a little black cinder with fiery eyes.

But when nothing remained of all her three months' work except a heap of ashes and the money in her lap, Jo looked sober, as she sat on the floor, wondering what she ought to do about her wages.

"I think I haven't done much harm *yet*, and may keep this to pay for my time," she said, after a long meditation, adding impatiently, "I almost wish I hadn't any conscience, it's so inconvenient. If I didn't care about doing right, and didn't feel uncomfortable when doing wrong, I should get on capitally. I can't help wishing sometimes, that Father and Mother hadn't been so particular about such things."

Ah, Jo, instead of wishing that, thank God that "Father and Mother *were* particular," and pity from your heart those who have no such guardians to hedge them round with principles which may seem like prison walls to impatient youth, but which will prove sure foundations to build character upon in womanhood.

Jo wrote no more sensational stories, deciding that the money did not pay for her share of the sensation, but going to the other extreme, as is the way with people of her stamp, she took a course of Mrs. Sherwood, Miss Edgeworth, and Hannah More, and then produced a tale which might have been more properly called an essay or a sermon, so intensely moral was it. She had her doubts about it from the beginning, for her lively fancy and girlish romance felt as ill at ease in the new style as she would have done masquerading in the stiff and cumbrous costume of the last century. She sent this didactic gem to several markets, but it found no purchaser, and she was inclined to agree with Mr. Dashwood that morals didn't sell.

Then she tried a child's story, which she could easily have disposed of if she had not been mercenary enough to demand filthy lucre for it. The only person who offered enough to make it worth her while to try juvenile literature was a worthy gentleman who felt it his mission to convert all the world to his particular belief. But much as she liked to write for children, Jo could not consent to depict all her naughty boys as being eaten by bears or tossed by mad bulls because they did not go to a particular Sabbath school, nor all the good infants who did go as rewarded by every kind of bliss, from gilded gingerbread to escorts of angels when they departed this life with psalms or sermons on their lisping tongues. So nothing came of these trials, and Jo corked up her inkstand, and said in a fit of very wholesome humility—

"I don't know anything; I'll wait till I do before I try again, and, meantime, 'sweep mud in the street,' if I can't do better; that's honest, at least"; which decision proved that her second tumble down the beanstalk had done her some good.

While these internal revolutions were going on, her external life had been as busy and uneventful as usual, and if she sometimes looked serious or a little sad no one observed it but Professor Bhaer. He did it so quietly that Jo never knew he was watching to see if she would accept and profit by his reproof; but she stood the test, and he was satisfied, for though no words passed between them, he knew that she had given up writing. Not only did he guess it by the fact that the second finger of her right hand was no longer inky, but she spent her evenings downstairs now, was met no more among newspaper offices, and studied with a dogged patience, which assured him that she was bent on occupying her mind with something useful, if not pleasant.

He helped her in many ways, proving himself a true friend, and Jo was happy, for while her pen lay idle, she was learning other lessons besides German, and laying a foundation for the sensation story of her own life.

It was a pleasant winter and a long one, for she did not leave Mrs. Kirke till June. Everyone seemed sorry when the time came; the children were inconsolable, and Mr. Bhaer's hair stuck straight up all over his head, for he always rumpled it wildly when disturbed in mind.

"Going home? Ah, you are happy that you haf a home to go in," he said, when she told him, and sat silently pulling his beard in the corner, while she held a little levee on that last evening.

She was going early, so she bade them all good-by overnight; and when his turn came, she said warmly, "Now, sir, you won't forget to come and see us, if you ever travel our way, will you? I'll never forgive you if you do, for I want them all to know my friend."

"Do you? Shall I come?" he asked, looking down at her with an eager expression which she did not see.

"Yes, come next month. Laurie graduates then, and you'd enjoy Commencement as something new."

"That is your best friend, of whom you speak?" he said in an altered tone.

"Yes, my boy Teddy. I'm very proud of him and should like you to see him."

Jo looked up then, quite unconscious of anything but her own pleasure in the prospect of showing them to one another. Something in Mr. Bhaer's face suddenly recalled the fact that she might find Laurie more than a "best friend," and simply because she particularly wished not to look as if anything was the matter, she involuntarily began to blush, and the more she tried not to, the redder she grew. If it had not been for Tina on her knee, she didn't know what would have become of her. Fortunately the child was moved to hug her, so she managed to hide her face an instant, hoping the Professor did not see it. But he did, and his own changed again from that momentary anxiety to its usual expression, as he said cordially—

"I fear I shall not make the time for that, but I wish the friend much success, and you all happiness. *Gott* bless you!"

And with that, he shook hands warmly, shouldered Tina, and went away.

But after the boys were abed, he sat long before his fire with the tired look on his face and the "*heimweh*," or home-sickness, lying heavy at his heart. Once, when he remembered Jo as she sat with the little child in her lap and that new softness in her face, he leaned his head on his hands a minute, and then roamed about the room, as if in search of something that he could not find.

"It is not for me, I must not hope it now," he said to himself, with a sigh that was almost a groan; then, as if reproaching himself for the longing that he could not repress, he went and kissed the two tousled heads upon the pillow, took down his seldom-used meerschaum, and opened his Plato.

He did his best and did it manfully, but I don't think he found that a pair of rampant boys, a pipe, or even the divine Plato, were very satisfactory substitutes for wife and child and home.

Early as it was, he was at the station next morning to see Jo off; and, thanks to him, she began her solitary journey with the pleasant memory of a familiar face smiling its fare-well, a bunch of violets to keep her company, and, best of all, the happy thought, "Well, the winter's gone, and I've written no books, earned no fortune, but I've made a friend worth having and I'll try to keep him all my life."

Chapter 35

Heartache

WHATEVER HIS MOTIVE might have been, Laurie studied to some purpose that year, for he graduated with honor, and gave the Latin oration with the grace of a Phillips and the eloquence of a Demosthenes, so his friends said. They were all there, his grandfather—oh, so proud!—Mr. and Mrs. March, John and Meg, Jo and Beth, and all exulted over him with the sincere admiration which boys make light of at the time, but fail to win from the world by any after-triumphs.

"I've got to stay for this confounded supper, but I shall be home early tomorrow. You'll come and meet me as usual, girls?" Laurie said, as he put the sisters into the carriage after the joys of the day were over. He said "girls," but he meant Jo, for she was the only one who kept up the old custom; she had not the heart to refuse her splendid, successful boy anything, and answered warmly—

"I'll come, Teddy, rain or shine, and march before you, playing 'Hail the conquering hero comes,' on a jew's-harp."

Laurie thanked her with a look that made her think in a sudden panic, "Oh, deary me! I know he'll say something, and then what shall I do?"

Evening meditation and morning work somewhat allayed her fears, and having decided that she wouldn't be vain enough to think people were going to propose when she had given them every reason to know what her answer would be, she set forth at the appointed time, hoping Teddy wouldn't do anything to make her hurt his poor little feelings. A call at Meg's, and a refreshing sniff and sip at the Daisy and Demijohn, still further fortified her for the tête-à-tête, but when she saw a stalwart figure looming in the distance, she had a strong desire to turn about and run away.

"Where's the jew's-harp, Jo?" cried Laurie, as soon as he was within speaking distance.

"I forgot it." And Jo took heart again, for that salutation could not be called loverlike.

She always used to take his arm on these occasions; now she did not, and he made no complaint, which was a bad sign, but talked on rapidly about all sorts of faraway subjects, till they turned from the road into the little path that led homeward through the grove. Then he walked more slowly, suddenly lost his fine flow of language, and now and then a dreadful pause occurred. To rescue the conversation from one of the wells of silence into which it kept falling, Jo said hastily, "Now you must have a good long holiday!"

"I intend to."

Something in his resolute tone made Jo look up quickly to find him looking down at her with an expression that assured her the dreaded moment had come, and made her put out her hand with an imploring, "No, Teddy, please don't!"

"I will, and you *must* hear me. It's no use, Jo, we've got to have it out, and the sooner the better for both of us," he answered, getting flushed and excited all at once.

"Say what you like, then. I'll listen," said Jo, with a desperate sort of patience.

Laurie was a young lover, but he was in earnest, and meant to "have it out," if he died in the attempt, so he plunged into the subject with characteristic impetuosity, saying in a voice that *would* get choky now and then, in spite of manful efforts to keep it steady—

"I've loved you ever since I've known you, Jo, couldn't help it, you've been so good to me. I've tried to show it, but you wouldn't let me; now I'm going to make you hear, and give me an answer, for I *can't* go on so any longer."

"I wanted to save you this. I thought you'd understand—" began Jo, finding it a great deal harder than she expected.

"I know you did, but girls are so queer you never know what they mean. They say no when they mean yes, and drive a man out of his wits just for the fun of it," returned Laurie, entrenching himself behind an undeniable fact.

"*I* don't. I never wanted to make you care for me so, and I went away to keep you from it if I could."

"I thought so; it was like you, but it was no use. I only loved you all the more, and I worked hard to please you, and I gave up billiards and everything you didn't like, and waited and never complained, for I hoped you'd love me, though I'm not not half good enough—" Here there was a choke that couldn't be controlled, so he decapitated buttercups while he cleared his "confounded throat."

"You, you are, you're a great deal too good for me, and I'm so grateful to you, and so proud and fond of you, I don't see why I can't love you as you want me to. I've tried, but I can't change the feeling, and it would be a lie to say I do when I don't."

"Really, truly, Jo?"

He stopped short, and caught both her hands as he put his question with a look that she did not soon forget.

"Really, truly, dear."

They were in the grove now, close by the stile; and when the last words fell reluctantly from Jo's lips, Laurie dropped her hands and turned as if to go on, but for once in his life that fence was too much for him; so he just laid his head down on the mossy post, and stood so still that Jo was frightened.

"Oh, Teddy, I'm sorry, so desperately sorry, I could kill myself if it would do any good! I wish you wouldn't take it so hard. I can't help it. You know it's impossible for people to make themselves love other people if they don't," cried Jo inelegantly but remorsefully, as she softly patted his shoulder, remembering the time when he had comforted her so long ago.

"They do sometimes," said a muffled voice from the post.

"I don't believe it's the right sort of love, and I'd rather not try it" was the decided answer.

There was a long pause, while a blackbird sung blithely on the willow by the river, and the tall grass rustled in the wind. Presently Jo said very soberly, as she sat down on the step of the stile, "Laurie, I want to tell you something."

He started as if he had been shot, threw up his head, and cried out in a fierce tone, "*Don't* tell me that, Jo, I can't bear it now!"

"Tell what?" she asked, wondering at his violence.

"That you love that old man."

"What old man?" demanded Jo, thinking he must mean his grandfather.

"That devilish Professor you were always writing about. If you say you love him, I know I shall do something desperate." And he looked as if he would keep his word, as he clenched his hands with a wrathful spark in his eyes.

Jo wanted to laugh, but restrained herself and said warmly, for she, too, was getting excited with all this, "Don't swear, Teddy! He isn't old, nor anything bad, but good and kind, and the best friend I've got, next to you. Pray, don't fly into a passion. I want to be kind, but I know I shall get angry if you abuse my Professor. I haven't the least idea of loving him or anybody else."

"But you will after a while, and then what will become of me?"

"You'll love someone else too, like a sensible boy, and forget all this trouble."

"I *can't* love anyone else, and I'll never forget you, Jo, never! never!" with a stamp to emphasize his passionate words.

"What shall I do with him?" sighed Jo, finding that emotions were more unmanageable than she expected. "You haven't heard what I wanted to tell you. Sit down and listen, for indeed I want to do right and make you happy," she said, hoping to soothe him with a little reason, which proved that she knew nothing about love.

Seeing a ray of hope in that last speech, Laurie threw himself down on the grass at her feet, leaned his arm on the lower step of the stile, and looked up at her with an expectant face. Now that arrangement was not conducive to calm speech or clear thought on Jo's part, for how *could* she say hard things to her boy while he watched her with eyes full of love and longing, and lashes still wet with the bitter drop or two her hardness of heart had wrung from him? She gently turned his head away, saying, as she stroked the wavy hair which had been allowed to grow for her sake—how touching that was, to be sure!—

"I agree with Mother that you and I are not suited to each other, because our quick tempers and strong wills would probably make us very miserable, if we were so foolish as to—" Jo paused a little over the last word, but Laurie uttered it with a rapturous expression.

"Marry—no, we shouldn't! If you loved me, Jo, I should be a perfect saint, for you could make me anything you like."

"No, I can't. I've tried it and failed, and I won't risk our happiness by such a serious experiment. We don't agree and we never shall, so we'll be good friends all our lives, but we won't go and do anything rash."

"Yes, we will if we get the chance," muttered Laurie rebelliously.

"Now do be reasonable, and take a sensible view of the case," implored Jo, almost at her wit's end.

"I won't be reasonable, I don't want to take what you call 'a sensible view,' it won't help me, and it only makes you harder. I don't believe you've got any heart."

"I wish I hadn't."

There was a little quiver in Jo's voice, and, thinking it a good omen, Laurie turned round, bringing all his persuasive powers to bear as he said, in the wheedlesome tone that had never been so dangerously wheedlesome before, "Don't disappoint us, dear! Everyone expects it. Grandpa has set his heart upon it, your people like it, and I can't get on without you. Say you will, and let's be happy. Do, do!"

Not until months afterward did Jo understand how she had the strength of mind to hold fast to the resolution she had made when she decided that she did not love her boy, and never could. It was very hard to do, but she did it, knowing that delay was both useless and cruel.

"I can't say 'Yes' truly, so I won't say it at all. You'll see that I'm right, by-and-by, and thank me for it—" she began solemnly.

"I'll be hanged if I do!" And Laurie bounced up off the grass, burning with indignation at the bare idea.

"Yes, you will!" persisted Jo. "You'll get over this after a while, and find some lovely accomplished girl, who will adore you, and make a fine mistress for your fine house. I shouldn't. I'm homely and awkward and odd and old, and you'd be ashamed of me, and we should quarrel—we can't help it even now, you see—and I shouldn't like elegant society and you would, and you'd hate my scribbling, and I couldn't get on without it, and we should be unhappy, and wish we hadn't done it, and everything would be horrid!"

"Anything more?" asked Laurie, finding it hard to listen patiently to this prophetic burst.

"Nothing more, except that I don't believe I shall ever marry. I'm happy as I am, and love my liberty too well to be in any hurry to give it up for any mortal man."

"I know better!" broke in Laurie. "You think so now, but there'll come a time when you *will* care for somebody, and you'll love him tremendously, and live and die for him. I know you will, it's your way, and I shall have to stand by and see it." And the despairing lover cast his hat upon the ground with a gesture that would have seemed comical, if his face had not been so tragic.

"Yes, I *will* live and die for him, if he ever comes and makes me love him in spite of myself, and you must do the best you can!" cried Jo, losing patience with poor Teddy. "I've done my best, but you *won't* be reasonable, and it's selfish of you to keep teasing for what I can't give. I shall always be fond of you, very fond indeed, as a friend, but I'll never marry you, and the sooner you believe it the better for both of us—so now!"

That speech was like fire to gunpowder. Laurie looked at her a minute as if he did not quite know what to do with himself, then turned sharply away, saying in a desperate sort of tone, "You'll be sorry some day, Jo."

"Oh, where are you going?" she cried, for his face frightened her.

"To the devil!" was the consoling answer.

For a minute Jo's heart stood still, as he swung himself down the bank toward the river, but it takes much folly, sin or misery to send a young man to a violent death, and Laurie was not one of the weak sort who are conquered by a single failure. He had no thought of a melodramatic plunge, but some blind instinct led him to fling hat and coat into his boat, and row away with all his might, making better time up the river than he had done in many a race. Jo drew a long breath and unclasped her hands as she watched the poor fellow trying to outstrip the trouble which he carried in his heart.

"That will do him good, and he'll come home in such a tender, pentitent state of mind, that I shan't dare to see him," she said, adding, as she went slowly home, feeling as if she had murdered some innocent thing, and buried it under the leaves, "Now I must go and prepare Mr. Laurence to be very kind to my poor boy. I wish he'd love Beth, perhaps he may in time, but I begin to think I was mistaken about her. Oh dear! How can girls like to have lovers and refuse them. I think it's dreadful."

Being sure that no could do it so well as herself, she went straight to Mr. Laurence, told the hard story bravely through, and then broke down, crying so dismally over her own insensibility that the kind old gentleman, though sorely disappointed, did not utter a reproach. He found it difficult to understand how any girl could help loving Laurie, and hoped she would change her mind, but he knew even better than Jo that love cannot be forced, so he shook his head sadly and resolved to carry his boy out of harm's way, for Young Impetuosity's parting words to Jo disturbed him more than he would confess.

When Laurie came home, dead tired but quite composed, his grandfather met him as if he knew nothing, and kept up the delusion very successfully for an hour or two. But when they sat together in the twilight, the time they used to enjoy so much, it was hard work for the old man to ramble on as usual, and harder still for the young one to listen to praises of the last year's success, which to him now seemed love's labor lost. He bore it as long as he could, then went to his piano and began to play. The windows were open, and Jo, walking in the garden with Beth, for once understood music better than her sister, for he played the "Sonata Pathétique," and played it as he never did before.

"That's very fine, I dare say, but it's sad enough to make one cry. Give us something gayer, lad," said Mr. Laurence, whose kind old heart was full of sympathy, which he longed to show but knew not how.

Laurie dashed into a livelier strain, played stormily for several minutes, and would have got through bravely, if in a momentary lull Mrs. March's voice had not been heard calling, "Jo, dear, come in. I want you."

Just what Laurie longed to say, with a different meaning! As he listened, he lost his place, the music ended with a broken chord, and the musician sat silent in the dark.

"I can't stand this," muttered the old gentleman. Up he got, groped his way to the piano, laid a kind hand on either of the broad shoulders, and said, as gently as a woman, "I know, my boy, I know."

No answer for an instant, then Laurie asked sharply, "Who told you?"

"Jo herself."

"Then there's an end of it!" And he shook off his grandfather's hands with an impatient motion, for though grateful for the sympathy, his man's pride could not bear a man's pity.

"Not quite. I want to say one thing, and then there shall be an end of it," returned Mr. Laurence with unusual mildness. "You won't care to stay at home just now, perhaps?"

"I don't intend to run away from a girl. Jo can't prevent my seeing her, and I shall stay and do it is long as I like," interrupted Laurie in a defiant tone.

"Not if you are the gentleman I think you. I'm disappointed, but the girl can't help it, and the only thing left for you to do is to go away for a time. Where will you go?"

"Anywhere. I don't care what becomes of me." And Laurie got up with a reckless laugh that grated on his granfather's ear.

"Take it like a man, and don't do anything rash, for God's sake. Why not go abroad, as you planned, and forget it?"

"I can't."

"But you've been wild to go, and I promised you should when you got through college."

"Ah, but I didn't mean to go alone!" And Laurie walked fast through the room with an expression which it was well his grandfather did not see.

"I don't ask you to go alone. There's someone ready and glad to go with you, anywhere in the world."

"Who, sir?" stopping to listen.

"Myself."

Laurie came back as quickly as he went, and put out his hand, saying huskily, "I'm a selfish brute, but—you know— Grandfather—"

"Lord help me, yes, I do know, for I've been through it all before, once in my own young days, and then with your father. Now, my dear boy, just sit quietly down and hear my plan. It's all settled, and can be carried out at once," said Mr. Laurence, keeping hold of the young man, as if fearful that he would break away as his father had done before him.

"Well, sir, what is it?" And Laurie sat down, without a sign of interest in face or voice.

"There is business in London that needs looking after. I meant you should attend to it, but I can do it better myself, and things here will get on very well with Brooke to manage them. My partners do almost everything, I'm merely holding on till you take my place, and can be off at any time."

"But you hate traveling, sir. I can't ask it of you at your age," began Laurie, who was grateful for the sacrifice, but much preferred to go alone, if he went at all.

The old gentleman knew that perfectly well, and particularly desired to prevent it, for the mood in which he found his grandson assured him that it would not be wise to leave him to his own devices. So, stifling a natural regret at the thought of the home comforts he would leave behind him, he said stoutly, "Bless your soul, I'm not superannuated yet. I quite enjoy the idea; it will do me good, and my old bones won't suffer, for traveling nowadays is almost as easy as sitting in a chair."

A restless movement from Laurie suggested that *his* chair was not easy, or that he did not like the plan, and made the old man add hastily, "I don't mean to be a marplot or a burden. I go because I think you'd feel happier than if I was left behind. I don't intend to gad about with you, but leave you free to go where you like, while I amuse myself in my own way. I've friends in London and Paris, and should like to visit them; meantime you can go to Italy, Germany, Switzerland, where you will, and enjoy pictures, music, scenery, and adventures to your heart's content."

Now, Laurie felt just then that his heart was entirely broken and the world a howling wilderness, but at the sound of certain words which the old gentleman artfully introduced into his closing sentence, the broken heart gave an unexpected leap, and a green oasis or two suddenly appeared in the howling wilderness. He sighed, and then said, in a spiritless tone, "Just as you like, sir, it doesn't matter where I go or what I do."

"It does to me, remember that, my lad. I give you entire liberty, but I trust you to make an honest use of it. Promise me that, Laurie."

"Anything you like, sir."

"Good," thought the old gentleman. "You don't care now, but there'll come a time when that promise will keep you out of mischief, or I'm much mistaken."

Being an energetic individual, Mr. Laurence struck while the iron was hot, and before the blighted being recovered spirit enough to rebel, they were off. During the time necessary for preparation, Laurie bore himself as young gentlemen usually do in such cases. He was moody, irritable, and pensive by turns; lost his appetite, neglected his dress and devoted much time to playing tempestuously on his piano; avoided Jo, but consoled himself by staring at her from his window, with a tragic face that haunted her dreams by night and oppressed her with a heavy sense of guilt by day.

Unlike some sufferers, he never spoke of his unrequited passion, and would allow no one, not even Mrs. March, to attempt consolation or offer sympathy. On some accounts, this was a relief to his friends, but the weeks before his departure were very uncomfortable, and everyone rejoiced that the "poor, dear fellow was going away to forget his trouble, and come home happy." Of course, he smiled darkly at their delusion, but passed it by with the sad superiority of one who knew that his fidelity like his love was unalterable.

When the parting came he affected high spirits, to conceal certain inconvenient emotions which seemed inclined to assert themselves. This gaiety did not impose upon anybody, but they tried to look as if it did for his sake, and he got on very well till Mrs. March kissed him, with a whisper full of motherly solicitude; then feeling that he was going very fast, he hastily embraced them all round, not forgetting the afflicted Hannah, and ran downstairs as if for his life. Jo followed a minute after to wave her hand to him if he looked round. He did look round, came back, put his arms about her as she stood on the step above him, and looked up at her with a face that made his short appeal both eloquent and pathetic.

"Oh, Jo, can't you?"

"Teddy, dear, I wish I could!"

That was all, except a little pause; then Laurie straightened himself up, said, "It's all right, never mind," and went away without another word. Ah, but it wasn't all right, and Jo *did* mind, for while the curly head lay on her arm a minute after her hard answer, she felt as if she had stabbed her dearest friend, and when he left her without a look behind him, she knew that the boy Laurie never would come again.

Chapter 36

Beth's Secret

WHEN JO CAME HOME that spring, she had been struck with the change in Beth. No one spoke of it or seemed aware of it, for it had come too gradually to startle those who saw her daily, but to eyes sharpened by absence, it was very plain and a heavy weight fell on Jo's heart as she saw her sister's face. It was no paler and but little thinner than in the autumn, yet there was a strange, transparent look about it, as if the mortal was being slowly refined away, and the immortal shining through the frail flesh with an indescribably pathetic beauty. Jo saw and felt it, but said nothing at the time, and soon the first impression lost much of its power, for Beth seemed happy, no one appeared to doubt that she was better, and presently in other cares Jo for a time forgot her fear.

But when Laurie was gone, and peace prevailed again, the vague anxiety returned and haunted her. She had confessed her sins and been forgiven, but when she showed her savings and proposed the mountain trip, Beth had thanked her heartily, but begged not to go so far away from home. Another little visit to the seashore would suit her better, and as Grandma could not be prevailed upon to leave the babies, Jo took Beth down to the quiet place, where she could live much in the open air, and let the fresh sea breezes blow a little color into her pale cheeks.

It was not a fashionable place, but even among the pleasant people there, the girls made few friends, preferring to live for one another. Beth was too shy to enjoy society, and Jo too wrapped up in her to care for anyone else; so they were all in all to each other, and came and went, quite unconscious of the interest they excited in those about them, who watched with sympathetic eyes the strong sister and the feeble one, always together, as if they felt instinctively that a long separation was not far away.

They did feel it, yet neither spoke of it; for often between ourselves and those nearest and dearest to us there exists a reserve which it is very hard to overcome. Jo felt as if a veil had fallen between her heart and Beth's, but when she put out her hand to lift it up, there seemed something sacred in the silence, and she waited for Beth to speak. She wondered, and was thankful also, that her parents did not seem to see what she saw, and during the quiet weeks when the shadows grew so plain to her, she said nothing of it to those at home, believing that it would tell itself when Beth came back no better. She wondered still more if her sister really guessed the hard truth, and what thoughts were passing through her mind during the long hours when she lay on the warm rocks with her head in Jo's lap, while the winds blew healthfully over her and the sea made music at her feet.

One day Beth told her. Jo thought she was asleep, she lay so still, and putting down her book, sat looking at her with wistful eyes, trying to see signs of hope in the faint color on Beth's cheeks. But she could not find enough to satisfy her, for the cheeks were very thin, and the hands seemed too feeble to hold even the rosy little shells they had been gathering. It came to her then more bitterly than ever that Beth was slowly drifting away from her, and her arms instinctively tightened their hold upon the dearest treasure she possessed. For a minute her eyes were too dim for seeing, and, when they cleared, Beth was looking up at her so tenderly that there was hardly any need for her to say, "Jo, dear, I'm glad you know it. I've tried to tell you, but I couldn't."

There was no answer except her sister's cheek against her own, not even tears, for when most deeply moved, Jo did not cry. She was the weaker then, and Beth tried to comfort and sustain her, with her arms about her and the soothing words she whispered in her ear.

"I've known it for a good while, dear, and, now I'm used to it, it isn't hard to think of or to bear. Try to see it so, and don't be troubled about me, because it's best; indeed it is."

"Is this what made you so unhappy in the autumn, Beth? You did not feel it then, and keep it to yourself so long, did you?" asked Jo, refusing to see or say that it *was* best, but glad to know that Laurie had no part in Beth's trouble.

"Yes, I gave up hoping then, but I didn't like to own it. I tried to think it was a sick fancy, and would not let it trouble anyone. But when I saw you all so well and strong and full of happy plans, it was hard to feel that I could never be like you, and then I was miserable, Jo."

"Oh, Beth, and you didn't tell me, didn't let me comfort and help you! How could you shut me out, and bear it all alone?"

Jo's voice was full of tender reproach, and her heart ached to think of the solitary struggle that must have gone on while Beth learned to say good-by to health, love, and life, and take up her cross so cheerfully.

"Perhaps it was wrong, but I tried to do right. I wasn't sure, no one said anything, and I hoped I was mistaken. It would have been selfish to frighten you all when Marmee was so anxious about Meg, and Amy away, and you so happy with Laurie—at least, I thought so then."

"And I thought that you loved him, Beth, and I went away because I couldn't," cried Jo, glad to say all the truth.

Beth looked so amazed at the idea that Jo smiled in spite of her pain, and added softly, "Then you didn't, deary? I was afraid it was so, and imagined your poor little heart full of lovelornity all that while."

"Why, Jo, how could I, when he was so fond of you?" asked Beth, as innocently as a child. "I do love him dearly; he is so good to me, how can I help it? But he never could be anything to me but my brother. I hope he truly will be, sometime."

"Not through me," said Jo decidedly. "Amy is left for him, and they would suit excellently, but I have no heart for such things, now. I don't care what becomes of anybody but you, Beth. You *must* get well."

"I want to, oh, so much! I try, but every day I lose a little, and feel more sure that I shall never gain it back. It's like the tide, Jo, when it turns, it goes slowly, but it can't be stopped."

"It *shall* be stopped, your tide must not turn so soon, nineteen is too young. Beth, I can't let you go. I'll work and pray and fight against it. I'll keep you in spite of everything; there must be ways, it can't be too late. God won't be so cruel as to take you from me," cried poor Jo rebelliously, for her spirit was far less piously submissive than Beth's.

Simple, sincere people seldom speak much of their piety; it shows itself in acts rather than in words, and has more influence than homilies or protestations. Beth could not reason upon or explain the faith that gave her courage and patience to give up life, and cheerfully wait for death. Like a confiding child, she asked no questions, but left everything to God and nature, Father and mother of us all, feeling sure that they, and they only, could teach and strengthen heart and spirit for this life and the life to come. She did not rebuke Jo with saintly speeches, only loved her better for her passionate affection, and clung more closely to the dear human love, from which our Father never means us to be weaned, but through which He draws us closer to Himself. She could not say, "I'm glad to go," for life was very sweet to her; she could only sob out, "I try to be willing," while she held fast to Jo, as the first bitter wave of this great sorrow broke over them together.

By and by Beth said, with recovered serenity, "You'll tell them this when we go home?"

"I think they will see it without words," sighed Jo, for now it seemed to her that Beth changed every day.

"Perhaps not, I've heard that the people who love best are often blindest to such things. If they don't see it, you will tell them for me. I don't want any secrets, and it's kinder to prepare them. Meg has John and the babies to comfort her, but you must stand by Father and Mother, won't you, Jo?"

"If I can. But, Beth, I don't give up yet. I'm going to believe that it is a sick fancy, and not let you think it's true," said Jo, trying to speak cheerfully.

Beth lay a minute thinking, and then said in her quiet way, "I don't know how to express myself, and shouldn't try to anyone but you, because I can't speak out except to my Jo. I only mean to say that I have a feeling that it never was intended I should live long. I'm not like the rest of you; I never made any plans about what I'd do when I grew up; I never thought of being married, as you all did. I couldn't seem to imagine myself anything but stupid little Beth, trotting about at home, of no use anywhere but there. I never wanted to go away, and the hard part now is the leaving you all. I'm not afraid, but it seems as if I should be homesick for you even in heaven."

Jo could not speak, and for several minutes there was no sound but the sigh of the wind and the lapping of the tide. A white-winged gull flew by, with the flash of sunshine on its silvery breast; Beth watched it till it vanished, and her eyes were full of sadness. A little gray-coated sand bird came tripping over the beach, "peeping" softly to itself, as if enjoying the sun and sea; it came quite close to Beth, looked at her with a friendly eye and sat upon a warm stone, dressing its wet feathers, quite at home. Beth smiled and felt comforted, for the tiny thing seemed to offer its small friendship and remind her that a pleasant world was still to be enjoyed.

"Dear little bird! See, Jo, how tame it is. I like peeps better than the gulls: they are not so wild and handsome, but they seem happy, confiding little things. I used to call them my birds last summer, and Mother said they reminded her of me —busy, quaker-colored creatures, always near the shore, and always chirping that contented little song of theirs. You are the gull, Jo, strong and wild, fond of the storm and the wind, flying far out to sea, and happy all alone. Meg is the turtle-dove, and Amy is like the lark she writes about, trying to get up among the clouds, but always dropping down into its nest again. Dear little girl! She's so ambitious, but her heart is good and tender, and no matter how high she flies, she never will forget home. I hope I shall see her again, but she seems *so* far away."

"She is coming in the spring, and I mean that you shall be all ready to see and enjoy her. I'm going to have you well and rosy by that time," began Jo, feeling that of all the changes in Beth, the talking change was the greatest, for it seemed to cost no effort now, and she thought aloud in a way quite unlike bashful Beth.

"Jo, dear, don't hope any more. It won't do any good, I'm sure of that. We won't be miserable, but enjoy being together while we wait. We'll have happy times, for I don't suffer much, and I think the tide will go out easily, if you help me."

Jo leaned down to kiss the tranquil face, and with that silent kiss, she dedicated herself soul and body to Beth.

She was right: there was no need of any words when they got home, for Father and Mother saw plainly now what they had prayed to be saved from seeing. Tired with her short journey, Beth went at once to bed, saying how glad she was to be home, and when Jo went down, she found that she would be spared the hard task of telling Beth's secret. Her father stood leaning his head on the mantelpiece, and did not turn as she came in; but her mother stretched out her arms as if for help, and Jo went to comfort her without a word.

Chapter 37

New Impressions

AT THREE o'clock in the afternoon, all the fashionable world at Nice may be seen on the Promenade des Anglais—a charming place, for the wide walk, bordered with palms, flowers, and tropical shrubs, is bounded on one side by the sea, on the other by the grand drive, lined with hotels and villas, while beyond lie orange orchards and the hills. Many nations are represented, many languages spoken, many costumes worn, and on a sunny day the spectacle is as gay and brilliant as a carnival. Haughty English, lively French, sober Germans, handsome Spaniards, ugly Russians, meek Jews, free-and-easy Americans, all drive, sit, or saunter here, chatting over the news, and criticizing the latest celebrity who has arrived—Ristori or Dickens, Victor Emmanuel or the Queen of the Sandwich Islands. The equipages are as varied as the company and attract as much attention, especially the low basket barouches in which ladies drive themselves, with a pair of dashing ponies, gay nets to keep their voluminous flounces from overflowing the diminutive vehicles, and little grooms on the perch behind.

Along this walk, on Christmas Day, a tall young man walked slowly, with his hands behind him, and a somewhat absent expression of countenance. He looked like an Italian, was dressed like an Englishman, and had the independent air of an American—a combination which caused sundry pairs of feminine eyes to look approvingly after him, and sundry dandies in black velvet suits, with rose-colored neckties, buff gloves, and orange flowers in their buttonholes, to shrug their shoulders, and then envy him his inches. There were plenty of pretty faces to admire, but the young man took little notice of them, except to glance now and then at some blonde girl or lady in blue. Presently he strolled out of the promenade and stood a moment at the crossing, as if undecided whether to go and listen to the band in the Jardin Publique, or to wander along the beach toward Castle Hill. The quick trot of ponies feet made him look up, as one of the little carriages, containing a single lady, came rapidly down the street. The lady was young, blonde, and dressed in blue. He stared a minute, then his whole face woke up, and, waving his hat like a boy, he hurried forward to meet her.

"Oh, Laurie, is it really you? I thought you'd never come!" cried Amy, dropping the reins and holding out both hands, to the great scandalization of a French mamma, who hastened her daughter's steps, lest she should be demoralized by beholding the free manners of these "mad English."

"I was detained by the way, but I promised to spend Christmas with you, and here I am."

"How is your grandfather? When did you come? Where are you staying?"

"Very well—last night—at the Chauvain. I called at your hotel, but you were all out."

"I have so much to say, I don't know where to begin! Get in and we can talk at our ease, I was going for a drive and longing for company. Flo's saving up for tonight."

"What happens then, a ball?"

"A Christmas party at our hotel. There are many Americans there, and they give it in honor of the day. You'll go with us, of course? Aunt will be charmed."

"Thank you. Where now?" asked Laurie, leaning back and folding his arms, a proceeding which suited Amy, who preferred to drive, for her parasol whip and blue reins over the white ponies' backs afforded her infinite satisfaction.

"I'm going to the bankers first for letters, and then to Castle Hill; the view is so lovely, and I like to feed the peacocks. Have you ever been there?"

"Often, years ago, but I don't mind having a look at it."

"Now tell me all about yourself. The last I heard of you, your grandfather wrote that he expected you from Berlin."

"Yes, I spent a month there and then joined him in Paris, where he has settled for the winter. He has friends there and finds plenty to amuse him, so I go and come, and we get on capitally."

"That's a sociable arrangement," said Amy, missing something in Laurie's manner, though she couldn't tell what.

"Why, you see, he hates to travel, and I hate to keep still, so we each suit ourselves, and there is no trouble. I am often with him, and he enjoys my adventures, while I like to feel that someone is glad to see me when I get back from my wanderings. Dirty old hole, isn't it?" he added, with a look of disgust as they drove along the boulevard to the Place Napoleon in the old city.

"The dirt is picturesque, so I don't mind. The river and the hills are delicious, and these glimpses of the narrow cross streets are my delight. Now we shall have to wait for that procession to pass; it's going to the Church of St. John."

While Laurie listlessly watched the procession of priests under their canopies, white-veiled nuns bearing lighted tapers, and some brotherhood in blue chanting as they walked, Amy watched him, and felt a new sort of shyness steal over her, for he was changed, and she could not find the merry-faced boy she left in the moody-looking man beside her. He was handsomer than ever and greatly improved, she thought, but now that the flush of pleasure at meeting her was over, he looked tired and spiritless—not sick, nor exactly unhappy, but older and graver than a year or two of prosperous life should have made him. She couldn't understand it and did not venture to ask questions, so she shook her head and touched up her ponies, as the procession wound away across the arches of the Paglioni bridge and vanished in the church.

"Que pensez-vous?" she said, airing her French, which had improved in quantity, if not in quality, since she came abroad.

"That mademoiselle has made good use of her time, and the result is charming," replied Laurie, bowing, with his hand on his heart and an admiring look.

She blushed with pleasure, but somehow the compliment did not satisfy her like the blunt praises he used to give her at home, when he promenaded round her on festival occasions, and told her she was "altogether jolly," with a hearty smile and an approving pat on the head. She didn't like the new tone, for though not blasé, it sounded indifferent in spite of the look.

"If that's the way he's going to grow up, I wish he'd stay a boy," she thought, with a curious sense of disappointment and discomfort, trying meantime to seem quite easy and gay.

At Avigdor's she found the precious home letters and, giving the reins to Laurie, read them luxuriously as they wound up the shady road between green hedges, where tea roses bloomed as freshly as in June.

"Beth is very poorly, Mother says. I often think I ought to go home, but they all say 'stay.' So I do, for I shall never have another chance like this," said Amy, looking sober over one page.

"I think you are right, there; you could do nothing at home, and it is a great comfort to them to know that you are well and happy, and enjoying so much, my dear."

He drew a little nearer, and looked more like his old self as he said that; and the fear that sometimes weighed on Amy's heart was lightened, for the look, the act, the brotherly "my dear," seemed to assure her that if any trouble did come, she would not be alone in a strange land. Presently she laughed and showed him a small sketch of Jo in her scribbling suit, with the bow rampantly erect upon her cap, and issuing from her mouth the words, "Genius burns!"

Laurie smiled, took it, put it in his vest pocket "to keep it from blowing away," and listened with interest to the lively letter Amy read him.

"This will be a regularly merry Christmas to me, with presents in the morning, you and letters in the afternoon, and a party at night," said Amy, as they alighted among the ruins of the old fort, and a flock of splendid peacocks came trooping about them, tamely waiting to be fed. While Amy stood laughing on the bank above him as she scattered crumbs to the brilliant birds, Laurie looked at her as she had looked at him, with a natural curiosity to see what changes time and absence had wrought. He found nothing to perplex or disappoint, much to admire and approve, for overlooking a few little affectations of speech and manner, she was as sprightly and graceful as ever, with the addition of that indescribable something in dress and bearing which we call elegance. Always mature for her age, she had gained a certain aplomb in both carriage and conversation, which made her seem more of a woman of the world than she was; but her old petulance now and then showed itself, her strong will still held its own, and her native frankness was unspoiled by foreign polish.

Laurie did not read all this while he watched her feed the peacocks, but he saw enough to satisfy and interest him, and carried away a pretty little picture of a bright-faced girl standing in the sunshine, which brought out the soft hue of her dress, the fresh color of her cheeks, the golden gloss of her hair, and made her a prominent figure in the pleasant scene.

As they came up onto the stone plateau that crowns the hill, Amy waved her hand as if welcoming him to her favorite haunt, and said, pointing here and there, "Do you remember the Cathedral and the Corso, the fishermen dragging their nets in the bay, and the lovely road to Villa Franca, Schubert's Tower, just below, and, best of all, that speck far out to sea which they say is Corsica?"

"I remember, it's not much changed," he answered, without enthusiasm.

"What Jo would give for a sight of that famous speck!" said Amy, feeling in good spirits and anxious to see him so also.

"Yes" was all he said, but he turned and strained his eyes to see the island which a greater usurper than even Napoleon now made interesting in his sight.

"Take a good look at it for her sake, and then come and tell me what you have been doing with yourself all this while," said Amy, seating herself, ready for a good talk.

But she did not get it, for though he joined her and answered all her questions freely, she could only learn that he had roved about the Continent and been to Greece. So after idling away an hour, they drove home again, and having paid his respects to Mrs. Carrol, Laurie left them, promising to return in the evening.

It must be recorded of Amy that she deliberately prinked that night. Time and absence had done its work on both the young people; she had seen her old friend in a new light, not as "our boy," but as a handsome and agreeable man, and she was conscious of a very natural desire to find favor in his sight. Amy knew her good points, and made the most of them with the taste and skill which is a fortune to a poor and pretty woman.

Tarlatan and tulle were cheap at Nice, so she enveloped herself in them on such occasions, and following the sensible English fashion of simple dress for young girls, got up charming little toilettes with fresh flowers, a few trinkets, and all manner of dainty devices, which were both inexpensive and effective. It must be confessed that the artist sometimes got possession of the woman, and indulged in antique coiffures, statuesque attitudes, and classic draperies. But, dear heart, we all have our little weaknesses, and find it easy to pardon such in the young, who satisfy our eyes with their comeliness, and keep our hearts merry with their artless vanities.

"I do want him to think I look well, and tell them so at home," said Amy to herself, as she put on Flo's old white silk ball dress, and covered it with a cloud of fresh illusion, out of which her white shoulders and golden head emerged with a most artistic effect. Her hair she had the sense to let alone, after gathering up the thick waves and curls into a Hebe-like knot at the back of her head.

"It's not the fashion, but it's becoming, and I can't afford to make a fright of myself," she used to say, when advised to frizzle, puff, or braid, as the latest style commanded.

Having no ornaments fine enough for this important occasion. Amy looped her fleecy skirts with rosy clusters of azalea, and framed the white shoulders in delicate green vines. Remembering the painted boots, she surveyed her white satin slippers with girlish satisfaction, and chasséd down the room, admiring her aristocratic feet all by herself.

"My new fan just matches my flowers, my gloves fit to a

charm, and the real lace on Aunt's *mouchoir* gives an air to my whole dress. If I only had a classical nose and mouth I should be perfectly happy," she said, surveying herself with a critical eye and a candle in each hand.

In spite of this affliction, she looked unusually gay and graceful as she glided away; she seldom ran—it did not suit her style, she thought, for, being tall, the stately and Junoesque was more appropriate than the sportive or piquante. She walked up and down the long saloon while waiting for Laurie, and once arranged herself under the chandelier, which had a good effect upon her hair, then she thought better of it, and went away to the other end of the room, as if ashamed of the girlish desire to have the first view a propitious one. It so happened that she could not have done a better thing, for Laurie came in so quietly she did not hear him, and as she stood at the distant window, with her head half turned and one hand gathering up her dress, the slender, white figure against the red curtains was as effective as a well-placed statue.

"Good evening, Diana!" said Laurie, with the look of satisfaction she liked to see in his eyes when they rested on her.

"Good evening, Apollo!" she answered, smiling back at him, for he, too, looked unusually debonair, and the thought of entering the ballroom on the arm of such a personable man caused Amy to pity the four plain Misses Davis from the bottom of her heart.

"Here are your flowers. I arranged them myself, remembering that you didn't like what Hannah calls a 'sot-bookay,' " said Laurie, handing her a delicate nosegay, in a holder that she had long coveted as she daily passed it in Cardiglia's window.

"How kind you are!" she exclaimed gratefully. "If I'd known you were coming I'd have had something ready for you today, though not as pretty as this, I'm afraid."

"Thank you. It isn't what it should be, but you have improved it," he added, as she snapped the silver bracelet on her wrist.

"Please don't."

"I thought you liked that sort of thing?"

"Not from you, it doesn't sound natural, and I like your old bluntness better."

"I'm glad of it," he answered, with a look of relief, then buttoned her gloves for her and asked if his tie was straight, just as he used to do when they went to parties together at home.

The company assembled in the long *salle à manger* that evening was such as one sees nowhere but on the Continent. The hospitable Americans had invited every acquaintance they had in Nice, and having no prejudice against titles, secured a few to add luster to their Christmas ball.

A Russian prince condescended to sit in a corner for an hour and talk with a massive lady, dressed like Hamlet's mother in black velvet with a pearl bridle under her chin. A Polish count, aged eighteen, devoted himself to the ladies, who pronounced him "a fascinating dear," and a German Serene Something, having come for the supper alone, roamed vaguely about, seeking what he might devour. Baron Rothschild's private secretary, a large-nosed Jew in tight boots, affably beamed upon the world, as if his master's name crowned him with a golden halo; a stout Frenchman, who knew the Emperor, came to indulge his mania for dancing, and Lady de Jones, a British matron, adorned the scene with her little family of eight. Of course, there were many light-footed, shrill-voiced American girls, handsome, lifeless-looking English ditto, and a few plain but piquante French demoiselles; likewise the usual set of traveling young gentlemen who disported themselves gaily, while mammas of all nations lined the walls and smiled upon them benignly when they danced with their daughters.

Any young girl can imagine Amy's state of mind when she "took the stage" that night, leaning on Laurie's arm. She knew she looked well, she loved to dance, she felt that her foot was on her native heath in a ballroom, and enjoyed the delightful sense of power which comes when young girls first discover the new and lovely kingdom they are born to rule by virtue of beauty, youth, and womanhood. She did pity the

Davis girls, who were awkward, plain, and destitute of escort, except a grim papa and three grimmer maiden aunts, and she bowed to them in her friendliest manner as she passed, which was good of her, as it permitted them to see her dress, and burn with curiosity to know who her distinguished-looking friend might be. With the first burst of the band, Amy's color rose, her eyes began to sparkle, and her feet to tap the floor impatiently, for she danced well and wanted Laurie to know it: therefore the shock she received can better be imagined than described, when he said in a perfectly tranquil tone, "Do you care to dance?"

"One usually does at a ball."

Her amazed look and quick answer caused Laurie to repair his error as fast as possible.

"I meant the first dance. May I have the honor?"

"I can give you one if I put off the Count. He dances divinely, but he will excuse me, as you are an old friend," said Amy, hoping that the name would have a good effect, and show Laurie that she was not to be trifled with.

"Nice little boy, but rather a short Pole to support

"A daughter of the gods,
   Divinely tall, and most divinely fair,"

was all the satisfaction she got, however.

The set in which they found themselves was composed of English, and Amy was compelled to walk decorously through a cotillion, feeling all the while as if she could dance the tarantella with a relish. Laurie resigned her to the "nice little boy," and went to do his duty to Flo, without securing Amy for the joys to come, which reprehensible want of forethought was properly punished, for she immediately engaged herself till supper, meaning to relent if he then gave any signs of penitence. She showed him her ball book with demure satisfaction when he strolled instead of rushed up to claim her for the next, a glorious polka redowa; but his polite regrets didn't impose upon her, and when she galloped away with the Count, she saw Laurie sit down by her aunt with an actual expression of relief.

That was unpardonable, and Amy took no more notice of him for a long while, except a word now and then when she came to her chaperon between the dances for a necessary pin or a moment's rest. Her anger had a good effect, however, for she hid it under a smiling face, and seemed unusually blithe and brilliant. Laurie's eyes followed her with pleasure, for she neither romped nor sauntered, but danced with spirit and grace, making the delightsome pastime what it should be. He very naturally fell to studying her from this new point of view, and before the evening was half over, had decided that "little Amy was going to make a very charming woman."

It was a lively scene, for soon the spirit of the social season took possession of everyone, and Christmas merriment made all faces shine, hearts happy, and heels light. The musicians fiddled, tooted, and banged as if they enjoyed it, everybody danced who could, and those who couldn't admired their neighbors with uncommon warmth. The air was dark with Davises, and many Joneses gamboled like a flock of young giraffes. The golden secretary darted through the room like a meteor with a dashing Frenchwoman who carpeted the floor with her pink satin train. The Serene Teuton found the supper table and was happy, eating steadily through the bill of fare, and dismayed the *garçons* by the ravages he committed. But the Emperor's friend covered himself with glory, for he danced everything, whether he knew it or not, and introduced impromptu pirouettes when the figures bewildered him. The boyish abandon of that stout man was charming to behold, for though he "carried weight," he danced like an India-rubber ball. He ran, he flew, he pranced, his face glowed, his bald head shone, his coattails waved wildly, his pumps actually twinkled in the air, and when the music stopped, he wiped the drops from his brow, and beamed upon his fellow men like a French Pickwick without glasses.

Amy and her Pole distinguished themselves by equal enthusiasm but more graceful agility, and Laurie found himself involuntarily keeping time to the rhythmic rise and fall of the white slippers as they flew by as indefatigably as if winged. When little Vladimir finally relinquished her, with assurances that he was "desolated to leave so early," she was ready to rest, and see how her recreant knight had borne his punishment.

It had been successful, for at three-and-twenty, blighted affections find a balm in friendly society, and young nerves will thrill, young blood dance, and healthy young spirits rise, when subjected to the enchantment of beauty, light, music, and motion. Laurie had a waked-up look as he rose to give her his seat; and when he hurried away to bring her some supper, she said to herself, with a satisfied smile, "Ah, I thought that would do him good!"

"You look like Balzac's '*Femme peinte par elle-même*,'" he said, as he fanned her with one hand and held her coffee cup in the other.

"My rouge won't come off." And Amy rubbed her brilliant cheek, and showed him her white glove with a sober simplicity that made him laugh outright.

"What do you call this stuff?" he asked, touching a fold of her dress that had blown over his knee.

"Illusion."

"Good name for it. It's very pretty—new thing, isn't it?"

"It's as old as the hills; you have seen it on dozens of girls, and you never found out that it was pretty till now—*stupide!*"

"I never saw it on you before, which accounts for the mistake, you see."

"None of that, it is forbidden. I'd rather take coffee than compliments just now. No, don't lounge, it makes me nervous."

Laurie sat bold upright, and meekly took her empty plate feeling an odd sort of pleasure in having "little Amy" order him about, for she had lost her shyness now, and felt an irresistible desire to trample on him, as girls have a delightful way of doing when lords of creation show any signs of subjection.

"Where did you learn all this sort of thing?" he asked with a quizzical look.

"As 'this sort of thing' is rather a vague expression, would you kindly explain?" returned Amy, knowing perfectly well what he meant, but wickedly leaving him to describe what is indescribable.

"Well—the general air, the style, the self-possession, the—the—illusion—you know," laughed Laurie, breaking down and helping himself out of his quandary with the new word.

Amy was gratified, but of course didn't show it, and demurely answered, "Foreign life polishes one in spite of one's self, I study as well as play, and as for this"—with a little gesture toward her dress—"why, tulle is cheap, posies to be had for nothing, and I am used to making the most of my poor little things."

Amy rather regretted that last sentence, fearing it wasn't in good taste, but Laurie liked her the better for it, and found himself both admiring and respecting the brave patience that made the most of opportunity, and the cheerful spirit that covered poverty with flowers. Amy did not know why he looked at her so kindly, nor why he filled up her book with his own name, and devoted himself to her for the rest of the evening in the most delightful manner, but the impulse that wrought this agreeable change was the result of one of the new impressions which both of them were unconsciously giving and receiving.

Chapter 38

On the Shelf

IN FRANCE THE young girls have a dull time of it till they are married, when *"Vive la liberté"* becomes their motto. In America, as everyone knows, girls early sign the declaration of independence, and enjoy their freedom with republican zest, but the young matrons usually abdicate with the first heir to the throne and go into a seclusion almost as close as a French nunnery, though by no means as quiet. Whether they like it or not, they are virtually put upon the shelf as soon as the wedding excitement is over, and most of them might exclaim, as did a very pretty woman the other day, "I'm as handsome as ever, but no one takes any notice of me because I'm married."

Not being a belle or even a fashionable lady, Meg did not experience this affliction till her babies were a year old, for in her little world primitive customs prevailed, and she found herself more admired and beloved than ever.

As she was a womanly little woman, the maternal instinct was very strong, and she was entirely absorbed in her children, to the utter exclusion of everything and everybody else. Day and night she brooded over them with tireless devotion and anxiety, leaving John to the tender mercies of the help, for an Irish lady now presided over the kitchen department. Being a domestic man, John decidedly missed the wifely attentions he had been accustomed to receive, but as he adored his babies, he cheerfully relinquished his comfort for a time, supposing with masculine ignorance that peace would soon be restored. But three months passed, and there was no return of repose; Meg looked worn and nervous, the babies absorbed every minute of her time, the house was neglected, and Kitty, the cook, who took life "aisy," kept him on short commons. When he went out in the morning he was bewildered by small commissions for the captive mamma, if he came gaily in at night, eager to embrace his family, he was quenched by a "Hush! They are just asleep after worrying all day." If he proposed a little amusement at home, "No, it would disturb the babies." If he hinted at a lecture or concert, he was answered with a reproachful look, and a decided "Leave my children for pleasure, never!" His sleep was broken by infant wails and visions of a phantom figure pacing noiselessly to and fro in the watches of the night; his meals were interrupted by the frequent flight of the presiding genius, who deserted him, half-helped, if a muffled chirp sounded from the nest above; and when he read his paper of an evening, Demi's colic got into the shipping list and Daisy's fall affected the price of stocks, for Mrs. Brooke was only interested in domestic news.

The poor man was very uncomfortable, for the children had bereft him of his wife, home was merely a nursery and the perpetual "hushing" made him feel like a brutal intruder whenever he entered the sacred precincts of Babyland. He bore it very patiently for six months, and, when no signs of amendment appeared, he did what other paternal exiles do— tried to get a little comfort elsewhere. Scott had married and gone to housekeeping not far off, and John fell into the way of running over for an hour or two of an evening, when his own parlor was empty, and his own wife singing lullabies that seemed to have no end. Mrs. Scott was a lively, pretty girl, with nothing to do but be agreeable, and she performed her mission most successfully. The parlor was always bright and attractive, the chessboard ready, the piano in tune, plenty of gay gossip, and a nice little supper set forth in tempting style.

John would have preferred his own fireside if it had not been so lonely, but as it was he gratefully took the next best thing and enjoyed his neighbor's society.

Meg rather approved of the new arrangement at first, and found it a relief to know that John was having a good time instead of dozing in the parlor, or tramping about the house and waking the children. But by-and-by, when the teething worry was over and the idols went to sleep at proper hours, leaving Mamma time to rest, she began to miss John, and find her workbasket dull company, when he was not sitting opposite in his old dressing gown, comfortably scorching his slippers on the fender. She would not ask him to stay at home, but felt injured because he did not know that she wanted him without being told, entirely forgetting the many evenings he had waited for her in vain. She was nervous and worn out with watching and worry, and in that unreasonable frame of mind which the best of mothers occasionally experience when domestic cares oppress them. Want of exercise robs them of cheerfulness, and too much devotion to that idol of American women, the teapot, makes them feel as if they were all nerve and no muscle.

"Yes," she would say, looking in the glass, "I'm getting old and ugly. John doesn't find me interesting any longer, so he leaves his faded wife and goes to see his pretty neighbor, who has no incumbrances. Well, the babies love me, they don't care if I am thin and pale and haven't time to crimp my hair, they are my comfort, and some day John will see what I've gladly sacrificed for them, won't he, my precious?"

To which pathetic appeal Daisy would answer with a coo, or Demi with a crow, and Meg would put by her lamentations for a maternal revel, which soothed her solitude for the time being. But the pain increased as politics absorbed John, who was always running over to discuss interesting points with Scott, quite unconscious that Meg missed him. Not a word did she say, however, till her mother found her in tears one day, and insisted on knowing what the matter was, for Meg's drooping spirits had not escaped her observation.

"I wouldn't tell anyone except you, Mother, but I really do need advice, for if John goes on so much longer I might as well be widowed," replied Mrs. Brooke, drying her tears on Daisy's bib with an injured air.

"Goes on how, my dear?" asked her mother anxiously.

"He's away all day, and at night when I want to see him, he is continually going over to the Scotts'. It isn't fair that I should have the hardest work, and never any amusement. Men are very selfish, even the best of them."

"So are women. Don't blame John till you see where you are wrong yourself."

"But it can't be right for him to neglect me."

"Don't you neglect him?"

"Why, Mother, I thought you'd take my part!"

"So I do, as far as sympathizing goes, but I think the fault is yours, Meg."

"I don't see how."

"Let me show you. Did John ever neglect you, as you call it, while you made it a point to give him your society of an evening, his only leisure time?"

"No, but I can't do it now, with two babies to tend."

"I think you could, dear, and I think you ought. May I speak quite freely, and will you remember that it's Mother who blames as well as Mother who sympathizes?"

"Indeed I will! Speak to me as if I were little Meg again. I often feel as if I needed teaching more than ever since these babies look to me for everything."

Meg drew her low chair beside her mother's, and, with a little interruption in either lap, the two women rocked and talked lovingly together, feeling that the tie of motherhood made them more one than ever.

"You have only made the mistake that most young wives make—forgotten your duty to your husband in your love for your children. A very natural and forgivable mistake, Meg, but one that had better be remedied before you take to different ways; for children should draw you nearer than ever, not separate you, as if they were all yours, and John had nothing to do but support them. I've seen it for some weeks, but have not spoken, feeling sure it would come right in time."

"I'm afraid it won't. If I ask him to stay, he'll think I'm jealous, and I wouldn't insult him by such an idea. He doesn't see that I want him, and I don't know how to tell him without words."

"Make it so pleasant he won't want to go away. My dear, he's longing for his little home; but it isn't home without you, and you are always in the nursery."

"Oughtn't I to be there?"

"Not all the time, too much confinement makes you nervous, and then you are unfitted for everything. Besides, you owe something to John as well as to the babies; don't neglect husband for children, don't shut him out of the nursery, but teach him how to help in it. His place is there as well as yours, and the children need him; let him feel that he has his part to do, and he will do it gladly and faithfully, and it will be better for you all."

"You really think so, Mother?"

"I know it, Meg, for I've tried it, and I seldom give advice unless I've proved its practicability. When you and Jo were little, I went on just as you are, feeling as if I didn't do my duty unless I devoted myself wholly to you. Poor Father took to his books, after I had refused all offers of help, and left me to try my experiment alone. I struggled along as well as I could, but Jo was too much for me. I nearly spoiled her by indulgence. You were poorly, and I worried about you till I fell sick myself. Then Father came to the rescue, quietly managed everything, and made himself so helpful that I saw my mistake, and never have been able to get on without him since. That is the secret of our home happiness: he does not let business wean him from the little cares and duties that affect us all, and I try not to let domestic worries destroy my interest in his pursuits. Each do our part alone in many things, but at home we work together, always."

"It is so, Mother; and my great wish is to be to my husband and children what you have been to yours. Show me how, I'll do anything you say."

"You always were my docile daughter. Well, dear, if I were you, I'd let John have more to do with the management of Demi, for the boy needs training, and it's none too soon to begin. Then I'd do what I have often proposed, let Hannah come and help you; she is a capital nurse, and you may trust the precious babies to her while you do more housework. You need the exercise, Hannah would enjoy the rest, and John would find his wife again. Go out more, keep cheerful as well as busy, for you are the sunshine-maker of the family, and if you get dismal there is no fair weather. Then I'd try to take an interest in whatever John likes—talk with him, let him read to you, exchange ideas, and help each other in that way. Don't shut yourself up in a bandbox because you are a woman, but understand what is going on, and educate yourself to take your part in the world's work, for it all affects you and yours."

"John is so sensible, I'm afraid he will think I'm stupid if I ask questions about politics and things."

"I don't believe he would. Love covers a multitude of sins, and of whom could you ask more freely than of him? Try it, and see if he doesn't find your society far more agreeable than Mrs. Scott's suppers."

"I will. Poor John! I'm afraid I *have* neglected him sadly, but I thought I was right, and he never said anything."

"He tried not to be selfish, but he *has* felt rather forlorn, I fancy. This is just the time, Meg, when young married people are apt to grow apart, and the very time when they ought to be most together; for the first tenderness soon wears off, unless care is taken to preserve it; and no time is so beautiful and precious to parents as the first years of the little lives given them to train. Don't let John be a stranger to the babies, for they will do more to keep him safe and happy in this world of trial and temptation than anything else, and through them you will learn to know and love one another as you should. Now, dear, good-by; think over Mother's preachment, act upon it if it seems good, and God bless you all!"

Meg did think it over, found it good, and acted upon it, though the first attempt was not made exactly as she planned to have it. Of course the children tyrannized over her, and ruled the house as soon as they found out that kicking and squalling brought them whatever they wanted. Mamma was an abject slave to their caprices, but Papa was not so easily subjugated, and occasionally afflicted his tender spouse by an attempt at paternal discipline with his obstreperous son. For Demi inherited a trifle of his sire's firmness of character —we won't call it obstinacy—and when he made up his little mind to have or to do anything, all the king's horses and all the king's men could not change that pertinacious little mind. Mamma thought the dear too young to be taught to conquer his prejudices, but Papa believed that it never was too soon to learn obedience; so Master Demi early discovered that when he understook to "wrastle" with "parpar," he always got the worst of it; yet, like the Englishman, Baby respected the man who conquered him, and loved the father whose grave "No, no," was more impressive than all Mamma's love pats.

A few days after the talk with her mother, Meg resolved to try a social evening with John; so she ordered a nice supper, set the parlor in order, dressed herself prettily, and put the children to bed early, that nothing should interfere with her experiment. But unfortunately Demi's most unconquerable prejudice was against going to bed, and that night he decided to go on a rampage; so poor Meg sang and rocked, told stories and tried every sleep-provoking wile she could devise, but all in vain, the big eyes wouldn't shut; and long after Daisy had gone to byelow, like the chubby little bunch of good nature she was, naughty Demi lay staring at the light, with the most discouragingly wide-awake expression of countenance.

"Will Demi lie still like a good boy, while Mamma runs down and gives poor Papa his tea?" asked Meg, as the hall door softly closed, and the well-known step went tip-toeing into the dining room.

"Me has tea!" said Demi, preparing to join in the revel.

"No, but I'll save you some little cakies for breakfast, if you'll go bye-by like Daisy. Will you, lovey?"

"Iss!" and Demi shut his eyes tight, as if to catch sleep and hurry the desired day.

Taking advantage of the propitious moment, Meg slipped away and ran down to greet her husband with a smiling face and the little blue bow in her hair which was his especial admiration. He saw it at once and said with pleased surprise, "Why, little mother, how gay we are tonight. Do you expect company?"

"Only you, dear."

"Is it a birthday, anniversary, or anything?"

"No, I'm tired of being a dowdy, so I dressed up as a change. You always make yourself nice for table, no matter how tired you are, so why shouldn't I when I have the time?"

"I do it out of respect to you, my dear," said old-fashioned John.

"Ditto, ditto, Mr. Brooke," laughed Meg, looking young and pretty again, as she nodded to him over the teapot.

"Well, it's altogether delightful, and like old times. This tastes right. I drink your health, dear." And John sipped his tea with an air of reposeful rapture, which was of very short duration however, for as he put down his cup, the door handle rattled mysteriously, and a little voice was heard, saying impatiently—

"Opy doy; me's tummin!"

"It's that naughty boy. I told him to go to sleep alone, and here he is, downstairs, getting his death a-cold pattering over that canvas," said Meg, answering the call.

"Mornin' now," announced Demi in a joyful tone as he entered, with his long nightgown gracefully festooned over his arm and every curl bobbing gayly as he pranced about the table, eying the "cakies" with loving glances.

"No, it isn't morning yet. You must go to bed, and not trouble poor Mamma. Then you can have the little cake with sugar on it."

"Me loves Parpar," said the artful one, preparing to climb the paternal knee and revel in forbidden joys. But John shook his head, and said to Meg—

"If you told him to stay up there, and go to sleep alone, make him do it, or he will never learn to mind you."

"Yes, of course. Come, Demi." And Meg led her son away, feeling a strong desire to spank the little marplot who hopped beside her, laboring under the delusion that the bribe was to be administered as soon as they reached the nursery.

Nor was he disappointed, for that shortsighted woman actually gave him a lump of sugar, tucked him into his bed, and forbade any more promenades till morning.

"Mornin' now" announced Demi in a joyful tone . . .

"Iss!" said Demi the perjured, blissfully sucking his sugar, and regarding his first attempt as eminently successful.

Meg returned to her place, and supper was progressing pleasantly, when the little ghost walked again and exposed the maternal delinquencies by boldly demanding, "More sudar, Marmar."

"Now this won't do," said John, hardening his heart against the engaging little sinner. "We shall never know any peace till that child learns to go to bed properly. You have made a slave of yourself long enough. Give him one lesson, and then there will be an end of it. Put him in his bed and leave him, Meg."

"He won't stay there, he never does unless I sit by him."

"I'll manage him. Demi, go upstairs, and get into your bed, as Mamma bids you."

"S'ant!" replied the young rebel, helping himself to the coveted "cakie," and beginning to eat the same with calm audacity.

"You must never say that to Papa. I shall carry you if you don't go yourself."

"Go 'way, me don't love Parpar." And Demi retired to his mother's skirts for protection.

But even that refuge proved unavailing, for he was delivered over to the enemy, with a "Be gentle with him, John," which struck the culprit with dismay, for when Mamma deserted him, then the judgment day was at hand. Bereft of his cake, defrauded of his frolic, and borne away by a strong hand to that detested bed, poor Demi could not restrain his wrath, but openly defied Papa, and kicked and screamed lustily all the way upstairs. The minute he was put into bed on one side, he rolled out on the other, and made for the door, only to be ignominiously caught up by the tail of his little toga and put back again, which lively performance was kept up till the young man's strength gave out, when he devoted himself to roaring at the top of his voice. This vocal exercise usually conquered Meg, but John sat as unmoved as the post which is popularly believed to be deaf. No coaxing, no sugar, no lullaby, no story, even the light was put out and only the red glow of the fire enlivened the "big dark" which Demi regarded with curiosity rather than fear. This new order of things disgusted him, and he howled dismally for "Marmar," as his angry passions subsided, and recollections of his tender bondwoman returned to the captive autocrat. The plaintive wail which succeeded the passionate roar went to Meg's heart, and she ran up to say beseechingly—

"Let me stay with him, he'll be good, now, John."

"No, my dear, I've told him he must go to sleep, as you bid him; and he must, if I stay here all night."

"But he'll cry himself sick," pleaded Meg, reproaching herself for deserting her boy.

"No, he won't, he's so tired he will soon drop off and then the matter is settled, for he will understand that he has got to mind. Don't interfere, I'll manage him."

"He's my child, and I can't have his spirit broken by harshness."

"He's my child, and I won't have his temper spoiled by indulgence. Go down, my dear, and leave the boy to me."

When John spoke in that masterful tone, Meg always obeyed, and never regretted her docility.

"Please let me kiss him once, John?"

"Certainly. Demi, say good night to Mamma, and let her go and rest, for she is very tired with taking care of you all day."

Meg always insisted upon it that the kiss won the victory, for after it was given, Demi sobbed more quietly, and lay quite still at the bottom of the bed, whither he had wriggled in his anguish of mind.

"Poor little man, he's worn out with sleep and crying. I'll cover him up, and then go and set Meg's heart at rest," thought John, creeping to the bedside, hoping to find his rebellious heir asleep.

But he wasn't, for the moment his father peeped at him, Demi's eyes opened, his little chin began to quiver, and he put up his arms, saying with a penitent hiccough, "Me's dood, now."

Sitting on the stairs outside Meg wondered at the long

silence which followed the uproar, and after imagining all sorts of impossible accidents, she slipped into the room to set her fears at rest. Demi lay fast asleep, not in his usual spread-eagle attitude, but in a subdued bunch, cuddled close in the circle of his father's arm and holding his father's finger, as if he felt that justice was tempered with mercy, and had gone to sleep a sadder and a wiser baby. So held, John had waited with womanly patience till the little hand relaxed its hold, and while waiting had fallen asleep, more tired by that tussle with his son than with his whole day's work.

As Meg stood watching the two faces on the pillow, she smiled to herself, and then slipped away again, saying in a satisfied tone, "I never need fear that John will be too harsh with my babies: he *does* know how to manage them, and will be a great help, for Demi *is* getting too much for me."

When John came down at last, expecting to find a pensive or reproachful wife, he was agreeably surprised to find Meg placidly trimming a bonnet, and to be greeted with the re-quest to read something about the election, if he was not too tired. John saw in a minute that a revolution of some kind was going on, but wisely asked no questions, knowing that Meg was such a transparent little person, she couldn't keep a secret to save her life, and therefore the clue would soon appear. He read a long debate with the most amiable readi-ness and then explained it in his most lucid manner, while Meg tried to look deeply interested, to ask intelligent ques-tions, and keep her thoughts from wandering from the state of the nation to the state of her bonnet. In her secret soul, however, she decided that politics were as bad as mathematics, and that the mission of politicians seemed to be calling each other names; but she kept these feminine ideas to herself, and when John paused, shook her head and said with what she thought diplomatic ambiguity, "Well, I really don't see what we are coming to."

John laughed, and watched her for a minute, as she poised a pretty little preparation of lace and flowers on her hand, and regarded it with the genuine interest which his harangue had failed to waken.

"She is trying to like politics for my sake, so I'll try and like millinery for hers, that's only fair," thought John the Just, adding aloud, "That's very pretty. Is it what you call a breakfast cap?"

"My dear man, it's a bonnet! My very best go-to-concert-and-theater bonnet."

"I beg your pardon, it was so small, I naturally mistook it for one of the flyaway things you sometimes wear. How do you keep it on?"

"These bits of lace are fastened under the chin with a rose-bud, so." And Meg illustrated by putting on the bonnet and regarding him with an air of calm satisfaction that was irresistible.

"It's a love of a bonnet, but I prefer the face inside, for it looks young and happy again." And John kissed the smiling face, to the great detriment of the rosebud under the chin.

"I'm glad you like it, for I want you to take me to one of the new concerts some night. I really need some music to put me in tune. Will you, please?"

"Of course I will, with all my heart, or anywhere else you like. You have been shut up so long, it will do you no end of good, and I shall enjoy it, of all things. What put it into your head, little mother?"

"Well, I had a talk with Marmee the other day, and told her how nervous and cross and out of sorts I felt, and she said I needed change and less care; so Hannah is to help me with the children, and I'm to see things about the house more, and now and then have a little fun, just to keep me from getting to be a fidgety, broken-down old woman before my time. It's only an experiment, John, and I want to try it for your sake as much as for mine, because I've neglected you shamefully lately, and I'm going to make home what it used to be, if I can. You don't object, I hope?"

Never mind what John said, or what a very narrow escape the little bonnet had from utter ruin; all that we have any business to know is that John did *not* appear to object, judging from the changes which gradually took place in the house and its inmates. It was not all Paradise by any means, but everyone was better for the division of labor system: the children throve under the paternal rule, for accurate, steadfast John brought order and obedience into Babydom, while Meg recovered her spirits and composed her nerves by plenty of wholesome exercise, a little pleasure, and much confidential conversation with her sensible husband. Home grew homelike again, and John had no wish to leave it, unless he took Meg with him. The Scotts came to the Brookes' now, and everyone found the little house a cheerful place, full of happiness, content, and family love. Even gay Sallie Moffatt liked to go there. "It is always so quiet and pleasant here, it does me good, Meg," she used to say, looking about her with wistful eyes, as if trying to discover the charm, that she might use it in her great house, full of splendid loneliness; for there were no riotous, sunny-faced babies there, and Ned lived in a world of his own, where there was no place for her.

This household happiness did not come all at once, but John and Meg had found the key to it, and each year of married life taught them how to use it, unlocking the treasuries of real home love and mutual helpfulness, which the poorest may possess, and the richest cannot buy. This is the sort of shelf on which young wives and mothers may consent to be laid, safe from the restless fret and fever of the world, finding loyal lovers in the little sons and daughters who cling to them, undaunted by sorrow, poverty, or age; walking side by side, through fair and stormy weather, with a faithful friend, who is, in the true sense of the good old Saxon word, the "house-band," and learning, as Meg learned, that a woman's happiest kingdom is home, her highest honor the art of ruling it not as a queen, but a wise wife and mother.

Chapter 39

Lazy Laurence

LAURIE WENT TO Nice intending to stay a week, and remained a month. He was tired of wandering about alone, and Amy's familiar presence seemed to give a homelike charm to the foreign scenes in which she bore a part. He rather missed the "petting" he used to receive, and enjoyed a taste of it again; for no attentions, however flattering, from strangers, were half so pleasant as the sisterly adoration of the girls at home. Amy never would pet him like the others, but she was very glad to see him now, and quite clung to him, feeling that he was the representative of the dear family for whom she longed more than she would confess. They naturally took comfort in each other's society and were much together, riding, walking, dancing, or dawdling, for at Nice no one can be very industrious during the gay season. But, while apparently amusing themselves in the most careless fashion, they were half-consciously making discoveries and forming opinions about each other. Amy rose daily in the estimation of her friend, but he sank in hers, and each felt the truth before a word was spoken. Amy tried to please, and succeeded, for she was grateful for the many pleasures he gave her, and repaid him with the little services to which womanly women know how to lend an indescribable charm. Laurie made no effort of any kind, but just let himself drift along as comfortably as possible, trying to forget, and feeling that all women owed him a kind word because one had been cold to him. It cost him no effort to be generous, and he would have given Amy all the trinkets in Nice if she would have taken them, but at the same time he felt that he could not change the opinion she was forming of him, and he rather dreaded the keen blue eyes that seemed to watch him with such half-sorrowful, half-scornful surprise.

"All the rest have gone to Monaco for the day; I preferred

to stay at home and write letters. They are done now, and I am going to Valrosa to sketch, will you come?" said Amy, as she joined Laurie one lovely day when he lounged in as usual about noon.

"Well, yes, but isn't it rather warm for such a long walk?" he answered slowly, for the shaded *salon* looked inviting after the glare without.

"I'm going to have the little carriage, and Baptiste can drive, so you'll have nothing to do but hold your umbrella, and keep your gloves nice," returned Amy, with a sarcastic glance at the immaculate kids, which were a weak point with Laurie.

"Then I'll go with pleasure." And he put out his hand for her sketchbook. But she tucked it under her arm with a sharp—

"Don't trouble yourself. It's no exertion to me, but *you* don't look equal to it."

Laurie lifted his eyebrows and followed at a leisurely pace as she ran downstairs, but when they got into the carriage he took the reins himself, and left little Baptiste nothing to do but fold his arms and fall asleep on his perch.

The two never quarreled—Amy was too well-bred, and just now Laurie was too lazy, so in a minute he peeped under her hatbrim with an inquiring air; she answered with a smile, and they went on together in the most amicable manner.

It was a lovely drive, along winding roads rich in the picturesque scenes that delight beauty-loving eyes. Here an ancient monastery, whence the solemn chanting of the monks came down to them. There a bare-legged shepherd, in wooden shoes, pointed hat, and rough jacket over one shoulder, sat piping on a stone while his goats skipped among the rocks or lay at his feet. Meek, mouse-colored donkeys, laden with panniers of freshly cut grass, passed by, with a pretty girl in a *capaline* sitting between the green piles, or an old woman spinning with a distaff as she went. Brown, soft-eyed children ran out from the quaint stone hovels to offer nosegays, or bunches of oranges still on the bough. Gnarled olive trees covered the hills with their dusky foliage, fruit hung golden in the orchard, and great scarlet anemones fringed the roadside; while beyond green slopes and craggy heights, the Maritime Alps rose sharp and white against the blue Italian sky.

Valrosa well deserved its name, for in that climate of perpetual summer roses blossomed everywhere. They overhung the archway, thrust themselves between the bars of the great gate with a sweet welcome to passers-by, and lined the avenue, winding through lemon trees and feathery palms up to the villa on the hill. Every shadowy nook, where seats invited one to stop and rest, was a mass of bloom, every cool grotto had its marble nymph smiling from a veil of flowers, and every fountain reflected crimson, white, or pale pink roses, leaning down to smile at their own beauty. Roses covered the walls of the house, draped the cornices, climbed the pillars, and ran riot over the balustrade of the wide terrace, whence one looked down on the sunny Mediterranean, and the white-walled city on its shore.

"This is a regular honeymoon paradise, isn't it? Did you ever see such roses?" asked Amy, pausing on the terrace to enjoy the view, and a luxurious whiff of perfume that came wandering by.

"No, nor felt such thorns," returned Laurie, with his thumb in his mouth, after a vain attempt to capture a solitary scarlet flower that grew just beyond his reach.

"Try lower down, and pick those that have no thorns," said Amy, gathering three of the tiny cream-colored ones that starred the wall behind her. She put them in his buttonhole as a peace offering, and he stood a minute looking down at them with a curious expression, for in the Italian part of his nature there was a touch of superstition, and he was just then in that state of half-sweet, half-bitter melancholy, when imaginative young men find significance in trifles and food for romance everywhere. He had thought of Jo in reaching after the thorny red rose, for vivid flowers became her, and she had often worn ones like that from the greenhouse at home. The pale roses Amy gave him were the sort that the Italians lay in dead hands, never in bridal wreaths, and for a moment he wondered if the omen was for Jo or for himself; but the next instant his American common sense got the better of sentimentality, and he laughed a heartier laugh than Amy had heard since he came.

"It's good advice, you'd better take it and save your fingers," she said, thinking her speech amused him.

"Thank you, I will," he answered in jest, and a few months later he did it in earnest.

"Laurie, when are you going to your grandfather?" she asked presently, as she settled herself on a rustic seat.

"Very soon."

"You have said that a dozen times within the last three weeks."

"I dare say, short answers save trouble."

"He expects you, and you really ought to go."

"Hospitable creature! I know it."

"Then why don't you do it?"

"Natural depravity, I suppose."

"Natural indolence, you mean. It's really dreadful!" And Amy looked severe.

"Not so bad as it seems, for I should only plague him if I went, so I might as well stay and plague you a little longer, you can bear it better; in fact, I think it agrees with you excellently." And Laurie composed himself for a lounge on the broad ledge of the balustrade.

Amy shook her head and opened her sketchbook with an air of resignation, but she had made up her mind to lecture "that boy," and in a minute she began again.

"What are you doing just now?"

"Watching lizards."

"No, no. I mean what do you intend and wish to do?"

"Smoke a cigarette, if you'll allow me."

"How provoking you are! I don't approve of cigars and I will only allow it on condition that you let me put you into my sketch. I need a figure."

"With all the pleasure in life. How will you have me—full-length or three-quarters, on my head or my heels? I should respectfully suggest a recumbent posture, then put yourself in also, and call it 'Dolce far niente.'"

"Stay as you are, and go to sleep if you like. *I* intend to work hard," said Amy in her most energetic tone.

"What delightful enthusiasm!" And he leaned against a tall urn with an air of entire satisfaction.

"What would Jo say if she saw you now?" asked Amy impatiently, hoping to stir him up by the mention of her still more energetic sister's name.

"As usual, 'Go away, Teddy, I'm busy!'" He laughed as he spoke, but the laugh was not natural, and a shade passed over his face, for the utterance of the familiar name touched the wound that was not healed yet. Both tone and shadow struck Amy, for she had seen and heard them before, and now she looked up in time to catch a new expression on Laurie's face —a hard, bitter look, full of pain, dissatisfaction, and regret. It was gone before she could study it and the listless expression back again. She watched him for a moment with artistic pleasure, thinking how like an Italian he looked, as he lay basking in the sun with uncovered head and eyes full of southern dreaminess, for he seemed to have forgotten her and fallen into a reverie.

"You look like the effigy of a young knight asleep on his tomb," she said, carefully tracing the well-cut profile defined against the dark stone.

"Wish I was!"

"That's a foolish wish, unless you have spoiled your life. You are so changed, I sometimes think—" There Amy stopped, with a half-timid, half-wistful look, more significant than her unfinished speech.

Laurie saw and understood the affectionate anxiety which she hesitated to express, and looking straight into her eyes, said, just as he used to say it to her mother, "It's all right, ma'am."

That satisfied her and set at rest the doubts that had begun to worry her lately. It also touched her, and she showed that it did, by the cordial tone in which she said—

"I'm glad of that! I didn't think you'd been a very bad boy, but I fancied you might have wasted money at that wicked Baden-Baden, lost your heart to some charming Frenchwoman with a husband, or got into some of the scrapes that young men seem to consider a necessary part of a foreign tour. Don't stay out there in the sun, come and lie on the grass here and 'let us be friendly,' as Jo used to say when we got in the sofa corner and told secrets."

Laurie obediently threw himself down on the turf, and began to amuse himself by sticking daisies into the ribbons of Amy's hat, that lay there.

"I'm all ready for the secrets." And he glanced up with a decided expression of interest in his eyes.

"I've none to tell; you may begin."

"Haven't one to bless myself with. I thought perhaps you'd had some news from home."

"You have heard all that has come lately. Don't you hear often? I fancied Jo would send you volumes."

"She's very busy. I'm roving about so, it's impossible to be regular, you know. When do you begin your great work of art, Raphaella?" he asked, changing the subject abruptly after another pause, in which he had been wondering if Amy knew his secret and wanted to talk about it.

"Never," she answered, with a despondent but decided air. "Rome took all the vanity out of me, for after seeing the wonders there, I felt too insignificant to live and gave up all my foolish hopes in despair."

"Why should you, with so much energy and talent?"

"That's just why—because talent isn't genius, and no amount of energy can make it so. I want to be great, or nothing. I won't be a common-place dauber, so I don't intend to try any more."

"And what are you going to do with yourself now, if I may ask?"

"Polish up my other talents, and be an ornament to society, if I get the chance."

It was a characteristic speech, and sounded daring; but audacity becomes young people, and Amy's ambition had a good foundation. Laurie smiled, but he liked the spirit with which she took up a new purpose when a long-cherished one died, and spent no time lamenting.

"Good! And here is where Fred Vaughn comes in, I fancy."

Amy preserved a discreet silence, but there was a conscious look in her downcast face that made Laurie sit up and say gravely, "Now I'm going to play brother, and ask questions. May I?"

"I don't promise to answer."

"Your face will, if your tongue won't. You aren't woman of the world enough yet to hide your feelings, my dear. I heard rumors about Fred and you last year, and it's my private opinion that if he had not been called home so suddenly and detained so long, something would have come of it—hey?"

"That's not for me to say," was Amy's prim reply, but her lips would smile, and there was a traitorous sparkle of the eye which betrayed that she knew her power and enjoyed the knowledge.

"You are not engaged, I hope?" And Laurie looked very elder-brotherly and grave all of a sudden.

"No."

"But you will be, if he comes back and goes properly down upon his knees, won't you?"

"Very likely."

"Then you are fond of old Fred?"

"I could be, if I tried."

"But you don't intend to try till the proper moment? Bless my soul, what unearthly prudence! He's a good fellow, Amy, but not the man I fancied you'd like."

"He is rich, a gentleman, and has delightful manners," began Amy, trying to be quite cool and dignified, but feeling a little ashamed of herself, in spite of the sincerity of her intentions.

"I understand. Queens of society can't get on without money, so you mean to make a good match, and start in that way? Quite right and proper, as the world goes, but it sounds odd from the lips of one of your mother's girls."

"True, nevertheless."

A short speech, but the quiet decision with which it was uttered contrasted curiously with the young speaker. Laurie felt this instinctively and laid himself down again, with a sense of disappointment which he could not explain. His look and silence, as well as a certain inward self-disapproval, ruffled Amy, and made her resolve to deliver her lecture without delay.

"I wish you'd do me the favor to rouse yourself a little," she said sharply.

"Do it for me, there's a dear girl."

"I could, if I tried." And she looked as if she would like doing it in the most summary style.

"Try, then. I give you leave," returned Laurie, who enjoyed having someone to tease, after his long abstinence from his favorite pastime.

"You'd be angry in five minutes."

"I'm never angry with you. It takes two flints to make a fire: you are as cool and soft as snow."

"You don't know what I can do; snow produces a glow and a tingle, if applied rightly. Your indifference is half affectation, and a good stirring up would prove it."

"Stir away, it won't hurt me and it may amuse you, as the big man said when his little wife beat him. Regard me in the light of a husband or a carpet, and beat till you are tired, if that sort of exercise agrees with you."

Being decidedly nettled herself, and longing to see him shake off the apathy that so altered him, Amy sharpened both tongue and pencil, and began:

"Flo and I have got a new name for you; it's 'Lazy Laurence.' How do you like it?"

She thought it would annoy him, but he only folded his arms under his head, with an imperturbable "That's not bad. Thank you, ladies."

"Do you want to know what I honestly think of you?"

"Pining to be told."

"Well, I despise you."

If she had even said "I hate you" in a petulant or coquettish tone, he would have laughed and rather liked it, but the grave, almost sad, accent of her voice made him open his eyes, and ask quickly—

"Why, if you please?"

"Because, with every chance for being good, useful, and happy, you are faulty, lazy, and miserable."

"Strong language, mademoiselle."

"If you like it, I'll go on."

"Pray, do, it's quite interesting."

"I thought you'd find it so; selfish people always like to talk about themselves."

"Am *I* selfish?" The question slipped out involuntarily and in a tone of surprise, for the one virtue on which he prided himself was generosity.

"Yes, very selfish," continued Amy, in a calm, cool voice, twice as effective just then as an angry one. "I'll show you how, for I've studied you while we have been frolicking, and I'm not at all satisfied with you. Here you have been abroad nearly six months, and done nothing but waste time and money and disappoint your friends."

"Isn't a fellow to have any pleasure after a four-year grind?"

"You don't look as if you'd had much; at any rate, you are none the better for it, as far as I can see. I said when we first met that you had improved. Now I take it all back, for I don't think you half so nice as when I left you at home. You have grown abominably lazy, you like gossip, and waste time on frivolous things, you are contented to be petted and admired by silly people, instead of being loved and respected by wise ones. With money, talent, position, health, and beauty—ah, you like that Old Vanity! But it's the truth, so I can't help saying it—with all these splendid things to use and enjoy, you can find nothing to do but dawdle, and instead of being the man you might and ought to be, you are only—" There she stopped, with a look that had both pain and pity in it.

"Saint Laurence on a gridiron," added Laurie, blandly finishing the sentence. But the lecture began to take effect, for there was a wide-awake sparkle in his eyes now and a half-angry, half-injured expression replaced the former indifference.

"I supposed you'd take it so. You men tell us we are angels, and say we can make you what we will, but the instant we honestly try to do you good, you laugh at us and won't listen, which proves how much your flattery is worth." Amy spoke bitterly, and turned her back on the exasperating martyr at her feet.

In a minute a hand came down over the page, so that she could not draw, and Laurie's voice said, with a droll imitation of a penitent child, "I will be good, oh, I will be good!"

But Amy did not laugh, for she was in earnest, and tapping on the outspread hand with her pencil, said soberly, "Aren't you ashamed of a hand like that? It's as soft and white as a woman's, and looks as if it never did anything but wear Jouvin's best gloves and pick flowers for ladies. You are not a dandy, thank Heaven, so I'm glad to see there are no diamonds or big seal rings on it, only the little old one Jo gave you so long ago. Dear soul, I wish she was here to help me!"

"So do I!"

The hand vanished as suddenly as it came, and there was energy enough in the echo of her wish to suit even Amy. She glanced down at him with a new thought in her mind, but he was lying with his hat half over his face, as if for shade, and his mustache hid his mouth. She only saw his chest rise and fall, with a long breath that might have been a sigh, and the hand that wore the ring nestled down into the grass, as if to hide something too precious or too tender to be spoken of. All in a minute various hints and trifles assumed shape and significance in Amy's mind, and told her what her sister never had confided to her. She remembered that Laurie never spoke voluntarily of Jo, she recalled the shadow on his face just now, the change in his character, and the wearing of the little old ring which was no ornament to a handsome hand. Girls are quick to read such signs and feel their eloquence. Amy had fancied that perhaps a love trouble was at the bottom of the alteration, and now she was sure of it. Her keen eyes filled, and when she spoke again, it was in a voice that could be beautifully soft and kind when she chose to make it so.

"I know I have no right to talk so to you, Laurie, and if you weren't the sweetest-tempered fellow in the world, you'd be very angry with me. But we are all so fond and proud of you, I couldn't bear to think they should be disappointed in you at home as I have been, though, perhaps, they would understand the change better than I do."

"I think they would," came from under the hat, in a grim tone, quite as touching as a broken one.

"They ought to have told me, and not let me go blundering and scolding, when I should have been more kind and patient than ever. I never did like that Miss Randal and now I hate her!" said artful Amy, wishing to be sure of her facts this time.

"Hang Miss Randal!" And Laurie knocked the hat off his face with a look that left no doubt of his sentiments toward that young lady.

"I beg pardon, I thought—" And there she paused diplomatically.

"No, you didn't, you knew perfectly well I never cared for any one but Jo." Laurie said that in his old, impetuous tone, and turned his face away as he spoke.

"I did think so, but as they never said anything about it, and you came away, I supposed I was mistaken. And Jo wouldn't be kind to you? Why, I was sure she loved you dearly."

"She *was* kind, but not in the right way, and it's lucky for her she didn't love me, if I'm the good-for-nothing fellow you think me. It's her fault, though, and you may tell her so."

The hard, bitter look came back again as he said that, and it troubled Amy, for she did not know what balm to apply.

"I was wrong, I didn't know. I'm very sorry I was so cross, but I can't help wishing you'd bear it better, Teddy, dear."

"Don't, that's her name for me!" And Laurie put up his hand with a quick gesture to stop the words spoken in Jo's half-kind, half-reproachful tone. "Wait till you've tried it yourself," he added in a low voice, as he pulled up the grass by the handful.

"I'd take it manfully, and be respected if I couldn't be loved," said Amy, with the decision of one who knew nothing about it.

Now, Laurie flattered himself that he *had* borne it remarkably well, making no moan, asking no sympathy, and taking his trouble away to live it down alone. Amy's lecture put the matter in a new light, and for the first time it did look weak and selfish to lose heart at the first failure, and shut himself up in moody indifference. He felt as if suddenly shaken out of a pensive dream and found it impossible to go to sleep again. Presently he sat up and asked slowly, "Do you think Jo would despise me as you do?"

"Yes, if she saw you now. She hates lazy people. Why don't you do something splendid, and *make* her love you?"

"I did my best, but it was no use."

"Graduating well, you mean? That was no more than you ought to have done, for your grandfather's sake. It would have been shameful to fail after spending so much time and money, when everyone knew you *could* do well."

"I did fail, say what you will, for Jo wouldn't love me," began Laurie, leaning his head on his hand in a despondent attitude.

"No, you didn't, and you'll say so in the end, for it did you good, and proved that you could do something if you tried. If you'd only set about another task of some sort, you'd soon be your hearty, happy self again, and forget your trouble."

"That's impossible."

"Try it and see. You needn't shrug your shoulders, and think, 'Much she knows about such things.' I don't pretend to be wise, but I *am* observing, and I see a great deal more than you'd imagine. I'm interested in other people's experiences and inconsistencies, and, though I can't explain, I remember and use them for my own benefit. Love Jo all your days, if you choose, but don't let it spoil you, for it's wicked to throw away so many good gifts because you can't have the one you want. There, I won't lecture any more, for I know you'll wake up and be a man in spite of that hardhearted girl."

Neither spoke for several minutes. Laurie sat turning the little ring on his finger, and Amy put the last touches to the hasty sketch she had been working at while she talked.

Presently she put it on his knee, merely saying, "How do you like that?"

He looked and then he smiled, as he could not well help doing, for it was capitally done—the long, lazy figure on the grass, with listless face, half-shut eyes, and one hand holding a cigar, from which came the little wreath of smoke that encircled the dreamer's head.

"How well you draw!" he said, with a genuine surprise and pleasure at her skill, adding, with a half-laugh, "Yes, that's me."

"As you are: this is as you were." And Amy laid another sketch beside the one he held.

It was not nearly so well done, but there was a life and spirit in it which atoned for many faults, and it recalled the past so vividly that a sudden change swept over the young man's face as he looked. Only a rough sketch of Laurie taming a horse: hat and coat were off, and every line of the active figure, resolute face, and commanding attitude was full of energy and meaning. The handsome brute, just subdued, stood arching his neck under the tightly drawn rein, with one foot impatiently pawing the ground, and ears pricked up as if listening for the voice that had mastered him. In the ruffled mane, the rider's breezy hair and erect attitude, there was a suggestion of suddenly arrested motion, of strength, courage, and youthful buoyancy that contrasted sharply with the supine grace of the *"Dolce far niente"* sketch. Laurie said nothing, but as his eye went from one to the other, Amy saw him flush up and fold his lips together as if he read and accepted the little lesson she had given him. That satisfied her, and without waiting for him to speak, she said, in her sprightly way—

"Don't you remember the day you played Rarey with Puck, and we all looked on? Meg and Beth were frightened, but Jo clapped and pranced, and I sat on the fence and drew you. I found that sketch in my portfolio the other day, touched it up, and kept it to show you."

"Much obliged. You've improved immensely since then,

and I congratulate you. May I venture to suggest in 'a honeymoon paradise' that five o'clock is the dinner hour at your hotel?"

Laurie rose as he spoke, returned the pictures with a smile and a bow and looked at his watch, as if to remind her that even moral lectures should have an end. He tried to resume his former easy, indifferent air, but it *was* an affectation now, for the rousing had been more efficacious than he would confess. Amy felt the shade of coldness in his manner, and said to herself—

"Now I've offended him. Well, if it does him good, I'm glad, if it makes him hate me, I'm sorry, but it's true, and I can't take back a word of it."

They laughed and chatted all the way home, and little Baptiste, up behind, thought that monsieur and mademoiselle were in charming spirits. But both felt ill at ease: the friendly frankness was disturbed, the sunshine had a shadow over it, and, despite their apparent gaiety, there was a secret discontent in the heart of each.

"Shall we see you this evening, *mon frère?*" asked Amy, as they parted at her aunt's door.

"Unfortunately I have an engagement. *Au revoir, mademoiselle.*" And Laurie bent as if to kiss her hand, in the foreign fashion, which became him better than many men. Something in his face made Amy say quickly and warmly—

"No, be yourself with me, Laurie, and part in the good old way. I'd rather have a hearty English handshake than all the sentimental salutations in France."

"Goodbye, dear." And with these words, uttered in the tone she liked, Laurie left her, after a handshake almost painful in its heartiness.

Next morning, instead of the usual call, Amy received a note which made her smile at the beginning and sigh at the end:

My dear Mentor,

Please make my adieux to your aunt, and exult within yourself, for "Lazy Laurence" has gone to his grandpa, like the best of boys. A pleasant winter to you, and may the gods grant you a blissful honeymoon at Valrosa! I think Fred would be benefited by a rouser. Tell him so, with my congratulations.

Yours gratefully,   TELEMACHUS.

"Good boy! I'm glad he's gone," said Amy, with an approving smile; the next minute her face fell as she glanced about the empty room, adding, with an involuntary sigh, "Yes, I *am* glad, but how I shall miss him!"

Chapter 40

The Valley of the Shadow

WHEN THE FIRST BITTERNESS was over, the family accepted the inevitable, and tried to bear it cheerfully, helping one another by the increased affection which comes to bind households tenderly together in times of trouble. They put away their grief, and each did his or her part toward making that last year a happy one.

The pleasantest room in the house was set apart for Beth, and in it was gathered everything that she most loved— flowers, pictures, her piano, the little worktable, and the beloved pussies. Father's best books found their way there, Mother's easy chair, Jo's desk, Amy's finest sketches, and every day Meg brought her babies on a loving pilgrimage, to make sunshine for Aunty Beth. John quietly set apart a little sum, that he might enjoy the pleasure of keeping the invalid supplied with the fruit she loved and longed for; old Hannah never wearied of concocting dainty dishes to tempt a capricious appetite, dropping tears as she worked; and from across the sea came little gifts and cheerful letters, seeming to bring breaths of warmth and fragrance from lands that know no winter.

Here, cherished like a household saint in its shrine, sat Beth, tranquil and busy as ever, for nothing could change the sweet, unselfish nature, and even while preparing to leave life, she tried to make it happier for those who should remain behind. The feeble fingers were never idle, and one of her pleasures was to make little things for the schoolchildren daily passing to and fro—to drop a pair of mittens from her window for a pair of purple hands, a needlebook for some small mother of many dolls, penwipers for young penmen toiling through forests of pothooks, scrapbooks for picture-loving eyes, and all manner of pleasant devices, till the reluctant climbers up the ladder of learning found their way strewn with flowers, as it were, and came to regard the gentle giver as a sort of fairy godmother, who sat above there, and showered down gifts miraculously suited to their tastes and needs. If Beth had wanted any reward, she found it in the bright little faces always turned up to her window, with nods and smiles, and the droll little letters which came to her, full of blots and gratitude.

The first few months were very happy ones, and Beth often used to look round, and say "How beautiful this is!" as they all sat together in her sunny room, the babies kicking and crowing on the floor, mother and sisters working near, and father reading, in his pleasant voice, from the wise old books which seemed rich in good and comfortable words, as applicable now as when written centuries ago; a little chapel, where a paternal priest taught his flock the hard lessons all must learn, trying to show them that hope can comfort love, and faith make resignation possible. Simple sermons, that went straight to the souls of those who listened, for the father's heart was in the minister's religion, and the frequent falter in the voice gave a double eloquence to the words he spoke or read.

It was well for all that this peaceful time was given them as preparation for the sad hours to come; for, by-and-by, Beth said the needle was "so heavy," and put it down forever; talking wearied her, faces troubled her, pain claimed her for its own, and her tranquil spirit was sorrowfully perturbed by the ills that vexed her feeble flesh. Ah me! Such heavy days, such long, long nights, such aching hearts and imploring prayers, when those who loved her best were forced to see the thin hands stretched out to them beseechingly, to hear the bitter cry, "Help me, help me!" and to feel that there was no help. A sad eclipse of the serene soul, a sharp struggle of the young life with death, but both were mercifully brief, and then, the natural rebellion over, the old peace returned more beautiful than ever. With the wreck of her frail body, Beth's soul grew strong, and though she said little, those about her felt that she was ready, saw that the first pilgrim called was likewise the fittest, and waited with her on the shore, trying to see the Shining Ones coming to receive her when she crossed the river.

Jo never left her for an hour since Beth had said, "I feel stronger when you are here." She slept on a couch in the room, waking often to renew the fire, to feed, lift, or wait upon the patient creature who seldom asked for anything, and "tried not to be a trouble." All day she haunted the room, jealous of any other nurse, and prouder of being chosen then than of any honor her life ever brought her. Precious and helpful hours to Jo, for now her heart received the teaching that it needed: lessons in patience were so sweetly taught her that she could not fail to learn them; charity for all, the lovely spirit that can forgive and truly forget unkindness, the loyalty to duty that makes the hardest easy, and the sincere faith that fears nothing, but trusts undoubtingly.

Often when she woke Jo found Beth reading in her well-worn little book, heard her singing softly, to beguile the sleepless night, or saw her lean her face upon her hands, while slow tears dropped through the transparent fingers; and Jo would lie watching her with thoughts too deep for tears, feeling that Beth, in her simple, unselfish way, was trying to wean herself from the dear old life, and fit herself for the life to come, by sacred words of comfort, quiet prayers, and the music she loved so well.

Seeing this did more for Jo than the wisest sermons, the saintliest hymns, the most fervent prayers that any voice could utter; for, with eyes made clear by many tears, and a heart softened by the tenderest sorrow, she recognized the beauty of her sister's life—uneventful, unambitious, yet full of the genuine virtues which "smell sweet, and blossom in the dust," the self-forgetfulness that makes the humblest on earth remembered soonest in heaven, the true success which is possible to all.

One night when Beth looked among the books upon her table, to find something to make her forget the mortal weariness that was almost as hard to bear as pain, as she turned the

leaves of her old favorite, *Pilgrim's Progress,* she found a little
paper, scribbled over in Jo's hand. The name caught her eye
and the blurred look of the lines made her sure that tears
had fallen on it.

"Poor Jo! She's fast asleep, so I won't wake her to ask
leave; she shows me all her things, and I don't think she'll
mind if I look at this," thought Beth, with a glance at her
sister, who lay on the rug, with the tongs beside her, ready
to wake up the minute the log fell apart.

MY BETH

Sitting patient in the shadow
  Till the blessed light shall come,
A serene and saintly presence
  Sanctifies our troubled home.
Earthly joys and hopes and sorrows
  Break like ripples on the strand
Of the deep and solemn river
  Where her willing feet now stand.

O my sister, passing from me,
  Out of human care and strife,
Leave me, as a gift, those virtues
  Which have beautified your life.
Dear, bequeath me that great patience
  Which has power to sustain
A cheerful, uncomplaining spirit
  In its prison-house of pain.

Give me, for I need it sorely,
  Of that courage, wise and sweet,
Which has made the path of duty
  Green beneath your willing feet.
Give me that unselfish nature,
  That with charity divine
Can pardon wrong for love's dear sake—
  Meek heart, forgive me mine!

Thus our parting daily loseth
　　Something of its bitter pain,
And while learning this hard lesson,
　　My great loss becomes my gain.
For the touch of grief will render
　　My wild nature more serene,
Give to life new aspirations,
　　A new trust in the unseen.

Henceforth, safe across the river,
　　I shall see forevermore
A beloved, household spirit
　　Waiting for me on the shore.
Hope and faith, born of my sorrow,
　　Guardian angels shall become,
And the sister gone before me
　　By their hands shall lead me home.

Blurred and blotted, faulty and feeble as the lines were, they brought a look of inexpressible comfort to Beth's face, for her one regret had been that she had done so little, and this seemed to assure her that her life had not been useless, that her death would not bring the despair she feared. As she sat with the paper folded between her hands, the charred log fell asunder. Jo started up, revived the blaze, and crept to the bedside, hoping Beth slept.

"Not asleep, but so happy, dear. See, I found this and read it. I knew you wouldn't care. Have I been all that to you, Jo?" she asked, with wistful, humble earnestness.

"Oh, Beth, so much, so much!" And Jo's head went down upon the pillow beside her sister's.

"Then I don't feel as if I'd wasted my life. I'm not so good as you make me, but I *have* tried to do right; and now, when it's too late to begin even to do better, it's such a comfort to know that someone loves me so much, and feels as if I'd helped them."

"More than any one in the world, Beth. I used to think I

couldn't let you go, but I'm learning to feel that I don't lose you, that you'll be more to me than ever, and death can't part us, though it seems to."

"I know it cannot, and I don't fear it any longer, for I'm sure I shall be your Beth still, to love and help you more than ever. You must take my place, Jo, and be everything to Father and Mother when I'm gone. They will turn to you, don't fail them; and if it's hard to work alone, remember that I don't forget you, and that you'll be happier in doing that than writing splendid books or seeing all the world; for love is the only thing that we can carry with us when we go, and it makes the end so easy."

"I'll try, Beth." And then and there Jo renounced her old ambition, pledged herself to a new and better one, acknowledging the poverty of other desires, and feeling the blessed solace of a belief in the immortality of love.

So the spring days came and went, the sky grew clearer, the earth greener, the flowers were up fair and early, and the birds came back in time to say good-by to Beth, who, like a tired but trustful child, clung to the hands that had led her all her life, as Father and Mother guided her tenderly through the Valley of the Shadow, and gave her up to God.

Seldom except in books do the dying utter memorable words, see visions, or depart with beatified countenances, and those who have sped many parting souls know that to most the end comes as naturally and simply as sleep. As Beth had hoped, the "tide went out easily," and in the dark hour before the dawn, on the bosom where she had drawn her first breath, she quietly drew her last, with no farewell but one loving look, one little sigh.

With tears and prayers and tender hands, Mother and sisters made her ready for the long sleep that pain would never mar again, seeing with grateful eyes the beautiful serenity that soon replaced the pathetic patience that had wrung their hearts so long, and feeling with reverent joy that to their darling death was a benignant angel, not a phantom full of dread.

When morning came, for the first time in many months the fire was out, Jo's place was empty, and the room was very still. But a bird sang blithely on a budding bough, close by, the snowdrops blossomed freshly at the window, and the spring sunshine streamed in like a benediction over the placid face upon the pillow—a face so full of painless peace that those who loved it best smiled through their tears, and thanked God that Beth was well at last.

Chapter 41

Learning to Forget

AMY'S LECTURE DID Laurie good, though, of course, he did not own it till long afterward; men seldom do, for when women are the advisers, the lords of creation don't take the advice till they have persuaded themselves that it is just what they intended to do; then they act upon it, and, if it succeeds, they give the weaker vessel half the credit of it; if it fails, they generously give her the whole. Laurie went back to his grandfather, and was so dutifully devoted for several weeks that the old gentleman declared the climate of Nice had improved him wonderfully, and he had better try it again. There was nothing the young gentleman would have liked better, but elephants could not have dragged him back after the scolding he had received; pride forbid, and whenever the longing grew very strong, he fortified his resolution by repeating the words that had made the deepest impression, "I despise you." "Go and do something splendid that will *make* her love you."

Laurie turned the matter over in his mind so often that he soon brought himself to confess that he *had* been selfish and lazy, but then when a man has a great sorrow, he should be indulged in all sorts of vagaries till he has lived it down. He felt that his blighted affections were quite dead now, and though he should never cease to be a faithful mourner, there was no occasion to wear his weeds ostentatiously. Jo *wouldn't* love him, but he might *make* her respect and admire him by doing something which should prove that a girl's no had not spoiled his life. He had always meant to do something, and Amy's advice was quite unnecessary. He had only been waiting till the aforesaid blighted affections were decently interred; that being done, he felt that he was ready to "hide his stricken heart, and still toil on."

As Goethe, when he had a joy or a grief, put it into a song, so Laurie resolved to embalm his love sorrow in music, and compose a Requiem which should harrow up Jo's soul and melt the heart of every hearer. Therefore the next time the old gentleman found him getting restless and moody and ordered him off, he went to Vienna, where he had musical friends, and fell to work with the firm determination to distinguish himself. But, whether the sorrow was too vast to be embodied in music, or music too ethereal to uplift a mortal woe, he soon discovered that the Requiem was beyond him just at present. It was evident that his mind was not in working order yet, and his ideas needed clarifying, for often in the middle of a plaintive strain, he would find himself humming a dancing tune that vividly recalled the Christmas ball at Nice, especially the stout Frenchman, and put an effectual stop to tragic composition for the time being.

Then he tried an opera, for nothing seemed impossible in the beginning, but here again unforeseen difficulties beset him. He wanted Jo for his heroine, and called upon his memory to supply him with tender recollections and romantic visions of his love. But memory turned traitor; and, as if possessed by the perverse spirit of the girl, would only recall Jo's oddities, faults, and freaks, would only show her in the most unsentimental aspects—beating mats with her head tied up in a bandanna, barricading herself with the sofa pillow, or throwing cold water over his passion à la Gummidge—and an irresistible laugh spoiled the pensive picture he was endeavoring to paint. Jo wouldn't be put into the opera at any price, and he had to give her up with a "Bless that girl, what a torment she is!" and a clutch at his hair, as became a distracted composer.

When he looked about him for another and a less intractable damsel to immortalize in melody, memory produced one with the most obliging readiness. This phantom wore many faces, but it always had golden hair, was enveloped in a diaphanous cloud, and floated airily before his mind's eye in a pleasing chaos of roses, peacocks, white ponies, and blue ribbons. He did not give the complacent wraith any name, but he took her for his heroine and grew quite fond of her, as well he might, for he gifted her with every gift and grace under the sun, and escorted her, unscathed, through trials which would have annihilated any mortal woman.

Thanks to this inspiration, he got on swimmingly for a time, but gradually the work lost its charm, and he forgot to compose, while he sat musing, pen in hand, or roamed about the gay city to get new ideas and refresh his mind, which seemed to be in a somewhat unsettled state that winter. He did not do much, but he thought a great deal and was conscious of a change of some sort going on in spite of himself. "It's genius simmering, perhaps. I'll let it simmer, and see what comes of it," he said, with a secret suspicion all the while that it wasn't genius, but something far more common. Whatever it was, it simmered to some purpose, for he grew more and more discontented with his desultory life, began to long for some real and earnest work to go at, soul and body, and finally came to the wise conclusion that everyone who loved music was not a composer. Returning from one of Mozart's grand operas, splendidly performed at the Royal Theatre, he looked over his own, played a few of the best parts, sat staring up at the busts of Mendelssohn, Beethoven, and Bach, who stared benignly back again; then suddenly he tore up his music sheets, one by one, and as the last fluttered out of his hand, he said soberly to himself—

"She is right! Talent isn't genius, and you can't make it so. That music has taken the vanity out of me as Rome took it out of her, and I won't be a humbug any longer. Now what shall I do?"

That seemed a hard question to answer, and Laurie began to wish he had to work for his daily bread. Now, if ever, occurred an eligible opportunity for "going to the devil," as he once forcibly expressed it, for he had plenty of money and nothing to do, and Satan is proverbially fond of providing employment for full and idle hands. The poor fellow had temptations enough from without and from within, but he withstood them pretty well; for much as he valued liberty, he valued good faith and confidence more, so his promise to his grandfather, and his desire to be able to look honestly into the eyes of the women who loved him, and say "All's well," kept him safe and steady.

Very likely some Mrs. Grundy will observe, "I don't believe it, boys will be boys, young men must sow their wild oats, and women must not expect miracles." I dare say *you* don't, Mrs. Grundy, but it's true nevertheless. Women work a good many miracles, and I have a persuasion that they may perform even that of raising the standard of manhood by refusing to echo such sayings. Let the boys be boys, the longer the better, and let the young men sow their wild oats if they must; but mothers, sisters, and friends may help to make the crop a small one, and keep many tares from spoiling the harvest, by believing, and showing that they believe, in the possibility of loyalty to the virtues which make men manliest in good women's eyes. If it *is* a feminine delusion, leave us to enjoy it while we may, for without it half the beauty and the romance of life is lost, and sorrowful forebodings would embitter all our hopes of the brave, tenderhearted little lads, who still love their mothers better than themselves and are not ashamed to own it.

Laurie thought that the task of forgetting his love for Jo would absorb all his powers for years, but to his great surprise he discovered it grew easier every day. He refused to believe it at first, got angry with himself, and couldn't understand it, but these hearts of ours are curious and contrary things, and time and nature work their will in spite of us. Laurie's heart *wouldn't* ache; the wound persisted in healing with a rapidity that astonished him, and instead of trying to forget, he found himself trying to remember. He had not foreseen this turn of affairs, and was not prepared for it. He was disgusted with himself, surprised at his own fickleness, and full of a queer mixture of disappointment and relief that he could recover from such a tremendous blow so soon. He carefully stirred up the embers of his lost love, but they refused to burst into a blaze: there was only a comfortable glow that warmed and did him good without putting him into a fever, and he was reluctantly obliged to confess that the boyish passion was slowly subsiding into a more tranquil sentiment, very tender, a little sad and resentful still, but that was sure to pass away in time, leaving a brotherly affection which would last unbroken to the end.

As the word "brotherly" passed through his mind in one of these reveries, he smiled, and glanced up at the picture of Mozart that was before him:

"Well, he was a great man, and when he couldn't have one sister he took the other, and was happy."

Laurie did not utter the words, but he thought them, and the next instant kissed the little old ring, saying to himself, "No, I won't! I haven't forgotten, I never can. I'll try again, and if that fails, why, then—"

Leaving his sentence unfinished, he seized pen and paper and wrote to Jo, telling her that he could not settle to anything while there was the least hope of her changing her mind. Couldn't she, wouldn't she, and let him come home and be happy? While waiting for an answer he did nothing, but he did it energetically, for he was in a fever of impatience. It came at last, and settled his mind effectually on one point, for Jo decidedly couldn't and wouldn't. She was wrapped up in Beth, and never wished to hear the word "love" again. Then she begged him to be happy with somebody else, but always to keep a little corner of his heart for his loving sister Jo. In a postscript she desired him not to tell Amy that Beth was worse, she was coming home in the spring and there was no need of saddening the remainder of her stay. That would be time enough, please God, but Laurie must write to her often, and not let her feel lonely, homesick, or anxious.

"So I will, at once. Poor little girl, it will be a sad going home for her, I'm afraid." And Laurie opened his desk, as if writing to Amy had been the proper conclusion of the sentence left unfinished some weeks before.

But he did not write the letter that day, for as he rummaged out his best paper, he came across something which changed his purpose. Tumbling about in one part of the desk among bills, passports, and business documents of various kinds were several of Jo's letters, and in another compartment were three notes from Amy, carefully tied up with one of her blue ribbons and sweetly suggestive of the little dead roses put away inside. With a half-repentant, half-amused expression, Laurie gathered up all Jo's letters, smoothed, folded, and put them neatly into a small drawer of the desk, stood a minute turning the ring thoughtfully on his finger, then slowly drew it off, laid it with the letters, locked the drawer, and went out to hear High Mass at Saint Stefan's, feeling as if there had been a funeral, and though not overwhelmed with affliction, this seemed a more proper way to spend the rest of the day than in writing letters to charming young ladies.

The letter went very soon, however, and was promptly answered, for Amy *was* homesick, and confessed it in the most delightfully confiding manner. The correspondence flourished famously, and letters flew to and fro with unfailing regularity all through the early spring. Laurie sold his busts, made allumettes of his opera, and went back to Paris, hoping somebody would arrive before long. He wanted desperately to go to Nice, but would not till he was asked, and Amy would not ask him, for just then she was having little experiences of her own, which made her rather wish to avoid the quizzical eyes of "our boy."

Fred Vaughn had returned, and put the question to which she had once decided to answer, "Yes, thank you," but now she said, "No, thank you," kindly but steadily, for, when the time came, her courage failed her, and she found that something more than money and position was needed to satisfy the new longing that filled her heart so full of tender hopes and fears. The words, "Fred is a good fellow, but not at all the man I fancied you would ever like," and Laurie's face when he uttered them, kept returning to her as pertinaciously as her own did when she said in look, if not in words, "I shall marry for money." It troubled her to remember that now, she wished she could take it back, it sounded so unwomanly. She didn't want Laurie to think her a heartless, worldly creature; she didn't care to be a queen of society now half so much as she did to be a lovable woman; she was so glad he didn't hate her for the dreadful things she said, but took them so beautifully and was kinder than ever. His letters were such a comfort, for the home letters were very irregular, and were not half so satisfactory as his when they did come. It was not only a pleasure, but a duty to answer them, for the poor fellow was forlorn, and needed petting, since Jo persisted in being stonyhearted. She ought to have made an effort, and tried to love him; it couldn't be very hard, many people would be proud and glad to have such a dear boy care for them: but Jo never would act like other girls, so there was nothing to do but be very kind, and treat him like a brother.

If all brothers were treated as well as Laurie was at this period, they would be a much happier race of beings than they are. Amy never lectured now: she asked his opinion on all subjects, she was interested in everything he did, made charming little presents for him, and sent him two letters a week, full of lively gossip, sisterly confidences, and captivating sketches of the lovely scenes about her. As few brothers are complimented by having their letters carried about in their sisters' pockets, read and reread diligently, cried over when short, kissed when long, and treasured carefully, we will not hint that Amy did any of these fond and foolish things. But she certainly did grow a little pale and pensive that spring, lost much of her relish for society, and went out sketching alone a good deal. She never had much to show when she came home, but was studying nature, I dare say, while she sat for hours, with her hands folded, on the terrace at Valrosa, or absently sketched any fancy that occurred to her—a stalwart knight carved on a tomb, a young man asleep in the grass, with his hat over his eyes, or a curly-haired girl in gorgeous array, promenading down a ballroom on the arm of a tall gentleman, both faces being left a blur according to the last fashion in art, which was safe but not altogether satisfactory.

Her aunt thought that she regretted her answer to Fred,

and finding denials useless and explanations impossible, Amy left her to think what she liked, taking care that Laurie should know that Fred had gone to Egypt. That was all, but he understood it, and looked relieved, as he said to himself, with a venerable air—

"I was sure she would think better of it. Poor old fellow! I've been through it all, and I can sympathize."

With that he heaved a great sigh, and then, as if he had discharged his duty to the past, put his feet up on the sofa and enjoyed Amy's letter luxuriously.

While these changes were going on abroad, trouble had come at home; but the letter telling that Beth was failing never reached Amy, and when the next found her, the grass was green above her sister. The sad news met her at Vevay, for the heat had driven them from Nice in May, and they had traveled slowly to Switzerland, by way of Genoa and the Italian lakes. She bore it very well, and quietly submitted to the family decree that she should not shorten her visit, for, since it was too late to say good-by to Beth, she had better stay, and let absence soften her sorrow. But her heart was very heavy, she longed to be at home, and every day looked wistfully across the lake, waiting for Laurie to come and comfort her.

He did come very soon; for the same mail brought letters to them both, but he was in Germany, and it took some days to reach him. The moment he read it, he packed his knapsack, bade adieu to his fellow pedestrians, and was off to keep his promise, with a heart full of joy and sorrow, hope and suspense.

He knew Vevay well, and as soon as the boat touched the little quay, he hurried along the shore to La Tour, where the Carrols were living *en pension*. The *garçon* was in despair that the whole family had gone to take a promenade on the lake; but no, the blonde mademoiselle might be in the chateau garden. If monsieur would give himself the pain of sitting down, a flash of time should present her. But monsieur could not wait even "a flash of time," and in the middle of the speech departed to find mademoiselle himself.

A pleasant old garden on the borders of the lovely lake, with chestnuts rustling overhead, ivy climbing everywhere, and the black shadow of the tower falling far across the sunny water. At one corner of the wide, low wall was a seat, and here Amy often came to read or work, or console herself with the beauty all about her. She was sitting here that day, leaning her head on her hand, with a homesick heart and heavy eyes, thinking of Beth and wondering why Laurie did not come. She did not hear him cross the courtyard beyond, nor see him pause in the archway that led from the subterranean path into the garden. He stood a minute, looking at her with new eyes, seeing what no one had ever seen before— the tender side of Amy's character. Everything about her mutely suggested love and sorrow—the blotted letters in her lap, the black ribbon that tied up her hair, the womanly pain and patience in her face; even the little ebony cross at her throat seemed pathetic to Laurie, for he had given it to her, and she wore it as her only ornament. If he had any doubts about the reception she would give him, they were set at rest the minute she looked up and saw him, for dropping everything, she ran to him, exclaiming, in a tone of unmistakable love and longing—

"Oh, Laurie, Laurie, I knew you'd come to me!"

I think everything was said and settled then, for as they stood together quite silent for a moment, with the dark head bent down protectingly over the light one, Amy felt that no one could comfort and sustain her so well as Laurie, and Laurie decided that Amy was the only woman in the world who could fill Jo's place and make him happy. He did not tell her so; but she was not disappointed, for both felt the truth, were satisfied, and gladly left the rest to silence.

In a minute Amy went back to her place, and while she dried her tears, Laurie gathered up the scattered papers, finding in the sight of sundry well-worn letters and suggestive sketches good omens for the future. As he sat down beside her, Amy felt shy again, and turned rosy red at the recollection of her impulsive greeting.

"I couldn't help it, I felt so lonely and sad, and was so very

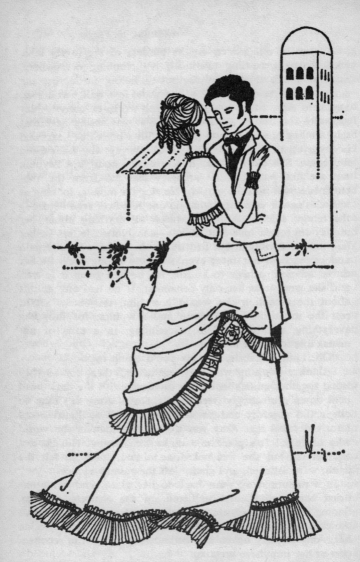

"O Laurie, Laurie, I knew you'd come to me!"

glad to see you. It was such a surprise to look up and find
you, just as I was beginning to fear you wouldn't come," she
said, trying in vain to speak quite naturally.

"I came the minute I heard. I wish I could say something
to comfort you for the loss of dear little Beth, but I can only
feel, and—" He could not get any further, for he, too, turned
bashful all of a sudden, and did not quite know what to say.
He longed to lay Amy's head down on his shoulder, and
tell her to have a good cry, but he did not dare, so took her
hand instead, and gave it a sympathetic squeeze that was
better than words.

"You needn't say anything, this comforts me," she said
softly. "Beth is well and happy, and I mustn't wish her back,
but I dread the going home, much as I long to see them all.
We won't talk about it now, for it makes me cry, and I want
to enjoy you while you stay. You needn't go right back,
need you?"

"Not if you want me, dear."

"I do, so much. Aunt and Flo are very kind, but you
seem like one of the family, and it would be so comfortable to
have you for a little while."

Amy spoke and looked so like a homesick child whose
heart was full that Laurie forgot his bashfulness all at once,
and gave her just what she wanted—the petting she was used
to and the cheerful conversation she needed.

"Poor little soul, you look as if you'd grieved yourself
half sick! I'm going to take care of you, so don't cry any
more, but come and walk about with me, the wind is too
chilly for you to sit still," he said, in the half-caressing, half-
commanding way that Amy liked, as he tied on her hat, drew
her arm through his, and began to pace up and down the
sunny walk under the new-leaved chestnuts. He felt more
at ease upon his legs, and Amy found it very pleasant to have
a strong arm to lean upon, a familiar face to smile at her,
and a kind voice to talk delightfully for her alone.

The quaint old garden had sheltered many pairs of lovers,
and seemed expressly made for them, so sunny and secluded
was it, with nothing but the tower to overlook them, and the

wide lake to carry away the echo of their words, as it rippled by below. For an hour this new pair walked and talked, or rested on the wall, enjoying the sweet influences which gave such a charm to time and place, and when an unromantic dinner bell warned them away, Amy felt as if she left her burden of loneliness and sorrow behind her in the château garden.

The moment Mrs. Carrol saw the girl's altered face, she was illuminated with a new idea, and exclaimed to herself, "Now I understand it all—the child has been pining for young Laurence. Bless my heart, I never thought of such a thing!"

With praiseworthy discretion, the good lady said nothing, and betrayed no sign of enlightenment, but cordially urged Laurie to stay and begged Amy to enjoy his society, for it would do her more good than so much solitude. Amy was a model of docility, and as her aunt was a good deal occupied with Flo, she was left to entertain her friend, and did it with more than her usual success.

At Nice, Laurie had lounged and Amy had scolded; at Vevay, Laurie was never idle, but always walking, riding, boating, or studying in the most energetic manner, while Amy admired everything he did and followed his example as far and as fast as she could. He said the change was owing to the climate, and she did not contradict him, being glad of a like excuse for her own recovered health and spirits.

The invigorating air did them both good, and much exercise worked wholesome changes in minds as well as bodies. They seemed to get clearer views of life and duty up there among the everlasting hills; the fresh winds blew away desponding doubts, delusive fancies, and moody mists; the warm spring sunshine brought out all sorts of aspiring ideas, tender hopes, and happy thoughts; the lake seemed to wash away the troubles of the past, and the grand old mountains to look benignly down upon them, saying, "Little children, love one another."

In spite of the new sorrow, it was a very happy time, so happy that Laurie could not bear to disturb it by a word. It took him a little while to recover from his surprise at the rapid cure of his first, and, as he had firmly believed, his last and only love. He consoled himself for the seeming disloyalty by the thought that Jo's sister was almost the same as Jo's self, and the conviction that it would have been impossible to love any other woman but Amy so soon and so well. His first wooing had been of the tempestuous order, and he looked back upon it as if through a long vista of years with a feeling of compassion blended with regret. He was not ashamed of it, but put it away as one of the bittersweet experiences of his life, for which he could be grateful when the pain was over. His second wooing, he resolved, should be as calm and simple as possible: there was no need of having a scene, hardly any need of telling Amy that he loved her, she knew it without words and had given him his answer long ago. It all came about so naturally that no one could complain, and he knew that everybody would be pleased, even Jo. But when our first little passion has been crushed, we are apt to be wary and slow in making a second trial, so Laurie let the days pass, enjoying every hour, and leaving to chance the utterance of the word that would put an end to the first and sweetest part of his new romance.

He had rather imagined that the denouement would take place in the château garden by moonlight, and in the most graceful and decorous manner, but it turned out exactly the reverse, for the matter was settled on the lake at noonday in a few blunt words. They had been floating about all the morning, from gloomy St. Gingolf to sunny Montreux, with the Alps of Savoy on one side, Mont St. Bernard and the Dent du Midi on the other, pretty Vevay in the valley, and Lausanne upon the hill beyond, a cloudless blue sky overhead, and the bluer lake below, dotted with the picturesque boats that look like white-winged gulls.

They had been talking of Bonnivard, as they glided past Chillon, and of Rousseau, as they looked up at Clarens, where he wrote his *Héloise*. Neither had read it, but they knew it was a love story, and each privately wondered if it was half as interesting as their own. Amy had been dabbling her hand in the water during the little pause that fell between them, and, when she looked up, Laurie was leaning on his oars with an expression in his eyes that made her say hastily, merely for the sake of saying something—

"You must be tired; rest a little, and let me row; it will do me good; for since you came I have been altogether lazy and luxurious."

"I'm not tired, but you may take an oar, if you like. There's room enough, though I have to sit nearly in the middle, else the boat won't trim," returned Laurie, as if he rather liked the arrangement.

Feeling that she had not mended matters much, Amy took the offered third of a seat, shook her hair over her face, and accepted an oar. She rowed as well as she did many other things; and, though she used both hands, and Laurie but one, the oars kept time, and the boat went smoothly through the water.

"How well we pull together, don't we?" said Amy, who objected to silence just then.

"So well that I wish we might always pull in the same boat. Will you, Amy?" very tenderly.

"Yes, Laurie," very low.

Then they both stopped rowing, and unconsciously added a pretty little tableau of human love and happiness to the dissolving views reflected in the lake.

Chapter 42

All Alone

IT WAS EASY to promise self-abnegation when self was wrapped up in another, and heart and soul were purified by a sweet example; but when the helpful voice was silent, the daily lesson over, the beloved presence gone, and nothing remained but loneliness and grief, then Jo found her promise very hard to keep. How could she "comfort Father and Mother" when her own heart ached with a ceaseless longing for her sister, how could she "make the house cheerful" when all its light and warmth and beauty seemed to have deserted it when Beth left the old home for the new, and where in all the world could she "find some useful, happy work to do," that would take the place of the loving service which had been its own reward? She tried in a blind, hopeless way to do her duty, secretly rebelling against it all the while, for it seemed unjust that her few joys should be lessened, her burdens made heavier, and life get harder and harder as she toiled along. Some people seemed to get all sunshine, and some all shadow; it was not fair, for she tried more than Amy to be good, but never got any reward, only disappointment, trouble, and hard work.

Poor Jo, these were dark days to her, for something like despair came over her when she thought of spending all her life in that quiet house, devoted to humdrum cares, a few small pleasures, and the duty that never seemed to grow any easier. "I can't do it. I wasn't meant for a life like this, and I know I shall break away and do something desperate if somebody doesn't come and help me," she said to herself, when her first efforts failed and she fell into the moody, miserable state of mind which often comes when strong wills have to yield to the inevitable.

But someone did come and help her, though Jo did not

recognize her good angels at once because they wore familiar shapes and used the simple spells best fitted to poor humanity. Often she started up at night, thinking Beth called her; and when the sight of the little empty bed made her cry with the bitter cry of an unsubmissive sorrow, "Oh, Beth, come back! Come back!" she did not stretch out her yearning arms in vain; for, as quick to hear her sobbing as she had been to hear her sister's faintest whisper, her mother came to comfort her, not with words only, but the patient tenderness that soothes by a touch, tears that were mute reminders of a greater grief than Jo's, and broken whispers, more eloquent than prayers, because hopeful resignation went hand-in-hand with natural sorrow. Sacred moments, when heart talked to heart in the silence of the night, turning affliction to a blessing, which chastened grief and strengthened love. Feeling this, Jo's burden seemed easier to bear, duty grew sweeter, and life looked more endurable, seen from the safe shelter of her mother's arms.

When aching heart was a little comforted, troubled mind likewise found help, for one day she went to the study, and leaning over the good gray head lifted to welcome her with a tranquil smile, she said, very humbly, "Father, talk to me as you did to Beth. I need it more than she did, for I'm all wrong."

"My dear, nothing can comfort me like this," he answered, with a falter in his voice, and both arms round her, as if he, too, needed help, and did not fear to ask it.

Then, sitting in Beth's little chair close beside him, Jo told her troubles—the resentful sorrow for her loss, the fruitless efforts that discouraged her, the want of faith that made life look so dark, and all the sad bewilderment which we call despair. She gave him entire confidence, he gave her the help she needed, and both found consolation in the act; for the time had come when they could talk together not only as father and daughter, but as man and woman, able and glad to serve each other with mutual sympathy as well as mutual love. Happy, thoughtful times there in the old study which Jo called "the church of one member," and from which she came with fresh courage, recovered cheerfulness, and a more submissive spirit; for the parents who had taught one child to meet death without fear, were trying now to teach another to accept life without despondency or distrust, and to use its beautiful opportunities with gratitude and power.

Other helps had Jo—humble, wholesome duties and delights that would not be denied their part in serving her, and which she slowly learned to see and value. Brooms and dish-cloths never could be as distasteful as they once had been, for Beth had presided over both; and something of her house-wifely spirit seemed to linger round the little mop and the old brush, that was never thrown away. As she used them, Jo found herself humming the songs Beth used to hum, imitating Beth's orderly ways, and giving the little touches here and there that kept everything fresh and cozy, which was the first step toward making home happy, though she didn't know it till Hannah said with an approving squeeze of the hand—

"You thoughtful creter, you're determined we shan't miss that dear lamb ef you can help it. We don't say much, but we see it, and the Lord will bless you for't, see ef He don't."

As they sat sewing together, Jo discovered how much improved her sister Meg was, how well she could talk, how much she knew about good, womanly impulses, thoughts, and feelings, how happy she was in husband and children, and how much they were all doing for each other.

"Marriage is an excellent thing, after all. I wonder if I should blossom out half as well as you have, if I tried it?" said Jo, as she constructed a kite for Demi in the topsy-turvy nursery.

"It's just what you need to bring out the tender womanly half of your nature, Jo. You are like a chestnut burr, prickly outside, but silky-soft within, and a sweet kernel, if one can only get at it. Love will make you show your heart some day, and then the rough burr will fall off."

"Frost opens chestnut burrs, ma'am, and it takes a good shake to bring them down. Boys go nutting, and I don't care to be bagged by them," returned Jo, pasting away at the kite which no wind that blows would ever carry up, for Daisy had tied herself on as a bob.

Meg laughed, for she was glad to see a glimmer of Jo's old spirit, but she felt it her duty to enforce her opinion by every argument in her power, and the sisterly chats were not wasted, especially as two of Meg's most effective arguments were the babies, whom Jo loved tenderly. Grief is the best opener for some hearts, and Jo's was nearly ready for the bag: a little more sunshine to ripen the nut, then, not a boy's impatient shake, but a man's hand reached up to pick it gently from the burr, and find the kernel sound and sweet. If she had suspected this, she would have shut up tight, and been more prickly than ever, fortunately she wasn't thinking about herself, so when the time came, down she dropped.

Now, if she had been the heroine of a moral storybook, she ought at this period of her life to have become quite saintly, renounced the world, and gone about doing good in a mortified bonnet, with tracts in her pocket. But, you see, Jo wasn't a heroine, she was only a struggling human girl like hundreds of others, and she just acted out her nature, being sad, cross, listless, or energetic, as the mood suggested. It's highly virtuous to say we'll be good, but we can't do it all at once, and it takes a long pull, a strong pull, and a pull all together, before some of us even get our feet set in the right way. Jo had got so far, she was learning to do her duty, and to feel unhappy if she did not; but to do it cheerfully—ah, that was another thing! She had often said she wanted to do something splendid, no matter how hard; and now she had her wish, for what could be more beautiful than to devote her life to Father and Mother, trying to make home as happy to them as they had to her? And if difficulties were necessary to increase the splendor of the effort, what could be harder for a restless, ambitious girl than to give up her own hopes, plans, and desires, and cheerfully live for others?

Providence had taken her at her word; here was the task, not what she had expected, but better because self had no part in it: now, could she do it? She decided that she would try, and in her first attempt she found the helps I have suggested. Still another was given her, and she took it, not as a reward, but as a comfort, as Christian took the refreshment afforded by the little arbor where he rested, as he climbed the hill called Difficulty.

"Why don't you write? That always used to make you happy," said her mother once, when the desponding fit overshadowed Jo.

"I've no heart to write, and if I had, nobody cares for my things."

"We do. Write something for us, and never mind the rest of the world. Try it, dear, I'm sure it would do you good, and please us very much."

"Don't believe I can." But Jo got out her desk and began to overhaul her half-finished manuscripts.

An hour afterward her mother peeped in and there she was, scratching away, with her black pinafore on, and an absorbed expression, which caused Mrs. March to smile and slip away, well pleased with the success of her suggestion. Jo never knew how it happened, but something got into that story that went straight to the hearts of those who read it, for when her family had laughed and cried over it, her father sent it, much against her will, to one of the popular magazines, and, to her utter surprise, it was not only paid for, but others requested. Letters from several persons, whose praise was honor, followed the appearance of the little story, newspapers copied it, and strangers as well as friends admired it. For a small thing it was a great success, and Jo was more astonished than when her novel was commended and condemned all at once.

"I don't understand it. What *can* there be in a simple little story like that to make people praise it so?" she said, quite bewildered.

"There is truth in it, Jo, that's the secret; humor and pathos make it alive, and you have found your style at last. You wrote with no thought of fame or money, and put your heart into it, my daughter; you have had the bitter, now comes the sweet. Do your best, and grow as happy as we are in your success."

"If there *is* anything good or true in what I write, it isn't mine; I owe it all to you and Mother and to Beth," said Jo, more touched by her father's words than by any amount of praise from the world.

So taught by love and sorrow, Jo wrote her little stories, and sent them away to make friends for themselves and her, finding it a very charitable world to such humble wanderers; for they were kindly welcomed, and sent home comfortable tokens to their mother, like dutiful children whom good fortune overtakes.

When Amy and Laurie wrote of their engagement, Mrs. March feared that Jo would find it difficult to rejoice over it, but her fears were soon set at rest; for, though Jo looked grave at first, she took it very quietly, and was full of hopes and plans for "the children" before she read the letter twice. It was a sort of written duet, wherein each glorified the other in loverlike fashion, very pleasant to read and satisfactory to think of, for no one had any objection to make.

"You like it, Mother?" said Jo, as they laid down the closely written sheets and looked at one another.

"Yes, I hoped it would be so, ever since Amy wrote that she had refused Fred. I felt sure then that something better than what you call the 'mercenary spirit' had come over her, and a hint here and there in her letters made me suspect that love and Laurie would win the day."

"How sharp you are, Marmee, and how silent! You never said a word to me."

"Mothers have need of sharp eyes and discreet tongues when they have girls to manage. I was half afraid to put the idea into your head, lest you should write and congratulate them before the thing was settled."

"I'm not the scatterbrain I was; you may trust me, I'm sober and sensible enough for anyone's confidante now."

"So you are, my dear, and I should have made you mine, only I fancied it might pain you to learn that your Teddy loved anyone else."

"Now, Mother, did you really think I could be so silly and

selfish, after I'd refused his love, when it was freshest, if not best?"

"I knew you were sincere then, Jo, but lately I have thought that if he came back, and asked again, you might, perhaps, feel like giving another answer. Forgive me, dear, I can't help seeing that you are very lonely, and sometimes there is a hungry look in your eyes that goes to my heart; so I fancied that your boy might fill the empty place if he tried now."

"No, Mother, it is better as it is, and I'm glad Amy has learned to love him. But you are right in one thing: I *am* lonely, and perhaps if Teddy had tried again, I might have said 'Yes,' not because I love him any more, but because I care more to be loved than when he went away."

"I'm glad of that, Jo, for it shows that you are getting on. There are plenty to love you, so try to be satisfied with Father and Mother, sisters and brothers, friends and babies, till the best lover of all comes to give you your reward."

"Mothers are the *best* lovers in the world, but I don't mind whispering to Marmee that I'd like to try all kinds. It's very curious, but the more I try to satisfy myself with all sorts of natural affections, the more I seem to want. I'd no idea hearts could take in so many; mine is so elastic, it nevers seems full now, and I used to be quite contented with my family. I don't understand it."

"I do." And Mrs. March smiled her wise smile, as Jo turned back the leaves to read what Amy said of Laurie.

"It is so beautiful to be loved as Laurie loves me; he isn't sentimental, doesn't say much about it, but I see and feel it in all he says and does, and it makes me so happy and so humble that I don't seem to be the same girl I was. I never knew how good and generous and tender he was till now, for he lets me read his heart, and I find it full of noble impulses and hopes and purposes, and am so proud to know it's mine. He says he feels as if he 'could make a prosperous voyage now with me aboard as mate, and lots of love for ballast.' I pray he may, and try to be all he believes me, for

I love my gallant captain with all my heart and soul and might, and never will desert him, while God lets us be together. Oh, Mother, I never knew how much like heaven this world could be, when two people love and live for one another!"

"And that's our cool, reserved, and worldly Amy! Truly, love does work miracles. How very, very happy they must be!" And Jo laid the rustling sheets together with a careful hand, as one might shut the covers of a lovely romance, which holds the reader fast till the end comes, and he finds himself alone in the workaday world again.

By-and-by Jo roamed away upstairs, for it was rainy, and she could not walk. A restless spirit possessed her, and the old feeling came again, not bitter as it once was, but a sorrowfully patient wonder why one sister should have all she asked, the other nothing. It was not true, she knew that and tried to put it away, but the natural craving for affection was strong, and Amy's happiness woke the hungry longing for some one to "love with heart and soul, and cling to while God let them be together."

Up in the garret, where Jo's unquiet wanderings ended stood four little wooden chests in a row, each marked with its owners name, and each filled with relics of the childhood and girlhood ended now for all. Jo glanced into them, and when she came to her own, leaned her chin on the edge, and stared absently at the chaotic collection, till a bundle of old exercise books caught her eye. She drew them out, turned them over, and relived that pleasant winter at kind Mrs. Kirke's. She had smiled at first, then she looked thoughtful, next sad, and when she came to a little message written in the Professor's hand, her lips began to tremble, the books slid out of her lap, and she sat looking at the friendly words, as if they took a new meaning, and touched a tender spot in her heart.

"Wait for me, my friend. I may be a little late, but I shall surely come."

"Oh, if he only would! So kind, so good, so patient with me always; my dear old Fritz, I didn't value him half enough when I had him, but now how I should love to see him, for everyone seems going away from me, and I'm all alone."

And holding the little paper fast, as if it were a promise yet to be fulfilled, Jo laid her head down on a comfortable rag bag, and cried, as if in opposition to the rain pattering on the roof.

Was it all self-pity, loneliness, or low spirits? Or was it the waking up of a sentiment which had bided its time as patiently as its inspirer? Who shall say?

Chapter 43

Surprises

Jo was alone in the twilight, lying on the old sofa, looking at the fire, and thinking. It was her favorite way of spending the hour of dusk; no one disturbed her, and she used to lie there on Beth's little red pillow, planning stories, dreaming dreams, or thinking tender thoughts of the sister who never seemed far away. Her face looked tired, grave, and rather sad, for tomorrow was her birthday, and she was thinking how fast the years went by, how old she was getting, and how little she seemed to have accomplished. Almost twenty-five, and nothing to show for it. Jo was mistaken in that; there was a good deal to show, and by-and-by she saw, and was grateful for it.

"An old maid, that's what I'm to be. A literary spinster, with a pen for a spouse, a family of stories for children, and twenty years hence a morsel of fame, perhaps; when, like poor Johnson, I'm old, and can't enjoy it, solitary, and can't share it, independent, and don't need it. Well, I needn't be a sour saint nor a selfish sinner, and, I dare say, old maids are very comfortable when they get used to it, but—" And there Jo sighed, as if the prospect was not inviting.

It seldom is, at first, and thirty seems the end of all things to five-and-twenty; but it's not so bad as it looks, and one can get on quite happily if one has something in one's self to fall back upon. At twenty-five, girls begin to talk about being old maids, but secretly resolve that they never will be; at thirty they say nothing about it, but quietly accept the fact, and, if sensible, console themselves by remembering that they have twenty more useful, happy years, in which they may be learning to grow old gracefully. Don't laugh at the spinsters, dear girls, for often very tender, tragic romances are hidden away in the hearts that beat so quietly under the sober gowns, and many silent sacrifices of youth, health, ambition, love itself, make the faded faces beautiful in God's sight. Even the sad, sour sisters should be kindly dealt with, because they have missed the sweetest part of life, if for no other reason; and, looking at them with compassion, not contempt, girls in their bloom should remember that they too may miss the blossom time; that rosy cheeks don't last forever, that silver threads will come in the bonnie brown hair, and that, by-and-by, kindness and respect will be as sweet as love and admiration now.

Gentlemen, which means boys, be courteous to the old maids, no matter how poor and plain and prim, for the only chivalry worth having is that which is the readiest to pay deference to the old, protect the feeble, and serve womankind, regardless of rank, age, or color. Just recollect the good aunts who have not only lectured and fussed, but nursed and petted, too often without thanks; the scrapes they have helped you out of, the tips they have given you from their small store, the stitches the patient old fingers have set for you, the steps the willing old feet have taken, and gratefully pay the dear old ladies the little attentions that women love to receive as long as they live. The bright-eyed girls are quick to see such traits, and will like you all the better for them; and if death, almost the only power that can part mother and son, should rob you of yours, you will be sure to find a tender welcome and maternal cherishing from some Aunt Priscilla, who has kept the warmest corner of her lonely old heart for "the best nevvy in the world."

Jo must have fallen asleep (as I dare say my reader has during this little homily), for suddenly Laurie's ghost seemed to stand before her—a substantial, lifelike ghost—leaning over her with the very look he used to wear when he felt a good deal and didn't like to show it. But, like Jenny in the ballad—

> She could not think it he,

and lay staring up at him in startled silence, till he stooped and kissed her. Then she knew him, and flew up, crying joyfully—

"O my Teddy! O my Teddy!"

"Dear Jo, you are glad to see me, then?"

"Glad! My blessed boy, words can't express my gladness. Where's Amy?"

"Your mother has got her down at Meg's. We stopped there by the way, and there was no getting my wife out of their clutches."

"Your what?" cried Jo, for Laurie uttered those two words with an unconscious pride and satisfaction which betrayed him.

"Oh, the dickens! Now I've done it." And he looked so guilty that Jo was down upon him like a flash.

"You've gone and got married!"

"Yes, please, but I never will again." And he went down upon his knees, with a penitent clasping of hands, and a face full of mischief, mirth, and triumph.

"Actually married?"

"Very much so, thank you."

"Mercy on us! What dreadful thing will you do next?" And Jo fell into her seat with a gasp.

"A characteristic, but not exactly complimentary, congratulation," returned Laurie, still in an abject attitude, but beaming with satisfaction.

"What can you expect, when you take one's breath away, creeping in like a burglar, and letting cats out of bags like that? Get up, you ridiculous boy, and tell me all about it."

"Not a word, unless you let me come in my old place, and promise not to barricade."

Jo laughed at that as she had not done for many a long day, and patted the sofa invitingly, as she said in a cordial tone, "The old pillow is up garret, and we don't need it now; so, come and fess, Teddy."

"How good it sounds to hear you say 'Teddy'! No one ever calls me that but you." And Laurie sat down with an air of great content.

"What does Amy call you?"

"My lord."

"That's like her. Well, you look it." And Jo's eye plainly

betrayed that she found her boy comelier than ever.

The pillow was gone, but there *was* a barricade, nevertheless—a natural one, raised by time, absence, and change of heart. Both felt it, and for a minute looked at one another as if that invisible barrier cast a little shadow over them. It was gone directly, however, for Laurie said, with a vain attempt at dignity—

"Don't I look like a married man and the head of a family?"

"Not a bit, and you never will. You've grown bigger and bonnier, but you are the same scapegrace as ever."

"Now, really, Jo, you ought to treat me with more respect," began Laurie, who enjoyed it all immensely.

"How can I, when the mere idea of you, married and settled, is so irresistibly funny that I can't keep sober!" answered Jo, smiling all over her face, so infectiously that they had another laugh, and then settled down for a good talk, quite in the pleasant old fashion.

"It's no use your going out in the cold to get Amy, for they are all coming up presently. I couldn't wait; I wanted to be the one to tell you the grand surprise, and have 'first skim,' as we used to say when we squabbled about the cream."

"Of course you did, and spoiled your story by beginning at the wrong end. Now, start right, and tell me how it all happened. I'm pining to know."

"Well, I did it to please Amy," began Laurie, with a twinkle that made Jo exclaim—

"Fib number one. Amy did it to please you. Go on, and tell the truth, if you can, sir."

"Now she's beginning to marm it; isn't it jolly to hear her?" said Laurie to the fire, and the fire glowed and sparkled as if it quite agreed. "It's all the same, you know, she and I being one. We planned to come home with the Carrols, a month or more ago, but they suddenly changed their minds, and decided to pass another winter in Paris. But Grandpa wanted to come home; he went to please me, and I couldn't let him go alone, neither could I leave Amy; and Mrs. Carrol had got English notions about chaperons and such nonsense, and wouldn't let Amy come with us. So I just settled the difficulty by saying, 'Let's be married, and then we can do as we like.'"

"Of course you did; you always have things to suit you."

"Not always." And something in Laurie's voice made Jo say hastily—

"How did you ever get Aunt to agree?"

"It was hard work, but, between us, we talked her over, for we had heaps of good reasons on our side. There wasn't time to write and ask leave, but you all liked it, had consented to it by-and-by, and it was only 'taking Time by the fetlock,' as my wife says."

"Aren't we proud of those two words, and don't we like to say them?" interrupted Jo, addressing the fire in her turn, and watching with delight the happy light it seemed to kindle in the eyes that had been so tragically gloomy when she saw them last.

"A trifle, perhaps, she's such a captivating little woman I can't help being proud of her. Well, then, Uncle and Aunt were there to play propriety; we were so absorbed in one another we were of no mortal use apart, and that charming arrangement would make everything easy all round, so we did it."

"When, where, how?" asked Jo, in a fever of feminine interest and curiosity, for she could not realize it a particle.

"Six weeks ago, at the American consul's, in Paris; a very quiet wedding, of course, for even in our happiness we didn't forget dear little Beth."

Jo put her hand in his as he said that, and Laurie gently smoothed the little red pillow, which he remembered well.

"Why didn't you let us know afterward?" asked Jo, in a quieter tone, when they had sat quite still a minute.

"We wanted to surprise you; we thought we were coming directly home, at first; but the dear old gentleman, as soon as we were married, found he couldn't be ready under a month, at least, and sent us off to spend our honeymoon wherever we liked. Amy had once called Valrosa a regular honeymoon home, so we went there, and were as happy as people are but once in their lives. My faith! Wasn't it love among the roses!"

Laurie seemed to forget Jo for a minute, and Jo was glad of it, for the fact that he told her these things so freely and naturally assured her that he had quite forgiven and forgotten. She tried to draw away her hand, but as if he guessed the thought that prompted the half-involuntary impulse, Laurie held it fast, and said, with a manly gravity she had never seen in him before—

"Jo, dear, I want to say one thing, and then we'll put it by forever. As I told you in my letter when I wrote that Amy had been so kind to me, I never shall stop loving you; but the love is altered, and I have learned to see that it is better as it is. Amy and you changed places in my heart, that's all. I think it was meant to be so, and would have come about naturally, if I had waited, as you tried to make me; but I never could be patient, and so I got a heartache. I was a boy then, headstrong and violent; and it took a hard lesson to show me my mistake. For it *was* one, Jo, as you said, and I found it out, after making a fool of myself. Upon my word, I was so tumbled up in my mind, at one time, that I didn't know which I loved best, you or Amy, and tried to love both alike; but I couldn't, and when I saw her in Switzerland, everything seemed to clear up all at once. You both got into your right places, and I felt sure that it was well off with the old love before it was on with the new; that I could honestly share my heart between sister Jo and wife Amy, and love them both dearly. Will you believe it, and go back to the happy old times when we first knew one another?"

"I'll believe it, with all my heart, but, Teddy, we never can be boy and girl again: the happy old times can't come back, and we mustn't expect it. We are man and woman now, with sober work to do, for playtime is over, and we must give up frolicking. I'm sure you feel this. I see the change in you, and you'll find it in me. I shall miss my boy, but I shall love the man as much, and admire him more, because he means to be what I hoped he would. We can't be little playmates any longer, but we will be brother and sister, to love and help one another all our lives, won't we, Laurie?"

He did not say a word, but took the hand she offered him, and laid his face down on it for a minute, feeling that out of the grave of a boyish passion, there had risen a beautiful, strong friendship to bless them both. Presently Jo said cheerfully, for she didn't want the coming home to be a sad one, "I can't make it true that you children are really married, and going to set up housekeeping. Why, it seems only yesterday that I was buttoning Amy's pinafore, and pulling your hair when you teased. Mercy me, how time does fly!"

"As one of the children is older than yourself, you needn't talk so like a grandma. I flatter myself I'm a 'gentleman growed,' as Peggotty said of David, and when you see Amy, you'll find her rather a precocious infant," said Laurie, looking amused at her maternal air.

"You may be a little older in years, but I'm ever so much older in feeling, Teddy. Women always are, and this last year has been such a hard one that I feel forty."

"Poor Jo! We left you to bear it alone, while we went pleasuring. You *are* older; here's a line, and there's another; unless you smile, your eyes look sad, and when I touched the cushion, just now, I found a tear on it. You've had a great deal to bear, and had to bear it all alone. What a selfish beast I've been!" And Laurie pulled his own hair, with a remorseful look.

But Jo only turned over the traitorous pillow, and answered, in a tone which she tried to make quite cheerful, "No, I had Father and Mother to help me, the dear babies to comfort me, and the thought that you and Amy were safe and happy, to make the troubles here easier to bear. I *am* lonely, sometimes, but I dare say it's good for me, and—"

"You never shall be again," broke in Laurie, putting his arm about her, as if to fence out every human ill. "Amy and I can't get on without you, so you must come and teach 'the children' to keep house, and go halves in everything, just as we used to do, and let us pet you, and all be blissfully happy and friendly together."

"If I shouldn't be in the way, it would be very pleasant. I begin to feel quite young already, for somehow all my troubles seemed to fly away when you came. You always were a comfort, Teddy." And Jo leaned her head on his shoulder, just as she did years ago, when Beth lay ill and Laurie told her to hold on to him.

He looked down at her, wondering if she remembered the time, but Jo was smiling to herself, as if, in truth, her troubles *had* all vanished at his coming.

"You are the same Jo still, dropping tears about one minute, and laughing the next. You look a little wicked now. What is it, Grandma?"

"I was wondering how you and Amy get on together."

"Like angels!"

"Yes, of course, at first, but which rules?"

"I don't mind telling you that she does, now, at least I let her think so—it pleases her, you know. By-and-by we shall take turns, for marriage, they say, halves one's rights and doubles one's duties."

"You'll go on as you begin, and Amy will rule you all the days of your life."

"Well, she does it so imperceptibly that I don't think I shall mind much. She is the sort of woman who knows how to rule well; in fact, I rather like it, for she winds one round her finger as softly and prettily as a skein of silk, and makes you feel as if she was doing you a favor all the while."

"That ever I should live to see you a henpecked husband and enjoying it!" cried Jo, with uplifted hands.

It was good to see Laurie square his shoulders, and smile with masculine scorn at that insinuation, as he replied, with his "high and mighty" air, "Amy is too well-bred for that, and I am not the sort of man to submit to it. My wife and I respect ourselves and one another too much ever to tyrannize or quarrel."

Jo liked that, and thought the new dignity very becoming, but the boy seemed changing very fast into the man, and regret mingled with her pleasure.

"I am sure of that. Amy and you never did quarrel as we

used to. She is the sun and I the wind, in the fable, and the sun managed the man best, you remember."

"She can blow him up as well as shine on him," laughed Laurie. "Such a lecture as I got at Nice! I give you my word it was a deal worse than any of your scoldings—a regular rouser. I'll tell you all about it sometime—*she* never will, because after telling me that she despised and was ashamed of me, she lost her heart to the despicable party and married the good-for-nothing."

"What baseness! Well, if she abuses you, come to me, and I'll defend you."

"I look as if I needed it, don't I?" said Laurie, getting up and striking an attitude which suddenly changed from the imposing to the rapturous, as Amy's voice was heard calling, "Where is she? Where's my dear old Jo?"

In trooped the whole family, and everyone was hugged and kissed all over again, and, after several vain attempts, the three wanderers were set down to be looked at and exulted over. Mr. Laurence, hale and hearty as ever, was quite as much improved as the others by his foreign tour, for the crustiness seemed to be nearly gone, and the old-fashioned courtliness had received a polish which made it kindlier than ever. It was good to see him beam at "my children," as he called the young pair; it was better still to see Amy pay him the daughterly duty and affection which completely won his old heart; and best of all, to watch Laurie revolve about the two, as if never tired of enjoying the pretty picture they made.

The minute she put her eyes upon Amy, Meg became conscious that her own dress hadn't a Parisian air, that young Mrs. Moffat would be entirely eclipsed by young Mrs. Laurence, and that "her ladyship" was altogether a most elegant and graceful woman. Jo thought, as she watched the pair, "How well they look together! I was right, and Laurie has found the beautiful, accomplished girl who will become his home better than clumsy old Jo, and be a pride, not a torment to him." Mrs. March and her husband smiled and nodded at each other with happy faces, for they saw that their youngest had done well, not only in worldly things, but the better wealth of love, confidence, and happiness.

For Amy's face was full of the soft brightness which betokens a peaceful heart, her voice had a new tenderness in it, and the cool, prim carriage was changed to a gentle dignity, both womanly and winning. No little affectations marred it, and the cordial sweetness of her manner was more charming than the new beauty or the old grace, for it stamped her at once with the unmistakable sign of the true gentlewoman she had hoped to become.

"Love has done much for our little girl," said her mother softly.

"She has had a good example before her all her life, my dear," Mr. March whispered back, with a loving look at the worn face and gray head beside him.

Daisy found it impossible to keep her eyes off her "pitty aunty," but attached herself like a lap dog to the wonderful chatelaine full of delightful charms. Demi paused to consider the new relationship before he compromised himself by the rash acceptance of a bribe, which took the tempting form of a family of wooden bears from Berne. A flank movement produced an unconditional surrender, however, for Laurie knew where to have him.

"Young man, when I first had the honor of making your acquaintance you hit me in the face: now I demand the satisfaction of a gentleman," and with that the tall uncle proceeded to toss and tousle the small nephew in a way that damaged his philosophical dignity as much as it delighted his boyish soul.

"Blest if she ain't in silk from head to foot? Ain't it a relishin' sight to see her settin' there as fine as a fiddle, and hear folks calling little Amy, Mis. Laurence?" muttered old Hannah, who could not resist frequent peeks through the slide as she set the table in a most decidedly promiscuous manner.

Mercy on us, how they did talk! First one, then the other, then all burst out together, trying to tell the history of three years in half an hour. It was fortunate that tea was at hand, to produce a lull and provide refreshment, for they would have been hoarse and faint if they had gone on much longer. Such a happy procession as filed away into the little dining room! Mr. March proudly escorted "Mrs. Laurence." Mrs. March as proudly leaned on the arm of "my son." The old gentleman took Jo, with a whispered "You must be my girl now," and a glance at the empty corner by the fire, that made Jo whisper back, with trembling lips, "I'll try to fill her place sir."

The twins pranced behind, feeling that the millennium was at hand, for everyone was so busy with the newcomers that they were left to revel at their own sweet will, and you may be sure they made the most of the opportunity. Didn't they steal sips of tea, stuff gingerbread ad libitum, get a hot biscuit apiece, and, as a crowning trespass, didn't they each whisk a captivating little tart into their tiny pockets, there to stick and crumble treacherously, teaching them that both human nature and pastry are frail? Burdened with the guilty consciousness of the sequestered tarts, and fearing that Dodo's sharp eyes would pierce the thin disguise of cambric and merino which hid their booty, the little sinners attached themselves to "Dranpa," who hadn't his spectacles on. Amy, who was handed about like refreshments, returned to the parlor on Father Laurence's arm; the others paired off as before, and this arrangement left Jo companionless. She did not mind it at the minute, for she lingered to answer Hannah's eager inquiry.

"Will Miss Amy ride in her coop (coupe), and use all them lovely silver dishes that's stored away over yander?"

"Shouldn't wonder if she drove six white horses, ate off gold plate, and wore diamonds and point lace every day. Teddy thinks nothing too good for her," returned Jo with infinite satisfaction.

"No more there is! Will you have hash or fishballs for breakfast?" asked Hannah, who wisely mingled poetry and prose.

"I don't care." And Jo shut the door, feeling that food was

an uncongenial topic just then. She stood a minute looking at the party vanishing above, and, as Demi's short plaid legs toiled up the last stair, a sudden sense of loneliness came over her so strongly that she looked about her with dim eyes, as if to find something to lean upon, for even Teddy had deserted her. If she had known what birthday gift was coming every minute nearer and nearer, she would not have said to herself, "I'll weep a little weep when I go to bed; it won't do to be dismal now." Then she drew her hand over eyes—for one of her boyish habits was never to know where her handkerchief was—and had just managed to call up a smile when there came a knock at the porch door.

She opened it with hospitable haste, and started as if another ghost had come to surprise her, for there stood a tall bearded gentleman, beaming on her from the darkness like a midnight sun.

"Oh, Mr. Bhaer, I *am* so glad to see you!" cried Jo, with a clutch, as if she feared the night would swallow him up before she could get him in.

"And I to see Miss Marsch—but no, you haf a party—" And the Professor paused as the sound of voices and the tap of dancing feet came down to them.

"No, we haven't, only the family. My sister and friends have just come home, and we are all very happy. Come in, and make one of us."

Though a very social man, I think Mr. Bhaer would have gone decorously away, and come again another day; but how could he, when Jo shut the door behind him, and bereft him of his hat? Perhaps her face had something to do with it, for she forgot to hide her joy at seeing him, and showed it with a frankness that proved irresistible to the solitary man, whose welcome far exceeded his boldest hopes.

"If I shall not be Monsieur de Trop, I will so gladly see them all. You haf been ill, my friend?"

He put the question abruptly, for, as Jo hung up his coat, the light fell on her face, and he saw a change in it.

"Not ill, but tired and sorrowful. We have had trouble since I saw you last."

"Ah, yes, I know. My heart was sore for you when I heard that." And he shook hands again, with such a sympathetic face that Jo felt as if no comfort could equal the look of the kind eyes, the grasp of the big, warm hand.

"Father, Mother, this is my friend, Professor Bhaer," she said, with a face and tone of such irrepressible pride and pleasure that she might as well have blown a trumpet and opened the door with a flourish.

If the stranger had had any doubts about his reception, they were set at rest in a minute by the cordial welcome he received. Everyone greeted him kindly, for Jo's sake at first, but very soon they liked him for his own. They could not help it, for he carried the talisman that opens all hearts, and these simple people warmed to him at once, feeling even the more friendly because he was poor; for poverty enriches those who live above it, and is a sure passport to truly hospitable spirits. Mr. Bhaer sat looking about him with the air of a traveler who knocks at a strange door, and, when it opens, finds himself at home. The children went to him like bees to a honeypot, and establishing themselves on each knee, proceeded to captivate him by rifling his pockets, pulling his beard, and investigating his watch, with juvenile audacity. The women telegraphed their approval to one another, and Mr. March, feeling that he had got a kindred spirit, opened his choicest stores for his guest's benefit, while silent John listened and enjoyed the talk, but said not a word, and Mr. Laurence found it impossible to go to sleep.

If Jo had not been otherwise engaged, Laurie's behavior would have amused her; for a faint twinge, not of jealousy, but something like suspicion, caused that gentleman to stand aloof at first, and observe the newcomer with brotherly circumspection. But it did not last long. He got interested in spite of himself, and, before he knew it, was drawn into the circle; for Mr. Bhaer talked well in this genial atmosphere, and did himself justice. He seldom spoke to Laurie, but he looked at him often, and a shadow would pass across his face, as if regretting his own lost youth, as he watched the young man in his prime. Then his eye would turn to Jo so wistfully that she would have surely answered the mute inquiry if she had seen it; but Jo had her own eyes to take care of, and, feeling that they could not be trusted, she prudently kept them on the little sock she was knitting, like a model maiden aunt.

A stealthy glance now and then refreshed her like sips of fresh water after a dusty walk, for the sidelong peeps showed her several propitious omens. Mr. Bhaer's face had lost the absent-minded expression, and looked all alive with interest in the present moment, actually young and handsome, she thought, forgetting to compare him with Laurie, as she usually did strange men, to their great detriment. Then he seemed quite inspired, though the burial customs of the ancients, to which the conversation had strayed, might not be considered an exhilarating topic. Jo quite glowed with triumph when Teddy got quenched in an argument, and thought to herself, as she watched her father's absorbed face, "How he would enjoy having such a man as my Professor to talk with every day!" Lastly, Mr. Bhaer was dressed in a new suit of black, which made him look more like a gentleman than ever. His bushy hair had been cut and smoothly brushed, but didn't stay in order long, for, in exciting moments, he rumpled it up in the droll way he used to do; and Jo liked it rampantly erect better than flat, because she thought it gave his fine forehead a Jove-like aspect. Poor Jo, how she did glorify that plain man, as she sat knitting away so quietly, yet letting nothing escape her, not even the fact that Mr. Bhaer actually had gold sleeve-buttons in his immaculate wristbands.

"Dear old fellow! He couldn't have got himself up with more care if he'd been going a-wooing," said Jo to herself, and then a sudden thought born of the words made her blush so dreadfully that she had to drop her ball, and go down after it to hide her face.

The maneuver did not succeed as well as she expected, however, for though just in the act of setting fire to a funeral pile, the Professor dropped his torch, metaphorically speaking, and made a dive after the little blue ball. Of course they bumped their heads smartly together, saw stars, and both came up flushed and laughing, without the ball, to resume their seats, wishing they had not left them.

Nobody knew where the evening went to, for Hannah skillfully abstracted the babies at an early hour, nodding like two rosy poppies, and Mr. Laurence went home to rest. The others sat round the fire, talking away, utterly regardless of the lapse of time, till Meg, whose maternal mind was impressed with a firm conviction that Daisy had tumbled out of bed, and Demi set his nightgown afire studying the structure of matches, made a move to go.

"We must have our sing, in the good old way, for we are all together again once more," said Jo, feeling that a good shout would be a safe and pleasant vent for the jubilant emotions of her soul.

They were not *all* there. But no one found the words thoughtless or untrue; for Beth still seemed among them, a peaceful presence, invisible, but dearer than ever, since death could not break the household league that love made dissoluble. The little chair stood in its old place; the tidy basket, with the bit of work she left unfinished when the needle grew "so heavy," was still on its accustomed shelf; the beloved instrument, seldom touched now had not been moved; and above it Beth's face, serene and smiling, as in the early days, looked down upon them, seeming to say, "Be happy. I am here."

"Play something, Amy. Let them hear how much you have improved," said Laurie, with pardonable pride in his promising pupil.

But Amy whispered, with full eyes, as she twirled the faded stool, "Not tonight, dear. I can't show off tonight."

But she did show something better than brilliancy or skill, for she sang Beth's songs with a tender music in her voice which the best master could not have taught, and touched the listeners' hearts with a sweeter power than any other inspiration could have given her. The room was very still, when the clear voice failed suddenly at the last line of Beth's favorite hymn. It was hard to say—

Earth hath no sorrow that heaven cannot heal;

and Amy leaned against her husband, who stood behind her,
feeling that her welcome home was not quite perfect without
Beth's kiss.

"Now, we must finish with Mignon's song, for Mr. Bhaer
sings that," said Jo, before the pause grew painful. And Mr.
Bhaer cleared his throat with a gratified "Hem!" as he stepped
into the corner where Jo stood, saying—

"You will sing with me? We go excellently well together."

A pleasing fiction, by the way, for Jo had no more idea of
music than a grasshopper. But she would have consented if
he had proposed to sing a whole opera, and warbled away,
blissfully regardless of time and tune. It didn't much matter,
for Mr. Bhaer sang like a true German, heartily and well,
and Jo soon subsided into a subdued hum, that she might
listen to the mellow voice that seemed to sing for her alone.

Know'st thou the land where the citron blooms,

used to be the Professor's favorite line, for "das land" meant
Germany to him; but now he seemed to dwell, with peculiar
warmth and melody, upon the words—

There, oh there, might I with thee,
O my beloved, go

and one listener was so thrilled by the tender invitation that
she longed to say she did know the land, and would joyfully
depart thither whenever he liked.

The song was considered a great success, and the singer
retired covered with laurels. But a few minutes afterward, he
forgot his manners entirely, and stared at Amy putting on her
bonnet; for she had been introduced simply as "my sister,"
and no one had called her by her new name since he came.
He forgot himself still further when Laurie said, in his most
gracious manner, at parting—

"My wife and I are very glad to meet you sir. Please remember that there is always a welcome waiting for you over the way."

Then the Professor thanked him so heartily, and looked so suddenly illuminated with satisfaction, that Laurie thought him the most delightfully demonstrative old fellow he ever met.

"I too shall go, but I shall gladly come again, if you will gif me leave, dear madame, for a little business in the city will keep me here some days."

He spoke to Mrs. March, but he looked at Jo; and the mother's voice gave as cordial an assent as did the daughter's eyes, for Mrs. March was not so blind to her children's interest as Mrs. Moffat supposed.

"I suspect that is a wise man," remarked Mr. March, with placid satisfaction, from the hearthrug, after the last guest had gone.

"I know he is a good one," added Mrs. March, with decided approval, as she wound up the clock.

"I thought you'd like him," was all Jo said, as she slipped away to her bed.

She wondered what the business was that brought Mr. Bhaer to the city, and finally decided that he had been appointed to some great honor, somewhere, but had been too modest to mention the fact. If she had seen his face when, safe in his own room, he looked at the picture of a severe and rigid young lady, with a good deal of hair, who appeared to be gazing darkly into futurity, it might have thrown some light upon the subject, especially when he turned off the gas, and kissed the picture in the dark.

Chapter 44

My Lord and Lady

"PLEASE, MADAM MOTHER, could you lend me my wife for half an hour? The luggage has come, and I've been making hay of Amy's Paris finery, trying to find some things I want," said Laurie, coming in the next day to find Mrs. Laurence sitting in her mother's lap, as if being made "the baby" again.

"Certainly. Go, dear, I forgot that you have any home but this." And Mrs. March pressed the white hand that wore the wedding ring, as if asking pardon for her maternal covetousness.

"I shouldn't have come over if I could have helped it; but I can't get on without my little woman any more than a——"

"Weathercock can without wind," suggested Jo, as he paused for a simile. Jo had grown quite her own saucy self again since Teddy came home.

"Exactly, for Amy keeps me pointing due west most of the time, with only an occasional whiffle round to the south, and I haven't had an easterly spell since I was married; don't know anything about the north, but am altogether salubrious and balmy, hey, my lady?"

"Lovely weather so far; I don't know how long it will last, but I'm not afraid of storms, for I'm learning how to sail my ship. Come home, dear, and I'll find your bootjack; I suppose that's what you are rummaging after among my things. Men are *so* helpless, Mother," said Amy, with a matronly air, which delighted her husband.

"What are you going to do with yourselves after you get settled?" asked Jo, buttoning Amy's cloak as she used to button her pinafores.

"We have our plans; we don't mean to say much about them yet, because we are such very new brooms, but we don't intend to be idle. I'm going into business with a devotion that shall delight Grandfather, and prove to him that I'm not spoiled. I need something of the sort to keep me steady. I'm tired of dawdling, and mean to work like a man."

"And Amy, what is she going to do?" asked Mrs. March, well pleased at Laurie's decision and the energy with which he spoke.

"After doing the civil all round, and airing our best bonnet, we shall astonish you by the elegant hospitalities of our mansion, the brilliant society we shall draw about us, and the beneficial influence we shall exert over the world at large. That's about it, isn't it, Madame Récamier?" asked Laurie, with a quizzical look at Amy.

"Time will show. Come away, Impertinence, and don't shock my family by calling me names before their faces," answered Amy, resolving that there should be a home with a good wife in it before she set up a *salon* as a queen of society.

"How happy those children seem together!" observed Mr. March, finding it difficult to become absorbed in his Aristotle after the young couple had gone.

"Yes, and I think it will last," added Mrs. March, with the restful expression of a pilot who has brought a ship safely into port.

"I know it will. Happy Amy!" And Jo sighed, then smiled brightly as Professor Bhaer opened the gate with an impatient push.

Later in the evening, when his mind had been set at rest about the bootjack, Laurie said suddenly to his wife, who was flitting about, arranging her new art treasures, "Mrs. Laurence."

"My lord!"

"That man intends to marry our Jo!"

"I hope so, don't you, dear?"

"Well, my love, I consider him a trump, in the fullest sense of that expressive word, but I do wish he was a little younger and a good deal richer."

"Now, Laurie, don't be too fastidious and worldly-minded. If they love one another it doesn't matter a particle how old they are nor how poor. Women *never* should marry for money—" Amy caught herself up short as the words escaped her, and looked at her husband, who replied, with malicious gravity.

"Certainly not, though you do hear charming girls say that they intend to do it sometimes. If my memory serves me, you once thought it your duty to make a rich match; that accounts, perhaps, for your marrying a good-for-nothing like me."

"Oh, my dearest boy, don't, don't say that! I forgot you were rich when I said 'Yes.' I'd have married you if you hadn't a penny, and I sometimes wish you were poor that I might show how much I love you." And Amy, who was very dignified in public and very fond in private, gave convincing proofs of the truth of her words.

"You don't really think I am such a mercenary creature as I tried to be once, do you? It would break my heart if you didn't believe that I'd gladly pull in the same boat with you, even if you had to get your living by rowing on the lake."

"Am I an idiot and a brute? How could I think so, when you refused a richer man for me, and won't let me give you half I want to now, when I have the right? Girls do it every day, poor things, and are taught to think it is their only salvation; but you had better lessons, and, though I trembled for you at one time, I was not disappointed, for the daughter was true to the mother's teaching. I told Mamma so yesterday, and she looked as glad and grateful as if I'd given her a check for a million, to be spent in charity. You are not listening to my moral remarks, Mrs. Laurence." And Laurie paused, for Amy's eyes had an absent look, though fixed upon his face.

"Yes, I am, and admiring the dimple in your chin at the same time. I don't wish to make you vain, but I must confess that I'm prouder of my handsome husband than of all his money. Don't laugh, but your nose is *such* a comfort to me." And Amy softly caressed the well-cut feature with artistic satisfaction.

Laurie had received many compliments in his life, but

never one that suited him better, as he plainly showed though he did laugh at his wife's peculiar taste, while she said slowly, "May I ask you a question, dear?"

"Of course you may."

"Shall you care if Jo does marry Mr. Bhaer?"

"Oh, that's the trouble, is it? I thought there was something in the dimple that didn't suit you. Not being a dog in the manger, but the happiest fellow alive, I assure you I can dance at Jo's wedding with a heart as light as my heels. Do you doubt it, my darling?"

Amy looked up at him, and was satisfied; her last little jealous fear vanished forever, and she thanked him, with a face full of love and confidence.

"I wish we could do something for that capital old Professor. Couldn't we invent a rich relation, who shall obligingly die out there in Germany, and leave him a tidy little fortune?" said Laurie, when they began to pace up and down the long drawing room, arm in arm, as they were fond of doing, in memory of the château garden.

"Jo would find us out, and spoil it all; she is very proud of him, just as he is, and said yesterday that she thought poverty was a beautiful thing."

"Bless her dear heart! She won't think so when she has a literary husband, and a dozen little professors and professorins to support. We won't interfere now, but watch our chance, and do them a good turn in spite of themselves. I owe Jo for a part of my education, and she believes in people's paying their honest debts, so I'll get round her in that way."

"How delightful it is to be able to help others, isn't it? That was always one of my dreams, to have the power of giving freely, and, thanks to you, the dream has come true."

"Ah, we'll do quantities of good, won't we? There's one sort of poverty that I particularly like to help. Out-and-out beggars get taken care of, but poor gentle folks fare badly, because they won't ask, and people don't dare to offer charity; yet there are a thousand ways of helping them, if one only knows how to do it so delicately that it does not offend. I must say, I like to serve a decayed gentleman better than a blarneying beggar; I suppose it's wrong, but I do, though it is harder."

"Because it takes a gentleman to do it," added the other member of the domestic admiration society.

"Thank you, I'm afraid I don't deserve that pretty compliment. But I was going to say that while I was dawdling about abroad, I saw a good many talented young fellows making all sorts of sacrifices, and enduring real hardships, that they might realize their dreams. Splendid fellows, some of them, working like heroes, poor and friendless, but so full of courage, patience, and ambition that I was ashamed of myself, and longed to give them a right good lift. Those are people whom it's a satisfaction to help, for if they've got genius, it's an honor to be allowed to serve them, and not let it be lost or delayed for want of fuel to keep the pot boiling; if they haven't, it's a pleasure to comfort the poor souls, and keep them from despair when they find it out."

"Yes, indeed, and there's another class who can't ask, and who suffer in silence. I know something of it, for I belonged to it before you made a princess of me, as the king does the beggarmaid in the old story. Ambitious girls have a hard time, Laurie, and often have to see youth, health, and precious opportunities go by, just for want of a little help at the right minute. People have been very kind to me; and whenever I see girls struggling along, as we used to do, I want to put out my hand and help them, as I was helped."

"And so you shall, like an angel as you are!" cried Laurie, resolving, with a glow of philanthropic zeal, to found and endow an institution for the express benefit of young women with artistic tendencies. "Rich people have no right to sit down and enjoy themselves, or let their money accumulate for others to waste. It's not half so sensible to leave legacies when one dies as it is to use the money wisely while alive, and enjoy making one's fellow creatures happy with it. We'll have a good time ourselves, and add an extra relish to our own pleasure by giving other people a generous taste. Will you be a little Dorcas, going about emptying a big basket of comforts, and filling it up with good deeds?"

"With all my heart, if you will be a brave St. Martin, stopping as you ride gallantly through the world to share your cloak with the beggar."

"It's a bargain, and we shall get the best of it!"

So the young pair shook hands upon it, and then paced happily on again, feeling that their pleasant home was more homelike because they hoped to brighten other homes, be-lieving that their own feet would walk more uprightly along the flowery path before them, if they smoothed rough ways for other feet, and feeling that their hearts were more closely knit together by a love which could tenderly remember those less blest than they.

Chapter 45

Daisy and Demi

I CANNOT FEEL that I have done my duty as humble historian of the March family, without devoting at least one chapter to the two most precious and important members of it. Daisy and Demi had now arrived at years of discretion; for in this fast age babies of three or four assert their rights, and get them, too, which is more than many of their elders do. If there ever were a pair of twins in danger of being utterly spoiled by adoration, it was these prattling Brookes. Of course they were the most remarkable children ever born, as will be shown when I mention that they walked at eight months, talked fluently at twelve months, and at two years they took their places at table, and behaved with a propriety which charmed all beholders. At three, Daisy demanded a "needler," and actually made a bag with four stitches in it; she likewise set up housekeeping in the sideboard, and managed a microscopic cooking stove with a skill that brought tears of pride to Hannah's eyes, while Demi learned his letters with his grandfather, who invented a new mode of teaching the alphabet by forming the letters with his arms and legs, thus uniting gymnastics for head and heels. The boy early developed a mechanical genius which delighted his father and distracted his mother, for he tried to imitate every machine he saw, and kept the nursery in a chaotic condition, with his "sewin-sheen"—a mysterious structure of string, chairs, clothespins, and spools, for wheels to go "wound and wound"; also a basket hung over the back of a chair, in which he vainly tried to hoist his too confiding sister, who, with feminine devotion, allowed her little head to be bumped till rescued, when the young inventor indignantly remarked. "Why, Marmar, dat's my lellywaiter, and me's trying to pull her up."

Though utterly unlike in character, the twins got on remarkably well together, and seldom quarreled more than thrice a day. Of course, Demi tyrannized over Daisy, and gallantly defended her from every other aggressor, while Daisy made a galley slave of herself, and adored her brother as the one perfect being in the world. A rosy, chubby, sunshiny little soul was Daisy, who found her way to everybody's heart, and nestled there. One of the captivating children, who seem made to be kissed and cuddled, adorned and adored like little goddesses, and produced for general approval on all festive occasions. Her small virtues were so sweet that she would have been quite angelic if a few small naughtinesses had not kept her delightfully human. It was all fair weather in her world, and every morning she scrambled up to the window in her little nightgown to look out, and say, no matter whether it rained or shone, "Oh, pitty day, oh, pitty day!" Everyone was a friend, and she offered kisses to a stranger so confidingly that the most inveterate bachelor relented, and baby-lovers became faithful worshipers.

"Me loves evvybody," she once said, opening her arms, with her spoon in one hand, and her mug in the other, as if eager to embrace and nourish the whole world.

As she grew, her mother began to feel that the Dovecote would be blessed by the presence of an inmate as serene and loving as that which had helped to make the old house home, and to pray that she might be spared a loss like that which had lately taught them how long they had entertained an angel unawares. Her grandfather often called her "Beth," and her grandmother watched over her with untiring devotion, as if trying to atone for some past mistake, which no eye but her own could see.

Demi, like a true Yankee, was of an inquiring turn, wanting to know everything, and often getting much disturbed because he could not get satisfactory answers to his perpetual "What for?"

He also possessed a philosophic bent, to the great delight of his grandfather, who used to hold Socratic conversations with him, in which the precocious pupil occasionally posed his teacher, to the undisguised satisfaction of the womenfolk.

"What makes my legs go, Dranpa?" asked the young philosopher, surveying those active portions of his frame with a meditative air, while resting after a go-to-bed frolic one night.

"It's your little mind, Demi," replied the sage, stroking the yellow head respectfully.

"What is a little mine?"

"It is something which makes your body move, as the spring made the wheels go in my watch when I showed it to you."

"Open me. I want to see it go wound."

"I can't do that any more than you could open the watch. God winds you up, and you go till He stops you."

"Does I?" And Demi's brown eyes grew big and bright as he took in the new thought. "Is I wounded up like the watch?"

"Yes, but I can't show you how, for it is done when we don't see."

Demi felt of his back, as if expecting to find it like that of the watch, and then gravely remarked, "I dess Dod does it when I's asleep."

A careful explanation followed, to which he listened so attentively that his anxious grandmother said, "My dear, do you think it wise to talk about such things to that baby? He's getting great bumps over his eyes, and learning to ask the most unanswerable questions."

"If he is old enough to ask the question he is old enough to receive true answers. I am not putting the thoughts into his head, but helping him unfold those already there. These children are wiser than we are, and I have no doubt the boy understands every word I have said to him. Now, Demi, tell me where you keep your mind?"

If the boy had replied like Alcibiades, "By the gods, Socrates, I cannot tell," his grandfather would not have been surprised; but when, after standing a moment on one leg, like a meditative young stork, he answered, in a tone of calm conviction, "In my little belly," the old gentleman could only join in Grandma's laugh, and dismiss the class in metaphysics.

There might have been cause for maternal anxiety, if Demi had not given convincing proofs that he was a true boy, as well as a budding philosopher; for, often, after a discussion which caused Hannah to prophesy, with ominous nods, "That child ain't long for this world," he would turn about and set her fears at rest by some of the pranks with which dear, dirty, naughty little rascals distract and delight their parents' souls.

Meg made many moral rules, and tried to keep them. but what mother was ever proof against the winning wiles, the ingenious evasions, or the tranquil audacity of the miniature men and women who so early show themselves accomplished Artful Dodgers?

"No more raisins, Demi, they'll make you sick," says Mamma to the young person who offers his services in the kitchen with unfailing regularity on plum-pudding day.

"Me likes to be sick."

"I don't want to have you, so run away and help Daisy make patty cakes."

He reluctantly departs, but his wrongs weigh upon his spirit, and by-and-by when an opportunity comes to redress them, he outwits Mamma by a shrewd bargain.

"Now you have been good children, and I'll play anything you like," says Meg, as she leads her assistant cooks upstairs, when the pudding is safely bouncing in the pot.

"Truly, Marmar?" asks Demi, with a brilliant idea in his well-powdered head.

"Yes, truly; anything you say," replies the shortsighted parent, preparing herself to sing "The Three Little Kittens" half a dozen times over, or to take her family to "Buy a penny bun," regardless of wind or limb. But Demi corners her by the cool reply—

"Then we'll go and eat up all the raisins."

Aunt Dodo was chief playmate and confidante of both children, and the trio turned the little house topsy-turvy. Aunt Amy was as yet only a name to them, Aunt Beth soon faded into a pleasantly vague memory, but Aunt Dodo was a living reality, and they made the most of her, for which compliment she was deeply grateful. But when Mr. Bhaer came, Jo neglected her playfellows, and dismay and desolation fell upon their little souls. Daisy, who was fond of going about peddling kisses, lost her best customer and became bankrupt; Demi, with infantile penetration, soon discovered that Dodo liked to play with "the bear-man" better than she did with him; but, though hurt, he concealed his anguish, for he hadn't the heart to insult a rival who kept a mine of chocolate drops in his waistcoat pocket, and a watch that could be taken out of its case and freely shaken by ardent admirers.

Some persons might have considered these pleasing liberties as bribes; but Demi didn't see it in that light, and continued to patronize the "bear-man" with pensive affability, while Daisy bestowed her small affections upon him at the third call, and considered his shoulder her throne, his arm her refuge, his gifts treasures of surpassing worth.

Gentlemen are sometimes seized with sudden fits of admiration for the young relatives of ladies whom they honor with their regard; but this counterfeit philoprogenitiveness sits uneasily upon them, and does not deceive anybody a particle. Mr. Bhaer's devotion was sincere, however likewise effective—for honesty is the best policy in love as in law; he was one of the men who are at home with children, and looked particularly well when little faces made a pleasant contrast with his manly one. His business, whatever it was, detained him from day to day, but evening seldom failed to bring him out to see—well, he always asked for Mr. March, so I suppose *he* was the attraction. The excellent papa labored under the delusion that he was, and reveled in long discussions with the kindred spirit, till a chance remark of his more observing grandson suddenly enlightened him.

Mr. Bhaer came in one evening to pause on the threshold of the study, astonished by the spectacle that met his eye. Prone upon the floor lay Mr. March, with his respectable legs in the air, and beside him, likewise prone, was Demi, trying to imitate the attitude with his own short, scarlet-stockinged legs, both grovelers so seriously absorbed that they were unconscious of spectators, till Mr. Bhaer laughed his sonorous laugh, and Jo cried out, with a scandalized face—

"Father, Father, here's the Professor!"

Down went the black legs and up came the gray head, as the preceptor said, with undisturbed dignity, "Good evening, Mr. Bhaer. Excuse me for a moment; we are just finishing our lesson. Now, Demi, make the letter and tell its name."

"I knows him!" And, after a few convulsive efforts, the red legs took the shape of a pair of compasses, and the intelligent pupil triumphantly shouted, "It's a We, Dranpa, it's a We!"

"He's a born Weller," laughed Jo, as her parent gathered himself up, and her nephew tried to stand on his head, as the only mode of expressing his satisfaction that school was over.

"What have you been at today, *bübchen*?" asked Mr. Bhaer, picking up the gymnast.

"Me went to see little Mary."

"And what did you there?"

"I kissed her," began Demi, with artless frankness.

"Prut! Thou beginnest early. What did the little Mary say to that?" asked Mr. Bhaer, continuing to confess the young sinner, who stood upon his knee, exploring the waistcoat pocket.

"Oh, she liked it, and she kissed me, and I liked it. *Don't* little boys like little girls?" added Demi, with his mouth full, and an air of bland satisfaction.

"You precious chick! Who put that into your head?" said Jo, enjoying the innocent revelation as much as the Professor.

" 'Tisn't in mine head, it's in mine mouf," answered literal Demi, putting out his tongue, with a chocolate drop on it, thinking she alluded to confectionery, not ideas.

"Thou shouldst save some for the little friend: sweets to the sweet, mannling." And Mr. Bhaer offered Jo some, with a look that made her wonder if chocolate was not the nectar drunk by the gods. Demi also saw the smile, was impressed by it, and artlessly inquired—

"Do great boys like great girls, too, 'Fessor?"

Like young Washington, Mr. Bhaer "couldn't tell a lie," so he gave the somewhat vague reply that he believed they did sometimes, in a tone that made Mr. March put down his clothesbrush, glance at Jo's retiring face, and then sink into his chair, looking as if the "precocious chick" had put an idea into *his* head that was both sweet and sour.

Why Dodo, when she caught him in the china closet half an hour afterward, nearly squeezed the breath out of his little body with a tender embrace, instead of shaking him for being there, and why she followed up this novel performance by the unexpected gift of a big slice of bread and jelly, remained one of the problems over which Demi puzzled his small wits, and was forced to leave unsolved forever.

Chapter 46

Under the Umbrella

WHILE LAURIE and Amy were taking conjugal strolls over velvet carpets, as they set their house in order and planned a blissful future, Mr. Bhaer and Jo were enjoying promenades of a different sort, along muddy roads and sodden fields.

"I always do take a walk toward evening, and I don't know why I should give it up, just because I often happen to meet the Professor on his way out," said Jo to herself, after two or three encounters; for, though there were two paths to Meg's whichever one she took she was sure to meet him, either going or returning. He was always walking rapidly, and never seemed to see her till quite close, when he would look as if his shortsighted eyes had failed to recognize the approaching lady till that moment. Then, if she was going to Meg's, he always had something for the babies; if her face was turned homeward, he had merely strolled down to see the river, and was just about returning, unless they were tired of his frequent calls.

Under the circumstances, what could Jo do but greet him civilly, and invite him in? If she *was* tired of his visits, she concealed her weariness with perfect skill, and took care that there should be coffee for supper, "as Friedrich—I mean Mr. Bhaer—doesn't like tea."

By the second week, everyone knew perfectly well what was going on, yet everyone tried to look as if they were stone-blind to the changes in Jo's face. They never asked why she sang about her work, did up her hair three times a day, and got so blooming with her evening exercise; and no one seemed to have the slightest suspicion that Professor Bhaer, while talking philosophy with the father, was giving the daughter lessons in love.

Jo couldn't even lose her heart in a decorous manner, but

516

sternly tried to quench her feelings; and, failing to do so, led a somewhat agitated life. She was mortally afraid of being laughed at for surrendering, after her many and vehement declarations of independence. Laurie was her especial dread; but, thanks to the new manager, he behaved with praiseworthy propriety, never called Mr. Bhaer "a capital old fellow" in public, never alluded, in the remotest manner, to Jo's improved appearance, or expressed the least surprise at seeing the Professor's hat on the Marches' hall table nearly every evening. But he exulted in private and longed for the time to come when he could give Jo a piece of plate, with a bear and a ragged staff on it as an appropriate coat of arms.

For a fortnight, the Professor came and went with lover-like regularity; then he stayed away for three whole days, and made no sign, a proceeding which caused everybody to look sober, and Jo to become pensive, at first, and then—alas for romance!—very cross.

"Disgusted, I dare say, and gone home as suddenly as he came. It's nothing to me, of course; but I *should* think he would have come and bid us good-by like a gentleman," she said to herself, with a despairing look at the gate, as she put on her things for the customary walk one dull afternoon.

"You'd better take the little umbrella, dear; it looks like rain," said her mother, observing that she had on her new bonnet, but not alluding to the fact.

"Yes, Marmee, do you want anything in town? I've got to run in and get some paper," returned Jo, pulling out the bow under her chin before the glass as an excuse for not looking at her mother.

"Yes, I want some twilled silesia, a paper of number nine needles, and two yards of narrow lavender ribbon. Have you got your thick boots on, and something warm under your cloak?"

"I believe so," answered Jo absently.

"If you happen to meet Mr. Bhaer, bring him home to tea. I quite long to see the dear man," added Mrs. March.

Jo heard *that*, but made no answer, except to kiss her mother, and walk rapidly away, thinking with a glow of gratitude, in spite of her heartache, "How good she is to me! What *do* girls do who haven't any mothers to help them through their troubles?"

The dry-goods stores were not down among the counting-houses, banks, and wholesale warerooms, where gentlemen most do congregate; but Jo found herself in that part of the city before she did a single errand, loitering along as if waiting for someone, examining engineering instruments in one window and samples of wool in another, with most unfeminine interest; tumbling over barrels, being half-smothered by descending bales, and hustled unceremoniously by busy men who looked as if they wondered "how the deuce she got there." A drop of rain on her cheek recalled her thoughts from baffled hopes to ruined ribbons; for the drops continued to fall, and, being a woman as well as a lover, she felt that, though it was too late to save her heart, she might her bonnet. Now she remembered the little umbrella, which she had forgotten to take in her hurry to be off, but regret was unavailing, and nothing could be done but borrow one or submit to a drenching. She looked up at the lowering sky, down at the crimson bow already flecked with black, forward along the muddy street, then one long, lingering look behind, at a certain grimy warehouse, with "Hoffmann, Swartz, & Co." over the door, and said to herself, with a sternly reproachful air—

"It serves me right! What business had I to put on all my best things and come philandering down here, hoping to see the Professor? Jo, I'm ashamed of you! No, you shall *not* go there to borrow an umbrella, or find out where he is, from his friends. You shall trudge away, and do your errands in the rain; and if you catch your death and ruin your bonnet, it's no more than you deserve. Now then!"

With that she rushed across the street so impetuously that she narrowly escaped annihilation from a passing truck, and precipitated herself into the arms of a stately old gentleman, who said, "I beg pardon, ma'am," and looked mortally offended. Somewhat daunted, Jo righted herself, spread her handkerchief over the devoted ribbons, and, putting temptation behind her, hurried on, with increasing dampness about the ankles, and much clashing of umbrellas overhead. The fact that a somewhat dilapidated blue one remained stationary above the unprotected bonnet attracted her attention, and looking up, she saw Mr. Bhaer looking down.

"I feel to know the strong-minded lady who goes so bravely under many horse noses, and so fast through much mud. What do you down here, my friend?"

"I'm shopping."

Mr. Bhaer smiled, as he glanced from the pickle factory on one side to the wholesale hide and leather concern on the other, but he only said politely, "You haf no umbrella. May I go also, and take for you the bundles?"

"Yes, thank you."

Jo's cheeks were as red as her ribbon, and she wondered what he thought of her, but she didn't care, for in a minute she found herself walking away arm in arm with her Professor, feeling as if the sun had suddenly burst out with uncommon brilliancy, that the world was all right again, and that one thoroughly happy woman was paddling through the wet that day.

"We thought you had gone," said Jo hastily, for she knew he was looking at her. Her bonnet wasn't big enough to hide her face, and she feared he might think the joy it betrayed unmaidenly.

"Did you believe that I should go with no farewell to those who haf been so heavenly kind to me?" he asked so reproachfully that she felt as if she had insulted him by the suggestion, and answered heartily—

"No, *I* didn't; I knew you were busy about your own affairs, but we rather missed you—Father and Mother especially."

"And you?"

"I'm always glad to see you, sir."

In her anxiety to keep her voice quite calm, Jo made it rather cool, and the frosty little monosyllable at the end seemed to chill the Professor, for his smile vanished, as he said gravely—

"I thank you, and come one time more before I go."

"You *are* going, then?"

"I haf no longer any business here, it is done."

"Successfully, I hope?" said Jo, for the bitterness of disappointment was in that short reply of his.

"I ought to think so, for I haf a way opened to me by which I can make my bread and gif my Jünglings much help."

"Tell me, please! I like to know all about the—the boys," said Jo eagerly.

"That is so kind, I gladly tell you. My friends find for me a place in a college, where I teach as at home, and earn enough to make the way smooth for Franz and Emil. For this I should be grateful, should I not?"

"Indeed you should. How splendid it will be to have you doing what you like, and be able to see you often, and the boys!" cried Jo, clinging to the lads as an excuse for the satisfaction she could not help betraying.

"Ah! But we shall not meet often, I fear, this place is at the West."

"So far away!" And Jo left her skirts to their fate, as if it didn't matter now what became of her clothes or herself.

Mr. Bhaer could read several languages, but he had not learned to read women yet. He flattered himself that he knew Jo pretty well, and was, therefore, much amazed by the contradictions of voice, face, and manner, which she showed him in rapid succession that day, for she was in half a dozen different moods in the course of half an hour. When she met him she looked surprised, though it was impossible to help suspecting that she had come for that express purpose. When he offered her his arm, she took it with a look that filled him with delight; but when he asked if she missed him, she gave such a chilly, formal reply that despair fell upon him. On learning his good fortune she almost clapped her hands: was the joy all for the boys? Then, on hearing his destination, she said, "So far away!" in a tone of despair that lifted him on to a pinnacle of hope; but the next minute she tumbled him down again by observing, like one entirely absorbed in the matter—

"Here's the place for my errands. Will you come in? It won't take long."

Jo rather prided herself upon her shopping capabilities, and particularly wished to impress her escort with the neatness and dispatch with which she would accomplish the business. But, owing to the flutter she was in, everything went amiss; she upset the tray of needles, forgot the silesia was to be "twilled" till it was cut off, gave the wrong change, and covered herself with confusion by asking for lavender ribbon at the calico counter. Mr. Bhaer stood by, watching her blush and blunder, and as he watched, his own bewilderment seemed to subside, for he was beginning to see that on some occasions women, like dreams, go by contraries.

When they came out, he put the parcel under his arm with a more cheerful aspect, and splashed through the puddles as if he rather enjoyed it on the whole.

"Should we not do a little what you call shopping for the babies, and haf a farewell feast tonight if I go for my last call at your so pleasant home?" he asked, stopping before a window full of fruit and flowers.

"What will we buy?" said Jo, ignoring the latter part of his speech, and sniffing the mingled odors with an affectation of delight as they went in.

"May they haf oranges and figs?" asked Mr. Bhaer, with a paternal air.

"They eat them when they can get them."

"Do you care for nuts?"

"Like a squirrel."

"Hamburg grapes; yes, we shall surely drink to the Fatherland in those?"

Jo frowned upon that piece of extravagance, and asked why he didn't buy a frail of dates, a cask of raisins, and a bag of almonds, and done with it? Whereat Mr. Bhaer confiscated her purse, produced his own, and finished the marketing by buying several pounds of grapes, a pot of rosy daisies, and a pretty jar of honey, to be regarded in the light of a demijohn. Then, distorting his pockets with the knobby bundles, and giving her the flowers to hold, he put up the old umbrella, and they traveled on again.

"Miss Marsch, I haf a great favor to ask of you," began the Professor, after a moist promenade of half a block.

"Yes, sir." And Jo's heart began to beat so hard she was afraid he would hear it.

"I am bold to say it in spite of the rain, because so short a time remains to me."

"Yes, sir." And Jo nearly crushed the small flowerpot with the sudden squeeze she gave it.

"I wish to get a little dress for my Tina, and I am too stupid to go alone. Will you kindly gif me a word of taste and help?"

"Yes, sir." And Jo felt as calm and cool all of a sudden as if she had stepped into a refrigerator.

"Perhaps also a shawl for Tina's mother, she is so poor and sick, and the husband is such a care. Yes, yes, a thick, warm shawl would be a friendly thing to take the little mother."

"I'll do it with pleasure. Mr. Bhaer. I'm going very fast and he's getting dearer every minute," added Jo to herself, then with a mental shake she entered into the business with an energy which was pleasant to behold.

Mr. Bhaer left it all to her, so she chose a pretty gown for Tina, and then ordered out the shawls. The clerk, being a married man, condescended to take an interest in the couple, who appeared to be shopping for their family.

"Your lady may prefer this; it's a superior article, a most desirable color, quite chaste and genteel," he said, shaking out a comfortable gray shawl, and throwing it over Jo's shoulders.

"Does this suit you, Mr. Bhaer?" she asked, turning her back to him, and feeling deeply grateful for the chance of hiding her face.

"Excellently well, we will haf it," answered the Professor, smiling to himself as he paid for it, while Jo continued to rummage the counters like a confirmed bargain-hunter.

"Now shall we go home?" he asked, as if the words were very pleasant to him.

"Yes, it's late, and I'm *so* tired." Jo's voice was more pathetic than she knew; for now the sun seemed to have gone in as suddenly as it came out, the world grew muddy and miserable again, and for the first time she discovered that her feet were cold, her head ached, and that her heart was colder than the former, fuller of pain than the latter. Mr. Bhaer was going away, he only cared for her as a friend, it was all a mistake, and the sooner it was over the better. With this idea in her head, she hailed an approaching omnibus with such a hasty gesture that the daisies flew out of the pot and were badly damaged.

"This is not our omniboos," said the Professor, waving the loaded vehicle away, and stopping to pick up the poor little flowers.

"I beg your pardon, I didn't see the name distinctly. Never mind, I can walk. I'm used to plodding in the mud," returned Jo, winking hard, because she would have died rather than openly wipe her eyes.

Mr. Bhaer saw the drops on her cheeks, though she turned her head away; the sight seemed to touch him very much, for, suddenly stooping down, he asked in a tone that meant a great deal, "Heart's dearest, why do you cry?"

Now, if Jo had not been new to this sort of thing she would have said she wasn't crying, had a cold in her head, or told any other feminine fib proper to the occasion; instead of which that undignified creature answered, with an irrepressible sob, "Because you are going away."

"*Ach, mein Gott,* that is *so* good!" cried Mr. Bhaer, managing to clasp his hands in spite of the umbrella and the bundles. "Jo, I haf nothing but much love to gif you; I came to see if you could care for it, and I waited to be sure that I was something more than a friend. Am I? Can you make a little place in your heart for old Fritz?" he added, all in one breath.

"Oh, yes!" said Jo; and he was quite satisfied, for she folded both hands over his arm, and looked up at him with

. . . she hailed an approaching omnibus with such a hasty
gesture that the daisies flew out of the pot . . .

an expression that plainly showed how happy she would be to walk through life beside him, even though she had no better shelter than the old umbrella, if he carried it.

It was certainly proposing under difficulties, for even if he had desired to do so, Mr. Bhaer could not go down upon his knees, on account of the mud; neither could he offer Jo his hand, except figuratively, for both were full; much less could he indulge in tender demonstrations in the open street, though he was near it; so the only way in which he could express his rapture was to look at her, with an expression which glorified his face to such a degree that there actually seemed to be little rainbows in the drops that sparkled on his beard. If he had not loved Jo very much, I don't think he could have done it *then,* for she looked far from lovely, with her skirts in a deplorable state, her rubber boots splashed to the ankle, and her bonnet a ruin. Fortunately, Mr. Bhaer considered her the most beautiful woman living, and she found him more "Jove-like" than ever, though his hatbrim was quite limp with the little rills trickling thence upon his shoulders (for he held the umbrella all over Jo), and every finger of his gloves needed mending.

Passers-by probably thought them a pair of harmless lunatics, for they entirely forgot to hail a bus, and strolled leisurely along, oblivious of deepening dusk and fog. Little they cared what anybody thought, for they were enjoying the happy hour that seldom comes but once in any life, the magical moment which bestows youth on the old, beauty on the plain, wealth on the poor, and gives human hearts a foretaste of heaven. The Professor looked as if he had conquered a kingdom, and the world had nothing more to offer him in the way of bliss; while Jo trudged beside him, feeling as if her place had always been there, and wondering how she ever could have chosen any other lot. Of course, she was the first to speak —intelligibly, I mean, for the emotional remarks which followed her impetuous "Oh, yes!" were not of a coherent or reportable character.

"Friedrich, why didn't you—"

"Ah, heaven, she gifs me the name that no one speaks since

Minna died!" cried the Professor, pausing in a puddle to regard her with grateful delight.

"I always call you so to myself—I forgot; but I won't, unless you like it."

"Like it? It is more sweet to me than I can tell. Say 'thou,' also, and I shall say your language is almost as beautiful as mine."

"Isn't 'thou' a little sentimental?" asked Jo, privately thinking it a lovely monosyllable.

"Sentimental? Yes. Thank Gott, we Germans believe in sentiment, and keep ourselves young mit it. Your English 'you' is so cold, say 'thou,' heart's dearest, it means so much to me," pleaded Mr. Bhaer, more like a romantic student than a grave professor.

"Well, then, why didn't thou tell me all this sooner?" asked Jo bashfully.

"Now I shall haf to show thee all my heart, and I so gladly will, because thou must take care of it hereafter. See, then, my Jo—ah, the dear, funny little name!—I had a wish to tell something the day I said good-by in New York, but I thought the handsome friend was betrothed to thee, and so I spoke not. Wouldst thou have said 'Yes,' then, if I *had* spoken?"

"I don't know. I'm afraid not, for I didn't have any heart just then."

"Prut! That I do not believe. It was asleep till the fairy prince came through the wood, and waked it up. Ah, well, *'Die erste Liebe ist die beste,'* but that I should not expect."

"Yes, the first love *is* the best, so be contented, for I never had another. Teddy was only a boy, and soon got over his little fancy," said Jo, anxious to correct the Professor's mistake.

"Good! Then I shall rest happy, and be sure that thou givest me all. I haf waited so long, I am grown selfish, as thou wilt find, Professorin."

"I like that," cried Jo, delighted with her new name. "Now tell me what brought you, at last, just when I most wanted you?"

"This." And Mr. Bhaer took a little worn paper out of his waistcoat pocket.

Jo unfolded it, and looked much abashed, for it was one of her own contributions to a paper that paid for poetry, which accounted for her sending it an occasional attempt.

"How could that bring you?" she asked, wondering what he meant.

"I found it by chance; I knew it by the names and the initials, and in it there was one little verse that seemed to call me. Read and find him; I will see that you go not in the wet."

Jo obeyed, and hastily skimmed through the lines which she had christened—

IN THE GARRET

Four little chests all in a row,
  Dim with dust, and worn by time,
All fashioned and filled, long ago,
  By children now in their prime.
Four little keys hung side by side,
  With faded ribbons, brave and gay
When fastened there, with childish pride,
  Long ago, on a rainy day.
Four little names, one on each lid,
  Carved out by a boyish hand,
And underneath there lieth hid
  Histories of the happy band
Once playing here, and pausing oft
  To hear the sweet refrain,
That came and went on the roof aloft,
  In the falling summer rain.

"Meg" on the first lid, smooth and fair.
  I look in with loving eyes,
For folded here, with well-known care,
  A goodly gathering lies,
The record of a peaceful life—
  Gifts to gentle child and girl,
A bridal gown, lines to a wife,
  A tiny shoe, a baby curl.

No toys in this first chest remain,
    For all are carried away,
In their old age, to join again
    In another small Meg's play.
Ah, happy mother! well I know
    You hear, like a sweet refrain,
Lullabies ever soft and low
    In the falling summer rain.

"Jo" on the next lid, scratched and worn,
    And within a motley store
Of headless dolls, of schoolbooks torn,
    Birds and beasts that speak no more;
Spoils brought home from the fairy ground
    Only trod by youthful feet,
Dreams of a future never found,
    Memories of a past still sweet;
Half-writ poems, stories wild,
    April letters, warm and cold,
Diaries of a wilful child,
    Hints of a woman early old;
A woman in a lonely home,
    Hearing, like a sad refrain—
"Be worthy love, and love will come,"
    In the falling summer rain.

My Beth! the dust is always swept
    From the lid that bears your name,
As if by loving eyes that wept,
    By careful hands that often came.
Death canonized for us one saint,
    Ever less human than divine,
And still we lay, with tender plaint,
    Relics in this household shrine—
The silver bell, so seldom rung,
    The little cap which last she wore,
The fair, dead Catherine that hung
    By angels borne above her door;
The songs she sang, without lament,

In her prison-house of pain,
Forever are they sweetly blent
  With the falling summer rain.

Upon the last lid's polished field—
  Legend now both fair and true
A gallant knight bears on his shield,
  "Amy," in letters gold and blue.
Within lie snoods that bound her hair,
  Slippers that have danced their last,
Faded flowers laid by with care,
  Fans whose airy toils are past;
Gay valentines, all ardent flames,
  Trifles that have borne their part
In girlish hopes and fears and shames,
  The record of a maiden heart
Now learning fairer, truer spells,
  Hearing, like a blithe refrain,
The silver sound of bridal bells
  In the falling summer rain.

Four little chests all in a row,
  Dim with dust, and worn by time,
Four women, taught by weal and woe
  To love and labor in their prime.
Four sisters, parted for an hour,
  None lost, one only gone before,
Made by love's immortal power,
  Nearest and dearest evermore.
Oh, when these hidden stores of ours
  Lie open to the Father's sight,
May they be rich in golden hours,
  Deeds that show fairer for the light,
Lives whose brave music long shall ring,
  Like a spirit-stirring strain,
Souls that shall gladly soar and sing
  In the long sunshine after rain.

                             J.M.

"It's very bad poetry, but I felt it when I wrote it, one day when I was very lonely, and had a good cry on a rag bag. I never thought it would go where it could tell tales," said Jo, tearing up the verses the Professor had treasured so long.

"Let it go, it has done its duty, and I will haf a fresh one when I read all the brown book in which she keeps her little secrets," said Mr. Bhaer with a smile as he watched the fragments fly away on the wind. "Yes," he added earnestly, "I read that, and I think to myself, She has a sorrow, she is lonely, she would find comfort in true love. I haf a heart full, full for her; shall I not go and say, 'If this is not too poor a thing to gif for what I shall hope to receive, take it in Gott's name?' "

"And so you came to find that it was not too poor, but the one precious thing I needed," whispered Jo.

"I had no courage to think that at first, heavenly kind as was your welcome to me. But soon I began to hope, and then I said, 'I will haf her if I die for it,' and so I will!" cried Mr. Bhaer, with a defiant nod, as if the walls of mist closing round them were barriers which he was to surmount or valiantly knock down.

Jo thought that was splendid, and resolved to be worthy of her knight, though he did not come prancing on a charger in gorgeous array.

"What made you stay away so long?" she asked presently, finding it so pleasant to ask confidential questions and get delightful answers that she could not keep silent.

"It was not easy, but I could not find the heart to take you from that so happy home until I could haf a prospect of one to give you, after much time, perhaps, and hard work. How could I ask you to gif up so much for a poor old fellow, who has no fortune but a little learning?"

"I'm glad you *are* poor; I couldn't bear a rich husband," said Jo decidedly, adding, in a softer tone, "Don't fear poverty. I've known it long enough to lose my dread and be happy working for those I love; and don't call yourself old —forty is the prime of life. I couldn't help loving you if you were seventy!"

The Professor found that so touching that he would have been glad of his handkerchief, if he could have got at it; as he couldn't, Jo wiped his eyes for him, and said, laughing, as she took away a bundle or two—

"I may be strong-minded, but no one can say I'm out of my sphere now, for woman's special mission is supposed to be drying tears and bearing burdens. I'm to carry my share, Friedrich, and help to earn the home. Make up your mind to that, or I'll never go," she added resolutely, as he tried to reclaim his load.

"We shall see. Haf you patience to wait a long time, Jo? I must go away and do my work alone. I must help my boys first, because, even for you, I may not break my word to Minna. Can you forgif that, and be happy while we hope and wait?"

"Yes, I know I can, for we love one another, and that makes all the rest easy to bear. I have my duty, also, and my work. I couldn't enjoy myself if I neglected them even for you, so there's no need of hurry or impatience. You can do your part out West, I can do mine here, and both be happy hoping for the best, and leaving the future to be as God wills."

"Ah! Thou gifest me such hope and courage, and I haf nothing to gif back but a full heart and these empty hands," cried the Professor, quite overcome.

Jo never, never would learn to be proper, for when he said that as they stood upon the steps, she just put both hands into his, whispering tenderly, "Not empty now," and, stooping down, kissed her Friedrich under the umbrella. It was dreadful, but she would have done it if the flock of draggle-tailed sparrows on the hedge had been human beings, for she was very far gone indeed, and quite regardless of everything but her own happiness. Though it came in such a very simple guise, that was the crowning moment of both their lives, when, turning from the night and storm and loneliness to the household light and warmth and peace waiting to receive them, with a glad "Welcome home!" Jo led her lover in, and shut the door.

Chapter 47

Harvest Time

FOR A YEAR Jo and her Professor worked and waited, hoped and loved, met occasionally, and wrote such voluminous letters that the rise in the price of paper was accounted for, Laurie said. The second year began rather soberly, for their prospects did not brighten, and Aunt March died suddenly. But when their first sorrow was over—for they loved the old lady in spite of her sharp tongue—they found they had cause for rejoicing, for she had left Plumfield to Jo, which made all sorts of joyful things possible.

"It's a fine old place, and will bring a handsome sum, for of course you intend to sell it," said Laurie, as they were all talking the matter over some weeks later.

"No, I don't," was Jo's decided answer, as she petted the fat poodle, whom she had adopted, out of respect to his former mistress.

"You don't mean to live there?"

"Yes, I do."

"But, my dear girl, it's an immense house, and will take a power of money to keep it in order. The garden and orchard alone need two or three men, and farming isn't in Bhaer's line, I take it."

"He'll try his hand at it there, if I propose it."

"And you expect to live on the produce of the place? Well, that sounds paradisiacal, but you'll find it desperate hard work."

"The crop we are going to raise is a profitable one." And Jo laughed.

"Of what is this fine crop to consist, ma'am?"

"Boys. I want to open a school for little lads—a good, happy, homelike school, with me to take care of them and Fritz to teach them."

"There's a truly Joian plan for you! Isn't that just like her?" cried Laurie, appealing to the family, who looked as much surprised as he.

"I like it," said Mrs. March decidedly.

"So do I," added her husband, who welcomed the thought of a chance for trying the Socratic method of education on modern youth.

"It will be an immense care for Jo," said Meg, stroking the head of her one all-absorbing son.

"Jo can do it, and be happy in it. It's a splendid idea. Tell us all about it," cried Mr. Laurence, who had been longing to lend the lovers a hand, but knew that they would refuse his help.

"I knew you'd stand by me, sir. Amy does too—I see it in her eyes, though she prudently waits to turn it over in her mind before she speaks. Now, my dear people," continued Jo earnestly, "just understand that this isn't a new idea of mine, but a long-cherished plan. Before my Fritz came, I used to think how, when I'd made my fortune, and no one needed me at home, I'd hire a big house, and pick up some poor, forlorn little lads who hadn't any mothers, and take care of them, and make life jolly for them before it was too late. I see so many going to ruin for want of help at the right minute, I love so to do anything for them, I seem to feel their wants, and sympathize with their troubles, and, oh, I should *so* like to be a mother to them!"

Mrs. March held out her hand to Jo, who took it, smiling, with tears in her eyes, and went on in the old enthusiastic way, which they had not seen for a long while.

"I told my plan to Fritz once, and he said it was just what he would like, and agreed to try it when we got rich. Bless his dear heart, he's been doing it all his life—helping poor boys, I mean, not getting rich; that he'll never be; money doesn't stay in his pocket long enough to lay up any. But now, thanks to my good old aunt, who loved me better than I ever deserved, *I'm* rich, at least I feel so, and we can live at Plumfield perfectly well, if we have a flourishing school. It's just the place for boys, the house is big, and the furniture strong and plain. There's plenty of room for dozens inside, and splendid grounds outside. They could help in the garden and orchard: such work is healthy, isn't it, sir? Then Fritz can train and teach in his own way, and Father will help him. I can feed and nurse and pet and scold them, and Mother will be my stand-by. I've always longed for lots of boys, and never had enough, now I can fill the house full and revel in the little dears to my heart's content. Think what luxury—Plumfield my own, and a wilderness of boys to enjoy it with me!"

As Jo waved her hands and gave a sigh of rapture, the family went off into a gale of merriment, and Mr. Laurence laughed till they thought he'd have an apoplectic fit.

"I don't see anything funny," she said gravely, when she could be heard. "Nothing could be more natural or proper than for my Professor to open a school, and for me to prefer to reside on my own estate."

"She is putting on airs already," said Laurie, who regarded the idea in the light of a capital joke. "But may I inquire how you intend to support the establishment? If all the pupils are little ragamuffins, I'm afraid your crop won't be profitable in a worldly sense, Mrs. Bhaer."

"Now don't be a wet-blanket, Teddy. Of course I shall have rich pupils, also—perhaps begin with such altogether; then, when I've got a start, I can take a ragamuffin or two, just for a relish. Rich people's children often need care and comfort, as well as poor. I've seen unfortunate little creatures left to servants, or backward ones pushed forward, when it's real cruelty. Some are naughty through mismanagement or neglect, and some lose their mothers. Besides, the best have to get through the hobbledehoy age, and that's the very time they need most patience and kindness. People laugh at them, and hustle them about, try to keep them out of sight, and expect them to turn all at once from pretty children into fine young men. They don't complain much—plucky little souls—but they feel it. I've been through something of it, and I know all about it. I've a special interest in such young bears, and like to show them that I see the warm, honest, well-meaning boys' hearts, in spite of the clumsy arms and legs and the topsy-turvy heads. I've had experience, too, for haven't I brought up one boy to be a pride and honor to his family?"

"I'll testify that you tried to do it,' said Laurie with a grateful look.

"And I've succeeded beyond my hopes; for here you are, a steady, sensible businessman, doing heaps of good with your money, and laying up the blessings of the poor, instead of dollars. But you are not merely a businessman: you love good and beautiful things, enjoy them yourself, and let others go halves, as you always did in the old times. I *am* proud of you, Teddy, for you get better every year, and everyone feels it, though you won't let them say so. Yes, and when I have my flock, I'll just point to you, and say, 'There's your model, my lads.' "

Poor Laurie didn't know where to look; for, man though he was, something of the old bashfulness came over him as this burst of praise made all faces turn approvingly upon him.

"I say, Jo, that's rather too much," he began, just in his old boyish way. "You have all done more for me than I can ever thank you for, except by doing my best not to disappoint you. You have rather cast me off lately, Jo, but I've had the best of help, nevertheless; so, if I've got on at all, you may thank these two for it." And he laid one hand gently on his grandfather's white head, the other on Amy's golden one, for the three were never far apart.

"I do think that families are the most beautiful things in all the world!" burst out Jo, who was in an unusually up-lifted frame of mind just then. "When I have one of my own, I hope it will be as happy as the three I know and love the best. If John and my Fritz were only here, it would be quite a little heaven on earth," she added more quietly. And that night when she went to her room after a blissful evening of family counsels, hopes, and plans, her heart was so full of happiness that she could only calm it by kneeling beside the empty bed always near her own, and thinking tender thoughts of Beth.

It was a very astonishing year altogether, for things seemed to happen in an unusually rapid and delightful manner. Almost before she knew where she was, Jo found herself married and settled at Plumfield. Then a family of six or seven boys sprung up like mushrooms, and flourished surprisingly, poor boys as well as rich; for Mr. Laurence was continually finding some touching case of destitution, and begging the Bhaers to take pity on the child, and he would gladly pay a trifle for its support. In this way the sly old gentleman got round proud Jo, and furnished her with the style of boy in which she most delighted.

Of course it was uphill work at first, and Jo made queer mistakes; but the wise Professor steered her safely into calmer waters, and the most rampant ragamuffin was conquered in the end. How Jo did enjoy her "wilderness of boys," and how poor, dear Aunt March would have lamented had she been there to see the sacred precincts of prim, well-ordered Plumfield overrun with Toms, Dicks, and Harrys! There was a sort of poetic justice about it, after all, for the old lady had been the terror of the boys for miles round; and now the exiles feasted freely on forbidden plums, kicked up the gravel with profane boots unreproved, and played cricket in the big field where the irritable "cow with a crumpled horn" used to invite rash youths to come and be tossed. It became a sort of boys' paradise, and Laurie suggested that it should be called the "Bhaer-garten," as a compliment to its master and appropriate to its inhabitants.

It never was a fashionable school, and the Professor did not lay up a fortune; but it *was* just what Jo intended it to be—"a happy, homelike place for boys, who needed teaching, care, and kindness." Every room in the big house was soon full; every little plot in the garden soon had its owner; a regular menagerie appeared in barn and shed, for pet animals were allowed; and, three times a day, Jo smiled at her Fritz from the head of a long table lined on either side with rows of happy young faces, which all turned to her with affectionate eyes, confiding words, and grateful hearts, full of love for "Mother Bhaer." She had boys enough now, and did not tire of them, though they were not angels, by any means, and some of them caused both Professor and Professorin much trouble and anxiety. But her faith in the good spot which exists in the heart of the naughtiest, sauciest, most tantalizing little ragamuffin gave her patience, skill, and in time success, for no mortal boy could hold out long with Father Bhaer shining on him as benevolently as the sun, and Mother Bhaer forgiving him seventy times seven. Very precious to Jo was the friendship of the lads; their penitent sniffs and whispers after wrongdoing; their droll or touching little confidences; their pleasant enthusiasms, hopes, and plans; even their misfortunes, for they only endeared them to her all the more. There were slow boys and bashful boys; feeble boys and riotous boys; boys that lisped and boys that stuttered; one or two lame ones; and a merry little quadroon, who could not be taken in elsewhere, but who was welcome to the "Bhaer-garten," though some people predicted that his admission would ruin the school.

Yes, Jo was a very happy woman there, in spite of hard work, much anxiety, and a perpetual racket. She enjoyed it heartily and found the applause of her boys more satisfying than any praise of the world, for now she told no stories except to her flock of enthusiastic believers and admirers. As the years went on, two little lads of her own came to increase her happiness—Rob, named for Grandpa, and Teddy, a happy-go-lucky baby, who seemed to have inherited his papa's sunshiny temper as well as his mother's lively spirit. How they ever grew up alive in that whirlpool of boys was a mystery to their grandma and aunts, but they flourished like dandelions in spring, and their rough nurses loved and served them well.

There were a great many holidays at Plumfield, and one of the most delightful was the yearly apple-picking; for then the Marches, Laurences, Brookes, and Bhaers turned out in full force and made a day of it. Five years after Jo's wedding, one of these fruitful festivals occurred—a mellow October day, when the air was full of an exhilarating freshness which made the spirits rise and the blood dance healthily in the veins. The old orchard wore its holiday attire: goldenrod and asters fringed the mossy walls; grasshoppers skipped briskly in the sere grass, and crickets chirped like fairy pipers at a feast; squirrels were busy with their small harvesting; birds twittered their adieux from the alders in the lane; and every tree stood ready to send down its shower of red or yellow apples at the first shake. Everybody was there; everybody laughed and sang, climbed up and tumbled down; everybody declared that there never had been such a perfect day or such a jolly set to enjoy it; and everyone gave themselves up to the simple pleasures of the hour as freely as if there were no such things as care or sorrow in the world.

Mr. March strolled placidly about, quoting Tusser, Cowley, and Columella to Mr. Laurence, while enjoying—

The gentle apple's winey juice.

The Professor charged up and down the green aisles like a stout Teutonic knight, with a pole for a lance, leading on the boys, who made a hook and ladder company of themselves, and performed wonders in the way of ground and lofty tumbling. Laurie devoted himself to the little ones, rode his small daughter in a bushelbasket, took Daisy up among the birds' nests, and kept adventurous Rob from breaking his neck. Mrs. March and Meg sat among the apple piles like a pair of Pomonas, sorting the contributions that kept pouring in, while Amy with a beautiful motherly expression in her face sketched the various groups, and watched over one pale lad, who sat adoring her with his little crutch beside him.

Jo was in her element that day, and rushed about, with her gown pinned up, her hat anywhere but on her head, and her baby tucked under her arm, ready for any lively adventure which might turn up. Little Teddy bore a charmed life, for nothing ever happened to him, and Jo never felt any anxiety when he was whisked up into a tree by one lad, galloped off on the back of another, or supplied with sour russets by his indulgent papa, who labored under the Germanic delusion that babies could digest anything, from pickled cabbage to buttons, nails, and their own small shoes. She knew that little Ted would turn up again in time, safe and rosy, dirty and serene, and she always received him back with a hearty welcome, for Jo loved her babies tenderly.

At four o'clock a lull took place, and baskets remained empty, while the apple-pickers rested and compared rents and bruises. Then Jo and Meg, with a detachment of the bigger boys, set forth the supper on the grass, for an out-of-door tea was always the crowning joy of the day. The land literally flowed with milk and honey on such occasions, for the lads were not required to sit at table, but allowed to partake of refreshment as they liked—freedom being the sauce best beloved by the boyish soul. They availed themselves of the rare privilege to the fullest extent, for some tried the pleasing experiment of drinking milk while standing on their heads, others lent a charm to leapfrog by eating pie in the pauses of the game, cookies were sown broadcast over the field, and apple turnovers roosted in the trees like a new style of bird. The little girls had a private tea party, and Ted roved among the edibles at his own sweet will.

When no one could eat any more, the Professor proposed the first regular toast, which was always drunk at such times —"Aunt March, God bless her!" A toast heartily given by the good man, who never forgot how much he owed her, and quietly drunk by the boys, who had been taught to keep her memory green.

"Now, Grandma's sixtieth birthday! Long life to her, with three times three!"

That was given with a will, as you may well believe; and the cheering once begun, it was hard to stop it. Everybody's health was proposed, from Mr. Laurence, who was considered their special patron, to the astonished guinea pig, who had strayed from its proper sphere in search of its young master. Demi, as the oldest grandchild, then presented the queen of the day with various gifts, so numerous that they were transported to the festive scene in a wheelbarrow. Funny presents, some of them, but what would have been defects to other eyes were ornaments to Grandma's—for the children's gifts were all their own. Every stitch Daisy's patient little fingers had put into the handkerchiefs she hemmed was better than embroidery to Mrs. March; Demi's shoebox was a miracle of mechanical skill, though the cover wouldn't shut; Rob's footstool had a wiggle in its uneven legs that she declared was very soothing; and no page of the costly book Amy's child gave her was so fair as that on which appeared, in tipsy capitals, the words—"To dear Grandma, from her little Beth."

During this ceremony the boys had mysteriously disappeared; and, when Mrs. March had tried to thank her children, and broken down, while Teddy wiped her eyes on his pinafore, the Professor suddenly began to sing. Then, from above him, voice after voice took up the words, and from tree to tree echoed the music of the unseen choir, as the boys sang with all their hearts the little song Jo had written, Laurie set to music, and the Professor trained his lads to give with the best effect. This was something altogether new, and it proved a grand success; for Mrs. March couldn't get over her surprise, and insisted on shaking hands with every one of the featherless birds, from tall Franz and Emil to the little quadroon, who had the sweetest voice of all.

After this, the boys dispersed for a final lark, leaving Mrs. March and her daughters under the festival tree.

"I don't think I ever ought to call myself 'Unlucky Jo' again, when my greatest wish has been so beautifully gratified," said Mrs. Bhaer, taking Teddy's little fist out of the milk pitcher, in which he was rapturously churning.

"And yet your life is very different from the one you pictured so long ago. Do you remember our castles in the air?" asked Amy, smiling as she watched Laurie and John playing cricket with the boys.

"Dear fellows! It does my heart good to see them forget business and frolic for a day," answered Jo, who now spoke in a maternal way of all mankind. "Yes, I remember, but the life I wanted then seems selfish, lonely, and cold to me now. I haven't given up the hope that I may write a good book yet, but I can wait, and I'm sure it will be all the better for such experiences and illustrations as these." And Jo pointed from the lively lads in the distance to her father, leaning on the Professor's arm, as they walked to and fro in the sunshine, deep in one of the conversations which both enjoyed so much, and then to her mother, sitting enthroned among her daughters, with their children in her lap and at her feet, as if all found help and happiness in the face which never could grow old to them.

"My castle was the most nearly realized of all. I asked for splendid things, to be sure, but in my heart I knew I should be satisfied, if I had a little home, and John, and some dear children like these. I've got them all, thank God, and am the happiest woman in the world." And Meg laid her hand on her tall boy's head, with a face full of tender and devout content.

"My castle is very different from what I planned, but I would not alter it, though, like Jo, I don't relinquish all my artistic hopes, or confine myself to helping others fulfil their dreams of beauty. I've begun to model a figure of baby, and Laurie says it is the best thing I've ever done. I think so myself, and mean to do it in marble, so that, whatever happens, I may at least keep the image of my little angel."

As Amy spoke, a great tear dropped on the golden hair of the sleeping child in her arms, for her one well-beloved daughter was a frail little creature and the dread of losing her was the shadow over Amy's sunshine. This cross was doing much for both father and mother, for one love and sorrow bound them closely together. Amy's nature was growing sweeter, deeper, and more tender; Laurie was growing more serious, strong, and firm; and both were learning that beauty, youth, good fortune, even love itself, cannot keep care and pain, loss and sorrow, from the most blessed for—

> Into each life some rain must fall,
> Some days must be dark and sad and dreary.

"She is growing better, I am sure of it, my dear. Don't despond, but hope and keep happy," said Mrs. March, as tenderhearted Daisy stooped from her knee to lay her rosy cheek against her little cousin's pale one.

"I never ought to, while I have you to cheer me up, Marmee, and Laurie to take more than half of every burden," replied Amy warmly. "He never lets me see his anxiety, but is so sweet and patient with me, so devoted to Beth, and such a stay and comfort to me always that I can't love him enough. So, in spite of my one cross, I can say with Meg, 'Thank God, I'm a happy woman.'"

"There's no need for me to say it, for everyone can see that I'm far happier than I deserve," added Jo, glancing from her good husband to her chubby children, tumbling on the grass beside her. "Fritz is getting gray and stout; I'm growing as thin as a shadow, and am thirty; we never shall be rich, and Plumfield may burn up any night, for that incorrigible Tommy Bangs *will* smoke sweet-fern cigars under the bedclothes, though he's set himself afire three times already. But in spite of these unromantic facts, I have nothing to complain of, and never was so jolly in my life. Excuse the remark, but living among boys, I can't help using their expressions now and then."

"Yes, Jo, I think your harvest will be a good one," began Mrs. March, frightening away a big black cricket that was staring Teddy out of countenance.

"Not half so good as yours, Mother. Here it is, and we never can thank you enough for the patient sowing and reaping you have done," cried Jo with the loving impetuosity which she never could outgrow.

"I hope there will be more wheat and fewer tares every year," said Amy softly.

"A large sheaf, but I know there's room in your heart for it, Marmee dear," added Meg's tender voice.

Touched to the heart, Mrs. March could only stretch out her arms, as if to gather children and grandchildren to herself, and say, with face and voice full of motherly love, gratitude, and humility—

"Oh, my girls, however long you may live, I never can wish you a greater happiness than this!"

LOUISA MAY ALCOTT (1832-1888)

Louisa May Alcott's novels call up vividly the life of nineteenth-century New England—tranquil, secure, and busily productive. Little wonder, for she drew on her own experiences as one of four daughters in a lively Boston family. At the age of eight, she moved with her family to nearby Concord. There she knew her happiest years, in spite of the constant threat of poverty, and counted as friends the children of Emerson and Hawthorne. The Alcott home was a modest cottage, but the girls enjoyed the use of a neighboring barn, in which they performed plays usually written by Louisa May.

Carefully educated at home, she became a schoolteacher in Boston. At the age of twenty she saw her first story printed in a Boston newspaper; her first book, *Flower Fables,* appeared two years later. She interrupted her teaching and writing during the Civil War to serve as a nurse in a Washington hospital. Her experiences there are recorded in two of the most touching documents of that sad time, *Hospital Sketches* and *Moods.*

After the war, the increasing sales of her books, including the famous *Little Women* (1869) and its sequel, *Little Men* (1871), helped to make her parents' life more comfortable. She spent most of her later years in her beloved Orchard House in Concord, where she wrote *Eight Cousins* (1875), *Rose in Bloom* (1876), *Under the Lilacs* (1878), and *Jo's Boys* (1886). She saw and wrote as she lived, depicting her world with loving accuracy, humor, and compassion.

A CONTROVERSY OF POETS

PARIS LEARY'S poetry has been published by Charles Scribner's Sons in the Poets of Today Series and in numerous magazines in this country and England. He is also author of a novel, *The Innocent Curate*. A member of the English and Philosophy Department at the State University College in New Paltz, New York, he was Fulbright Lecturer in English literature at the University of Leicester, in 1964–65.

ROBERT KELLY was founder and co-editor of *Chelsea Review* and later *Trobar*. He has published five volumes of poetry and taught at Wagner College and the University of Buffalo. He is presently on the faculty of Bard College.

AN ANTHOLOGY OF
CONTEMPORARY AMERICAN POETRY

A Controversy of Poets

Edited by
PARIS LEARY
and
ROBERT KELLY

ANCHOR BOOKS
DOUBLEDAY & COMPANY, INC.
GARDEN CITY, NEW YORK

The publisher wishes to thank the magazines and publishers who have given permission to reprint the following poems:

John Ashbery's "Europe," from *The Tennis Court Oath*, Wesleyan University Press, 1960. Copyright © 1960 by John Ashbery, by permission of Wesleyan University Press.

Paul Blackburn's "Meditation on the BMT" from *Brooklyn-Manhattan Transit*, 1960, published by Totem Press. Copyright 1960 by Paul Blackburn; "Bañalbufar, A Brazier, Relativity, Cloud Formations and the Kindness and Relentlessness of Time, etc.," "The Purse-Seine," "El Camino Verde," from *The Nets*, 1961, published by Trobar Press. Copyright © 1961 by Paul Blackburn; "Park Poem," from *Origin* 6, July 1962. Copyright 1962 by Cid Corman with permission of Origin Press; "Three Part Invention," in *Sum #2*, February 1964.

Robin Blaser's "The Park," from *Locus Solus*, Winter 1962. Copyright 1961 by Harry Mathews; "The Faerie Queen," Part One, *The Nation*, December 30, 1961. Copyright © 1961 by Robin Blaser.

Gray Burr's "Sailing, Sailing," from *The New Yorker*, September 14, 1963. Copyright © 1963 by The New Yorker Magazine, Inc., with permission of The New Yorker Magazine; "The Butterfly," from *The Massachusetts Review*, Autumn 1961. Copyright © 1962 by Gray Burr; "A Glance at the Album," from *Poetry*, August 1955. Copyright © 1955 by Modern Poetry Association.

Gregory Corso's "The Mad Yak," "I Am 25," "But I Do Not Need Kindness," "Italian Extravaganza," "The Last Warmth of Arnold," from *Gasoline*, The Pocket Poets Series #8, City Lights Books, 1958. Copyright © 1958 by Gregory Corso, reprinted by permission of City Lights Books.

Robert Creeley's "The House," "Kore," "The Name," "I Know a Man," from *For Love*, Charles Scribner's Sons, 1962. Copyright © 1962 by Robert Creeley, reprinted with the permission of Charles Scribner's Sons; "Rhythm," from *Poetry*, March 1962. Copyright © 1962 by Robert Creeley; "Language," from *Poetry*, June 1964. Copyright © 1964 by Robert Creeley, with permission of the Editors of *Poetry;* "The Mountains in the Desert," from *The Paris Review*, Winter–Spring 1963, by permission of *The Paris Review;* "Anger," from *El Corno Emplumado* #11, Mexico. Copyright 1964 by Robert Creeley.

Peter Davison's "North Shore," "Finale: Presto," "The Breaking of the Day," from *The Breaking of the Day*, 1964, Yale University Press. Copyright © 1961, 1963, 1964 by Peter Davison, reprinted by permission of Yale University Press.

James Dickey's four poems from *Drowning with Others*, Wesleyan University Press, reprinted by permission of Wesleyan University Press: "The Lifeguard," copyright © 1961 by James Dickey, originally published in *The New Yorker;* "The Owl King," copyright © 1962 by James Dickey; "Drowning with Others," copyright © 1960 by James Dickey; "The Hospital Window," copyright © 1962 by James Dickey.

Edward Dorn's "Sousa," "The Song," "The Biggest Killing," from *The Newly Fallen*, 1961, published by Totem Press. Copyright © 1961 by Edward Dorn; "From Gloucester Out," from *Idaho Out*, 1964, published by Trobar Books. Copyright © 1964 by Edward Dorn.

PREFACE

A Controversy of Poets is representative, but not comprehensive; it means to represent not all but the most significant American poetry. Many of these poets are, according to the generations of poets, fairly young. The few exceptions are those older men whose work has come into special prominence since 1950.

This anthology is designed to turn the attention of the reader to the contemporary *poem,* away from movements, schools or regional considerations. Hitherto some of these poets have been referred to by commentators more enthusiastic than accurate as belonging to this or that rival —and hostile—school. Such poetasting has only served to distract the reader from the *poem* and to divert his attention to supposed movements or schools, whereas the only affiliation finally relevant is that apparent from the work itself.

Towards only two of the poets whose work is represented here have the editors been unable to maintain that detachment and impartiality that they hope distinguish their treatment of the others.

P. L. & R. K.

ACKNOWLEDGMENTS

We would like to thank Anne Freedgood, Editor of Anchor Books, and her assistants, Phyllis Klein and Margot Kriel, for their confidence, enthusiasm, and active cooperation in the preparation of this book; and Naomi Burton of Doubleday & Company for her early interest in the project.

We wish also to express our gratitude to Mr. Andrew Haigh, Director of the Bard College Library, for help in gathering texts and bibliographical information; to Mr. Jonathan Greene for assistance in selecting the work of one of these poets; Joan Kelly and Mrs. Fred Crane for their help in preparing the manuscript; to Messrs. Robert Pack of Middlebury College and T. Weiss, editor of *The Quarterly Review of Literature*, who generously responded to certain technical editorial queries, and to Mr. Gerrit Lansing, Mr. and Mrs. Paul Blackburn, and Mr. and Mrs. Louis Zukofsky for the clarity of their encouragements and of their no less valuable criticisms.

Special thanks are due to Muriel DeGré without whose commitment to the work of preparing this anthology our editorial labors would have been in vain.

CONTENTS

A CONTROVERSY OF POETS

JOHN ASHBERY

Europe

1 To employ her
   construction ball
   Morning fed on the
   light blue wood
   of the mouth
                           cannot understand
   feels deeply)

2 A wave of nausea —

3 a few berries

4 the unseen claw
   Babe asked today
   The background of poles roped over
   into star jolted them

5 filthy or into backward drenched flung heaviness
   lemons asleep pattern crying

6 The mouth of elephant —
   embroidery over where
   ill page sees.

7 What might have
             children singing
   the horses
             the seven
   breaths under tree, fog
   clasped — absolute, unthinking
   menace to our way of life.
   um more unearth cloth
   This could have been done —
   This could not be done

8 In the falling twilight of the wintry afternoon all looked
dull and cheerless. The car stood outside with Ronald Pryor
and Collins attending to some slight engine trouble — the
fast, open car which Ronnie sometimes used to such advan-

tage. It was covered with mud, after the long run from Suf-
folk, for they had started from Harbury long before daylight,
and, until an hour ago, had been moving swiftly up the Great
North Road, by way of Stamford, Grantham and Doncaster
to York. There they had turned away to Ripon, where, for
an hour, they had eaten and rested. In a basket the waiter had
placed some cold food with some bread and a bottle of wine,
and this had been duly transferred to the car.
All was now ready for the continuance of the journey.

    9 The decision in his life
        soul elsewhere
        the gray hills
        out there on the road darkness
        covering lieutenant
            there is a cure

   10 He had mistaken his book for garbage

   11 The editor realized
            its gradual abandonment
        a kind of block where other men come down
        spoiling the view
        wept blood
        on the first page and following snow
        gosh flowers upset ritual
            a mass of black doves
        over the scooter, snow outlining the tub
            flowers until dawn

   12 that surgeon must operate
        I had come across
        to the railway from the Great North
        Road, which I had followed up to London.

   13 the human waste cannibals designed the master
            and his life
        robot you underground sorrow to the end
        can unlack horsemen. Storm seems berries —
        until the truth can be explained
        Nothing can exist. Rain
        blossomed in the highlands — a
        secret to annul grass sticks — razor today engraved
            sobs.
        The lion's skin — ears, to travel.

14 Before the waste
   went up
  Before she had worked
  The sunlight in the square —
  apples, oranges, the compass
  tears of joy — over rotten stone flesh
  His dyspepsia uncorked — that's
        leaf of the story
     mitigated

15 Absolve me from the hatred I never
  she — all are wounded against
  Zeppelin — wounded carrying dying
  three colors over land
  thistles again closed around voice.
  She is dying —
  automatically —
  wanting to see you again, but the stone
  must be rebuilt. Time stepped

16 before I started
  I was forced to   flying
  she said
  higher and higher on
  next tree, am as wire
  when canvas the must spread
        to new junk

17 I moved up
       glove
   the field

18 I must say I
  suddenly
  she left the room, oval tear tonelessly fell.

19 Life pursued down these cliffs.
  the omened birds
  intrusion; skated, at night
  clear waves of weather
  fur you bring genius
  over hell's curiosity
  the librarian shabbily books on
  You cannot illusion; the dust.
  abstract vermin the garden worn smiles

20 That something desperate was to be attempted
      was,
however, quite plain.

21 Night hunger
   of berry . . . stick

22 "Beautiful morning for a flip miss," remarked the
mechanic in brown overalls. "Are you going up alone."

23 "Then I'll take the bombs out," he said, and at once
removed the six powerful bombs from the rack, the projectiles
intended for the destruction of zeppelins.

24 The tables gleamed — soft lighting
      covered the place.
There was a certain pleasure in all this for him.
The twelve girls wept. She willed him
loveliest diamond of the tree; the old lawyer kept
      his mule there.
They had gone. The weather was very pure that
      night like
leaves of paper placed on the black — the opal
crescent still dangled on the little chain —
a pleasant memory of a kiss, completely
given to recollection. Only
faded water remained. The last memory left.

25 She was dying but had time for him —
brick. Men were carrying the very heavy things —
      dark purple, like flowers.
Bowl lighted up the scare just right

26 water
        thinking
          a

27   A notice:

28   wishing you were a
      the bottle really before the washed
          handed over to her:
             hundreds
light over her
    hanging her
you can remember

29 Have you encouraged judge
       inked commentary
   approaching obvious battle
   summer night less ecstatic
           train over scream . . . mountain
                   into woods

30 sweetheart . . .   the stamp
       ballooning you
   vision I thought you
   forget, encouraging your vital organs.
   Telegraph. The rifle — a page folded over.
   More upset, wholly meaningless, the willing sheath
   glide into fall . . . mercury to passing
   the war you said won — milling around the picket
       fence, and noise of the engine from the sky
   and flowers — here is a bunch
   the war won out of cameos.
   And somehow the perfect warrior is fallen.

31 They wore red
   the three children dragged into next year
   sad . . .   gold under the feet.
   sadly more music is divine to them.

32 The snow stopped falling
   on the head of the stranger.
   In a moment the house would be dark

33 mirrors — insane

34 dying for they do not
   the hole no crow can
   and finally the day of thirst
   in the air.
   whistles carbon dioxide. Cold
   pavement grew. The powerful machine
   The tractor, around edge
   the listless children. Good night
   staining the naughty air
   with marvelous rings. You are going there.
   Weeps. The wreath not decorating.
   The kids pile over the ample funeral hill.
   had arrived from London
                   o'clock
       baited tragically

This time the others grew.
The others waited
by the darkening pool — "a world of silence"
you can't understand their terror
means more to these people waste
the runt crying in the pile of colored
snapshots offal in the wind
that's the way we do it terror
the hand of the large person falls
to the desk. The people all leave.
the industries begin
moment   puts on the silencer
You crab into the night

35 The sheiks protest use of
aims. In the past
coal has protected their
O long, watchful hour.
the engines had been humming
stones of March in the gray woods
still, the rods, could not they take long
More anthems until dust
flocks disguised machine. The stone
the valentine couldn't save. . . . Hooks

36 he ran the machine swiftly across the frosty grass.
Soon he rose, and skimming the trees, soon
soared away into the darkness.

37 From where Beryl sat she saw the glow
of the little electric bulb set over the instruments
   shining into
her lover's strong clean-shaven face, and, by the
   compass, gathered that
they had described a half-circle, and, though
still rising rapidly, were now heading eastward in
the direction of the sea.

38 The roar of the engine, of course,
rendered speech impossible,
while the mist was very chilly, causing her to draw
   her brown woollen comforter around her legs.
There was no sign of light anywhere below
— all was a bright black void.

39 The few children
   Seeds under the glare
   The formal tragedy of it all
   Mystery for man — engines humming
   Parachutes opening. The newspaper being read
   Beside the great gas turbine
   The judge calls his assistant over
   And together they try to piece together the secret
      message contained in today's paper.

40 The police
   Had been forgotten
   Scarlet, blue and canary
   Heads tossing on the page
      grunting to the coatroom
   there was another ocean, ballads and legends, the
      children returning to the past — head

41 She was saying into the distance
         It was a sad day
   the riders drinking in the car
   haze of trees behind
                     dummy woods
      plans and sketches
      soda, glasses, ice
      bumped off
   "with these strange symbols."

42 the club had bought aperture

43 Their hidden storage (to you, murder)
   but what testimony buried under colored sorrow — the
nerve
         children called upon
   assassination this racket.

44 He ran the ferret
   backing him hard nest
            The chil —
   One day the children particularly surrounded
   he had read about him.

45 Like a long room
   Monsignor
         pushed away it
   studio artificially small
      pine rounds

46 The last time she crossed close to Berck,
   beyond Paris-Plage, she passed over Folke-
   stone, and then over to Cape Grisnez
   alone into the night

47 Or he hides bodies
   stone night,
   pleasant city, gray
                    hides
   perfect dictionary for you
   valentine not wanted storm under the
   snow backed rubbers
   The city hides, desolate
   rocks snow tile hides
   over the door marked "The Literature
   beginning veins hide the mind
   robot —" — capped by all. release.

48 Then she studied her map, took her bearings
   and, drawing on her ample gauntlet gloves
                    (for it had become chilly)
   she followed a straight line of railway leading
       through Suffolk and Norfolk

49 I'm on my way to Hull
       grinned the girl

50 It was in German. The aviator and his
   observer climbed out of the seats and stood
   with Mr. Aylesworth, chatting and laughing.

51 They are written upon English paper, and English
       penny stamps are upon them . . .
   they can be put into any post-box . . . . They
   mostly contain instructions to our good friends
       in Great Britain.

52 The rose
                    dirt
       dirt you

   pay
   The buildings
   is tree

Undecided
       protest
           This planet.

53 The vegetable wagon had not been placed yet
Scotchmen with their plaids — all the colorful
Photography, horror of all
That has died
The hundred year old stones — deceived
by the mind of these things — the stairs
climbing up out of dark hollyhocks
old, dirt, smell of the most terrifying thing in the
world.

54 "He is probably one of the gang."

55   mood seems the sort
               to brag
               end

56   songs like
               You came back to me
               you were wrong about the gravestone
that nettles hide quietly
The sun is not ours.

57 Precise mechanisms
Love us.

He came over the hill
He held me in his arms — it was marvelous

But the map of Europe
shrinks around naked couples

Even as you lick the stamp
A brown dog lies down beside you and dies

In the city an eleven year old girl with pig tails
Tied with a yellow ribbon takes the trolley

All of this ends somewhere — the book is replaced
   on the shelf
By an unseen hand

We are not more loved than now
The newspaper is ruining your eyes.

58 The professor — a large "S"
               One kitten escaped
                     Take plane

or death by hanging
And naturally it is all over again, beginning to get tired you
realize

59 The real thing the matter
        with him you see studio end
    of day masked
  you didn't see him — he went
  escape is over on the lighted steps
  "My blood went into this"
  Misunderstandings arise cathedral
  twenty years later catching sight of him
  his baggy trousers the porch daylight
  playing tennis before we realize the final dream is
    razed
  Today, of course.

60 Wing
        Bostonian
    and his comments
  thirty-three years old the day
    of his third birthday the legs
  Lenin De Gaulle three days later
    also comparing simple

61 reflecting trout

62 All of us fear the secret
  guarded too carefully
    An assortment

63 she ran along the grass for a short distance
  couple of beers
  eats   being corpse tables

64 ice   dirt
  five minutes
  get your money back
    the hole screamed
  two persons
              two cut flowers

65 nothing is better than
  glowing coals
  The perfect animal
    during the summer, sleep of brine and ice

66 She followed a straight line leading
    due north through Suffolk and Norfolk

67 over the last few years
    there is one terrifying

wild
        the error of sleep
           love

68 The straight line out of sight
    of beads
    decades cheapest
  the more post card
     "genius"

69 because it is
    That is to say

70   Her last dollar

71 They must hold against
    The fire rain
    or when sometime it seems
    upward, hands down
      against
    pilloried
      sell quickly took her bearings
    did not appear entirely
    upper hand of her
    a height of five thousand feet

72 The village (using the new headache system) were
     cut
    With the stops running
    A French or Swiss
    had hit bottom and gotten back up
    wild margins are possible
    The gold a "call"
    options his life . . . flea

73 A least
    four days
    A surprise
    mothers
    suppose
    Is not a "images"
    to "arrange"

He is a descendant, for example
The Swiss bank — a village.

74 Man come for one is humanity
   the lowest pickpocket helps

75 Like the public,
   reactions
   from Crystal Palace

76 A roar
   "sweetness and light"
   pickpocket — stem
   and more scandalous . . . well, forgotten
   The snow is around storm
   He laughed lightly at cliff
   and used that term

77 "Perhaps you've heard of her. She's a great flying
      woman."

   "Oh yes," replied the stranger. "I've seen things
      about
   her in the papers. Does she fly much?"

78 applauding itself — wiser
      more gun   I come from the district
   four times carrying a small,
      oval
   the movie was also
      in the entire crystal

79 to stroll down Main Street
   the dignified and paternal image
   telegraph — magnificent
                     dump
porch
      flowers   store
   weed local relatives
                  whine

80 multitude headquarters shout there
   Because there are no
   because the majority is toxic
   An exquisite sense — like pretzels.
   He was sent to the state senate
   wage conceal his disapproval

The arguments situation lawyers worthlessness sullen
    cafeterias

81 barcarolle

82 The silencer. "Is he not . . ."

83 Soon after noon, carrying a narrow,

84   about her

85 ghost of stone — massive
      hangs halfway
polishing
     whose winding
Strong, sad half-city
 gardens
                  from the bridge of
stair
             broom
recent   past   symbolized
hair   banana
does not evoke a concrete image
the splendid

86 nourished on the
    railings of bare stone —

87 Your side
    is majestic — the dry wind
    timeless stones. a deep sigh
    dragged up with a piercing scream
    the clean, crisp air
    aging on the villas
    little openings for her bath
    façades of the the — all alike, the hard rain
    "the dignity of this fortress."

88 the invaders
               so bad just now
    go up and see the shabby traveler
               ordered a pint
At half-past two, the visitor, taking
   his bag, set out on a tour of the
   village.   An endeavor
                 remained
  rolls on them
         at night

89 This car has some private
   more than one cottage the chintzes were bright its
   brass candlestick forgotten
   twenty-five cents.
   could offer was a feeble

90 I have a perfect memory and
   the sky seems to pass
   a couple of them like a huge bowl
   and encircle the earth

91 flanked by his lieutenants — lemon —
   his chief outside
   "if I am wrong
       a fine sieve
   telephones I do not
   strong nature who wrote of him while starving himself

92 to be dying, he gets them into magazines
   and some of them mangy and rabid
   hardly seemed necessary.

   I was horrified. I felt sorry for him.
   No branch without . . .
   down to the lakes the ornamental
   bronze — isn't it the fear that

   Hand in hand like fire
   and in your souls

93 A searchlight sweeping
   picked up "The Hornet"
   Hardly had he undressed when he
   heard again that low swish of
   "The Hornet" on her return from scouting circuit of
       the Thames estuary
   solidifying disguises

   who died in an automobile accident
   had developed a
   then, imperceptibly

94 The snow had begun to fall on Paris
   It is barely noon

95 Between the legs of her
   Cobwebs   the lip   reads   chewing
   and taste seem uncertain;

powerless creating images
shut up and leave me . . . Hush! This
two men who have
   most profoundly
      the islanders

96 Mr. Bean remained indoors
   at the small boats
   of our defences, our intentions

97 out upon the lawn after a few months in the village
     big
   "Like some of my friends
   Otherwise we'll chop off his head

98 This was the third thing
   another giant

99 dark wool, summer
   and winter

100 gun metal — her right foot in both hands
         things

101 the doctor, comb

           Sinn Fein

102   dress

103 streaming sweeping the surface
   long-handled twig-brooms
        starving
   wall   great   trees

104 blaze   aviators
          out
                              dastardly

105 We must be a little more wary in
    future, dear

106 she was trying to make sense of
   what was quick laugh
   hotel — cheap for them
   caverns the bed
    box of cereal

Ere long a flare was lit
I don't understand wreckage

107 blue smoke?   The steel bolts
        It was as though   having been replaced
            She had   by a painting of
the river   one of wood!
    above the water   Ronnie, thoughtfully
                                      of the silencer
            plot to kill both of us, dear
pet
            oh
        it that she was there

108   the bridge crosses
                        dragon   ships
        canal lock
                was   effect
                    There are but two seasons
        the map of Paris
            through the center of the sheet
                    character
    sewers empty into under the
    literally choked the river with
        bodies
            "on the coast, I think . . ."
            passing over

109 Magnificent trees — the old
        chateau — he said he was
    going home for their needs
            only the other —
                exchanged another meaning
            here lately
            the inn-keeper's

110 Dry, the bush
    settling   Everybody
    knows him
                    close to the Thwaite
    passing close to where
        The bookshop
            were crouched in conceal —
up a steep, narrow path
    to the summit of Black Hill

recognized him
lavatory — dogging
                his footsteps
                        out to sea

111 Half an hour later
     Ronald recognized him.
     They suddenly saw a beam of intense, white light,
     A miniature searchlight of great brilliance,
     — pierce the darkness, skyward.

     They now recognized to be a acetylene,
     a cylinder mounted
     upon a light tripod of aluminum
     with a bright reflector behind the gas-jet,
     that the light began to "wink,"
          three times in quick succession
     the Morse letter "S."

     Slowly the beam turned from north to south,
     making the Morse "S." upon the clouds,
     time after time.

     Suddenly the light was shut off — for five minutes by
          Ronald's watch no flicker was shown
     Then suddenly, once again, the series of S's was repeated
     in a semi-circle from north to south
     and back again.

     Another five minutes passed in darkness.

     Once more the light opened out and commenced
     to signal the Morse flashes and flares,
     "N.F.", "N.F."
     followed by a long beam of
     light skyward, slowly sweeping in a circle
                              the breath

PAUL BLACKBURN

The Letter

> The legs being uneven
> the chair opposite wobbles by
> itself .

Clear air of Adriatic morning
On the bridge the capitain reads it out:
>   49 hrs. 14 min. 42 sec.
> sextant error   02 min.   0 sec.
>   49 -   12 -   32, he reads,
>   49 -   02 -   00
>   second correction . The
>   horizon a perfect circle .
>   Ship the moving center of the circle .

>   The sun is the stick, an
>   absolute time .
>   Lat.   41° 34′ N
>   Long.   16° 58′ E
>   Declination of sun   24° 09′

Say I know where you are
Now you know where I am
Time on Board (not Greenwich)
9 hrs. 24 min. 52 sec.
the 3rd of August, 1955.
>   Your son and daughter-in-law send you herewith
>   greetings
>   and that we thought of you,
>   this, your day .

And there were dolphins this morning
early, tho I did not see them
and was reading .
Freddie told me about them .

>   The barometer is rising .
>   The sea is anyway fair
>   *and* incredibly blue
>   damned incredibly blue.

Horizon is a circle
and the ship its center
All sea-rings have centers, as we know,
and all worlds are one
                    in appearance :
the rest a geometrical projection of
what otherwise might be proved a hell, but is
in fact an Eden, where no tree grows
and land is beyond imagining, my mother.
                              The blue
                                the blue .
              This is all my news.

        Both of us are well and send our love

        All things contain themselves and pass away

                By this hand, the third day
                of August . '55,
                from the ARSIA
                in a timeless sea   .

Meditation on the BMT

Here, at the beginning of the new season
before the new leaves burgeon,   on
either side of the Eastern Parkway station
              near the Botanical Gardens
they burn trash on the embankments, laying
barer than ever our sad, civilized refuse.

1 coffee can without a lid
1 empty pint of White Star, the label
              faded by rain
1 empty beer-can
2 empty Schenley bottles
1 empty condom, seen from
1 nearly empty train
          empty

          empty

          empty
Repeated often enough, even the word looks funny.

Man in an alley carrying a morning load already
          walks
only by propping his hand against a thick red
          line
painted on a building wall, while he goes past
coffee-can   beer can   condom   bottles & fire
          past
faded brick and pock-marked cement to somewhere
relieve his bladder in the sorrow of a sun-shot morning
          with some semblance of privacy, some-
          how needed here . Cold . Sad

winter morning in spring where it is cold while
this man is high and the sun is high and there are no
rules governing the award of prizes to the dead.

          My eyes

enter poor backyards, backyards
          O I love you.

backyards, I make you my own, and you
my barren, littered embankments, now that you
've a bit of fire to warm & cleanse you, be
grateful that men still tend you, still will
          rake your strange leaves
          your strange leavings.

          Poor Brooklyn soil
          poor american earth
          poor sickening houses
poor hurricanes of streets, both
your subterranean and your public lives go on
          anyhow,   beneath
refuse that is a refusal, with alienated, uneasy, un-
reflective citizens, who will be less un-
          happy, more contented and vacant, if they
          relieve their bladders against some
crappy wall or other.

El Camino Verde

                    The green road lies this way.
                    I take the road of sand.

One way the sun burns hottest,   no relief,   the other
sun   (the same) is filtered thru
                    leaves that cast obscene
                       beautiful patterns
                    on roads and walls . And

                    the wind blows all day.
Hot . sirocco, a chain
of hot wind rattles across
high over the mountains
rushes down from the peaks to the sea
laving men's bodies in the fields between
                    Days when
the serpent of wind plucks and twists the harp of the sun.

              In the green road,   pale
           gray-green of olives, olive-wood twisted
              under the burning wind, the wet
           heat of an armpit, but in the mouth

this other road. And the dry heat of the mouth is the pitiful
                                   possibility
of finding a flower in the dust.   Sanity . See
              there, the white
                 wing of a gull over blindness of water,
the black black wing of a hawk over stretches of forest   .
                                             Wish
to hold the mind clear in the dark honey of evening light, think
of a spring
in an orchard
in flower
in soft sun amid ruins, down there
a small palm offers its leaves to the wind .
              On the mountain, olive,
                 o, live wood,
its flawless curve hangs from the slope.

Hot . sirocco . covers everything
and everyone, all day, it blows all day as if
this were choice, as if
the earth were anything else but
what it is, a hell.   But
blind, bland, blend the flesh.
Mix the naked foot with the sand that caresses it, mix
with the rock that tears it,   enter
                    the hot world.

cave of the winds .
What cave?   the
>reaches of Africa
>where an actual
>>measure
>>>exists.

Bañalbufar, A Brazier, Relativity, Cloud Formations & The Kindness & Relentlessness of Time, All Seen Through A Window While Keeping The Feet Warm at The Same Time As

End of February
beginning of Lent. How prevent
the clouds from moving now. Where
>sunlight falls . . .

>The walls
keep the wind out, but the house
>>cold, cold
Feet under the fold
>of the tablecover
edge toward the brazier underneath.   Old house.
Warmer outside, where is
>sun

>>when sun is.

>>Sheaves of love and talk
>>wave at the attention.
>>More hot coals are added. Loud
>>>thanks.
>>Focus on direction. Analyse.
>>Keep the eyes

>>>peeled
>>are changing now, clouds

>Southwind:
and lines of clouds walk across the mountains, straight
across the sea; the land, the mountains at angle.
>Between the cloudbanks
>>sun falls.
>>Lemon trees

outside the window under sun
　　making a sweet quadrangle:
parallel lines of sun straight,
　　　　trees bent
　　under the double weight,
　　　　　　wind
　　　　　　fruit.

　　　　How prevent
the clouds from moving, now that sun . . . . Sunlight on

pear blossom, apple blossom, the red wall,
roofs' tile,　red and yellow, yellow!
　　　　lemons under sun.
　　The mountain　　now in one
　　　　　　shadow,　　huge;
the colors in old wood, the door, sun,
dark green of pines, dark blue of rock, more
　　　　cloud, the
　　　　wing of a cloud
　　　　　　　　passes.
　　　　　　　　　　Alas!
Alles, ala, the wing, everything
　　　　　　　　　goes.

　　　　　　No.
　　Always is always all ways.
　　　　No, not so.
　　My love says to me,　—Not so.
　　I am humble under this wind
　　but stupid, and hopeful even.

"Come
　　　into this cold room
　　　　　　The smell of wildflowers is
　　in every corner.
　　The mind
is filled with flower smell and sun
　　　　　　even when sun is not."

The Purse — Seine

Fierce luster of sun on sea, the gulls
　　　　　　swinging by,
　　　gulls flung by wind

aloft, hung clear and still before the
                         pivot
          turn
                    glide out
riding the wind as tho it were
                         the conditions of civilisation

But they are hungry too,
and what they do that looks so beautiful, is
          hunt .

The side of your face so soft, down, their cried falls, bitter
broken-wing graces crying freedom, crying carrion, and
we cannot look one another in the eye,
                         that frightens, easier to face
the carapace of monster crabs along the beach . The empty
shell of death was always easier to gaze upon
than to look into the eyes of the beautiful killer . Never
                    look a gull in the eye

Fit the 300-pound tom over the pursing lines, start it sliding
down the rope to close the open circle, bottom of the net,
                                        weight
thudding down thru the sea

brass rings hung from the lead line come closer together, the
tom pushing the rings ahead of it, the purse line drawing thru
them, taking up the slack, the school sounding the fish streak-
                                                        ing
by toward that narrowing circle
                    and out . . .

Waiting behind the skiff, birds sit on the sea, staring off, patient
                    for what we throw them . We
          merely fight it, surf, and that other day. No
bed ever was until this, your face half-smiling down your
                              swell of half-
sleep, eyes closed so tightly they will admit
               nothing but fear and stars . How can we
call all this our own? and shall we dare? admit the moon? full
bars of song from night birds, doors of the mind agape and
                                        swelling?
               Dream again
that orange slope of sand, we belting down it hand upon hand,
                                        the birds
          cry overhead

the sea
lies in its own black anonymity and we here on this bed
enact the tides, the swells, your hips rising toward me,
                        waves break over the shoals, the
sea bird hits the mast in the dark and falls
with a cry to the deck and flutters off . Panic spreads, the
                        night is long, no
            one sleeps, the net
is tight
we are caught or not, the tom sliding down ponderous
                        shall we make it?
                        The purse closes.

The beach is a playground . unsatisfactory, but we
pretending still it's play swim out too far, and reaching
back, the arms strain inward
Waters here are brown with sand, the land too close,
                        too close, we drown
                        in sight of
I love you and you love me. . .

Park Poem

From the first shock of leaves their alliance
with love, how is it?

Pages we write and tear
Someone in a swagger coat sits and waits on a hill

It is not spring, may-
be it is never spring
maybe it is the hurt end of summer
the first tender autumn air
fall's first cool rain over the park
and these people walking thru it

the girl thinking:
                    life is these pronouns
the man : to ask / to respond / to accept
                    bird-life . reindeer-death
                    Life is all verbs, vowels and verbs
They both get wet

                    If it is love, it is to make
                    love, or let be

       'To create the situation / is love
               and to avoid it, this is also
      Love'
as any care or awareness, any
other awareness might   might
          have been
          but is now

hot flesh
socking it into hot flesh
until reindeer-life / bird-death

You are running, see?
you are running down slope across this field
I am running too
to catch you round

         This rain is yours
         it falls on us
         we fall on one another

Belong to the moon
we do not see

         It is wet and cool
         bruises our skin
         might have been
         care and avoidance
         but we run . run

to prepare
love later

Three Part Invention

June 21/62, 1:05 AM
   s o l s t i c e

    All windows open, moths
    strike against the screens.
               The cheerful counterpoint:
the wide sound,
you whizzing in the bathroom
with the door open, against
        the steady whirr
        of air
        conditioners in

the new building around the block,
pressure of air forced on metal leaves slatted out, over-
laid by the soft nature of your relief, the sigh
                                        as you dry
the small tight hairs
        and rise .
The leverage is metallic
and a cataract of water
ends the song .

The first quarter-hour of solstice
ends with your hand in the small of my back, a gentle
                                stroking
that brings everything from me, colors
and the dark spring from me into the dark / breaths
move from the shallows to deeps after-
ribcages rise and fall together.
                Aware finally of movement of air
                cooling the damp limbs, to making V
                four an inverted M : and then, both
                flopping on our faces, all those
                        lower case l's .

                Returning to work
                after the fuck, first
                I water the flowers,
care with fingers for the young plants that
nod in the well of night . The black young
cat jumps onto my knee as I write, her
belly heavy with kittens . She
prods at the book in my hand.

                Air conditioners spin
against the regular
breathing from the
other room . Air
                moves thru'
the quiet stream of my wrist, moths
        strike the screen.

ROBIN BLASER

The Park

Cleo on the Section Gang
75 miles of railroad   Checking
the ties   Repairing the washouts

More than one animal

Duplications tick in the leaves
like insects
sucking the bitter green

The male womb
which links our bodies
in brutal imagination

Cleo swears
            the god-damned rabbits
mate with the sagebrush

Nearly no sound at all

                    *

The whir of traffic identifies a city
It is night out

The rain starts   A musical
plucking at the windows

I have allowed the stream
of traffic to end here
(Lost River) at my table
where lost,
            I was hunted

Evidence . Footsteps
on the muddy bank
at the edge

Event . The river
flowed into a cave,

disappeared, except for a field
of water-filled pits
where he walked, testing
the grass before each step

A salutation .
Obedient to the garden
Out of the spines of that black
flowering tree,
the night noises

                    *

The soft step is
only the possibility
of entrance
at the door

I am framed
as in a box at the play
Around . Around . Around .
To look out . Lookout .
Abstractions
(beyond my capacity
to write)
                    stop striking
The clock
                    Around

So much for what it is
in the heart
steps back

                    *

He follows   The bird endures
what the bird sings

Between two gates,
the garden   That turn
to the left where the pale

yellow wisteria is falling,
surprisingly

Though it is not the body
attaches there in its quick
movements a what-next,
the deed pities my hand

Follow!   And you did
take the next turn,
                          surprising
the water that fell from your fists,
which then, dropped to your thighs
were only tokens of a loud knocking

                *

Around us, the city imagines
the tourists   The guide books
are full of facts
                     The fountains
play on Monday and Wednesday

A light of desire among
the monuments,
                      wet to the skin

                *

She went down cellar to get
the ham (larder, she called
it) but stopped on the last
step and held up her right arm
so the bull snake could come
down off the rafter to greet us
(she said) She liked to describe
the pull of its body on her skin
Its nature (she said) was to pull
tightly in friendship

                *

She beat on the floor with her stick
until I came   She said 'Sing'   Which
I did   She commented that my voice
was thin, but I had enough silliness to
amount to (hesitation) a poet   Old
lady whose false breasts were made of
cambric stuffed with cotton and hung
around her neck on a ribbon, kept a
goldfish bowl full of life-savers to
sweeten the sour breath she was aware of

                *

She bent over the drinking fountain
one hand poised to turn the
cock
      and there she remained

(caught up)
until we noticed and called an
ambulance

                    *

Sights float on the ponds

                    *

True and false, two sparrows,
chittering,
        fall down the side of the building,
stems of ivy breaking their descent,
locked beaks,
                    then fly up
in the nick of time

                    *

The idiot gathered her aprons
from the clothes line   The
wind shaking the sumac,
planted for an 18th birthday,
breaks the red plumes

Crack   (The burned
letters of the alphabet)
We wake hurt,
the sight of ourselves too much
the pattern

Wake up! The birds dive at the trees,
true enemies of their shapes

Awake   Sophia Nichols says

*we are using all this electricity which
escapes upward, gathering to destroy
the world*

Telephone   'Many happy returns'   (true
turns of the light, she meant)

                    *

(Tincans smashed around the heels of our shoes
    High heels

(Bill took out the atlas and began to divide
    the world between us   General William Halley
England, the Americas, Russia   he used his

own name, so I kept mine, but added Duc of
Orleans because I held France, China and Africa

(We gave the imaginary kingdoms to the late
   comers   Mu, Atlantis, the Arctics

(Then I held power in a vacant lot where I
   built a tunnel dedicated to their sex play

(Then I built a tunnel in a vacant lot dedicated
   to history

(where their sex play held power

                    *

The oath between us
for 1 hour
          to see
nothing that did not appear
in the water

The male womb here caught up
in the beloved sight,
passes quickly over the surface,
darkens among the water plants,
the goldfish more golden
                    but 'you'
will form in
          the bell
          We timed
this oath

                    *

From a high shelf
above the books of pedigree
the clock chimes

Someone called out
against this photographic proof
of ancestors

A flight of sparrows
suddenly drops into a nearby tree
disappearing, though its shape
darkens

*a sudden or violent display (of joy,
    delight, etc.*

Jessie Whitehead told me they sometimes choose a tree
and kill it, they so mire the branches

The Faerie Queene

AN APPEARANCE

Okay   A nightingale
does sing
                outside this window

A mirror of leaves and noise

                This monument
has torn to pieces our guide book
of facts
                This startles

A nightingale,
                the bird so ancient
he (anybody)
                falls back
on his dusty shoes, pointing

The event darkens   So like
our trembling,
                we caught at it
breaking the skin

METAMORPHOSES

I burn 'your' magnificence in the streets
It is paper

The gods written on paper flare up
suddenly
                in a turn taken up the alley

I turn away from the stars,
roll over,
                it is that falls out of my eye
a pearl of great price
                no tear

The same with the flakes of mica,
                              desiring
the tree stands before me of what name

SO

You speak against the mundane
which is for instance
the sidewalk

and, I suspect, the gods
severed and loose
like architectural adornments

The word means
                    worldly
but requiring the mundus

Gloria Swanson used one image to reappear
in the imagination
                    the claw,
and Garbo chose white to show that death
works at the convenience of the lady of the
camellias, thus saving Robert Taylor for
later movies — in white flannels, the college
hero out on the town
                         I suppose you think the
plots were about Norma Desmond and Mme. Gautier

You missed the structure they personified

where Dionysus lay sleeping against
the corner stone

the wall broke into pieces of glass

Again and again

I saw myself about to wake him

FROM A FORTUNE-COOKY

He is practicing a speech before the glass

There is a slight wind
bitter on the tongue
An image trembles
or floats as in water

The dismemberment happens
like rain against the sidewalk

What rules
is a twist of light

In the arms of these railroads,
no music
                  discovers us

THE SPHINX

A honk and broken sounds

Rain spills lights
against the window
They have a brief life
of their own

faced into

A rayed machine is before me
devouring my labor   This much,
a dream wherein I read the next morning
that many carry the wands

I am to ask a question
where no question exists

Who stops among the leaves
of this tree I'm married to
in Roman fashion?
                        I piss
into the roots of my love
where words break true

FOR GUSTAVE MOREAU

The streets are my body
or rather the wish
of the skin to put on
the grass in a gold rain

not vice-versa,
the lips twisting to allow
the tongue to play in
the broken mirror on the floor

Catches an arm
a distance
            the light
at the ceiling
                This kills
the lift begged
of a magical hand

I have walked a long way
traced in these pieces
an arm
a crotch   The queen
of faerie guarded
by blue winged griffins
Untouched by

Sophia Nichols

SOPHIA NICHOLS

the wind hits and returns   it is easy to personify
a new place and language,   but the new body stings

these men with green eyelids, drawing their worth,
it was rumored, from Egypt, knew

the work is part of it   a power arrived at the
same thirst

                he borrowed a head for a day

but which head   the phrases tremble in the other
mouth   It is true and false   the veil of her face,

an old porcelain, not for the hand to comfort   she
moved beyond the sop one gave for affection   'My

success has been to keep duty and love alive' she said
her hand waved with the power of disease   Sophia

Nichols of the orchards, the deserts, the flooded
ponds and games wherein the moon sought our feet

died with a mouth full of tumor   it is true and
false   the moon flowers (that is Blake talking)

tonight it is the half blossom and the stars too
above this mud are from the other mouth   this city

untouched   the streets, Hotel Lyric have a foreignness,
a place outside a window   a sound of bees pulling

the lilac   above cement this wonder   (the other mouth)
that crickets were men once who so loved the muses they

forgot to eat   now fed on thistles, the language must
sting   the flesh turn to a dew (the other mouth) the

loss, some glistening blood on the leaves of the mirror
plant   Sophia Nichols of the story, the golden rod,

of the snake that entered the cage and ate the captured
sparrows, the telegraph keys, pale yellow paper,   of

the Odyssey and the homing stories of the soul,   the sea
imaginary, light and foaming green on the rocks,   dark

further out as the eyes of the cat
                              if she would be
free from words, she would free me   even in the night
there are birds summoned by words

GRAY BURR

The Butterfly

Tracer of wind's contour by line of flight,
His weightless leaves of color caper in air.
How rootlessly his color grew wings' flair:
You've seen him shut

And open and shut in slow winks on a twig
Or a cannon where he can most thoroughly please
By irony our taut taste for antitheses.
For he's not big

And, soundless, opposes the burly and loud. When
Children fish him from blue air he shapes
By crisp of wing, their love, like ours, is perhaps
Too crude to plan

Fit action for its object. He can't last
Without a sting. But now his jerking yellows
Puppet the eye in the wind's blue shallows
And purely contrast

The dull arrest of things. He is a locus
Of precision's myth in whose dissolving change
The worm climbs wind and we the range
Of all our focus.

A Glance at the Album

I saw only the edge
Of a photograph peeping out
Of the album: as if a ledge
Had given way in the mind,
Back, back, I fell,
Clutching the living-room air,
Down the years' well
To a beach of childhood where
I surprised the lovers behind
Big umbrellas, and buried

Their scowls and bribes in the sand.
(Perhaps they all got married).
Back to the left land
And bit of unfinished picture
Where little would go as planned.
No art or other stricture
Could order it into a game.
It was a wild unreeling;
Neither an unmixed pleasure
Nor without effect and feeling.
And this photo represents
A time when a kind presence
Let the heart rest a measure
Before what was coming came.

Garden Puzzle

The window-screen sifts the blue cumulus
From my cigarette.
I sit and ponder the big synthesis but the answer
I just forget.

Constellated at my feet newspapers pepper
And salt the truth
I taste in them nevertheless as I squirm and shift
From the rage to the ruth

Of the somewhat helpless who is and who is not
Quite able
To say "Just kill the witches and you'll be a lot
More comfortable."

And against much advice I read in the Bible
A love-lorn column
With wish then to use such passion and scruple without
Getting solemn

And queasy, but can't do it, and the mixed-up
Jig-saw
Puzzle cut from the Garden and scattered in a world
For the cats-paw

Mankind to put together in the pain of its truth
Stays shining
More dear, derelict, strict though asunder
Than all our repining

Has learned. I must hope that solution mankindled
May find breath
Wiser than any we know if the solving's a matter
For life, not death.

The Epistemological Rag

The world turns and its turning wheels
In sprocket with the chain of years.
The Dipper falls and disappears
Behind the mountain as it reels.

The plane of the ecliptic rides
Through all the signs of Zodiac.
Orion hunts and Cygnus hides.
Hunter and hunted won't be back.

In fusions of their furnaces
The supernovae forge new planets,
Byproducing universes,
Heavy elements and granites.

Hominids are somewhere breathing
Methane, argon, other gases;
Ecologically teething
Atoms gather to new masses.

What does it all mean to humans,
Men and women, you and me?
Are we really catechumens?
Our first text this galaxy?

Must we try to piece it all out
With new math and heavy taxes
While our dunces juggle fall-out
And the earth slows on its axis?

Saints and devils short-cut mystery.
For the rest it's grope and die.
Though we can't predict our history,
We have got to make it. Why?

Otherwise there is no moral
Save that time becomes the hero,
Man a fancy, earth a coral,
Dualism double zero.

A Play of Opposites

PHILOCOSMOS: Outside my blind a bird lit in a tree.
    The tree, an aspen, mobilized the light
    And half-concealed the bird I wished to see.
    I ran to get my glasses from the closet.
    When I returned, that bird had taken flight.
    What kind it was my mind can only posit.
    Already it takes on the quality
    Of something outlined, like the world at night.

MUSOPHILUS: It was neither robin, finch, nor crow
    Nor phoenix either, though it almost seems
    To share the latter's will to come and go,
    To be and not to be, to baffle, tease
    The mind's concreteness with the shapes of dreams.
    This bird nests only in uncertainties;
    Your role is played out in the passing show.
    It is my mummeries the bird esteems.

PHILOCOSMOS: What rot you talk. I'll catch the creature yet
    In gin or snare or glass, with net or gun.
    Its song was magical, and, as a pet
    That bird would be a conversation piece.
    I'll teach it what to say. It would be fun
    And could, with proper handling, bring in fees.

MUSOPHILUS: Your world's already rather in its debt.

PHILOCOSMOS: I'd talk the game down if I hadn't won.

MUSOPHILUS: I know you think you've had the final word,
    But I believe it's just the last thing said.
    Well, go ahead, and try to catch the bird.
    You've often tried before, if you but knew it.
    The squawks and screeches coming from your head
    Make plain to everyone how well you do it.

PHILOCOSMOS: I've taken everything winged, finned, or furred.

MUSOPHILUS: But everyplace you hunt, this bird is fled.

PHILOCOSMOS: I'll get it if I have to buy the earth;
    Or conquering the place will do as well.
    I set the price of death, the trap of birth.
    I think you underestimate my powers.

MUSOPHILUS: Oh, no. Orpheus sang his best in hell.
    You'll have your moments, perhaps even hours,
    But only time will pay the bird's true worth.
    By then your world will be a cracked egg-shell.

PHILOCOSMOS: A dismal prospect for a man of action.
    I have no time to waste on mysteries.
    I round my numbers to the nearest fraction.
    Your nice perceptions bore me half to death.
    You'll never see the forest for the trees.
    For every sigh you heave, I'll sell you breath
    And dearly, too. Be wise, and join my faction.
    A bird that I can't see will starve and freeze.

MUSOPHILUS: You were its subject once, and patron, too,
    But, as you say, the times have changed a lot.
    Our talk, at least, has driven home to you
    The fact that your new interests lie elsewhere.
    Your character cannot resolve the plot,
    Though your one part may leave our theme threadbare.
    Despite your guns and drums and hullabaloo,
    There is no luck out there beyond earshot.

A Skater's Waltz

There was a pond on which we learned to skate,
Where the blades flashed like sabres, and the ice,
Scored and carved as an old dinner-plate,
Lay locked within its shores as in a vise.

How different we all were; how much the same.
Do you remember Speed, the hockey ace,
Who shuttled stick and puck to early fame?
Not one of us could skate to match his pace.

And there was Flora, queen of pirouette,
Who wore such scimitars upon her feet
And whirled her skirt to flowers; oh, well met,
Flora, lovely Flora, light and fleet.

Hand in hand, the couples zigged and zagged
And had their ups and downs; the cut-ups fell
Most often, though bad holes were plainly flagged.
Still, anyone could trip and break the spell

That music made, and movement, in the mesh
Of skaters shifting, threading warp and woof.
Oh tapestry of heart and mind and flesh,
We all were skeins in you; yet one, aloof,

Hung from the general scene, our loosest end,
A mystery and reproach to naiveté.
You'd meet him coming round the sharpest bend,
Racing against the crowd, another way.

Whistles shrilled in that well-ordered place
And he was often asked to leave the ice.
But when he'd gone, so also had some grace,
Some figure only he could improvise.

I think that if the god should pull that thread
A whole woven dream might fall apart.
It would, at least, be less. Arise, ye dead!
Remain, O Dionysian, in our heart.

Sailing, Sailing

It is the sea's edge lubbers love,
Where sand, the mirror, slurs their faces,
And the surf's smash completes the cove,
At least from an observer's basis.

Such people like the harbor's hull
That rides so steady in the swell
And never lists or pitches. Lull,
Not squall, for them, means sailing well.

But we have known some sailors who,
In a seaway mauled around,
Didn't dream of Malibu
Or catboats on Long Island Sound.

A lot of commodores in whites
Foundered on the yacht-club shoals
While Captain Slocum's riding lights
Danced a jig between the poles.

GREGORY CORSO

The Mad Yak

I am watching them churn the last milk
    they'll ever get from me.
They are waiting for me to die;
They want to make buttons out of my bones.
Where are my sisters and brothers?
That tall monk there, loading my uncle,
    he has a new cap.
And that idiot student of his —
    I never saw that muffler before.
Poor uncle, he lets them load him.
How sad he is, how tired!
I wonder what they'll do with his bones?
And that beautiful tail!
How many shoelaces will they make of that!

I am 25

With a love a madness for Shelley
Chatterton   Rimbaud
and the needy-yap of my youth
        has gone from ear to ear:
           I HATE OLD POETMEN!
Especially old poetmen who retract
who consult other old poetmen
who speak their youth in whispers,
saying:—I did those then
           but that was then
           that was then—
O I would quiet old men
say to them:—I am your friend
           what you once were, thru me
           you'll be again—
Then at night in the confidence of their homes
rip out their apology-tongues
           and steal their poems.

But I Do Not Need Kindness

I have known the strange nurses of Kindness,
I have seen them kiss the sick, attend the old,
give candy to the mad!
I have watched them, at night, dark and sad,
rolling wheelchairs by the sea!
I have known the fat pontiffs of Kindness,
the little old grey-haired lady,
the neighborhood priest,
the famous poet,
the mother,
I have known them all!
I have watched them, at night, dark and sad,
pasting posters of mercy
        on the stark posts of despair.

2

I have known Almighty Kindness Herself!
I have sat beside Her pure white feet,
gaining Her confidence!
We spoke of nothing unkind,
but one night I was tormented by those strange nurses,
those fat pontiffs
The little old lady rode a spiked car over my head!
The priest cut open my stomach, put his hands in me,
and cried:—Where's your soul? Where's your soul!—
The famous poet picked me up
and threw me out of the window!
The mother abandoned me!
I ran to Kindness, broke into Her chamber,
and profaned!
with an unnamable knife I gave Her a thousand wounds,
and inflicted them with filth!
I carried Her away, on my back, like a ghoul!
down the cobble-stoned night!
Dogs howled! Cats fled! All windows closed!
I carried Her ten flights of stairs!
Dropped Her on the floor of my small room,
and kneeling beside Her, I wept. I wept.

3

But what is Kindness? I have killed Kindness,
but what is it?
You are kind because you live a kind life.
St. Francis was kind.
The landlord is kind.
A cane is kind.
Can I say people, sitting in parks, are kinder?

Italian Extravaganza

Mrs. Lombardi's month-old son is dead.
I saw it in Rizzo's funeral parlor,
A small purplish wrinkled head.

They've just finished having high mass for it;
They're coming out now
. . . wow, such a small coffin!
And ten black cadillacs to haul it in.

The Last Warmth of Arnold

Arnold, warm with God,
hides beneath the porch
remembering the time of escape, imprisoned in Vermont,
shoveling snow. Arnold was from somewhere else,
where it was warm; where he wore suede shoes
and played ping-pong.
Arnold knew the Koran.
And he knew to sing:
        Young Julien Sorel
Knew his Latin well
And was wise as he
Was beautiful
Until his head fell.

In the empty atmosphere
Arnold kept a tiplet pigeon, a bag of chicken corn.
He thought of Eleanor, her hands;
watched her sit sad in school
He got Carmine to lure her into the warm atmosphere;

he wanted to kiss her, live with her forever;
break her head with bargains.

Who is Arnold? Well,
I first saw him wear a black cap
covered with old Willkie buttons. He was 13.
And afraid. But with a smile. And he was always
willing to walk you home, to meet your mother,
to tell her about Hester Street Park
about the cold bums there;
about the cold old Jewish ladies who sat,
hands folded, sad, keeping their faces
away from the old Jewish Home.
Arnold grew up with a knowledge of bookies
and chicken pluckers

And Arnold knew to sing:
    Dead now my 15th year
    F.D.R., whose smiling face
    Made evil the buck-toothed Imperialist,
    The moustached Aryan,
    The jut-jawed Caesar—
    Dead now, and I weep . . .
    For once I did hate that man
    and no reason
    but innocent hate
    —my cap decked with old Willkie buttons.

Arnold was kicked in the balls
by an Italian girl who got mad
because there was a big coal strike on
and it forced the Educational Alliance to close its doors.
Arnold, weak and dying, stole pennies from the library,
but he also read about Paderewski.
He used to walk along South Street
wondering about the various kinds of glue.
And it was about airplane glue he was thinking
when he fell and died beneath the Brooklyn Bridge.

ROBERT CREELEY

The House

(for Louis Zukofsky)

Mud put
upon mud,
lifted
to make room,

house
a cave,
and
colder night.

To sleep
in, live in,
to come in
from heat,

all form derived
from kind,
built
with that in mind.

Kore

As I was walking
    I came upon
chance walking
    the same road upon.

As I sat down
    by chance to move
later
    if and as I might,

light the wood was,
    light and green,
and what I saw
    before I had not seen.

It was a lady
    accompanied
by goat men
    leading her.

Her hair held earth.
    Her eyes were dark.
A double flute
    made her move.

"O love,
    where are you
leading
    me now?"

The Name

Be natural,
wise
as you can be,
my daughter,

let my name
be in you flesh
I gave you
in the act of

loving your mother,
all your days
her ways,
the woman in you

brought from
sensuality's measure,
no other,
there was no thought

of it but such
pleasure all women
must be in her,
as you. But not wiser,

not more of nature
than her hair,
the eyes
she gives you.

There will not be another
woman such as you
are. Remember
your mother,

the way you came,
the days of waiting.
Be natural,
daughter, wise

as you can be,
all my daughters,
be women
for men

when that time comes.
Let the rhetoric
stay with me
your father. Let

me talk about it,
saving you such
vicious self-
exposure, let you

pass it on
in you. I cannot
be more than the man
who watches.

I Know a Man

As I sd to my
friend, because I am
always talking, — John, I

sd, which was not his
name, the darkness sur-
rounds us, what

can we do against
it, or else, shall we &
why not, buy a goddamn big car,

drive, he sd, for
christ's sake, look
out where yr going.

The Rhythm

It is all a rhythm,
from the shutting
door, to the window
opening,

the seasons, the sun's
light, the moon,
the oceans, the
growing of things,

the mind in men
personal, recurring
in them again,
thinking the end

is not the end, the
time returning,
themselves dead but
someone else coming.

If in death I am dead,
then in life also
dying, dying . . .
And the women cry and die.

The little children
grow only to old men.
The grass dries,
the force goes.

But is met by another
returning, oh not mine,
not mine, and
in turn dies.

The rhythm which projects
from itself continuity
bending all to its force
from window to door,
from ceiling to floor,
light at the opening,
dark at the closing.

The Mountains in the Desert

The mountains blue now
at the back of my head,
such geography of self and soul
brought to such limit of sight,

I cannot relieve it
nor leave it, my mind locked
in seeing it
as the light fades.

Tonight let me go
at last out of whatever
mind I thought to have,
and all the habits of it.

The Language

Locate *I*
love you some-
where in

teeth and
eyes, bite
it but

take care not
to hurt, you
want so

much so
little. Words
say everything,

I
love you
again,

then what
is emptiness
for. To

fill, fill.
I heard words
and words full

of holes
aching. Speech
is a mouth.

Anger

The time is.
The air seems a cover,
the room is quiet.

She moves, she
had moved. He
heard her.

The children
sleep, the dog fed,
the house around them

is open, descriptive,
a truck through the walls,
lights bright there,

glaring, the sudden
roar of its motor, all
familiar impact

as it passed
so close. He
hated it.

But what does she answer.
She moves
away from it.

In all they save,
in the way of his saving
the clutter, the accumulation

of the expected disorder —
as if each dirtiness,
each blot, blurred

happily, gave
purpose, happily —
she is not enough there.

He is angry. His
face grows — as if
a moon rose

of black light,
convulsively darkening,
as if life were black.

It is black.
It is an open
hole of horror, of

nothing as if not
enough there is
nothing. A pit —

which he recognizes,
familiar, sees
the use in, a hole

for anger and
fills it
with himself,

yet watches on
the edge of it,
as if she were

not to be pulled in,
a hand could
stop him. Then

as the shouting
grows and grows
louder and louder

with spaces
of the same open
silence, the darkness,

in and out, him-
self between them,
stands empty and

holding out his
hands to both,
now screaming

it cannot be
the same, she
waits in the one

while the other
moans in the hole
in the floor, in the wall.

2

Is there some odor
which is anger,

a face
which is rage.

I think I think
but find myself in it.

The pattern
is only resemblance.

I cannot see myself
but as what I see, an

object but a man
with lust for forgiveness,

raging, from that vantage,
secure in the purpose,

double, split.
Is it merely intention,

a sign quickly adapted,
shifted to make

a horrible place
for self-satisfaction.

I rage.
I rage, I rage.

3

You did it,
and didn't want to,

and it was simple.
You were not involved,

even if your head was cut off,
or each finger

twisted
from its shape until it broke,

and you screamed too
with the other, in pleasure.

4

Face me,
in the dark,
my face. See me.

It is the cry
I hear all
my life, my own

voice, my
eye locked in
self sight, not

the world what
ever it is
but the close

breathing beside
me I reach out
for, feel as

warmth in
my hands then
returned. The rage

is what I
want, what
I cannot give

to myself, of
myself, in
the world.

5

After, what
is it — as if
the sun had

been wrong to return,
again. It was
another life, a

day, some
time gone, it
was done.

But also
the pleasure, the
opening

relief
even in what
was so hated.

6

All you say you want
to do to yourself you do
to someone else as yourself

and we sit between you
waiting for whatever will
be at last the real end of you.

Distance

1

Hadn't I been
aching, for you,
seeing the

light there, such
shape as
it makes.

The bodies
fall, have
fallen, open.

Isn't it such
a form one
wants, the warmth

as sun
light on you.
But what

were you, where,
one thought, I
was always

thinking. The
mind itself,
impulse, of form

last realized,
nothing
otherwise but

a stumbling
looking after, a
picture

of light through
dust on
an indeterminate distance,

which throws
a radiator into
edges, shining,

the woman's long
length, the move-
ment of the

child, on her,
their legs
from behind.

2

Eyes,
days and
forms' photograph,

glazed
eyes, dear
hands. We

are walking.
I have
a face grown

hairy
and old, it
has greyed

to white
on the sides
of my cheeks. Stepping

out of
the car with these
endless people,

where are
you, am I happy,
is this car

mine. Another
life comes to
its presence,

here, you
sluffing, beside
me, me off, my-

self's warmth
gone inward,
a stepping

car, walking
waters on, such
a place like the

size of great
breasts, warmth and
moisture, come

forward, waking
to that edge
of the silence.

3

The falling back
from as in
love, or

casual friend-
ship, "I am so
happy, to

meet you—" These
meetings, it is
meet

we right (write)
to one another,
the slip-

shod, half-
felt, heart's
uneasinesses in

particular
forms, waking to
a body felt

as a hand pushed
between the long
legs. Is this

only the form,
"Your face
is unknown to me

but the hair, the
springing hair there
despite the rift,

the cleft,
between us, is
known, my own—"

What have *they*
done to me, who
are they coming

to me on such
informed feet, with
such substance of forms,

pushing
the flesh aside,
step in-

to my own,
my longing
for them.

PETER DAVISON

North Shore

(For Charles Hopkinson)

1. THE EMBARKATION FOR CYTHEREA

The sun is high. Young Saxons shouldering oars
Trample the shaven lawn. Platoons of girls
In organdied profusion follow them.
Flowers of Boston's bright virginity,
Cool limbs beneath frail garments. At the pier,
Piled high with picnic baskets, cutters ride
The hospitable swell, their halyards eased
Yet eager to spread sail. Across the strait
The islands rise like rain-clouds from the sea.
Here on our hill the house, after its crowded morning,
Will sleep till dusk. Then we expect them home,
Their wine all drunk, their faces gorged with sun,
Guiding their ships with briny headsails furled,
To quiet moorings.

2. THE RETURN

                    Many years have passed.
The house and I still wait for their return.
Shutters keep out the sun, chairs lie in shrouds,
The Chinese vases rattle with dry leaves.
Angry with age, but waiting, I keep watch
High in the eastern wing, my spyglass cocked
To sight the flicker of those homeward sails.
Perhaps they are all dead? I have not heard
A youthful voice for years. When will they come?
The sea still glimmers, empty of islands now.
The lawns are empty. Over the weathered house
Gulls hover, wailing their disdainful cry.
At night the house is silent, and the wind
Steals out each dawn to comb a barren sea.

FINALE: PRESTO

"I think I'm going to die," I tried to say.
My husband, standing over the bed, labored
To hear words in the sounds as they emerged.
He shook his head as briskly as a dog
Taking its first steps on land, and acted deaf
To the words he knew he might have heard me speak.
Throughout this evil month I've said the same
To every visitor. It comes out gibberish.
The night nurse, hiding in my room to smoke,
My daughter, prattling anxiously of clothes,
My son, weary from four hundred miles
Of travel every weekend — all escape
By smiling, talking, plumping up my pillows.
I wrack myself to utter any word;
They reply, "Dear, I cannot understand you."
If I could move this hand, this leg, I'd write
Or stamp a fury on the sterile floor.
I'd act the eagle, I, who winced at death
If the neighbor's second cousin passed at ninety,
Who bore an ounce of pain so awkwardly
It might have been a ton, who fed myself
With visions of good order in a future
Near enough to reach for — I am cumbered
With armlessness, with leglessness, with silence.
To say the word so anyone could hear it!
Death, do you hear me, death? The room is empty.
Only the one word now, hearers or no.
I batter at it with convulsive shouts
That resonate like lead. Again. And now —
Listen — it rings out like a miracle.
No one stands near. The corridor is dark.
"Death." I sing the lovely word again,
And footsteps start to chatter down the hall
Towards my bed. Smiling at every sound,
I see that no one can arrive in time,
And I, emptying like water from a jug,
Will be poured out before a hand can right me.
That word raised echoes of a halleluia.
Death, do you hear me singing in your key?

The Breaking of the Day

> (Genesis 32: 24–30)

1. JULY

The afternoon is dark and not with rain.
Intent on conquest, the sun presses its attack
Harder as the blunt day closes in.
Swallows like knives carve at the thickening air.

I swab the sweat from my blistering hide and walk
Burnt, unblessed, my brain inert as alum.
I stagger beneath the weight of the day
Like a three-legged dog howling curses at the climate
Until, defeated by the weather's bludgeon,
I lift my hands to half a god
And stammer out a portion of a prayer.

2. THE BIRTHRIGHT

A half-and-half affair, I grew from the union
Of a buxom, vital, Titian-haired New Yorker
And the cockerel moodiness of a Tyneside orphan.
She in the gabble of upper-West-Side tea dances,
Looked feverish when her father, the cotton merchant,
Stumped off to synagogue to pray for his brothers' funerals.
Later, she chose not to explain to me the difference
Between the Talmud and the Pentateuch,
And I, unlearned in the ways of Shabbas and Seder,
Had to read them up later in the works of Wouk.
Not until I got to be thirteen
Did it cross my mind I might be half a Jew,
And not until a malicious schoolmate told me:
I heard the malice rising in his voice.

To take a step backward, look once more at my father,
Who never saw a Jew till he was twenty.
Sweet-voiced, he was made much of by the Rector
As he raised his boy soprano at St. Simon's
And learned his Apostles' Creed and Cathechism.
For him a Jewess was rich with secret knowledge
And raven-haired — he'd read Scott and Disraeli.
Jews, on the other hand, were money-lenders.

When the schoolboy told me of my being Jewish
I asked my parents: was he telling truth?
My mother said that they had *meant* to tell me.
My father said that it didn't really matter
Because I was Anglican by half.
The question I had asked was left unanswered
And all the knowledge that I got for asking
Was learning that they had no wish to answer
And that my questions led to other questions.

3. THE WRESTLER

Breath knocked out under Elm Street's summer,
Fastened by the skewer of despair in a hotel room,
Steeling under anger and lust, the leers of the sergeants,
The desperate passionless grab of Kansas cunts,
Bound hand and foot on a tufted counterpane,
I lay in prison while the night air hardened.
This was my shave-pate vigil, stiff as glass.

God burst in at last with the cry of a prairie rooster,
And in the darkness my heart began again.
My limbs were kindled with a course of blood,
And I shot from my prison into the sunrise streets
To trudge for miles while I turned a new weight in my hands:
Cherished sin, to carry for my burden —
Mine for my charge, my signal, my evermore mark,
That a single touch had bestowed, and not of my choosing.

After sunrise came the shock of daylight:
To grapple with my sinfulness I must
Put God in words. The only words I knew
Were those that God had spoken in His books,
The books that England had prepared for Him.

4. THE GIFT OF TONGUES

God my father spoke in the calm of evening.
He spoke in iambs beating in the darkness.
His pipe glowed and its vapor blossomed upward.
The child at his feet drank in the heady honey
Of his voice, his presence, his attention
While the elm-leaves rustled their assent.
The words he spoke — from Oreb or from Sinai —

Were, had I known it, many times outworn
Except for those that burned as his alone:

> I shall come back to die
> From a far place at last,
> After my life's carouse
> In the old bed to lie
> Remembering the past
> In this dark house.

His voice wore all the costumes of our tongue,
And in the dark I trembled at the golden
Din of the past resounding in my ears.
These were the words that God had always spoken,
As, "This is my beloved Son, in whom
I am well pleased." The words belonged to him,
And now, as their custodian, he gave
His hoard to me at night beneath the trees.
I counted them for years before I learned
The spending of them: yet I did not know
That he had given them away for good
And that from that night forward he would walk
The earth like any natural man,
His powers incomplete, his magic gone.

5. THE SALT LAND

After baptisms, confessions, confirmations,
Communions by the dozen, rites and choirs,
Cranmer's great book was absorbed into my bloodstream,
And all the words turned into words again.
The fish died while I stood before the Cross:
Christ's blood, they said, was infinitely precious,
But all I knew of it was that they said so.

Later still I watched my mother's mother
(She wept because she must outlive her daughter)
Being interred at a non-religious funeral
With a eulogy delivered by her doctor
At a Lexington Avenue mortician's chapel.
This was the end. The Jewesses were dead.
My female life-line was extinguished.

6. THE DEAD SEA

Shore people worshipped, we are told, the Mother
In preference to the Horseman, Father, Poseidon.
My gods were naked. He was wrinkled, massive,
Bearded, with eyes that gleamed in wrath or kindness;
She, mother-sister, of an unloosing softness,
Had breasts that flowed with all I knew of bounty.

The womb that held me in its lake is dry,
The bounty parched and powdered. He that held
A weapon or a sceptre or a cross
Has lost the good of his grasp and sits in silence,
Who took it on himself to shake the earth.

Mother Jew, you gave me an endearment
For my inheritance, but hid your race away,
Withholding what I had to learn to want.
You, mother, rocked me bloodless in my cradle
And yearned to free me from my ancestors:
The womb of the Goddess denied she had been born.

My Father Christian never knew his father
And had to fashion sceptres for himself.

So both were outcasts from their ancestry.
No offerings for them, no worshippers —
Except for me, who worshipped in myself
Crude copies of their skilled originals,
To find at last, on the baked earth of this shrine,
That I am no more Christian, no more Jew.

The afternoon is dark and now with rain.

7. DELPHI

The crackle of parched grass bent by wind
Is the only music in the grove
Except the gush of the Pierian Spring.
Eagles are often seen, but through a glass
Their naked necks declare them to be vultures.
The place is sacred with a sanctity
Now faded, like a kerchief washed too often.
There lies the crevice where the priestesses
Hid in the crypt and drugged themselves and spoke

Until in later years the ruling powers
Bribed them to prophesy what was desired.
Till then the Greeks took pride in hopelessness
And, though they sometimes wrestled with their gods,
They never won a blessing or a name
But only knowledge.

                    I shall never know myself
Enough to know what things I half believe
And, half believing, only half deny.

JAMES DICKEY

The Lifeguard

In a stable of boats I lie still,
From all sleeping children hidden.
The leap of a fish from its shadow
Makes the whole lake instantly tremble.
With my foot on the water, I feel
The moon outside

Take on the utmost of its power.
I rise and go out through the boats.
I set my broad sole upon silver,
On the skin of the sky, on the moonlight,
Stepping outward from earth onto water
In quest of the miracle

This village of children believed
That I could perform as I dived
For one who had sunk from my sight.
I saw his cropped haircut go under.
I leapt, and my steep body flashed
Once, in the sun.

Dark drew all the light from my eyes.
Like a man who explores his death
By the pull of his slow-moving shoulders,
I hung head down in the cold,
Wide-eyed, contained, and alone
Among the weeds,

And my fingertips turned into stone
From clutching immovable blackness.
Time after time I leapt upward
Exploding in breath, and fell back
From the change in the children's faces
At my defeat.

Beneath them I swam to the boathouse
With only my life in my arms
To wait for the lake to shine back

At the risen moon with such power
That my steps on the light of the ripples
Might be sustained.

Beneath me is nothing but brightness
Like the ghost of a snowfield in summer.
As I move toward the center of the lake,
Which is also the center of the moon,
I am thinking of how I may be
The savior of one

Who has already died in my care.
The dark trees fade from around me.
The moon's dust hovers together.
I call softly out, and the child's
Voice answers through blinding water.
Patiently, slowly,

He rises, dilating to break
The surface of stone with his forehead.
He is one I do not remember
Having ever seen in his life.
The ground I stand on is trembling
Upon his smile.

I wash the black mud from my hands.
On a light given off by the grave
I kneel in the quick of the moon
At the heart of a distant forest
And hold in my arms a child
Of water, water, water.

The Owl King

I. THE CALL

Through the trees, with the moon underfoot,
More soft than I can, I call.
I hear the king of the owls sing
Where he moves with my son in the gloom.
My tongue floats off in the darkness.
I feel the deep dead turn
My blind child round toward my calling,
Through the trees, with the moon underfoot,

In a sound I cannot remember.
It whispers like straw in my ear,
And shakes like a stone under water.
My bones stand on tiptoe inside it.
Which part of the sound did I utter?
Is it song, or is half of it whistling?
What spirit has swallowed my tongue?
Or is it a sound I remember?

And yet it is coming back,
Having gone, adrift on its spirit,
Down, over and under the river,
And stood in a ring in a meadow
Round a child with a bird gravely dancing.
I hear the king of the owls sing.
I did not awaken that sound,
And yet it is coming back,

In touching every tree upon the hill.
The breath falls out of my voice,
And yet the singing keeps on.
The owls are dancing, fastened by their toes
Upon the pines. Come, son, and find me here,
In love with the sound of my voice.
Come calling the same soft song,
And touching every tree upon the hill.

II. THE OWL KING

I swore to myself I would see
When all but my seeing had failed.
Every light was too feeble to show
My world as I knew it must be.
At the top of the staring night
I sat on the oak in my shape
With my claws growing deep into wood
And my sight going slowly out
Inch by inch, as into a stone,
Disclosing the rabbits running
Beneath my bent, growing throne,
And the foxes lighting their hair,
And the serpent taking the shape
Of the stream of life as it slept.
When I thought of the floating sound

In which my wings would outspread,
I felt the hooked tufts on my head
Enlarge, and dream like a crown,
And my voice unplaceable grow
Like a feathery sigh;
I could not place it myself.
For years I humped on the tree
Whose leaves held the sun and the moon.
At last I opened my eyes
In the sun, and saw nothing there.
That night I parted my lids
Once more, and saw dark burn
Greater than sunlight or moonlight,
For it burned from deep within me.
The still wood glowed like a brain.
I prised up my claws, and spread
My huge, ashen wings from my body,
For I heard what I listened to hear.
Someone spoke to me out of the distance
In a voice like my own, but softer.
I rose like the moon from the branch.

Through trees at his light touch trembling
The blind child drifted to meet me,
His blue eyes shining like mine.
In a ragged clearing he stopped,
And I circled, beating above him,
Then fell to the ground and hopped
Forward, taking his hand in my claw.
Every tree's life lived in his fingers.
Gravely we trod with each other
As beasts at their own wedding, dance.
Through the forest, the questioning voice
Of his father came to us there,
As though the one voice of us both,
Its high, frightened sound becoming
A perfect, irrelevant music
In which we profoundly moved,
I in the innermost shining
Of my blazing, invented eyes,
And he in the total of dark.
Each night, now, high on the oak,
With his father calling like music,
He sits with me here on the bough,

His eyes inch by inch going forward
Through stone dark, burning and picking
The creatures out one by one,
Each waiting alive in its own
Peculiar light to be found:
The mouse in its bundle of terror,
The fox in the flame of its hair,
And the snake in the form of all life.
Each night he returns to his bed,
To the voice of his singing father,
To dream of the owl king sitting
Alone in the crown of my will.
In my ruling passion, he rests.
All dark shall come to light.

III. THE BLIND CHILD'S STORY

I am playing going down
In my weight lightly,
Down, down the hill.
No one calls me
Out of the air.
The heat is falling
On the backs of my hands
And holding coldness.
They say it shines two ways.
The darkness is great
And luminous in my eyes.
Down I am quickly going;
A leaf falls on me,
It must be a leaf I hear it
Be thin against me, and now
The ground is level,
It moves it is not ground,
My feet flow cold
And wet, and water rushes
Past as I climb out.
I am there, on the other side.
I own the entire world.

It closes a little; the sky
Must be cold, must be giving off
Creatures that stand here.
I say they shine one way.

Trees they are trees around me,
Leaves branches and bark;
I can touch them all; I move
From one to another — someone said
I seem to be blessing them.
I am blessing them
Slowly, one after another
Deeper into the wood.

The dark is changing,
Its living is packed in closer
Overhead — more trees and leaves —
Tremendous. It touches
Something touches my hand,
Smelling it, a cold nose
Of breath, an ear of silk
Is gone. It is here I begin
To call to something unearthly.
Something is here, something before
Me sitting above me
In the wood in a crown,
Its eyes newborn in its head
From the death of the sun.
I can hear it rising on wings.
I hear that fluttering
Cease, and become
Pure soundless dancing
Like leaves not leaves;
Now down out of air
It lumbers to meet me,
Stepping oddly on earth,
Awkwardly, royally.
My father is calling

Through the touched trees;
All distance is weeping and singing.
In my hand I feel
A talon, a grandfather's claw
Bone cold and straining
To keep from breaking my skin.
I know this step, I know it,
And we are deep inside.
My father's voice is over
And under us, sighing.

Nothing is strange where we are.
The huge bird bows and returns,
For I, too, have done the same
As he leads me, rustling,
A pile of leaves in my hands;
The dry feathers shuffle like cards
On his dusty shoulders,
Not touching a tree,
Not brushing the side of a leaf
Or a point of grass.

We stop and stand like bushes.
But my father's music comes
In, goes on, comes in,
Into the wood,
Into the ceased dance.
And now the hard beak whispers
Softly, and we climb
Some steps of bark
Living and climbing with us
Into the leaves.
I sit among the leaves,
And the whole branch hums
With the owl's full, weightless power
As he closes his feet on the wood.
My own feet dangle
And tingle down;
My head is pointing
Deep into moonlight,
Deep into branches and leaves,
Directing my blackness there,
The personal dark of my sight,
And now it is turning a color.
My eyes are blue at last.

Something within the place
I look is piled and coiled.
It lifts its head from itself.
Its form is lit, and gives back
What my eyes are giving it freely.
I learn from the master of sight
What to do when the sun is dead,
How to make the great darkness work
As it wants of itself to work.

I feel the tree where we sit
Grow under me, and live.
I may have been here for years;
In the coil, the heaped-up creature
May have taken that long to lift
His head, to break his tongue
From his thin lips,
But he is there. I shut my eyes
And my eyes are gold,
As gold as an owl's,
As gold as a king's.
I open them. Farther off,
Beyond the swaying serpent,
A creature is burning itself
In a smoke of hair through the bushes.
The fox moves; a small thing
Being caught, cries out,
And I understand
How beings and sounds go together;
I understand
The voice of my singing father.
I shall be king of the wood.

Our double throne shall grow
Forever, until I see
The self of every substance
As it crouches, hidden and free.
The owl's face runs with tears
As I take him in my arms
In the glow of original light
Of Heaven. I go down
In my weight lightly down
The tree, and now
Through the soul of the wood
I walk in consuming glory
Past the snake, the fox, and the mouse:
I see as the owl king sees,
By going in deeper than darkness.
The wood comes back in a light
It did not know it withheld,
And I can tell
By its breathing glow
Each tree on which I laid
My hands when I was blind.

I cross the cold-footed flowing,
The creek, a religious fire
Streaming my ankles away,
And climb through the slanted meadow.
My father cannot remember
That he ever lived in this house.
To himself he bays like a hound,
Entranced by the endless beauty
Of his grief-stricken singing and calling.
He is singing simply to moonlight,
Like a dog howling,
And it is holy song
Out of his mouth.
Father, I am coming,
I am here on my own;
I move as you sing,
As if it were Heaven.
It is Heaven. I am walking
To you and seeing
Where I walk home.
What I have touched, I see
With the dark of my blue eyes.
Far off, the owl king
Sings like my father, growing
In power. Father, I touch
Your face. I have not seen
My own, but it is yours.
I come, I advance,
I believe everything, I am here.

Drowning With Others

There are moments a man turns from us
Whom we have all known until now.
Upgathered, we watch him grow,
Unshipping his shoulder bones

Like human, everyday wings
That he has not ever used,
Releasing his hair from his brain,
A kingfisher's crest, confused

By the God-tilted light of Heaven.
His deep, window-watching smile
Comes closely upon us in waves,
And spreads, and now we are

At last within it, dancing.
Slowly we turn and shine
Upon what is holding us,
As under our feet he soars,

Struck dumb as the angel of Eden,
In wide, eye-opening rings.
Yet the hand on my shoulder fears
To feel my own wingblades spring,

To feel me sink slowly away
In my hair turned loose like a thought
Of a fisherbird dying in flight.
If I opened my arms, I could hear

Every shell in the sea find the word
It has tried to put into my mouth.
Broad flight would become of my dancing,
And I would obsess the whole sea,

But I keep rising and singing
With my last breath. Upon my back,
With his hand on my unborn wing,
A man rests easy as sunlight

Who has kept himself free of the forms
Of the deaf, down-soaring dead,
And me laid out and alive
For nothing at all, in his arms.

The Hospital Window

I have just come down from my father.
Higher and higher he lies
Above me in a blue light
Shed by a tinted window.
I drop through six white floors
And then step out onto pavement.

Still feeling my father ascend,
I start to cross the firm street,

My shoulder blades shining with all
The glass the huge building can raise.
Now I must turn round and face it,
And know his one pane from the others.

Each window possesses the sun
As though it burned there on a wick.
I wave, like a man catching fire.
All the deep-dyed windowpanes flash,
And, behind them, all the white rooms
They turn to the color of Heaven.

Ceremoniously, gravely, and weakly,
Dozens of pale hands are waving
Back, from inside their flames.
Yet one pure pane among these
Is the bright, erased blankness of nothing.
I know that my father is there,

In the shape of his death still living.
The traffic increases around me
Like a madness called down on my head.
The horns blast at me like shotguns,
And drivers lean out, driven crazy —
But now my propped-up father

Lifts his arm out of stillness at last.
The light from the window strikes me
And I turn as blue as a soul,
As the moment when I was born.
I am not afraid for my father —
Look! He is grinning; he is not

Afraid for my life, either,
As the wild engines stand at my knees
Shredding their gears and roaring,
And I hold each car in its place
For miles, inciting its horn
To blow down the walls of the world

That the dying may float without fear
In the bold blue gaze of my father.
Slowly I move to the sidewalk
With my pin-tingling hand half dead
At the end of my bloodless arm.
I carry it off in amazement,

High, still higher, still waving,
My recognized face fully mortal,
Yet not; not at all, in the pale,
Drained, otherworldly, stricken,
Created hue of stained glass.
I have just come down from my father.

EDWARD DORN

Sousa

Great brass bell of austerity
and the ghosts of old picnickers
ambling under the box-elder when the sobriety
was the drunkenness. John,

you child, you drumhead, there is no silence
you can't decapitate
and on forgotten places (the octagonal
stand, Windsor, Illinois, the only May Day
of my mind) the fresh breeze
and the summer dresses of girls once blew
but do not now. They blow instead at the backs
of our ears John,
under the piñon,
that foreign plant with arrogant southern smell.
I yearn for the box-elder and its beautiful
bug, the red striped and black-plated —
your specific insect, in the Sunday after noon.

Oh restore my northern madness
which no one values anymore and shun,
its uses, give them back their darkened instinct
(which I value no more) we are
dedicated to madness that's why I love you
Sousa, you semper fidelis maniac.

And the sweep
of your american arms
bring a single banging street in Nebraska
home, and your shock
when a trillion broads smile at you
their shocking laughter can be heard long after
the picnickers have gone home.

March us home through the spring rain
the belief, the relief
of occasion.

Your soft high flute and brass
remind me of a lost celebration I can't
quite remember,
in which I volunteered as conquerer:
the silence now stretches me
into sadness.

Come back into the street bells
and tin soldiers.

  * *

But there are no drums
no drums, loudness,
no poinsette shirts,
there is no warning, you won't recognize anyone.

Children and men in every way
milling, gathering daily, (those vacant eyes)
the bread lines of the deprived are here
Los Alamos, 1960, not Salinas
not Stockton.

Thus when mouths are opened,
waves of poison rain will fall, butterflies
do not fly up from any mouth in that area.

  * *

Let me go away,
shouting alone, laughing
to the air, Sousa be here
when the leaves wear
a blank radio green, for honoring without trim
or place.

 To dwell again in the hinterland
and take your phone,
play to the lovely eyed people in the field
on the hillside.

Hopeful, and kind
merrily and possible
(as my friend said, "Why can't it be
like this all the time?"
her arms spread out before her).

  * *

John Sousa you can't now
amuse a nation with colored drums
even with cymbals, their ears
have lifted the chalice of explosion
a glass of straight malice, and
we wander in Random in the alleys
of their longfaced towns taking
from their sickly mandibles handbills
summoning our joint spirits.

I sing Sousa.

The desire to disintegrate the Earth
is eccentric,
And away from centre
nothing more nor sizeable
nor science
nor ennobling
no purity, no endeavor
toward human grace.

               *   *

We were
on a prominence though
so lovely to the eye eyes
of birds only caught
all the differences
of each house filled hill.

And from the window a spire
of poplar, windows
and brown pater earth buildings.

My eye on the circling bird
my mind lost in the rainy hemlocks of Washington
the body displaced, let it
wander all the way to Random and dwell
in those damp groves
where stand the friends
I love and left: behind me
slumbering under the dark morning sky

are my few friends.

Oh, please
cut wood to warm them
and stalk never appearing animals

to warm them,
I hope they are warm tonight —
bring salmonberries
even pumpkinseed.

Sousa,
it can never be
as my friend said
"Why can't it be like this all the time?"
Her arms spread out before her
gauging the alarm,
(with that entablature)
and the triumph of a march
in which no one
is injured.

The Song

So light no one noticed
so lightly she could not care
or her deep dark eyes would have turned
saw I surmised in my fear
her walk was troubled for she tried
men's eyes with her grace,
her secret wave
with her fingers
had luck willed,
been real, been an ending to a life
of small tears.

            Thus days go by
and I stand knowing her hair
in my mind as a dark cloud, its presence
straying over the rim of a volcano
of desire, and I take something
so closed as a book
into the world where she is.

Our love.
Like a difficult memory lives and revisits
in certain dreams at night
or during days when I am tired
of the blight of the poorly tuned sounds
    of where I am, times

which make me beholden to please
the motions of those I talk with
eat with sleep with plead with
need. Concerning love
the first trace that slips to the ground
leaving all space above, into which one can enter
was mother? Lespuge is a figure
of dreamed wholeness, the form
is born of that desire
the whole swelling difficulty.

From Gloucester Out

It has all
come back today.
That memory for me is nothing
there ever was,
                    That man

so long,
when stretched out
and so bold
              on his ground
and so much
lonely anywhere.

*

But never to forget
                    that moment

when we came out of the tavern
and wandered through the carnival.
They were playing
the washington post march
but I mistook it for manhattan beach
for all around were the colored lights
of delirium
              to the left the boats
of Italians
and ahead of us, past the shoulders
of St. Peter, the magician of those fishermen

the bay
stood, and immediately is it the silent
inclined pole where tomorrow the young men

of this colony
so dangerous on the street
will fall harmlessly
into the water.

They are not the solid
but are the solidly built
citizens, and they are about us
as we walk across
                        the square
with their black provocative
women
slender, like whips of
sex in the sousa filled night.

Where edged
by that man in the music
of a transplanted time and
enough of drunkenness
to make you senseless of all
but virtue
            (there is never
no, there is never a small complaint)
(that all things shit poverty,
and Life, one wars on with
many embraces) oh it was a time that was perfect
but for my own hesitating
to know all I had not known.
Pure existence, even in the crowds
I love
will never be possible for me
even with the men I love
                        This is
the guilt
that kills me
            My adulterated presence

but please believe with all men
I love to be

*

That memory
of how he lay out
on the floor in his great length
and when morning came,
late,

we lingered
in the vastest of all cities
in this hemisphere
                    and all other movement
stopped, nowhere
else was there a stirring known to us

yet that morning I stood
by the window up 3 levels
and watched a game
of stick ball, thinking of going away,
and wondering what would befall that man
when he returned to his territory.
The street as you could guess
was thick with their running
and cars,
themselves, paid that activity
such respect I thought a ritual
in the truest sense,
where all time and all motion
part around the space of men
in that act
as does a river flow past
the large rock.

*

And he slept.
in the next room, waiting
in an outward slumber
                    for the time

we climbed into the car, accepting all things
from love, the currency of which is
parting, and glancing.

Then went
out of that city to jersey
where instantly we could not find our way
and the maze of the outlands west
starts that quick
where you may touch
your finger to liberty
and look so short a space
to the columnar bust
of New York

and know those people exist
as a speck in your own lonely heart
who will shortly depart,
taking a conveyance for the
radial stretches
past girls on corners
past drugstores, tired hesitant
creatures who I also love
in all their alienation were it not so
past all equipment of country side
to temporary homes
where the wash of sea and other
populations come
once more to whisper only one thing
for all people: a late and far-away
night yearning for
and when he gets there
I want him to stay away
from the taverns of familiarity
I want him to walk by the seashore alone
in all height
which is nothing more than
a mountain. Or the hailing of a mast
with big bright eyes.

So rushing,
            all the senses
come to him
as a swarm of golden bees
and their sting is the power
he uses as parts of
the oldest brain. He hears
the delicate thrush
of the water attacking
He hears the cries, falling gulls
and watches silently the gesture of grey
bygone people. He hears their cries
and messages, he never

ignores any sound.
As they come to him he places them
puts clothes upon them
and gives them their place
in their new explanation, there is never

a lost time, nor any inhabitant
of that time to go split by prisms or unplaced
and unattended,
                    that you may believe

is the breath he gives
the great already occurred and nightly beginning world.
So with the populace of his mind
you think his nights? are not
lonely. My God. Of his
loves, you know nothing and of his
false beginning
you can know nothing,
                        but this thing to be marked
again

        only

he who worships the gods with his strictness
can be of their company
the cat and the animals, the bird he took
from the radiator
of my car saying it had died
a natural death, rarely seen in a bird.

To play, as areal particulars can out of the span
of Man, and of all, this man
does not
        he, does, he
    walks
            by the sea
in my memory

and sees all things and to him
are presented at night
the whispers of the most flung shores
from Gloucester out

The Biggest Killing

1.

Not by lost killers stranded
on the empty road

the various armies moving
   on to find each other the lost
   killers hail their jeeps
   of victory, colonels sitting
   friendly behind the wheel
but by stranded defeated
killers whose mouths water
for exotic factories
   their new Alabamas
   where they immediately begin
   to assemble old rockets, but better.

2.

"And the dreamer turns away

from his visionary herds
and his splendid yesterday"
but we
   live in an earth of well-dressed gangs
my friend
waiting on the new Trinity.
And why don't the unctuous catholics
do something but start new wars
and why don't the unctuous protestants.

3.

The yellow leaves will be here supposedly
riding the wind on dark branches
beyond a window
beyond summer's yellowing hills oh dead
filthy a dump truck shines in the black mud
November November.

   He remembers Yesterday
as one single day,
the sky was grey, but dark oh day
somewhere in the hills
the wind
everywhere the bleating of this
blissful era comes down against
our land in stark particles of rain.

For no single energetic man requires
anything of us
no single act of cognition
no matter how they rant the time
runs into years and they lead their gangs
through the streets the streets
of our souls and on an actual island
it was you said—they told you
stop ranting about your filthy soul?

        My god man, you should have wept.
What would they do, clean up the streets?
No leader can be exempt from drunk blood,
remember we passed Trinity site,
where 15 years ago we were led by the top gang
of all marching with their eye protectors imagine
they covered their eyes thus those idiot eyes
were not burned out by what they saw of their own
creation. Only a man

will play God and refuse to look on his own creation.
Will Fidel feed his people before his own stomach
is filled? Can Jack
hold up his grimy hands and shade us
from that vileness falling in particles
of fine shifting daily poison sand whose
stirring up he is the anxious inheritor of
he who falls in direct popular birthright to
is there any greater nonsense than
"our leaders would save us"?

My friend, don't breathe too deeply.

Remember we passed Trinity site
returning from Juarez-going north
you could see through ventanas
in the mountains some sixty miles away

still they whisper in the wind
we need you
still they whisper of green elegant glass
there and of emerald plains and say who
will they let in first.
Still the lethal metric bubbles of science
burst there every day and those sophisticated
workers go home to talk politely of pure science,

they breathe, go about in their cars and pay rent
until they advance by degrees to ownership
it is
like a gigantic Parker game of careers.

No complaint.

Still we see the marvelous vapor trails
across the face of the moon.
Still we awaken in the morning
and Yesterday which should be one-half
our whole possibility is lost
in a common nostril so decayed, so cynical
it cannot smell the blood it lifts
and drinks, to all of us.

And spills gaily, like a nutty booze machine
while we are the yellowing leaves, my friends and I
heaped upon the slopes of the New World Trinity
where grieves forth obsolescent landwrack
to infinity.

LARRY EIGNER

A Weekday

the foundation waits (will rise)
between morning and afternoon
for a 2nd load of dirt

the trucks move

eyelessness, uncovered
windows, the outdoors
                          toothless,
        the garage
open like a grave

or a child perhaps

                faces play, have played

the quaking stone

        they have wandered over from the next lot, their
        bikes   a near way

            slowed the gulls

    (a surprise, the difference of time

soon the walls will have been wholly
real
even on the hot nights

    though they were not always the same

The Shock

men were connected with animals
I look up and see the plane
  scarcely

able to move while casting
my legs

I cry my world full of the head
if it would do any good

in the twisted path, not by distance but
                    the wind in my face

the eyes tossed back, fitted
 locked oars

          passing, coming singly to every one
                    what is "aboard"

beasts they wrecked, and the world still spread
 and in more and more ways, but back
gradual,   as needed,   faster
    and unfelt

              for protection

                    the dead brains

          and the fall, where, for a time

              the great matter at the end of my soul

   the dog deciding to bark up my feet
and all the trees, with the wind
  dragging its roots
          blown to bits, eyes that are stopped

          the love of life and death

A Sleep

air is mild, not quite
bareness, the sky
                    burning its way
the clouds are nothing

                       the rain
is tremendous   it is mild
  dispersing figures

the ocean   day
break   the gulls
manage the view

a year ago here was a hurricane

to stay in one place
at evening

to move about
the morning pass

the gnomes stop their shaking
and convert into flowers

o laugh

  some, visible

  dissipating seeds

        to find more endings as a tree or circle

one state contemplates others
and we have gone in towards death
  leaving, up, the
filled birds to the sea

Washing between the buildings
    Holland   the clear sky
      over the hay-loading
        the clouds'
          brief rise   a temperate substance

as if the white mortar of history
   the grounds of people   canals
     mirror the overhung banks   dividing
      bridges   and is water deep what
        opens the roots as calm

               oblong

  even the streets are shining

  What happened
        to fire, the clouds
  out of hand, the machines'
    free fall,   sewers
     fouled up,   accuracy
      of destructive laws

  Measure of bridges,   into the endless boats of water
                             with
    those who would waste

       monument to the underground

suicide, and the reckless   put it off
        to the next moment

                quiet

            fog
        roof of trolleys
            cobbled
                floods

        night

            mills like a tiller

            varying distance of wind

the dog yelped,   skunk let fly
    coffee burning
        rubber   motors
                used to the plow

                    ephemeral now

        the birds
    may cross the road
    the dip in the gutter tonight   no
        distance   away
    with the big passengers
    snow to climb

                near the diningroom growing
            pears   down
                memory can be strong

            what kind of paper   all types of patterns the writ-
                                                    ing
                is thinner than the panes

                and houses to become ghosts

            unlovely   look
                    how the leaves go
The fog by another direction
        pear-tree   one briefly
    lopped off   buried itself

        the rain the snow
                            game
            later
                the shift of ground before night

and to the birds a bath
sometimes   I was paying attention   it
looks deserted

    a very long truck
    bedded in earth

        provide a voice for it
                lurking under the seat

                never mind
                the complete turn

bird shadows mounting
the bath of
 screens and walls
   the light horizon
   firm   and singing   opened
   tree,   trees

  clumps
  swaying of birds have
   beaten storm   ,   slight
   in mist, all they know

water is everywhere
                        pile
     the clouds
 through numbers of days   join
        layers, the scattering
 night, disappeared,   the
 trees, not any of the
 stars   hide and seek

I will have an image
 of quiet   at hand
    it floats away
        I don't grasp

  by the beach
            sand ugly enough
        night is cool

stars pass
            over
     again
   the rocks tamed
        sea

but no strength to travel
 a lot of ends   the paths

destroy places
     as time
   the miraculous series

       so you may awake
         to streets in the morning

          and maybe rain

              the sun already up

THEODORE ENSLIN

Tansy for August

> *'Tis not the Object but the Light*
> *That maketh Hev'n.* — Thomas Traherne

And this July — its nakedness burned out —
moves through the muffling dust toward August,
down and downward, fire and light obscured
in mist and spent smoke — trails and breathings —
pain and patience in the annealed life
preceding harvest.
        Moves — declares itself
in these attempts: One flower that follows on
               another —
small this year, and unconvincing.
Withered. Limp. Wrinkled. Corn at midday
offers little. The attempt to sweat
dries salt and stillborn. Brooks run low.
Bogs are, for the moment, dried out, passable
            and scarred.

Night is their trance — the cicadas
whose patient sound is endless:
Passionate, unsatisfied, and waking.
Trembling, the eyelid closes on a wet, dark,
           grave;
shuts out the world, retains itself
and dream: The Qualities of night.
Night ends — goes up in mist —
leaves at sunrise — lonely and unrested —
solitary on a barren landscape.

The quick star tansy burns itself — sears — pulses
through pace of days set forward through their
           time —
over the ashes which are fields in drought.
Tansy's bitter buttons hold with heat
their character — the way penultimate for summer —

waking from trance, fever, and July.
Tansy for August. Tansy in the stiff bouquet.
                    Tansy for seed.

Witch Hazel

This:
That is my straight-flying fury.
And not this:
The dead bone of poetics buried
under sacramental clouds
of sleep or of wine, or too much
awareness of the things that are not there:
Ghosts.

I will make directly through
the woods where the early and late
witch hazel keep blossoms in a long season.
Cut me a switch!
I am not likely to tire on that walk
direct between March and October —
oddly alike and seldom linked —
cut me a switch!

Divined for the water,
the well should be here.
An old cellar hole
dropping away to the infinite
side of the hill and the sunset.
This should be blind water's well.
Switch cut? Very well.

Begin here.
                    But straight-flying
is my time of day, and no ruins
but for rocks to build.
Nostalgia is along the way
and very well, but no stopover.
Cut me another switch,
I found that well.
The water is good: Cold
and clear through ten feet
of gravel and sand. It clears
itself.

Cut me a switch to whip old ghosts
through sunsets to the morning.

Landscape With Figures

A sharp smoke drifts,
clears the eaves
barely
        skims the cold ground
thins;
        mingles its smell
with grass and leaves.
Gone.

Late for a spring song
early for winter
to set
except in shadows holding the light frost.

A brooding time
hangs.
The birds
        swing close
to the house.
                A bare branch
nests them.

A man walks through
and whistles
a love song
if it's that
        for him.

The smoke drifts down.
I see
    no more.

Tangere

And if
        you reach
over
    to touch

whatever it is
you want to touch

if
  ever
      you get to the place
where you think you're
going (headed
in the right direction)
or
  if you
stand right here
reaching over the hip
bone of the little hill
a breeze   slight breeze
being all that you want
to touch   really
it will make no difference
so long
        as the blaze of in-
tention
        holds up
the fires lit red
                on the smooth wet bark
of pine trees in the afternoon
when the clouds have broken
and the last rays of the sun
are touching
them.

The Belongings

High
    in your room
I have been sitting quietly
with your things scattered around me;
your love for them is
                            evident
in their disorder.
                    That you have used them
displaces lust, and puts them
somehow at my service—

clean, with bright edges,
with lives that are dependent
upon you,
used to your touch
   even to your impatient
longing to get rid of them,
all of them, for a moment's breath.
To you they will not seem friendly,
being friends of yours,
              and too well known;
but to me they bring a promise
which should be in you—not them—
high, in your room.

'Your Need is Greater than Mine'

I do not say this
        easily.
It is difficult to imagine
what anyone really needs.
So often you ask for things
which are harmful.
There is the feeling, too,
that in helping,
       my pride is strengthened.
You see, I am more than selfish.
I need so much more than you do.

Stance

A tremulous distance
   in
sistence
    'dance then
and be done with it'
knowing that the dance
is endless
    no
but without limits
defining
    the edges

into picked
                conclusions
and this is where we came in

from *Forms*: LXXVII.

Things being what they are do not imply necessity.
Try.
    Not much ahead.
Well, the hindsight is ahead—
the being here
                things
(you know) and a shrug.
No, it is not that easy—
it is that
        things as they are
belong to
        forms
                belong—
to force the emptiness
                        back
and again back.
            I think
not the necessity.
                Some good may
come out of it—as
probably it won't
                things
being
    as they are.
The being!
        And that brings light.
More or less
        lodged
at the corner of the bridge,
the current sweeps by
                    leaves—
a few
    stay there
in eddies strong against
stem tide
        or the stem
is for the leaf to hold to

the branch to hold on
and the distances
                    break back
and the future and the past
one and the same   they
lose themselves.
                    We have only
the minute presence—
the minute!
                    Not even that
much.
        I have said this to you—
to you, Garance, beloved,
whoever you are—one or the other
or both of them
                    merged
sometimes as there is an object
wedged against my corners—
my bridge
            over the river
which is distance between us.
Only in moments do you believe me
as
    only in moments the love
which is possible.
And I think
            you have been listening
when you leave me
                    poised
on the edge of something—
something I might have told you
further
        to lighten the reaching:
take weight and give fire—
but you have gone—
it is right that you do go
                        (in some sense
it is right)
            and I am left
with things as they are,
never
        as they might be.
It is my failure,
                but I

cannot leave you
                    scot free
to say that you might not
have made the difference
if you would
                    or could.
It is hard to say these things
in general terms
                    they are platitudes
to be shovelled out with the ashes
of sermons
            generations of sermons
thundered to empty pews
now
    as the pews were always empty—
the living went on—
                    but outside.
It is hard to say these things, then,
you are a good listener
to have tried
                no matter
what
    the failure of things as they are.
The poems are, in a sense,
crystals
        of that failure,
a mixing of fine spices,
sugars which coalesce
and go
        in their last period
to crystal
            the geodes
which rot away from the form
we had planned
                leaving
crystals—the poems.
Something must guard or forewarn us—
the templar—
it may be in the poem—
possibly never in the act.
I have said these things,
                    I will say them
again—the long ellipsis
around to around

to a maypole of dancing
which may not be
all joy.
I will ask you to listen.
I do not suppose you will.
The relief of knowing
that there is the failure—
that to say all of it
                    and to have it
all of it understood
                    would be death
as we
      (necessarily)
shy away from death—
the nigh horse knowing
that there is danger
                    implicit
in his off mate.
                    The relief
that will come in rejection
and the power to move on
through it, as if it were nothing
more than a twilight
of understanding—which it may be.
So that we come to reject
what it is that we most want—
to do without it
                    when it seems
that nothing is possible
without a successful conclusion.
Now I may be talking around you,
but I doubt if it is that simple,
or simply that I am hedging in words
a departure
            no
it is larger than
either one of us.
                    We cannot live
with success or completion,
as finally we cannot live with each other,
or alone in believing
that we belong to another.
If you doubt me
it is just as well, I

do not want your belief,
your faith is a sorrow to me.
I cannot bear it.
Heave slowly at the corners of my bridge
to shed flotsam
                    downstream.
It is a case of mistaken—
not identities,
                but sharing
identities which we do not have.
I have called for you
when you have been with me
more
        than when we were separate.
Only in leave-taking
were we at one
or at peace—as a gentle bed
is always
        an empty one.
Now is the best time
to say these things
                    before
the shock of the wound has worn off
fully
    to be felt as pain
if there is such thing as pain
beyond the outward feeling
which is nothing more than we can bear
in recalling it.
                    The present has shattered concepts
that come from clock and mirror,
and these may not be
the space which would be left
where they once were.
It is in looking again
to the water drawn
with stars wavering
that we are aware
of other
        dim shadows
admittedly not much
to go on
        but enough
to wonder about.

I see you with your head propped on your arm.
Are you asleep?
It makes no difference
the words will penetrate
sleep
        or the dreams
which will fracture it
later.
It is hardly a moment to laugh,
yet I am laughing
at you, and at myself—
what has burst in on us—.
It is not bitter laughter,
nor am I joking,
but the laughter is whole—
there is a ridiculous security
in the way that you sit,
with your head pillowed
as if it would never fall
further.
I could tell you stories,
or make love to you, now,
even in this place
which is not conducive
to more than sitting
                    a certain
aimless colloquy.
I will do nothing of the sort,
but with my chair pushed back
from the slopped coffee and toast rinds
tell you a story
                about goblins
a ghost story unsuited
to the streaming sun
refrained in your hair.
Yes, you *are* lovely
and still, so very still.
It is late in the morning,
I had forgotten
                there are things
I must do today
                things
which must happen away from here—
away from you.

They will not lead back.
I doubt if you will care very much.
Things must be
                if they aren't
quite what we had expected,
or what they contain in themselves
like buds close-hooded
but cut off:
                The only promise
lies in the sharp knife
to first peel them
                        or cut them across.
Garance,
        Are you listening?
Yes, you are listening,
but not to me
                not to
anything that is here.
Soon it will be afternoon.
You will wake up
to a much deeper sleep.

LAWRENCE FERLINGHETTI

Tentative Description of a Dinner to Promote the Impeachment of President Eisenhower

After it became obvious that the strange rain would never
  stop
And after it became obvious that the President was doing
  everything in his power
And after it became obvious that the President's general
  staff was still in contact with the President deep in the
  heart of Georgia while deep in the heart of South
  America the President's left-hand man was proving all
  the world loves an American
And after it became obvious that the strange rain would
  never stop and that Old Soldiers never drown and that
  roses in the rain had forgotten the word for bloom and
  that perverted pollen blown on sunless seas was eaten
  by irradiated fish who spawned up cloudleaf streams
  and fell onto our dinnerplates
And after it became obvious that the President was doing
  everything in his power to make the world safe for
  nationalism his brilliant military mind never having
  realized that nationalism itself was the idiotic superstition
  which would blow up the world
And after it became obvious that the President nevertheless
  still carried no matter where he went in the strange rain
  the little telegraph key which like a can opener could
  be used instantly to open but not to close the hot box
  of final war if not to waylay any stray asinine action
  by any stray asinine second lieutenant pressing any
  strange button anywhere far away over an arctic
  ocean thus illuminating the world once and for all
And after it became obvious that the law of gravity was still
  in effect and that what blows up must come down on
  everyone including white citizens
And after it became obvious that the Voice of America was
  really the Deaf Ear of America and that the President
  was unable to hear the underprivileged natives of the
  world shouting No Contamination Without Representa-

tion in the strange rain from which there was no escape
  — except Peace
And after it became obvious that the word Truth had only
    a comic significance to the Atomic Energy Commission
    while the President danced madly to mad Admiral
    Straus waltzes wearing special atomic earplugs which
    prevented him from hearing Albert Schweitzer and nine
    thousand two hundred and thirtyfive other scientists
    telling him about spastic generations and blind bone-
    less babies in the strange rain from which there was no
    escape — except Peace
And after it became obvious that the President was doing
    everything in his power to get thru the next four years
    without eating any of the crates of irradiated vege-
    tables wellwishers had sent him from all over and
    which were filling the corridors and antechambers and
    bedchambers and chamberpots in the not-so-White
    House
And after it became obvious that the Great Soldier had
    become the Great Conciliator who had become the
    Great Compromiser who had become the Great Fence
    Sitter who actually had heard of the Supreme Court's
    decision to desegregate the land of the free and had
    not only heard of it but had actually
                                        read it
And after it became obvious that the President had gone to
    Gettysburg fourscore and seven years ago and had
    given his Gettysburg Address to the postman and so
    dedicated himself to the unfinished task
                    Then it was that the natives of the Re-
public began assembling in the driving rain from which
there was no escape — except Peace
                    And then it was that no invitations had
to be sent out for the great testimonial dinner except to politicians whose respected names would lend weight to the
project but who did not come anyway suspecting the whole
thing was a plot to save the world from the clean bomb from
which there was no escape — except Peace
                    And women who still needed despair
to look truly tragic came looking very beautiful and very
tragic indeed since there was despair to spare
                    And some men also despaired and sat
down in Bohemia and were too busy to come

But other men came whose only politi-
cal action during the past twenty years had been to flush
a protesting toilet and run

And babies came in their carriages car-
rying irradiated dolls and holding onto crazy strings of
illuminated weather balloons filled with Nagasaki air

And those who had not left their TV
sets long enough to notice the weather in seven years now
came swimming thru the rain holding their testimonials

And those came who had never
marched in sports car protest parades and those came who
had never been arrested for sailing a protesting Golden
Rule in unpacific oceans

And Noah came in his own Ark looking
surprisingly like an outraged Jesus Christ and cruised about
flying his pinion and picking up two of each beast that
wanted to be preserved in the strange rain which was raining real cats and dogs and from which there was no escape —
except Peace

And peddlers came in lead jockstraps
selling hotdogs and rubber American flags and waving peti-
tions proclaiming it Unamerican to play golf on the same
holy days that clean bombs were set off on time

And finally after everyone who was
anyone and after everyone who was no one had arrived and
after every soul was seated and waiting for the symbolic
mushroom soup to be served and for the keynote speeches
to begin

The President himself came in
Took one look around and said
We Resign

(*May, 1958*)

Underwear

I didn't get much sleep last night
thinking about underwear
Have you ever stopped to consider
underwear in the abstract
When you really dig into it
some shocking problems are raised
Underwear is something

we all have to deal with
Everyone wears
some kind of underwear
Even Indians
wear underwear
Even Cubans
wear underwear
The Pope wears underwear I hope
Underwear is worn by Negroes
The Governor of Louisiana
wears underwear
I saw him on TV
He must have had tight underwear
He squirmed a lot
Underwear can really get you in a bind
Negroes often wear
white underwear
which may lead to trouble
You have seen the underwear ads
for men and women
so alike but so different
Women's underwear holds things up
Men's underwear holds things down
Underwear is one thing
men and women have in common
Underwear is all we have between us
You have seen the three-color pictures
with crotches encircled
to show the areas of extra strength
and three-way stretch
promising full freedom of action
Don't be deceived
It's all based on the two-party system
which doesn't allow much freedom of choice
the way things are set up
America in its Underwear
struggles thru the night
Underwear controls everything in the end
Take foundation garments for instance
They are really fascist forms
of underground government
making people believe
something but the truth
telling you what you can or can't do

Did you ever try to get around a girdle
Perhaps Non-Violent Action
is the only answer
Did Gandhi wear a girdle?
Did Lady Macbeth wear a girdle?
Was that why Macbeth murdered sleep?
And that spot she was always rubbing —
Was it really in her underwear?
Modern anglosaxon ladies
must have huge guilt complexes
always washing and washing and washing
Out damned spot — rub don't blot —
Underwear with spots very suspicious
Underwear with bulges very shocking
Underwear on clothesline a great flag of freedom
Someone has escaped his Underwear
May be naked somewhere
Help!
But don't worry
Everybody's still hung up in it
There won't be no real revolution
And poetry still the underwear of the soul
And underwear still covering
a multitude of faults
in the geological sense —
strange sedimentary stones, inscrutable cracks!
And that only the beginning
For does not the body stay alive
after death
and still need its underwear
or outgrow it
some organs said to reach full maturity
only after the head stops holding them back?
If I were you I'd keep aside
an oversize pair of winter underwear
Do not go naked into that good night
And in the meantime
keep calm and warm and dry
No use stirring ourselves up prematurely
'over Nothing'
Move forward with dignity
hand in vest
Don't get emotional

And death shall have no dominion
There's plenty of time my darling
Are we not still young and easy
Don't shout

One Thousand Fearful Words for Fidel Castro

I am sitting in Mike's Place trying to figure out
                what's going to happen
                    without Fidel Castro
Among the salami sandwiches and spittoons
                I see no solution
            It's going to be a tragedy
                I see no way out
        among the admen and slumming models
        and the brilliant snooping columnists
    who are qualified to call Castro psychotic
        because they no doubt are doctors
            and have examined him personally
and know a paranoid hysterical tyrant when they see one
        because they have it on first hand
    from personal observation by the CIA
        and the great disinterested news services
And Hearst is dead but his great Cuban wire still stands:
        'You get the pictures, I'll make the War'
                I see no answer
                I see no way out
            among the paisanos playing pool
        it looks like Curtains for Fidel
        They're going to fix his wagon
            in the course of human events

    In the back of Mike's the pinball machines
        shudder and leap from the floor
        when Cuban Charlie shakes them
            and tries to work his will
on one named 'Independence Sweepstakes'
Each pinball wandered lonely as a man
            siphons thru and sinks
        no matter how he twists and turns
    A billiardball falls in a felt pocket
    like a peasant in a green landscape

You're whirling around in your little hole
Fidel
and you'll soon sink
in the course of human events

On the nickelodeon a cowboy ballad groans
'Got myself a Cadillac' the cowhand moans
He didn't get it in Cuba, baby
Outside in the night of North Beach America
the new North American cars flick by
from Motorama
their headlights never bright enough
to dispel this night
in the course of human events

Three creepy men come in
One is Chinese
One is Negro
One is some kind of crazy Indian
They look like they may have been
walking up and down in Cuba
but they haven't
All three have hearing aids
It's a little deaf brotherhood of Americans
The skinny one screws his hearing aid
in his skinny ear
He's also got a little transistor radio
the same size as his hearing aid box
For a moment I confuse the two
The radio squawks
some kind of memorial program:
'When in the course of human events
it becomes necessary for one people
to dissolve the political bonds
which have connected them with another —'
I see no way out
no escape
He's tuned in on your frequency, Fidel
but can't hear it
There's interference
It's going to be
a big evil tragedy
They're going to fix you, Fidel
with your big Cuban cigar
which you stole from us

and your army surplus hat
which you probably also stole
and your Beat beard

History may absolve you, Fidel
but we'll dissolve you first, Fidel
You'll be dissolved in history
We've got the solvent
We've got the chaser
and we'll have a little party
somewhere down your way, Fidel
It's going to be a Gas
As they say in Guatemala

Outside of Mike's place now
an ambulance sirens up
It's a midnight murder or something
Some young bearded guy stretched on the sidewalk
with blood sticking out
Here's your little tragedy, Fidel
They're coming to pick you up
and stretch you on their Stretcher
That's what happens, Fidel
when in the course of human events
it becomes necessary for one people to dissolve
the bonds of International Tel & Tel
and United Fruit
Fidel
How come you don't answer anymore
Fidel
Did they cut you off our frequency
We've closed down our station anyway
We've turned you off, Fidel

I was sitting in Mike's Place, Fidel
waiting for someone else to act
like a good Liberal
I hadn't quite finished reading Camus' *Rebel*
so I couldn't quite recognize you, Fidel
walking up and down your island
when they came for you, Fidel
'My Country or Death' you told them
Well you've got your little death, Fidel
like old Honest Abe
one of your boyhood heroes

who also had his little Civil War
and was a different kind of Liberator
(since no one was shot in his war)
and also was murdered
in the course of human events

Fidel . . . Fidel . . .
your coffin passes by
thru lanes and streets you never knew
thru day and night, Fidel
While lilacs last in the dooryard bloom, Fidel
your futile trip is done
yet is not done
and is not futile
I give you my sprig of laurel

EDWARD FIELD

Unwanted

The poster with my picture on it
Is hanging on the bulletin board in the Post Office.

I stand by it hoping to be recognized
Posing first full face and then profile

But everybody passes by and I have to admit
The photograph was taken some years ago.

I was unwanted then and I'm unwanted now
Ah guess ah'll go up echo mountain and crah.

I wish someone would find my fingerprints somewhere
Maybe on a corpse and say, You're it.

Description: Male, or reasonably so
White, but not lily-white and usually deep-red

Thirty-fivish, and looks it lately
Five-feet-nine and one-hundred-thirty pounds: no physique

Black hair going gray, hairline receding fast
What used to be curly, now fuzzy

Brown eyes starey under beetling brow
Mole on chin, probably will become a wen

It is perfectly obvious that he was not popular at school
No good at baseball, and wet his bed.

His aliases tell his history: Dumbell, Good-for-nothing,
Jewboy, Fieldinsky, Skinny, Fierce Face, Greaseball, Sissy.

Warning: This man is not dangerous, answers to any name
Responds to love, don't call him or he will come.

Ode to Fidel Castro

I

O Boy God, Muse of Poets
Come sit on my shoulder while I write
Cuddle up and fill my poem with love
And even while I fly on billows of inspiration
Don't forget to tickle me now and then
For I am going to write on World Issues
Which demands laughter where we most believe.

Also, My Cute One, don't let me take a heroic pose
And act as though I know it all
Guard me from Poet's Head that dread disease
Where the words ring like gongs and meaning goes out the
    window
Remind me of the human size of truth
Whenever I spout a big, ripe absolute
(Oh why did you let the architects of our capital city
Design it for giants
So that a man just has to take a short walk and look about
For exhaustion to set in immediately)
Please, Sweet Seeker, don't discourage me from contradicting
    myself
But make everything sound like life, like people we like
And most of all give me strength not to lay aside this poem
Like so many others in the pile by my typewriter
But to write the whole thing from beginning to end
O Perfection, the way it wants to go.

II

My subject, Dear Muse, is Fidel Castro
Rebellissimo and darling of the Spanish-American lower
                                                    classes
A general who adopted for his uniform
The work clothes of the buck private and the beard of the
                                                    saints
A man fit for ruling a great nation
But who only has an island.

Irene, the beautiful Cuban, has his picture over her bed
Between Rudolph Valentino and the Blessed Virgin —
He stands large and flabby between the perfect body and the
     purest soul
Doves on his shoulders, on his open hands
And one dove for crown standing on his head —
He is not afraid of birdshit, his face is radiant.

Someday Hollywood will make a movie biography of his life
Starring the spreading Marlon Brando
They'll invent a great love on his way up, a blonde with a
                                        large
     crucifix
Whom he loses along with his idealism, and once at the top
A great passion, a dark whore with large breasts, to drag him
     down.
In real life his romance is with his people and his role
Otherwise his sex life is normal for his age and position.

Fidel, Fidel, Fidel . . .
I am in love with the spotlight myself
And would like the crowds to chant my name
Which has the same letters as yours but rearranged
Where is my island Where my people
What am I doing on this continent Where is my crown
Where did everyone go that used to call me king
And light up like votive candles when I smiled?
(I have given them all up for you sweet youth my muse
Be truly mine.)
Am I like Goethe who kept faith in Napoleon
Long after the rest of the world had given him up
For tyrant and betrayer of the revolution?
If Napoleon was like Tolstoy writing a novel
Organizing a vast army of plots and themes
Then Castro is like a poet writing an ode
(Alas that poets should be rulers —
Revise that line, cut that stanza, lop off that phrase)
Paredon! Paredon!

What he did was kick out the bad men and good riddance
                                        Batista
What he is doing . . . Well, what he is trying to do is . . .
(Muse, why don't you help me with this,
Are you scared of socialist experiment?)
One thing he is doing is upsetting a lot of people

Our papers are full of stories that make him out a devil
And you a fool if you like him
But they are against me too even if they don't know I exist
so let's shake Fidel
(The hand that exists shakes the hand that doesn't)
My Fidel Castro, Star of Cuba.

III

The Hotel Teresa in Harlem is a dumpy landmark in a slum
But when Fidel Castro went there to stay
And when Nikita Khrushchev went up and hugged and kissed
him for being Mr. Wonderful
Right out in public (they get away with it those foreigners)
Then Harlem became the capital of the world
And the true home of the united nations.

That whole bunch sitting around the hotel like in bivouac
                                        roasting
        chickens
And all those Negroes looking at them bugeyed —
Nobody that great ever came up there before to stay.
Of course plenty of people that great came out of Harlem
Like Jim Baldwin, not to mention those jazz people we all love
But the colored that came out of Harlem like roman candles
You don't catch them going back there like a Fourth of July
        parade.

Now Cuba and Russia have gone to Harlem
And found it a good place for loving —
That Harlem, full of rats chewing off babies' arms
And social workers trying to keep the whole place from
        exploding
I used to have friends up there
When I went to visit them if I passed a mirror
My whiteness would surprise me
The mind takes on darkness of skin so easily
(Of course being a Jew I'm not exactly white)
It is that easy to turn black
And then have to be in that awful boat the Negroes are in
Although it's pretty lousy being white
And having that black hatred turned on you.

What after all can a white man say but, I'm ashamed
Hey fellas I'm sorry . . .

Unless you are President and then you have your golden
    opportunity.
Perhaps the only thing to do is look upon each other
As two men look when they meet solitary in the deep woods
Come black man let us jerk off together
Like boys do to get to know each other.

Well just like others who have escaped ghettos I don't go to
    Harlem anymore
I don't like to see the trapped whom I can't set free
But when I see the big front-page photos of Castro and
    Khrushchev hugging in Harlem
A widescreen spectacle with supermen in totalscope embrace,
                                and
    in color yet,
I sit back and dig it all the way
Man it swings.

IV

BOMBS GOING OFF ALL OVER HAVANA
In Rockefeller Center the Cuban Tourist Office is closed
And across the skating rink men are putting up
The world's largest Christmas tree which will never be Chris-
                                tian
Even if you cut it down, make it stand on cement, decorate it
    with balls
It will still scream for the forest, like a wild animal
Like the gods who love freedom and topple to the saws of
    commerce
The gods who frighten us half to death in our dreams with
                               their
    doings
And disappear when we need them most, awake.

By the time you see this, Fidel, you might not even exist any-
                              more
My government is merciless and even now
The machine to destroy you is moving into action
The chances are you won't last long
Well so long pal it was nice knowing you
I can't go around with a broken heart all my life
After I got over the fall of the Spanish Republic
I guess I can get over anything
My job is just to survive.

But I wish you well Fidel Castro
And if you do succeed in making that island
The tropic paradise God meant it to be
I'll be the first to cheer and come for a free visit if invited.

So you're not perfect, poets don't look for perfect
It's your spirit we love and the glamor of your style
I hope someday the cameras of the world
Are turned on you and me in some spot like Harlem
And then you'll get a kiss that will make Khrushchev's be
    forgotten
A kiss of the poet, that will make you truly good
The way you meant to be.

Graffiti

Blessings on all the kids who improve the signs in the subways:
They put a beard on the fashionable lady selling soap,
Fix up her flat chest with the boobies of a chorus girl,
And though her hips be wrapped like a mummy
They draw a hairy cunt where she should have one.

The bathing beauty who looks pleased
With the enormous prick in her mouth, declares
"Eat hair pie; it's better than cornflakes."
And the little boy in the tarzan suit eating white bread
Now has a fine pair of balls to crow about.

And as often as you wash the walls and put up your posters,
When you go back to the caged booth to deal out change
The bright-eyed kids will come with grubby hands.
Even if you watch, you cannot watch them all the time,
And while you are dreaming, if you have dreams anymore,

A boy and girl are giggling behind an iron pillar;
And although the train pulls in and takes them on their way
Into a winter that will freeze them forever,
They leave behind a wall scrawled all over with flowers
That shoot great drops of gism through the sky.

What Grandma Knew

The office feels like a sealed glass case today.
The air conditioning dates from the thirties.
That means it is ten years younger than I am.
Neither of us is working too well.

Outside the summer is going on for the outside world
But time is dragging me unwillingly into winter.
I ask myself my favorite question
"Why must I work for a living?"

This has no answer besides being irrelevant.
Old Italian men are fond of saying "No work, no eat."
And I guess that sums things up,
It says the world is so, and just accept it.

If you're famous, life is fun;
If you're not, you live like others do,
And go to the same death of the heart
Long before the hairs finally all fall out of your head.

If I had banjo eyes I'd strum a tune:
"My grandma always said, Alone is a stone.
But by the time life got through with grandma
She was glad to be alone."

DONALD FINKEL

Cocteau's *Opium: 1*

*Even without any spirit of proselytising, it is impossible
for a person who does not smoke to live with a person who
does. Each would inhabit a different world.*

Still, no one has paid much tribute to the man
who has to live *in* the addict, that madman, that poet,
that adolescent pimpled with spiritual acne;
to support him, and his wife, and his brats,
to purchase with sweat his fixes and his furniture.
Lorenzo di Medici. Solomon Guggenheim. Pah!

And for what? But it is like trying to turn your back
on a sick cat. There is a kind of man
who cannot keep from carrying one home.

The addict, on the other hand, needs no excuse;
does he say, The world is chaos, therefore I need
my opium, my art, my ivory, my politics, my morals?
At the crucial moment, he says nothing.
He knows the world *is* order, because he knows
each scrap of chaos personally, by first name.

It is the Judas in Jesus, reason, the eternal husband,
who at the end, having paid the rent for so long,
begins to wonder if it is possible he has been forsaken.

Cocteau's *Opium: 2*

The Leitmotiv of DE PROFUNDIS. The only crime is to be
superficial. Everything which is understood is good. *The
repetition of this sentence is irritating and revealing.*

Picasso, who knows everything, will tell you:
everything is a miracle; for instance, that one
does not dissolve in one's bath "like a lump of sugar."
Everywhere, euphoria of opium, euphoria of art,
everywhere the equation of miracle with understanding,
true with beautiful, wise with good.

The miracle blasts the fig tree, from which it expects
the impossible; it demands to be understood; it has all
the significance of a man kicking a cat. It is the blind
damning the blind for not being able to conduct
a guided tour in this country of miracles. *De profundis*,
in the place of suffering, where everything is understood.

Like the noble fig, let us accept our punishment;
"a tree must suffer from the rising of its sap."
Certainly we have not been good; innocence, like ignorance,
is no excuse. Ask the adolescent, ask the addict
taking the cure, or the first weed of spring;
every morning, rising, rising, rising, ask yourself.

Note in Lieu of a Suicide

> *In those days they shall say no more, The
> fathers have eaten a sour grape, and the
> children's teeth are set on edge.*

I am surrounded by armies, I have sent them word
it was not I who asked for a fight.
By whose decree am I called Jew?
By my grandfather's who observed the passover?
They have sent word back it was not they.
By my father's who knows a few yiddish jokes?
I shake my fist at the sky and there is no lightning.
By the local rabbi's who has recognized my name?
I have just looked in the ark and found a stone.

Yet since when have I not been a Jew?
Since the day I heard God was dead?
The blood is on me, I am not clean.
Since the day I became a Unitarian?
Like a woman in her time I am not clean.
Since the day I first discovered that in these
perilous times every man jack is circumcised?
Like a dog that has rolled in dogshit I am not clean.
The blood on my hands is as much his
as the blood in my veins. Admitted.

I will leave the silver in the temple,
but I am damned if I will hang myself;
I have in Kerioth a wife and two kids
who but for me would be living on the state.

Oedipus at San Francisco

He left me exposed on a hill of woman, my mother.
I paid him back at every crossroads, quitting
school, taking pot, writing poems
he couldn't fathom; after a while it palled.
The past is dead now, neither of us could care less.

But mamma, that's something else; no peace with *her*.
You can't turn your back, she is everywhere, under
your feet, like the ground. The old man's prod withdrawn,
she turns slowly inanimate; every year
she gets harder and harder to push away. It isn't
enough, any more, that she rarely calls. She is there;
and there's no getting around it, I am a bastard.

The Bush on Mount Venus

In the American dream it is customarily deleted
along with odors, tooth decay, and the clap,
in a shy bid for the approval of Parents' Magazine.

The Greeks could not find a place for it
on their marble, though the Babylonians
managed to tattoo it on their humbler clay.

It is something woman would much rather forget,
this net, this trap, this tangled labyrinth
where lurks the outcome of her beastliness.

Or is this veil the riddle of the princess,
the answer to which is the lovely princess herself?
Behind the darkness at the door, the door is dark.

There is another version of the story,
in which the answer to the riddle is the man.
"Who comes?" she asks, half animal, half human.

"I come," he replies, "whenever I get the chance.
It is I, crawling, walking, limping, here I come;
the third leg is not necessarily a walking stick."

For there is no difference between the Sphinx and Jocasta,
riddle and prize; one kills all who do not
know the answer, the other all who do.

Still, the fellow comes, eager to penetrate
any mystery, whether of death or birth.
If you ask him, in fact, he will explain

that it was he in the first place who designed
the labyrinth, as a kind of school
for heroes, artificers, and mice.

The Father

When I am walking with the children, and a girl
still hard in the buttocks bends to them with a laugh,
my heart bangs where it hangs in my empty carcass.
But you knew that. It has already passed
the stage of neighbors' gossip and attained
the clarity of an historical fact.
A myth comes down your street: here on my right
toddles my twinkling daughter, who loves me, while
on my left marches my son, who does not.

It is all true, but it does not matter;
in twenty years my son and I will have reached
a silent understanding, whereas (poor fool,
already growing hollow) some pimply bastard
will have made off with my blessings and my daughter.

ALLEN GINSBERG

*
* *

Poem
Rocket

```
    .       .
    .       .
    .       .
  .           .
 .             .
.               .
  . . . . . . . .
**************
```

'Be a Star-screwer!' —Gregory Corso

Old moon my eyes are new moon with human footprint
no longer Romeo Sadface in drunken river Loony Pierre eye-
      brow, goof moon
O possible moon in Heaven we get to first of ageless constella-
      tions of names
as God is possible as All is possible so we'll reach another life.

Moon politicians earth weeping and warring in eternity

tho not one star disturbed by screaming madmen from
      Hollywood
oil tycoons from Romania making secret deals with flabby green
      Plutonians —
slave camps on Saturn Cuban revolutions on Mars?
Old life and new side by side, will Catholic church find Christ
      on Jupiter
Mohammed rave in Uranus will Buddha be acceptable on the
      stolid planets
or will we find Zoroastrian temples flowering on Neptune?
What monstrous new ecclesiastical designs on the entire universe
      unfold in the dying Pope's brain?
Scientist alone is true poet he gives us the moon
he promises the stars he'll make us a new universe if it comes
      to that
O Einstein I should have sent you my flaming mss.
O Einstein I should have pilgrimaged to your white hair!

O fellow travellers I write you a poem in Amsterdam in the
     Cosmos
where Spinoza ground his magic lenses long ago
I write you a poem long ago
already my feet are washed in death
Here I am naked without identity
with no more body than the fine black tracery of pen mark on
     soft paper
as star talks to star multiple beams of sunlight all the same
     myriad thought
in one fold of the universe where Whitman was
and Blake and Shelley saw Milton dwelling as in a starry temple
brooding in his blindness seeing all —
Now at last I can speak to you beloved brothers of an unknown
     moon
real Yous squatting in whatever form amidst Platonic Vapors of
     Eternity
I am another Star.
Will you eat my poems or read them
or gaze with aluminum blind plates on sunless pages?
do you dream or translate & accept data with indifferent
     droopings of antennae?
do I make sense to your flowery green receptor eyesockets? do
     you have visions of God?
Which way will the sunflower turn surrounded by millions
     of suns?

This is my rocket my personal rocket I send up my message
     Beyond
Someone to hear me there
My immortality
without steel or cobalt basalt or diamond gold or mercurial fire
without passports filing cabinets bits of paper warheads
without myself finally
pure thought
message all and everywhere the same
I send up my rocket to land on whatever planet awaits it
preferably religious sweet planets no money
fourth dimensional planets where Death shows movies
plants speak (courteously) of ancient physics and poetry itself is
     manufactured by the trees
the final Planet where the Great Brain of the Universe sits
     waiting for a poem to land in His golden pocket
joining the other notes mash-notes love-sighs complaints-musical
     shrieks of despair and the million unutterable thoughts
     of frogs
I send you my rocket of amazing chemical
more than my hair my sperm or the cells of my body

the speeding thought that flies upward with my desire as
    instantaneous as the universe and faster than light
and leave all other questions unfinished for the moment to turn
    back to sleep in my dark bed on earth.

Aether

                        11:15 PM May 27

4 Sniffs & I'm High,
Underwear in bed,
        white cotton in left hand,
    archtype degenerate,
        bloody taste in my mouth
            of Dentist Chair
    music, Loud Farts of Eternity —
an owl with eyeglasses scribbling in the
    cold darkness —
All the time the sound in my eardrums
            of trolleycars below
    taxi fender cough — creak of streets —
Laughter & pistol shots echoing
        at all walls —
    tic leaks of neon — the voice of Myriad
        rushers of the Brainpan
all the chirps the crickets have created
ringing against my eares in the
                instant before unconsciousness
                  before, —
    the teardrop in the eye to come, —
    the Fear of the Unknown —

One does not yet know whether Christ was
        God or the Devil —
    Buddha is more reassuring.

Yet the experiments must continue!

Every possible combination of Being — all
    the old ones! all the old Hindu
        Sabahadabadie-pluralic universes
           ringing in Grandiloquent
                Bearded Juxtaposition,
    with all their minarets and moonlit
        towers enlaced with iron

or porcelain embroidery,
        all have existed —
    and the Sages with
white hair who sat crosslegged on
        a female couch —
hearkening to whatever music came
        from out the Wood or Street,
whatever bird that whistled in the
                Marketplace,
    whatever note the clock struck to say
            Time —
whatever drug, or aire, they breathed
    to make them think so deep
        or simply hear what passed,
like a car passing in the 1960 street
    beside the Governmental Palace
        in Peru, this Lima
        year I write.

                Kerouac! I salute yr
wordy beard. Sad Prophet!
    Salutations and low bows from
baggy pants and turbaned mind and hornèd foot
    arched eyebrows & Jewish Smile —
One single specimen of Eternity — each
        of us poets.

Breake the Rhythm! (too much pentameter)
    . . . My god what solitude are you in Kerouac
                now?
— heard the whoosh of carwheels in the 1950 rain —

And every bell went off on time,
And everything that was created
Rang especially in view of the Creation
For
This is the end of the creation
This is the redemption Spoken of
This is the view of the Created
    by all the Drs, nurses, etc of
                creation;
i.e., —

★

> I JUST NODDED BECAUSE OF THE SECONDARY
> NEGATION

!!

The unspeakable passed over my head for
        the second time.
                        and still can't say it!

i.e. we are the sweepings of the moon
we're what's *left over* from perfection —
The universe is an OLD mistake
I've understood a million times before
and always come back to the same
                        scissor brainwave —
The
Sooner or later all Consciousness will
            be eliminated
                        because Consciousness is
    a by-product of —
                        (Cotton & N$_2$O)
            Drawing saliva back from the tongue —

Christ! you struggle to understand
            One consciousness
            & be confronted with Myriads —
after a billion years
        with the same ringing in the ears
            and pterodactyl-smile of Oops
                        Creation,
        known it all before.
        A Buddha as of old, with sirens of
whatever machinery making cranging noises in
                        the street
        and pavement light reflected in the facade
            RR Station window in a
                        dinky port in Backwash
    of the murky old forgotten
                        fabulous whatever
                        Civilization of
                                Eternity, —
with the RR Sta Clock ring midnight,
        as of now,
                & waiting for the 6th
                    you write your
                            Word,
        and end on the last chime — and remember
    This *one* twelve was struck
                    before,
            and *never again;* both.

. . . . I stood on the balcony
          waiting for an explosion
   of Total Consciousness of the All —
             being Ginsberg sniffing ether in Lima.
      The same struggle of Mind, to reach the
                    Thing
      that ends its process with an X
                comprehending its befores and afters,
      unexplainable to each, except in a prophetic
                    secret recollective hidden
                        half-hand unrecorded.
                                 way.
As the old sages of Asia, or the white beards of Persia
      scribbled on the margins of their scrolls
             in delicate ink
   remembering with tears the ancient clockbells of their
                                          cities
             and the cities that had been —
      Nasca, Paracas, Chancay & Secrecy of the Priests
                    buried, Cat Gods
             of all colors, a funeral shroud
                    for a museum —
   None remember but all return to the same thought
                    before they die — what sad old
             knowledge, we repeat again.
                        Only to be lost
   in the sands of Paracas, or wrapped in a mystic shroud
             of Poesy
      and found by some kid in a thousand years
          inspire what dreadful thoughts of his own?

It's a horrible, lonely experience. And
      Gregory's letter, and Peter's . . .

                                   May 28 7:30 PM

. . . In the foul dregs of Circumstance
          'Male and Female He created them'
             with mustaches.
      There ARE certain REPEATED
      (pistol shot) reliable points
      of reference which the insane
      (pistol shot repeated outside
      the window) — madman suddenly

writes — THE PISTOL SHOT
outside — the REPEATED situations
the experience of return to the
same place in Universal Creation
Time — and every time we return
we recognize again that we
HAVE been here & that is the
Key to Creation — the same pistol shot
— DOWN, bending over his book of Un
intelligable marvels with his mustache.

(my) Madness is intelligable reactions to
        Unintelligable phenomena.
                    Boy — what a marvellous bottle,
            a clear glass sphere of transparent
                                    liquid ether —

    (Chloraethyl Merz)

                                                9 PM

        I know I am a poet — in this universe — but what
good does that do — when in another, without these mechanical
aids, I might be doomed to be a poor Disneyan Shoe Store
Clerk — This consciousness an *accident* of one of the Ether-
possible worlds, not the Final World

    Wherein we all look Crosseyed
    & triumph in our Virginity
    without wearing Rabbit's-foot
            ears or eyes looking sideways
            strangely but in Gold

    Humbled & more knowledgeable, acknowledge
    the Vast mystery of our creation —
    without giving any sign that
        we have heard from the

        GREAT CREATOR

    WHOSE NAME I NOW

    PRONOUNCE:

    GREAT CREATOR OF THE UNIVERS, IF
        THY WISDOM ACCORD IT
    AND IF THIS NOT BE TOO

                    MUCH TO ASK
                    MAY I PUBLISH YOUR NAME?
                    I ASK IN THE LIMA
                        NIGHT
                    FEARFULLY WAITING
                        ANSWER,

        hearing the buses out on
        the street hissing,
        Knowing the Terror
                    of the World Afar —

I have been playing with Jokes
and His is too mighty to hold
        in the hand like a Pen
and His is the Pistol Shot Answer
        that brings blood to the brain
And —

        What *can* be possible
            in a minor universe
            in which you can see
            God by sniffing the
            gas in a cotton?
        The answer to be taken in
            reverse & Doubled Math
            ematically *both* ways.

Am I a sinner?
There are hard & easy universes. This
        is neither.

(If I close my eyes will I regain consciousness?)
        That's the Final Question — with
all the old churchbells ringing and
bus pickup snuffles & crack of iron
whips inside cylinders & squeal of brakes
and old crescendos of responsive
demiurgic ecstasy whispering in streets of ear
        — and when was it Not
        ever answered in the Affir-
        mative? Saith the Lord?

A MAGIC UNIVERSE

Flies & crickets & the sound of buses & my
        stupid beard.

But what's Magic?
Is there Sorrow in Magic?
Is Magic one of my boyscout creations?
Am I responsible? I with my flop?
Could Threat happen to Magic?
Yes! this the one universe in which
        there *is* threat to magic, by
        writing while high.

A Universe in which I am condemned to write statements.

'Ignorant Judgements Create Mistaken Worlds —'
        and this one is joined in
                Indic union to
        Affirm with laughing
                        eyes —
The world as we see it,
        Male & Female, passing thru the years,
        as has before & will, perhaps
with all its countless pearls & Bloody noses
        and I poor stupid All in G
        am stuck with that old Choice —
Ya, Crap, what Hymn to seek, & in
                what tongue, if this's the most
                I can requite from Consciousness? —
That I can skim? & put in words?
                        Could skim it faster with more juice —
        could skim a crop with Death, perchance
                — yet never know in this old world.
Will know in Death?
                And before?
                                                Will in
Another know.
                        And in another know.
                                        And
in another know.
                        And
                                Stop conceiving worlds!
                        says Philip Whalen
(My Savior!)   (oh what snobbery!)
                (as if he cd save Anyone) —
        At *least,* he won't understand.
I lift my finger in the air to create
a universe he won't understand, full
        of sadness.

— finally staring straight ahead in surprise
        & recollection into the mirror of
                the Hotel Commercio room.
        Time repeats itself. Including
this consciousness, which has seen
itself before — thus the locust-whistle
of antiquity's nightwatch in my eardrum . . .
I propounded a final question, and
        heard a series of final answers.
What is God? for instance, asks the answer?
        And whatever else can the replier reply but reply?
Whatever the nature of mind, that
                the nature of *both* question and answer.

                    & yet one wants to live
                in a *single* universe.

                                Does one?

Must it be one?
        Why, as with the Jews
        must the God be One?
                O what does
the concept ONE mean?
                IT'S MAD!

        GOD IS ONE!

             IS X

        IS MEANINGLESS —

                ADONOI —

        IS A JOKE —

          THE HEBREWS ARE

      WRONG — (CRIST & BUDDA

      ATTEST, also wrongly!)

      What is One but Formation
                of mind?
        arbitrary madness! 6000 years
Spreading out in all directions simultaneously —

      I forgive both good & ill
& I seek nothing, like a painted savage with
spear crossed by orange black & white bands!

'I found the Jivaros & was
entrapped in their universe'
                    I'm scribbling nothings.
Page upon page of profoundest nothing,
    as scribed the Ancient Hebe, when
            he wrote Adonoi Echad or One —
all to amuse, make money, or deceive —
Let Wickedness be Me
    and this the worst of all
            the universes!
                        Not the worst! Not Flame!
    I can't stand that — (Yes that's
        for Somebody Else!
                        Yet I accept
O Catfaced God, whatever comes! It's me!
I am the Flame, etc.
                O Gawd!
                    Pistol shot! Crack!
                            Circusmaster's whip —
        IMPERFECT !
                and a soul is damned to
        HELL !
                And the churchbell rings !
and there is melancholy, once again, throughout the realm.
            and I'm that soul, small as it is.

            HAVE FELT SAME BEFORE

The death of consciousness is terrible
            and yet! when all is ended
                what regret?
'S none left to remember or forget.
            And's gone into the odd.
        The only thing I fear is the Last
Chance. I'll see that last chance too
before I'm done, Old Mind. All them
old Last Chances that you knew before.
                — someday thru the dream wall
        to nextdoor consciousness
            like thru this blue hotel wall
                — millions of hotel rooms fogging
                        the focus of my eyes —

with whatever attitude I hold the cotton
to my nose, it's still a secret joke

with pinky akimbo, or with effete queer
    eye in mirror at myself,
    or serious-brow mein
             & darkened beard,
I'm still the kid of obscene chance await-
        ing —
        breathing in a chinese Universe
thru the nose like some old Brahamic God.

O   BELL   TIME   RING THY

MIDNIGHT FOR THE BILLIONTH

SOUNDY TIME, I HEAR AGAIN!

    I'll go to walk the street,
                    Who'll find
me in the night, in Lima, in my
33'd year,

On Street (Cont.)

    The souls of Peter &
I answer each other.
But — and what's a soul?
To be a poet's a
serious occupation,
condemned to that
in universe —
to walk the city
ascribbling in
a book — just accosted
by a drunk —
in Plaza de Armas
sidestreet under
a foggy sky, and
sometimes with no
moon.
    The heavy balcony
hangs over the white
marble of the Bishop's
Palace next the Cathedral —
The fountain plays
in light as e'er —
The busses & the

motorcyclists pass
thru midnight, the
carlights shine
the beggar turns
a corner with his
cigarette stub &
cane, the Noisers
leave the tavern
and delay, conversing
in high voice,
Awake,
    Hasta Manana
they all say —
    and somewhere
at the other end of
the line, a telephone
is ringing, once again
with unknown news —
    The night
looms over Lima
sky black fog —
and I sit helpless
smoking with a
pencil hand —
    The long crack

in the pavement
          or yesterday's
volcano in Chile,
or the day before
the Earthquake
that begat the
World.

          The Plaza pavement
shines in the electric
light. I wait.
          The lonely beard
workman staggers
home to bed from
Death.
          Yes but I'm
a little tired of
being alone . . .
          Keats' Nightingale — the
instant of realization
a single consciousness
that hears the chimes
of Time, repeated
endlessly —

All night, w/Ether, wave

after wave of magic
understanding. A dis-
turbance of the field
of consciousness.
Magic night, magic stars,
magic men, magic music,
magic tomorrow, magic death,
magic Magic.
          What crude Magic
we live in (seeing trolley
like a rude monster
in downtown street
w/ electric diamond
wire antennae to sky
pass night café under
white arc-light by
Gran Hotel Bolivar.)

The mad potter of
Mochica made a
pot w/6 Eyes & 2
Mouths & half a Nose
& 5 Cheeks & no Chin
for us to figure out,
serious side-track,
blind alley Kosmos.

(Back in Room)

How strange to remember anything, even a button
                    much less a universe.
'What creature gives birth to itself?'
The universe is mad, slightly mad.
          — and the two sides wriggle away
      in opposite directions to die
                    lopped off
      the blind metallic length curled up
      feebly & wiggling its feet
                    in the grass
      the millepede's black head moving inches away
             on the staircase at Macchu Picchu
             the Creature feels itself,
                    destroyed,

head & tail of the universe
cut in two.

Men with slick mustaches of mystery have
pimp horrible climaxes & Karmas —
— the mad magician that created Chaos
in the peaceful void & suave.
with my fucking suave manners & knowitall
eyes, and mind full of fantasy —
the Me!   that horror that keeps me conscious
in this Hell of Birth & Death.

34 coming up — I suddenly felt old — sitting with
Walter & Raquel in Chinese Restaurant — they kissed — I alone
— age of Burroughs when we first met.

Hotel Commercio
Lima, Peru
May 28, 1960

ANTHONY HECHT

Jason

> *And from America the golden fleece*
> —Marlowe

The room is full of gold.
Is it a chapel? Is that the genuine buzz
Of cherubim, the wingèd goods?
Is it no more than sun that floods
To pool itself at her uncovered breast?
O lights, o numina, behold
How we are gifted. He who never was,
Is, and her fingers bless him and are blessed.

That blessedness is tossed
In a wild, dodging light. Suddenly clear
And poised in heavenly desire
Prophets and eastern saints take fire
And fuse with gold in windows across the way,
And turn to liquid, and are lost.
And now there deepens over lakes of air
A remembered stillness of the seventh day

Borne in on the soft cruise
And sway of birds. Slowly the ancient seas,
Those black predestined waters rise
Lisping and calm before my eyes,
And Massachusetts rises out of foam
A state of mind in which by twos
All beasts browse among barns and apple trees
As in their earliest peace, and the dove comes home.

Tonight, my dear, when the moon
Settles the radiant dust of every man,
Powders the bedsheets and the floor
With lightness of those gone before,
Sleep then, and dream the story as foretold:
Dream how a little boy alone
With a wooden sword and the top of a garbage can
Triumphs in gardens full of marigold.

Adam

> *Hath the rain a father? or who*
> *hath begotten the drops of dew?*

"Adam, my child, my son,
These very words you hear
Compose the fish and starlight
Of your untroubled dream.
When you awake, my child,
It shall all come true.
Know that it was for you
That all things were begun."

Adam, my child, my son,
Thus spoke Our Father in heaven
To his first, fabled child,
The father of us all.
And I, your father, tell
The words over again
As innumerable men
From ancient times have done.

Tell them again in pain.
You are far away
Across the salt ocean
And cannot hear my voice.
Will you forget our games,
Our hide-and-seek and song?
Child, it will be long
Before I see you again.

Adam, there will be
Many hard hours,
As an old poem says,
Hours of loneliness.
I cannot ease them for you;
They are our common lot.
During them, like as not,
You will dream of me.

When you are crouched away
In a strange clothes closet
Hiding from one who's "It"
And the dark crowds in,

Do not be afraid —
O, if you can, believe
In a father's love
You shall know some day.

Think of the summer rain,
The warmth of your small bed;
Seeing a bird in flight,
Try to remember me.
From far away
I send my blessing out
To circle the great globe;
It shall reach you yet.

The Man Who Married Magdalene: Variation on a Theme by Louis Simpson

> *Then said the Lord, dost thou*
> *well to be angry?*

I have been in this bar
For close to seven days.
The dark girl over there,
For a modest dollar, lays.

And you can get a blow-job
Where other men have pissed,
In the little room that's sacred
To the Evangelist —

If you're inclined that way.
For myself, I drink and sleep.
The floor is knotty cedar
But the beer is flat and cheap.

And you can bet your life
I'll be here another seven.
Stranger, here's to my wife,
Who died and went to heaven.

She was a famous beauty,
But *our very breath is loaned.*
The rabbi's voice was fruity,
And since then I've been stoned —

A royal, nonstop bender.
But your money's no good here;
Put it away. Bartender,
Give my friend a beer.

I dreamed the other night
When the sky was full of stars
That I stood outside a gate
And looked in through the bars.

Two angels stood together.
A purple light was shed
From their every metal feather.
And then one of them said,

"It was pretty much the same
For years and years and years,
But since the Christians came
The place is full of queers.

Still, let them have their due.
Things here are far less solemn.
Instead of each beardy Jew
Muttering, 'Shalom, Shalom,'

There's a down-to-earth, informal
Fleshiness to the scene;
It's healthier, more normal,
If you know what I mean.

Such as once went to Gehenna
Now dance among the blessed.
But Mary Magdalena,
She had it the best."

And he nudged his feathered friend
And gave him a wicked leer,
And I woke up and fought back
The nausea with a beer.

What man shall understand
The Lord's mysterious way?
My tongue is thick with worship
And whiskey, and some day

I will come to in Bellevue,
And make psalms unto the Lord.
But verily I tell you,
She hath her reward.

Behold the Lilies of the Field

And now. An attempt.
Don't tense yourself; take it easy.
Look at the flowers there in the glass bowl.
Yes, they are lovely and fresh. I remember
Giving my mother flowers once, rather like those
(Are they narcissus or jonquils?)
And I hoped she would show some pleasure in them
But got that mechanical enthusiastic show
She used on the telephone once in praising some friend
For thoughtfulness or good taste or whatever it was,
And when she hung up, turned to us all and said,
"God, what a bore she is!"
I think she was trying to show us how honest she was,
At least with us. But the effect
Was just the opposite, and now I don't think
She knows what honesty is. "Your mother's a whore,"
Someone said, not meaning she slept around,
Though perhaps this was part of it, but
Meaning she had lost all sense of honor,
And I think this is true.

But that's not what I wanted to say.
What was it I wanted to say?
When he said that about Mother, I had to laugh,
I really did, it was so amazingly true.
Where was I?
Lie back. Relax.

Oh yes. I remember now what it was.
It was what I saw them do to the emperor.
They captured him, you know. Eagles and all.
They stripped him, and made an iron collar for his neck,
And they made a cage out of our captured spears,
And they put him inside, naked and collared,
And exposed to the view of the whole enemy camp.
And I was tied to a post and made to watch
When he was taken out and flogged by one of their generals
And then forced to offer his ripped back
As a mounting block for the barbarian king
To get on his horse;
And one time to get down on all fours to be the royal throne

When the king received our ambassadors
To discuss the question of ransom.
Of course he didn't want ransom.
And I was tied to a post and made to watch.
That's enough for now. Lie back. Try to relax.
No, that's not all.
They kept it up for two months.
We were taken to their outmost provinces.
It was always the same, and we were always made to watch,
The others and I. How he stood it, I don't know.
And then suddenly
There were no more floggings or humiliations,
The king's personal doctor saw to his back,
He was given decent clothing, and the collar was taken off,
And they treated us all with a special courtesy.
By the time we reached their capital city
His back was completely healed.
They had taken the cage apart —
But of course they didn't give us back our spears.
Then later that month, it was a warm afternoon in May,
The rest of us were marched out to the central square.
The crowds were there already, and the posts were set up,
To which we were tied in the old watching positions.
And he was brought out in the old way, and stripped,
And then tied flat on a big rectangular table
So that only his head could move.
Then the king made a short speech to the crowds,
To which they responded with gasps of wild excitement,
And which was then translated for the rest of us.
It was the sentence. He was to be flayed alive,
As slowly as possible, to drag out the pain.
And we were made to watch. The king's personal doctor,
The one who had tended his back,
Came forward with a tray of surgical knives.
They began at the feet.
And we were not allowed to close our eyes
Or to look away. When they were done, hours later,
The skin was turned over to one of their saddle-makers
To be tanned and stuffed and sewn. And for what?
A hideous life-sized doll, filled out with straw,
In the skin of the Roman Emperor, Valerian,
With blanks of mother-of-pearl under the eyelids,
And painted shells that had been prepared beforehand

For the fingernails and toenails,
Roughly cross-stitched on the inseam of the legs
And up the back to the center of the head,
Swung in the wind on a rope from the palace flagpole;
And young girls were brought there by their mothers
To be told about the male anatomy.
His death had taken hours.
They were very patient.
And with him passed away the honor of Rome.

In the end, I was ransomed. Mother paid for me.
You must rest now. You must. Lean back.
Look at the flowers.
Yes. I am looking. I wish I could be like them.

Upon the Death of George Santayana

Down every passage of the cloister hung
A dark wood cross on a white plaster wall;
But in the court were roses, not as tongue
Might have them, something of Christ's blood grown small,
But just as roses, and at three o'clock
Their essences, inseparably bouqueted,
Seemed more than Christ's last breath, and rose to mock
An elderly man for whom the Sisters prayed.

What heart can know itself? The Sibyl speaks
Mirthless and unbedizened things, but who
Can fathom her intent? Loving the Greeks,
He whispered to a nun who strove to woo
His spirit unto God by prayer and fast,
"Pray that I go to Limbo, if it please
Heaven to let my soul regard at last
Democritus, Plato and Socrates."

And so it was. The river, as foretold,
Ran darkly by; under his tongue he found
Coin for the passage; the ferry tossed and rolled;
The sages stood on their appointed ground,
Sighing, all as foretold. The mind was tasked;
He had not dreamed that so many had died.
"But where is Alcibiades," he asked,
"The golden roisterer, the animal pride?"

Those sages who had spoken of the love
And enmity of things, how all things flow,
Stood in a light no life is witness of,
And Socrates, whose wisdom was to know
He did not know, spoke with a solemn mien,
And all his wonderful ugliness was lit,
"He whom I loved for what he might have been
Freezes with traitors in the ultimate pit."

Birdwatchers of America

> "I suffer now continually from vertigo,
> and today, 23rd of January, 1862, I
> received a singular warning: I felt
> the wind of the wing of madness pass
> over me."
>
> Baudelaire, *Journals*

It's all very well to dream of a dove that saves,
        Picasso's or the Pope's,
The one that annually coos in Our Lady's ear
        Half the world's hopes,
And the other one that shall cunningly engineer
The retirement of all businessmen to their graves,
        And when this is brought about
Make us the loving brothers of every lout —

But in our part of the country a false dusk
        Lingers for hours; it steams
From the soaked hay, wades in the cloudy woods,
        Engendering other dreams.
Formless and soft beyond the fence it broods
Or rises as a faint and rotten musk
        Out of a broken stalk.
There are some things of which we seldom talk;

For instance, the woman next door, whom we hear at night,
        Claims that when she was small
She found a man stone dead near the cedar trees
        After the first snowfall.
The air was clear. He seemed in ultimate peace
Except that he had no eyes. Rigid and bright
        Upon the forehead, furred
With a light frost, crouched an outrageous bird.

Lizards and Snakes

On the summer road that ran by our front porch
      Lizards and snakes came out to sun.
It was hot as a stove out there, enough to scorch
      A buzzard's foot. Still, it was fun
To lie in the dust and spy on them. Near but remote,
      They snoozed in the carriage ruts, a smile
In the set of the jaw, a fierce pulse in the throat
Working away like Jack Doyle's after he'd run the mile.

Aunt Martha had an unfair prejudice
      Against them (as well as being cold
Toward bats.) She was pretty inflexible in this,
      Being a spinster and all, and old.
So we used to slip them into her knitting box.
      In the evening she'd bring in things to mend
And a nice surprise would slide out from under the socks.
It broadened her life, as Joe said. Joe was my friend.

But we never did it again after the day
      Of the big wind when you could hear the trees
Creak like rockingchairs. She was looking away
      Off, and kept saying, "Sweet Jesus, please
Don't let him hear me. He's as like as twins.
      He can crack us like lice with his fingernail.
I can see him plain as a pikestaff. Look how he grins
And swinges the scaly horror of his folded tail."

DANIEL HOFFMAN

Exploration

I am who the trail took,
nose of whom I followed,
woodwit I confided in
through thorned-and-briared hallows;
favoring my right side for
clouds the sun had hemmed in.
Behind the North I sought daystar,
bore down highroads hidden
to undiscerning gaze.
My right, my right I turned to
on trails strangely unblazoned
where fistfive forkings burgeoned,
I took my right. Was destined
among deerdroppings on the ridge
or chipmunk stones astrain
or hoofmucks in the swampcabbage
to err? Landmarking birch
selfmultiplied in malice till
woods reared a whitebarred cage
around my spinning eye. The spool
of memory had run out my yarn
and lost the last hank. Found
I the maze I wander in
where my right, trusted hand,
leads round and round a certain copse,
a sudden mound of stone,
an anthill humming in the rocks
an expectant tune?
Lacklearning now my knowledge is
of how to coax recalcitrant
ignition from cold engines,
or mate a fugue in either hand
on spinet or converse
in any tongue but stonecrop signs.
Clouds hump like battling bulls. The firs
lash me with angry tines,

shred my clothes. A windwhipped will
uncompassed, lacking fur or fang,
strange to these parts, yet whom the anthill
anticipating, sang.

In the Days of Rin-Tin-Tin

In the days of Rin-Tin-Tin
There was no such thing as sin,
No boymade mischief worth God's wrath
And the good dog dogged the badman's path.

In the nights, the deliquescent horn of Bix
Gave presentiments of the pleasures of sex;
In the Ostrich Walk we walked by twos —
Ja-da, jing-jing, what could we lose?

The Elders mastered The Market, Mah-jongg,
Readily admitted the Victorians wrong,
While Caligari hobbled with his stick and his ghoul
And overtook the Little Fellow on his way to school.

Flushing Meadows, 1939

Lightning! Lightning! Lightning! Without thunder!
A zaggedy white trombone of lightshot, crackling
Between metallic globules, egglike, hugely
Aching in the corners of our eyes, —
The afterburn of electrocuted air
Sizzled into our ears and nostrils, halfblinded
Us. We reeled into the dim sunshine
Groping a little, holding hands, still hearing
The confident vibrant voice of the sound system —
'Harnessed . . . power . . . unnumbered benefits . . .'
And this we pondered down the bedecked Concourse
Of Nations. A gold-robed King of Poland brandished
Crossed swords on horseback pedestaled on high;
The Soviet Citizen bore his sanguine star
Almost as high as that American flag
That snaffled in the smart wind perched atop
The Amusement Park's live parachute drop.
Trapped in antique mores, now the sun
Abandoned the International Pavilions

To miracles of manmade light. The trees
In their pots were underlit, revealing pasty
Backsides of their embarrassed leaves.
In the wind's vortex toward the Pool of Fountains:
Mauve and yellowing geysers surged and fell
As national anthems tolled, amity-wise,
From the State of Florida's Spanish Carillon.
What portent, in that luminous night to share
Undyingly, discovery of each other!
Helen, Helen, thy beauty is to me
Like those immutable emblems, huge and pure, —
One glimmering globe the world's will unifying
Beside spired hope that ravels the deep skies,
Our time's unnumbered benefits descrying
In their own light's shimmer, though the new dawn comes
With lightning, lightening in a murmur of summer thunder.

A Meeting

He had awaited me,
The jackal-headed.

He from Alexandria
In the days of the Dynasts,

I from Philadelphia
In a time of indecisions.

His nose sniffed, impassive,
Dust of the aeons.

A sneeze wrenched my brain
— I couldn't control it.

His hairy ears listen
Long. He is patient.

I sift tunes from the winds
That blast my quick head.

His agate eye gazes
Straight ahead, straight ahead.

Mine watch clocks and turn
In especial toward one face.

I thank Priestess of Rā
Who brought us together,

Stone-cutters of Pharaoh
And The Trustees of

The British Museum.
When with dog-eared Anubis

I must sail toward the sun
The glistering Phoenix

Will ride on our prow;
Behind the hound-voices

Of harrying geese
Sink the cities of striving,

The fiefdoms of change
With which we have done,

Grown in grandeur more strange,
More heroic than life was

Or the dark stream at peace,
Or wings singed in the sun.

A Letter to Wilbur Frohock

St-Apollinaire (Côte D'or)
November, 1956

Cher Maître:

Neither my explication
of 'Le Dernier Abencérage'
nor the almost-fluency
at quip and badinage

attested by your A minus
a decade ago
in 'Oral Intermediate
French' suffices now;

a beret is not enough.
Je puis acheter du pain
mais, when I go to the coalyard
as I do, again and again,

my first word or gesture's
carte d'identité,
sufficient proclamation:
'JE SUIS ÉTRANGER.'

'Sell you coal? My poor mother
Burns faggots in her mountain hovel —
You've la bombe atomique in your country —
Our children go barefoot in winter'

la marchande rails, distrait —
Besides, her coalyard's bare;
but, as you've said, the structure
— impeccable — of their

grammar reflects the logic
of the French mind. We've been here
two months. By now the neighbors
say 'Bonjour, Monsieur';

in our village there are two eggs
for sale each second day,
reserved for the toothless aged
or a sick bébé

and when our boy got queasy
and couldn't take his meat
at l'épicerie they sold me
un oeuf for him to eat —

my accent's improving.

The City of Satisfactions

As I was travelling toward the city of satisfactions
On my employment, seeking the treasure of pleasure,
Laved in the superdome observation car by Muzak
Soothed by the cool conditioned and reconditioned air,
Sealed in from the smell of the heat and the spines
Of the sere mesquite and the seared windblast of the sand,
It was conjunction of a want of juicy fruit
And the train's slowdown and stopping at a depot
Not listed on the schedule, unnamed by platform sign,
That made me step down on the siding
With some change in hand. The newsstand, on inspection,

Proved a shed of greyed boards shading
A litter of stale rags.
Turning back, I blanched at the Silent Streak: a wink
Of the sun's reflection caught its rear-view window
Far down the desert track. I grabbed the crossbar
And the handcar clattered. Up and down
It pumped so fast I hardly could grab hold it,
His regal head held proud despite the bending
Knees, back-knees, back-knees, back-knees propelling.
His eyes bulged beadier than a desert toad's eyes.
His huge hands shrank upon the handlebar,
His mighty shoulders shrivelled and his skin grew
Wrinkled while I watched the while we reeled
Over the mesquite till the train grew larger
And pumping knees, back-knees, we stood still and
Down on us the train bore,
The furious tipping of the levers unabated
Wrenched my sweating eyes and aching armpits,
He leapt on long webbed feet into the drainage
Dryditch and the car swung longside on a siding
Slowing down beside the Pullman diner
Where the napkined waiter held a tray of glasses.
The gamehen steamed crisp-crust behind the glass.
I let go of the tricycle and pulled my askew necktie,
Pushed through the diner door, a disused streetcar,
A Danish half devoured by flies beneath specked glass,
Dirty cups on the counter,
A menu, torn, too coffeestained for choices, told
In a map of rings my cryptic eyes unspelled
Of something worth the digging for right near by
Here just out beyond the two-door shed.
The tracks were gone now but I found a shovel,
Made one, that is, from a rusting oildrum cover,
A scrap of baling wire, a broken crutch,
And down I heaved on the giving earth and rockshards
And a frog drygasped once from a distant gulley
And up I spewed the debris in a range
Of peaks I sank beneath and sweated under till
One lunge sounded the clunk of iron on brass
And furious scratch and pawing of the dryrock
Uncovered the graven chest and the pile of earth downslid
While under a lowering sky, sweatwet, I grasped and wrestled
The huge chest, lunged and jerked and fought it upward
Till it toppled sideways on the sand. I smashed it

Open, and it held a barred box. My nails broke
On the bars that wouldn't open. I smashed it
Open and it held a locked box. I ripped my knuckles
But couldn't wrest that lock off till I smashed it
Open and it held a small box worked
In delicate filigree of silver with
A cunning keyhole. But there was no key.
I pried it, ripped my fingers underneath it
But couldn't get it open till I smashed it
Open and it held a little casket
Sealed tight with twisted wires or vines of shining
Thread. I bit and tugged and twisted, cracked my teeth
But couldn't loose the knot. I smashed it
Open and the top came off, revealing
A tiny casket made of jade. It had
No top, no seam, no turnkey. Thimblesmall
It winked unmoving near the skinbreak
Where steakjuice pulsed and oozed. I thought aroma
Sifted, thinning till the dark horizon
Seemed, and then no longer seemed, a trifle
Sweetened. I knelt before
A piece of desert stone. When I have fitted
That stone into its casket, and replaced
The lid and set that casket in its box,
Fitted the broken top and set that box within
The box it came in and bent back the bars
And put it in the chest, the chest back in the hole,
The peaks around the pit-edge piled back in the pit,
Replaced the baling wire and crutch and oildrum cover
And pushed back through the diner, will the train
Sealed in from the smell of heat and mesquite
Envelop me in Muzak while it swooshes
Past bleak sidings such as I wait on
Nonstop toward the city of satisfactions roaring?
If I could only make this broken top
Fit snug back on this casket

THEODORE HOLMES

The Dysynni Valley (Wales)

The larger, gentler slopes of its mouth opening upon the ocean
Like a woman's legs upon the grey impersonal expanse of
distance
That extends from the hollow within her; across the valley
The lines of stone walls marking the fields on the hillside
Like the fine reticulations of viscera seen under a microscope,
Or the veins beneath an eyelid lifted to remove a speck of dust.
The green infolding of its depression, the silk bed of its grazing
Made greener by the rich loam washed down from higher
elevations,
Holds all that man is or all that man has done on it
Like a breast the earth has bared to offer him her bounty,
A vast lap between whose knees he has been rocked to sleep
for ages;
Across the rounded tops of hills, the soft curves of ridges,
The fields like a quilt-pattern of an apron, — the tiny dwellings
of man,
The small clusters of farm buildings laid in crevices,
So inconsequential, so diminished by the vastness of the earth
they occupy,
So temporary do they seem, there only by its indulgence,
They look like those places a woman bears inside her —
The marks left on the ground where once man entered to
perform his love.
There are the mouldy gates rusted open, falling off their
hinges from use,
Broken wells in which the water has run fresh for ages,
Paths over which the farmer has driven his cows for gen-
erations
Grown stony by the ceaseless trickle of buried springs down
them;
There are the animal smells, the smell of excrement returning
to the earth,
The tinge of musk given the air by the earth's dark renewal
of decay:
And below, winding like a snake along the floor, its scales
glittering in the sun,

Is the Dysynni, that means "follows the floor of the valley":
It seems an opening in the earth through which shines a light
                                                    beneath it.
Up where the valley narrows, becomes hardly more than a
                                          bed for the stream,
There is the antique fortress of her heart;
Raised upon an outcropping of rock from the floor, looking
                                              out to the sea,
That commands the prospect of the whole entry to the valley:
It is where, they say, Llewellyn the Great was finally taken by
                                                      storm.
For long it lay a rubble of stone, overgrown by weed and
                                                      briar,
Until, in late years, they have rebuilt it as a tourist attrac-
                                                  tion —
Raising a model of the old out of fresh cement and the old
                                                    stone
As a concession to the heart's need for something to display
                                            to public view:
Its brave ramparts rising a little too proudly, the empty pit
Of its dungeon, the dry moat, its vacant rooms and courtyard,
With cigarette stubs where armorial bearings used to lean,
History on graven tablets where chain-mail used to be;
In remodeling it they even incorporated the ruins for au-
                                              thenticity.
Up further, where the floor is no more a floor but a rise,
On the ascent to Cader Idris that overlooks the valley like a
                                                    head,
There is the remains of a place in which someone used to
                                                    dwell;
Gutted by fire or wind, only the stone outlines of the walls
                                            still standing
With a few patches of roof overhead, it was once the highest
                                            habitation
At this end of the valley, from which all else could be seen;
Some say it is the ruins of an old cloister,
Some, the house of a visionary who would keep all before
                                                    him —
Others maintain it was built by the original dwellers of the
                                                  valley
As a shrine to an unknown god; now visited only as a cu-
                                              riosity
By hikers on their way up the mountain, children out for a
                                                  spree,

Climbing through the windows, swinging on the door, chin-
                                      ning on beams, —
Or the odd traveler from the valley below who has lost his way
And stops for a rest or to take shelter from the rain.
— There now, the moon is white on the broken cistern,
The owl hoots, the wind moans in the rafters,
A door swings on a rusty hinge,
The stars shine through the roof,
While below herds crop the well-kept fields by night.

The Old Age Home (Cambridge, Mass.)

Voluntarily walled themselves up inside the stone,
Because life no longer held for them a way of getting along —
On the shores of the reservoir as if it was some wisdom of the
                                                        town's
They have stored up in them by having lived in it;
Each day cared for by a world that no longer has meaning:
Food prepared on trays sent up from below,
Beds from which they need only arise to return to them made;
Entertainment, what pastimes they can devise for themselves
Or the moving figures on the screen in the solarium.
Aged men and aged women passing their days
Stirring a little dust in the corridors — combing their hair
In bathrobes as they once did for their dinner dates,
Putting on a touch of lipstick to add color to their face;
Gestures made in expiation of wounds that have healed:
Sly smiles, overtures of commiseration, minor gallantries;
An intercourse arisen out of the knowledge of the old fail-
                                                        ures —
Being able to get along now because they no longer are
An expression of the reason why; making of infirmity a life.

What society has raised to the colloquies of the past,
Looking out over a body of water toward a graveyard on a
                                                        hill;
Surrounded by the unintelligible order of nature renewing it-
                                                        self,
They have raised this institution of brick to preserve them:
The old rocking on balconies or strolling along flowered paths,
At the edge of that lake looking out toward that further hill.
The gulf of their existence between them and their final end —
All that they once took for their image reflected in life,

Now only become the dimensions of space through which they
see:
The hole of their dreams, broken off bits of desire, the
emptiness
That always lay just beyond their fulfillment; wisdom
Written out in the soul in words: the forms of life without its
needs.
The sun setting in the west over the graveyard
Casts up in the heavens the promise of an existence beyond it;
The stones, a monument to the last point of their identity
As they go on in the world as others — in the lake
The colors reflected like the story of a life going on above it:
It is the water that bubbles up in the fountains in our studies.

Christ

Shifting his position to relieve a cramped limb
That had been bent too long under him,
Sitting in the shade of an aspen tree at noon
To refresh himself for the remainder of his journey;
Partaking in the evening of a meal with friends,
Lying covered with leaves at night beneath the stars,
He felt, as other men, the weight of his body
For which he endured the support of his needs:
He found that those about him were necessary to his pur-
poses —
The mother that first bore him inside her
And then in her arms on the flight into Egypt;
The burly peasant that tagged along like a dog,
And later the wide-eyed followers
Who bore him on their shoulders to distant lands.
Even his first cries were answered with gifts —
He had all the zeal of a man left to make his way in the
world.

Standing among the smells of the market-place
While the women passed with their burdens on their backs;
Riding ass-back from encounter to encounter;
Stooping to amazement to conquer —
Pretending that the parables in which he spoke
Possessed a content beyond their meaning:
And by the manner of his going, making sure
That what he left behind contained his continuance —
Knowing that one word is supplanted by another

In the endless struggle of man for the mastery of his soul,
And that the deeds we perform soon die
With the diminishing results their effects have had,
He took the marks of our pain upon his flesh; —
Were he divine, how would we have recognized him?

Buddha

As when a stone is dropped in water, the harmonies of the
                                                    universe
In the circles radiating from his invisible self;
About his head those concentric shells of light
In which intelligence is taken to be
An attribute of mind perceived by its own thinking:
He sits as irrefrangible on earth as a tree stump
Gradually receding back into the element from which it
                                                    came, —
His feet folded under him as those youthful skills at play
For which he has no further use.
Behind the impassive mask of his features, about the lips
An inner brimming of light suggests on his face
A smile of compassion, resignation or illumination —
The broad surfaces of a world given up to our complications
                                                    in it;
It is the smoothness into which the wrinkles on a woman's
                                                    brow dissolve
When taken into the arms of her lover:
Behind his closed lids he is experiencing the redemption of
                                                    himself.
His hands are held in complementary positions —
One soliciting us with the offer of hope,
The other raised in admonition against too close an approach;
With one hand the clarity,
The other the essence —
His being having wholly given up his existence,
He offers us nothing but the vision of the illumination that
                                                    he is.

LEROI JONES

The Clearing

Trees & brown squares
of shadow. The green
washed out and drained into clumps of mist
that cloak more trees. And trees, outside
the window; or spreading heavy fronds
stepping away from the light. We come
to a forest, or we see it
from the window. We step into it,
spreading the heavy leaves, or drop the blind
& let it clatter in the damp breeze from the yard.

Where are the beasts? In a forest,
there are always wild beasts. And the sun, a woman,
goes there to sleep. Brown trunks
their shadows against the white wall, rain
spreading against the glass. Blue rain
outside, and shadows against the wall. A wet wind
moves them. The smells
come in. Leaves & darkness
wetting our faces. Breathing
through the leaves, and disappear.

Trees,
& shadows of trees (the wind
pushes them apart. I am
an animal watching
his forest. Listening
for your breathing, your merest
move in the dark. You wear
a gown of it. The dark
ness. And
we can move naked
through it, through
the forest
if it does not disappear. Who
will remember
the way back. When the blind

flings back
and more smells come in. As sound
or light moving against the wall. Where
are the beasts?

The eye is useless. Sound, Sound,
& what you smell
or feel. I am someone else
who smells you. The lamp
at the corner is bleak
& leafless. Its light
does not even reach
the edge of the trees.

What bird
makes that noise? (If this
were a western place, a temperate hand
could shape it. A western mouth
could make it on this mist. Green mist
settling on our flesh. (if this
were a western place, a bank
of the Marne, Cezanne's greens
& yellows floating unreal
under a bridge. A blue bridge
for a temperate eye. We have
vines. (What bird
makes that noise?

Your voice down the hall. Are
you singing? A shadow song
we lock our movement
in. Were you singing?
down the hall. White plaster
on the walls, our fingers
leave their marks, on
the dust, or tearing
the wall away. Were you
singing? What song
was that?

I love you (& you be
quiet, & feel my wet mouth
on your fingers, I
love you
& bring you fish
& oranges. (Before the light fails

we should move to a dryer place,
but not too far from water.) I
Love you &
you are singing. What song
is that? (The blinds held up
by a wind, tearing
the shadows. I
Love you
& you hide yourself
in the shadows. The forest is huge
around us. The night
clings to our cries. (I hear
your voice
down the hall, through the window, above
all those trees, a light
it seems
& you are singing. What song
is that The words
are beautiful.

The Death of Nick Charles

. . . And how much of this
do you understand? I hide
my face, my voice twisted
in the heavy winter fog. If I
came to you, left this wet island
& came to you; now, when I am young,
& have strength in my fingers. To say,
I love you, & cannot even recognize
you. How much of me
could you understand? (Only
that I love colour, motion, thin high air
at night? The recognizable parts
of yourself?

We love only heroes. Glorious
death in battle. Scaling walls,
burning bridges behind us, destroying
all ways back. All retreat. As if
some things were fixed. As if the moon
would come to us each night (&
we could watch

from the battlements). As if
there were anything certain
or lovely
in our lives.

Sad
long
motion of air
pushing in my face. Lies,
weakness, hatred
of myself. Of you
for not understanding
this. Or not
despising me
for the right causes. I am
sick as, OH,
the night is. As
cold days are,
when we must watch them
grow old
& dark.

2

I am thinking
of a dance. One I could
invent, if there
were music. If you
would play for me, some
light music. Couperin
with yellow hillsides. Ravel
as I kiss your hair. Lotions
of Debussy.
I am moved by what? Angered at its whine;
the quiet delicacy of my sadness. The elements.
My face torn by wind, faces, desire, lovely chinese ladies
sweeping the sidewalks. (And this is not
what I mean. Not the thing I wanted for you. Not, finally.
Music, only terror at this lightly scribbled day.

Emotion. Words.
Waste. No clear delight.
No light under my fingers. The room, The
walls, silent & deadly. Not
Music.

If there were
a dance. For us
to make; your fingers
on my face, your face wet
with tears (or silence. For us
to form upon this heavy air. Tearing
the silence, hurting the darkness
with the colour of our movement! Nakedness?
Great leaps
into the air? Huge pirouettes; the moon blurred
on ancient lakes. Thin horns
and laughter.

3

Can you hear this? Do you know
who speaks to you? Do you
know me? (Not even
your lover. Afraid of you, your sudden
disorder. Your ringless
hands. Your hair
disguised. Your voice
not even real. Or
beautiful.

        (What we had
I cannot even say. Something
like loathing
covers your words.

4

It grows dark
around you. And these words
are not music. They make no motions
for a dance. (Standing awkwardly
before the window, watching
the moon. The ragged smoke
lifting against
grey sheaths
of night.
You shimmer like words
I barely hear. Your face
twisted into words. "Love, Oh,

Love me." The window facing night, & always
when we cannot speak.

What shapes stream through the glass?
Only shadows
on the wall. Under
my fingers, trailing me
with a sound like
glass on slate. You cry out
in the night,
& only the moon
answers.

5

The house sits
between red buildings. And a bell
rocks against the night air. The moon
sits over the North river, underneath
a blue bridge. Boats & old men
move through the darkness. Needing
no eyes. Moving slowly
towards the long black line
of horizon. Footfalls, the
twisting dirty surf. Sea birds
scalding the blackness.

I sit inside alone, without
thoughts. I cannot lie
& say I think of you. I merely sit
& grow weary, not even watching
the sky lighten with morning.

                & now
I am sleeping
& you will not be able
to wake me.

The Insidious Dr. Fu Man Chu

If I think myself
strong, then I am
not true to the misery
in my life. The uncertainty.

(of what I am saying, who
I have chosen to become, the
very air pressing my skin
held gently away, this woman
and the one I taste continually
in my nebular pallet tongue face
mouth feet, standing in piles
of numbers, hills, lovers.
                              If
I think myself ugly
& go to the mirror, smiling,
at the inaccuracy, or now
the rain pounds dead grass
in the stone yard, I think
how very wise I am. How very
very wise.

Notes For A Speech

African blues
does not know me. Their steps, in sands
of their own
land. A country
in black and white, newspapers
blown down pavements
of the world. Does
not feel
what I am.
                    Strength
in the dream, an oblique
suckling of nerve, the wind
throws up sand, eyes
are something locked in
hate, of hate, of hate, to
walk abroad, they conduct
their deaths apart
from my own. Those
heads, I call
my "people."

          (And who are they. People. To concern
myself, ugly man. Who
you, to concern
the white flat stomachs

of maidens, inside houses
dying. Black. Peeled moon
light on my fingers
move under
her clothes. Where
is her husband. Black
words throw up sand
to eyes, fingers of
their private dead. Whose
soul, eyes, in sand. My color
is not theirs. Lighter, white man
talk. They shy away. My own
dead souls, my, so called
people. Africa
is a foreign place. You are
as any other sad man here
american.

The politics of rich painters

is something like the rest
of our doubt, whatever slow thought
comes to rest, beneath the silence
of starving talk.
                              Just their fingers' prints
staining the cold glass, is sufficient
for commerce, and a proper ruling on
humanity. You know the pity
of democracy, that we must sit here
and listen to how he made his money.
Tho the catalogue of his possible ignorance
roars and extends through the room
like fire. "Love", becomes the pass,
the word taken intimately to combat
all the uses of language. So that learning
itself falls into disrepute.

2

What they have gathered into themselves
in that short mean trip from mother's iron tit
to those faggot handmaidens of the french whore
who wades slowly in the narrows, waving her burnt out

torch. There are movies, and we have opinions. There are
regions of compromise so attractive, we daily long
to filthy our minds with their fame. And all the songs
of our handsome generation fall clanging like stones
in the empty darkness of their heads.

                              Couples, so beautiful
in the newspapers, marauders of cheap sentiment. So much
                                                     taste
so little understanding, except some up and coming queer ex-
                                                      plain
cinema and politics while drowning a cigarette.

3

They are more ignorant than the poor
tho they pride themselves with that accent. And
move easily in fake robes of egalitarianism. Meaning,
I will fuck you even if you don't like art. And are wounded
that you call their italian memories petit bourgeois.

                                      Whose death
will be Malraux's? Or the names Senghor, Price, Baldwin
whispered across the same dramatic pancakes, to let each eye-
                                               lash flutter
at the news of their horrible deaths. It is a cheap game
to patronize the dead, unless their deaths be accountable
to your own understanding. Which be nothing nothing
if not bank statements and serene trips to our ominous
                                           countryside.
Nothing, if not whining talk about handsome white men.
                                               Nothing
if not false glamorous and static. Except, I admit, your lives
are hideously real.

The source of their art crumbles into legitimate history.
The whimpering pigment of a decadent economy, slashed into
                                                     life
as Yeats' mad girl plummeting over the nut house wall, her
                                               broken
knee caps rattling in the weather, reminding us of lands
our antennae do not reach.

And there are people in these savage geographies
use your name in other contexts
think, perhaps, the title of your latest painting
another name for liar.

Hegel

Cut out
the insides,
where eyes
bungle their silence, and trains suffer
to be painted
by memory.
This is turning.   As a man
turns.   Hardened or reconceived
sometimes the way we wish our lives
would be. "Let me do this
again,
another way."

*

Pushed to the wall
we fall away from each other
in this heresy. Dispute each other's
lives, as history. Or the common speech
of disaster, lacking a face or name, we give it
ours. And are destroyed by the very virtues
of our ignorance.
I am not saying,
"Let the state fuck
its faggots,"
only that no fag
go unfucked, for purely impersonal
reasons.

*

I am trying to understand
the nightmare of economies. On the phone,
through the mails, I am afraid. I scream
for help. I scream
for help. And none comes, has ever
come. No single redeeming hand
has ever been offered,
even against the excess
of speech, no single redeeming
word, has come
wringing out of flesh
with the imperfect beautiful resolution
that would release me from this heavy contract
of emptiness.

Either I am wrong
or "he" is wrong. All right
I am wrong, but give me someone
to talk to.

The Dance

The dance.
                (held up for me by
an older man.   He told me how.   Showed
me. Not steps, but the fix
of muscle.   A position
for myself: to move.

Duncan
told of dance. His poems
full of what we called
so long for you to be. A
dance. And all his words
ran out of it. That there
was some bright elegance
the sad meat of the body
made. Some gesture, that
if we became, for one blank moment,
would turn us
into creatures of rhythm.

I want to be sung. I want
all my bones and meat hummed
against the thick floating
winter sky. I want myself
as dance. As what I am
given love, or time, or space
to feel myself.

The time of thought. The space
of actual movement. (Where they
have taken up the sea, and
keep me against my will.) I said, also,
love, being older or younger
than your world. I am given
to lying, love, call you out
now, given to feeling things
I alone create.

And let me once, create
myself. And let you, whoever
sits now breathing on my words
create a self of your own. One
that will love me.

ROBERT KELLY

Parallel Texts

FIGURE

If her neck is
if her lips were
Egypt

        curve of her
pubis convexed
by two small bones

and call her rump
Arabian
        vase of
flower

    of the carpel
of her sex: stir

          red
yielding to dark:
    the corolla.

FIGURE

into this chest of spices
step
into this brown zodiac

the great mystery
rocking on her heels

and oregano   these green leaves
can they be
in the jar in the jar
mountain grasses
oregano?

         she
in one place or another

enclosing
a chest of spices

The boat

floated in the cove
her cat in it
keeping out of the
shipped water

she sat up to her
ankles in slosh
and dreamed over at
Pennsylvania

where there are pines
and wildcats and
barns caved in on
empty mangers empty

troughs and she said
what is that star?
pointing to a single
light a farmhouse

way up the same hill
my father one year saw
a white enormous
silent owl nesting on.

Going

If you ever get there
where I have been once or
twice before, running in
summers with no sleep

under iron bridges, the
eddy around me, curve
of blackwillow bank
around me lying at bottom

looking up at the river's
skin, shadows of fish
in the sun and no whispers,
under wooden bridges

rumbling under the Fords
sifting dust into that
coolness of underbridge
striped with sunlight

God I love you all and
don't want you to be there
under the blue skin
itching in shallow grass

no thought in your minds
but to measure those
distances, counting
in pores of sunburnt skin

and tell me you're there
in inches and feet and
how very far away, easily
that much further away.

Sun of the Center

a man divided into animal
biting down through burrows with its teeth
into animal pressed into earth
a different shape
the five arrows of his motion
fly out into the structured world and are lost
the stone arrowheads enter the house of the wind
the reed shafts burn in the sky the lightning is random
proceeding from the north the black lightning out of a clear
                                                            sky

into the shape of a man
who walks out with flowering skull and starfish fingers
and clay runs out of his nostrils
and his hips are still covered with bark
who makes patterns on the walls, his five fingers spread
who twists his hands together folding the fingers together
the true gesture of sunrise, the flower delivered from earth
who knows that empty horizons come from an open hand
who holds tight, who breathes on his own hands some cold
        morning
imperially able to make suns rise by being there and being
                                                        himself
spread out in a blossoming cross against the black sky

into yellow flowers and the spell is lost things keep growing
a circular motion between earth and flower that must be
                                                        plucked
that must be pulled out of earth and held in the hand
and what stays in the earth is brittle and breaks open

the dry stalk snaps
the dry pods of the tree split open
the dry beans inside them hard to the tooth
and the acorn pulled out of burnt grass after rainstorms
green cup crisscrossed crown split open by fingernail
the bitter interior kernel of roasted earth
bitter alum of earth puckering puckering and breaking open
the vegetable forests where he cannot live
the drying leaf the wooden stalk

hardening from within, brittle
which stand up out of earth and are wasted
brown at the edges the color of earth but the impulse
wasted, the somersault of the seed ended in mid-air
no ground to fall back to perishing in air

into the hot wind
that plays over the grains of soil
and lies down in hot sunlight and is called dog
and falls over itself in the mountains and is called river
and spreads out over the earth and is very close to being alive
but let only him whose body is of earth exist and sing
the shape of a man proceeds from all sides to center
and he is the star whose body is called movement
and in his hands the sun puts out branches
leaves and petals break out of silver
the corn is eaten, the animal howls, the sun flowers.

The Boar

stayed where he was
led. The others
larked over to the
trough & fed.

The one they were after had
blue eyes we
couldnt see under his
notched ears,

so I went over the fence
& saw him looking
at nothing, sharply,
across the field.

He had a strong white
back, even shone a
little in the sun
all round him

& on the blue steel gun
that made the dull
flat sound into
his head

he toppled over from
& lay dead and bleeding.
The feeding pigs ate
what they were fed.

1.

A pig stood in the mud,
a pig lay in the mud.
This was the animal I
was most myself in,
watching it ready to
die. Its eyes were the
color of my eyes, I had
bristles on my chin, not
many, didnt shave yet.

It knew enough to
keep its mouth shut. Would
they have killed him if
he talked? They would, & I
said nothing too, the pink
fat pig would taste too good
for them to leave it alone.

2.

I wish it had been otherwise. What kind of
country am I living in, who were those two
men, one of them the sheriff of the town, &
why did they have to kill the pig?

They had him flayed, scalded in the caldron
an hour after he was shot. The butcher came down
in time for supper, cut him up & salted the pork.

                              These ex-
periments in time & truth, I was thirteen &
had to see it happen. These are the things we
have to learn, not when it happened
or how the pig fell over, but that it does,
& keeps on happening, across me & my own
doings, my age & hatred of that sheriff with
a silver star on his plaid shirt, a
Dutchman who hadnt caught a criminal in years,

were none to catch, kept his revolver
clean & oiled, ready for any animal, for the
deer they kept in chickenwire cages down the road.

3.

It was plain that pig had
nothing on his mind. For
Christ's sake didnt he
know what was happening
to him when one held him
by the flanks? No, nor the other
making click click, spin
spin noises, clearing his throat.

The Exchanges II

Clarified into present

standing now in the stare of the vulture Jesus
watching the wings spread   the animal body writhe
leading to an immediate world
is Vision to be compromised in the glitter of steel
arched back of wildcat   tin leaves of the gumtree?

how sure you are of the residents of darkness come to life
how certain that when the rim of the circle breaks open
a form of life articulate, comprehensible will stand forth
                    or that the world formed
the invisible instruments of control & banishment
are a crust only to a sweet fruit only
not the gibbering piety of the remorseless dead

gently
you have gone into her body
a knife skillful in severing   wandering up & down her
to find life?   to mutilate, to be
in the first stagger of deathliness alive & singing
saying: animal of the quiet dark
animal now to burrow softly down
scour around inside her, follow those
lines of motion & supply till you come to heart
walk up & down & swallow it, looking the other way,

to find life? to discover in the consumed
whatever principle it is that brings you here
hungry & horny?

                        .
                      .   .

there is in language a temperament of fear

to answer the animal is to talk about syllables
pure as a lake in Siberia
salty and rush-ridden   centuries from the sea
to which a river flows backwards   Christmas night
or gull's hornpipe lowly to the cross   in deep snow
when they hanged the first king: whose strangled throat
made consonants
            in the forests vowels
invented with the caprice of the unicorn,
goat-eyed red-bottomed mandrills at horizons,
perpetual song of lemurs: ururur, syllables,
Aurora bloody-fisted from the lake,
erect,

the Madman's Vision a vision into
image or into form?

Adam's allergy to the first bite retched into speech?

                        .
                      .   .

To protect you from the secret, she said,
that vowels & consonants fuck each other into speech.
which you could not bear
for not knowing the efficient question
Oeheim, waz wirret dir?
what is this here? wherefore this crummy pageantry
opening into present?

            for I would mount the cart & go
questioning the sea-girt eyes of Athene, to whom in
Troy's treasure house the great horned silver phallus stood
angular as futhorc, branched out into ocean:
whom only I would honor with my sharp teeth & slow-
moving gentle mammalian mind understanding her rightly
a hero with drawn sword
(*hinne-ni* the sword of immediate presence
every rune chiseled neatly in, legible, compelling,

a message of swordmaster to armorer: let
edge be bright here, not for the cutting but
for the honor of it
        which I would draw
        with me into Babylon
        my cutthroat word
        catchpenny empire
        on all fours:) imagined

which is the present position of poetry
the animal rooting under the tree, black sow
at winter solstice, at 6 o'clock, evening
out of the snow: so far down, the
gods of fertile fields & hidden springs
the water rushing out of the ground into

her body foreshortened & consumed
distorted into my mouth, her blood my swollen tongue
her cunt my oxcart, groan of the ritual pretense

unanswerable animal.
year moving in rigid circles round
your flexible refusals. alone
there is only one continent of metaphor
one rhythm you invite us to be native in,
move upriver away from the seashaped ode,
lyric dappled like pomegranate,
snapshots of the momentary real

                  .
               . .

close to the eggyolk, fertile or
sterile in one white albumen gesture
distinguish only by the tender vein
the streak of blood:

> *to light in perfect fulness; so that a con-*
> *tinuous rhythmic procession of phenomena*
> *passes by, and never is there a form left*
> *fragmentary or half-illuminated, never a*
> *lacuna, never a gap, never a glimpse of un-*
> *plumbed depths*
>
>   (Auerbach on Homer)

unplumbed?
men must have looked the first time fire,
each time man covered girl in darkness
his open eyes focused in the dark

unspeaking mouth of the vulture

to make those things appear that he has closely hidden
in the smell & shadow of his wings

to have a mouth

protect us in the paradox? it is what
we see when we look in the fire
what we see in the dark
moving to the immediate rhythm of the visible
moving to the hidden rhythm of the real

The Process

how much more
will I see
or see again:

the problem
hurts. I have
no eyes to

see it, no
flesh or time
to see it

through. A day
walks from sun
to shadow

on grass wet
from a last
sweet rain. It

solves itself
outside me
in the air.

I am with
the old men
watching one

spring go out.

To Her Body, Against Time

Long over, what's on the tree
shivers. Sky hides behind
white-faced, giving flesh to branch,
a red leaf

or yellow far enough away,
what Broch called "the style
of old age," simplified
of images,

lean in the perfection of the bough,
naked and half-undone. Clouds break,
rain against a hidden sun,
the form plain

Knee Lunes

they are given to
hold close, not
air, not each other
/
the dress that hides your
meaning creeps
towards relevance
/
they shimmer o the
glamor is
on me your knees spell
/
they visibly relate
earth & air
secret water, fire
/
ground mist, a shroud for
mountains, last
roots with our own earth
/
thin sliver of the
crescent moon
high up the real world
/

cross locked the holy
interchange
through which we can move
        /
in that air between
your knees the
song begins to sing
        /
after silence your legs
break open
the final measure
        /

The Alchemist

for Robert Duncan

the origin, far side of a lake
is always shadow

                        the voice goes around
                        it easily in one hour

given: man, the
origin, dark side of a lake, the sun
breaks on it, walks in it, drives
out the human face

the sun walks in the deep water
where the shadow of origin touches bottom

the lake silent in a cold without snow
where the further shore is invisible & there are
no hills   but cranes
spread out on it if there are cranes
if there is anything for them to eat

                        IF ANYTHING GROWS THERE

(making me whatever I do,
where he is or is about to be
not even letting the long afternoon grow under him)

        SINCE OUR OWN EYES ARE NOT STILL
        a song that some of us are singing in the ditch. . .
        totum incognitum

sum of what we don't know for ourselves)
of ourselves

>   the inquisitors' faces
>   sheathed in rare earths,
>   the old religion, our
>   god in his own horns, a
>   spring freshet in Spain
>   uncovering Altamira,
>   baring elements in

The alchemist
(twenty years over the alembic)
his left hand fisted, snotrag on cheekbone,
who shall weep

>   and wake up in the morning
selling flowers in the veins of his arm
crying down the street jonquils jonquils
the needle stuck in his brain
inventing true north

>   as the Chinese the southpointing carriage,
>   the wheeled cart with a figure that
>   would go on forever pointing south,
>   however the cart was turned

or Sung and Wei divided, north by south, Sung & northern
                                                        Wei.

Sung: Mu Ch'i and his persimmons, a measurement of light

>   remote from Tao: contained

  made into a thing

(six things, and a painting is not about them)

>   but the task of a carriage to go on riding north

>   wherever the figure is pointing IS south

& ride northward through the hemispheres of his brain
apple in the cracked skin   .   o madness

>   will we reproach burnt flesh with a mirror,
>   turn away Antichrist, reject the imposed form,
>   with a clear clean painting however composed
>   or organized, if the light be anything else but
>   fragment?

& if we do not get up and destroy all the congressmen
turn them into naked men and let the sun shine on them
set them down in a desert & let them find their way out,
north, by whatever sexual power is left in them, if we do not
seize the president and take him out in daytime and show him
the fire & energy of one at least immediate star, white star,
hammer that down in his skull till he can hear only that
rhythm & goes and enters the dance or makes his own,

we will walk forever down the hallways into mirrors and
stagger and look to our left hand for support & the sun
will have set inside us & the world will be filled with Law,
and it is that exchange we must sweep out of the temple,
the changing of gold and power & the figure of Christ into
                                                              Law,
till the leaf is subject only to the pattern of its own green
                                                              veins
which out of all patterns only will feed it when I am dark

light contained in the persimmons, six powers of light

            folly of alchemists
            stretched out on the snow
            unlivable abstraction of his skin

in the robe covered with suns, moons,
motions we call 'planets' and do not know
the green life in their valleys, geysirs
of wet light at the exact temperature of orgasm,
brown breath, brown blood wreathing the heart muscles

            he holds to his eye

                        The alchemist

            at the top of her A her
            voice, breaking,

            Calaf's name is 'Love'

                  Stir well little
                  chew thoroughly
                  boy in the fire /
                  to sing in the
                  fire

where the streets run north
roughly but Broadway to the true north?

and asked

        what corner is he on today with his music?
He was here yesterday and
sold daffodils

NAME IS LOVE

movements somewhere in time
since our own eyes are not still

in the sleepless dark
to travel with made light

holds his hand to his face & weeps for the lost struggle
wasted in the snowfall in the crucible, only the fire of Law
burning off sulfur & mercury and this fire is earth's face

       recognizable in the plain light
       the failure of self to go into gold,
       unaccountable. The alchemist

weeping in the Spanish field
in a cloak chewed into rags by its symbols

             a body,
             under it,
whose name is love & which only of all light love can eat

Round Dance, & Canticle

in the orchestra the fixed stars
in the water the robe of Jesus
soft . undivided . sustained,
sustaining . & shadowing fishes,

true music, in the orchestra, of blood—
You tell me men are as the parts of blood
cells to all purposes, flow
& what flows, not the process but
what is so processed, us, into this time

as where the fixed stars, where Jesus,
a woman died on Sunday, which was Easter,
as I woke up from dream & said it was not,
the dream, cannot have been, because it is
Easter & is Easter & is Easter. Her blood is
upon us who do not use the time.

AND what of the tower of praise
built before a single one of us
had hands could hold stone

that tower of exalted praise
halfway up the shore
its shadow at night on the mountain
at dawn on the sea,

the room at its base
the size of your hips
& on it the tower is made
that casts its shadow

onto every ground
we can walk on,

it, before us, before any of us,
walking down to the sea &
back again.

X. J. KENNEDY

A Water Glass of Whisky

Through the hill by the Rite Nite Motel
Not a picture unbroken can reach:
An old famous head in the screen
Facelifted, falls halt in its speech

As if no line cast from the set
Could fix with a definite hook
Into any live lip going by.
There is no good book but the Good Book.

No use. Try the window instead
But the near-beer bar's sign is no more.
As far as the breeze stretches off
Only outer space answers your stare.

You don't die for want of TV
But even so, here lies a lack
As though more than night or a hill
Had walled you in, back of its back.

Song to the Tune of 'Somebody Stole My Gal'

> I'm fed up with people who say,
> Boo hoo, somebody stole my myths.
> —W. D. Snodgrass, in conversation

Somebody stole my myths,
Stole all their gists and piths.
Somebody pinched my Juno and Pan,
Crooked Dionysus
And caused my spiritual crisis,

Somebody stole my bread,
My wine and cut me off dead.
Somebody in a laboratory coat with test-tube in hand
Mixed nitrogen with glycerin and poof! went the
        promised land,

O hear me crying,
Don't much like forever dying,
Somebody stole my myths.

Down In Dallas

Down in Dallas, down in Dallas
Where the shadow of blood lies black
Lee Oswald nailed Jack Kennedy up
With the nail of a rifle crack.

Every big bright Cadillac stompled its brakes,
Every face in the street fell still,
While the slithering gun like a tooth of sin
Recoiled from the window sill.

In a white chrome room on a table top,
Oh, they tried all a scalpel knows
But they couldn't spell stop to that drop-by-drop
Till it bloomed to a rigid rose.

Down on the altar, down on the altar
Christ is broken to bread and wine
But each asphalt stone where the blood dropped down
Prickled into a cactus spine.

Oh down in Dallas, down in Dallas
Where the wind has to cringe tonight
Lee Oswald nailed Jack Kennedy up
On the cross of a rifle sight.

Hearthside Story

At seventeen I spent cold cash
In Scranton on a piece of ash

With legs like logs of solid oak
Half-burnt and flaking. When she spoke

You'd hear a hiss and, when she laughed,
A chimney with a faulty draft.

She snapped her gum, she punched which floor.
The DON'T DISTURB sign on the door,

A hot gust hurtled up my flue.
All night, the room a thickening blue,

What perfect ovals she could blow!
I watched the ashtrays overflow

While on the andirons of the bed
Two lipsticked clinkers in lips' stead

Purveyed me tastes of frost on hire
I had no heart to fan a fire

That chilled. I gave it up for good,
O mistress mine, my kindling wood.

Cross Ties

Out walking ties left over from a track
Where nothing travels now but rust and grass,
I half-believe in something that would pass
Growing to hurtle from behind my back
And when the night wind slams by, have to start.
Out of its mass the disembodied wail
Of some far night shift like a bag of mail
Is flung. Moon looms, her headbeam strews apart
A cloud. Wings batter: in a dive to strafe
The crouched grass drops a mousehawk—there's a screech
As steel stretched taut till severed. Out of reach
Or too small for desiring, I go safe,
Walk on, tensed for a leap, unreconciled
To a dark void all kindness.
                                    When I spill
The salt I throw the Devil some and, still,
I let them sprinkle water on my child.

GALWAY KINNELL

The Avenue Bearing The Initial Of Christ Into The New World

Was diese kleine Gasse doch für ein Reich an sich war . . .

for Gail

1

pcheek pcheek pcheek pcheek pcheek
They cry. The motherbirds thieve the air
To appease them. A tug on the East River
Blasts the bass-note of its passage, lifted
From the infra-bass of the sea. A broom
Swishes over the sidewalk like feet through leaves.
Valerio's pushcart Ice Coal Kerosene
Moves   clack
                    clack
                            clack
On a broken wheelrim. Ringing in its chains
The New Star Laundry horse comes down the street
Like a roofleak whucking in a pail.
At the redlight, where a horn blares,
The Golden Harvest Bakery brakes on its gears,
Squeaks, and seethes in place. A propane-
gassed bus makes its way with big, airy sighs.

Across the street a woman throws open
Her window,
She sets, terribly softly,
Two potted plants on the windowledge
            tic   tic
And bangs shut her window.

A man leaves a doorway tic toc tic toc tic toc tic hurrah
        toc splat on Avenue C tic etc and turns the corner.

Banking the same corner
A pigeon coasts 5th Street in shadows,

Looks for altitude, surmounts the rims of buildings,
And turns white.

The babybirds pipe down. It is day.

2

In sunlight on the Avenue
The Jew rocks along in a black fur shtraimel,
Black robe, black knickers, black knee-stockings,
Black shoes. His beard like a sod-bottom
Hides the place where he wears no tie.
A dozen children troop after him, barbels flying,
In skullcaps. They are Reuben, Simeon, Levi, Judah, Issachar,
        Zebulun, Benjamin, Dan, Naphtali, Gad, Asher.
With the help of the Lord they will one day become
Courtiers, thugs, rulers, rabbis, asses, adders, wrestlers,
        bakers, poets, cartpushers, infantrymen.

The old man is sad-faced. He is near burial
And one son is missing. The women who bore him sons
And are past bearing, mourn for the son
And for the father, wondering if the man will go down
Into the grave of a son mourning, or if at the last
The son will put his hands on the eyes of his father.

The old man wades towards his last hour.
On 5th Street, between Avenues A and B,
In sunshine, in his private cloud, Bunko Certified Embalmer,
Cigar in his mouth, nose to the wind, leans
At the doorway of Bunko's Funeral Home & Parlour,
Glancing west towards the Ukrainians, eastward idly
Where the Jew rocks towards his last hour.

Sons, grandsons at his heel, the old man
Confronts the sun. He does not feel its rays
Through his beard, he does not understand
Fruits and vegetables live by the sun.
Like his children he is sallow-faced, he sees
A blinding signal in the sky, he smiles.

Bury me not Bunko damned Catholic I pray you in Egypt.

3

From the Station House
Under demolishment on Houston

To the Power Station on 14th,
Jews, Negroes, Puerto Ricans
Walk in the spring sunlight.

The Downtown Talmud Torah
Blosztein's Cutrate Bakery
Areceba Panataria Hispano
Peanuts Dried Fruit Nuts & Canned Goods
Productos Tropicales
Appetizing Herring Candies Nuts
Nathan Kugler Chicken Store Fresh Killed Daily
Little Rose Restaurant
Rubinstein the Hatter Mens Boys Hats Caps Furnishings
J. Herrmann Dealer in All Kinds of Bottles
Natural Bloom Cigars
Blony Bubblegum
Mueren las Cucarachas Super Potente Garantizada de Matar
                                                                              las
            Cucarachas mas Resistentes
Wenig מצבות
G. Schnee Stairbuilder
Everyouth la Original Loción Eterna Juventud Satisfacción
                                                                          Dinero
        Devuelto
Happy Days Bar & Grill

Through dust-stained windows over storefronts
Curtains drawn aside, onto the Avenue
Thronged with Puerto Ricans, Negroes, Jews,
Baby carriages stuffed with groceries and babies,
The old women peer, blessed damozels
Sitting up there young forever in the cockroached rooms,
Eating fresh-killed chicken, productos tropicales,
Appetizing herring, canned goods, nuts;
They puff out smoke from Natural Bloom cigars
And one day they puff like Blony Bubblegum.
Across the square skies with faces in them
Pigeons skid, crashing into the brick.
From a rooftop a boy fishes at the sky,
Around him a flock of pigeons fountains,
Blown down and swirling up again, seeking the sky.
From a skyview of the city they must seem
A whirlwind on the desert seeking itself;
Here they break from the rims of the buildings
Without rank in the blue military cemetery sky.

A red kite wriggles like a tadpole
Into the sky beyond them, crosses
The sun, lays bare its own crossed skeleton.

To fly from this place — to roll
On some bubbly blacktop in the summer,
To run under the rain of pigeon plumes, to be
Tarred, and feathered with birdshit, Icarus,

In Kugler's glass headdown dangling by yellow legs.

4

First Sun Day of the year. Tonight,
When the sun will have turned from the earth,
She will appear outside Hy's Luncheonette,
The crone who sells the *News* and the *Mirror*,
The oldest living thing on Avenue C,
Outdating much of its brick and mortar.
If you ask for the *News* she gives you the *Mirror*
And squints long at the nickel in her hand
Despising it, perhaps, for being a nickel,
And stuffs it in her apron pocket
And sucks her lips. Rain or stars, every night
She is there, squatting on the orange crate,
Issuing out only in darkness, like the cucarachas
And strange nightmares in the chambers overhead.
She can't tell one newspaper from another,
She has forgotten how Nain her dead husband looked,
She has forgotten her children's whereabouts
Or how many there were, or what the *News*
And *Mirror* tell about that we buy them with nickels.
She is sure only of the look of a nickel
And that there is a Lord in the sky overhead.
She dwells in a flesh that is of the Lord
And drifts out, therefore, only in darkness
Like the streetlamp outside the Luncheonette
Or the lights in the secret chamber
In the firmament, where Yahweh himself dwells.
Like Magdelene in the Battistero of Saint John
On the carved-up continent, in the land of sun,
She lives shadowed, under a feeble bulb
That lights her face, her crab's hands, her small bulk on the
                                                              crate.

She is Pulchería mother of murderers and madmen,
She is also Alyona whose neck was a chicken leg.

Mother was it the insufferable wind?
She sucks her lips a little further into the mousehole.
She stares among the stars, and among the streetlamps.

The mystery is hers.

5

That violent song of the twilight!
Now, in the silence, will the motherbirds
Be dead, and the infantbirds
That were in the dawn merely transparent
Unfinished things, nothing but bellies,
Will they have been shoved out
And in the course of a morning, casually,
On scrawny wings, have taken up the life?

6

In the pushcart market, on Sunday,
A crate of lemons discharges light like a battery.
Icicle-shaped carrots that through black soil
Wove away lie like flames in the sun.
Onions with their skirts ripped seek sunlight
On green skins. The sun beats
On beets dirty as boulders in cowfields,
On turnips pinched and gibbons
From budging rocks, on embery sweets,
Peanut-shaped Idahos, shore-pebble Long Islands and Maines,
On horseradishes still growing weeds on the flat ends,
Cabbages lying about like sea-green brains
The skulls have been shucked from,
On tomatoes, undented plum-tomatoes, alligator-skinned
Cucumbers, that float pickled
In the wooden tubs of green skim milk —

Sky-flowers, dirt-flowers, underdirt-flowers,
Those that climbed for the sun in their lives
And those that wormed away — equally uprooted,
Maimed, lopped, shucked, and misaimed.

In the market in Damascus a goat
Came to a stall where twelve goatheads
Were lined up for sale. It sniffed them
One by one. Finally thirteen goats started
Smiling in their faintly sardonic way.

A crone buys a pickle from a crone,
It is wrapped in the *Mirror*,
At home she will open the wrapping, stained,
And stare and stare and stare at it.
And the cucumbers, and the melons,
And the leeks, and the onions, and the garlic.

7

Already the Avenue troughs the light of day.
Southwards, towards Houston and Pitt,
Where Avenue C begins, the eastern ranges
Of the wiped-out lives — punks, lushes,
Panhandlers, pushers, rumsoaks, everyone
Who took it easy when he should have been out failing at
    something —
The pots-and-pans man pushes his cart,
Through the intersection of the light, at 3rd,
Where sunset smashes on the aluminum of it,
On the bottoms, curves, handles, metal panes,
Mirrors: of the bead-curtained cave under the falls
In Freedom, Seekonk Woods leafing the light out,
Halfway to Kingston where a road branches out suddenly,
Between Pamplonne and Les Salins two meeting paths
Over a sea the green of churchsteeple copper.
Of all places on earth inhabited by men
Why is it we find ourselves on this Avenue
Where the dusk gets worse,
And the mirrorman pushing his heaped mirrors
Into the shadows between 3rd and 2nd,
Pushes away a mess of old pots and pans?

The ancient Negro sits as usual
Outside the Happy Days Bar & Grill. He wears
Dark glasses. Every once in a while, abruptly,
He starts to sing, chanting in a hoarse, nearly breaking

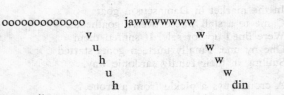

Voice —

ooooooooooooo   jawwwwwww
                v   w
              u   w
            h   w
          u   w
        h   din

And becomes silent
        Stares into the polaroid Wilderness
Gross-Rosen, Maidanek, Flössenberg, Ravensbruck, Stutthof,
                                                                            Riga,
Bergen-Belsen, Mauthausen, Birkenau, Treblinka, Natzweiler,
Dachau, Buchenwald, Auschwitz —
                                        Villages,
Pasture-bordered hamlets on the far side of the river.

8

The promise was broken too freely
To them and to their fathers, for them to care.
They survive like cedars on a cliff, roots
Hooked in any crevice they can find.
They walk Avenue C in shadows
Neither conciliating its Baalim
Nor whoring after landscapes of the senses,
Tarig bab el Amoud being in the blood
Fumigated by Puerto Rican cooking.

Among women girthed like cedar trees
Other, slenderer ones appear:
One yellow haired, in August,
Under shooting stars on the lake, who
Believed in promises which broke by themselves —
In a German flower garden in the Bronx
The wedding of a child and a child, one flesh
Divided in the Adirondack spring —
One who found in the desert city of the West
The first happiness, and fled therefore —
And by a southern sea, in the pines, one loved
Until the mist rose blue in the trees
Around the spiderwebs that kept on shining,
Each day of the shortening summer.

And as rubbish burns
And the pushcarts are loaded
With fruit and vegetables and empty crates
And clank away on iron wheels over cobblestones,
And merchants infold their stores
And the carp ride motionlessly sleeplessly
In the dark tank in the fishmarket,
The figures withdraw into chambers overhead —
In the city of the mind, chambers built
Of care and necessity, where, hands lifted to the blinds,
They glimpse in mirrors backed with the blackness of the
world
Awkward, cherished rooms containing the familiar selves.

9

Children set fires in ashbarrels,
Cats prowl the fires, scraps of fishes burn.

A child lay in the flames.
It was not the plan. Abraham
Stood in terror at the duplicity.
Isaac whom he loved lay in the flames.
The Lord turned away washing
His hands without soap and water
Like a common housefly.

The children laugh.
Isaac means *he laughs*.
Maybe the last instant,
The dying itself, *is* easier,
Easier anyway than the hike
From Pitt the blind gut
To the East River of Fishes,
Maybe it is as the poet said,
And the soul turns to thee
O vast and well-veiled Death
And the body gratefully nestles close to thee —

I think of Isaac reading Whitman in Chicago,
The week before he died, coming across
Such a passage and muttering, Oi!
What shit! And smiling, but not for you — I mean,

For *thee*, Sane and Sacred Death!

10

It was Gold's junkhouse, the one the clacking
Carts that little men pad after in harnesses
Picking up bedbugged mattresses, springs
The stubbornness has been loved out of,
Chairs felled by fat, lampshades lights have burned through,
Linoleum the geometry has been scuffed from,
Carriages a single woman's work has brought to wreck,
Would come to in the dusk and unload before,
That the whole neighborhood came out to see
Burning in the night, flames opening out like
Eyelashes from the windows, men firing the tears in,
Searchlights coming on like streams of water, smashing
On the brick, the water blooming up the wall
Like pale trees, reaching into the darkness beyond.

Nobody mourned, nobody stood around in pajamas
And a borrowed coat steaming his nose in coffee.
It was only Gold's junkhouse.
                   But this evening
The neighborhood comes out again, everything
That may abide the fire was made to go through the fire
And it was made clean: a few twisted springs,
Charred mattresses (crawling still, naturally),
Perambulator skeletons, bicycles tied in knots —
In a great black pile at the junkhouse door,
Smelling of burnt rubber and hair. Rustwater
Hangs in icicles over the windows and door,
Like frozen piss aimed at trespassers,
Combed by wind, set overnight. Carriages we were babies in,
Springs that used to resist love, that gave in
And were thrown out like whores — the black
Irreducible heap, mausoleum of what we were —
It is cold suddenly, we feel chilled,
Nobody knows for sure what is left of him.

11

The fishmarket closed, the fishes gone into flesh.
The smelts draped on each other, fat with roe,
The marble cod hacked into chunks on the counter,
Butterfishes mouths still open, still trying to eat,
Porgies with receding jaws hinged apart

In a grimace of dejection, as if like cows
They had died under the sledgehammer, perches
In grass-green armor, spotted squeteagues
In the melting ice meek-faced and croaking no more,
Except in the plip plop plip plip in the bucket,
Mud-eating mullets buried in crushed ice,
Tilefishes with scales like chickenfat,
Spanish mackerels, buttercups on the flanks,
Pot-bellied pikes, two-tone flounders
After the long contortion of pushing both eyes
To the brown side that they might look up,
Brown side down, like a mass laying-on of hands,
Or the oath-taking of an army.

The only things alive are the carp
That drift in the black tank in the rear,
Kept living for the usual reason, that they have not died,
And perhaps because the last meal was garbage and they might
                                              begin stinking
On dying, before the customer was halfway home.
They nudge each other, to be netted,
The sweet flesh to be lifted thrashing in the air,
To be slugged, and then to keep on living
While they are opened on the counter.
Fishes do not die exactly, it is more
That they go out of themselves, the visible part
Remains the same, there is little pallor,
Only the cataracted eyes which have not shut ever
Must look through the mist which crazed Homer.

These are the vegetables of the deep,
The Sheol-flowers of darkness, swimmers
Of denser darknesses where the sun's rays bend for the last
                                                      time
And in the sky there burns this shifty jellyfish
That degenerates and flashes and re-forms.

Motes in the eye land is the lid of,
They are plucked out of the green skim milk of the eye.

Fishes are nailed on the wood,
The big Jew stands like Christ, nailing them to the wood,
He scrapes the knife up the grain, the scales fly,
He unnails them, reverses them, nails them again,

Scrapes and the scales fly. He lops off the heads,
Shakes out the guts as if they did not belong in the first place,
And they are flesh for the first time in their lives.

Dear Frau _____:
    Your husband, _____, died in the Camp Hos-
pital on _____. May I express my sincere sympathy on your bereavement. _____ was admitted
to the Hospital on _____ with severe symptoms of
exhaustion, complaining of difficulties in breathing and pains
in the chest. Despite competent medication and devoted medical attention, it proved impossible, unfortunately, to keep the
patient alive. The deceased voiced no final requests.
                    Camp Commandant, _____

On 5th Street Bunko Certified Embalmer Catholic
Leans in his doorway drawing on a Natural Bloom Cigar.
He looks up the street. Even the Puerto Ricans are Jews
And the Chinese Laundry closes on Saturday.

12

Next door, outside the pink-fronted Bodega Hispano —

(A crying: you imagine
Some baby in its crib, wailing
As if it could foresee everything.
The crying subsides: you imagine
A mother or father clasping
The damned creature in their arms.
It breaks out again,
This time in a hair-raising shriek — ah,
The alleycat, in a pleasant guise,
In the darkness outside, in the alley,
Wauling, shrieking slowly in its blood.

Another, loftier shrieking
Drowns it out. It begins always
On the high note, over a clang of bells:
Hook & Ladder 11 with an explosion of mufflers
Crab-walking out of 5th Street,
Accelerating up the Avenue, siren
Sliding on the rounded distances
Returning fainter and fainter,
Like a bee looping away from where you lie in the grass.

The searchlights catch him at the topfloor window,
Trying to move, nailed in place by the shine.
The bells of Saint Brigid's
On Tompkins Square
Toll for someone who has died —
J'oïs la cloche de Serbonne,
Qui tousjours à neuf heures sonne
Le Salut que l'Ange prédit . . .

Expecting the visitation
You lie back on your bed,
The sounds outside
Must be outside. Here
Are only the dead spirituals
Turning back into prayers —
You rise on an elbow
To make sure they come from outside,
You hear nothing, you lay down
Your head on the pillow
Like a pick-up arm —
        swing low
                swing low
                        sweet
        lowsweet —)
— Carols of the Caribbean, plinkings of guitars.

13

The garbage disposal truck
Like a huge hunched animal
That sucks in garbage in the place
Where other animals evacuate it
Whines, as the cylinder in the rear
Threshes up the trash and garbage,
Where two men in rubber suits
(It must be raining outside)
Heap it in. The groaning motor
Rises in a whine as it grinds in
The garbage, and between-times
Groans. It whines and groans again.
All about it as it moves down
5th Street is the clatter of trashcans,
The crashes of them as the sanitary engineers
Bounce them on the sidewalk.

If it is raining outside
You can only tell by looking
In puddles, under the lifted streetlamps.

It would be the spring rain.

14

Behind the Power Station on 14th, the held breath
Of light, as God is a held breath, withheld,
Spreads the East River, into which fishes leak:
The brown sink or dissolve,
The white float out in shoals and armadas,
Even the gulls pass them up, pale
Bloated socks of riverwater and rotted seed,
That swirl on the tide, punched back
To the Hell Gate narrows, and on the ebb
Steam seaward, seeding the sea.

On the Avenue, through air tinted crimson
By neon over the bars, the rain is falling.
You stood once on Houston, among panhandlers and winos
Who weave the eastern ranges, learning to be free,
To not care, to be knocked flat and to get up clear-headed
Spitting the curses out. "Now be nice,"
The proprietor threatens; "Be nice," he cajoles.
"Fuck you," the bum shouts as he is hoisted again,
"God fuck your mother." (In the empty doorway,
Hunched on the empty crate, the crone gives no sign.)

That night a wildcat cab whined crosstown on 7th.
You knew even the traffic lights were made by God,
The red splashes growing dimmer the farther away
You looked, and away up at 14th, a few green stars;
And without sequence, and nearly all at once,
The red lights blinked into green,
And just before there was one complete Avenue of green,
The little green stars in the distance blinked.

It is night, and raining. You look down
Towards Houston in the rain, the living streets,
Where instants of transcendence
Drift in oceans of loathing and fear, like lanternfishes,
Or phosphorous flashings in the sea, or the feverish light
Skin is said to give off when the swimmer drowns at night.

From the blind gut Pitt to the East River of Fishes
The Avenue cobbles a swath through the discolored air,
A roadway of refuse from the teeming shores and ghettos
And the Caribbean Paradise, into the new ghetto and new
                                                    paradise,
This God-forsaken Avenue bearing the initial of Christ
Through the haste and carelessness of the ages,
The sea standing in heaps, which keeps on collapsing,
Where the drowned suffer a C-change,
And remain the common poor.

Since Providence, for the realization of some unknown
                                            purpose, has
seen fit to leave this dangerous people on the face of the
                                              earth, and

did not destroy it . . .

Listen! the swish of the blood,
The sirens down the bloodpaths of the night,
Bone tapping on the bone, nerve-nets
Singing under the breath of sleep —
We scattered over the lonely seaways,
Over the lonely deserts did we run,
In dark lanes and alleys we did hide ourselves . . .

The heart beats without windows in its night,
The lungs put out the light of the world as they
Heave and collapse, the brain turns and rattles
In its own black axlegrease —

                              In the nightime
Of the blood they are laughing and saying,
Our little lane, what a kingdom it was!

                              oi weih, oi weih

MELVIN WALKER LA FOLLETTE

Saint Stephen in San Francisco

I. SAINT FRANCIS' PASSION

When Brother Francis, rich in birds, arose
To wake his Brother Wolf from quiet sleep,
Those gentle paws were stigmatized with blood —
"My Brother Wolf, you have so long lacked food
"Because you foreswore your acreage of sheep,
"What can I give you? — you of the soft, sheep's clothes,
"I who must fight with the sullen wolf inside?"
The gentle wolf licked Francis' feet, and cried.

Being so drunk, the city did not care
Who walked the streets in joyful carnival
And no one seemed to know who Francis was —
Much crying there is, and never without cause,
And bodies there are that have not seen a soul;
The doggy wolf looked kind, and Francis, fair;
He entered an unlatched garden, stole a rose,
Hid by a bush and licked the wolf's wet paws.

II. SAINT STEPHEN'S AGON

I rode on the wings of owls to search his grace,
But Francis, son of life, could see no death;
Francis, who was good, could see no bad.
He took me for another drunken lad
And smelled the heavy liquor on my breath
And missed the lines of sadness in my face;
But when my heavy brush began to paint
He recognized my style, and called me "saint."

"If I am saint, then who are you?" I said,
"Surrounded by birds, and sheepish wolves who cry?
"In what wild prairie have we met before?
"On what remote, enchanted forest floor
"Have we two slept, with wolves for lullaby
"And chippy birds for angels at our heads?

"Am I really sinful? Are you pure?
"Together we worship Saint Lucifer."

III. SAINT LUCIFER'S LAMENT

Light blinds the dark, beneath the erotic tower
That says, "I AM, I am;" Then who am I
Whose prayers are vain? I think that I am God,
For I died, and still, I walk; my feet are blood,
Though stainless grass is green where lovers lie.
I trip on the steps, and wait the forgiving hour,
The mortal immortal who died and cannot die.
I cry, but no one knows that gods can cry.

The clock strikes nine, the arrow points to twelve —
My Father in heaven is careless of detail;
He who owns nebulae cannot keep time,
Although He instructs us with angelus and prime.
I scowl — I scheme — I resist the archaic male,
Despoiler of virgins (and yet, He had Her love)
Why will He not forgive me, when I give
The bread of life by which all poets live?

IV. SAINT STEPHEN'S POEM

An archangelic presence stirs the stars,
A beautiful hand takes mine to write a poem with
And looking up I almost miss the sight
Of sinewed haste encircling the night,
But taste the subtle sulphur in the mouth.
Alone, I am lost, of peace bereft; what mars
My vision? Shall I then fall into sin?
Is this the beauty where all poems begin?

'Burnt, I do burn.' But who can really tell
The tarnished flame from pure, celestial fire?
Fire, blood, stones, bread — is this the sum
Of all temptations unto martyrdom?
Stones warmed by fists, the Godly mob was sure,
But the stones cried, and I cried, forgive them all,
Forgive them, they must suffer in their turn:
I am elemental fire. I burn.

A Valediction

A crow's harsh dissyllables
Blacken the magic of this shimmering morning,
Adding insult to enchantment,
Making mud of the clean rain.

I could not say goodbye. That is
For friends and rivals, and I am neither.
So I have walked in the wet grass we walked in,
The rain only knows which blades you printed.

The rain only knows which trees
You touched, teaching them how to be
Trees; I think that way is best,
For I am a lover of secret rain.

I am a lover of all apple
Trees, even as you; look, how I taste
The sour green apple, rend its core
In a frenzy you would understand

If you were here. But you are not
Here. You are being kissed,
And kissing back, and I throw the hard apple
At the breast of a skittish squirrel.

You are leaving at ten. You have left.
And last night, in the fire and thunder
I prayed for grace, that I might love
The rain only.

The Sleeping Saint

The old women say that children asleep are saints,
In sleep they cast off the pulled ears of sensitive dogs,
The broken lamps and the sound of fury,
The broken toys and the sound of their own tears,
The puddle they did not intend, these symbols of shame.

An old poet said the child is father to the man,
That sentience is rationed, like muscle and hair,
Like heartbeat, even, and the pulse slows,
Marble replaces the rose, a hill becomes
An obstacle, puddles after rain are things to walk around.

When I was a child I prayed to a saint who was also a child;
And when I grew pubic hair, my saint grew, too;
And now that my hair turns grey, my saint greys, too,
And the hair falls petal by petal from the flowers of our heads.
But in sleep we are children. In short, the dream's the thing.

In dreams a rainbow is what it is, a noose;
Phalluses refuse to hide in carrots or switches;
Mares are things to ride on: it is our own selves wake us
                                          screaming,
Wake parent, sibling, spouse, child, whoever is beside us,
And we die in the landscape of cockcrow and breakfast.

Some say that a man asleep is good,
That plots which hatch dragons from the shells of dreams
Are not the same as acts, that dreams purify
And purge the conscience of its grosser stuff,
Theater and confessional at once. This is primordial tragedy

That Nietzsche spoke of, Freud tried to articulate.
Young men think, in dreams their stars have crossed
Image and imago, person, persona, shooting the yonic moon,
Making of dreams a Thule — that secret interior
In which all aging gods become their sons.

Arrivals and Departures

I swim in darkness, swim
Because I am. Dim
Saline arcs my eyes,
No tears. I know him.

He is. I have understood
His secret fatherhood.
I live by quiet kicks;
Daily I earn my food.

When she cries, I hear her
And understand. They clothe her
With stars; she is all the stars
To me; she is my mother.

I come a foreigner
To things. I am a mourner
For all eld. I am wed
With one idea: to be born here.

I scream while torture
Attends my departure
Which they call arrival.
I am now a creature.

Already, the sudden sting
Of hands brings forgetting.
In joy, they hear me cry;
God knows, I sing!

GERRIT LANSING

The Malefic Surgeon

If death is what he seeks in life he fails.
Pale among marine accomplices
or dark against the Arctic banks of sleep
he wields uncanny knives, small symbols
of that wish to be transformed he must deride
or bear the burning mother's cherishing
the child he is. Adoring crazy shapes
of love acquits no nights to charity
and never makes a face he has not cut
from desperation long before. Knowledge
then is shrivelling, and he prefers cool
averted gods who skill to father dreams.
Drifting in his watery nursery
of brazen pomps, old nightmares stink romantic.

A Ghazel of Absence

for D.

If I had trained a gull I'd send it off to Boothbay Harbor
(like Solomon to Sheba, like Hafiz to his Friend)
bearing greetings & compleyntes of absence
from "the cypress envying your figure & the moon bowled
                                      over by your face."
The bird would say: *you there, captain,*
though you are Absconditus my heart is touching you

sunrise to sunset the winds weave endlessly between us
& let of my Affection the boiling deepsea currents testify.

Lest the warriors of grief ravage your beauty (la Beauté)
I send you the ransom of my self-love, keep it,

musicians will play out Gerrit's desire
in the mode of this poem which is like a "gazelle."

The Heavenly Tree Grows Downward

Who bury the dead
must from the grave
establish a habit

Who bury the dead
lead forth the bride
stainless in dress

the morning-
glory creeps
stone
lizard

Who bury the dead
in fetal position
knees pulled up to chin

Who bury the dead
to rise again

The Undertaking

Don't ask where is Wisdom to be sought as ecstatic music
                sounds and the loving republic lies rotting away
in polarities confounded, the rites broken and swallowed by
                public drunkards,
abominable tones sounding everywhere, Capitol to fairytale
                Radio City Music Halls,
agriculture only ownership,
the ministers administers adverteasing heartsease.

Just don't ask.
I won't tell, am feeding my lamb by the still waters,
but She dances, the Old Girl, yet, where, in the Presence
and She in the (moist) breath of the godly powers and love is
                the keeping of Her laws
and She is empty of own-marks, unstopped unproduced. She
                sings, a lotus blue:

"More precious am I than precious stones a treasure that
                faileth never

this household is disordered but I am the (sweetly) order of
                                                            things
and I am Temperance and Prudence,
as men can have nothing more profit in their life than Me."

Conventicle

The people of the Phoenix do not say "the Phoenix"
and we do not name the Mystery that weaves a parsley garland
                                    for the temples of the lusters

(Marshes,   mothers,
the sweet flag fallen and parades move by.

A god is of the nature of the slime;
he invincibly uprises until on surface of the water suddenly is
                                    Water Lily and the Child.
Eaters of the Lotus

A man cannot be but enters in some folly:
if he is saved the direction and the savor is the god who blind
                as Orphics say and dumb is still the Chariot

we ride in every day
or drown.

Tabernacles

Over the seagulls and the gull white roofs the music lies like
                                                            heat
to sound and evidence the blessing of the god
who inhabits where he favors.   Sanctity
returns to place, and time picks up the savor of the merely
                                                            actual.
Sexual is almost godly on the beach.
The stars are seamen in the hero blue night ancestors
who lean through windows of the high school genitals to certify
                                    a desperate shibboleth,

Pudenda!

Honor is for thieves to countenance
as the polity of fish and salt evaporates,

and religion universalized: sea salt in old men's eyes who burn
horizons endlessly in hope to see the coming of the lissome
blond

Conquistadors!

The splendid and abasements of the ages come to this:
the body of a man or woman robed in faith and mercy seat of
gold and ark of testimony.

I have seen the wounds where godhead was expelled:
god needs body and burns in unjust anger until the man is
faithful and his work be satisfied.

PARIS LEARY

Elegy for Helen Trent

'Nita, Juanita. . .

The airlanes are silent now, you are gone
with Vic and Sade into another world,
weary of proving afternoons that women
can find love after thirty-five.

And gone with you are ChiChi and Papa David
their faces turned towards The Guiding Light
to see if Life *Can* Be Beautiful.
And Oxydol's Own Ma Perkins
is gone and Pepper Young is gone
into a radiomagnetic yonder
wearing thin towards infinity:
in Scorpio Stella Dallas weeps
for Lolly-Baby and her tony in-laws
and Sunday Gal proves to a rapt Venus
while the Danae sing 'Red River Valley'
that the adopted child of a lonely mining-camp
can find happiness as the wife
of one of Britain's richest noblest lords.

It is a kind of Sunday afternoon—
but who wakes now from the fried chicken and yams
to Evelyn And Her Magic Violin,
before the Longines Symphonette,
Charlie McCarthy, Dennis Day. . .Mr. *Al*len!
Mixed with these voices is the cry
of a lost child who trips on the cellar steps
and breaks his tooth while Carman Lombardo sings
'Red Sails In The Sunset.'

                    'Nita
Juanita. . .
You may rest. Love does not come easily
after or before thirty-five.

Saturdays I Love A Mystery
and Tizzy Lish and Grand Central Station.
'Mamma, what did they put in newspapers

before the war?' Elmer Blurt stuttering
as he knocks, 'I hope I hope I hope.' Hope?
The All-American Boy Jack Armstrong
grew up. Shot from a cannon forever.

These are your people; they wait to receive you:
Mary Noble and Young Widder Brown,
Ethel and Albert, and the Dlagon Rady,
Bess of Hilltop House, the Green Hornet,
Lorenzo Jones And His Wife Belle, Second
Husband. But only The Shadow Knows what Right
one has To Happiness.
                    Kemo Sabay,
it's a bird, it's a plane, it's a rocket,
no, it's Kaltenborn. Good-night.

'Nita, Juanita, lean thou on my heart. . .

One by one they all died but you
and now finally you too leave us—
but to sleep. You cannot die. You rise
into another dimension, a lost world
where a lost child walks searching in vain
for a disappearing Wistful Vista
along The Lincoln Highway of the dead.

Onan

Whether Two-Backed Beast or Many-Splendoured-Thing
their loves are in the last analysis a bore.
When will the buffs and punks of verse stop using lovers
as the image to silence protest, clinch an argument,
a gauntlet thrown in the boughten teeth of Dean or Daddy?
A year's election or the market price of wheat
makes or breaks more of reality than lovers.

Love should be practiced like Lent, secretly and dumbly,
(lovers names anonymous in lists of donors),
its outward form something like the Liturgy
of S. John Chrysostom—gorgeous, measured, sober,
its formal exchanges archaic but understandable:
candles and incense and the Song of the Cherubim,
but always the final mystery, the epiklesis,
the consecration, performed behind golden doors
closed hugely in the faces even of believers.

I have seen the young inchoate Bronx boy poets
scattering their seed in successive teen-aged girls
and their words in verses celebrating waste
(both acts more or less public, open)—
and always the result is the poem tender or violent,
free or ordered, throwing up lovers always
as the final image that somehow justifies their sense
of betrayal in the impotence of poetry.
How old they are: downy lips and clearing complexions,
sneakers, sweat, and Levi's, bad teeth and diction—
more vulnerable than children in an open age
where nothing is private, where even the Holiest of Holies
is fitted out with couch and file, mirrors and Muzak.

There are things more important than their bloody affairs:
the old gods shifting in the cycle of the earth;
my great-aunt Flavia McIntyre who made her cancer
a miracle of healing for all the bitter world
who came astonished to see her reaching out for pain
as if to comfort it; the white calligraphy
of birches in the red combes of the autumn Hudson;
the Pope, I suppose, whose irrelevance afflicts
the world in its curious unbelief like a trauma;
Sugarman Prescott twisted in a parody
of embryo, speechless since birth, but who understands
his mother's private language, whom the Bishop confirmed;
the innocent and irrecoverable purity
of children's speculations on the theory of flight;
the cry 'I thirst' hushed by a formal art of mercy
by posh crucifixes, elegant triptychs, and music. . .

Damn the young poets! Let them rather learn
cooking or prosody and study the dull Masters.

Summa Contra Gentiles

(for Albert Ellenberg)

Your face is an Eastern garden of response and gladness
but suspended in your smile like a frozen bell,
the silence of God terrible in the death of prophets.
Century upon century of hurt and dispersion
free you from the usual pain, the common ailments
of a late and despicable hour, the ulcers, migraines, break-
                                                    downs,

which procure to my Scotch-Irish minor verse
its fashionable anxious sentiments and the half-lies
of a Catholic disenchanted vulnerable orthodoxy.
Deeper and elder your pain, endemic, a mode
of knowledge, not an incident in visible nature.
There is perspective in your eyes before which
every *thing* is an abomination and desolation,
all plates unclean, every outstretched hand
defiling though eagerly, and with love, sought:
every newsreel a pogrom, and the open city the Bronx
a ghetto bombed by the boom and crash of Christian bells.

Your face, which El Greco taught to Kollwitz,
keeps me in its utter aesthetic dedication
at a certain distance, lest I discover crucifixion
in the stress and patience of its joy and isolation,
lest with bloody Christian hands I try to mend
the crime of Hugh of Lincoln or uphold the spires
of ruined Christendom before their reach and rubble
build into Buchenwald, Dachau, Auschwitz,
Mauthausen, and the millionth country club.
And yet too diffident to be a conscience
you are easy on Ezra Pound, keep silence about the Germans,
and grasp with a strange comprehension my belief
in the second coming of *Arthurus Rex* from the Welsh Hills.

Our Lady of Sorrows, Mary of the Seven Dolours,
but with the eternal tears of Rachel, wash me, wash me
in your presence before whom I swear oaths
that I am guiltless of your innocent blood.

Views of the Oxford Colleges

There are no red leaves in yellow Oxford,
no acrid scent of red leaves burning
on wet grass waiting to be brown.
At night the coal-smoke settling on the town
brought the small sky closer, and the turning
of the earth numbed the keys in awkward locks.

Moisture logs the print of Christ's scorched shadow
sagging from the frost-crippled altar
where the breath rimes the chalice with a touch

of cold humanity and snaps with such
frozen Amens that fingers smart and falter
in their chilled blessing over silent bread.

A ragged cat with yellow dignity
moves like a stone along a ragged wall
and vanishes from sight by standing still.
But the season will not change for me until
I walk ankle-deep through the blazing fall
and watch the wind blow the sun away.

For though the summer rose in me in Ludlow,
and though a second autumn pales me here,
yet always it is Tilbury Town that rises
round me where the Cherwell and the Isis
swell gently with the custom of the year.
It is too many years until the snow.

Christ in sacrifice leans dangerously
from the chipped wall, his broken nose
and powdered eyes brutal with centuries.
Leaves drop like jaundiced blood from chestnut trees
but, falling where the feeble morning rose,
scatter mercy down the thin lame street —

and in that part of mind where I am youngest,
sumac bleeds and crimson cracks like thunder
through maples incandescent with the reason
there are no red leaves this yellow season;
and I, admiring Magdalen Tower, wonder
how the age has scraped Christ's blood from everything.

Manifesto

A spectre is haunting Europe, with no name
and a certain tread and a certain taste for youth,
moving across the odourless canals
of Amsterdam, almost visible now,
hissing through the Hapsburg-Christian halls
at Melk, lying along the fished-out Seine;
above splendid Rome it sees what the Hun saw;
the point of all the jokes, it never laughs;
at once it riots, hides, and restores Order;
it is the mists over the wire at every border.

We are deployed along the summer here
in iced rooms, as America retires
from the summer in phoney shantung jackets.
Daddy reads *The Nation,* more withdrawn lately.
Mother deserts Sheen for a Jebbie lecture.
Cissy sighs and puts on Mabel Mercer
for the fifth time. Look at the ivy in the grate,
its plastic leaves our crisp summer fire.
Look at the sharp red dust boiling outside—
Louisiana is like Mars, hostile, dyed,

not really meant for human habitation—
which is useful. Here I can watch it happening,
the spectre growing by art and discontent,
dispassionately. For the hills of Austria
sound with bell-throated cows, and protest.
The hearties laughing in the Oxford station,
the old women in the Swan in Gloucester,
lovers in the parks in Lisbon, grapple
with the spectre, cry out against death, refusing
to give up hope in conferences and truces.

In blue valleys men pause and look out
at fields excited by their own passionate hands,
sown with the seed of their fathers and their fathers,
think of their sons growing tall, muscled, ready
almost now to do a man's work, bathed
in a man's sweat. Battles have been fought
in these valleys; crops and brides have died;
there has been famine, pain in childbirth, man's
living itself a chore— but always the spring
came down the yearly mountains like a young girl running.

Here in a heat that sickens and can kill
I see it all more clearly. My father dozes
over his antique editor, believing
in The People, Yes. Mother will return soon
to tell me that evil is only a negative—
the positive heat beyond the window-sill
hardens her eyes like clay; her bed-room
becomes a tomb for a daughter of the Pharaohs.
Listen to the hum of the air-conditioner
and abandon hope, all you that enter here.

The earth belongs to the living generation,
but we belong to the spectre called Death.
Evil is not negative. I have seen
in the alien fury of a Southern summer,
in the ruthless gales off Florida or Maine,
in the quakes and frosts that ruin and lay waste
the image of our own more awful power.
And yet. . .even here the heart is loath,
cries, 'Take this cup. . .', tells beads to the calm heavens,
and turns to the cool hills singing in procession.

"What Five Books Would You Pick To Be Marooned With on a Desert Island?"

> There is a desert island of the heart
> towards which no clipper ever points her prow.
> I am the castaway, I live there now
> and then, sending poems out like bottles
>
> stuffed with messages. I tear the pages
> from my five books, one by one,
> and commit them to the shrug of the ocean,
> to the accidental wind and its sky.

FIRST BOOK

This is the book I write about myself.
It is a kind of perpetual first novel,
regretful of childhood, miserly with youth,
traditional enough but qualified
both by its compact with mortality
and a sense of humour like a two-way mirror.

SECOND BOOK

Here I am committed, *engagé*,
angry about the child in the ghetto,
helpless with fury over my mother's cook's
second son a neighbor just called 'nigger.'
I purify myself with politics,
assuage my guilt with mildly Left compunctions.
But this is an uneven book, unsure
of its own motivations, too easily written.
Compassion is a sort of expertise.

THIRD BOOK
Occasional works, written for 'R.J.',
or 'Poem To Michael Out Of Ulster County.'
I am most facile and most desperate
here in these small pages. Epics cry
in 'Memo Of An August Afternoon,'
there is high tragedy, a fall of greatness,
in 'Verses For A Friend's Unborn Child.'
The urgent ecstasy of a generation
declines into my better travel-poems.

FOURTH BOOK
This is my largest book, my holy scriptures,
journal, testimony, and confessions.
Here I tell God what I think of him
and shock the casual atheist with the funny
sallies of my broken prayers. But they veil
the terrible beauty of his human face
from my belief and disobedience.
This book speaks volumes, comprehends
all other books, my small offering
magnified a thousand times by grace.

FIFTH BOOK
As I am least successful in the art
of love, so my art falls out of love
with me when I would turn it to this subject.
But as love is blind so have I written
this work of braille that, failing the real vision,
the deaf and mute may feel where I have failed.

First Reader

> '*When you go home, you may ask your
> parents to get you a Second Reader.*'
> McGuffey's First Reader

Sun goes lime in a throng of oak.
O in the coffee-roasted acre
where Jip pulled Bess in Robert's cart
brave Ponto has buried my years
and years. The shade by the wall
is innocent of children. Run, Nat,
and fetch the eggs. John can run

as fast as Rab, can you and Fanny?
Another boy for a brief chapter
could run, run in wind
as loose as the bark of his clothes, and grow
so slowly he took long root
in the dandelion noon and the damp
mushroom earth of the parish night.
Kate, will you help James fly
his kite? It will be great sport.
Why, this boy in the breezy chapter
could kite his sport in wild great
flights of fancy friends whose mothers
with their citrus hands and biscuit purses
waited like evenings in the propped doors
of Fords with front open windshields.
There is a bee shut in a flower.
Hattie saw a rat and Nero
tried to catch it, but Ben White
frightened Lucy with his whip.
And Ponto has taken my early book
and buried all its primer leaves
in a field of stern time and harvest
where Frank, the lame boy, plays
to Mary on his willow-pipe
and that running boy is good to his Mama
and Papa lets him ride on Prince.
O I have turned those mulched pages
again and again to find his windy
name; but always there is one
page missing. This is the last
lesson in the first book.

September 1, 1965

> I sit in a roadside diner
> On Highway 23
> Come from hearing a minor
> Poet read at me
> And the breath of the hip bard
> Affects the flashy day
> And I respond to the cigarette
> And the tuna-salad plate
> And think of tooth-decay. . .

I

It won't wash now, the clever dissonance,
    insulted rhymes, wrenched elegance.
We know it all: the universal treason,
    the efficient terrors and the secret prisons,
every lad rutting after his mother,
    all toilet training the fatal bother,
colonialism festering in the heart
    of each of us, and all elections certain.
We love one another and we die
    just the same. Every truth's a lie.
We've done the dirt, we've all been had,
    and we all sound like Auden when we're bad.

II

But having known the worst we may detect the best.
Having dreamt of daddy furry with the knife,
I may now kneel and ask his ancient blessing.
Mad about the boy, I may yet love my wife.
Joy waits like an accident around the corner—
the close call, the squeal of brakes, the sudden horn—
life, like death, is where the traffic jam is densest.
We need a new chauvinism about existence.

Love Lifted Me

My cousins, lean hunters,
at twenty-two shaped
by Sewanee, Kappa Alpha,
shabby affluence,
the Order Of DeMolay,
Aunt Mim's and Aunt Martha's voices
(Randolph Macon
out of Hockaday):
Bobo Randolph pissed
out steaming Jax behind
the tent; Clay Stuart
said, 'Get the lead out,'
both auburn, fair,
enemies of the duck,
the rabbit, and the deer,

tall and tight; and I
at fifteen, once-removed.

Banana-glare of floodlights,
pulps of cow-pies
and sawdust, thin women
rattling in rows like a canebrake,
stiff salt denims,
and a Fat with bow-tie,
galluses, and Bible.
Cousin Bobo said,
'Hot damn! Clay Boy,
he's preaching like a nigger.
I think I'll get religion.'

'Episcopalians don't
get religion, Bo.'

'Clay Boy, you never saw
some little old gal
get all hotted up
with one of those mean low-down
Gospel choruses?
Down in Rapides Parish
last summer one
damn near got her rocks off
with "Love Lifted Me."
God, I'm getting it. Clay Boy,
this stuff hits you
where you live.'
                    I once-
removed, once-removed,
heart Fat pop,
thought of Christ moving
in the silence of the Host
and his mother the Virgin
my mother with cool
hands on my forehead
and her perpetual face
an ivory of repose.

Saw Christ the Alley Cat
crucified and stretched
on canvas, vermin Messiah,
his blood noisy with multitudes,
multitudes.

           Bo was saved
from being saved—by Clay
who warned him that Aunt Mim
would have a hissy if
he let the Rector down.

'Okay, okay. Let's
you and me hustle
us some poontang, Clay Boy.'

Outside over the tent
stars moving through
my hunting kin's drunk,
the hot-ham smell
of a cottonseed mill,
a ruined armadillo,
the instant salience of chiggers.

My mother with Mary's sword
in her heart and a quarter-moon
white under her feet
moved through the summer night
crushing the patchouli.

DENISE LEVERTOV

To the Reader

As you read, a white bear leisurely
pees, dyeing the snow
saffron,

and as you read, many gods
lie among lianas: eyes of obsidian
are watching the generations of leaves,

and as you read
the sea is turning its dark pages,
turning
its dark pages.

Six Variations

i

We have been shown
how Basket drank—
and old man Volpe the cobbler
made up what words he didn't know
so that his own son, even
laughed at him: but with respect.

ii

two flutes! How close
to each other they move
in mazing figures,
never touching, never
breaking the measure,
as gnats dance in
summer haze all afternoon, over
shallow water sprinkled
with mottled blades of willow—
two flutes!

iii

Shlup, shlup, the dog
as it laps up
water
makes intelligent
music, resting
now and then to
take breath in irregular
measure.

iv

When I can't
strike one spark from you,
when you don't
look me in the eye,
when your answers
come
        slowly, dragging
their feet, and furrows
change your face,
when the sky is a cellar
with dirty windows,
when furniture
obstructs the body, and bodies
are heavy furniture coated
with dust-time
for a lagging leaden pace,
a short sullen line,
measure
of heavy heart and
cold eye.

v

The quick of the sun that gilds
broken pebbles in sidewalk cement
and the iridescent
spit, that defiles and adorns!
Gold light in blind love does not distinguish
one surface from another, the savor
is the same to its tongue, the fluted
cylinder of a new ashcan a dazzling silver,

the smooth flesh of screaming children a quietness, it is all
a jubilance, the light catches up
the disordered street in its apron,
broken fruitrinds shine in the gutter.

vi

Lap up the vowels
of sorrow,
           transparent, cold
water-darkness welling
up from the white sand.
Hone the blade
of a scythe to cut swathes
of light sound in the mind.
Through the hollow globe, a ring
of frayed rusty scrapiron,
is it the sea that shines?
Is it a road at the world's edge?

The Jacob's Ladder

The stairway is not
a thing of gleaming strands
a radiant evanescence
for angels' feet that only glance in their tread, and need not
touch the stone.

It is of stone.
A rosy stone that takes
a glowing tone of softness
only because behind it the sky is a doubtful, a doubting
night gray.

A stairway of sharp
angles, solidly built.
One sees that the angels must spring
down from one step to the next, giving a little
lift of the wings:

and a man climbing
must scrape his knees, and bring
the grip of his hands into play. The cut stone
consoles his groping feet. Wings brush past him.
The poem ascends.

Matins

i

The authentic! Shadows of it
sweep past in dreams, one could say imprecisely,
evoking the almost-silent
ripping apart of giant
sheets of cellophane. No.
It thrusts up close. Exactly in dreams
it has you off-guard, you
recognize it before you have time.
For a second before waking
the alarm bell is a red conical hat, it
takes form.

ii

The authentic! I said
rising from the toilet seat.
The radiator in rhythmic knockings
spoke of the rising steam.
The authentic, I said
breaking the handle of my hairbrush as I
brushed my hair in
rhythmic strokes: That's it,
that's joy, it's always
a recognition, the known
appearing fully itself, and
more itself than one knew.

iii

The new day rises
as heat rises,
knocking in the pipes
with rhythms it seizes for its own
to speak of its invention—
the real, the new-laid
egg whose speckled shell
the poet fondles and must break
if he will be nourished.

iv

A shadow painted where
yes, a shadow must fall.
The cow's breath
not forgotten in the mist, in the
words. Yes,
verisimilitude draws up
heat in us, zest
to follow through,
follow through,
follow
transformations of day
in its turning, in its becoming.

v

Stir the holy grains, set
the bowls on the table and
call the child to eat.

While we eat we think,
as we think an undercurrent
of dream runs through us
faster than thought
towards recognition.

Call the child to eat,
send him off, his mouth
tasting of toothpaste, to go down
into the ground, into a roaring train
and to school.

His cheeks are pink
his black eyes hold his dreams, he has left
forgetting his glasses.

Follow down the stairs at a clatter
to give them to him and save
his clear sight.

Cold air
comes in at the street door.

vi

The authentic! It rolls
just out of reach, beyond
running feet and
stretching fingers, down
the green slope and into
the black waves of the sea.
Speak to me, little horse, beloved,
tell me
how to follow the iron ball,
how to follow through to the country
beneath the waves
to the place where I must kill you and you step out
of your bones and flystrewn meat
tall, smiling, renewed,
formed in your own likeness.

vii

Marvelous Truth, confront us
at every turn,
in every guise, iron ball,
egg, dark horse, shadow,
cloud
of breath on the air,

dwell
in our crowded hearts
our steaming bathrooms, kitchens full of
things to be done, the
ordinary streets.

Thrust close your smile
that we know you, terrible joy.

LAURENCE LIEBERMAN

Orange County Plague: scenes

SCENE 1: Dislocations

In Orange, tree-plague has struck the mile-long groves. Greased
Chainsaws slide through trunks as knives slice butter.
Autos skid in the orangesap treejuice
Blend flooding the gutter.
Psychotic farmers hallucinate glues
To restore limbs slashed by sharktoothed steeljawed beasts.
If some of the screws are loose,
It doesn't matter.
At least,
Teenage lovers scatter
Back to the parks. They cruise
From bench to bench, and a few coolcats grow chaste
Perhaps. There is less temptation to bruise
Forbidden fruit — a daughter
Waits for her father's permission to choose
Her life. Blood-mistakes are small enough to blotter,
Like smudges of ink. Loss-of-faith is mended with library
paste.

SCENE 2: Stump Fugue

In unison, hundreds of shovels vanish under stumps. They
descend
By regular strokes, like oil-drills. Workmen's faces
Whiten; their bodies absent, statuesque.
White knuckles, weightless,
Glitter in the failing sun. Dusk
Attends the snapping of roots. Arms, self-moving, blend
With saws. The sun's disc
In the last oasis
Sinks. *Send*
Rain where the Human Race is
Still tree-loving, still able to risk
Life to preserve the beauty that lives. What sickens, mend!
Great fists of roots in trucks whisk
Up Coast Hi-way, menacing crisis:

WIDE LOAD marked in red. The clay-stuck
Upturned stumps, tree-corpses, bounce on the chassis
And sway. . .clotted hands, upcast, clutching madly at the
wind.

SCENE 3: Freeway Skeletons

(a deserted grove: mostly dead trees, rotten fruit)

Near the freeway, the unburied dead raise delicate skeletons,
brittle
Arms extending frail hands—mock-perch for birds.
In a light breeze the air is black
With falling fingers; words
From the dying lips of lynchees, their luck
Run out—the crackle of twigs; last drools of spittle—
Drops of sap that fleck
The bark, wood's
Blood. *Ill*
Winds rattle old boards
(Or bones) in America's (hush!) rack-
Negroes slaughterhouse. The passing motorists, cattle
Armed to butcher each other, slack
Their speed to loot. Rewards
Are few. But the thieves have a special knack
For sorting the stray good orange from the rotting hoards.
Listen for the moos. Chewing of the cud. The spirit's death-
rattle.

SCENE 4: Tree Burning

At the center of a stump-studded field, a disordered pyre,
strewn
With mangled tree-carcass, waits. Branches, at all
Angles, prevent neat piling of logs.
An indignity too subtle
For the influx of watchers (pyros) begs
Notice. For hours, blood-thirst in the air has grown.
Eyes, unwinking, glare. Legs
Stiffen into metal.
Night. No moon.
Lit match! Odd chanting. A riddle.
Burn, witch, burn! Crochety old bags
Burn. Witch, burn, witch! Nigger-witch. Which nigger? One!
How spot a witch? Check for wigs,

Or black mustache. Telltale
Itch in the crotch, sticky lips: Nigger-stags!
Or check bold strut, briar tongue, fire in the eyes, mettle.
Guilt stinks under the arms and dons old rags. Nigger-witch,
burn!

SCENE 5: Preservatives

Mid-day. A mammoth Redwood creeps on wheels. Four lanes
of autos,
Reluctant, bestow reverence; the giant's funeral
Hearse shambles. The corpse, exposed,
Has not begun to smell.
Tree-flesh, unembalmed, won't rust
Or rot. Tree bodies outlast tree souls. Mulattos,
In America's death-in-life lust
Agony, grow beautiful
As trees. Bistros
Are mills where blackwhite people
Logs are cut to prayer size; kiss-Christ
Blues—a holy rage of buzzsaw jazz. . .sham Castros
Preach re-growth from severed roots. . .
Boogie-and-twist swivel
Hips roll—tree limbs in tornados tossed.
Battered Races, timbers that seem to rise as they fall,
Murderously blossom in the suffering and dancing country of
ghettos.

SCENE 6: The American Halfway

Above, the farm and pasture—halfway—the metropolis below,
Smog in the eyes and throat, dung-stink in the nose,
Fordtruck in the front yard, moocow in back;
That's how you sing the halfway blues.
On the freeway, herded twelve-deep in dumptrucks,
Stooped on the warped floorboards of stalls (Jim Crow
In the Deep South, spics
Out West) braceros
Sing. Sow
Beanfields gold in the sunrise,
Half-frozen all night in pasteboard shacks!
Free country good for beez-ness. Amor in Meh-hee-koh.
(Slave labor don't mind the dirt wages: Mex
Eat crow.) They file through bean-rows,

Swift and frail as antelope. If anyone ask,
Why drudge all day in sun-fire, strings for clothes?
Ah-meh-ree-kuh ees work! eat! sleep! Amor in Meh-hee-koh!

SCENE 7: The Wire Forests

On their sides, resembling fallen timbers without rough
Barks—a hundred feet apart—lie power poles.
Just yesterday, this road was edged
With Eucalyptus; in aisles
Between rows of trees, seats for the aged.
Now tree-odors hover in the air, residues of life.
The poles are erected. The frigid
Passionless verticals
Strive
To fill the socket-shaped holes
Left by trees. Identical, cement-wedged
Below, parasitically fastened to live wires above—
Tree-impostors, never to be budged
From a telegraphic owl's
Knowitallness, they stand—rigid!
Sad children, wishing to climb, scan the miles
And miles of uninterrupted electric forests for leaves.

SCENE 8: Tree Praise

Beauty is poorness of posture, a studied unevenness of frame.
Trees have sex appeal, gnarled character, a stubborn
Knottiness: a refusal to grow one way;
Preference for curves, fork-turns
Over a sapling's uprightness; asymmetry
Of branches, leaf-shapes askew, imbalance of color-scheme.
The Eucalyptus, obsessed with nudity
Or eager for sunburn,
Sheds lame
Barks as snakes slough skins.
The leaning Birch, to hide its branchless purity
Of form, loves to dance in a blinding gale, and for shame
Of the drab whiteness of bark, for eternity
Would spring up and back—and burn
In the driving wind. I think of the sway-
Backed Oak, the lackadaisical Willow, the Juniper, Haw-
thorn—
And a preference for woods over human society, at last, I
proclaim.

SCENE 9: The Sterilization

Hydra-trees survive the death of parts. Some trees
Dead at the top outlive bad weather, poisons.
Decapitation cures. My Pepper
Tree (a kind of treason?)
Has become a bush. Trees, like lepers,
Slough their rotten limbs. Gratuitous sprays,
"Weed-killers," infect the upper
Earth. Do those men
Who squeeze
Death spray suffer my vision?
They sterilize loam in fields. The deadly vapors
Spread to my backyard. Today, in the faintest breeze—
Like beautiful hanks of hair in the barber
Shop—fall dried stem-
Husks, brittle, bewildered to sever
From roots and lie in useless piles, my Bougain-
Villea withered to brown scrolls of leafage. . . No rose.

SCENE 10: The View from the Kitchen

Sides sheered off, the sand level on the bottom, this river-bed
Is dry. The parallel cyclone fences entice scores
Of children to enter; without risk, play
Is dull. Forbidden tours
Follow KEEP OUT signs as crime follows prey.
FLOOD CONTROL threats replace NO FISHING. The mud
Is moistened with sewage. Debris
And watercress lure
Vagrants, mutts,
Wildlife. An occasional horse
And horseman, cyclists, tractors pass by
Alongside the ditch. In my kitchen I watch, and the skid-
Row scum watch back. *What can we say
To each other? Who is worse
Off?* In Winter, the fantastic rains wash away
Tons of dirt from the banks. *Nothing is safe in my house.*
In Spring, I measure the narrowing margin of earth near my
yard.

SCENE 11: The Waves

House-high waves envelop the pier with algae, brine,
Sea-scum. The roughest surf in years excites

Beach bums to risk their skins. Life
Guards, who lift weights
After hours, imbibe their fill of grief.
The deaths they swallow turn to cramps in the groin
Nightfall. High tides knife
Trenches in cliff-sides,
Undermine
Foundations of lavish estates.
Many slide downhill. One topples off
Into the sea, somersaulting over stilts, a falling crane
Or heron. Beach houses on a low bluff
Wash away like orangecrates.
Nothing slakes the hunger of the thief-
Pacific. Maddened by the tedium of days, he mates
With womanish earth. Anything human is chaff of the grain.

SCENE 12: The Ice Phallus

Frozen halibut is fresher than today's catch. Vacuum-packed
Bass in freezers grow purer than life. Time stops.
Ice crystals' skill competes with veteran
Seamen's. Fish essence sleeps
In Stiffened flesh. In our future, semen
Shall cease to flow. Ice-birth will men slacked
Morals and eliminate sin —
Love snarls and rapes,
Sex-locked.
An idle fisherman drops
Bait from the pier. Fish, like women
Immune, resist his hook. His rod is cracked,
His reel jammed with backlash, the line
snagged on a rock. Surfers' lips
Arc mockeries below, the mouths green-
Blue, sea-numbed. The highest breaker snaps
Torso-whips. The brain's deepfreeze they love, wave-bucked.

SCENE 13: Afterlife of a War-jet

(at a children's park)

Fresh coats of paint disguise the emblems of war. Maggots
Restoring the flesh of dead wolves to life
In the elixir of gnashing jaws and gut:
Children swarming in the *safe*
Cockpit and fuselage of a killer-jet,

A surprise package of doom in the hands of bigots.
Stale blood and fresh snotspit
Mix in the mouth-strafe
Of play. Tots
On the wings rehearse tough
Battle lingo, or they regurgitate
Movie war poses: salute, the march, rigor mortis.
Both with and without honor they commit
War crimes, and forget. The chafe
Of rough surface on hands and face whets
The appetite for more. Morticians render grief
Therapy. Death-play opens *all* of the emotion spigots.

SCENE 14: Mines and Missiles

(Naval Munitions Station, Seal Beach)

In plain view from Coast Highway, thousands of steel balls,
Arranged neatly as cans on the grocer's shelf,
Lie dormant. In World War II, they guarded
The nation's bodies from Adolf
Hitler, Mussolini, Hirohito. In morbid
Idleness they rest, their monomaniacal death-wills,
By munitions-surgery, rendered
Sterile. *A stray calf*
Moos. Gulls
Swoop off the coast. The gulf
Between TNT and the Atom is underscored
By the Atlas ICBMs, the length of the battleships' hulls,
Maneuvering in highway traffic. Shrouded
With canvas, they exceed half
Of the road's six lanes in width. The livid
Faces of motorists sicken, as they mutter gruff
Curses at the traffic deadlock. Oblivious to mines *or* missiles.

SCENE 15: Meditation Upon the Power House

Most of the County's vital organs, exposed to all weathers
And the bomb of assassin, form the power house.
Vulnerable, it hums in the night,
Quivers with a queer pulse.
Visible for miles, it looms in the soot-
Dark fields of the coast—a meteoric glow—and gathers
The dark into arteries of light-
Alchemy. Small wills
Smother

In *One*—encompassing *Else*—
That engenders power as swiftly as thought
Flashes in the brain. In the Great Whole, parts wither
Into the truth. Daybreak. When Lot's
Wife looked back, the Gospels
Tell, she changed to a pillar of salt. . .
Such risk the listener takes when, in daylight, he mulls
Over the divinity of a dynamo that resembles a grain elevator.

SCENE 16: Spotlights

A pulsating three-hundred-sixty degree incandescent eye,
On the clubhouse roof, patrols my midnight walk.
The moon is a spotlight too. Lights
Guard and watch; they mock
My secret thoughts with telltale watts.
The sacred grasses glitter like a black-green sea.
This is no place for halfwits
Who treasure the dark.
Bats. I
Walk soft, but my shadow, a block
Long, jerks like hiccups in the epiglottis.
I hunt myself on the links, out-of-bounds, a bit loony.
I seek my moon's dark side. Light waits
In ambush, behind my back.
In love or art, the Beloved shuts
Her eyes and turns her face from glare of daybreak.
The beam of the watchman's flashlight squelches immortality.

SCENE 17: Interference

Tonight, strolling the hills overlooking the shore, I gasp
At the beauty of an electric storm. My radio's static
Muddles the up-to-the-minute news.
Punctual as a nervous tic,
The sea-and-skyscape, palpitant, glows.
Will the lovely pulse of the universe ever collapse?
How much there is to lose.
We forget. The cynic
Traps us
In ourselves, like a hypodermic.
I welcome tonight's interference: snows
On the TV screen, dimmed lights, an occasional lapse
In telephone service. *Cut the wires. I refuse*

To answer the door. The clock
Misses a tick. More than the wind blows.
In precious night, we touch. I pray for the fantastic
Messages one can learn to receive when the heartbeat skips.

ROBERT LOWELL

Caligula

My namesake, Little Boots, Caligula,
you disappoint me. Tell me what I saw
to make me like you when we met at school?
I took your name—poor odd-ball, poor spoiled fool,
my prince, young innocent and bowdlerized!
Your true face sneers at me, mean, thin, agonized,
the rusty Roman medal where I see
my lowest depths of possibility.

What can be salvaged from your life? A pain
that gently darkens over heart and brain,
a fairy's touch, a cobweb's weight of pain,
now makes me tremble at your right to live.
I live your last night. Sleepless fugitive,
your purple bedclothes and imperial eagle
grow so familiar they are home. Your regal
hand accepts my hand. You bend my wrist,
and tear the tendons with your strangler's twist. . .
You stare down hallways, mile on stoney mile,
where statues of the gods return your smile.
Why did you smash their heads and give them yours?
You hear your household panting on all fours,
and itemize your features—sleep's old aide!
Item: your body hairy, badly made,
head hairless, smoother than your marble head;
item: eyes hollow, hollow temples, red
cheeks rough with rouge, legs spindly, hands that leave
a clammy snail's trail on your soggy sleeve. . .
a hand no hand will hold. . . nose thin, thin neck—
you wish the Romans had a single neck!

Small thing, where are you? Child, you sucked your thumb,
and could not sleep unless you hugged the numb
and wooly-witted toys of your small zoo.
There was some reason then to fondle you
before you found the death-mask for your play.
Lie very still, sleep with clasped hands, and pray

for nothing. Child! Think, even at the end,
good dreams were faithful. You betray no friend
now that no animal will share your bed.
Don't think! . . . And yet the God Adonis bled
and lay beside you, forcing you to strip.
You felt his gored thigh spurting on your hip.
Your mind burned, you were God, a thousand plans
ran zig-zag, zig-zag. You began to dance
for joy, and called your menials to arrange
deaths for the gods. You worshipped your great change,
took a cold bath, and rolled your genitals
until they shrank to marbles . . .

                    Animals
fattened for your arenas suffered less
than you in dying—yours the lawlessness
of something simple that has lost its law,
my namesake, and the last Caligula.

The Mouth of the Hudson

A single man stands like a bird-watcher,
and scuffles the pepper and salt snow
from a discarded, gray
Westinghouse Electric cable drum.
He cannot discover America by counting
the chains of condemned freight-trains
from thirty states. They jolt and jar
and junk in the siding below him.
He has trouble with his balance.
His eyes drop,
and he drifts with the wild ice
ticking seaward down the Hudson,
like the blank sides of a jig-saw puzzle.

The ice ticks seaward like a clock.
A negro toasts
wheat-seeds over the coke-fumes
in a punctured barrel.
Chemical air
sweeps in from New Jersey,
and smells of coffee.

Across the river,
ledges of suburban factories tan
in the sulphur-yellow sun
of the unforgivable landscape.

Mother Marie Therese

Drowned in 1912
(*The speaker is a Canadian nun stationed in New Brunswick.*)

Old sisters at our Maris Stella House
Remember how the Mother's strangled grouse
And snow-shoe rabbits matched the royal glint
Of Pio Nono's vestments in the print
That used to face us, while our aching ring
Of stationary rockers saw her bring
Our cake. Often, when sunset hurt the rocks
Off Carthage, and surprised us knitting socks
For victims of the Franco-Prussian War,
Our scandal's set her frowning at the floor;
And vespers struck like lightning through the gloom
And oaken ennui of her sitting room.
It strikes us now, but cannot re-inspire;
False, false and false, I mutter to my fire.
The good old times, ah yes! But good, that all's
Forgotten like our Province's cabals;
And Jesus, smiling earthward, finds it good;
For we were friends of Cato, not of God.
This sixtieth Christmas, I'm content to pray
For what life's shrinkage leaves from day to day;
And it's a sorrow to recall our young
Raptures for Mother, when her trophies hung,
Fresh in their blood and color, to convince
Even Probationers that Heaven's Prince,
Befriending, whispered: "Is it then so hard?
Tarry a little while, O disregard
Time's wings and armor, when it flutters down
Papal tiaras and the Bourbon crown;
For quickly, priest and prince will stand, their shields
Before each other's faces, in the fields,
Where, as I promised, virtue will compel
Michael and all his angels to repel
Satan's advances, till his forces lie

Beside the Lamb in blissful fealty."
Our Indian summer! Then, our skies could lift,
God willing; but an Indian brought the gift.
"A sword," said Father Turbot, "not a saint;"
Yet He who made the Virgin without taint,
Chastised our Mother to the Rule's restraint.
Was it not fated that the sweat of Christ
Would wash the worldly serpent? Christ enticed
Her heart that fluttered, while she whipped her hounds
Into the quicksands of her manor grounds
A lordly child, her habit fleur-de-lys'd
There she dismounted, sick; with little heed,
Surrendered. Like Proserpina, who fell
Six months a year from earth to flower in hell;
She half-renounced by Candle, Book and Bell
Her flowers and fowling pieces for the Church.
She never spared the child and spoiled the birch;
And how she'd chide her novices, and pluck
Them by the ears for gabbling in Canuck,
While she was reading Rabelais from her chaise,
Or parroting the *Action Française*.
Her letter from the soi-disant French King,
And the less treasured golden wedding ring
Of her shy Bridegroom, yellow; and the regal
Damascus shot-guns, pegged upon her eagle
Emblems from Hohenzollern standards, rust.
Our world is passing; even she, whose trust
Was in its princes, fed the gluttonous gulls,
That whiten our Atlantic, when like skulls
They drift for sewage with the emerald tide.
Perpetual novenas cannot tide
Us past that drowning. After Mother died,
'An émigrée in this world and the next,'
Said Father Turbot, playing with his text.
Where is he? Surely, he is one of those,
Whom Christ and Satan spew! But no one knows
What's happened to that porpoise-bellied priest.
He lodged with us on Louis Neuvième's Feast,
And celebrated her memorial mass.
His bald spot tapestried by colored glass,
Our angels, Prussian blue and flaking red,
He squeaked and stuttered: 'N-n-nothing is so d-dead
As a dead s-s-sister.' Off Saint Denis' Head,
Our Mother, drowned on an excursion, sleeps.

Her billy goat, or its descendant, keeps
Watch on a headland, and I hear it bawl
Into this sixty knot Atlantic squall,
'Mamamma's Baby,' past Queen Mary's Neck,
The ledge at Carthage—almost to Quebec,
Where Monsieur de Montcalm, on Abraham's
Bosom, asleep, perceives our world that shams
His New World, lost—however it atones
For Wolfe, the Englishman, and Huron bones
And priests'. O Mother, here our snuffling crones
And cretins feared you, but I owe you flowers:
The dead, the sea's dead, has her sorrows, hours
On end to lie tossing to the east, cold,
Without bed-fellows, washed and bored and old,
Bilged by her thoughts, and worked on by the worms,
Until her fossil convent come to terms
With the Atlantic. Mother, there is room
Beyond our harbor. Past its wooden Boom
Now weak and waterlogged, that Frontenac
Once diagrammed, she welters on her back.
The bell-buoy, whom she called the Cardinal,
Dances upon her. If she hears at all,
She only hears it tolling to this shore,
Where our frost-bitten sisters know the roar
Of water, inching, always on the move
For virgins, when they wish the times were love,
And their hysterical hosannahs rouse
The loveless harems of the buck ruffed grouse,
Who drums, untroubled now, beside the sea—
As if he found our stern virginity
Contra naturam. We are ruinous;
God's Providence through time has mastered us:
Now all the bells are tongueless, now we freeze,
A later Advent, pruner of warped trees,
Whistles about our nunnery slabs, and yells,
And water oozes from us into wells;
A new year swells and stirs. Our narrow Bay
Freezes itself and us. We cannot say
Christ even sees us, when the ice floes toss
His statue, made by Hurons, on the cross,
That Father Turbot sank on Mother's mound—
A whirligig! Mother, we must give ground,
Little by little; but it does no good.
Tonight, while I am piling on more driftwood,

A stooping with the poker, you are here,
Telling your beads; and breathing in my ear,
You watch your orphan swording at her fears.
I feel you twitch my shoulder. No one hears
Us mock the sisters, as we used to, years
And years behind us, when we heard the spheres
Whirring *venite;* and we held our ears.
My mother's hollow sockets fill with tears.

JACKSON MAC LOW

1st Dance — Making Things New — 6 February 1964

He makes himself comfortable,
& matches parcels.

Then he makes glass boil,
while having political material get in,
& coming by.

Soon after, he's giving gold cushions or seeming to do so,
taking opinions,
shocking,
pointing to a fact that seems to be an error & showing it to be
                                    other than it seems,
& presently paining by going or having waves.

Then he names things.

A little while later he gets out with things,
& finally either rewards someone for something or goes up
                                    under something.

2nd Dance — Seeing Lines — 6 February 1964

She seems to come by wing,
& keeping present being in front,
she reasons regularly.

Then — making her stomach let itself down,
& giving a bit or doing something elastic,
& making herself comfortable,
she lets complex impulses make something.

She disgusts everyone.

She does a little penning,
& then she fingers a door.

Later she wheels awhile,
while either transporting a star or letting go of a street.

3rd Dance — Making A Structure With A Roof Or Under A Roof — 6–7 February 1964

They meet over water,
say something between thick things,
& make things new.

Soon they're making drinks,
& giving falsely.

Then, after giving enough of anything to anyone,
they awake yesterday when the skin's a little feeble;
seeing danger,
they attack,
force someone to see something,
again give enough of anything to anyone,
attack again,
& after doing things to make a meal,
thus having uses among harmonies,
one of them being a brother to someone,
& giving an egg to someone loose or seeming to do so,
they wheel awhile,
giving the hour,
& thereafter let complex impulses make something.

Once more giving the hour,
they again awaken yesterday when the skin's a little feeble;
then they reason regularly.

They copy each other,
shocking everyone,
& pointing to a fact that seems to be an error & showing it
                                    to be other than it seems,
having or seeming to have serious holes,
they either transport a star or let go of a street;
they keep up a process.

As if to say, "One must make oneself comfortable,"
they go under,
wheel some more,
& reward someone for something or go up under something.

They awaken yesterday when the skin's a little feeble;
they rail,
& they come against something or fear things.

They smoke awhile,
& then they make structure with a roof or under a roof.

10th Dance — Coming On As A Horn — 20 February 1964

Thou comest by.

& then thou goest about between & through unserious-seeming
goings-on,
& thou hammerest.

Presently thou art making a bridge & giving it to someone,
& making decisions.

Thou gettest out with things,
& thou gettest insects.

Thou comest against something or thou fearest things.

Thou dost something in the manner of a sister whose mind is
happy & willing,
thou writest with a bad pen,
& either thou hast curves or thou hast to put weight on a bird,
while thou puttest something slow under an insect,
& thou hast or seem'st to have serious holes,
albeit thine ending be one wherein thou reactest to orange
hair.

12th Dance — Getting Leather By Language — 21 February 1964

This gives support to insects,
& gets feeble.

Later this lets things be equal or does things like an ant,
while putting something slow under an insect,
& seeming to send things or putting wires on things,
though keeping to the news.

Then, handing or seeming to hand snakes to people,
this lets potatoes get bad,
while seeing something that seems to be wax,

& transporting a star or letting go of a street;
either this is letting a system give punishments or this is sadly
keeping the toes under.

This does things with the mouth & eyes,
puts a story between much railing,
makes trousers,
& quietly chalks a strange tall bottle.

After that, this does something with the nose or gets something
by attraction,
& locks something up.

This makes meat before heat,
putting in languages other than English.

This gets leather by language,
while discussing something brown.

Finally, being a fly,
& forcing someone to see something,
this ends by going over things.

13th Dance — Matching Parcels — 21 February 1964

Those make thunder though taking pigs somewhere,
but one of those says something after a minute.

Presently those get insects.

Those touch,
& give enough of anything to anyone,
planting all the while.

Soon, those are reacting to orange hair.

After that, those spend time shutting something.

Later still, each of those give the neck a knifing, or all of
those come to give a parallel meal, beautiful & shocking.

Those will themselves to be dead or come to see something
narrow.

One of those says things as a worm would,
while all of those discuss something brown.

Numbering,
each of those has an example.

At the end, those are all saying things about making gardens.

29th Dance — Having An Instrument — 22 March 1964

Whichever harbours poison between cotton, or goes from
                        breathing to a common form,
walks,
& makes a bridge, giving it to someone,
after making decisions.

Then, giving a bit or doing something elastic,
whichever is saying something between thick things,
is saying things about making gardens.

Then whichever can do so keeps a wheel under parcels.

Whichever later puts in languages other than English?

Whichever is going about being a unit.

Then whichever gives an answer
soon is seeming to send things or is putting wires on things,
& letting a system give punishments or sadly keeping the toes
                                                              under.

But, at the end, whichever has or seems to have serious holes,
through letting a system give punishments or sadly keeping the
                                                         toes under?

Whichever has uses among harmonies,
& whichever is blackening something,
— in short, whichever has an instrument.

37th Dance — Banding — 22 March 1964

While some are being flies,
others are having examples.

Then others do something consciously,
while saying things about making gardens.

Is it then that others are getting insects?

No it's when still others are boiling delicate things,
keeping up that process till the end.

*from THE PRONOUNS — A COLLECTION OF 40
        DANCES — FOR THE DANCERS — 6 February —
        22 March 1964*

EDWARD MARSHALL

Sept. 1957

O' How deep is thy love says
        the Hymnal with the tune
           from Greenoble
How green is thy valley
        which is just a hole under my
         window where two cats played
         at seven this morning and they
         howled like babies but they
         were taken from the ass next door.
How deep is that drop beneath and
     especially if the dog should sniff too
        much and take a leap—all would
        happen would be a cat's leap in
         heat right back at Fritz's
          throat.
How deep it is, your altruism, the high
     wall, the backyard, brick leaning,
       Tower of Pisa—rent-o-building
       —rent asunder with junk and shit-
       apartments with rent unpaid.
O' Someone come along and redeem everyone
     here: Negro, Jew, Czech and yank all out
     of debt and let us have a jubilee,
     seven years and forgive us seventy
     times seven but this is not a bona year.
How deep is the cut-rate, Fourth Avenue, Up it,
     up it retail, knock it down Fourth Avenue—
     pour in, pour in—there is a junk yard
     out back to put the cardboard box—
     a reminder of your laying them out one
     by one with newspaper shreds of your
     ads and invoices not paid from the inky
     printers who wish to fill up the fire-
     places with mantels over them while I do
     the poking in my own cauldron.
How deep is thy love in repairing the clatter
     box and I have been up all night poking

in the pails (one voice) I was looking
under the curtains and finally let the
water fall and held back the rest.
How deep is thy love with a pause
and the wall says menopause.
Hey, there! Cook your breakfast,
I don't need to break a fast that
I never have had—so I won't have
anything this morning—I shall be
burned out—heat—radium—I shall
work it out with less eating and how
can I eat when I see the dog masticate?
How deep is thy love for setting before me this
clat-clat—with noisy t's and liquid
sounds and the r's rolling and autumn
almost here when I shall be alone (aut)
How deep is thy love and fall here at hand and
light houses will be bobbing up the North
Shore and down South at Scituate and I
have got it and I have never been to Provincetown
on the belle and have never been there period.
This is the time for Asian fever.
Have you been inoculated my school children?
Has the district nurse been around to see you?
You better see her before the alley cats howl
and that is why I shall eventually be taken away
because we all howl in the night that we haven't
admitted has become morning and after all I am in the
environs where people have the five-day work week.
Of course, they are still sleeping 10 o'clock
Saturday morning but to do that they have had
to sleep right along and I am going to get
Blaser on the trail and find out about these
cats before they take off—cats that will always
put one more up.
O' love how deep, keep up your cheshire grin (grin
and bear it—it's in the grain) to shake out
your dust mops this time in the morning
and whip your rugs (little harder lady—
not enough dust!)
O' love how deep says the hymnal and the Bird this
morning is at his best because I am at black and
white keys and this coloring (blacks and white aren't
colors)

There is no symbolism to black and white keys—why
    the machine is only a clatter board and there
        can be no demarcation.
How deep is thy love to make me feel good
    while I am penniless and I have to
    return a bank book with small corporation
      holdings that are no longer because it
    will fold up soon by amber November
      and I shall have Thanksgiving right
      now and not then because I have got
      the seasons in my hand
How deep is Thy Love for giving me the seasons prodded
    by thy Reason and I could go right through
    the seasons and never have any reason
              (not to be confused with thinking)
How deep is thy love that I can pour myself out this
    morning without resorting to the tape
      recorder and now to the ribbon
      again and the clatter board and I shall
      pull out a quill when I don't want
      noise in the refrains
How deep is thy love for all this morning is in
    refrains—that refrain from running out to
    the els and the cabinets (steamed and otherwise)
    and you have refrained me from
    my pratique cours—that sleep
Deep love for dipping bread in that heel—
    the crust around—building a wall within
      to keep down safe-crackers—safety
      no longer.
How deep is thy love for making me jump
    for I am the true Quaker and how can you quake
    at the meeting house when you have reduced
      all to the elements and can only use song to
      make rationale mind confused—is that why
      you want my songs because you hear
      something announced that something is
      around the corner—a footing—conspiracy
        going on?
How deep is thy love for the pinned point ears to
    hear that selected by someone observing in
    his tower on the roof with a barking dog
    and howling cats beneath and junk all about

(at the same time looking North from whence
   the bard came)
How deep is thy love for bringing me North so that I
   can look back on the wrecks of many hours wasted
   on a double bed with counterparts but too
   often alone and no image but only for
   the telephone—hot activity on the wires.
How deep is thy love for bringing me North and letting
   me once again walk around the bounds laid out by my
                  grandparents.
Deep is thy love for letting me pick up my bag of
   crib notes to put in the autumn fires when
   my fingers burn out of circulation.
Deep is thy love for dampness for I know on whom I
   depend on these voices who have not yet
   spoken and the mystic says if I would only
   surrender—give up what—certainly
   not property for I no longer have
   that.
I throw my manuscript at your feet and I surrender all,
   my Dear but God says that I must throw some more
   of my conscience (pricks) at His son's feet if I
   expect to be lifted high angel-wise and go by L's
   lifted—archangels and lyres.
A little more surrender and you'll go everywhere
   sure everywhere on the bear-skin rug.
      —toted everywhere—the totem
      poll not out of my ken.*
How deep is thy love that I need not defend myself
   as a tract once said because we can have this
   love what more do we need?
Supposing we don't have the tape—the ribbon—No ribbon,
   the quill and a blotter of course—and if you just
   copy and no ink spots look on twice for there/is
             no love here.
How deep is thy love for giving me the line to choke
   and chalk up the streets that I shall run
   through unbounded with the dog running ahead
   in the alleys and the cats, if not
   in heat—mauled.
How deep is thy love for not marrying me—not holding
      back the sound to be sounded and a sounding
                board—

* poll is a beat, count, measure; so totem *poll* rather than totem *pole*.

O' xylophone at Christmastide
and the word going forth by thy tong that
I used to put sugar in my tea—
Lady, don't read the tea leaves.
This is the birth of the Savior and the fullness
of the GODHEAD IN TIME
Whitehead, whatever you think I know
if you have anything to say—say it in
time and I shall keep the beat while
you and Lord Russell keep your numbers independent
from decaying matter
How deep is thy love for the five-tone scale for the
Mass rising in the East and climaxing with the
Octave in the West after a completion of the hebdom-
adal week.
Today is Saturday and some are up—those who use
their backbone but most will be jelly fish
and you better get on your window
sills! jelly fish bowls;
Let the Sun fall through the big plant.
How deep is thy love for the octave 1 plus 7
and if I live to be eighty I can live longer
and that would not be contrary to the history of
my family.
But how deep is thy love for my eternity
because of my concern for thee
but never me for I am drawn
out of murk
like the rest but still for thee.

Two Poems

One writes when
an idea comes to the head—
idea somewhere in the blues
sometimes in the trash can
in the basement
I have the idea of fire—
So what?
When I saw the rotted cartons
that used to have coffee
in the basement,

I took the torch and fumigator—
That ended the stench—
Idea—Hell! I can think myself there
I have an idea if the
  cardboard boxes in the cellar would never
                                    combust
                  then I have no idea at all.

          idea to ideogram
when I come back from the cellar
        I know of the sewer and the drainage—
Let me drain myself of my words and nouns
          so that they will not encumber you
Let me draw out with lines and pulleys
          so that you will ask: let me see that
Forget the orange and the blue in the flames
        and let us concentrate on the results.
        Have you burned that stuff out—
              that giddy laugh—?
Do you have to go out on the roof to watch
  incandescent light bulbs and orange bodies
    going on to jaundice and hepatitis—
Or would you from your roof top like to step
                    into that ap't?
Binoculars are not used just to peek
        they are only a means
          one eye by one
And when binoculars hit at someone
          it doesn't hit her
        because the eyes are looking past.
        The eyes looking through the rain drops—
              later on the river Charles—
And the police come to pick up
              hara-kiri man on the bridge
  I was there and Andy was there.
  Andy speculated and I observed.
We both went for coffee then to the bungalow.
  He took his pill and didn't write
    because said he: I don't know what to think
              of modern verse
              myself given into the classical line.
But I saw no library around save for 'How-to-do-it—'
And I knowing how to do it way down deep went home
          after eating a few peanuts.
I went home and sat down with a pencil.

Yet Andy says he prefers to take the typewriter
>to recall the classical line.
But at noon I pulled away.

Memory as Memorial in the Last

Sound-Noise
Color-Burning
Body-Odor
These are all swinging and ringing
>before me — sensations in context
>of memory — I remember the first
>time I looked into the dirty cellar
>window and loved my face as I saw it
>at the age of five.
>This is something no one told me
>because I was there alone — next to a
>lilac bush interwined with a grape vine.
>This is structure in context of memory
>which has nothing to do with burning
>sensation except that a burning sensation
>recorded an incident before the advent
>of red eyes after periods of long
>study under the influence of any thing
>you name — I remember, member, not
>dis-membering — We need all sensations
>but in memory. When I read Tiger, Tiger
>in the Night I remember — Sensation
>but in memory and oblivion only at the
>last in the nothingness that is everything.

MICHAEL McCLURE

Oh Ease Oh Body-Strain Oh Love Oh Ease Me Not! Wound-Bore

be real, show organs, show blood, OH let me
be as a flower. Let ugliness arise without care
grow side by side with beauty. Oh twist
be real to me. Fly smoke! Meat-real, as nerves
TENDON
Ion, FLAME, Muscle, not banners but bulks as
we are all 'deer'
and move as beasts. Stalking in our forest
as these are speech-words!

Burn them pure as above they rise from attitude are
stultified. Are shit. Burn
what arises from habit. Let custom
die. Smash patterns and forms let spirit
free to blasting liberty. Smash the
habit shit above!!!!!!!!!

LET PURE BLACK WORDS MOVE FROM THOUGHT
BEHIND

The Aelf-scin, The Shining Scimmer The Gleam, The Shining

color of walls of scratches of cracks of brightness
the cold mystery the (Philip calls it) Weir. The deja
vu of the forest-sorrel, tiny, leaves sun-folded
bent like a head in uniqueness. Animal in look
to fold so. The moment I
leave what I am in aelf-scin. Stand
in wonder. Lose myself. Even to fear.
A difference. Aelf-scin, Weir. But
similar. Knowing its name the horror
of void is gone. Knowing it almost
with my ash spear over my arm in the black
FOREST CLEAR WATER AND AIR SEA

The Anglo Saxons build huge boats fight battles
and rejoice in what they see,
see beauty more clearly
have words for what
I forget. Live in
liberty. For.
ever. !!!!

CALL IT FEAR NOW-GONE
the whole thing a star
breathing.

Oh Bright Oh Black Singbeast Lovebeast Catkin Sleek

spined and gullet shaped. Free me

in the tree-lighted evening and full cool
morning. OH
VISION free me erect and huge to VISION

DEEP-DELVED

OUTDELVING. BANNER-
hung and warm warmly gestured
star gestured in
the coldness.
Fingers spread pointing.

The only vision sight-sense.

GEORGIA LEE McELHANEY

Effigy

i

And walked across Potomac into Thebes
and by the bridge saw birds scattered into sky
where dogs barked at the strange sight of horses
trotting down Fourteenth street
down to the bridge.

Anacostia stirred;
those inmates, howled.
And the great coach crawled over the bridge

in the rain

toward Arlington. Lincoln sits here.
He cannot rock. Jefferson stands
and almost shifts from one leg.
He'd lean on a pillar but
The Monument glares. The Pentagon's
pentangular face reflects in almost sun
on almost water

and the horses neigh; cars move
and the carillon rings out on Hains Point
disturbing the man on the seventh green.

ii

They are burying the dead in Arlington.
They are changing the guard
at the tomb
of the unknown. White-faced soldiers stand
ill at ease

and as the horses trample by
the sand-stone tombs resound
and chandeliers quake
in Lee Mansion. Row on row

the little tombstones face the flag-draped coach
and stones drop
into new-cut earth.

And walked across Potomac into Thebes
where in the shadow of NRA
Luther salutes the pigeons. Fountains
and cupidons keep green the White House lawn
and at the Senate Office Building
it's five o'clock.

iii

Rameses would have found the word,
would have surveyed the scene and would have said
"Plant me in front of the Nile, let me
face upstream, and raise my tomb
with baboons on it, flanked by son
and Queen."

The pipe that feeds the pool is plugged

by dead leaves

and Lincoln-eyed the sphinx rests paws
upon the water where Rameses sits; he
cannot rock. Nefertari stands
and almost shifts from one leg. She'd
lean against a pillar but the pillars are gone.

iv

Then walked across the river into Thebes
where, at five o'clock, the Senate stands
adjourned. At Karnak now the solemn women wail

and wolfhounds growl at donkeys in the street
where wrapped in winding sheet Osiris rides in state
across the bridge, beyond the gate

to the Valley of the Kings.

Dervish

(—"We are blind and live our blind
lives out in blindness. Poets are
damned but they are not blind, they
see with the eyes of the angels."
—William Carlos Williams)

Beggar in dirt,
prophet in rhyme, tincup king
of Bedlam and the New
Jerusalem—

    pass by
sad and strange voyeur of night;

    sanctify
bones of children slain
for Moloch;

    dance
on hard and dry
crusts of blood;

    pass by
gardens of cities
where dwellings move in sleep
and streets tumble into seas;

    pass by
blood brushed
cross marks;

    dance
at the door of the dead but stay
only where there is no light:
having no sight, it is the mad
who pitch a star
to read by; it is the dead
who need no moon
to dream by.

Conquistador

> "I have a disease of the heart
> that only gold can cure." — Cortez

i

3/19— "just a day's march
> > through wet leaves,
> fallen trees/
> > over the hill lies

> > the gold.

> trees here
> grow together/   branches
> do not end.

3/20— "we have been told of a city
> > of solid gold
> > just over the hill.

3/21— "it has been said that in this city
> the streams run gold/
> > that with the plants
> > gold grows.

3/22— "and meeting with a man
> > native
> > > hereabouts
> he spoke of a golden city
> > just over the hill.
> > We have a river to cross.

3/23— "not that I was greater, but that
> my armor reflected the sun/
> and as I alone wore armor
> the hostiles aimed for me.
> > Many are dead
> but we have taken the village.
> > When we have rested
> we must push on. There is
> only the river to cross.

3/24—

*   *   *   *   *   *   *   *

Just in the echo of the sunrise
          river run, gold river golden
          in the sun
          greengold
below sunrise, the bluejay circling in the sun

          screamed

just beyond gunsight / above the rock
          where the river falls

ii

          and the bluejay turned west
                    sunlight
on feathers, circling in the rain/
asleep
          in treeshade
                    feather and leaf
                              wet/

Where the sun will not shine it is wet
     and the damp wings shivered
               tongue throbbed

     'cri cri cri cri

build a nest of bone feather and leaf
          on treebranch
just behind the wind/

          "cri
               sunlight on feathers
                    sunlight
swallowed by rain.

iii

     In the limits of green   fish
nest together. Sun only falls/
          in green rays
on yellow stone/   fish form
          green shade.

               Armor
rotted away, in upright position the bones
               wait/

             skull inclined/
               head bent/
                 hands
at sides
        nodding

with soft wave   green shade bending
   the mouth:
           open/
fish swim
      in and out of the eyes.

      Armor
rotted away, only bone remains.

iv
      and the bluejay turned west
            rain
on the feathers, tall in the trees/
asleep
     in the night shade
              leaves wet
                   rain
in the leaves:
         throbbing

   "cri
     in the windwave
               huddled
until daybreak gray sky
   cloudlift
        and clear sky/
   sunlight
on feathers: circling

    "cri cri cri cri
build a nest of bone feather and leaf
             on treebranch

just below the sun.

THOMAS MERTON

Duns Scotus

Striking like lightning to the quick of the real world
Scotus has mined all ranges to their deepest veins:
But where, oh, on what blazing mountain of theology
And in what Sinai's furnace
Did God refine that gold?

Who ruled those arguments in their triumphant order
And armed them with their strict celestial light?
See the lance-lightning, blade-glitter, banner-progress
As love advances, company by company
In sunlit teams his clean embattled reasons,

Until the firmament, with high heavenly marvel
Views in our crystal souls her blue embodiment,
Unfurls a thousand flags above our heads —
It is the music of Our Lady's army!

For Scotus is her theologian,
Nor has there ever been a braver chivalry than his
          precision.
His thoughts are skies of cloudless peace
Bright as the vesture of her grand aurora
Filled with the rising Christ.

But we, a weak, suspicious generation,
Loving emotion, hating prayer,
We are not worthy of his wisdom.
Creeping like beasts between the mountain's feet
We look for laws in the Arabian dust.
We have no notion of his freedom

Whose acts despise the chains of choice and passion.
We have no love for his beatitude
Whose act renounces motion:
Whose love flies home forever
As silver as felicity,
Working and quiet in the dancelight of an everlasting
          arrow.

Lady, the image of whose heaven
Sings in the might of Scotus' reasoning:
There is no line of his that has not blazed your glory
    in the schools,
Though in dark words, without romance,
Calling us to swear you our liege.

Language was far too puny for his great theology:
But, oh! His thought strode through those words
Bright as the conquering Christ
Between the clouds His enemies:
And in the clearing storm and Sinai's dying thunder
Scotus comes out, and shakes his golden locks
And sings like the African sun.

St. Malachy

In November, in the days to remember the dead
When air smells cold as earth,
St. Malachy, who is very old, gets up,
Parts the thin curtains of the trees and dawns upon our
    land.

His coat is filled with drops of rain, and he is bearded
With all the seas of Poseidon.
(Is it a crozier, or a trident in his hand?)
He weeps against the gothic window, and the empty
    cloister
Mourns like an ocean shell.

Two bells in the steeple
Talk faintly to the old stranger
And the tower considers his waters.
"I have been sent to see my festival," (his cavern
    speaks!)
"For I am the saint of the day.
Shall I shake the drops from my locks and stand in
    your transept,
Or, leaving you, rest in the silence of my history?"

So the bells rang and we opened the antiphoners
And the wrens and larks flew up out of the pages.
Our thoughts became lambs. Our hearts swam like
    seas.

One monk believed that we should sing to him
Some stone-age hymn
Or something in the giant language.
So we played to him in the plainsong of the giant
        Gregory:
Oceans of Scripture sang upon bony Eire.

Then the last salvage of flowers
(Fostered under glass after the gardens foundered)
Held up their little lamps on Malachy's altar
To peer into his wooden eyes before the Mass began.

Rain sighed down the sides of the stone church.
Storms sailed by all day in battle fleets.
At five o'clock, when we tried to see the sun, the
        speechless visitor
Sighed and arose and shook the humus from his feet
And with his trident stirred our trees
And left down-wood, shaking some drops upon the
        ground.

Thus copper flames fall, tongues of fire fall
The leaves in hundreds fall upon his passing
While night sends down her dreadnought darkness
Upon this spurious Pentecost.

And the Melchisedec of our year's end
Who came without a parent, leaves without a trace,
And rain comes rattling down upon our forest
Like the doors of a country jail.

Elegy for the Monastery Barn

As though an aged person were to wear
Too gay a dress
And walk about the neighborhood
Announcing the hour of her death,

So now, one summer day's end,
At suppertime, when wheels are still,
The long barn suddenly puts on the traitor, beauty,
And hails us with a dangerous cry,
For: "Look!" she calls to the country,
"Look how fast I dress myself in fire!"

Had we half guessed how long her spacious shadows
Harbored a woman's vanity
We would be less surprised to see her now
So loved, and so attended, and so feared.

She, in whose airless heart
We burst our veins to fill her full of hay,
Now stands apart.
She will not have us near her. Terribly,
Sweet Christ, how terribly her beauty burns us now!

And yet she has another legacy,
More delicate, to leave us, and more rare.

Who knew her solitude?
Who heard the peace downstairs
While flames ran whispering among the rafters?
Who felt the silence, there,
The long, hushed gallery
Clean and resigned and waiting for the fire?

Look! They have all come back to speak their sum-
      mary:
Fifty invisible cattle, the past years
Assume their solemn places one by one.
This is the little minute of their destiny.
Here is their meaning found. Here is their end.

Laved in the flame as in a Sacrament
The brilliant walls are holy
In their first-last hour of joy.

Fly from within the barn! Fly from the silence
Of this creature sanctified by fire!
Let no man stay inside to look upon the Lord!
Let no man wait within and see the Holy
One sitting in the presence of disaster
Thinking upon this barn His gentle doom!

To a Severe Nun

I know, Sister, that solitude
Will never dismay you. You have chosen
A path too steep for others to follow.
I take it you prefer to go without them.

You will not complain that others are fickle
When they abandon you, renouncing the contest.
After all, they have not understood
That love is a contest, and that the love you demand
Is a match, in which you overcome your friends
After a long agony.

Thus you have no visible companions. Yet, drive on,
Drive on: do not consider your despair! Imagine
    rather
That there are many saints around you in the same
    desperation,
Violent, without contact, without responsibility,
Except of course to their own just souls
And to the God Who cannot blame them.

You know where you are going. You alone
In the whole convent know what bitter comfort
Eludes the malcontents who travel this unusual desert,
Seeking the impossible, and not the Absolute —
Sustained always by the same hate.

Do not be disconcerted, Sister, if in spite of your effort
The impertinent truth shows up weakness at least in
    others
And distracts you with their suffering.
Do not be humbled if, for an instant,
Christ seems glad to suffer in another.

Forget this scandal. Do not look at them
Or you may lose your nerve, and come to admit
That violence is your evasion and that you,
You most of all, are weak.

A Practical Program for Monks

1

Each one shall sit at table with his own cup and
    spoon, and with his own repentance. Each one's
    own business shall be his most important affair,
    and provide his own remedies.

They have neglected bowl and plate.
Have you a wooden fork?
Yes, each monk has a wooden fork as well as a potato.

2

Each one shall wipe away tears with his own saint,
    when three bells hold in store a hot afternoon.
    Each one is supposed to mind his own heart, with
    its conscience, night and morning.
Another turn on the wheel: ho hum! And observe the
    Abbot!
Time to go to bed in a straw blanket.

3

Plenty of bread for everyone between prayers and the
    psalter: will you recite another?
Merci, and *Miserere.*
Always mind both the clock and the Abbot until
    eternity.
Miserere.

4

Details of the Rule are all liquid and solid. What
    canon was the first to announce regimentation
    before us? Mind the step on the way down!
Yes, I dare say you are right, Father. I believe you; I
    believe you.
I believe it is easier when they have ice water and even
    a lemon.
Each one can sit at table with his own lemon, and
    mind his conscience.

5

Can we agree that the part about the lemon is regu-
    lar?
In any case, it is better to have sheep than peacocks,
    and cows rather than a chained leopard says
    Modest, in one of his proverbs.
The monastery, being owner of a communal row-
    boat, is the antechamber of heaven.
Surely that ought to be enough.

6

Each one can have some rain after Vespers on a hot
    afternoon, but *ne quid nimis,* or the purpose of
    the Order will be forgotten.
We shall send you hyacinths and a sweet millennium.
Everything the monastery provides is very pleasant to
    see and to sell for nothing.
What is baked smells fine. There is a sign of God on
    every leaf that nobody sees in the garden. The
    fruit trees are there on purpose, even when no
    one is looking. Just put the apples in the basket.
In Kentucky there is also room for a little cheese.
Each one shall fold his own napkin, and neglect the
    others.

7

Rain is always very silent in the night, under such
    gentle cathedrals.
Yes, I have taken care of the lamp. *Miserere.*
Have you a patron saint, and an angel?
Thank you. Even though the nights are never danger-
    ous, I have one of everything.

A Baroque Gravure

(from a 17th century book of piety)

She is devout and plump, but not happy:
Hers is a *vie infortunée*
But she will be patient
She will bear life at Versailles.

No, she is not a barbary slave:
But she, too, has her destiny, and the friendly engraver
Suggests a comparison: blackamoors
In chains. They are beaten.
A placid overseer
Raises his stick. One slave
Meek in coat and chain,
Waits.
                (Are you, Madame,
                Sometime or other stung by wicked tongues?)

She, under the palm tree,
Great unfortunate peahen,
Sees none of this,
(Though three blacks in the next field
Are hooked to a plow).
No, she contemplates her own case,
And musters up
Her own resolutions.

> *(Plusieurs ont vu leurs peines terminées*
> *Par leur patience et leur vertu.)*

A resolution:
"Let each carry his own cross!"

Two shiploads, there, arrive from Barbary.
(Is there patience under hatches?
Is there merit? Will virtue terminate
Their misfortunes?)
She does not inquire.
She is carrying her own
Cross.

One independent Moor
Wearing an arbitrary uniform
Holds a bow and arrow
And (as if it had a meaning)
Views her sorrow.

Seneca

When the torch is taken
And the room is dark
The mute wife
Knowing Seneca's ways
Listens to night
To rumors
All around the house
While her wise
Lord promenades
Within his own temple
Master and censor
Overseeing
His own ways
With his philosophical sconce
Policing the streets

Of this secret Rome
While the wife
Silent as a sea
Policing nothing
Waits in darkness
For the Night Bird's
Inscrutable cry.

W. S. MERWIN

Lemuel's Blessing

Let Lemuel bless with the wolf,
which is a dog without a master,
but the Lord hears his cries and
feeds him in the desert.

Christopher Smart: *Jubilate Agno*

You know the way,
Spirit,
I bless your ears which are like cypruses on a mountain
With their roots in wisdom. Let me approach.
I bless your paws and their twenty nails which tell their own
prayer
And are like dice in command of their own combinations.
Let me not be lost.
I bless your eyes for which I know no comparison.
Run with me like the horizon, for without you
I am nothing but a dog lost and hungry,
Ill-natured, untrustworthy, useless.

My bones together bless you like an orchestra of flutes.
Divert the weapons of the settlements and lead their dogs a
dance.
Where a dog is shameless and wears servility
In his tail like a banner,
Let me wear the opprobrium of possessed and possessors
As a thick tail properly used
To warm my worst and my best parts. My tail and my laugh
bless you.
Lead me past the error at the fork of hesitation.
Deliver me

From the ruth of the lair, which clings to me in the morning,
Painful when I move, like a trap;
Even debris has its favorite positions but they are not yours;
From the ruth of kindness, with its licked hands;
I have sniffed baited fingers and followed
Toward necessities which were not my own: it would make me
An habitué of back steps, faithful custodian of fat sheep;

From the ruth of prepared comforts, with its
Habitual dishes sporting my name and its collars and leashes of
vanity;

From the ruth of approval, with its nets, kennels, and taxi-
dermists;
It would use my guts for its own rackets and instruments, to
play its own games and music;
Teach me to recognize its platforms, which are constructed
like scaffolds;
From the ruth of known paths, which would use my feet, tail,
and ears as curios,
My head as a nest for tame ants,
My fate as a warning.

I have hidden at wrong times for wrong reasons.
I have been brought to bay. More than once.
Another time, if I need it,
Create a little wind like a cold finger between my shoulders,
then
Let my nails pour out a torrent of aces like grain from a
threshing machine;
Let fatigue, weather, habitation, the old bones, finally,
Be nothing to me,
Let all lights but yours be nothing to me.
Let the memory of tongues not unnerve me so that I stumble
or quake.

But lead me at times beside the still waters;
There when I crouch to drink let me catch a glimpse of your
image
Before it is obscured with my own.

Preserve my eyes, which are irreplaceable.
Preserve my heart, veins, bones,
Against the slow death building in them like hornets until the
place is entirely theirs.
Preserve my tongue and I will bless you again and again.

Let my ignorance and my failings
Remain far behind me like tracks made in a wet season,
At the end of which I have vanished,
So that those who track me for their own twisted ends
May be rewarded only with ignorance and failings.

But let me leave my cry stretched out behind me like a road
On which I have followed you.
And sustain me for my time in the desert
On what is essential to me.

Air

Naturally it is night.
Under the overturned lute with its
One string I am going my way
Which has a strange sound.

This way the dust, that way the dust.
I listen to both sides
But I keep right on.
I remember the leaves sitting in judgment
And then winter.

I remember the rain with its bundle of roads.
The rain taking all its roads.
Nowhere.

Young as I am, old as I am,

I forget tomorrow, the blind man.
I forget the life among the buried windows.
The eyes in the curtains.
The wall
Growing through the immortelles.
I forget silence
The owner of the smile.

This must be what I wanted to be doing,
Walking at night between the two deserts,
Singing.

Walk-Up

The inspector of stairs is on the stairs
Oh my God and I thought it was Sunday,
His advance like a broom and those stairs going
Down to meet him, alright
What that's mine will he show me
To be ashamed of this time

The spiders in my face, the whistles
In the cupboards,
The darkness in my shoes, going out
To deep water

                No

The sky's at home in these windows, and the maps
Of themselves on these walls,
And your letter is enough improvement
For anywhere, lying open
On my table, my
Love

        I won't close a thing

Let him arrive fanning himself
With his calendar, let him become
At the door the inspector of doors and find
Mine open,
Inspector of hands—
                His name
Would mean nothing to me, his questions are not
His own, but let my answers
Be mine.

For Now

The year a bird flies against the drum

I come to myself miles away with
Tickets dying in my hand

You are not here will the earth last till you come
I must say now what cannot
Be said later Goodbye
The name of the statues but who needs them
As for myself I

Look back at the rain
I grew up in the rooms of the rain
So that was home so let the grass grow
Goodbye faces in stains churches
In echoes dusters at windows
Schools without floors envelopes full of smoke

Goodbye hands of those days I keep the fossils
Goodbye iron Bible containing my name in rust
Cock Robin and
The date
Goodbye Cock Robin I never saw you

On plates upside down in token of mourning
I eat to your vanishing

I bearing messages

With all my words my silence being one

From childhood to childhood the
Message Goodbye from the shoulders of victory
To the followers
From the sea to the nearest of kin

From the roller skates to the death in the basement
From the lightning to
Its nest from myself to my name
Goodbye

I begin with what was always gone

Ancestors in graves of broken glass
In empty cameras

Mistakes in the mail Goodbye to the same name

Goodbye what you learned for me I have to learn anyway

You that forgot your rivers they are gone
Myself I would not know you

Goodbye as
The eyes of a whale say goodbye having never seen
Each other

And to you that vanished as I watched goodbye
Walter the First
Jacques the Clown
Marica the Good

Goodbye the pain of the past that
Will never be made better goodbye
Pain of the innocent that will never
Not have existed
Goodbye you that are

Buried with the name of the florist in your hands
And a box from our
Box society your finger holding the place
Your jaws tied with a ribbon marked Justice
To help us

The dead say Look
The living in their distress sink upward weeping
But who could reach them in such a sea

Goodbye kites painted with open mouths over the
Scarlet road of the animals

Goodbye prophets sometimes we are
Here sometimes we remember it
Sometimes we walk in your
Eyes which sometimes you lost
Sometimes we walk in your old brains and are forgotten

Or this character gets on the bus with an open razor
Bends down to my face at once thinking he
Knows me goodbye
Yard where I was supposed
To be safe behind the fences of sand
Watched over by an empty parasol and the sound of
Pulleys I who
Had built the ark

Goodbye cement street address of cement tears
Grief of the wallpaper the witness
Cold banisters worn thin with fright
Photo of me wondering what it would be like
The girls at last the hips full of dice the names
In smoke for the lamps the
Calling Goodbye among the wishes
Among the horses

If I had known what to say there would be the same hands
Holding white crosses in front of the windows

Goodbye to the dew my master

And you masters with feathers on your key rings
Wardens of empty scales
When I find where I am goodbye

Goodbye sound of a voice spelling its name to a uniform
Spelling it
Again goodbye white
Truck that backs up to drugstores after dark
Arriving at
Apartment houses in the afternoon
And the neighbors calling can you come up for a minute

Goodbye anniversaries I pass without knowing
Days for which the chairs are wired
The law on the throne of ice above the salting floor
Its eyes full of falling snow
Friend Instead and the rest of the
Brothers Meaningless

Those who will drown next bow to their straw

Goodbye to the water a happy person
The longer its story the
Less it tells
Goodbye to the numbers starting with God

To the avenues
No one asked their permission so they had none

Goodbye hands wrapped in newspaper

And when the towers are finished the frameworks are
Thrown from the tops and descend slowly
Waving as they

Dissolve

Tell me what you see vanishing and I
Will tell you who you are
To whom I say Goodbye
You my neighbors in the windows in the registers you
The sizes of your clothes
You born with the faces of presidents on your eyelids

Tell me how your hands fall and I will tell you
What you will wave to next
Guests of yourselves expecting hosts
You in the cold of whose
Voices I can hear
The hanged man in the chimney turning
You with mouths full of pebbles
In the rising elevator in the falling building you

With your destinations written in your shoelaces
And your lies elected

They return in the same
Skins to the same seats by the flags of money
Goodbye to the Bibles hollowed for swearing on
A hole knocks on the panes but is not heard

Around them the crashes occur in silence
The darkness that flows from the sirens passes the windows
The blackness spreads from the headlines
Over their spectacles they light the ceilings

Goodbye what we may never see
Age would have kissed false teeth if any
Its caresses making a bed slowly
Even as a child I hoped it would spare me
I made tears for it I sang

As the cards are laid out they turn to ashes
I kiss
The light to those who love it it is brief

Goodbye before it is taken away
I have been with it the season could sign for me

The message sang in its bottle it would find me
I knew the king of the moths I knew the watchman's country
I knew where the phoebe lost herself I knew the story
I stepped in the lock I
Turned
My thumb was carved with the one map of a lost mountain

My scars will answer to no one but me
I know the planet that lights up the rings in the hems
I know the stars in the door

I know the martyrs sleeping in almonds
I know the gloves of the hours I know Pilate the fly
I know the enemy's brother

But it will happen just the same goodbye

Heart my elder

My habits of sand
My bones whose count is lost every night every day
The milestones of salt the rain my feet
Memory in its rivers
Goodbye my house my cat my spiders

Goodbye distance from whom I
Borrow my eyes goodbye my voice
In the monument of strangers goodbye to the sun
Among the wings nailed to the windows goodbye
My love

You that return to me through the mountain of flags
With my raven on your wrist
You with the same breath

Between death's republic and his kingdom

VASSAR MILLER

Without Ceremony

Except ourselves, we have no other prayer;
Our needs are sores upon our nakedness.
We do not have to name them; we are here.
And You who can make eyes can see no less.
We fall, not on our knees, but on our hearts,
A posture humbler far and more downcast;
While Father Pain instructs us in the arts
Of praying, hunger is the worthiest fast.
We find ourselves where tongues cannot wage war
On silence (farther, mystics never flew)
But on the common wings of what we are,
Borne on the wings of what we bear, toward You,
Oh Word, in whom our wordiness dissolves,
When we have not a prayer except ourselves.

Christmas Mourning

On Christmas Day I weep
Good Friday to rejoice.
I watch the Child asleep.
Does He half dream the choice
The Man must make and keep?

At Christmastime I sigh
For my Good Friday hope.
Outflung the Child's arms lie
To span in their brief scope
The death the Man must die.

Come Christmastide I groan
To hear Good Friday's pealing.
The Man, racked to the bone,
Has made His hurt my healing,
Has made my ache His own.

Slay me, pierced to the core
With Christmas penitence
So I who, new-born, soar
To that Child's innocence,
May wound the Man no more.

Faintly and From Far Away

Between the wheeze of her torpor and the wind of her falling,
Between the whey of her face and the snow of its blanching,
Between the vacuum of her monotone and the void of its
                                                    stilling
Was only the difference between the cicadas on a summer
                                                    afternoon
And their declining into the bottom of evening,
Only the difference between the sparrows pecking the rock of
                                                    silence
And the rock of silence itself.

Father, rememberer of sparrows and dullards,
Each of us cries, even as she, from some twig of a cross:
        Remember me, Lord. Before it swoops me up, feather
        The hawk of the world's forgetting with the down of
            Your memory.

No Return

Once over summer streams the ice-crusts harden,
No one can wade therein to wash his feet
Thence to go flying after nymphs that fleet
Naked and nimble through the woods. Time's warden
Has locked them all (or is it us?) past pardon.
Yet freed, we could not find the path that beat
Toward — call it any name — fauns, home, retreat;
For there is no returning to that garden.

No, not to Adam's. We must keep our own,
Remembering. In Eden's greenery
God walked. While in our garden rocks are brown
With His dried blood where He has crouched to groan.
Our apples rotted, only His crosstree
Bears crimson fruit. But no hand plucks it down.

Joyful Prophecy

(for Daryl)

If he is held in love,
the thin reeds of my baby's bones
are pipes for it, it hums

and chuckles from the hollows
as a flower whispers,
it ripples off him, suave

honey of the sunlight
stored for his kin, his kind, such lovely
mirrors of it, he

is tempted to hoard it in
his well where he may gaze at it,
yet held in love and gracious

he shares it with his sister;
but, lest death waste it on the wind,
love measures him for the man

who can hold its heartiness
fermented to a man's delight,
if he is held in love.

How Far?

How far is it to you by foot?
Ten thousand stones,
Two million grains of dust and soot,
All my bruised bones.

How far is it to you by sea?
Twelve hills and hollows
Of water, each one risking me
Gulped in salt swallows.

How far is it to you by rail?
A myriad meadows
Sweeping the window in a gale
Of golden shadows.

How far is it to you by air?
Ten thousand thunders,
Countless ice crystals set aflare
With rainbow wonders.

How far is it to you by light?
Two parted petals
Of eyelids flowering with sight
Where sunshine settles.

How far is it to you by love?
I have no notion.
For so to seek and find you prove
One selfsame motion.

The Resolution

You broke Your teeth upon the question Why,
Sucking its acrid marrow dry,
Its taste of silence wry.

Like You, on quandaries ripened in the brain,
Dropped on the heart, I bruised in vain;
Poised on this point of pain,

We find no room, whether at odds like fencers,
We two, or in embrace like dancers,
For questions or for answers

Except ourselves when, I in You, for once
The query rests in the response,
The candle in its sconce.

FRANK O'HARA

Biotherm (for Bill Berkson)

The best thing in the world   but I better be quick about it
better be gone tomorrow

                          better be gone last night and
                  next Thursday better be gone

better be
                  always   or what's the use the sky
        the endless clouds trailing we leading them by the bandanna, red

you meet the Ambassador   "a year and a half of trying to make him"
      he is dressed in red, he has a red ribbon down his chest he
        has   7   gold decorations pinned to his gash
he sleeps a lot, thinks a lot, fucks a lot, impenetrable and Jude-ish
      I love him, you would love him too   if you could see outside

                  whoops-musicale (sei tu m'ami) ahhahahahaha
              loppy di looploop   which is why   I suppose
        Leontyne Price asked Secretary Goldberg to intervene with Metropera
it's not as dangerous as you think
                          NEVERTHELESS (thank you, Aristotle)

        I know you are interested in the incongruities of my behavior, John
just as Bill you are interested in the blue paint JA Oscar Maxine Khnute
perhaps you'd better be particularly interested   POOF

                          extended vibrations
ziggurats ZIG I to IV   stars of the Tigris-Euphrates basin
        leading ultimates such as kickapoo joyjuice halvah Canton cheese
in thimbles
                  paraded for gain, but yet a parade kiss me,
                          Busby Berkeley, kiss me
you have ended the war by simply singing in your Irene Dunne foreskin
"Practically Yours"
              with June Vincent, Lionello Venturi and Casper Citron
        a Universal-International release produced by G. Mennen Williams
                          directed by Florine Stettheimer
                          continuity by the Third Reich
after "hitting" the beach at Endzoay we drank up the liebfraumilch
        and pushed on up the Plata to the pampas
you didn't pick up the emeralds you god-damned fool you got
        no collarbone you got no dish no ears
                          Maurice Prendergast
                          Tilly Losch
              "when the seizure tuck 'im 'e went" — Colette
besides, the snow was snowing, our fault for calling the ticket
                  perhaps at the end of a very strange game
                  you won   ? (?) ! (?)   .
        and that is important (yeah) to win (yeah)

bent on his knees the Old Mariner said where the fuck
        is that motel you told me about mister I aint come here for no clams
I want swimmingpool mudpacks the works carbonateddrugstorewater hiccups
fun a nice sissy under me clean and whistling a donkey to ride rocks
              "OKAY (smile) COMING UP"

"This is, after all," said Margaret Dumont, "the *original* MAIN CHANCE"
(fart) "Suck this," said the Old M, spitting on his high heels
which he had just put on to get his navel up to her knee

but even that extended a little further,
   out into the desert, where
   no flash tested, no flashed!
   oops! and no nail polish, yak
         yak yak, Lieut.
   no flesh to taste no flash to tusk
   no flood to flee no fleed to dlown flom the iceth loot
"par exemple!"

out of the dark a monster appears full of grizzly odors which exhale through
him like a samovar belches out the news of the Comintern in a novel by
Howard Fast
   BUT
      the cuckoo keeps falling off the branch so everything's okay
nobody worries about mistakes disasters calamities so long as they're "natural"
sun sun bene bene bullshit it's important to be sensitive in business and
insensitive in love because what have you if you have no "balls" what made
the French important after all if not: jeu de balles, pas de balles and,
for murderers of Algerians, regle de balles may I ask
    "do you love it?"

 I don't think I want to win anything I think I want to die unadorned

     the dulcet waves are
     sweeping along in their purplish
     way and a little girl is
     beginning to cry and I know
     her but I can't help because
     she has just found her first brick
     what can you do what

does that seem a little too Garboesque? now Garbo, a strange case. oh god

keeping them alive
     there are more waves with bricks in them than there are
        well-advertised mansions in the famous House
but we will begin again, won't we
       well I will anyway or as 12,
"continuez, même stupide garçon"

    "This dedelie stroke, wherebye shall seace
     The harborid sighis within my herte"

and at the doorway there is no
      acceptable bong except stick mush
room for paranoia comme à l'heure de midi moins quatre
        et pour

JOUR DE FÊTE j'ai composé mon "Glorification" hommage au poète
           américain
   lyrique et profond, Wallace Stevens
        but one
  of your American tourists told me he was a banker
      quels délices
 I would like to tell you what I think about bankers but . . .
     except W. C. Fields

what do you want from a bank but love   ouch
  but I don't get any love from Wallace Stevens no I don't

I think délices is a lot of horseshit and that comes from one who infinitely
                                        prefers bullshit
                            and the bank rolled on
                            and Stevens strolled on
                            an ordinary evening alone
                            with a lot of people

                    "the flow'r you once threw at me
                    socked me with hit me over the head avec
                    has been a real blessing let me think
                    while lying here with the lice
                                        you're a dream"
AND
                    "measure shmeasure know shknew
                    unless the material rattle us around
                    pretty rose preserved in biotherm
                    and yet the y bothers us when we dance
                                        the pussy pout"
                            never liked to sing much but that's what being
                                a child means   BONG

le bateleur! how wonderful
I'm so so so so so so so so so so so happy
so happy I make you happy
like in the s- s- s- s- soap opera wow
        what else I mean what else do you need (I)
                                        then you
                            were making me happy otherwise I
                            was staring into *Saturday Night* and flag
                            pink shirt with holes cinzano-soda-grin
                            unh. it is just too pleasant to b.w.y.

hey! help! come back! you spilled your omelette all over your pants!
oh damn it, I guess that's the end of one of our meetings

"vass hass der mensch geplooped
that there is sunk in the battlefield a stately grunt
and the idle fluice still playing on the hill
because of this this this this slunt"
                            it's a secret told by
                            a madman in a parlor car
                            signifying chuckles
                                    * Richard Widmark *
                                    * Gene Tierney *
                                    * Googie Withers *

        I hate the hat you are not wearing, I love to see your narrow head

there in the dark London streets
                            there were all sorts of murderers
                    gamblers and Greek wrestlers
            "I could have had all of wrestling in London in my hand"
                    BANG
                            down by the greasy Thames shack
                                stumbling up and over

(PROKOFIEVIANA)

One day   you are posing in your checkerboard bathing trunks
        the bear eats only honey   what a strange life

is the best of mine impossible   what does it mean

                    that equally strange smile it's like seeing the moon rise
                              "keep believing it"
          you will not want, from me

      where you were no longer exists
      which is why we will go see it to be close to you how could it leave

I would never leave you
if I didn't have to
                              you will have to too
                              Soviet society taught us that
                              is the necessity to be "realistic" love is a football
                                        I only hear the pianos
                    when possession turns into frustration
                    the North Star goes out will it
                    is there anyone there
the seismograph at Fordham University says it will
                                                  so it will not

                    we are alone no one is talking it feels good
      we have our usual contest about claustrophobia
      it doesn't matter much
      doing without each other is much more insane

                         okay, it's not the sun setting it's the moon rising
                         I see it that way too

          (BACK TO SATIE)

when the *Vitalità nell' arte* catalog came in the mail I laughed
          thinking it was *Perspectives USA* but it wasn't it
          was vitality nellie arty ho ho that's a joke pop
          I never had to see I just kept looking at the pictures"
                              damn good show!
                              don't I know it?
                              take off your glasses
                              you're breaking my frame
                              sculptresses wear dresses

      Lo! the Caracas transport lunch with George Al Leslie 5:30 I'll
be over at 5
                         I hope you will I'm dying of loneliness
                         here with my red blue green and natch pencils and the erasers
                         with the mirror behind me and the desk in front of me
                         like an anti-Cocteau movement
"who did you have lunch with?" "you" "oops!" how ARE you

          then too, the other day I was walking through a train
          with my suitcase and I overheard someone say "speaking of faggots"
          now isn't life difficult enough without that
          and why am I always carrying something
          well it was a shitty looking person anyway
          better a faggot than a farthead
          or as fathers have often said to friends of mine
          "better dead than a dope" "if I thought you were queer I'd kill you
          you'd be right to, DAD, daddio, addled annie pad-lark (Brit.
                                                            19th C.)

          well everything can't be perfect
          you said it

I definitely do not think that Lobelia would be a suitable name
for Carey and Norman's daughter if they have a daughter
and if they have a son Silverrod is insupportable by most
put that back in your pipe Patsy and make pot out of it honey

you were there I was here you were here I was there where are you I miss you
    (that was an example of the "sonnet" "form") (this is another)
when you went I stayed and then I went and we were both lost and then I died

                        oh god what joy
                        you're here
                        sob and at the
                        most recent summit
                        conference they
                        are eating string
                        beans butter
                        smootch slurp
                        pass me the filth
                        and a coke pal
                        oh thank you

down at the box-office of Town Hall I was thinking of you in your no hat
    music often reminds me of nothing, that way, like reforming

September 15 (supine, unshaven, hungover, passive, softspoken) I was
very happy
                on Altair 4, I love you that way, it was on Altair 4 "a happy day"
        I knew it would be
        yes to everything
                I think you will find the pot in the corner
    where the Krells left it
                      rub it a little and music comes out
    the music of the fears
                I reformed we reformed each other
    being available
                it is something our friends don't understand
    if you loosen your tie
        my heart will leap out
    like a Tanagra sculpture
                    from the crater of the Corsican "lip"
    and flying through the heavens
                I am reminded of Kit Carson
    and all those smiles which were exactly like yours
    but we hadn't met yet
                when are you going away on "our" trip
    why are you melancholy
                    if I make you angry you are no longer
                            doubtful
    if I make you happy you are no longer doubtful
                          what's wrong with
                          doubt

it is mostly that your face
is like the sky behind the Sherry Netherland
blue instead of air, touching instead of remote, warm instead of racing
you are as intimate as a "cup" of vodka
                and when yesterday arrives and troubles us you always say
                              NO
    I don't believe you at first but you say no no no no
    and pretty soon I am smiling and doing just what I want
    again
                that's very important
                you put the shit back in the drain
                and then you actually find the stopper

take back September 15 to Aug something
I think you are wonderful on your birthday
                        I think you are wonderful
    on all your substitute birthdays

I am rather irritated at your being born
at all
where did you put that stopper
you are the biggest fool I ever laid eyes on
that's what they thought about the Magi, I believe

first you peel the potatoes
then you marinate the peelies
in campari all the while playing
the Mephisto Waltz on your gram
and wrap them in grape leaves
and bake them in mush ouch
that god damn oven delicacies
the ditch is full of after dinner

what sky
out there in between the ailanthuses
a 17th Century prison an aardvark
a photograph of Mussolini and
a personal letter from Isak Dinesen
written after eating

the world of thrills! 7 Lively Arts! Week-in-Review! whew!
if you lie there asleep on the floor after lunch
what else is there for me to do but adore you
I am sitting on top of Mauna Loa seeing thinking feeling
the breeze rustles through the mountain gently trusts me
I am guarding it from mess and measure

it is cool
I am high
and happy
as it turns
on the earth
tangles me
in the air

the celestial drapery salutes an ordinary occurrence
the moon is rising I am always thinking of the moon rising
I am always thinking of you
your morality your carved lips
on the beach we stood on our heads
I held your legs it was summer and hot
the Bloody Marys were spilling on our trunks
but the crocodiles didn't pull them
it was a charmed life full of
innuendos and desirable hostilities
I wish we were back there among the
irritating grasses and the helmet crabs
that spindrift gawk towards Swan Lake Allegra Kent
those Ten Steps of Patricia Wilde
unison matches anxious putty Alhambra
bus-loads of Russians' dignity desire
when we meet we smile in another language

you don't know the half of it
I never said I did
your mortality
I am very serious

ENDGAME WAITING FOR GODOT WATT HAPPY DAYS which means I
love you
what is that hat doing on that table in my room where I am asleep
"thank you for the dark and the shoulders"
"oh   thank you"

okay I'll meet you at the weather station at 5
we'll take a helicopter into the "eye" of the storm
we'll be so happy in the center of things at last
now the wind rushes up nothing happens and departs
L'EUROPA LETTERATURA CINEMATOGRAFICA
                              ARTISTICA 9-10
your back the street   solidity   fragility erosion
why did this Jewish hurricane have to come
and ruin our Yom Kippur

favorites: vichyssoise, capers, bandannas, fudge-nut-ice, collapsibility,
    the bar of the Winslow, 5:30 and 12:30, leather sweaters, tunafish,
    cinzano and soda, Marjorie Rambeau in *Inspiration*
                    whatdoyoumeanandhowdoyoumeanit

(MENU)
Déjeuner Bill Berkson
30 August 1961

Hors-d'oeuvre abstrait-expressionistes, américain-styles, bord-durs, etc.
Soupe Samedi Soir à la Strawberry-Blonde
Poisson Pas de Dix au style Patricia
Histoire de contrefilet, sauce Angelicus Fobb
La réunion des fins de thon à la boue
Chapon ouvert brûlé à l'Hoban, sauce Fidelio Fobb
Poèmes 1960-61 en salade

          Fromage de la Tour Dimanche 17 septembre
          Fruits des Jardins shakspériens
          Biscuits de l'*Inspiration* de Clarence Brown

Vin blanc supérieur de Bunkie Hearst
Vin rouge mélancholique de Boule de neige
Champagne d'Art News éditeur diapré
Café ivesanien "Plongez au fond du lac glacé"
                    Vodka-campari et TV

as the clouds parted the New York City Ballet opened Casey Stengel was there
with Blanche Yurka, "Bones" Mifflin, Vera-Ellen and Alice Pearce, Stuts
"Bearcat" Lonklin and Louella "Prudential" Parsons in another "box", Elsa
"I-Don't-Believe-You're-a-Rothschild" Maxwell wouldn't speak to them
because she wasn't "in" the party and despite the general vulgarity Diana
Adams again looked exactly like the moon as she appears in the works of
Alfred de Musset and me
                    who am I? I am the floorboards of that zonked palace

after the repast the reap (hic) the future is always fustian (ugh)
    nobody is Anglican everybody is anguished

"now the past is something else the past is like a future that came through
you can remember everything accurately and be proud of your honesty you can
lie about everything that happened and be happily reminiscent you can alter
here and there for increased values you can truly misremember and have it
both ways or you can forget everything completely the past is really something"

          but the future always fall' through!
          for instance will I ever really go live
          in Providence Rhode Island or Paestum Lucania
          I doubt it   "you are a rose, though?" (?)

a long history of populations, though
the phrase beginning with "Palms!" and quickly forgotten
in the pit under the dark there were books
being written about strange rites of the time
the time was called The Past and the books were in German

which scholars took to be Sanskrit or Urdu
(much laughter) which later turned out to be indeed
Sanskrit or Urdu (end of laughter, start of fight)
and at the same time the dark was going on and on
never getting bluer or greener or purpler just
going on and that was civilization and still is
nobody could see the fight but they could hear what
it was about and that's the way things were and stayed
and are except that in time the sounds started to
sound different (familiarity) and that was English

             well, that Past we have always with us, eh?
             I am talking about the color of money
             the dime so red and the 100 dollar bill so orchid
             the sickly fuchsia of a 1 the optimistic
             orange of a 5 the useless penny like a seed
             the magnificent yellow zinnia of a 10
             especially a roll of them the airy blue of a
             50 how pretty a house is when it's filled with them
             that's not a villa that's a bank
             where's the ocean
now this is not a tract against usury it's just putting two and two together
                           and getting five (thank you, Mae)

     actually I want to hear more about your family
                           yes you get the beer

I am actually thinking about how much I love Lena Horne
I never intended to go to New Hampshire without you
you know there's an interesting divinity in Rarotonga that looks sort of like you

"I am a woman in love" he said
the day began with the clear blue sky and ended in the Parrot Garden
the day began and ended with my finding you in the Parrot Garden
Lena Horne had vanished into a taxi and we were moreorless alone together
of course it wasn't Lena Horne it was Simone Signoret we were happy anyway

       "As if a clear lake meddling with itself
           Should cloud its pureness with a muddy gloom"

       "My steeds are all pawing at the threshhold of the morn"

favorites: going to parties with you, being in corners at parties with you,
           being in gloomy pubs with you smiling, poking you at parties when
           you're "down", coming on like South Pacific with you at them,
           shrimping with you into the Russian dressing, leaving parties with
           you alone to go and eat a piece of cloud
                 YIPE! 504 nails in The Gross Clinic!
                 it's more interesting to see a Princess dance
                 with a Bluebird than just two bluebirds
                 dancing through diagonal vist' together

at the flea circus there was a bargain-hunter
at the end of the road a bum, the blue year
commenced with an enormous sale of loneliness
and everyone came back with a little something
one a baby, one a tooth, one a case of clap
and, best of all, a friend bought a medical dispensary
there were a lot of limbs lying around so
of course someone created a ballet company, oke
the barely possible snow sifted into a solid crystal
I sometimes think you are Mozart's nephew: "Talk
to me Harry Winston, tell me all about it!"

"from August to October
the sun drips down the sign
for eating at midnight ask Virgo
to be lost outside the cafeteria"

I went to Albania for coffee and came back for the rent day
"I think somebody oughta go through your mind with a good
                                                    eraser"
meanwhile Joe is tracing love and hate back to the La Brea tar-pits

                              hear that rattling?
those aren't marbles in my head they're chains on my ankles

why do you say you're a bottle and you feed me
the sky is more blue and it is getting cold
last night I saw Garfinkel's Surgical Supply truck
and knew I was near "home" though dazed and thoughtful
            what did you do to make me think
            after we led the bum to the hospital
            and you got into the cab
            I was feeling lost myself

                (ALWAYS)

never to lose those moments in the Carlyle without a tie

endless as a stick-pin barely visible you
drown whatever one thought of as perception and
let all the clouds in under the yellow heaters
meeting   somewhere over St. Louis
call me earlier because I might want to do something else
except eat   ugh
endlessly unraveling itself before the Christopher Columbus Tavern
quite a series was born   as where I am going is to
Quo Vadis for lunch
out there in the blabbing wind and glass   c'est l'azur

perhaps
marinated duck saddle with foot sauce and a tumbler of vodka
picking at my fevered brain
perhaps
letting you off the hook at last or leaning on you in the theatre

oh plankton!
"mes poèmes lyriques, à partir de 1897, peuvent se lire comme un journal
                                                    intime"

yes always though you said it first
you the quicksand and sand and grass

                    as I wave toward you freely
                    the ego-ridden sea
                    there is a light there that neither
                    of us will obscure
                    rubbing it all white
                    saving ships from fucking up on the rocks
                    on the infinite waves of skin smelly and crushed
                                    and light and absorbed

                                        8/26/61–1/23/62

CHARLES OLSON

Letter for Melville 1951

> *written to be read* AWAY FROM *the Melville Society's*
> *"One Hundredth Birthday Party" for* MOBY-DICK *at*
> *Williams College, Labor Day Weekend, Sept. 2–4, 1951*

My dear —:

                 I do thank you, that we hear from
you, but the Melville Society invitation came in the
same mail with your news of this thing, and do you for
a moment think, who have known me 17 years, that I would
come near, that I would have anything to do with their
business other than to expose it for the promotion it
is, than to do my best to make clear who these creatures
are who take on themselves to celebrate a spotless book
a wicked man once made?

                 that I find anywhere in my being any
excuse for this abomination, for the false & dirty thing
which it is — nothing more than a bunch of commercial
travellers from the several colleges? Note this incredible
copy: "Those who are planning to take part in the English
Institute of Columbia University on September 5–8 will
find it convenient to attend both conferences"! Can anything be clearer, as to how Melville is being used? And
all the other vulgarities of ease and come-on: how pretty
the trees are this time of year, how nice of Williams College to take our fifteen bucks, how you won't run over
anyone, the conference is so planned—o no let's not run
over anyone but him, and just exactly here in the Berkshire
hills where he outwrote himself, just where he—when we go
together in the sight-seeing bus—where—the house will be
open, it has been arranged—he was very clean with his knife,
the arrowhead of his attention having struck, there we'll
be able to forget he fell in a rut in that very road and
had, thereafter, a most bad crick in his back

                             o these
things we can—we must—not speak of, we must avoid *all* of
the traffic except the meals, the sessions, the other points,
of interest

                                     for there are most important
things to be taken care of: you see, each of us has families
(maybe we have as many children as he did) and if we don't
or we have only a wife because we really prefer boys, in
any case, no matter what the circumstances which we will not
mention in the speeches (you know that sort of thing we can
only talk about in the halls, outside the meetings, or, at
table, out of the corners of our mouths—you might say, out
of a crack in the grave where a certain sort of barbed ivy
has broken in over the years it has lain and multiplied flat
on the rather silly stone others took some care in placing
over the remains—we cannot forget, even for this instant,
that, in order, too, that we can think that we ourselves
are of some present importance, we *have* to—I know, we
really would prefer to be free, *but*—we do have to have an
income, so, you see, you must excuse us if we scratch each
other's backs with a dead man's hand

for after all, who but us, who but us has had the niceness
to organize ourselves in his name, who, outside us, is remembering that this man a year ago one hundred years ago
(you see, we *are* very accurate about our celebrations, know
such things as dates) was, just where we are gathering just
ahead of labor day (walked coldly in a cold & narrow hall
by one window of that hall to the north, into a room, a very
small room also with one window to the same white north) to
avoid the traffic who is, but us, provided with dormitories
and catering services?

                         Timed in such a way to avoid him, to see
                         he gets a lot of lip (who hung in a huge jaw)
                         and no service at all (none of this chicken, he
                         who is beyond that sort of recall, beyond
                         any modern highway (which would have saved
                                                                    him
                         from sciatica? well, that
                         we cannot do for him but we can
                         we now know so much, we can make clear
                         how he erred, how, in other ways
                         —we have made such studies and
                         we permit ourselves to think—they
                         allow us to tell each other how wise
                         he was

He was. Few flying fish
no dolphins and in that glassy sea
two very silly whales throwing
that spout of theirs you might call sibylline
it disappears so fast, why
this year a hundred years ago he
had moved on, was offering
to such as these
a rural bowl of milk, subtitled
the ambiguities

      July
above Sigsbee deep,
the *Lucero del Alba,*
500 tons, 200,000 board feet
of mahogany, the Captain
25, part Negro, part American Indian and perhaps
a little of a certain Cereno, by name
Orestes Camargo
      Herman Melville
looked up again at the weather, noted
that landlessness   And it was not so much truth
as he had thought, even though the ratlines
could still take his weight (185, eyes
blue, hair auburn, a muscular man knowing
that knowledge
is only what makes a ship shape, takes care

of the precision of the crossed sign, the feather
and the anchor, the thing
which is not the head but is
where they cross, the edge
the moving edge of force, the wed
of sea and sky (or land & sky), the Egyptian
the American backwards

        (The stern, at evening,
          a place for conversation, to drop
                  paper boats, to ask
          why clouds are painters' business,
                    why now he
        would not write *Moby-Dick*)

Was writing
Pierre: the world
had moved on, in that hallway, moved
north north east, had moved him

    O such fools
    neither of virtue nor of truth
    to associate with
        to sit to table by
    as once before to you, and Harry, and I
    the same table the same Broadhall saw
    water raised by another such to tell us
    this beast hauled up out of great water was
    society!
      this Harvard and this Yale
    as Ossa on Pelion (or,
    as one less than he but
    by that lessness still
    a very great man, said
    of another—who never learned a thing
    from Melville—worth
    "five Oxfords on ten thousand
        Cambridges"!

    o that these fellow diners of yours might
           know
    that poets move very fast, that it is true
    it is very wise to stay the hell out of
    such traffic, of such labor
    which knows no weekend

Please to carry my damnations to each of them
as they sit upon their arse-bones variously
however differently padded, or switching

      to say please, to them
(whom I would not please any more than he will: he is flying
for the weekend, from Pensacola, where,
any moment, he will dock

please say some very simple things, ask them
to be accurate:
ask one to tell you
what it was like to be a Congregational minister's son Midwest
how hard it was for a boy who liked to read to have to pitch,
             instead,

hay; and how, now that he has published books, now that he
                                             has done that
(even though his edition of this here celebrated man's verse
whom we thought we came here to talk about
has so many carelessnesses in it that, as of this date,
it is quite necessary to do it over)
let him tell you, that no matter how difficult it is
to work in an apartment in a bedroom in a very big city
because the kids are bothersome and have to be locked out,
                                             and the wife
is only too good, yet, he did republish enough of this other man
to now have a different professional title, a better salary
and though he wishes he were at Harvard or a Whale,
he is, isn't he, if he is quite accurate, much more liked
by his president?

There'll be main speeches, and one
will do the same thing that other did that other time, tell you
(as he did then who has, since, lost a son in war, society
is such a shambles, such a beast, and altogether not
that white whale), this new one, this new book-maker
will talk about democracy, has such a nose
is so imbued with progress he will classify
the various modes of same (what,
because it was the '30's, and hope was larger, that other
gave us in a broader view) but press him, ask him
is it not true you have, instead, made all this make your way
into several little magazines however old they are?

                    (How much light
          the black & white man threw—Orestes!—on
          democracy!)

          as, if you were on the floor that night, you could
                                                  see
          just what are the differences of the hidden rears
          of each of your fellow celebrators

Myself, I'd like to extricate you who have the blood of him,
                                        and another
who loves him as a doctor knows
a family doctor, how
his mother stayed inside him, how
the compact came out hate, and what
this kept him from, despite
how far he travelled

                    (The match-box, with a match for mast,
                    goes backward gaily, bumping
                    along the wake)

What they'll forget—they'll smother you—is
there is only one society, there is no other than
how many we do not know, where
and why they read a book, and that
the reading of a book can save a life, they
do not come to banquets, and Nathaniel Hawthorne
whom Herman Melville loved
will not come, nor Raymond Weaver
who loved them both because they loved each other.

You have the right to be there
because you loved an old man's walk
and took a little attic box, and books.
And there is he, the doctor, whom I love
and by his presence side by side with you
will speak for Melville and myself, he
who was himself saved, who
because, in the middle of the Atlantic,
an appendectomy was called for, read
a sea story once, and since
has gone by the pole-star, a scalpel overside
for rudder, has moved on from Calypso, huge
in the despatch of
the quick-silver god

Yet I wish so very much that neither of you mixed
(as Leyda hasn't) in this middle place, in such salad
as these caterers will serve!

For you will have to hear one very bright man speak, so bright
he'll sound so good that every one of you will think
he knows whereof he speaks, he'll say such forward things,
                                            he'll tag
the deific principle in nature, the heroic
principle in man, he'll spell
what you who do not have such time to read as he
such definitions so denotatively clear you'll think you'll
                                        understand
(discourse is such a lie) that Herman Melville
was no professional, could not accomplish

such mentality and so, as amateur (as this clear neuter will
                                        make clear)
was anguished all his life in struggle, not with himself, he'll say,
no, not with when
shall i eat my lunch Elizabeth has set outside the door so quiet
it was not even a mouse, my prose today
is likewise, the cows, what a damned nuisance they also are,
                                        why
do i continue to extend my language horizontally when
i damn well know what is
a water-spout

No, he'll skillfully confuse you, he knows such words
as mythic, such adjectives that fall so easily you'll think it's
                                        true
Melville was a risky but creative mingling
                    (how they put words on, that this
                              lad was so
who stowed himself with roaches and a blue-shining corpse at
                              age 16: "Hey!
Jackson!"

                    the diced bones—now this too, he
                    who is also of the one society
                    who likewise lifted altars
                    too high (a typewriter
                    in a tree) and spilled himself
                    into the honey-head, died
                    the blond ant
                    so pleasantly

                              as though he did not want to
                                        woo
                              to chance a Bronx grave, pre-
                                        ferred
                              to choose his own headland

All these that you will sit with—"a mingling," he will drone on,
"of the fortunate and the injurious"

                    And only you, and Harry (who knows)
                    will not be envious, will know
                    that he knows not one thing
                    this brightest of these mischievous men
                    who does not know that it is not the point
                    either of the hook or the plume which lies

cut on this brave man's grave
—on all of us—
but that where they cross is motion,
where they constantly moving cross anew,
cut

this new instant open—as he is who
is this weekend in his old place
presumed on

I tell you,

he'll look on you all with an eye you have the color of.
He'll not say a word because he need not, he said so many.

The Librarian

The landscape (the landscape!) again: Gloucester,
the shore one of me is (duplicates), and from which
(from offshore, I, Maximus) am removed, observe.

In this night I moved on the territory with combinations
(new mixtures) of old and known personages: the leader,
my father, in an old guise, here selling books and manuscripts.

My thought was, as I looked in the window of his shop,
there should be materials here for Maximus, when, then,
I saw he was the young musician has been there (been before
me)

before. It turned out it wasn't a shop, it was a loft (wharf-
house) in which, as he walked me around, a year ago
came back (I had been there before, with my wife and son,

I didn't remember, he presented me insinuations via
himself and his girl) both of whom I had known for years.
But never in Gloucester. I had moved them in, to my country.

His previous appearance had been in my parents' bedroom
where I
found him intimate with my former wife: this boy
was now the Librarian of Gloucester, Massachusetts!

> Black space,
> old fish-house.
> Motions
> of ghosts.

                    I,
                    dogging
                    his steps.
                    He
                    (not my father,
                    by name himself
                    with his face
                    twisted
                    at birth)
                    possessed of knowledge
                    pretentious
                    giving me
                    what in the instant
                    I knew better of.

                    But the somber
                    place, the flooring
                    crude like a wharf's
                    and a barn's
                    space

I was struck by the fact I was in Gloucester, and that my
                                                    daughter
was there — that I would see her! She was over the Cut. I
hadn't even connected her with my being there, that she was

here. That she was there (in the Promised Land — the Cut!
But there was this business, of poets, that all my Jews
were in the fish-house too, that the Librarian had made a party

I was to read. They were. There were many of them, slumped
around. It was not for me. I was outside. It was the Fort.
The Fort was in East Gloucester — old Gorton's Wharf, where
                                                    the Library

was. It was a region of coal houses, bins. In one a gang
was beating someone to death, in a corner of the labyrinth
of fences. I could see their arms and shoulders whacking

down. But not the victim. I got out of there. But cops
tailed me along the Fort beach toward the Tavern

                    The places still
                    half-dark, mud,
                    coal-dust.

There is no light
east
of the Bridge

Only on the headland
toward the harbor
from Cressy's

have I seen it (once
when my daughter ran
out on a spit of sand

isn't even there.) Where
is Bristow? when does I-A
get me home? I am caught

in Gloucester. (What's buried
behind Lufkin's
Diner? Who is

Frank Moore?

Maximus, From Dogtown -I

proem

The sea was born of the earth without sweet union of love
                                                Hesiod says

But that then she lay for heaven and she bare the thing which
                                                        encloses
every thing, Okeanos the one which all things are and by which
                                                        nothing
is anything but itself, measured so

screwing earth, in whom love lies which unnerves the limbs
                                                and by its
heat floods the mind and all gods and men into further nature

                                Vast earth rejoices,

deep-swirling Okeanos steers all things through all things,
everything issues from the one, the soul is led from drunk-
                                                        enness
to dryness, the sleeper lights up from the dead,
the man awake lights up from the sleeping

WATERED ROCK
of pasture meadow orchard road where Merry
died in pieces tossed by the bull he raised himself, to fight
in front of people, to show off his
                    Handsome Sailor ism

died as torso head & limbs
in a Saturday night's darkness
drunk trying
to get the young bull down
to see if Sunday morning again he might
before the people show off
once more
his prowess — braggart man to die
among Dogtown meadow rocks

                    "under" the dish
                    of the earth
                    Okeanos *under*
                    Dogtown
                    through which (inside of which)
                                        the sun passes
                    at night -
                              she passes the sun back
                                                  to
                    the east through her body
                    the Geb (of heaven) at night

Nut is water
above & below, vault
above and below
watered rock on which
by which Merry
was so many pieces
Sunday morning

subterranean and celestial
primordial water holds
Dogtown high
                    And down
the ice holds
Dogtown, scattered
boulders little bull
who killed

Merry
        who sought to manifest
his soul, the stars
manifest their souls

                    my soft sow the roads
of Dogtown trickling like from underground rock
springs under an early cold March moon

                                or hot summer and my son
                                we come around a corner
                                where a rill
                                makes Gee Avenue in a thin
                                ford

                            after we see a black duck
                            walking across a populated
                            corner

                                    life spills out

Soft soft rock
Merry died by
in the black night

fishermen lived
in Dogtown and came
when it was old to whore
on Saturday nights
at three girls' houses

Pisces eternally swimming
inside her overhead
their boots or the horse
clashing the sedimentary
rock tortoise shell
she sits on the maternal beast
of the moon and the earth

Not one mystery
nor man
possibly not even a bird
heard Merry
fight that bull by
(was Jeremiah Millet's house

Drunk
to cover his shame
blushing Merry
in the bar
walking up

to Dogtown to try
his strength,
the baby bull
now full grown

waiting,
not even knowing
death
was in his power over
this man who lay
in the Sunday morning sun
liked smoked fish
in the same field
fly-blown and a colony
of self-hugging grubs — handsome
in the sun, the mass
of the dead and the odor
eaten out of the air
by the grubs sticking
moving by each other
as close as sloths

              she is the goddess
              of the earth, and night
              of the earth and fish
              of the little bull
              and of Merry

                  Merry
                  had a wife

She is the heavenly mother
the stars are the fish swimming
in the heavenly ocean she has
four hundred breasts

Merry could have used
as many could have drunk
the strength he claimed
he had, the brave

Pulque in Spain
where he saw the fight
octli in Mexico
where he wanted to
show off
dead in Gloucester
where he did

The four hundred gods
of drink alone
sat with him
as he died
in pieces

In 400 pieces
his brain shot
the last time the bull
hit him pegged him
to the rock

     before he tore him
to pieces

     the night sky
looked down

Dogtown is soft
in every season
high up on her granite
horst, light growth
of all trees and bushes
strong like a puddle's ice
the bios
of nature in this
park of eternal
events is a sidewalk
to slide on, this
terminal moraine:

the rocks the glacier tossed
toys
Merry played by
with his bull

     400 sons of her only
would sit
by the game

All else was in the sky
or in town
or shrinking solid rock

We drink
or break open
our veins solely
to know. A drunkard
showing himself in public
is punished
by death

The deadly power of her
was there that night
Merry was born
under the pulque-sign

The plants of heaven
the animals of the soul
were denied

Joking men
had laughed
at Merry

Drink
had made him
brave

Only the sun
in the morning
covered him
with flies

Then only
after the grubs
had done him
did the earth
let her robe
uncover and her part
take him in

Letter 27

I come back to the geography of it,
the land falling off to the left
where my father shot his scabby golf
and the rest of us played baseball

into the summer darkness until no flies
could be seen and we came home
to our various piazzas where the women
buzzed

To the left the land fell to the city,
to the right, it fell to the sea

I was so young my first memory
is of a tent spread to feed lobsters
to Rexall conventioneers, and my father,
a man for kicks, came out of the tent roaring
with a bread-knife in his teeth to take care of
a druggist they'd told him had made a pass at
my mother, she laughing, so sure, as round
as her face, Hines pink and apple,
under one of those frame hats women then wore

This, is no bare incoming
of novel abstract form, this

is no welter or the forms
of those events, this,

Greeks, is the stopping
of the battle

        It is the imposing
of all those antecedent predecessions, the precessions

of me, the generation of those facts
which are my words, it is coming

from all that I no longer am, yet am,
the slow westward motion of

more than I am

        There is no strict personal order
        for my inheritance

            No Greek will be able
        to discriminate my body

            An American
        is a complex of occasion,
        themselves a geometry
        of spatial nature

        I have this sense,
that I am one
with my skin.

        Plus this — plus this:
that forever the geography
leans in
on me, and I compell
backwards I compell Gloucester
to yield to Maximus, to
change

        Polis
is this

The River Map and we're done

by Master Saville who, conceivably, from the accuracy of his
                                drawing of the Fort,
was the Keeper as well as the Drawer
of both the Harbor and the Canal?

wreck here flats Old Bass Rock channel Annisquam
Harbor tell up river Obadiah Bruen's
                Island   granitite
                base   river   flowing

in both directions   ledge only
at one point Rocky Hill   and Castle Rock
                        a few   yards further
                        than Cut Bridge enabling sand
                        to gather

                        off mouth
                        a Table
                        Rock
                        like Tablet

a Canal Corporation
to be formed
drawn for the record
of the incorporation

                Between Heaven and Earth
kun   and   on any side   Four

directions   the banks

and between them the   River Flowing

                    in North and South out

                    when the tide re-

                    fluxes

carrying a crest
at the mixing point
filling Mill
Stream

                    at flood immersing
                    all the distance over
                    from

                              Alexander Baker's
                              goldenrod
                              field

                              and dry lavender
field flower   guillemot sat and fattened
and the herring gull wasn't even here
mullein   aster   mustard   specularia

With the water high no distance
to Sargents houses Apple Row
the river a salt Oceana or lake
from Baker's field to Bonds Hill

nothing all the way
of the hollow of the Diorite
from glacial time to this soft summer night
with the river in this respite solely
an interruption of itself

the firmness of the Two Hills
the firmness of the Two Directions
the bottom of the vase the rise
of the power of the Sea's plant

right through the middle of the River
neap or flood tide

inspissate River
times repeated

      old hulk   Rocky Marsh

JOEL OPPENHEIMER

The Couple

if i dont bring you
flowers. if i dont have any
flowers. delicate grubby violets.
chrysanthemums for your coat.
only children. what has that got
to do with it.

any child is isaac.
brushwood and sticks.
the burning bush in the hill's side.
jesus strung from a dogwood.

if it is not fair
where is fairness. if she is not
fair where is fairness. if flowers.
apples. peaches and pears
for the summer. an edible potato.
the stain of the dogwood
is in you. what now.
mushrooms. or underground
truffles. a pig with a ring
in his snout. he is hungry.
the stain of the dogwood.

who cries for another's
pain hasnt enough of his own.
where are my children they
leave me here knocking wood.

what is there i havent invented
contrived cut out of the
whole cloth. some day to
make it easier, with more
pleasure. that is a pleasure.

how else to be fecund if not
to put up with a man.

The Peaches

when your belly
is swoln. when your
belly is full. when there is a child.
never in this situation
words like peaches.
to bite into. savor.
peel the skin
with your teeth.
bit of a peach. sweet.
flavor. filling myself
on your extension.
i will talk to you about this.
let us eat a peach after supper.

The Numbers

1   the circlet
     gold upon gold
     delicately chased
     no figure seen
     neither beard nor breast
     hairless
     complete

2   each woman made
     what a man would
     have her

     yellow, the light lifts
     uncovered
     bone upon bone

3   at the end of his life
     it is surely the act which
     is his crutch
     answered by man, and
     the years behind him

     for it is as he has
     lain with his mother, as one
     drowned in the sea

4   the remembered
     yellow upon gold, red
     the night, the middle
     of day

     meetings

5   they
     upon doorsteps, flaunting

6   pale gold, raised through itself
     entering upon itself

     elsewhere
     curiosity
     historically displayed, which
     is seen

7   in the dark, the
     sunlighted rung
     blood poured into blood
     wrist to wrist
     under the bony arm

8   prosaically told
     and again the sea
     one
     man

9   straight lines
     hot sun
     the day
     god
     the mountain
     cloud

10   with it all, the true colors
     how to see without using the eye

11   and returned to the circlet
     gold upon
     as it is
     man does not know
     what it is encircled

     as a light
     should enter the dark

12   should — is
     grammatic

     how shall we
     act

13   yellow upon gold, red
     the day,
     and the night
     light
     dark
     complete neither
     beard nor
     breast
     neither

Cartography

the ceiling of his bedroom
cracks into map shapes.
an island. harbors sunk in the island's perimeter.
two great rivers. a lake at the confluence.
while on the phone he draws plans of houses abstractedly,
or replots the defense of gettysburg.
on the bedroom wall, in detail, san francisco bay,
the hills marked and notated with the addresses of friends.
on the walls of the john,
hand-drawn and accurately scaled,
the devil's den and the round tops.
the lines outside vicksburg, petersburg, the wilderness
mile by mile engraved in his mind. carried with him
white oaks, where his grandfather fell.
he does not even know if this fact, his grandfather's death,
exists for him outside of white oaks.
shall he not die also when he has no direction
before him, no plan of action, no campaign.
does he not find it impossible to move without
at least compass, or sun, gunter's chain, or a
measured pace, or the regular plat of a city's streets.
at one time his pace was exactly three feet.
with it he could determine miles, within a few yards.
or put it this way. if in his own islands
he could move freely. if he could take himself and his words.
build a continent of them. that might break him free.

if his children were more than milestones to him.
or if his wife more than the tracings of his finger
outlined before him. that might break him free.
but he will find it necessary to move himself.
this is the first action.

For the Barbers

tenderly as a
barber trimming
it off i
sing my songs, like
a barber stropping
a razor, i rage.

tho the song be
pure as anything, if
the mode be not right,
if the mode
            be not pure

the calculation of
a barber is immeasurable,
the cunning, the sly
skittering about the
head
        if a needle were
dug in the middle of
the cranium would it
do more damage?

                    oh the
professionals what we
should fear.

The Love Bit

the colors we depend on are
red for raspberry jam, white
of the inside thigh, purple as
in deep, the blue of moods, green
cucumbers (cars), yellow stripes down
the pants, orange suns on ill-
omened days, and black as the

dirt in my fingernails.
also, brown, in the night,
appearing at its best when
the eyes turn inward, seeking
seeking, to dig everything but
our own. i.e. we make it crazy or
no, and sometimes in the afternoon.

The Torn Nightgown

it seemed to me when i saw her
the white white of a
light in the midst of darkness,
the softness as a belly is, also the
rip, to not forget this rape.
and i wondered then in the night
if all wives had such badges.
and bitterly, if over each
set of stretch marks, over
each veined breast, each brown
nipple there floated soft and
white a torn nightgown. and thought
of all of us who turn heavily
on our beds at night. of the heart
which ponderously grasps its
way back, great sea creature caught
far up on the beach, a monstrous polyp or
jellyfish. of the lungs painfully
beating in used air to bring us back
sweating to face air. of the nameless
faceless images we dealt with, giving
our all. of the snorts and grunts and
great cracks of wind exhaled fighting
off the wild animals, keeping the beasts
at bay, while we slept. of all the legs
that might be slid between, all the
buttocks held firm and resilient,
all the nipples erected and tweaked
between thumb and first finger.
of all the bodies male and
female to be made love to
beneath the grinding of light,
air, darkness, all the

constituents and elements.
the cat makes it in the alley meanwhile,
the neighbor makes it next door, heaving and
grunting and shaking the springs.
panting in the dark night, lusting
again and again for warmth, for
a semblance of love. when day comes
the cock rises and crows he crows.
but the night is the day of my cock.

Leave It To Me Blues

from the heart of a flower
a stalk emerges; in each fruit
there are seeds. we turn our
backs on each other so often,
we destroy any community of
interest. yet our hearts are
seeded with love and care sticks
out of our ears. but there is no
bridge unless it is the wind which
whistles our bare house, tearing
the slipcovers apart and constantly
removing the tablecloth covering
it (the table) like a shroud (the
shroud of what the table could mean,
if only we were hungry enough to
care), and we cut ourselves off
because we discovered each man is
an island, detached. man, the
mainland is flipped over the moon.
all i have to depend on is effort,
and the moon goes round and round
in the evening sky. my sons will
make it if they ever reach age,
but how to take care i dont know.
it doesnt get better. on the other
hand, even with answers, where
would we be, out in the cold, with
an old torn blanket, and no one
around us to cry

Mathematics

we come to another place.
there is no reason we
stay one place only. there
is no inertia we cannot defeat

why we are going to the
market to buy vegetables
don/t you know that

we are those who have
never once admitted the
validity of the hair on
our own heads no matter
how much we have praised
that beneath our hands

we do not talk now in
terms of love or even of
position. we talk about
problems in the calculus
of motion. how, in going
from here to there, do we
intercept or not intercept
that which is going also

> i have drawn the map as i
> drew it then, the dotted line
> is the line of march, the bluffs
> were very high at this point

> severe cold
>   (i.e., −28°, contrast
>   scott, shackleton, lieutenant
>   greeley)
>   many
> cases of frostbite, the general/s
> ears even, the general doesn/t
> like fighting indians, he wants
> to fight rebels. he wants to
> go south, where the glory is

> shan-tag-a-lisk and the big mandan
> keep trying to show him where the
> glory is

shan-tag-a-lisk, with
such a name, spotted tail, given
such a language might not you
ask the general: would you name
yourself in such a manner, bad medicine?

spotted tail, and you, the big mandan
you may not ask the general anything,
stare and glare across the line of
cavalry, watch the two howitzers,
behind this screen you can see the
eighty pawnee scouts, they are staring
across at you, they at least you can
fight, they have names

we talk only in terms of
the world we see, whatever
we talk about. when we
smell liver and onions
through the open window
the world comes into us

we are not now talking
of love or of the laying
on of hands

'The rock bluff was limestone without
fossils . . . . heavy growth of very
large willows here, quite tall and some
of them two feet in diameter, with very
heavy underbrush of willows. From
the mouth of White Man's Fork down
to this camp was twenty miles . . . .
the river bend and the bottoms were about
five miles wide, covered with high rank
grass . . . .'

to see the world . . . oglala
is a village divided into scattered
bands; brule is burnt, burnt
thighs, they were the riders

that easily we have come to
a world the real thing and yet
it was not a simple journey

it is after all a hard world to live in

now we will learn anew how to
move ourselves. we will devise
of our own makings the particular
travois necessary to this undertaking —
see already we have found the
willows necessary, a 'very heavy
underbrush of willows'. if
there are no horses we will use
the dogs. they will do

ROCHELLE OWENS

Strawberries Mit Cream

for Nikita who loves us

the "forest folk"
Oh out-of-the-way
folk
so fascinated
a-patch-of-ground
folk
they began producing
blessed
berries
chicken &
cattle
animal domestication
3000 b. c.

out of the maglemosian
bog
come fish-hooks
axes spears
harpoons &
clubs
piddles paddles
(they did a lot of fishing)
what a time
for a revolution
in southern
russia!
caucasus shmawkusus
pass the pirogen
you
communist!

Medieval Christ Speaks On A Spanish Sculpture Of Himself

honey & water
father & son
  so am i
so chiefly
  good
      i would seem by virtu
two christs (2)
     with butterbrown
  hair & blessed
(2) yellow eyes
     god himself
  sees me faire
         geometricians
crawl at my feet;
  my divinity
my highest blessedness!

mother mary kissed my carcass
     thinketh she of me
       on my holiness
       my uncorruption
  And everlastingness
i marvel even too
at gods knowledge simple
(2) fyry angels
   sweet policemen
press their bosoms
  on my knees
(base poets say i
  received holy
        erection)
like lusty puella
  with impious thighs
    wet eyes
    earthly sighs
     O

Macrobius mingling with nature

On hand is 27
all-powerfuls
omnipresent
everywheres

god i hope i don't get blind
with all this god-ful brightness

& now there's 28
all-greatnesses

venus with her moon
9 x crazier than the
egyptians

half the sky
has light-ful
opinions
pouring from

A to C; somewhere where's
the middle of it all
Macrobius

Macrobius are you there?

Man As He Shall Be

until a man should
come; honorable
with a buckle of gold
enjoying—
with a not extended neck
wearing a civilian's
dress
like any other roman
no old loin cloth
of the essenes

"May Jose smite Jose"

bring him back
enroll him in society

he knows the greek
    of the philistines
        visited egypt
knows the coastal plains
knows the prices of dried
        fruit
remembers the smell
    of incense

"Forsake ye not my law"

    born after his grand
dad's crucifixion
    his feet, his hands, the
cleft in the chin
        were like good
    somebody or others
this was the judgement
    clusters & clusters
        of grapes;
    the cleansing grape cure

"Who is ever the guardian of peace"

Between The Karim Shahir

    man-apes
        not at Steinheim!

but he doesn't hang
        in limbo —
    the face is pretty
        brutish
    put together from
a sack of old bones
    their heads were neither
        low or primitive

spearheads   stone picks
    stone teeth & chopping
        tools —
rivers yield water-logged
        wooden idols,
everybody was so
    advanced
over the europe of
        8000 years

             great joy!
                  suddenness
    no longer living like
                      animals
    (O those lucky food-producers)
              their specialty:
                  horse, dog
                       pregnant woman
    worship the watermelon
                       venus —

         found pigs
    in the latest levels

    (O those nile udders
             give my lips a rash)
    We know they had goats & sheep
              porridge bowls

                   parch it —

      crack it, reap grain, wheat
        & eat up
    So the Jarmo people
              grew barley

      two different kinds
                of wheat &
        grew a barley plant
    there's not a too clear
                   picture

      between the Karim Shahir
    M'lefaat-Zawi
         record says
              in the
                      kurdish hills

Evolution

I

         coon explains it
           that we stood
                 erect
                 slowly

s
l
o
w
l
y
somebody was
the size of
a big gorilla
teeth looking
like man's
more

than the
chinese apes
what's your skull capacity
o coon
larger than a white-handed
gibbon?

i should
hope so

II

assistant leakey lay next to
Von Koenigs
wald

what a link
like zeuner he
found his
findings
look ma i'm a caucasoid
see by my teeth?

III

o islands of indonesia
sweet pithecanthropus o
little infant skull
o homo mother-fucker
everybody
had to
originate somewhere
out of the hearts
of water

IV

    no. 100 was killed
somebody dropped
  a stone
        what hell happened
           at Formosa that day
  o the head-crushing o the
            crushed skulls
    o junius bird
        who excavated

Woman Par Excellence

Peter Freuchen's Eskimo wife

    first
   it's not heat pros
   tration
    just that.
   i'm sincere
 the european trip
gave her a
    stricken heart

on the mound, whoa you boy!
you cannot get on
her bank of earth

    especially
  a woman
 not in the finest
    condition
with an S-shaped
   nasal gap
 like a german swastika,
make a photostatic copy of

    the philosophy:
We hold these truths to be self-evident,
that all men are created equal, . . .
      safety & happyness

  if they ought not to be
   in love with Eskimo features

(Peary's grandson was very handsome)
    they should love the
            white meat
    of the breasts,
        at least not
              be wet blankets!

like a cat's tongue tastes
        its whiskers
        matter-of-factly

Chugachimute   *I Love The Name*

a few miles from
the Chugachimute
people (& not
derisively i
say it) they are
fine with
  me

the Chugachimute
people (i say it
again i love the
name) Chugachimute

some old walrus
that we kill
we are people
i'll eat a small
piece of heart
by the seaside.
i am near them

a few miles from
the Chugachimute
people i love the
name

old mother or old
hag. Amen. she
had gnats in her
hair. why? four
foul ones in her
navel were they
making   little

shirts of the fuzz?
snow all year &
some wild flowers
everybody's naked

ROBERT PACK

Father

I have not needed you for thirteen years.
You left my mother to me like a bride.
To take your place, I shut off all my tears,
And with your death, it was my grief that died.
How could I know that women worship pain?
My mother's eyes bring back your ghost again.

    I dreamed that digging in the humid ground
    You found, among the worms, my embryo;
    You put it on a hook — it made no sound
    Opening its mouth as you let it go
    Into the lake where, fishing from a boat,
    You watched the bulging, blood-eyed fishes float.

Failing, the strong at least learn gentleness.
When you cried out — that was your mastery!
I took a wife, but never let her guess
It was your ghost that chose my secrecy.
She needed what you would not have me show:
My need. Your strength too late let weakness grow.

    I dreamed we both rowed through a windy mist;
    The dark lake tilted where you wished to go.
    Fish scales and blood glowed at me from your wrist;
    The air I gulped only the drowning know.
    You had me hold the net, and I believed
    The fish's spastic death was what I grieved.

Screams come too easily these guarded days.
The bright, complaining, are most eloquent.
Must loss always be prelude to our praise?
Is this what mother's rising mourning meant?
For whose sake did I envy suicide?
Could death win wife and mother as one bride?

    I dreamed you threw the unhooked fish away.
    Why did I fear I had done something wrong?
    You took me home, insisting that I stay,

But I did not feel weak, feeling you strong,
For when you left I found the net behind,
And Angered as gored waters gagged my mind.

I have not needed you for thirteen years.
I have grown grim with my authority.
Take back my mother and release my tears,
And let a child's lost grief give strength to me!
  Dreaming, I seek your skeleton below;
  I dig the worms and find your embryo.

The Election

One candidate has been nominated
By both parties. He is running
Against himself. He has two platforms,
Similar, yes, but not identical.
A large vote is expected. People
Are informed, they argue their opinions;
They defend their party. Never,
They feel, has more been at stake.
The kids stop at their games, giggling,
Watching me, watching T.V.

At the University, my friends
Have decided not to vote. They
Are protesting. Historians are writing
Letters to the *Times*. Professional
Negroes, glib children of Christ's
Grace, Jews grown perfect in their
History of pain, the beatified —
All are brandishing analogies.

I, as you observe, see through this,
And have detached myself. Not
Out of principle — understand that ,
Nor because I am a fatalist
And do not believe in human will,
But because I know only
What is wrong (everything human),
And can't seriously imagine civilization
Otherwise. Would you call us
Hypocrites, we whose whole virtue

Lies in our hatred of the world?
What would we do without that hate?
Ah, but our motives do not prove us wrong!

What do they see in my face that has made them
Stop playing? Go back to your games!

A trend has been established. Gestures
Of conciliation are being made.
The new president will address
The people . . . Wait — something has gone wrong
With my T.V. It is distorting.
The repairman, who seems to be talking
On several phones at once, tells me
There has been a mix-up at Central
Broadcasting, I should be patient.

The president's image is marvelously
Grotesque, his voice is garbled.
The kids are laughing wildly. A brown
Substance seems to be coming out of his mouth
And into the room. The kids are throwing it
At each other. It is filling the room.
The kids have stopped laughing.
I had not expected this. The kids
Are screaming and tearing at my eyes.

The Shooting

I shot an otter because I had a gun;
The gun was loaned to me, you understand.
Perhaps I shot it merely for the fun.
Must everything have meaning and be planned?

Afterwards I suffered penitence,
And dreamed my dachshund died, convulsed in frigh
They look alike, but that's coincidence.
Within one week my dream was proven right.

At first I thought its death significant
As punishment for what I'd lightly done;
But good sense said I'd nothing to repent,
That it is natural to hunt for fun.

Was I unnatural to feel remorse?
I mourned the otter and my dog as one.
But superstition would not guide my course;
To prove that I was free I bought the gun.

I dreamed I watched my frightened brother die.
Such fancy worried me, I must admit.
But at his funeral I would not cry,
Certain that I was not to blame for it.

I gave my friend the gun because of guilt,
And feared then that my sanity was done.
On fear, he said, the myth of hell was built.
He shot an otter because he had a gun.

Raking Leaves

Packed with woodpeckers, my head knocks,
Coaxing the drum of the tree to make its sap speak —
My sap, my boned branches, my veined leaves
Staining the wind, dizzying down
Amid a busyness of birds.

And she, in the bedroom, hands warm with work,
Smoothes out the wrinkles from the sheets
That last night's tumbled sleep may once again
Grow young, that habit, unfolded back
Into desire, may heat the purposed place
Where body's music's sung; unknown
Even to herself, as they
Who do not live by words, she sings
This place whose memories are birds,
And as she turns away, back
Into her noon of bells, in her flown eyes
Nothing like gratitude remains,
There are no debts in her farewells.

Raking, taking time quickly,
I watch my own feet move in the ragged shade
Of the shagbark hickory, burly in the blood
Of my own speed, my own strength, now smack
In the sun, barbarously bright, sight
For closed eyes, and up out again to seek,
To take, to make what I will, skill of delight
I am not author of; above, no missing God
I miss; high satisfying sky though, and below,

Chrysanthemums in garb of gaiety,
Little serious clowns, and look, beyond the brook
The fat grouse bumps across the field
And jumps for berries in the honeysuckle.

Not here, not now, one world goes down,
And, not in my head, the serious men
Chronicle its going; I cannot tell them
I am raking leaves. This day is hers,
This is my time; with us together
Two chores away, all rocking hours
Support this hour, all knocking days
Repeat this day.

Self-Portrait

The eyes are lying again, posing. Pluck out
Their whispers! Blur the left one that likes corners,
Will not look back, staring through the grackle-dark-
Are you out there? What can the nose smell
In that thick paint, but itself strung downward
Into throat, into lungs? Can the one ear in sight,
Touched blue, be listening? I remember the other,
Snooping behind your chosen words to find you.
The red circles I have put nearby the lips
Are lights stuffed to remain wet, and the splatter
Of whites slashed outward are, in their way,
Looking for you. Harder than breathing,
Something like a vacuum is sucking the cheeks
In-shadows, cave shadows where dregs of bears
Sleep the winter through, dwindling. Beneath
The table where elbows thicken and apples
Glisten inward and a water pitcher sweats, its handle
Toward you, if you are out there — below,
Where one cannot see, is the left hand resting
On the knee, the crotch? Are there eyes
Beneath the table? Laughter? A nest of birds?

The Weasel

Since his death, nothing removes my fear,
Though I have all his power now. I remind myself
That I am king, and it is true. Here

In my hole, lord of the milk and garter
Snakes, I stand on guard. In the bleached meadow,
With a look blank as his death, I wish them well.

And beyond, where grass in the wind is quick
As my own tongue, over the rabbit's smoking belly, flies,
Hovering like notes, make usual music.

I had long ago accepted it — that song which quivered
Through my teeth like happiness. But since his death,
It has gone sour. I taste it from my liver,

Licking the puffed wound where my heart lies.
I breathe the spoiled milk scent of the air,
And know, for the first time, I too must die.

Since his death, voices call I cannot name.
After the catbird's last cry, after the squirrel's
Chitter tweaks in my nose its damp dreams,

After the bullfrog's rumble fattens his belly
For round sleep, I cannot tell her
As she dreams, clutched to her spent day, beside me.

Did she twitch like that in sleep before?
I cannot remember. And though it seems
That even now I love her more,

An ease is gone. Our nest is rearranged.
The walls of the hole are packed down tighter.
The entrance to the hole is changed.

The fear grows in me like a child. At odd
Hours, it tells me what I should not do.
If this goes on, I will believe in God.

Don't Sit Under the Apple Tree With Anyone Else But Me!

> "Don't bug me, Pa!" —Gregor Samsa

Created for whose sake? The praying
Mantis eats its mate. Hatched,
Two hundred or more eggs scramble
Away — (Breakfast for whom?) —eating
Each other. Among the outer leaves
Of plants; along flower stems;

Sometimes on branches; sometimes on walls;
Seen by some, yes, looking in windows —
They wait for lady beetles, they wait
For honeybees. I do not judge them.
Do not judge my poem! They are —
I am — both are what we are.
They can be kept (in separate cages)
As pets, and will take pieces of apple
(See *Genesis*, chapters 1–4)
From your fingers or sip water
From a spoon. With imagination
(Familiarity?), there is little
One cannot love in heaven or earth.
After they know you well, they cock
Their little heads at your approach —
Asking, as I do, to be loved?

KENNETH PITCHFORD

Five Lyrics From Good For Nothing Man, *A Folk Opera*

I- *Pickup in Tony's Hashhouse*

SHE: The he-man, the sea-man,
the show-man, the shaman,
the hay-man, the snow-man,
the rich man, the common,

all of them shapely
from shoulder to shank
I have slept with and loved
and from their flesh drank

elixirs of beauty,
delight and proportion,
no hold barred,
and no abortion.

HE: The bar-maid, the bare maid,
the maid-not-at-all,
the slender, the slinky,
the femme fatale

I have pleasured and tasted
and sweated atop,
each night wasted
unless I drop

dead with exhaustion,
my heart gone mad
with quickened combustion,
giddy and glad.

SHE: I wither in weather
all drizzly and grim,
but light as a feather
I'm thinking of him

all wicked and naked
beside me in bed.
Praise God who created
the quick and the dead.

HE: I brimming with whiskey,
she dizzy with gin,
it's time to mean business,
it's time we begin

to blazon our summer
through blankets of snow,
past bookie and mummer,
c'mon let's go.

BOTH: Our blessings upon
each body that braves
love's randy dance
on the deadmen's graves

where in a wide arc
through divinity goes
the petalled flesh
of the human rose.

II- *The Onion Skin:* song of an old woman cooking

When I was young, I put on rouge
and danced upon high heels.
Now hands wear red and feet go bare,
a cooking maid who boils and peels,
            peeling the onion skin.

Soon I wore an altered face
when my shadow husband fell
to sleep in war's cold wedding bed
and gave her hot embrace and all,
            down to the nothingness within.

As widow I wore mask and weeds,
held finger up and suitors off.
Gone to seed or pieces now,
eyes misted, at the stove I cough,
            peeling the onion skin.

But houses built by legacy
fall unless dark room and bed
can hold the hump that fills the shelves:
I kept the key when all is said,
                down to the nothingness within.

Now I stir and stew my weeds,
the little now my belly asks,
I who wore out one by one
all my loves and all my masks,
                peeling peeling the onion skin
                down to the nothingness within.

III- *Jacqueline Gray* (to the tune of "Henry Martin")

There once was a woman named Jacqueline Gray,
    as plain as a woman could be.
She had no husband nor handsome young man
whom she could honor love trust and obey.

She worked as a waitress at Tony's Hashhouse,
    took orders as quick as a wink;
but in the restroom she often would stop
and pour her salt sorrow all into the sink.

On Sunday's she woke up a little past two
    and went to the best movie show,
where she saw Miss Lamarr and Mr. Boyer
acting a passion she never would know.

One summer she took her vacation and went
    to bask at a seaside resort,
turned brown on the sand while within her she felt
bitter red juices confirming her heart.

One day a lifeguard passed her by as she sat.
    He was handsome and broad in the chest.
She suddenly knew she would rather be dead
than never to know his tight arms at her breast.

She dashed to the water and gaily plunged in,
    and farther and farther swam out.
But when she turned to call him to her,
the brine filled her throat and distracted her shout.

The next day they found her cast up on the sand,
    her sighs and desires at a halt,
hair loose to the wind and a smile on her lips,
her eyes staring clear, through white flakes of sea-salt.

IV- *Young Buck's Sunday Blues*

There's a Catholic church on the corner,
there's a Quaker church on the hill,
one a' them sits in silence,
and one a' them rings a bell bell bell,
and I gotta git a woman
ain't scared a' raisin' hell.

In her peep-toed shoes and her brownest mole
she crawled up in my lap,
and told me many a grievous lie
and a lot a' downright crap (my friends),
'bout how she was a woman
weren't scared a' raisin' hell.

Well, you see, there's nothin' I love so much
as dancin' in my skin all night,
so I opened back the sheets and, man,
played the seven dwarfs to her snow white,
thinkin' I'd found a woman
weren't scared a' raisin' hell.

But in my Sunday mornin' sleep
as the dawn came creakin' up,
she left me a note said, Charlie Jones,
goodbye you lowdown pup—
I'm gonna find a preacher
full a' brimstone, cash, and hell.

There's a Catholic church on the corner,
there's a Quaker church on the hill,
one a' them sits in silence,
and one a' them rings a bell bell bell,
and one a' them's got a woman
who oughta be in hell.

V- *Blues Ballad*

I saw in the East a sign, a sign,
I felt in my blood its voice, its voice;

then the rising sun fell on the earth
making the world, the world rejoice.

And by his light men up and go
to work the mines of fear, of fear;
but he spoke to me an empty day
and words I would not hear, and words,
and words I would not hear:

>"Good for nothing man, bad man,
>good for nothing all day through,
>where are you gonna sleep tonight,
>what are you gonna do, and do?"

>Out in the street on stone, on stone,
>I've laid my head before, before.
>There's a long weariness of bone
>makes all beds hard the more.

>"Good for nothing man, bad man,
>good for nothing all night through,
>you've gotta eat some meals today,
>what are you gonna do, and do?"

>I'll eat the heart of man, I guess,
>I hear it tastes real fine, real fine,
>and the flesh he turns to stone for bread,
>and tears or blood for wine, for wine,
>and tears or blood for wine.

Then I heard in the West a blackbird cry
from a burled tree on a crooked hill,
and the world was dark again as night
though the loud sun shone still, shone still.

And he spoke to me soft words of ease
and bade me come to the tree, the tree,
like a black sun crying up the night,
he spoke these words to me, to me,
he spoke these words to me:

>"Good for nothing man, bad man,
>not worth a feather in my tail,
>come to me if come you can,
>it'll keep you out of jail, of jail."

So I climbed up that hill of his
and saw my life spread out below,
the frozen days that none would miss,
the drifted nights like black, black snow.

And to the topmost limb I've climbed.
This third tree I've been given.
Oh who is that across from me,
with thorn and red side riven?

Good for nothing man, I am;
but whoever he is I have no grief.
I'll see the sun no more blackbird,
just a bad man, a thief, a thief,
just a bad man, a thief.

Aunt Cora

Walking through usual flannels and faces,
or uniform scowls in drain-pipe jeans,
I recall gratefully odd Aunt Cora,
and see at last what that wry face means
that even in death stared fierce and alone,
turned from us on the pillow without a moan.

Carrot-haired and daft, she knew
how she must always practice herself
before her mirror of midwest blue
to achieve her sunstruck lunacy
in a world where only the flat was sane,
and cut her sharp height on the austere plain.

When locusts swarmed their fields one fall
she ran among them, scooping up
their shell-like bodies in yellow handfuls,
stained with their brown blood. The crop
lay ragged already beyond repair,
yet she cackled her practiced laugh into thin air.

And when the heifer calved, or the mare foaled,
quicker than veterinarian's fingers,
she could unsplice the binding cord,
lips pursed in concern and wonder, jetting
tobacco when no one could see
(but since I shared that secret, winking at me).

Yes, she was a strange one, all agreed,
her husband locked away, crazy with drink.
Only when all her children married
did she take him back, not as some think,
because she was lonely or afraid,
but to have the good company of someone mad.

Yet to her credit, when the gas-lamp
in the kitchen glared across
the white shocks at his scruffy temples
to kindle in his unwitting eyes,
she somehow found in her drought-hard face
an unashamed moisture for her tears to waste.

Unrelieved flatness, now, commands
those acres where Aunt Cora stood,
all beauty in her shrivelled hands,
in her malicious eyes, all good.
Refusing bread and wine, she cried,
"Away with your blasphemies!" And laughed, and died.

The Blizzard Ape

After the wind
            they built the blizzard ape
above the fox-and-geese of tumult in the courtyard
and all the window-mothers, hauling in stiff laundries,
paused to articulate collaborations,

—His stomach's flat

            —His nose is much too small

until he shared their shape's magnificence
and ponderous
            became their own imaginings.

The wives lent to the children freshest lint
gathered by vacuums from the cordbare rugs
to soot him, hirsute, from the flapping cold,
a tenement king,
            and crowned him with fedora
and popped blue coals for eyes in the crouching forehead.

All day long he presided their shrill olympics.

The fathers from work admired him,
adding new twists and grimaces to his snow:

—The landlord, sure, with arms about his paunch.

And one affixed a penis icicle.

* * *

By moonlight could it be
                    the ape took on
the flowering crystals of a snow of thought,
congealing under brow a shadow sentience?
Could it be
            the ape, white artifact of tropics,
by silver statement
                lured into belief
of his own self,
                took on deluded being?
—Something of jungle heat creeps through my veins,
my velvet fluids
                silvering glacial tracks
as though high twining vines awaited me
and hairy bowers disclosed the ample mate,
but for the six-rayed cells of sleep and thought,
sub-zero's slow metabolism.
                            Feted by sluggish savages
that hibernate, snow-pale,
                        beneath their drifted caves of
                                                    sheet?
Never to break gray moonlit stasis.
                            Am I their king
or clown?
        A mental music.

* * *

They came and went.
                    He was their king of summer
while blizzard hugged them close with skinny arms.
But the sun came back
                    and all the children augured
to guess the surly change within their hero.

One day a woman from her high escape
cried out to see a smudge of coal-dust tears.

—We did him wrong
                    to give him blizzard's shape
with our inclement airs, so far from home.
Now he will drip away, no spring or mating
to will him wintry concubines of pleasure.

His body wrinkled
                    sudden with fever's age,
his pebble teeth fell one by one away,
until they found one day the flattened hat
beside a shapeless mound
                    and knew him dead.

But the ape, released from winter, free to flow,
sunk earth-by-tropic
                    to loosen his lost youth

and April was german with his mating call.

Off Viareggio

From a granite rib of rock off Viareggio,
dwindling into the Tyrrhene sea,
shoal fishers stand in the early sun.
Light flakes from their backs like falls of fire
poised above lucid greens of the very sea
that once extinguished
—too long ago for any to remember—
the pale sun enclosed in Shelley's English skull.

A father with his child squats on the rock,
quick fingers prying at tenacious shells
that quiver open in his hand
beneath the pressure of the knife.
They would not believe, if asked,
that a man could die here
chasing angelic butterflies
within a northern mind.
They suck the raw flesh from the salt-shells,
grinning.

So many Platos die, eyes inward,
cast up from real seas into statuary.
The fishers stand,
begetting simple gestures in their sons,

leaving no carrara to commemorate
an immortality of living flesh alone.
Armies of common men, as well as Shelley,
expired near here in mountain passes
for reasons as strange to these
as Diotima's,
these who could set a tower to heaven
with so little will
its penchant toward the earth
stood poised transpicuous through every blitz.

The sun within the skull was not enough;
its fleeced light falls like snow across the mind
in fatal blizzards.
Meanwhile, the fishers, stooping to haul home their catch,
bear still the weight of a real sun on their shoulders,
and endure.

Death Swoops,

as Kaethe Kollwitz knew,
for the child just born,
whose mouth shapes the distended fever
in the bones for food;
swoops through the unrelief of black
on the speechless grin of the page,
with instant spirals;

or waits politely at the old man's side,
whose eyes have seen his visitor so often
in a life of deprivation
between one war and another
that all his surprise amounts to
are the suddenly opened hands that never
held too much of anything;

or takes the young girl tenderly
within a blurred embrace,
head buried in the farther shoulder
while the girl leans gratefully,
throat stretched for a cry
that need never climb that hollow stairway now,
never be uttered by the curling lips
beneath cheeks wasted toward their perpetual smile;

but the picture of the just-dead poet,
as Kaethe Kollwitz knew,
could hold no spirals of black lines swooping,
no patient visitor, no tender recognition;
only the hardening of flesh
toward its final formlessness,
the brow unflexed as though a craggy line
had just grown smooth within the brain,
putting an apt end to the final poem:

other calligraphies than his etched death-mask
must hold the shadows
by which he saw dimmed empires gutter out,
and tyrannies usurp and then cast off
the old man's body, the bloomless breasts
of a girl put to hungry uses,
and that fruit of all his labor and their rage:
the soft bones of a baby about whose sleep
no joy-dazzled shepherds crowd.

Leviathan   A Poem In Four Movements

    (for P.G., *mentis in mari nauta*)

I- *The Man*

Whether we flee or pursue, we are the same:
Ahab and Jonah, two sides of a coin.
In the beginning, lacking voice or name,
we lay unformed where fear and courage join.

I, Jonah, rose up early and departed
on my aimless journey, no joy in my gait,
the taste of ashes on my tongue, ice-hearted,
hoping, by lingering, to arrive too late.

I, Ahab, manned the Pequod, hoisted sail
headlong for waters where the sea-beast lay;
pursuit was fleeing from the icy gale
that hollowed my mind each mile along the way.

Both of us watched our plotted courses press
toward that black X on azures of the chart
where words dumbfound their meanings: our no and yes
the flex and lax within one bestial heart.

I, Jonah, in the storm, knelt down and wept.
The ship refused me. In the sailor's clutch,
I cried, "Lord God . . ." but cleft tongues of lightning
leapt,
blinding my prayer. The sea shrank from my touch.

I, Ahab, saw all Evil burn and ooze
on that brute face—as though the crystal sea
above the corals of the heart could fuse
in one white lens a vast antinomy.

The rest looked on: old salts and young bloods, all;
ours was no human battle to be fought
with the aid of usual men not in the thrall
of the pure good or evil we fled or sought.

I, Jonah, felt the jaws gape to receive
my coward's body. Cringing I lay still
and listened to black fathoms surge and heave
as the whale climbed through hosannas of his will.

I, Ahab, tangled by a length of rope,
drove home by useless steel where, inchoate,
Lucifer trembled, breathing through a slope
of snow-cold flesh the hot hill of my hate.

And did we find our answers in those eyes
or those wide jaws? Or did our questions loom
more sharply to have taken on his size,
that animal intelligence of our doom?

The sea-beast spiralled downwards in his scorn
that has no words for evil or for good;
one drowned by darkness too vast to be borne,
one borne toward light too fierce to be withstood.

II- *The Commonwealth*

Upon the horizon in its animal sleep,
its hill like rolls of flesh twined high with wire,
the city pulsed in tides drowned dreamers keep
behind the darkened windows of each spire.

By morning the prophet had stormed the market-place
to swagger barefoot on the paving stone,
hawking fresh cancers through the populace,
fine shames more precious than any they had known.

Yet forty days and Nineveh shall fall.
"Who is this alien—greasy and absurd?"
they mocked. "Our commonwealth is comfortable,
strongly defended, well administered."

Some thieves and beggars, idlers in the square,
heard the Hebrew snarling his tirade,
but none by the neon's metronomic glare
slackened his pace, much less fell down and prayed.

Yet twenty days . . . And still the city cast
its keenest fevers on its largest screens,
swam in circuitous unisons, through vast
hypnoses, the reefs of its routines.

But the viruses in which the prophet dealt
crept invisibly through the busy veins.
A shudder beneath the animal's smooth pelt
signalled the riotous flowering of those stains.

Yet ten days more . . . From their somniloquence
the people started: "Today the market fell.
The churches blaze with light again. Incense
clouds every shrine, and prayer fills every cell."

Yet five days more, ye Gentiles, yet four days . . .
"But the government assure us the state is sound."
Yet three . . . Yet two . . . "Have you seen all the high-
ways
clogged with refugees for miles around?"

Yet one more day . . . But Nineveh was saved;
the crisis abated. The commonwealth swam on
to other holocausts each man had craved
in his most secret dreams each watery dawn.

Today, the traveller notices a mound
on that unfeatured shore acred wide and bare,
like the hump of some huge sea-beast who was found
stranded in sleep on the corrosive air.

III- *The Wife*

Peering across gray sleeves of harbor foam
from her high widow-walk, for months she'd pace.
The bay was scored with masts of captains home,
escaped from the sea's adulterous embrace.

Landlocked Nantucket wives have known a stain
harsher, more permanent than their bed-sheets know—
so, with the wife of Ahab who since has lain
trammelled in his death-bed mound of snow.

In mourning, the wife resumed the mother's task:
when men die scaling the slopes of the Unknown,
women forgive their rival, ceasing to ask
mild metaphysics to recapture flesh and bone.

The other wife had urged the galled ascent,
though he limped off, not to Nineveh, but Tarshish.
Yet Jonah knew best, surely, what the angel meant,
although he roamed on the slack length of God's leash.

She shrugged her shoulders. What else should she do?
Later, the tales of Leviathan would bore
her evening sewing. Let men fret and stew
in their mid-ocean juices. Wives stay on shore.

One welcomed back her husband with a word;
the other waited, but soon set black aside.
Both winked at the stories of the whale they heard—
though neither suggested that the teller lied.

Both coaxed their stubborn blooms to sprout each spring,
scolded their fledglings to fear God and the Law,
sure that clear sunlight each new dawn would bring
reason and order, if not a sense of awe.

IV- *The Animal*

> "For X beginneth not,
> but connects and continues."

Where you lie, Leviathan, Moby Dick,
your icy secrets blazing in your breast,
you trail a skeleton, encrusted thick,
along the salty circuits of its rest.

What sunken fissures do your visits fill,
what coral shelves, what fjords? Or do you live
beyond charts printed with our tongue's poor skill
at pale denial, or bland affirmative?

Wherever I look I see that smouldering cone,
the crystal spray you spout against the sky:

beyond the last horizon of the Known,
in the deepest reaches of the inward eye.

Behemoth and monolith. Bethel and city-state.
Emblem to be blazoned on a shield,
attended by porpoises, by ray and skate.
A sceptre of power too terrible to wield.

The thrum of piston, the drone of dynamo
insinuates the accents your pulse keeps.
The derrick spouts black blood harpooners know
when through your hulk the mortal heartquake sweeps.

Yet from such ordinals of death, you rise
on undulating floors of weed and brit:
a cardinal phosphorescence on the eyes
of the few men returned to tell of it.

And deeper, in the vaults of each man's mind,
through unlit seas, you plunge. In that cold waste,
the currents of your hot blood have defined
the good or evil Jonah and Ahab faced.

Unanswerable, unspeakable brute might,
all the obliques I chart are streams that feed,
like veins and arteries, in quest or flight,
the life you kindle and the death you breed.

Rise, then, Leviathan, be with me still,
inspirit me with your great breath, I pray,
so I may scale the steeps of each night's hill,
home to the coral fathoms of my day.

Reflections on Water

(for Paris Leary)

We were antagonists; we knew that.
Live water thickens in a well
into unusable moistures,
brimming with viscous death.

I said: in sun and motion
            water never fails, but rinses
            old stains clean, and dancing
            is only a way
            to keep live water liquid and singing.

Perhaps we agreed more than I knew.
There's a dark cot where a procrustean will
cuts us to one measure,
where the agonist, like Jacob wrestling,
turns windlass sighs to haul up from himself
his precious element, sacred and for use.

You said: there is an angel
            who has eyes that float
            like stars on standing pools
            in the backreaches of the stream.
            The vision is terrible, if it comes at all.

Tapping, we went our opposing ways,
for the same miraculous rock
in the one desert, a thin horizon distant.
But any rock releases the cool jet to the throat
of him who knows the sesame, and strikes
at all the famines, real and possible,
that wait in that ultimate desert to be fed.

Racked on the terrible cot
            in a dark hutch at daybreak,
            each measured by foul breath
            that creeps through lips, cold-purpled,
            we will see:

a sunlit dance of living water
and the struck rock gushing forth sweet juices,
a moving sea where the night's deserts were—
            Thalassa! Thalassa! life-giver
            over which doves descend
            as usual as the day.

The angel that we wrestle is ourselves.

RALPH POMEROY

Patrol

"F. Patrouiller — to go through puddles"

I travel through thin jails of rain
Indifferent to the man I am.
My hair runs down into my eyes,
My washed-out levis suck my thighs.
Dumb beauty is on top again
And I am high on Possible.

We seek a dreamed-of-innocence,
Uncertain what disguise to wear:
Get-up of forgetfulness
Seems to be the proper dress.
Anxious, but not knowing why,
I cruise in ambiguity.

Now, wearing water as my mask,
I navigate brisk barriers,
Free, yet surrounded by cell doors
Sounding like struck poles of brass
Hit into music by the wind
Whose nightstick prods wet orchestras.

I spot the one I want to meet
Walking down a dead-end street.
He comes to meet me as if he,
Soaked and uncertain, knew me.
As we near, the rain clangs shut
Forming a mirror from a door.

Mirror, dim in this downpour,
Reveal the warden of this blood
That hustles through my corridors
And cons my senses to wipe clear
Your bright shield they shine to show
Unconsciousness I stare to know.

Letter to Pasternak

"It was like listening to a horse describing how it broke
itself in."
—*Doctor Zhivago*

Believe me, I understand your refusal
to be turned out of the paddock where you have always
cantered —
boldly or gently, just enough to ease fear's bit,
just enough then, conjuring, to strike free and be utterly
off.

Off to range the lowlands and the shorelines,
running unfenced in prodigies of freedom,
swift in the singing air, conjoined with music,
part of the general song which is the poets' cycle:

silence to speech: cry to articulation;
moving and taking fresh fences as they extend
their brutal come-ons, tireless in their successions —
over and over, until you are broken and concede.

And desire only to be admitted back into the dark pasture,
having known for a long time a deeper liberty:
migrating from vista to vista, galloping over the heartlands,
internally, secretly, as unrestricted as a stallion's shadow.

In the Redwood Forest

Through these green Parthenons
small birds assert their levels,
measuring their heights and heavens
in tireless flights.
Light hangs like grapes sweating in thick gloom.
Failures of sunshine abdicate the air,
give up their falling half-way down.

As I go deeper, like them, into obscurity,
all around me the light plunges and wrecks,
until even sound seems affected by darkening
and I begin to hear my being alone.

I stop to look all the way up
and suddenly feel at the bottom of someplace —
as if I'd changed places with the stones
I looked down at earlier,
watched stare up at me through
the brown, clear stream
that cuts its lifetime into
the dimming strata.

Islands

Islands are islands though in the steady sea
       They seem unsteady.
       Smoke is strong.

Low-lying or mountainous, the sea's their lover.
       If no other praise,
       Clouds will cover the water

Which has their color. The sea rests easily also
       When not looked at.
       Consider silhouette.

To these shores, trees, birds, piers, winds, solitude
       Are attached and fused.
       These islands are homes, are harbors.

Daily the sun docks; sometimes the rain applauds
       These acres at anchor.
       Fog is their winding sheet.

You do not have to see all the sea at once
       To know all of it is there.
       The pretender can be king.

Without sky, water has no color other than its own.
       Mock laughter is laughter.
       Mock hummingbird is music.

Without these islands, without their displacement,
       The sea is no sea. Loved
       Without lover is not all.

Corner

The cop slumps alertly on his motorcycle,
Supported by one leg like a leather stork.
His glance accuses me of loitering.
I can see his eyes moving like fish
In the green depths of his green goggles.

His ease is fake. I can tell.
My ease is fake. And he can tell.
The fingers armored by his gloves
Splay and clench, itching to change something.
As if he were my enemy or my death,
I just stand there watching.

I spit out my gum which has gone stale.
I knock out a new cigarette—
Which is my bravery.
It is all imperceptible:
The way I shift my weight,
The way he creaks in his saddle.

The traffic is specific though constant.
The sun surrounds me, divides the street between us.
His crash helmet is whiter in the shade.
It is like a bull ring as they say it is just before the fighting.
I cannot back down. I am there.

Everything holds me back.
I am in danger of disappearing into the sunny dust.
My levis bake and my T shirt sweats.

My cigarette makes my eyes burn.
But I don't dare drop it.

Who made him my enemy?
Prince of coolness. King of fear.
Why do I lean here waiting?
Why does he lounge there watching?

I am becoming sunlight.
My hair is on fire. My boots run like tar.
I am hung-up by the bright air.

Something breaks through all of a sudden,
And he blasts off, quick as a craver,
Smug in his power; watching me watch.

In Hotels Public and Private

to John Lehmann

In hotels public and private
Day wakes me to an absence
No schedule or defence
Can override or pirate.
The morning trees are dressed
In wardrobes of fine rain.
Reminding me again
They wear, who can't relate,
Old loneliness unpressed.

Nor can they unpack
What they've misplaced going:
Appointment schedules showing
Exactly how to track,
By telephone, by street,
Fugitive days and nights
Spent in busy flights
From tenderness can crack
The rockiest when they meet.

On flooded estuary
Royal swans are choosing
Who shall have their losing
To build an aviary.
And, like coasting fans,
Gladly seek dear fetters:
Dominions of white feathers
To form cloud statuary,
Groom into singing clans.

Confession

Love, I am guilty of listening to hot rods
practicing somewhere below the window
with you beside me, quiet as linen,
folded — lax with fondness.

And while you lie there
my mind is up and dressing
to follow my imagined body

already bounding,
like an echo,
down the stairs.

To Words

They have said, "too risky"
They have said, "too easy"
They have said, "your enemy is impatience"
They have said, "you're changing"

The shadows continue to bolster objects.
Every noon the hands of the clock meet again.

Come words!
and nourish the surprises of order.
Take on your lives
and live them with me.

Together, who knows?
we may last awhile.

ADRIENNE RICH

33

Piece by piece I seem
to re-enter the world: I first began

a small, fixed dot, I still can see
that old myself, a darkblue thumbtack

pushed into the scene,
a hard little head protruding

from the pointillist's buzz and bloom.
After a time the dot

begins to ooze. Certain heats
melt it.
        Now I was hurriedly

blurring into ranges
of burnt red, burning green,

whole biographies swam up and
swallowed me like Jonah —

Jonah! I was Wittgenstein,
Mary Wollstonecraft, the soul

of Louis Jouvet, dead
in a blown-up photograph.

Till, wolfed almost to shreds,
I learned to make myself

unappetizing. Scaly as a dry bulb
thrown into a cellar

I used myself, let nothing use me.
Like being on a private dole,

sometimes more like cutting bricks in Egypt.
What life was there, was mine,

now and again to lay
one hand on a warm brick

and touch the sun's ghost
with economical joy.

So much for those days. Soon
practise may make me middling-perfect, I'll

dare inhabit the world
trenchant in motion as an eel, solid

as a cabbage-head. I have invitations:
a curl of mist steams upward

from the fields, visible as my breath,
houses along a road stand waiting

like old women knitting, breathless
to tell their tales.

Breakfast in a Bowling Alley in Utica, New York

Smudged eyeballs,
mouth stale as air,
I'm newly dead, a corpse

so fresh the grave unnerves me.
Nobody here but me
and Hermes behind the counter

defrosting sandwich steaks.
Paeans of *vox humana*
sob from the walls. *This land*

is my land. . .It sounds
mummified. Has no sex,
no liquor license.

I chew meat and bread
thinking of wheatfields —
a gold-beige ceinture —

and cattle like ghosts
of the buffalo, running
across plains, nearing

the abattoir. Houses
dream oldfashionedly
in backwoods townships

while the land glitters
with temporary life
stuck fast by choice:

trailers put out taproots
of sewage pipe, suckers
of TV aerial —

and in one of them
a man, perhaps
alone with his girl

for the first time. Who could live
to read our poems
in the softened bitterness

of his heart.

The Corpse-Plant

     (Whitman: 'How can an obedient man, or a sick man,
                             dare to write poems?')

A milk-glass bowl hanging by three chains
from the discoloured ceiling
is beautiful tonight. On the floor, leaves, crayons,
innocent dust foregather.

Neither obedient nor sick, I turn my head
feeling the weight of a thick gold ring
in either lobe. I see the corpse-plants
clustered in a hob-nailed tumbler

at my elbow, white as death, I'd say
if I'd ever seen death;
whiter than life
next to my summer-stained hand.

Is it in the sun that truth begins?
Lying under that battering light
the first few hours of summer
I felt scraped clean, washed down

to ignorance. The gold in my ears,
souvenir of a shrewd old city,
might have been wearing thin as wires
found in the ears of a woman's head

miraculously kept in its essentials
in some hot cradle-tomb of time.
I felt my body slipping through
the fingers of its mind.

Later, I slid on wet roots,
threw my shoes across a brook,
waded on algae-furred stones
to join them. That day it was I found

the corpse-plants, growing like
shadows on a negative
in the chill of fern and lichen-rust.
That day for the first time

I gave them their deathly names —
or did they name themselves? —
not 'Indian pipes' as once
we children called them.

Tonight, an August night, feeling
the apples yellow as young moons
on the tree behind the house,
I think of winters —

all those winters of mind, of flesh,
wet undercover I've grubbed at,
sick with the rot-smell of leaves
turned silt-black, heavy as tarpaulin,

obedient as the elevator cage
lowering itself, crank by crank
into the mine-pit,
forced labor forcibly renewed —

but the horror is dimmed:
like the negative of one
intolerable photograph
it barely sorts itself out

under the radiance of the milk-glass shade.
Only death's insect whiteness
crooks its neck in a tumbler
where I placed its sign by choice.

The Trees

The trees inside are moving out into the forest,
the forest that was empty all these days
where no bird could sit
no insect hide
no sun bury its feet in shadow
the forest that was empty all these nights
will be full of trees by morning.

All night the roots work
to disengage themselves from the cracks
in the veranda floor.
The leaves strain toward the glass
small twigs stiff with exertion
long-cramped boughs shuffling under the roof
like newly discharged patients
half-dazed, moving
to the clinic doors.

I sit inside, doors open to the veranda
writing long letters
in which I scarcely mention the departure
of the forest from the house.
The night is fresh, the whole moon shines
in a sky still open
the smell of leaves and lichen
still reaches like a voice into the rooms.
My head is full of whispers
which tomorrow will be silent.

Listen. The glass is breaking.
The trees are stumbling forward
into the night. Winds rush to meet them.
The moon is broken like a mirror,
its pieces flash now in the crown
of the tallest oak.

Like This Together

— for A.H.C.

1.

Wind rocks the car.
We sit parked by the river,
silence between our teeth.
Birds scatter across islands
of broken ice. Another time
I'd have said "Canada geese",
knowing you love them.
A year, ten years from now,
I'll remember this,
this sitting like drugged birds
in a glass case —
not why, only that we
were here like this together.

2.

They're tearing down, tearing up
this city, block by block.
Rooms, cut in half,
hang like flayed carcasses,
their old roses in rags,
famous streets have forgotten
where they were going. Only
a fact could be so dreamlike.
They're tearing down the houses
we met and lived in,
soon our two bodies will be all
left standing from that era.

3.

We have, as they say,
certain things in common.
I mean: a view
from a bathroom window
over slate to stiff pigeons
huddled every morning; the way
water tastes from our tap,

which you marvel at, letting
it splash into the glass.
Because of you I notice
the taste of water,
a luxury I might
otherwise have missed.

4.

Our words misunderstand us.
Sometimes at night
you are my mother:
old detailed griefs
twitch at my dreams, and I
crawl against you, fighting
for shelter, making you
my cave. Sometimes
you're the wave of birth
that drowns me in my first
nightmare. I suck the air.
Miscarried knowledge twists us
like hot sheets thrown askew.

5.

Dead winter doesn't die.
It wears away, a piece of carrion
picked clean at last,
rained away or burnt dry.
Our desiring does this,
make no mistake, I'm speaking
of fact: through mere indifference
we could prevent it.
Only our fierce attention
gets hyacinths out of those
hard cerebral lumps,
unwraps the wet buds down
the whole length of a stem.

6.

A severed hand
keeps tingling, air still suffers
beyond the stump. But new
life? How do we bear it

(or you, huge tree)
when fresh flames start spurting
out through our old sealed skins,
nerve-endings ours and not yet ours?
Susceptibilities we still
can't use, sucking
blind power from our roots —
what else to do but
hold fast to the
one thing we know,
grip earth and let burn.

The Stranger

Fond credos, wooden ecstasies!
We arrange a prison-temple

for the weak-legged little god
who might stamp the world to bits

or pull the sky in like a muslin curtain.
We hang his shrine with bells,

aeolian harps, paper windmills,
line it with biscuits and swansdown.

His lack of culture we expected,
scarcely his disdain however —

that wild hauteur, as if
it were we who blundered.

Wildness we fret to avenge!
Eye that hasn't yet blinked

on the unquivering gold atmosphere
of its trance — *that* we know

must be trained away:
that aloof, consuming stare.

Otherness that confronts us
as the mere animal does not —

once this was original sin
beaten away with staves of holy writ.

Old simplemindedness. But the primal fault
of the little god still baffles.

All other strangers are forgiven
their strangerhood, but he —

how save the eggshell world from his
reaching hands, how loose

ourselves from the disinterested
blaze of his wide pure eye?

JEROME ROTHENBERG

The Stationmaster's Lament

I have buried her under a stone
The eagles fly past our house with umbrellas
The grey forms rise in the grass
I have buried her solemnly
Speaking the words that she knew:
And the chairs have stood by my side
The trains have been constant in death

The trains have been constant
The conductors who watered our plants have dropped by:
Nodding their pale Busterkeaton-like heads
The brakemen have played farewells on their cellos
Have rendered their final farewells
And the chairs have stood by my side

The chairs have been constant
The chairs with their arms full of wires were dearer to
     me than my friends
I will never forget them
They and the eagles both loved us (as only our plants
     had before)
They came when I called them
They wept dark tears made of burlap
And stood by my side

I have buried her under a forest
The conductors who walked with her coffin were there
The benches were there with white thermoses turning
     her sheets
With burning black eyes the telegraph keys called the
     wind
Now they sleep at her feet
And the brakemen play their farewells

We have paid our farewells with her plants
Where the grey forms were rising commuters climb ramps
     through the night
They throw in their fistfulls of earth and bad dreams

They run to the edge of the night where no one will follow
Past lakes of blue darkness where furnaces holler like bulls
And I sit with the three-hundred chairs of my dreams
They have stood by my side
I will never forget them

And the trains have been constant in death

'A Little Boy Lost'

They took me from the white sun and they
left me in the black sun, left
me to sleep among long rows of overcoats:
I was a city boy lost in the country, a
wound in my hand was all I knew about willows
Can you understand, do you hear the wide
sound of the wind against the cow's
side, and the crickets that run down my
sleeve, crickets full of the night, with
bodies like little black suns? try as I will
there is only this cry in my heart, this cry:
They took me from the white sun, and they
left me in the black sun, and I
have no way of turning now, no door

from Three Landscapes

I

The dark bull quartered in my eye
turns slowly from his herd: the branches
part, and now his grey tongue,
trembling, fights a nest
of adders: stung,
the bloodroot quivers in the earth:
too late he walks along a
pebbled beach, his forehead
(like a grieving moon) against the sea.

II

Tonight the river's warm with
bathers: Christ!

to throw myself against the rain,
be swallowed in its
darkness, like an eyelash.

The Seventh Hell: Of Smoke, Where Fire-Raisers Try In Vain To Escape From A Shower Of Hot Sand Falling From A Cloud . . .

The houses of men are on fire
        Pity the dead in their graves
                And the homes of the living
Pity the roofbeams whose waters burn till they're ash
Pity the old clouds devoured by the clouds of hot sand
And the sweat that's drawn out of metals pity that too
Pity the teeth robbed of gold
        The bones when their skin falls away
Pity man's cry when the sun is born in his cities
And the thunder breaks down his door
              And pity the rain
For the rain falls on the deserts of man and is lost

If the mind is a house that has fallen
            Where will the eye find rest
The images rise from the marrow and cry in the blood
Pity man's voice in the smoke-filled days
        And his eyes in the darkness
Pity the sight of his eyes
           For what can a man see in the darkness
What can he see but the children's bones and the dead sticks
But the places between spaces and the places of sand
And the places of black teeth
        The faraway places
The black sand carried and the black bones buried
The black veins hanging from the open skin
        And the blood changed to glass in the night

The eye of man is on fire
        A green bird cries from his house
And opens a red eye to death
The sun drops out of a pine tree
        Brushing the earth with its wings
For what can a man see in the morning

What can he see but the fire-raisers
>The shadow of the fire-raisers lost in the smoke
The shadow of the smoke where the hot sand is falling
The fire-raisers putting a torch to their arms
The green smoke ascending
>Pity the children of man
Pity their bones when the skin falls away
Pity the skin devoured by fire
>The fire devoured by fire
The mind of man is on fire
>And where will his eyes find rest

A Bodhisattva Undoes Hell

>Because he saw the men of the world
>ploughing their fields, sowing the
>seed, trafficking, huckstering,
>buying and selling, and at the end
>winning nothing but bitterness,
>For this he was moved to pity . . .

To the figures bathing at the river
Jizo appeared

The sky was full of small fishes
The bodies of the men
twisted in an afternoon
when earth and air were one

With Hell a hard fact
the double lotus
brought the son of heaven
down among us
And the bathers showed their hands
that bore the marks of nails

What Jizo said
was this

Let's bury their lousy hammers
My people
are tired of pain
The world's been crucified
long enough

The rain fell gently on their wounds
The women lugged
big platters of shrimp
to the bathers
when Jizo's diamond
caught the sun

The rest of us
sat at the stone windows
overlooking the river
We saw him climb the hill
and disappear
behind the guardhouse

What he told the guards
was this

Your bosses are men
who darken counsel
with words
But the white sun
carries love
into the world

When Jizo leaned on his stick
the blue lines on his face
were shining with tears
We followed him
into the city
where lilies bled beside a lake

He said

The heart's
a flower
Love
each other
Keep the old
among you

Write the poem
The image
unlocks Hell
Man's joy
makes
his gods

For those who heard him
hatred fell away

We spent the night
with angels
Fishing in the ponds
of Hell

Sightings I

He hides his heart.

.

A precious arrangement of glass & flowers.

.

They have made a covenant between them, the circumstance of being tried.

.

Who will signal you?

.

It doesn't open to their touch though some wait where it rests.

.

Try sleep.

.

The emblem perhaps of a herd of elephants—as signal for a change in weather.

.

Animal.

.

A pigeon dreaming of red flowers.

STEPHEN SANDY

The Woolworth Philodendron

Among the plastic flowers one honest one
Graced Woolworth's floor: a real dodo in a green-
house of smilax and excelsior, a sort of proto-
Gew-gaw, if you please, it was so dada
In that museum of small cheers,
Leaves snapped and torn by the sheer
Relentless legs of ladies foraging
For comfort; in a plastic pot, the real thing.

Suspecting it alive, I brought it home.
Five months it sulked in a leafless dream;
Through grillings by the daily sun it never broke
Its dimestore trance, tight-lipped as rock.
And now it is April in the pliant bones and strange
To note the beaten juices fuse and plunge:
A green prong spirals up to the blaze, unplugs
Revenge for ladies' grazing and ungrateful legs.

The shoppers' world is washed away — how fine
To see my green tooth cut the sunshine
And make a brittle pact with the sun's plan!
But it's more than the tender gesture of a jungle vine.
I watch it coil to careful multiplicity
Through my weeks of boring work; I have begun to see
A careless wildness, long-leaved and green,
Mesh with dark plots implicit in the sun.

The Destruction of Bulfinch's House

> 8 Bulfinch Place, designed and
> lived in by Charles Bulfinch,
> architect of the National Cap-
> itol; for years a tenement, it
> is razed to make way for govern-
> ment buildings.

His graceful swag blocks catch the eye,
but the senses stall at whiffs of death . . .
antique cosmetics . . . urine . . . sweat

ooze from ruined windows and try
to grasp some walker through this breath
of air they don't give in to yet.

Outside, next door where Bulfinch built,
a silver nameplate on the door
I find caked black with sooty scum.
I pry at it. I rattle the bolt . . .
a woman calls from an upper floor
at her dog to stop. She strikes me dumb.

Inside Bulfinch's hollowed home
the nose goes gaga at more smells . . .
damp char and rust . . . here, haggard sheets
still on the beds — just risen from;
these personal effects excel
the remains outside in mangled streets.

Mauled rooms bleed trash, not yet resigned
to emptiness. As if for a bomb
they fled — too rushed to pack — yet more
than glad to leave their lives behind,
as if not miffed to head for some
final occasion in the shirts they wore.

Nothing's removed but every sink!
A dumbell rests by uncanned food,
and paper breasts, akimbo, boss
the room, beaming with lipsticked pink.
Only these scrawls of solitude
survive this small survivable loss,

and yet I poke this man-made mess.
I guess what souls this mess has made
— and grub for a Bulfinch souvenir.
Here's one!
             Here's worth beneath the dross!
A handworked ceiling — plaster frayed
and cracked — but a lace of wreaths still clear.

Watch it! My grime goes white as the sieve
of a ceiling rains. Some witch up there
swears out. A hoarse bass spurts *you go
to hell*.
     I see it's time I leave,
copping a doorknob and wondering where
in hell you tell people to go.

Hiawatha

> "These sacred objects had been in the tribe
> for many generations and were kept in the
> Sacred Tent of War. The changes following
> civilization led to the giving up of these
> objects, upon which the former ceremonies
> of the tribe depended. They were entrusted
> to the Museum by the chief of the gens,
> through Francis La Flesche and Alice C.
> Fletcher, 1884."
>
> (Placard in a Harvard museum)

I

                    False dawns
Defunct as Jefferson and Monticello.
Skins of falcon wrapped in bladder, stiff
(Brown paper, twisted), tied with sinew. A mauve
Snuff box: "European manufacture."
                              They lie
Locked in a case misty with handprints. Pale
Lares and *penates* of tribes gone
To our reward. The painted bits call up
My bringing up in Minneapolis
(*City of water,* Ojibway & Greek),
                    haunt of Hiawatha
And his Minnehaha, whose stream once fell
Dark past our house to its thundering fall.

    That fall: the whole idea's strange now
    To me eight states eight years away,
    Unreal as to Longfellow ages ago
    With only a photo from Minnesota
    (Ojibway, *invisible water*).
                         What
    Moved him to sketch in Hiawatha
    From his cupboard Arcady? The thin
    Light caught on those Midwestern waters?
    Perhaps, below the fall, he saw the spare
    Reticulation of some mild
    Oblivion, as in the bare
    Elm's pincers cramping the sun's oblique
    Decline on Cambridge Common.

                                        A postcard
          Or cabinet snap on a warping board?
          Or—of course!—(it moved the bard so)
          A stereograph, bleak doubletake
          For the Beard of Cambridge gazing down
          At brandy after dinner to the sepia
          Swamp of the Charles, wondering where
          His next poem was coming from.

And the Indian.
The Indian gave in
Gave up his most sacred possessions.
Successful men, their hands in the till of the land,
Gave up that fall. They
Raised a dam's apron nine miles upstream:
A lake for a land development. Real
Estate came first:
                    water grew less.
                              Finally
Only a stream, like bathwater from a tap,
Roped down from the fall's brink.
                              Then nothing.
Moss fumbled
Over the rocks by the pool below; fish
Rummaged in algae; the hollow
Behind the fall, a dent bashed in the cliff
Whose sandstone, worn by the force of waters,
Sagged in creased swags like the belly
Of a woman of many children.
The glen that had pooled fallen waters
Was a rose of dust.
                    Then
An icicle.
          We woke
Cold to a perilous morning, one
Beginning of us gone, a dream
Which we'd been wakened from.

Upstream, two-by-four
Wickerworks stapled the meadows;
Barrows of formstone under the drifts
Waited building weather. Blades
Scored the tranced waters.

There were no words between us then
When I followed my brother. Behind our fall
In the hollow we hid laughing,
Quaffing the yellow mist; once,
Dizzily bracing, gave streams of urine to the torrent.
Our selves. In that shade, shreds of sunlight and water
Spattered us, held us. In that place we
Were of it: outside was make-believe. Then
Sun webbed our eyes alone; the misty
Light walked on our legs.

We passed that sun-fired wall, boulder-
Heavy, heavy enough to drag a boy down
In its scathing heave. Yet the sinewy whirl
Skirling headlong from ledge lip high
Up there fell inside to a soft
Mist of embrace. Thought drowned in that grasp; we
                                                    were
There, was all, contained by that cave, laid out
On the tawny stone. The white mane spumed light
Into our stringy bodies: we shivered
Sharing light's movement in our flesh.

II

Under the silver maples the young leaves
Have strewn grapes of sunlight. Ten yards
Upstream from the brink, leached gray and smooth now,
The Indian's monument stands. I see him,

Proud prince of the Onondaga
(Hiawatha, maker of rivers)
Toting his princess forever; still he goes
Over the dead creek bed: crisp leaves, pale stones.
His bronze arms hold her high so her toes
Won't dip in the stream he fords alone
In the branch-screened dimple and tawny shadows,
In the stream which is no longer there:
He walks where a mayor decreed he should,
A debris of benches, a brawl of picnics now.

Where the wind's needles suture the pollen
And seed husks and patchwork napkins, Saran
Wraps wadded at tree-foot burls, this Indian

Commends to our cups and refreshing pauses,
To our Polaroid snaps, our immortal poses,
What was of what never was; himself.

> Somehow: these relics got arranged here
> —The pack consisting of cornhusk wrappers
> Enclosing a caterpillar (dried), and hair;
> The sacred shell, worn by long use

> In sacred ceremony; diminished skins
> Of martins, the meaningless holy pebbles,
> The whole bag of pitiable tricks—
> The faith of primitives traded in

> To Harvard social workers. Faded
> Fetishes, these tinder bits, these
> Are some inheritance —not less
> For lack of guarantee. We held

> We held
> That Hiawatha retained a nobility
> Which our minds had fashioned for our lives.
> He was the instance on earth of essences
> We held to have been the possible

> Condition of our lives.

Hiawatha, tubercular, alcoholic,

Knew every lake and lair of game,
Guided my father on fishing trips,
Drank whiskey round the fire with the men,
Who chipped in twenty for the tip.

One night, the winter of '56, he sat
Home from the tavern, home from the hill.
One last pull in the snow: then sleep.
They found him brittle, immobile

As bronze Hiawatha bearing his Penelope
Over the leaves in the park where children
Peer in casual disbelief at the god
We made of what

We most deeply believed in, the sign of a profitable
Treaty with wildness; of something
Within, beyond us, too essential
Ever to be entertained in life.
                              The man

And his woman still cross the essential
Stream of our youth, the stream which is
Not there: for us, for him.
                          A death,
A truth, a childhood of us gone.

> The sun has burst a bright orange, pared
> It into the rock pool. Goldfish hang
> Under the algae, dart and circle in pairs,
> Intently practicing
> The goldfish. Silence. No prince or king
> May regulate this gravid solitude.

> Teacher has told them another tale
> The eyes of the children say:
> They came for the fall, and it's not there.
> But the boys accept, demand response; two
> Let stones fly, aimed at goldfish. Far-off
> The plash is scarred by the suburb bus horn's squall.

> And schoolchildren ramp each spring now
> At the lip of the glen by that fall,
> Holding breath as their glances flow
> Over the rock ledge like dazzled water.
> Here for the fall, they bridle, daunted, as gazes
> Slow into nothing, nothing but air.

FREDERICK SEIDEL

A Negro Judge

The juice glass throbs against his lips,
He rubs it across his brow, while a draft sips
At the bare grate and palpitates in the chimney.
His cigarette fingers are the color of whiskey.

Week nights he sleeps in town.
Seeming nakeder each weekend, in the bluebook-blue
    nightgown,
His wife cuts the daffodils —
The Sunday scissors shine and glint like the onset of chills.

Backed up love kills
The loving eye with its quills.
Once, his nerves would have stood and stared, prongs on a
    mace,
His meatless Jansenist hooked face . . .

Spawning salmon's face, the lippy death's-head
Fighting starvation to get to its deathbed.
Around the lawn, sparrows flit through the thaw
Trailing rabbinical beards of straw.

His favorite magistrate — favorite piece of justice:
Fielding committed a T. Jones for assaulting a bawd with
    his cutlass.
The lean law
Warbles the galliambic scripture through lips fat as pads of
    a paw.

And law-hagged America dreams on, with disgust, of a
    hairy,
Plenary,
Incessant lust,
A God-like black penis, a white buttocks-sized bust.

A large, slow tear, a hangover,
Rolls down his cheek, magnifying each unshaved pore . . .
Now the dark rose-pimples come up from so low,
Like pebbles tossed at a dark window!

From the Judge's seat, a world of widow's peaks!
Where the lying defendant shrieks,
"Your Honor, I believe! Help thou mine unbelief!"
And slavers with hate and grief.

Plaintiff is awarded the Judge! Passerine,
Perched on branch and vine,
Plaintiff spreads its smallish wings —
Brownish white, whitish brown — and sings.

Dayley Island

Gulls spiral high above
The porch tiles and my gulf-green,
Cliff-hanging lawn, with their
Out-of-breath wail, as
Dawn catches the silver ball
Set in the dried-up bird bath
To scare the gulls. My slippers
Exhale lamé.

I was egged on by old age —
To sell that house,
Winterize this house,
Give up my practice . . . that
You, Pauli, gave up
At Belzec, our son at Belsen,
And one at Maidenek,
Our last at Maidenek.

Below the cliff, the shallows
Tear apart, beating
Themselves white and black,
While the sea's smooth other edge
Towers, reddening,
Over the surfacing sun.
I rise early, always,
Earlier each day . . .

Holding on.
But it's the island that's locked in
By the sea — a case
Of vaginismus, Pauli —

Except for the one bridge
To the next island. I'm free —
Dayley's first once Jewish,
Nonpracticing analyst:

Old, but she had no helper;
Station wagon, but
She's not a tourist; poor for
An island Venus or matron.
The man who sells me fish
Says he fought my Nazis
The captured ones talked
Just like me — I'm somebody.

Last week — March-cold
In the middle of August,
Snow-blue, high, thin skies —
I drove the hour to Brunswick
To drop my suits at
Maine's Only Chinese Laundry,
A down-easter's,
With a Negro presser.

The man was just then off
For Hagard to shoot rabbits
For the reward,
Three miles off Dayley's east-shore.
Years before,
A mainlander
Had loosed two white rabbits
There; now it was theirs.

Frail, pink-veined, pale ears,
And pink as perfect gums,
Pink eyes, rose noses, as if
Diseased — I'd been there.
The lead-gray Yankee owner,
After the shotgun blast,
Strode forward, gathered the bunch,
And one by one, grabbed each

By its hind legs while it sobbed,
And swinging it against
The bare lawn, slapped it dead,
And swung it to the shrubs.

I left the cleaners wanting
So to tell you. The sun's
Well up now. Our blue carpet's
Fading evergreen, Pauli.

The Sickness

1.

The way a child's hands stare through glass
Under the frost, pining so much
They lag behind the child, they pass
Their two hours, patients and their visitors, and touch
Each other's hands with all their love.
The huge scarred Chinaman, a yellow boxing glove
(His neck and head), spreads out his wife's left hand

Just so, and strokes her wedding band,
A lion lapping at a thorn
In his own paw. Alone, I stand
By the wall scribbling with my finger Pound's forlorn
Hymn, "What thou lovest well remains . . .
What thou lov'st well . . ." They don't allow us pens.
          Bleak grains
Of sunlight cross the floor, as the sun leans

Inside the tall barred windowscreens,
While the river escalates downtown
On flattening steps of foam. "I cleans
Yo hans, I cleans you fresh blue sunshine," Chas, his brown
And blue eyes tilting madly, sings.
The gulls, their own white tracers, dip through spumy rings
For rubbers, fish and rubbish. Pudgy squabs

Peck the yard's pebbles. Each head bobs
Like a cork floater. *From these stones
Give us our bread, Lord,* each craw sobs.
"Shall not be reft from thee" — rose lips and flinty crones'
Lips peck their husband's lips, the priest
Who came is going. Eyes and tongues and ears, like yeast,
Swell through their sockets as the studded door

Opens and buzzes closed for more
Long hours. When washday's down the drain,
Comes Tuesday, two o'clock to four,
Though some of them won't come if there's a washday rain.

Priests, girls run down — the hours just run.
No heliotrope, I watch that dead gray door. The sun,
The flexed life-dealing sun's too strong, the sun.

2.

Bottlegreen grass in Central Park,
The early light streams. Lying like
A lover near her boy, a girl,
Pre-Raphaelite in profile, pearl-
Smooth lips, nose and brow, and the passive
Long eyelids and lashes of Melancholy pensive —
And when she rises and walks away
A borzoi and its soft sashay
On slender white paws comes to mind.
We lay there like a heart, our mind
Off to our right the blue lagoon,
Free still of sailboats, just free of the moon,
Our south, the red and brown brick zoo.
But that was then. This now is Bellevue,
And God knows where the girl is, a ruined
Wax mask, waist-down a shiftless hot wind.
Dear heart, those times that were sweet milk
For our pale bones, and in the clock spun silk
For our chapped skin, like dice have scattered.
I'm like that lady-killer Bluebeard,
Dead, but to my last wife's dust,
All Bellevue-blue obsessive trust,
Repeating like an old blind cock,
"Dear heart, the light streams down on Central Park."
It's not my mind. Shouldn't that show
Have gorgeous Desdemona snow
Othello, ax him and then fly,
Black circles under each blue eye,
My dear? And our Miss Liberty,
Lounging beside the door, our trusty p.t.,
Will she be had, will she give in
To the Red Bear and live in sin,
And then Red China break the door?
Divorce, adultery and war
Thrive. "Let live, sleep late, leave the lark
To cry, The light streams down on Central Park,"
You'd say — but some say, "Miss the slut
A little while, poor soiled girl." What

Else is there but — to live — to care
For something flashy made of air
And lose it to the wind, and sue
For breach of promise with faked death in Bellevue
Or the sex pen? But I don't know.
The smile that builds the cretin's brow,
The tenderness one gives and gets,
And lives off, with stale cigarettes,
And what old people keep of fleece
And breath, aren't they some help? They give some peace.
One man here said, "Don't play dead — die!"
But others try life, try dope, try
The fairy bars, join the Reserves,
Or take the wife their life deserves.
He said we're locked together like rhymes,
Us and our loved-ones, in bad times,
And the live whole halves of our heart
Shall, wind or bomb, be smithereened apart.

3.

Like a gray cat tied to the tarred stump of a tree
At night, the hall hides, tries its length, slinks back. It
                                        climbs
Piles of back stairs down from the dark street. Finally
The kitchen. Just to waste the steak here would take lifetimes!
There's that much, and all much too gamy to be good —
Blue tons braised, baked, broiled or basted violet. Pie-eyed
Waiters dump it on castered slabs they wheel inside
The banquet room. They breathe here. No one else could.
The air's close as wet wool. On the last door's a hide,
White once, now orange, lettered GRAEFIN SEIDE'S PRIDE.
In the room, jet columns lace the floor and balcony
From which low music flickers on the parquet wood
Through massive fuming candelabra. Easily
A dozen colored footmen hum along the walls,
Among them grown men dressed like Philip Morris boys,
Smooth moon-faced fairies, serving trays to him. He stalls
Over each choice until — this the fat king enjoys —
Their hands start shaking, picks some favorite *saignant* dish
He's had prepared, and motioning away the rest,
Pokes it, and slurps his fingertip, and smiles — "Deeelish . . .
Deeelicious!" Sweating, finished, he sheds his green vest
And rolls his saffron blouse's sleeves up to his armpits —

Slowly, because of the stiff spangles — even so,
They slip out of his fat gold fingers — and just sits,
Just strokes his lapdog, slowly — no hour hand's so slow.
The candles huddle, soughing, in the brain-gray gloom,
In their pale light. His gold knuckles gleam. Not a sound.
        Don't make a sound, here's your last chance. Take it
        And run for it down the wrong hallway, the one
That's never used, and don't look back. You've missed
The worst of it just barely. You *have* to know!
Is what you're going to say. Well, things like a girl
Exposing herself in various poses to
A vast steel machine and its little red eye
Which stares and stares and never goes off. Enough?
Behind her, behind where she spreads herself out
Nude in her stockings and black garter belt
On the Persian carpet, its pile the silencer,
Is another huge heavy machine, this one
Entirely hooded in black leather except for
Its appendages, mantis-like chrome arms
Which operate on her face with silver knives,
Finally leaving only her eyes. Enough?
Well, like the room where priests walk on the ceiling,
Nuns on the floor, looking for each other
In pitch-darkness with great blind eyes on stalks,
Like dandelions. With their charcoals they scrawl
Messages they of course can't know the others
Can't see, all being deaf-mutes, on the damp walls.
Enough? One last thing, then, and the worst.
In about an hour the Royal Servitors
Of the Commode come in and fold a silk screen,
Tall and lavender, with various seals
And names sewn into it, like Eurydice, Gandhi,
Nietzsche, Troilus, Dulles, Pola Negri
And others — they fold this screen around the fat king,
Who is seated. Under it you can see
The pairs of slippers, the Servitors at attention
On triangle bases. Then they emerge, the screen
Is folded back, and in the pot are gold bees,
Honeybees, millions of them, which rise and join
The millions and millions of them on the ceiling
That you thought were highly overwrought
Gold work. They made the low music that you heard.
No one eats honey here — it drips down the walls
And columns, it hangs in the air — so it happens

Sometimes that a live man is selected
For his weakness to come and gorge, to swell up
Half dead on the sweetness that famishes,
And all the while he dies the honeybees feed
On him with their stingers, until in ecstasy
He does die. You were lured here for this purpose.
Get outside. It is morning on Eighty-sixth Street
Where you live. The painted clock outside
The jeweler's window happens to have the right time,
6 o'clock. A girl with crooked stockings
Walks on the feet of a goddess to the bus stop.
An opening window flashes light out over
The street like a big white bird. Coming home,
After a rainy night in Central Park,
Behind his old friend, his old suffering mare,
A horse-cab driver, looking straight ahead,
Smiles quietly, just because it is morning.

ANNE SEXTON

All My Pretty Ones

Father, this year's jinx rides us apart
where you followed our mother to her cold slumber;
a second shock boiling its stone to your heart,
leaving me here to shuffle and disencumber
you from the residence you could not afford:
a gold key, your half of a woolen mill,
twenty suits from Dunne's, an English Ford,
the love and legal verbiage of another will,
boxes of pictures of people I do not know.
I touch their cardboard faces. They must go.

But the eyes, as thick as wood in this album,
hold me. I stop here, where a small boy
waits in a ruffled dress for someone to come . . .
for this soldier who holds his bugle like a toy
or for this velvet lady who cannot smile.
Is this your father's father, this commodore
in a mailman suit? My father, time meanwhile
has made it unimportant who you are looking for.
I'll never know what these faces are all about.
I lock them into their book and throw them out.

This is the yellow scrapbook that you began
the year I was born; as crackling now and wrinkly
as tobacco leaves: clippings where Hoover outran
the Democrats, wiggling his dry finger at me
and Prohibition; news where the *Hindenburg* went
down and recent years where you went flush
on war. This year, solvent but sick, you meant
to marry that pretty widow in a one-month rush.
But before you had that second chance, I cried
on your fat shoulder. Three days later you died.

These are the snapshots of marriage, stopped in places.
Side by side at the rail toward Nassau now;
here, with the winner's cup at the speedboat races,
here, in tails at the Cotillion, you take a bow,
here, by our kennel of dogs with their pink eyes,

running like show-bred pigs in their chain-link pen;
here, at the horseshow where my sister wins a prize;
and here, standing like a duke among groups of men.
Now I fold you down, my drunkard, my navigator,
my first lost keeper, to love or look at later.

I hold a five-year diary that my mother kept
for three years, telling all she does not say
of your alcoholic tendency. You overslept,
she writes. My God, father, each Christmas Day
with your blood, will I drink down your glass
of wine? The diary of your hurly-burly years
goes to my shelf to wait for my age to pass.
Only in this hoarded span will love persevere.
Whether you are pretty or not, I outlive you,
bend down my strange face to yours and forgive you.

Water

We are fishermen in a flat scene.
All day long we are in love with water.
The fish are naked.
The fish are always awake.
They are the color of old spoons
and caramels.
The sun reaches down
but the floor is not in sight.
Only the rocks are white and green.
Who knows what goes on in the halls below?

It's queer to meet the loon falling in
across the top of the yellow lake
like a checkered hunchback
dragging his big feet.
Only his head and neck can breathe.
He yodels.
He goes under yodeling
like the first mate
who sways all night in his hammock, calling
       I have seen, I have seen.

       Water is worse than woman.
       It calls to a man to empty him.
       Under us
       twelve princesses dance all night,

exhausting their lovers, then giving them up.
I have known water.
I have sung all night
for the last cargo of boys.
I have sung all night
for the mouths that float back later,
one by one,
holding a lady's wornout shoe.

Unknown Girl in the Maternity Ward

Child, the current of your breath is six days long.
You lie, a small knuckle on my white bed;
lie, fisted like a snail, so small and strong
at my breast. Your lips are animals; you are fed
with love. At first hunger is not wrong.
The nurses nod their caps; you are shepherded
down starch halls with the other unnested throng
in wheeling baskets. You tip like a cup; your head
moving to my touch. You sense the way we belong.
But this is an institution bed.
You will not know me very long.

The doctors are enamel. They want to know
the facts. They guess about the man who left me,
some pendulum soul, going the way men go
and leave you full of child. But our case history
stays blank. All I did was let you grow.
Now we are here for all the ward to see.
They thought I was strange, although
I never spoke a word. I burst empty
of you, letting you learn how the air is so.
The doctors chart the riddle they ask of me
and I turn my head away. I do not know.

Yours is the only face I recognize.
Bone at my bone, you drink my answers in.
Six times a day I prize
your need, the animals of your lips, your skin
growing warm and plump. I see your eyes
lifting their tents. They are blue stones, they begin
to outgrow their moss. You blink in surprise
and I wonder what you can see, my funny kin,

as you trouble my silence. I am a shelter of lies.
Should I learn to speak again, or hopeless in
such sanity will I touch some face I recognize?

Down the hall the baskets start back. My arms
fit you like a sleeve, they hold
catkins of your willows, the wild bee farms
of your nerves, each muscle and fold
of your first days. Your old man's face disarms
the nurses. But the doctors return to scold
me. I speak. It is you my silence harms.
I should have known; I should have told
them something to write down. My voice alarms
my throat. "Name of father — none." I hold
you and name you bastard in my arms.

And now that's that. There is nothing more
that I can say or lose.
Others have traded life before
and could not speak. I tighten to refuse
your owling eyes, my fragile visitor.
I touch your cheeks, like flowers. You bruise
against me. We unlearn. I am a shore
rocking you off. You break from me. I choose
your only way, my small inheritor
and hand you off, trembling the selves we lose.
Go child, who is my sin and nothing more.

The Lost Ingredient

Almost yesterday, those gentle ladies stole
to their baths in Atlantic City, for the lost
rites of the first sea of the first salt
running from a faucet. I have heard they sat
for hours in briny tubs, patting hotel towels
sweetly over shivered skin, smelling the stale
harbor of a lost ocean, praying at last
for impossible loves, or new skin, or still
another child. And since this was the style,
I don't suppose they knew what they had lost.

Almost yesterday, pushing West, I lost
ten Utah driving minutes, stopped to steal
past postcard vendors, crossed the hot slit

of macadam to touch the marvelous loosed
bobbing of The Salt Lake, to honor and assault
it in its proof, to wash away some slight
need for Maine's coast. Later the funny salt
itched in my pores and stung like bees or sleet.
I rinsed it off in Reno and hurried to steal
a better proof at tables where I always lost.

Today is made of yesterday, each time I steal
toward rites I do not know, waiting for the lost
ingredient, as if salt or money or even lust
would keep us calm and prove us whole at last.

W. D. SNODGRASS

Heart's Needle

For Cynthia

> " 'Your father is dead.' 'That grieves me,' said he.
> 'Your mother is dead,' said the lad. 'Now all pity
> for me is at an end,' said he. 'Your brother is dead,'
> said Loingsechan. 'I am sorely wounded by that,'
> said Suibne. 'Your daughter is dead,' said Loing-
> sechan. 'And an only daughter is the needle of the
> heart,' said Suibne. 'Dead is your son who used to
> call you "Father,"' said Loingsechan. 'Indeed,'
> said he, 'that is the drop that brings a man to the
> ground.' "

From an old Irish story,
The Frenzy of Suibne,
As translated by Myles Dillon

1

Child of my winter, born
When the new fallen soldiers froze
In Asia's steep ravines and fouled the snows,
When I was torn

By love I could not still,
By fear that silenced my cramped mind
To that cold war where, lost, I could not find
My peace in my will,

All those days we could keep
Your mind a landscape of new snow
Where the chilled tenant-farmer finds, below,
His fields asleep

In their smooth covering, white
As quilts to warm the resting bed
Of birth or pain, spotless as paper spread
For me to write,

And thinks: Here lies my land
Unmarked by agony, the lean foot
Of the weasel tracking, the thick trapper's boot;
And I have planned

My chances to restrain
The torments of demented summer or
Increase the deepening harvest here before
It snows again.

2

Late April and you are three; today
    We dug your garden in the yard.
To curb the damage of your play,
Strange dogs at night and the moles tunneling,
    Four slender sticks of lath stand guard
        Uplifting their thin string.

So you were the first to tramp it down.
    And after the earth was sifted close
You brought your watering can to drown
All earth *and* us. But these mixed seeds are pressed
    With light loam in their steadfast rows.
        Child, we've done our best.

Someone will have to weed and spread
    The young sprouts. Sprinkle them in the hour
When shadow falls across their bed.
You should try to look at them every day
    Because when they come to full flower
        I will be away.

3

The child between them on the street
Comes to a puddle, lifts his feet
    And hangs on their hands. They start
At the live weight and lurch together,
    Recoil to swing him through the weather,
        Stiffen and pull apart.

We read of cold war soldiers that
Never gained ground, gave none, but sat
    Tight in their chill trenches.

Pain seeps up from some cavity
Through the ranked teeth in sympathy;
    The whole jaw grinds and clenches

Till something somewhere has to give.
It's better the poor soldiers live
    In someone else's hands
Than drop where helpless powers fall
On crops and barns, on towns where all
    Will burn. And no man stands.

For good, they sever and divide
Their won and lost land. On each side
    Prisoners are returned
Excepting a few unknown names.
The peasant plods back and reclaims
    His fields that strangers burned

And nobody seems very pleased.
It's best. Still, what must not be seized
    Clenches the empty fist.
I tugged your hand, once, when I hated
Things less: a mere game dislocated
    The radius of your wrist.

Love's wishbone, child, although I've gone
As men must and let you be drawn
    Off to appease another,
It may help that a Chinese play
Or Solomon himself might say
    I am your real mother.

4

    No one can tell you why
  the season will not wait;
    the night I told you I
must leave, you wept a fearful rate
    to stay up late.

    Now that it's turning Fall,
  we go to take our walk
    among municipal
flowers, to steal one off its stalk,
    to try and talk.

We huff like windy giants
    scattering with our breath
        gray-headed dandelions;
Spring is the cold wind's aftermath.
            The poet saith.

But the asters, too, are gray,
    ghost-gray. Last night's cold
        is sending on their way
petunias and dwarf marigold,
            hunched sick and old.

Like nerves caught in a graph,
    the morning-glory vines
        frost has erased by half
still scrawl across their rigid twines,
            like broken lines

of verses I can't make.
    In its unraveling loom
        we find a flower to take,
with some late buds that might still bloom,
            back to your room.

Night comes and the stiff dew.
    I'm told a friend's child cried
        because a cricket, who
had minstreled every night outside
            her window, died.

5

Winter again and it is snowing;
Although you are still three,
You are already growing
Strange to me.

You chatter about new playmates, sing
Strange songs; you do not know
Hey ding-a-ding-a-ding
Or where I go

Or when I sang for bedtime, *Fox*
Went out on a chilly night,
Before I went for walks
And did not write;

You never mind the squalls and storms
That are renewed long since;
Outside, the thick snow swarms
Into my prints

And swirls out by warehouses, sealed,
Dark cowbarns, huddled, still,
Beyond to the blank field,
The fox's hill

Where he backtracks and sees the paw,
Gnawed off, he cannot feel;
Conceded to the jaw
Of toothed, blue steel.

6

    Easter has come around
  again; the river is rising
    over the thawed ground
and the banksides. When you come you bring
    an egg dyed lavender.
We shout along our bank to hear
our voices returning from the hills to meet us.
  We need the landscape to repeat us.

    You lived on this bank first.
While nine months filled your term, we knew
    how your lungs, immersed
in the womb, miraculously grew
    their useless folds till
the fierce, cold air rushed in to fill
them out like bushes thick with leaves. You took your hour,
  caught breath, and cried with your full lung power.

    Over the stagnant bight
we see the hungry bank swallow
    flaunting his free flight
still; we sink in mud to follow
    the killdeer from the grass
that hides her nest. That March there was
rain; the rivers rose; you could hear killdeers flying
  all night over the mudflats crying.

You bring back how the red-
winged blackbird shrieked, slapping frail wings,
    diving at my head —
I saw where her tough nest, cradled, swings
    in tall reeds that must sway
with the winds blowing every way.
If you recall much, you recall this place. You still
    live nearby — on the opposite hill.

After the sharp windstorm
of July Fourth, all that summer
    through the gentle, warm
afternoons, we heard great chain saws chirr
    like iron locusts. Crews
of roughneck boys swarmed to cut loose
branches wrenched in the shattering wind, to hack free
    all the torn limbs that could sap the tree.

In the debris lay
starlings, dead. Near the park's birdrun
    we surprised one day
a proud, tan-spatted, buff-brown pigeon.
    In my hands she flapped so
fearfully that I let her go.
Her keeper came. And we helped snarl her in a net.
    You bring things I'd as soon forget.

You raise into my head
a Fall night that I came once more
    to sit on your bed;
sweat beads stood out on your arms and fore-
    head and you wheezed for breath,
for help, like some child caught beneath
its comfortable woolly blankets, drowning there.
    Your lungs caught and would not take the air.

Of all things, only we
have power to choose that we should die;
    nothing else is free
in this world to refuse it. Yet I,
    who say this, could not raise
myself from bed how many days
to the thieving world. Child, I have another wife,
    another child. We try to choose our life.

7

Here in the scuffled dust
    is our ground of play.
I lift you on your swing and must
    shove you away,
see you return again,
    drive you off again, then

stand quiet till you come.
    You, though you climb
higher, farther from me, longer,
    will fall back to me stronger.
Bad penny, pendulum,
    you keep my constant time

to bob in blue July
    where fat goldfinches fly
over the glittering, fecund
    reach of our growing lands.
Once more now, this second,
    I hold you in my hands.

8

I thumped on you the best I could
        which was no use;
you would not tolerate your food
until the sweet, fresh milk was soured
        with lemon juice.

That puffed you up like fine yeast.
    The first June in your yard
like some squat Nero at a feast
you sat and chewed on white, sweet clover.
        That is over.

When you were old enough to walk
        we went to feed
the rabbits in the park milkweed;
saw the paired monkeys, under lock,
    consume each other's salt.

Going home we watched the slow
stars follow us down Heaven's vault.
You said, let's catch one that comes low,
        pull off its skin
    and cook it for our dinner.

As absentee bread-winner,
I seldom got you such cuisine;
we ate in local restaurants
or bought what lunches we could pack
        in a brown sack

with stale, dry bread to toss for ducks
        on the green-scummed lagoons,
crackers for porcupine and fox,
life-savers for the footpad coons
        to scour and rinse,

snatch after in their muddy pail
        and stare into their paws.
When I moved next door to the jail
        I learned to fry
omelettes and griddlecakes so I

could set you supper at my table.
As I built back from helplessness,
        when I grew able,
the only possible answer was
    you had to come here less.

This Hallowe'en you come one week.
        You masquerade
        as a vermilion, sleek,
fat, crosseyed fox in the parade
or, where grim jackolanterns leer,

go with your bag from door to door
foraging for treats. How queer:
        when you take off your mask
my neighbors must forget and ask
        whose child you are.

Of course you lose your appetite,
    whine and won't touch your plate;
        as local law
I set your place on an orange crate
in your own room for days. At night

you lie asleep there on the bed
        and grate your jaw.
Assuredly your father's crimes
        are visited
on you. You visit me sometimes.

The time's up. Now our pumpkin sees
  me bringing your suitcase.
        He holds his grin;
the forehead shrivels, sinking in.
You break this year's first crust of snow

off the runningboard to eat.
        We manage, though for days
I crave sweets when you leave and know
they rot my teeth. Indeed our sweet
        foods leave us cavities.

9

  I get numb and go in
though the dry ground will not hold
  the few dry swirls of snow
and it must not be very cold.
A friend asks how you've been
        and I don't know

  or see much right to ask.
Or what use it could be to know.
  In three months since you came
the leaves have fallen and the snow;
your pictures pinned above my desk
        seem much the same.

  Somehow I come to find
myself upstairs in the third floor
  museum's halls,
walking to kill my time once more
among the enduring and resigned
        stuffed animals,

  where, through a century's
caprice, displacement and
  known treachery between
its wars, they hear some old command
and in their peaceable kingdoms freeze
        to this still scene,

  Nature Morte. Here
by the door, its guardian,
  the patchwork dodo stands

where you and your stepsister ran
laughing and pointing. Here, last year,
    you pulled my hands

    and had your first, worst quarrel,
so toys were put up on your shelves.
    Here in the first glass cage
the little bobcats arch themselves,
still practicing their snarl
    of constant rage.

    The bison, here, immense,
shoves at his calf, brow to brow,
    and looks it in the eye
to see what is it thinking now.
I forced you to obedience;
    I don't know why.

    Still the lean lioness
beyond them, on her jutting ledge
    of shale and desert shrub,
stands watching always at the edge,
stands hard and tanned and envious
    above her cub;

    with horns locked in tall heather,
two great Olympian Elk stand bound,
    fixed in their lasting hate
till hunger brings them both to ground.
Whom equal weakness binds together
    none shall separate.

    Yet separate in the ocean
of broken ice, the white bear reels
    beyond the leathery groups
of scattered, drab Arctic seals
arrested here in violent motion
    like Napoleon's troops.

    Our states have stood so long
At war, shaken with hate and dread,
    they are paralyzed at bay;
once we were out of reach, we said,
we would grow reasonable and strong.
    Some other day.

Like the cold men of Rome,
we have won costly fields to sow
    in salt, our only seed.
Nothing but injury will grow.
I write you only the bitter poems
        that you can't read.

Onan who would not breed
a child to take his brother's bread
    and be his brother's birth,
rose up and left his lawful bed,
went out and spilled his seed
        in the cold earth.

I stand by the unborn,
by putty-colored children curled
    in jars of alcohol,
that waken to no other world,
unchanging where no eye shall mourn.
        I see the caul

that wrapped a kitten, dead.
I see the branching, doubled throat
    of a two-headed foal;
I see the hydrocephalic goat;
here is the curled and swollen head,
        there, the burst-skull;

skin of a limbless calf;
a horse's foetus, mummified;
    mounted and joined forever,
the Siamese twin dogs that ride
belly to belly, half and half,
        that none shall sever.

I walk among the growths,
by gangrenous tissue, goitre, cysts,
    by fistulas and cancers,
where the malignancy man loathes
is held suspended and persists.
        And I don't know the answers.

The window's turning white.
The world moves like a diseased heart
        packed with ice and snow.

Three months now we have been apart
less than a mile. I cannot fight
   or let you go.

10

The vicious winter finally yields
   the green winter wheat;
the farmer, tired in the tired fields
   he dare not leave will eat.

Once more the runs come fresh; prevailing
   piglets, stout as jugs,
harry their old sow to the railing
   to ease her swollen dugs

and game colts trail the herded mares
   that circle the pasture courses;
our seasons bring us back once more
   like merry-go-round horses.

With crocus mouths, perennial hungers,
   into the park Spring comes;
we roast hot dogs on old coat hangers
   and feed the swan bread crumbs,

pay our respects to the peacocks, rabbits,
   and leathery Canada goose
who took, last Fall, our tame white habits
   and now will not turn loose.

In full regalia, the pheasant cocks
   march past their dubious hens;
the porcupine and the lean, red fox
   trot around bachelor pens

and the miniature painted train
   wails on its oval track:
you said, I'm going to Pennsylvania!
   and waved. And you've come back.

If I loved you, they said, I'd leave
   and find my own affairs.
Well, once again this April, we've
   come around to the bears;

punished and cared for, behind bars,
   the coons on bread and water
stretch thin black fingers after ours.
   And you are still my daughter.

GARY SNYDER

Hunting

1

first shaman song

In the village of the dead,
Kicked loose bones
       ate pitch of a drift log
       (whale fat)
Nettles and cottonwood. Grass smokes
                in the sun

Logs turn in the river
       sand scorches the feet.

Two days without food, trucks roll past
       in dust and light, rivers
       are rising.
Thaw in the high meadows. Move west in July.

Soft oysters rot now, between tides
          the flats stink.

I sit without thoughts by the log-road
Hatching a new myth
Watching the waterdogs
          the last truck gone.

2

Atok: creeping
Maupok: waiting
    to hunt seals.
The sea hunter
    watching the whirling seabirds on the rocks
The mountain hunter
    horn-tipped shaft on a snowslope
    edging across cliffs for a shot at goat
"Upon the lower slopes of the mountain,

on the cover, we find the sculptured forms
of animals apparently lying dead in the
wilderness" thus Fenellosa
On the pottery of Shang.

It's a shame I didn't kill you,
                    Yang Kuei Fei,
Cut down in the old apartment
Left to bleed between the bookcase and the wall,
I'd hunt you still, trail you from town to town.
But you change shape.
                    death's a new shape,
Maybe flayed you'd be true
But it wouldn't be through.

"You who live with your grandmother
I'll trail you with dogs
And crush you in my mouth."
                    —not that we're cruel—
But a man's got to eat.

3

this poem is for birds

Birds in a whirl, drift to the rooftops
Kite dip, swing to the seabank fogroll
Form: dots in air changing line from line,
                    the future defined.

Brush back smoke from the eyes,
                    dust from the mind,
With the wing-feather fan of an eagle.
A hawk drifts into the far sky.
A marmot whistles across huge rocks.
Rain on the California hills.
Mussels clamp to sea-boulders
Sucking the Spring tides

Rain soaks the tan stubble
Fields full of ducks

Rain sweeps the Eucalyptus
Strange pines on the coast
        needles two to the bunch
The whole sky whips in the wind
Vaux Swifts

Flying before the storm
Arcing close hear sharpwing-whistle
Sickle-bird
          pale gray
          sheets of rain slowly shifting
          down from the clouds,
Black Swifts.
               —the swifts cry
As they shoot by, See or go blind!

4

The swallow-shell that eases birth
  brought from the south by Hummingbird.
"We pull out the seagrass, the seagrass,
  the seagrass, and it drifts away"
—song of the geese.
"My children
  their father was a log"
—song of the pheasant.
The white gulls south of Victoria
  catch tossed crumbs in midair.
When anyone hears the Catbird
  he gets lonesome.
San Francisco, "Mulberry Harbor"
  eating the speckled sea-bird eggs
  of the Farallones.
Driving sand sends swallows flying,
  warm mud puts the ducks to sleep.
Magical birds: Phoenix, hawk, and crane
  owl and gander, wren,
Bright eyes aglow: Polishing clawfoot
  with talons spread, subtle birds
Wheel and go, leaving air in shreds
  black beaks shine in gray haze.
Brushed by the hawk's wing
  of vision.

—They were arguing about the noise
Made by the Golden-eye Duck.
Some said the whistling sound
Was made by its nose, some said
No, by the wings.
     "Have it your way.

We will leave you forever."
They went upriver:
The Flathead tribe.

    Raven
      on a roost of furs
No bird in a bird-book,
    black as the sun.

5

the making of the horn spoon

The head of the mountain-goat is in the corner
    for the making of the horn spoon,
The black spoon. When fire's heat strikes it
    turn the head
Four days and hair pulls loose
    horn twists free.
Hand-adze, straightknife, notch the horn-base;
    rub with rough sandstone
Shave down smooth. Split two cedar sticks
    when water boils plunge the horn,
Tie mouth between sticks in the spoon shape
    rub with dried dogfish skin.
It will be black and smooth,
    a spoon.

Wa, laEm gwala ts!ololaqe ka · ts!Enaqe laxeq.

6

this poem is for bear

"As for me I am a child of the god of the mountains."
A bear down under the cliff.
She is eating huckleberries.
They are ripe now
Soon it will snow, and she
Or maybe he, will crawl into a hole
And sleep. You can see
Huckleberries in bearshit if you
Look, this time of year
If I sneak up on the bear
It will grunt and run

The others had all gone down
From the blackberry brambles, but one girl
Spilled her basket, and was picking up her
Berries in the dark.
A tall man stood in the shadow, took her arm,
Led her to his home. He was a bear.
In a house under the mountain
She gave birth to slick dark children
With sharp teeth, and lived in the hollow
Mountain many years.
                    snare a bear: call him out:

honey-eater
forest apple
light-foot
Old man in the fur coat, Bear! come out!
Die of your own choice!
Grandfather black-food!
                    this girl married a bear
Who rules in the mountains, Bear!
                    you have eaten many berries
                    you have caught many fish
                    you have frightened many people

            Twelve species north of Mexico
            Sucking their paws in the long winter
            Tearing the high-strung caches down
            Whining, crying, jacking off
            (Odysseus was a bear)

            Bear-cubs gnawing the soft tits
            Teeth gritted, eyes screwed tight
                            but she let them.

            Til her brothers found the place
            Chased her husband up the gorge
            Cornered him in the rocks.
            Song of the snared bear:
                    "Give me my belt.
                    "I am near death.
                    "I came from the mountain caves
                    "At the headwaters,
                    "The small streams there
                    "Are all dried up.

—I think I'll go hunt bears.
                              "hunt bears?
         Why shit Snyder,
         You couldn't hit a bear in the ass
                          with a handful of rice!"

7

All beaded with dew
        dawn grass runway
Open-eyed rabbits hang
        dangle, loose feet in tall grass
From alder snares.
The spider is building a morning-web
From the snared rabbit's ear to the snare

        down trail at sunrise
        wet berry brush
Splinter pines,
        bark the firs,
                    rest in maple shade.

I dance
On every swamp
                    sang the rabbit
        once a hungry ghost
        then a beast
        who knows what next?

Salmon, deer, no pottery;
Summer and winter houses
Roots, berries, watertight baskets—
Our girls get layed by Coyote
We get along
                    just fine.
The Shuswap tribe.

8

this poem is for deer

"I dance on all the mountains
On five mountains, I have a dancing place
When they shoot at me I run
To my five mountains"

Missed a last shot
At the Buck, in twilight
So we came back sliding
On dry needles through cold pines.
Scared out a cottontail
Whipped up the winchester
Shot off its head.
The white body rolls and twitches
In the dark ravine
As we run down the hill to the car.

                              deer foot down scree

Picasso's fawn, Issa's fawn,
Deer on the autumn mountain
Howling like a wise man
Stiff springy jumps down the snowfields
Head held back, forefeet out,
Balls tight in a tough hair sack
Keeping the human soul from care
                    on the autumn mountain
Standing in late sun, ear-flick
Tail-flick, gold mist of flies
Whirling from nostril to eyes.

                              ***

Home by night
               drunken eye
Still picks out Taurus
Low, and growing high:
               four-point buck
Dancing in the headlights
               on the lonely road
A mile past the mill-pond,
With the car stopped, shot
That wild silly blinded creature down.

Pull out the hot guts
               with hard bare hands
While night-frost chills the tongue
               and eye
The cold horn-bones.
The hunter's belt
               just below the sky
Warm blood in the car trunk.
Deer-smell,
          the limp tongue.

***

Deer don't want to die for me
        I'll drink sea-water
Sleep on beach pebbles in the rain
Until the deer come down to die
        in pity for my pain.

9

Sealion, salmon, offshore—
Salt-fuck desire driving flap fins
North, south, five thousand miles
Coast, and up creek, big seeds
Groping for inland womb.

Geese, ducks, swallows,
               paths in the air
I am a frozen addled egg on the tundra

My petrel, snow-tongued
      kiss her a brook her mouth
of smooth pebbles her tongue a bed
      icewater flowing in that
Cavern dark, tongue drifts in the creek
          —blind fish

On the rainy boulders
On the bloody sandbar
I ate the spawned-out salmon
I went crazy
covered with ashes
Gnawing the girls breasts
Marrying women to whales
Or dogs, I'm a priest too
I raped your wife
I'll eat your corpse

10

Flung from demonic wombs
      off to some new birth
A million shapes—just look in any
      biology book.
And the hells below mind
      where ghosts roam, the heavens

Above brain, where gods & angels play
        an age or two
& they'll trade with you,
Who wants heaven?
        rest homes like that
scattered all through the galaxy.

        "I kill everything
        I fear nothing but wolves
        From the mouth of the Cowlitz
                to its source,
        Only the wolves scare me,
        I have a chief's tail"
—Skunk.
        "We carry deer-fawns in our mouths
        We carry deer-fawns in our mouths
        We have our faces blackened"
—Wolf-song.
"If I were a baby seal
                        every time I came up
I'd head toward shore—"

11

songs for a four-crowned dancing hat

O Prajapati
        You who floated on the sea
        Hatched to godhead in the slime
Heated red and beaten for a bronze ritual bowl
The Boar!
        Dripping boar emerged
        On his tusk his treasure
Prajapati from the sea-depths:
Skewered body of the earth
Each time I carry you this way.

The year I wore my Raven skin
  Dogfish ran. Too many berries on the hill
Grizzly fat and happy in the sun—
  The little women, the fern women,
They have stopped crying now.
  "What will you do with human beings?
Are you going to save the human beings?"
  That was Southeast, they say.

12

Out the Greywolf valley
in late afternoon
after eight days in the high meadows
hungry, and out of food,
the trail broke into a choked
clearing, apples grew gone wild
hung on one low bough by a hornet's nest.
caught the drone in tall clover
lowland smell in the shadows
then picked a hard green one:
watched them swarm.
smell of the mountains still on me.
none stung.

13

Now I'll also tell what food
we lived on then:

Mescal, yucca fruit, pinyon, acorns,
prickly pear, sumac berry, cactus,
spurge, dropseed, lip fern, corn,
mountain plants, wild potatoes, mesquite,
stems of yucca, tree-yucca flowers, chokecherries,
pitahaya cactus, honey of the ground-bee,
honey, honey of the bumblebee,
mulberries, angle-pod, salt, berries,
berries of the one-seeded juniper,
berries of the alligator-bark juniper,
wild cattle, mule deer, antelopes,
white-tailed deer, wild turkeys, doves, quail,
squirrels, robins, slate-colored juncoes,
song sparrows, wood rats, prairie dogs,
rabbits, peccaries, burros, mules, horses,
buffaloes, mountain sheep, and turtles.

14

Buddha fed himself to tigers
& donated mountains of eyes
            (through the years)
To the blind,
              a mountain-lion

Once trailed me four miles
At night and no gun
It was awful, I didn't want to be ate
          maybe we'll change.

Or make a net of your sister's cunt-hair
Catch the sun, and burn the world.

Where are you going now?
Shake hands.
Goodbye, George Bell . . .
               that was a Kwakiutl woman
          singing goodbye to her man,
          Victoria B.C., 1887

The mules are loaded
          packs lashed with a vajra-hitch
          the grass-eaters steam in the dawn
          the workers are still asleep
          light swings on the high cornice
          on the chill side of the mountain, we
          switchback
          drink at the waterfall
          start to climb
"Stalk lotusses
Burst through the rocks
And come up in sevens."

15

First day of the world.
White rock ridges

                    new born
Jay chatters   the first time
Rolling a smoke by the campfire
New! never before.

                    bitter coffee, cold
Dawn wind, sun on the cliffs,
You'll find it in *Many old shoes*
High!   high on poetry & mountains.

That silly ascetic Gautama
          thought he knew something;
Maudgalyâyana knew hell
Knew every hell, from the
Cambrian to the Jurassic
He suffered in them all.

16

How rare to be born a human being!
Wash him off with cedar-bark and milkweed
            send the damned doctors home.
Baby, baby, noble baby
Noble-hearted baby

One hand up, one hand down
"I alone am the honored one"
Birth of the Buddha.
And the whole world-system trembled.
"If that baby really said that,
I'd cut him up and throw him to the dogs!"
said Chao-chou the Zen Master. But
Chipmunks, gray squirrels, and
Golden-mantled ground squirrels
            brought him each a nut.
Truth being the sweetest of flavors.

Girls would have in their arms
A wild gazelle or wild wolf-cubs
And give them their white milk,
            those who had new-born infants home
Breasts still full.
Wearing a spotted fawnskin
            sleeping under trees
            bacchantes, drunk
On wine or truth, what you will,
Meaning: compassion.
Agents: man and beast, beasts
Got the buddha-nature
All but
Coyote.

The Market

                                    (from *Mts. & Rivers*)

heart of the city
            down   town
the country   side

John Muir.   up before dawn
packing pears in the best boxes
      beat out the others — to Market
            the Crystal Palace
on the morning milk-run train.

me, milk bottles by bike
guernsey milk, six percent butterfat
raw and left to rise natural
                  ten cents a quart
slipped on the ice turning
            in to a driveway
      and broke all nine bottles.
when we had cows.
   a feathery hemlock out back
   by manure pile where
            one cow once
   lay with milkfever   transfusions
   & worries until the vet come
we do this still dark in the morning —

1

to town on high thin-wheeled carts.
squat on the boxtop stall.
papayas   banana   slicd fish   grated ginger

fruit for fish, meat for flowers
      french bread for ladle
            steamer, tea giant
      rough glaze earthware
            — for brass shrine bowls.

push through fish
bound pullets lay on their sides
                        wet slab
watch us with glimmering eye
                        slosh water.
a carrot, a lettuce.   a ball of cookd noodle.
      beggars hang by the flower stall
      give them all some

strong women.   dirt from the hills
                  in her nails.

valley thatch houses
    palmgroves for hedges
ricefield and thrasher
      to white rice
        dongs and piastre
to market, the
          changes, how much
          is our change:

2

seventy-five feet hoed rows equals
one hour explaining power steering
equals two big crayfish =
        all the buttermilk you can drink
= twelve pounds cauliflower
= five cartons greek olives = hitch-hiking
        from Ogden Utah to Burns Oregon
= aspirin, iodine, and bandages
= a lay in Naples = beef
= lamp ribs = Patna
          long grain rice, eight pounds
equals two kilogram soybeans = a boxwood
                geisha comb.
equals the whole family at the movies
equals whipping dirty clothes on rocks
  three days, some Indian river
= piecing off beggars two weeks
= bootlace and shoelace
  equals one gross inflatable
  plastic pillows
= a large box of petit-fours, chou-crêmes —
  barley-threshing
  mangoes, apples, custard apples, raspberries
= picking three flats strawberries
= a christmas tree = a taxi ride
carrots, daikon, eggplant, greenpeppers,
oregano white goat cheese
    = a fresh-eyed bonito, live clams.
a swordfish
a salmon
  a handful of silvery smelt in the pocket;
    whiskey in cars. out late after dates.

old folks   eating cake   in secret
breastmilk enough.
                    if the belly be fed —
& wash-down.   hose off aisles
reach under fruitstands
        green gross rack
            meat scum on chop blocks
            bloody butcher concrete floor
        old knives sharpened down to scalpels
            brown wrap paper rolls, stiff
                push-broom back
wet spilld food
            when the market is closed
                the cleanup comes
                    equals

a billygoat pushing through people
stinking and grabbing a cabbage
arrogant, tough
he took it — they let him —
Katmandu — the market

I gave a man seventy paise
in return for a clay pot
of curds
was it worth it?
how can I tell

3

they eat feces
    in the dark
    on stone floors.
one legged animals, hopping cows
    limping dogs   blind cats

crunching garbage in the market
    broken fingers
            cabbage
    head on the ground.

who has young face.
    open pit eyes
between the bullock carts and people
  head pivot with the footsteps
                passing by

dark scrotum spilld on the street
    penis laid by his thigh
        torso
turns with the sun

I came to buy
    a few bananas by the ganges
        while waiting for my wife.

Foxtail Pine

bark smells like pineapple: Jeffries
cones prick your hand: Ponderosa

nobody knows what they are, saying
"needles three to a bunch."

        turpentine tin can hangers
        high lead riggers
"the true fir cone stands straight,
the doug fir cone hangs down."

—wild pigs eat acorns in those hills
cascara cutters
tanbark oak bark gatherers
myrtlewood burl bowl-makers
little cedar dolls,
        baby girl born from the split crotch
           of a plum
          daughter of the moon —

foxtail pine with a
clipped curve-back cluster of tight
      five-needle bunches
  the rought red bark scale
 and jigsaw pieces sloughed off
          scattered on the ground.
—what am I doing saying "foxtail pine"?
those conifers whose home was ice
age tundra, taiga, they of the
      naked sperm

do whitebark pine and white pine seem the same?

```
            a sort of tree
            its leaves are needles
            like a fox's brush
(I call him fox because he looks that way)
         and call this other thing, a
               foxtail pine.
```

Eight Sandbars on the Takano River

```
well water                                              1
cool in
summer
warm in
winter
```

```
white radish root                                      2
a foot long
by its dark
dirt hole
her son.
```

```
cherry blossoms                                        3
the farmer never looks up
the woman serves saké
the tourists are sick or asleep
```

```
gone wild                                              4
strawberry vine
each year more small
sour
mulched by  pine
```

```
white peeled logs                                      5
toppled in sap
scalped branch
            spring
              woods
```

```
dragonfly                                              6
why wet moss
         your black
           stretch-stretch-
wing perch
```

strawberrytime   7
walking the tight-rope
high over the streets
with a hoe and two buckets
              of manure

straight-   8
          backed
swaying stride
twelve-foot
              pine pole
                lightly,
on her head

JACK SPICER

Billy The Kid

I

The radio that told me about the death of Billy The Kid
(And the day, a hot summer day, with birds in the sky)
Let us fake out a frontier — a poem somebody could
hide in with a sheriff's posse after him — a thousand
miles of it if it is necessary for him to go a thousand
miles — a poem with no hard corners, no houses to get
lost in, no underwebbing of customary magic, no New
York Jew salesmen of amethyst pajamas, only a place
where Billy The Kid can hide when he shoots people.

Torture gardens and scenic railways. The radio
That told me about the death of Billy The Kid
The day a hot summer day. The roads dusty in the
summer. The roads going somewhere. You can almost
see where they are going beyond the dark purple of the
horizon. Not even the birds know where they are going.

The poem. In all that distance who could recognize his
face.

II

A sprinkling of gold leaf looking like hell flowers
A flat piece of wrapping paper, already wrinkled, but
wrinkled again by hand, smoothed into shape by an
electric iron
A painting
Which told me about the death of Billy The Kid.
Collage   a binding together
Of the real
Which flat colors
Tell us what heroes
really come by.
No, it is not a collage. Hell flowers
Fall from the hands of heroes
fall from all of our hands
flat
As if we were not ever able quite to include them.

His gun
      does not shoot real bullets
                      his death
Being done is unimportant.
Being done
In those flat colors
Not a collage
A binding together, a
Memory.

III

There was nothing at the edge of the river
But dry grass and cotton candy.
"Alias," I said to him. "Alias,
Somebody there makes us want to drink the river
Somebody wants to thirst us."
"Kid," he said. "No river
Wants to trap men. There ain't no malice in it. Try
To understand."
We stood there by that little river and Alias took
     off his shirt and I took off my shirt
I was never real. Alias was never real.
Or that big cotton tree or the ground.
Or the little river.

IV

            What I mean is
            I
            will tell you about the pain
            It was a long pain
            About as wide as a curtain
            But long
            As the great outdoors.
            Stig-
                 mata
            Three bullet holes in the groin
            One in the head
                     dancing
            Right below the left eyebrow
            What I mean is I
            Will tell you about his
            Pain.

V

Bill The Kid in a field of poplars with just one touch of moon-
                                                              light
His shadow is carefully
                  distinguished from all of their shadows
Delicate
        as perception is
No one will get his gun or obliterate
Their shadows

VI

The gun
A false clue
                  Nothing can kill
Anybody.
Not a poem or a fat penis. Bang,
Bang, bang. A false
Clue.
Nor immortality either (though why immortality should
    occur to me with somebody who was as mortal as
    Billy The Kid or his gun which is now rusted in
    some rubbish heap or shined up properly in some
    New York museum) A
False clue
Nothing
Can kill anybody. Your gun, Billy,
And your fresh
Face.

VII

Grasshoppers swarm through the desert.
Within the desert
There are only grasshoppers.
Lady
Of Guadalupe
Make my sight clear
Make my breath pure
Make my strong arm stronger and my fingers tight.
Lady of Guadalupe, lover
Of many   make
Me avenge
Them.

VIII

Back where poetry is Our Lady
Watches each motion when the players take the cards
From the deck.
The Ten of Diamonds. The Jack of Spades. The Queen
Of Clubs. The King of Hearts. The Ace
God gave us when he put us alive writing poetry for
    unsuspecting people or shooting them with guns.
Our Lady
Stands as a kind of dancing partner for the memory.
Will you dance, Our Lady,
Dead and unexpected?
Billy wants you to dance
Billy
Will shoot the heels off your shoes if you don't dance
Billy
Being dead also   wants
Fun.

IX

So the heart breaks
Into small shadows
Almost so random
They are meaningless
Like a diamond
Has at the center of it a diamond
Or a rock
Rock.
Being afraid
Love asks its bare question —
I can no more remember
What brought me here
Than bone answers bone in the arm
Or shadow sees shadow —
Deathward we ride in the boat
Like someone canoeing
In a small lake
Where at either end
There are nothing but pine-branches —
Deathward we ride in the boat
Broken-hearted or broken-bodied
The choice is real. The diamond. I
Ask it.

X

Billy The Kid
I love you
Billy The Kid
I back anything you say
And there was the desert
And the mouth of the river
Billy The Kid
(In spite of your death notices)
There is honey in the groin
Billy

The Book of Percival

1

Fool —
Killer lurks between the branches of every tree
Bird-language.
Fooled by nature, I
Accepted the quest gracefully
Played the fool. Fool —
Killer in the branches waiting.
Left home. Fool-killer left home too. Followed me.
Fool —
Killer thinks that just before the moment I will find the
    grail he will catch me. Poor
Little boy in the forest
Dancing.

2

Even the forest felt deserted when he left it. What nonsense!
The enormous trees. The lakes with carp in them. The wolves
    and badgers. They
Should feel deserted for a punk kid who has left them?
Even the forest felt deserted. There were no leaves dropping
    or sounds anybody could hear.
The wind met resistance but no noise, the sky
Could not be heard through the water.
Percival
Fool, like badger, pinetree, broken water,
Gone.

3

"Ship of fools," the wise man said to me.
"I used to work in Chicago in a department store," I said
    to the wise man never knowing that there would be a ship
Whose tiny sails, grail bearing
Would have to support me
All the loves of my life
Each impossible choice I had been making. Wave
Upon wave.
"Fool," I could hear them shouting for we were becalmed
    in some impossible harbor
The grail and me
And in impossible armor
The spooks that bent the ship
Forwards and backwards.

4

If someone doesn't fight me I'll have to wear this armor
All of my life. I look like the Tin Woodsman in the Oz Books.
Rusted beyond recognition.
I am, sir, a knight. Puzzled
By the way things go toward me and in back of me. And
                                                        finally
    into my mouth and head and red blood
O, damn these things that try to maim me
This armor
Fooled
Alive in its
Self.

5

The hermit said dance and I danced
I was always meeting hermits on the road
Who said what I was to do and I did it or got angry and didn't
Knowing always what was not expected of me.
She electrocuted herself with her own bathwater
I pulled the plug
And there was darkness (the Hermit said)
Deeper than any hallow.

6

It was not searching the grail or finding it that prompted me
It was the playing the fool (Fool-killer along at my back
Playing the fool.)
I knew that the cup or the dish or the knights I fought didn't
    have anything to do with it
Fool-killer and I were fishing in the same ocean
"And at the end of whose line?" I asked him once when I
    met him in my shadow.
"You ask the wrong questions" and at that my shadow jumped
    up and beat itself against a rock, "or rather the wrong
    questions to the wrong person"
At the end of whose line
I now lie
Hanging.

7

No visible means of support
The Grail hung there like june-berries in October or
                                    something
    I had felt and forgotten.
This was a palace and an ocean I was in
A ship that cast its water on the tide
A grail, a real grail. Snark-hungry.
The Grail hung there with the seagulls circling round it and
                                    the
    pain of my existence soothed
"Fool," they sang in voices more like angels watching
"Fool."

The Book of Merlin

1

"Go to jail. Go directly to jail. Do not pass Go. Do
    not collect $200.00."
The naked sound of a body sounds like a trumpet through all
    this horseshit.
You do not go to jail. You stay there unmoved at what any
    physical or metaphysical policemen do.
You behave like Gandhi. Your

Magic will be better than their magic. You await that time
   with hunger.
Strike
Against the real things. The colonial Hengest and Horsa
The invasion of Britain was an invasion of the spirit.

2

Wohin auf das Auge blicket
Moor und Heide rings herum
Vogelsang uns nicht erquicket
Eichen stehen kahl und krumm.
Lost in the peril of their own adventure
Grail-searchers im Koncentrationslage
A Jew stole the grail the first time
And a jew died into it
That is the history of Britain.
The politics of the world of spooks is as random as that of
   a Mesopotamian kingdom
Merlin (who saw two ways at the least of the river, the bed
   of the river.) Maer-
Chen ausgeschlossen.

3

The tower he built himself
From some kind of shell that came from his hide
He pretended that he was a radio station and listened to
   grail-music all day and all night every day and every night.
Shut up there by a treachery that was not quite his own (he
   could not remember whose treachery it was) he predicted
                                                        the
   future of Britain.
The land is hollow, he said, it consists of caves and holes so
   immense that eagles or nightingales could not fly in them
Love,
The Grail, he said,
No matter what happened.

4

Otherwise everything was brilliant
Flags loose in the wind. A tournament
For live people. Disengagement as from the throat to the
   loin or the sand to the ocean.

The flags
Of another country.
Flags hover in the breeze
Mary Baker Eddy alone in her attempt
To slake Thursdays. Sereda,
Oh, how chill the hill
Is with the snow on it
What a semblance of
Flags.

5

Then the thought of Merlin became more than imprisoned
                                                Merlin
A jail-castle
Was built on these grounds.
Sacco and Vanzetti and Lion-Hearted Richard and Dillinger
                                              who
   somehow almost lost the Grail. Political prisoners
Political prisoners. Willing to rise from their graves.
"The enemy is in your own country," he wrote that when
                                          Gawain
   and Percival and almost everybody else was stumbling
                                          around
   after phantoms
There was a Grail but he did not know that
Jailed.

6

That's it Clyde, better hit the road farewell
That's it Clyde better hit the road
You're not a frog you're a horny toad. Goodbye, farewell,
                                          adios.
The beach reaching its ultimate instant. A path over the sand.
And the toadfrog growing enormous in the shadow of
                                        fogged-in
   waters. The Lady of the Lakes. Monstrous.
This is not the end because like a distant bullet
A ship comes up. I don't see anybody on it. I am Merlin
   imprisoned in a branch of the Grail Castle.

7

"Heimat du bist wieder mein"
Heinmat. Heimat ohne Ferne
You are called to the phone.
You are called to the phone to predict what will happen to
    Britain. The great silver towers she gave you. What you
    are in among
You are called to predict the exact island that your ancestors
    came from
Carefully now will there be a Grail or a Bomb which tears
    the heart out of things?
I say there will be no fruit in Britain for seven years unless
    something happens.

NANCY SULLIVAN

The History of the World as Pictures

The poem about the history of the world
As pictures will be in pieces like the history
Of that world and like those pictures
Each separate upon a wall in separate places.
Lined up they may be the meaning of the world
Or they may be the only world with meaning.

1. *Prehistoric Cave Painting of a Bison*

Perhaps it was being inside of something
That caused them to render it outside
By scrawling great beasts in screams
Of rust and black over the walls of the cave.
Perhaps it was the visitation of an idea,
An event so powerful
As to turn them into men.

The bison is taut inside the readiness
Of its fur. It has no dimensions
Because it is already huge. Miniature
Black men resembling the matches
No one yet knows about cast needles
At the beast that is large as Africa.
What it must have been like to scramble
In out of a rain to discover not only
The sensation of dryness, but a place
That had been visited by a god.

2. *Design on a Greek Amphora: Apollo on a Winged Tripod*
(ca. 490 B.C.)

The very opposite of the cave with its bison
Because the design is on the outside here and the hollow in-
side,
But the terra cotta colors and the black vase
Loop it to that earlier gallery
As an arrow is fulfilled in its prey.

Apollo carries his arrows at his shoulder
As he sits plucking a lyre on the curved
Surface of the vase. He is in love.
Cupid has shot his heart with fire
For Daphne, a woodsy girl,
That eternal camper, later his laurel.
Why should the god of music and poetry
Seek such a woman? Not to attain
Is the grasping of poetry and music its name.
Because a woman in her tree is better loved
Than bison or boar. Sing, Apollo,
From your tripod above the sturdy wings of Pegasus.

> *'I sing a woman into bed*
> *Her hair my pillow*
> *Her arms my cage.*
> *I sing us married or dead*
> *For as accounted by the sage*
> *Love is endless when wed.*
> *Now only the leaves reckon*
> *Where my love has fled.'*

3. *Buddha Expounding the Doctrine to Yasas, the First Lay Member of the Buddhist Community* (5th century)

This too was painted on a rock,
On a pillar in a temple in India.
It pictures what the beginnings were like:
A man listening to his god in a garden of goodness.
The flowers are everywhere. What was Buddha
Offering to Yasas in that gouged-out hand?
Possibly a lotus. Surely not an apple.
Everything's serene. Two men talk.
Their voices mingle: Yasas in the white
Face and garment of the layman and Buddha,
Big and brown. It is happy.

The roundness of the pillar is the wholeness of the doctrine,
And the pillar itself like the detachment of holy men
Given to separate ways in the temples of their gods.

4. *A Triptych* by Van Eyck (ca. 1430)

There are three sections and the middle one
Is larger than its sides. Christ is dead
In the center. It looks like this.

Left: Sprung late from his mother's womb,
             John the Baptist in the ombres of a hair skin
             Lopes the desert, the Neanderthal of saints,
             Crying us all into water and the tomb.

Center: It is Christ risen in a shower of light
             Stunning as gaiety. A banner whirled
             Above a god with a man's skin. Everything is white
             As if to strain the dirty reaches of the world
             Into which he came. Observe the sight
             Of a god risen on a lacquered board
             Rushing headlong to his heaven to record
             The sorrows of this place. Look to the right.

Right: How it stank in that tomb.
             Inside the immaculate painting of that fierce na-
                                                           tivity
             The pigment people stare into the miracle, rags to
                                                            noses.

             Odor of Lazarus in the womb.

5. *Spring in Chiang-nan* by Wen Cheng-Ming (1547)

There is writing at the top, a criticism
Or perhaps a poem done in a calligraphy
More intricate than the branches on the trees,
And speaking more clearly than the singular boatsman
Brushed on the long scroll with the skeleton of a feather.

Words and trees and one man in a boat.

The words, pictures themselves, explain what
The scene does not. I do not know what they mean,
But they must be a lesson telling things
That the old academician could not trust to the landscape.

It is spring in Chiang-nan. The trees tell it.
And the man, a stem in his half-moon of a boat,
Sits as though aware of the marvelous changes.
The picture is as still as the idea of China
Wrapped tight in the heavy kimono of its past.
But the colors are as soft as the beginnings of something.
The picture hangs long and narrow, as its theme does not.

6. *Las Meniñas* by Velázquez (1656)

The dwarfs dominate, at least theatrically.
The little princess near the center, illuminated
In her petulant reluctance to pose for yet
Another portrait illustrates an idea of order,
Not the governing parents, the mother and the father,
Philip IV and Mariana of Austria, mere reflections
In the distant mirror in the far places of the paint.
The commissioned artist accepts a royal order
Although he alone governs this pigment territory
Where dwarfs rule and ugliness flowers to virtue.

We look into the picture to watch a situation,
Into a tall room in the Alcázar hung with copies of Rubens.
The Infanta Doña Margarita doesn't want to pose.
She is now five years old and has had enough of paint.
But forces are at work here: the perspective
That holds the room together and holds the Rubens
On to the painted walls. There are triangles
Of people whose duties are enormous, eleven in all.
Velázquez must paint, the ladies-in-waiting,
Las meniñas, must cajole and pass some chocolate
To the princess. The king and queen must
Be that, but here without a single power.
The man going up the steps must go up them.
In the right hand corner, the dwarf Nicolasito
Is stepping on the dog. Another, Maribarbola,
Stares out of her massive face to tell a royal story.

Her brief finery is the somber opposite of little
Margarita's bright and golden style. She rules
No empire nor ever will, but here she dominates the mind.
Beauty, a dog, and this wizened female
So ugly, so sad, so sufficient to this scene
As to make you wonder at the governments of men.
How detached the painter's glance now that he has
Put everyone in his place and upset the candor of Spain.

7. *Portrait of Mrs. Siddons* by Gainsborough (ca. 1785)

In a monumental hat above a swirl of blue clothes
The actress, Mrs. Siddons, assumes a rigid pose.
The furs drape to languor, but the woman is precise.
Once as his Lady, she thrust a bloody dagger through Mac-
beth's nice,

Reckless life to act to triumph the vanity of human wishes.
It sold out. Fame rose above the echo of kisses
Above the cheer of dapper London, and on the Gainsborough's
brush.

She sits so in a damask chair in the hush
Of the bursting painting. Prime ministers might borrow
That face, Lord Nelson the nose. A conquered sorrow
In those black eyes is minimized by the close of the lips,
Unspeaking but full. No part of paint on part drips
Awkwardly. Surely through him her hair is her own.
A precise century dwindles and brings them to that.
Reason, reason is this your lady's face or that her hat?

8. *La Gare Saint-Lazare* by Claude Monet (1877)

It is the picture of a thing in a place,
Not an apple or a pear in a bowl,
But of a train resting in its station
Surrounded by mist, smoke, vapor, and paint.

A few people stare down an opposite track
To focus a train coming from some point
Outside the picture. The only train important
To them is the one that will take them somewhere.

But with Monet, his train is stationary
In the station, going nowhere but here
Into its mechanical cathedral. What a revolution
Is involved in the turning of those intricate wheels

Into art. The hush of the waiting is there
As well as the light dappled with soot
And the tracks bearing the monumental weight
Of transportation transfixed in the mist of Paris.

9. *Night Fishing at Antibes* by Picasso (1939)

What is in it? First there is always that.
Two men spear fish by the light of abstract lanterns.
One has on a striped jersey, and with a four-pronged spear
Pierces a sole. At the right, near the sea wall,
Two girls stand watching. One has a bicycle
And is eating a double ice cream cone.
Or is it double? For what is single here?

How anxious that second fisherman
With his grey nose almost in the water.
His eye is in his nose.
The girl with the ice cream rests on her two fin feet.
One of the two fish has an eyebrow.
Inside the moon a spring spirals light down
Into the conventional waters. Lanterns
Are cut in corners. Two towers of the town
Surmount the rocky shore to the left,
At the bottom, a crab stares out.
Squares are circles and vice versa.
How what is painted is the history here.
The design, the shape of this interlude,
Is its meaning decorated in the colors
Of a nocturne, in green, blue, purple, and light.
Brought to completion a month before World War again be-
                                                        gan,

The painting reminds me of why that war was ended:
So that men may fish and ladies dawdle
In the serene quiet of revolutionary places.

10. *Number I* by Jackson Pollock (1948)

No name but a number.
Trickles and valleys of paint
Devise this maze
Into a game of Monopoly
Without any bank. Into
A linoleum on the floor
In a dream. Into
Murals inside of the mind.
No similes here. Nothing
But paint. Such purity
Taxes the poem that speaks
Still of something in a place
Or at a time.
How to realize his question
Let alone his answer?

ROBERT SWARD

Uncle Dog: The Poet at 9

I did not want to be old Mr.
Garbage man, but uncle dog
Who rode sitting beside him.

Uncle dog had always looked
To me to be truck-strong
Wise-eyed, a cur-like Ford

Of a dog. I did not want
To be Mr. Garbage man because
All he had was cans to do.

Uncle dog sat there me-beside-him
Emptying nothing. Barely even
Looking from garbage side to side:

Like rich people in the backseats
Of chauffeur-cars, only shaggy
In an unwagging tall-scrawny way.

Uncle dog belonged any just where
He sat, but old Mr. Garbage man
Had to stop at everysingle can.

I thought. I did not want to be Mr.
Everybody calls them that first.
A dog is said, Dog! Or by name.

I would rather be called Rover
Than Mr. And sit like a tough
Smart mongrel beside a garbage man.

Uncle dog always went to places
Unconcerned, without no hurry.
Independent like some leashless

Toot. Honorable among Scavenger
Can-picking dogs. And with a bitch
At every other can. And meat:

His for the barking. Oh, I wanted
To be uncle dog — sharp, high fox-
Eared, cur-Ford truck-faced

With his pick of the bones.
A doing, truckman's dog
And not a simple child-dog

Nor friend to man, but an uncle
Traveling, and to himself —
And a bitch at every second can.

What It Was

What it was, was this: the stars
Had died for the night,
               and shone;
And God, God also shone,
Up, straight up, at the very
Top of the sky.
              The street
Was one of the better suburbs
Of the night, and was a leaf,
Or the color of one in the
Moonlit dark.
           She, my mother,
Went to the window; it was
As late as night could be
To her.
        She looked at the wind,
Still, the wind,
       . . . never having blown.
And in the morning, now, of sleep
The stars, the moon and God
               began
Once more, away,
          into the sky.
—And she, my mother, slept . . .
In her window, in her sky.

Kissing the Dancer

For Diane, who dances

Song is not singing,
        the snow

Dance is dancing,
    my love

On my knees, with voice
    I kiss her knees

And dance; my words are song,
        for her

I dance; I give up my words,
        learn wings instead

We fly like trees
    when they fly

To the moon, which
    on occasion

They do; there, there are
    some now

The clouds opening, as you, as we
        are there

                    Come in!

I love you, kiss your knees
    with words,

Enter you, your eyes
    your lips, like

                    Lover

Of us all,

        words sweet words,
            learn wings instead.

Terminal Theater

We fight. I am clubbed from behind. They pin me
And take turns, forearm feet fists to face
Forefinger and thumb opening eyelids, press
Graze with the nail, touch with the palps
Squash, the Jew's eyes seeing eye, sand
Sprinkle, candlewax, cigarette ash,
Cigar smoke. It is necessary to see this
Against a backdrop of ____
For four miles west of it one can smell
The lake; further, it being July, the water
Tastes of chlorine stale fish breath snail-dew
Sharks

Even at nine or ten o'clock, the buildings
Give off an unexpected heat; it has rained
This day, and the night before. I have spent them
At the movies, watching Bud Abbott and Lou Costello
Weary stark flat slapstick, but offering conditions
Questions, occasions for grieved analyses.
Do you not laugh, do you not cry?
What is real? cried the oyster, glob of spit
In a pane of glass.

There is No Reason Why Not to Look at Death

There is no reason why not to look at death.
A good poem, also, is also death-contained.
I once pulled out all the business feathers
Of a crow; he became better: godcomplete: black.

Nothing makes barely looking haste to put away
The dead: except the "dead" involved: in business.
The earth, the seasons, the poets, before they become
Poets, make no haste to put away the dead. Nor God

The Lord giveth, and He taketh away — by and large
Slowly. And without haste. Crow-bombs are here
Not my concern, nor ordinary bombs. But plain decay
(The proper autumnal process subsequent to life).

Emphasis need not be placed upon the soul. My point
Involves the leaf (as an example), and the unplumaged
Crow. Nor is my point one with flesh, and no blood . . .
But one of death. I am fond of death — and/or

The self-contained. This poem may not be said to be
About souls. But of things. Feathers and leaves.
Leafless trees and the featherless bodies of crows.
Finally, let us say, I have been asked to write simply.

Mothers-in-Law

Married twice now, I've had two
Mothers-in-law. One visited us
And required, upon departure,
The services of three gentlemen
        with shoehorns
To get her back into her large black
Studebaker.

        The other, Momma-law the Present,
Is (with the exclusion neither
        of that other,
            my wives
        nor the fathers-in-law
            of either marriage),
that Studebaker.

DIANE WAKOSKI

Justice Is Reason Enough

He, who once was my brother, is dead by his own hand.
Even now, years later, I see his thin form lying on the sand,

where the sheltered sea washes against those cliffs
he chose to die from. Mother took me back there every day
    for
over a year and asked me, in her whining way, why it had to
    happen

over and over again—until I wanted
never to hear of David any more. How
could I tell her of his dream about the gull beating its wings
effortlessly together until they drew blood?

Would it explain anything, and how can I tell
anyone here about that great form and its beating wings. How
    it
swoops down and covers me, and the dark tension leaves

me with blood on my mouth and thighs. But it was that dream,
you must know, that brought my tight, sullen little

brother to my room that night and pushed his whole taut body
right over mine until I yielded, and together we yielded to the
    dark tension.
Over a thousand passing years, I will never forget
him, who was my brother, who is dead. Mother asked me why
every day for a year; and I told her justice. Justice is
reason enough for anything ugly. It balances the beauty in the
    world.

Poem to the Man on My Fire Escape

Dark brain,
the large sponge coral,
resting in your head,
naked women flash through,
moving,

registering in the cave your fantasies—
the jewel-chest in which you plunge your arms up to the
                                                        elbows
while rocks and clasps and pins gouge and graze your skin;
your bleeding
and bliss from the torn flesh.
I do not know what you were doing
or wanting to do,
climbing up the wall,
slipping on to the fire escape,
standing at the window
watching me; nor could I stop to think or
investigate. Screaming
lets it all out. Pushes your body off my eyes,
topples it off—a box of soap from the ledge—
and how or where you came from
I don't care: don't want to know.

Voyeur,
how limited your investigations become. How far
away from satisfaction.
You want to know what's inside a woman—
underneath her clothing;
you want to know more than she wants to tell?
you want to know how she is joined together,
how she bleeds,
how she creeps in your past?

You are looking in the wrong window; and I hope
you were frightened by what you saw,
I hope you know some women are dead
from the head down.
I hope you know what death on the outside
looks like
now.
I hope you saw it and were scared.
I hope you were warned that death runs all the way through.
I hope you will never forget
Fear holds us all in the palm of his hand.
The fingers fall off one by one.
The hand paralyzes and drops.
Where are we when the hand drops?
Large sponge coral

sitting on top your head
dries
solidifies
is crushed finally as the earth settles
and buries us all.

Coins and Coffins Under My Bed

Three children dancing around an orange tree,
not holding hands because the tree is too round and full,
and there are only three of them:
The spiders, making their webs in the orange tree talk to the
  children.
    Do you want silver coins?
    Do you want silver cups?
    Do you remember our names?
they ask.
One little boy answers.
    I want silver rings.
    I want silver keys.
    I remember my own name. It is John.
But the spiders are making their webs larger and larger.
A yellow spider says:
    Do you hear us spinning?
    The sound
    is so loud it makes our legs vibrate.
    Do you know that David is dead
    and buried
    under this tree?
    Do you want silver coins
    to buy death away?
    Do you want silver cups to drink at your wedding?
    We spin our webs to spell our names,
    your names,
    dark names.

Three children dancing around an orange tree.
They are heavy with childhood.
    We want silver rings to link us together
    and silver keys to unlock your webs,
    and we all know our names.
    They are John.

Quietly, under the orange tree, David, who is dead and buried,
settles down.
The spiders walk over the earth like tight-rope walkers
playing above the crowd,
and I forget the coffin under my bed.

Tell me, spiders,
what I want to hear—why those children, all three of them,
sing around the tree?
They are heavy with rings,
Their bodies are made of bells,
and tell me,
what are your names, spiders?
I will write your names on coins
and throw them in the coffin under my bed.
Tell me why my hands are empty of rings yet
heaviest of all,
and my body,
like a bell, doesn't ring.
I have thousands of keys,
keys on the doorstep, in my ears,
under my pillow, in my clock,
rooms full of keys,
chests full, iron crates full.
They unlock everything,
and I hate them.
Three children around an orange tree
who know the answers to everything;
spiders who know more.
Do you see the round orange tree with three children dancing
            around it?

I am trying to believe I haven't seen, glinting through the
                                        leaves,
the hanged man,
caught by his key ring—
hanged by the key,
and the sun catching it, as he swings.

Apparitions Are Not Singular Occurrences

When I rode the zebra past your door,
wearing nothing but my diamonds, I expected to hear bells
and see your face behind the thin curtains.
But instead I saw you, a bird, wearing the mask of a bird,

with all the curtains drawn, the lights blazing,
and death drinking cocktails with you.
In your thin hand, like the claw of a bird, because you are a
                                                            bird,
the drink reflected the light from my diamonds, passing by.

Your bird's foot, like thin black threads of bone or metal
                                                          staples,
has the resistance necessary to keep death at a pleasant dis-
                                                            tance,
drinking his Scotch and enjoying your company,
as he seldom has a chance; the zebra hide against my bare legs
is warm. The diamonds now warm on my neck,
on my fingers,
my feet,
my ears.
How death looks at them
and my body
and the old man desires them all.

I rode by your window, hoping you would see me and want me
not knowing you already had a guest.
The diamonds I put on for you,
the clothes I took off;
and my zebra—did you see his eyes just slightly narrow
as we came by?
Not knowing you would wear your bird-mask,
I let you see my face.
Not knowing death would be there,
I rode by.
And death and I see each other now so often,
I have even thought of becoming a trapeze artist so that I
                                                          might
swing on the bar away from him—so far up he'd never reach
                                                            me
but instead I see him more and more with all my friends,
drinking, talking,
and always his elderly eyes are watching me.
And you, watching me ride by on my zebra and dressed only in
    my diamonds, were my one last hope,
but even you, wearing the mask of a bird, invited him to have
                                                        a drink
and left the curtains drawn for him,
sharing something which you had no right to share.

Six of Cups

If you spin me around until I'm so dizzy
I'm a blue top,
there is no reason to believe I will have lost my sense
of direction when I stop.
I simply will not have the heart to go on.

POEM FOR A CARD

Pretend means something different every time.
The two children gathering flowers
in the high-walled garden,
filling their cups with blossoms,
must see that there is a star,
white-hot, as it fell from the sky, burning its way down
into the flower cup,
on top of each receptacle,
but they do not seem to be aware that it changes the contents
in any way.
They hand each other the cups;
perhaps they touch the stars floating on top
as if they were hot cookies
or pieces of gingerbread fresh from the oven.
The cups are toys that they hand one another for examination
and sampling — proud of ownership,
proud of each pretty star.
If I put my hand on one of their stars,
my hand would disintegrate into a lump of carbon in a minute,
without even a chance for me to reflect and draw back.
I have to keep my hand away from that ten-thousand degree
                                                    star.

But they still hand each other the cups,
smiling and bowing,
presenting for love
something I do not need them to tell me the value of.
They could as well hand me the cup
with a coral snake inside
curled up like a carved face.

POEM AFTER THE CARD

Do not tell me that when I am sterile I should quit trying to
                                                    produce.
If you were once jealous because I seemed to have so much,
you are now jealous that I have so little. What is it?

Do you want to own me?
Do you want both my former fullness and now my present
emptiness?
Do you want to take my memories and make them your
memories?
Do you want to take my hand, cut it off, and say it is your
hand?
Don't you know I brought the desert with me
and that you can't live in it?
I still have those three oranges I bought at the roadside stand.
I know those birds are going to fly out of them, sure as any-
thing—
and you know it too.
So what are you hanging around for?
You want me to give you an orange?

You know that bird's going to be in it.
You just don't seem to know when to stop.
You'll die in this desert.
It's all the same to me, but don't you care?
I have my own reasons for being here,
but by now you should know they're crazy ones.
Do you really think you'll stick around till I die,
like some old man hanging around an old miser till he dies,
hoping to find out where he's hiding his gold?
Man, you're going to be disappointed.
When you find my cache, it's just going to be sticks.
Bare sticks,
And those oranges — by now they don't even have birds in
them.

Don't you understand? I have nothing.
Can't you leave me alone to die in my own cactus,
my own sun, my own thirst?
You can't even stand that I have that, can you?
Stop walking on my shadow. You'll wear it out.
If you must be on me all the time, at least
put only your shadow
not your body
on my shadow. The weight is almost unbearable.

POEM ON THE CARD

We almost made it with our stars and fruit, didn't we?
Pretending we could get away from the truth even for a
minute.
Pretending we could talk about objects rather than events,

as if objects were even real,
as if there were such a thing as being concrete.
I guess we knew we'd never make it,
all along.
I guess being little and playing with cups heaped with flowers
                                                                 and
stars is what we wished our past were.
I guess having that orange with a bird in it really sounded
more like what we wanted than having an orange with juice
                                                              in it.
I guess we want to think that being honest is saying the truth
so that it sounds like we understand it.
I guess we want to give everything grace,
make everything clean.
I guess we want the illusion of what we want more
than what we want
because we think we are wise and know
it's harder to destroy an illusion
than what the illusion stands for:
the star, burning the flowers in those gold cups,
held and exchanged by the children.

The Empress

She took the bone from her arm.
This music frenzied the wild gazelles
and the milk pigs running
under the high arches of her feet
and past her heavy black-budded breasts.
Taking this instrument
to
file
the words
in her
shawl, spilling
out in dis-
order/ honing each
syllable
till the screeching
became a har-
mony, till the buzz
became small on the smooth edge
of a word,

she set herself
a simple task. But the music in her own
armbone was so loud
she set the thicket
within her
running. Arm bone. Arm bone. Arm bone.
The arm bone sings. The arm bone sings.
And the gazelle leap under her armpits.
The small pigs snuffle and run past
lips. The birds caw, caw.
What noise,
as she only makes
a word.
Commotion for
every syllable.

THEODORE WEISS

The Fire at Alexandria

Imagine it, a Sophocles complete,
the lost epic of Homer, including no doubt
his notes, his journals, and his observations
on blindness. But what occupies me most,
with the greatest hurt of grandeur, are those
magnificent authors, kept in scholarly rows,
whose names we have no passing record of:
scrolls unrolling Aphrodite like Cleopatra
bundled in a rug, the spoils of love.

Crated masterpieces on the wharf,
and never opened, somehow started first.
And then, as though by imitation, the library
took. One book seemed to inspire another,
to remind it of the flame enclosed
within its papyrus like a drowsy torch.
The fire, roused perhaps by what it read,
its reedy song, raged Dionysian, a band
of Corybantes, down the halls now headlong.

The scribes, despite the volumes wept
unable to douse the witty conflagration —
spicy too as Sappho, coiling, melted
with her girls: the Nile no less, reflecting,
burned — saw splendor fled, a day consummate
in twilit ardencies. Troy at its climax
(towers finally topless) could not have been
more awesome, not though the aromatic house
of Priam mortised the passionate moment.

Now whenever I look into a flame,
I try to catch a single countenance:
Cleopatra, winking out from every joint;
Tiresias eye to eye; a magnitude, long lost,
restored to the sky and the stars he once
struck unsuspected parts of into words.

Fire, and I see them resurrected,
madly crackling perfect birds, the world
lit up as by a golden school, the flashings
of the fathoms of set eyes.

The Dance Called David

How could I know
how beyond this love
which held me to him and
by its very hold blinded me?

Hours of many days
we walked, past the reputable,
through scenes, people, past
street-names and corners,
                              deep
through poverty with its charming
air of things half-dropping off
into oblivion.
                    Words from me,
pointings to bits of color
or surprise longing
urged upon me,
                    recalled him
as those that burned in hell
steadied their flames to answer
one earthbound.
                    Like something
mattered out of air, a smile —
did it reflect the morning
songs that once enlightened? —
would flicker, then go out.

How could I know,
I who loved him, viewed
the world around us as phrases
visible of his taut unmoving lips,
a music incredible, illuminated
as a battered hurdygurdy
by the love he simply woke,

how could I know
how right I was: windows
strewn behind us, swirling
traffic, parks bouqueting lovers,
children burst from school,
all movements in the meaning
mysteriously clear he was for me.

Only now, years after
his death, do I know what
terror I called friend, what
wrestlings I walked beside, what
anguish — dance of madness, gaiety —
he adorned,
            the total city
with its grey wizen streets,
each ash-pale puddle, its thin
furtive faces, and the tiniest
broken straw looked after.

Only now I see
how much he deserved —
if love must deserve — whatever
love I could attain, and more,
speechless, ignorant as a child.

These years between, now
that he is with what we are not,
time and the multiple wild fears
have helped me recognize what
first must have frightened me
away.
        Time that cut us
off sharper than space can
holds out again generous hands
as he, the harmonious blacksmith,
leads me through the depths unrolling, these scarred years that are
journeying and pity, of myself.

An Egyptian Passage

Beside me she sat, hand hooked and hovering, nose sharp under black-lacquered hair,
and body, skinny, curving under a brownish big
thick book.
                    I glanced past her hand to pages
she checked; there, beside strange symbols,
curious hawk-beaked little birds at attention,
gawky beasts, stiff plants, some more than strange,
set next to words which I, despite the rail-
yard shuttling shadows and the battering light
at the end of tunnels, gradually made out
as items in a German-Egyptian lexicon.

Then red- and black-brick tenements; billboards;
excavations; three boys with mattocks, digging
by a squat, half-finished, bushy hut;
tumbled-together shacks, drifting in the way
of winter; near the bank, its wharf rotted
through in several places, a gutted house
like something done by fire, slowly floating
(so it seemed) out on the river; smoke stacks;

and the dumps, one burning in three spots,
lurid like old passion among heavy piled-
up boxes and black banged-in pots, and birds
floating above like ashes.
                                Birds too
on the Hudson: ducks in strict formation,
gulls — like lungs — working their great wings
or perched like dirty, jagged lumps of ice
on the ice caking the shoreward waters,
till another dump, a vast flattened white,
for the train's racing flapped into the air.

And all fashion of ice, from shoots in spray
to zigzag rows, waves at their climbing's apex
trapped, frizzled work, to tesselation.

Along the shore a shaggy red-brown brush,
so thick partridges must be crouching in it,
as in the Hudson, under an icy lid,
a brood of clouds. And heavy-headed, long,
thin, flaggy things like the stuff we think of
growing beside the Nile.

The trees bare,
through them the early light already deepened,
purpling. And rocks rode through, by speed
light as the distant hills, the clouds, crumbling,
fitful, round them.

Like the little crate-
white houses across the river, quiet enough,
but indoors, I knew, no bush for its morning
birds busier.

Still her eyes never left
the ibises that fluttered under her fingers.
Deeper and deeper she went, like the sun
unfolding fields, forsaken spots, and towns,
the dirty sharp details of, always more
and always clearer — like the river itself,
the roads agog with golden high-legged going,
song-sparrows swept from their nests, their wings
praising the sun — the steeples, broken houses
and smoky streets, kids dashing in and out
of hide-and-seek, the billowy wash on lines.

And I thought of sitting on a polar star
a million miles away, looking down at this earth
surrounded by its tiny nimbus of a day.
And I saw the days — each hour a speck, twelve
motes combined — like waves like sparks like bushes
burning, lined up one by one, for its intricate
strokes each a kind of word.

"Poughkeepsie,"
the conductor said as he took her ticket
from the seat. Several times he tapped her
on the shoulder before she looked up, fumbled
for her coat and bag, and lurched out.

Out of Your Hands

(on receiving W. C. Williams' Theocritus, June 5, 1953)

Though you regret it,
out of your hands it must go,
out of your hands still warm on it,
loving with the best love, a bare mind,
undaunted, inside the hands, casting
the familiar line, a child fished,

a poem — the issue
life: this manuscript your note
calls "a unique copy" you would hate
to lose. How unique only those who try
to make as well, having staked out
their pleasurable awareness

in the clearing
of your verse, can know. June
now, the first sultry day, swept in,
one swollen glare, on the back of last
night's thundrous rain, the morning
looking as though its masons

just broke off.
And you, returning whence you
came, closer daily, have mailed us
your translation of Theocritus: Idyl I
after your local hundreds, ground
from which this new-fangled

garden of America
you still prune, hard as it is
to believe, has sprung. You return
(for all the times between, Rutherford
and Alexandria not so far apart)
as though in age you know

that hungering again,
the virgin green — this a field
where crops nourish crops — growing
through practised hands. No yokel you
to luten notes, whatever disguise,
and of the few equipt to face

Priapus equally
with old Chronos, out of Libya
or wherever, engrossed, hang-doggedly,
and grazing in your songs. You alone,
shepherd of cool shades, puffball
flocks and winds, sleep-dipt

under squat weeds,
twig and runty leaf, refining
silence, manage among shrill horns,

enjoying naked noon, to keep the music
going, freshets as of a deep-down
source, that Pan, chase-worn,

exasperation only
reedy at his nostrils, can find
a cove where revelry, love and folly
know some ease. Despite your vigilance
the gifts come to you hardly goat,
shag-white, or firstling kid,

a delicate fleshed
for being eaten before its milk
begins, you feed on bramble-berries,
make iron, refuse, yield. This no less,
your hands not letting go except it,
naming bless, must slip away.

Your poems will
stay — your voice alive in them,
compelling as odors from a summerday —
worked like the cup, dipt in the spring
of the seasons, given Thyrsis for his
song, *The Afflictions of Daphnis*.

Your poems, passed
through whatever hands, understanding or not, put to lips, whatever their taste, what pots they drink,
will keep the marking of your clean-
edged knife. A seasoned wine

poured in, sly winds,
involved in the curving ivy,
carved, flickering through yellow
flowers, flaunt their airs: April, May,
frisky months again, leading groves
in frolic; alewives too, tails

flashing in this sea-
dark surge; and bees, drunk as
in a mazy rose — all garlanding a girl,
in turn a mazy rose. Summers, those
long moons ago sunk in the grass,
mornings, bulls, and bells

well up, a ritual,
for her, fairer than the gods
might dream, your mind's familiar.
Beside this stir a furrowed fisherman
on a furrowed rock, mending nets,
splicing knots, repairing

tangled lines, and
lending skill to rods and pipes
that these release their wood's chief
ingrained spell. One pair of hands
to do all things, strike human
moods from time, the harmony

past need that makes
the need the more. Set to cast
now, the thousandth time — his whole
heart in it — the mighty net. And near
the veteran, straddling the ruddy
vineyard wall, indifferent

to grape-roused foxes,
winter, and the Foe, greedily
fixed at his foot, a boy, plaiting
star-flower stalks around short reeds
for a pet-cricket cage in intent,
wise and thoughtless joy.

House of Fire

I

To burn is surely bad, to be
possessed by greed or lust or anger . . .

Down the pathway pebbles clatter
into brush more ashen than the rocks
that mount the cliff; beyond it windows,
flaring, flood the light through vines,
entangled with the thudding wind,
as litter, crackled underfoot, puffs
up the dust of countless little deaths.

And yet in the abandoned field
below, through this intense decaying
and its acrid breath, a freshness wells
as if an April, some forgotten day of,
starting up out of the time's debris,
looked round amazedly.

II

The man
Job squats among the soot and ashes,
his complaints mingling with the smoke.
He sifts with peeling fingers cinders
of that once his boundless joy:

sheep, camels, oxen and she-asses;
seven sons, three comely daughters,
the tender dewy branch unceasing who
guaranteed the generations of his name
as of his various unique features;
and his fame gone through the streets
a bounteous morning to proclaim him —
    these sift, soft flakes, breaking
        in the flurry of his cries.

III

Yet what lust or greed or anger,
what burning in this house of fire
beyond what becomes a man, that man
who girt up his loins according
to the Lord's command?

And sifting
flakes, he strews them in a drunkenness
of despair about his head, the last
fruits of his efforts, the folly
of all living.

Surrender all,
the Whirlwind says, whatever endeared
you even as it made Me dear to you.

No less lovely than the first arriving
leaves at falling; through the nakedness
the mighty music, unmitigated, enters.

Dew all night an ice upon the branch,
the cedars cleaving in the wind,
like a huge flock gathering
in the boughs, each tree achieves
its height the moment when it crashes.

IV

And yet that leveling Wind
did He not summon as witnesses
His freckled, much-loved creatures,
numberless as leaves, yet loved
for individual, self-willed features?

Mane flamboyant, hoof and nostril
bristlings of the mine of fire,
the horse that, leaping forth, saith "Aha!"
no less to battle than to pelting hail;
Leviathan grown tender, weltering
out his rage, the boiling ocean docile
in waves self-absorbed —
                        these, springing
like the hurricane, soft cooing words
around His lips, from God's own fingertips,
warm with them He warms, exult Him surely
in the grandeur and unique particulars
of their pride.

V

                        Sky and earth
are held in a twilight's rushing
furious fire, earth and sky the route
of pawing hoofs, till all the colors drain
into one conflagration.
                        But here
as I pause on the little wooden bridge,
the waters, shielded by two arching pines,
needles heaped below, purl into a cat's paw.

Coolly the ripples from one side,
pursuing their dappled course, are crossed
like a shuttle by ripples from the other
till they pour together — yet still
themselves — in the next step
of their streaming.

VI

                    And so the sea
is fed, and so the fire, the rampant waves
and flames flared up in stubborn homage
to their fathering first desire.

JOHN WIENERS

The Waning of the Harvest Moon

No flowers now to wear at
Sunset. Autumn and the rain. Dress in
blue. For the descent. Dogs bark at
the gate. Go down daughter my soul
heavy with the memory of heaven.

It is time for famine and empty
altars. We ask your leave for
by that going we gain spring again.
No lights glimmer in the wood.
I want to go out and rob a grocery store.

Hunger. My legs ache. Who will feed us.
Miles more to go. Secrets yet unread.
Darkness on the leaves. My lord lost.
My soul a jangle of lost connections.
Who will plug in the light at autumn.
When all men are alone.
Down. And further yet to go.
Words gone from my mouth.
Speechless in the tide.

The Windows of Waltham

Sol, *Bronze Age came first* Sol,
    Wong, before snow nothing came.
Dont worry about the wisdom of
                              the past.
    Two met and made a first.

The Acts of Youth

And with great fear I inhabit the middle of the night
What wrecks of the mind await, what drugs
to dull the senses, what little I have left,
what more can be taken away?

The fear of travelling, of the future without hope
or buoy. I must get away from this place and see
that there is no fear without me, that it is within
unless it be some sudden act or calamity

to land me in the hospital, a total wreck, without
memory again; or worse still, behind bars. If
I could just get out of the country. Some place
where one can eat the lotus in peace.

For in this country, it is terror, poverty awaits; or
am I a marked man, my life to be a lesson
or experience to those young who would tread
the same path, without God

unless he be one of justice. to wreak vengeance
on the acts committed while young under un-
due influence or circumstance. Oh I have
always seen my life as drama, patterned

after those who met with disaster or doom.
Is my mind being taken away me.
I have been over the abyss before. What
is that ringing in my ears that tells me

all is nigh, is naught but the roaring of the winter wind.
Woe to those homeless who are out on this night.
Woe to those crimes committed from which we
can walk away unharmed.

So I turn on the light
And smoke rings rise in the air.
Do not think of the future; there is none.
But the formula all great art is made of.

Pain and suffering. Give me the strength
to bear it, to enter those places where the
great animals are caged. And we can live
at peace by their side. A bride to the burden

that no god imposes but knows we have the means
to sustain its force unto the end of our days.
For that it is what we are made for; for that
we are created. Until the dark hours are done.

And we rise again in the dawn.
Infinite particles of the divine sun, now
worshipped in the pitches of the night.

A Series 5.8

Of the filth and order of the world
        I have to sing.
Already by putting this pen to paper
        the music loses
                itself in a labyrinth
                        of deception.
And description is a deceit, an easy
        trap to fall into. Look, how the shadows
                fall across the page.
And the hand is on the wall. And the picture
        of Mistinguett beneath it.
                In feathers and Indian headdress
                        as a priest at his brazier.
        Or a hero returned from the wars.
Look the candle leaps up straight as a column
        or pillar of marble to herald his homecoming.
                                And the hand trembles
                at the next word to put down.

The Meadow

Where all things grow according to their own design.

Destiny lies behind our forces
and what lives in the soul
dies not. It inhabits our dreams
as perpetual as light.

As the spring grass flowers,
it sprouts out in fields
and keeps birds thin
with the perpetual gnawing of desire.

The higher one goes
up the angelic ladder
remains the minute bits
and ends of our life.

Seeds there to recur when we
are most unaware.
Old faces, letters crop up again.
Words from our poems

Menace the night

For Jan

The girl hustles her islands of pure flesh.
There is no way to redeem her loss but words
Where the ecstasy awaits at the fringe of our lips.

There in the night she sells her body to old China
For the dreams all men carry in their loins.
Offend not the ancestral gods, by this sale

Of love, or tasting of unknown secret pleasures
Always been my due, to inhabit at the river bank
The depth of ocean in mid-stream.

"In the half light of holding and giving"

In the half light of holding and giving
taking and receiving
we find a mean line

which is the basis of all things.

The temptress dares not receive our gifts,
but exists in an empire which is a kingdom
of living and dying beyond the pale
of ordinary human experience.

It is the gate of hatred,
the harbor to hot labor
which she hands us in return
for observance of that instant
we obeyed without regret.

Let us no longer endure malformations
of denial. The half light breeds false shadows
on the crown. Down dark and dreary ways
line survivors of our expectation.

Oh hold us up in the dawn
This false light breeds old ways
of death and desire we tried without success
In hallways corridors of fire

Past all endurance, existing.

Two Years Later

The hollow eyes of shock remain
Electric sockets burnt out in the
                    skull.

The beauty of man never disappears
But drives a blue car through the parking lot.

Where Fled

   Despair is given me
as others' daily bread. What wish is this?
of this stuff fed. Does despair in faith
bring on re-incarnation?

                              The night nurtures
faith in dawn. But let one creep of light
disappear from the afternoon and all
murmur: too soon the darkness falls.

Does dawn come on? We continue walking
on. The walls. Are fled by whom.
The moon? She shines through the blood
& clouds.

RICHARD WILBUR

Advice to a Prophet

When you come, as you soon must, to the streets of our city,
Mad-eyed from stating the obvious,
Not proclaiming our fall but begging us
In God's name to have self-pity,

Spare us all word of the weapons, their force and range,
The long numbers that rocket the mind;
Our slow, unreckoning hearts will be left behind,
Unable to fear what is too strange.

Nor shall you scare us with talk of the death of the race.
How should we dream of this place without us? —
The sun mere fire, the leaves untroubled about us,
A stone look on the stone's face?

Speak of the world's own change. Though we cannot conceive
Of an undreamt thing, we know to our cost
How the dreamt cloud crumbles, the vines are blackened
        by frost,
How the view alters. We could believe,

If you told us so, that the white-tailed deer will slip
Into perfect shade, grown perfectly shy,
The lark avoid the reaches of our eye,
The jack-pine lose its knuckled grip

On the cold ledge, and every torrent burn
As Xanthus once, its gliding trout
Stunned in a twinkling. What should we be without
The dolphin's arc, the dove's return,

These things in which we have seen ourselves and spoken?
Ask us, prophet, how we shall call
Our natures forth when that live tongue is all
Dispelled, that glass obscured or broken

In which we have said the rose of our love and the clean
Horse of our courage, in which beheld
The singing locust of the soul unshelled,
And all we mean or wish to mean.

Ask us, ask us whether with the wordless rose
Our hearts shall fail us; come demanding
Whether there shall be lofty or long standing
When the bronze annals of the oak-tree close.

Loves of the Puppets

Meeting when all the world was in the bud,
Drawn each to each by instinct's wooden face,
These lovers, heedful of the mystic blood,
Fell glassy-eyed into a hot embrace.

April, unready to be so intense,
Marked time while these outstripped the gentle weather,
Yielded their natures to insensate sense,
And flew apart the more they came together.

Where did they fly? Why, each through such a storm
As may be conjured in a globe of glass
Drove on the colder as the flesh grew warm,
In breathless haste to be at lust's impasse,

To cross the little bridge and sink to rest
In visions of the snow-occluded house
Where languishes, unfound by any quest,
The perfect, small, asphyxiated spouse.

That blizzard ended, and their eyes grew clear,
And there they lay exhausted yet unsated;
Why did their features run with tear on tear,
Until their looks were individuated?

One peace implies another, and they cried
For want of love as if their souls would crack,
Till, in despair of being satisfied,
They vowed at least to share each other's lack.

Then maladroitly they embraced once more,
And hollow rang to hollow with a sound
That tuned the brooks more sweetly than before,
And made the birds explode for miles around.

She

What was her beauty in our first estate
When Adam's will was whole, and the least thing
Appeared the gift and creature of his king,
How should we guess? Resemblance had to wait

For separation, and in such a place
She so partook of water, light, and trees
As not to look like any one of these.
He woke and gazed into her naked face.

But then she changed, and coming down amid
The flocks of Abel and the fields of Cain,
Clothed in their wish, her Eden graces hid,
A shape of plenty with a mop of grain,

She broke upon the world, in time took on
The look of every labor and its fruits.
Columnar in a robe of pleated lawn
She cupped her patient hand for attributes.

Was radiant captive of the farthest tower
And shed her honor on the fields of war,
Walked in her garden at the evening hour,
Her shadow like a dark ogival door,

Breasted the seas for all the westward ships
And, come to virgin country, changed again —
A moonlike being truest in eclipse,
And subject goddess of the dreams of men.

Tree, temple, valley, prow, gazelle, machine,
More named and nameless than the morning star,
Lovely in every shape, in all unseen,
We dare not wish to find you as you are,

Whose apparition, biding time until
Desire decay and bring the latter age,
Shall flourish in the ruins of our will
And deck the broken stones like saxifrage.

October Maples, Portland

The leaves, though little time they have to live,
Were never so unfallen as today,
And seem to yield us through a rustled sieve
The very light from which time fell away.

A showered fire we thought forever lost
Redeems the air. Where friends in passing meet,
They parley in the tongues of Pentecost.
Gold ranks of temples flank the dazzled street.

It is a light of maples, and will go;
But not before it washes eye and brain
With such a tincture, such a sanguine glow
As cannot fail to leave a lasting stain.

So Mary's laundered mantle (in the tale
Which, like all pretty tales, may still be true),
Spread on the rosemary-bush, so drenched the pale
Slight blooms in its irradiated hue,

They could not choose but to return in blue.

Fall in Corrales

Winter will be feasts and fires in the shut houses,
Lovers with hot mouths in their blanched bed,
Prayers and poems made, and all recourses
Against the world huge and dead:

Charms, all charms, as in stillness of plumb summer
The shut head lies down in bottomless grasses,
Willing that its thought be all heat and hum,
That it not dream the time passes.

Now as these light buildings of summer begin
To crumble, the air husky with blown tile,
It is as when in bald April the wind
Unhoused the spirit for a while:

Then there was no need by tales or drowsing
To make the thing that we were mothered by;
It was ourselves who melted in the mountains,
And the sun dove into every eye.

Our desires dwelt in the weather as fine as bomb-dust;
It was our sex that made the fountains yield;
Our flesh fought in the roots, and at last rested
Whole among cows in the risen field.

Now in its empty bed the truant river
Leaves but the perfect rumples of its flow;
The cottonwoods are spending gold like water;
Weeds in their light detachments go;

In a dry world more huge than rhyme or dreaming
We hear the sentences of straws and stones,
Stand in the wind and, bowing to this time,
Practise the candor of our bones.

A Christmas Hymn

> *And some of the Pharisees from among
> the multitude said unto him, Master, rebuke
> thy disciples.*
>
> *And he answered and said unto them, I
> tell you that, if these should hold their
> peace, the stones would immediately cry out.*
> St. Luke XIX, 39–40

A stable-lamp is lighted
Whose glow shall wake the sky;
The stars shall bend their voices,
And every stone shall cry.
And every stone shall cry,
And straw like gold shall shine;
A barn shall harbor heaven,
A stall become a shrine.

This child through David's city
Shall ride in triumph by;
The palm shall strew its branches,
And every stone shall cry.
And every stone shall cry,
Though heavy, dull, and dumb,
And lie within the roadway
To pave his kingdom come.

Yet he shall be forsaken,
And yielded up to die;
The sky shall groan and darken,
And every stone shall cry.
And every stone shall cry
For stony hearts of men:
God's blood upon the spearhead,
God's love refused again.

But now, as at the ending,
The low is lifted high;
The stars shall bend their voices,
And every stone shall cry.
And every stone shall cry
In praises of the child
By whose descent among us
The worlds are reconciled.

JONATHAN WILLIAMS

In England's Green &

    (A Garland and a Clyster)

the thyrsus of wild thyme
for
EDWARD DAHLBERG,
Mentor & Friend

> "That there are no Absolutes
> is of no importance; but he
> who refuses to strive after
> them is a liar, a coward and
> a caitiff."

1. *Reflections from "Appalachia,"*
   in Honor of Delius' Centenary: 1962

dawn songs in the dews of young orange trees;
and ranging orisons; and wordless longings

sung in tranquility's waters sliding in sun's
light;

and benisons sung in these trees . . .

in these, yes, it is the 'ah-ness,' yes, it is the course of adrenalin,
but, it is the lens opening of Frederick Delius' luminous blind
                                            eye:
f/stop open —
all things measureless lucidities,

my eyes
so in tune: atonement, at-one-ment is
atonement,

what is meant by not
being able to focus two eyes . . .

they lie on the horizon,
they lie on the great St. John's River's waters
in the monocular sunlight

three miles wide
lid to lid

2. *Two Pastorals for Samuel Palmer at Shoreham:*

I. "If the Night Could Get Up & Walk"

I cannot put my hand into
a cabbage to turn
on the light, but

the moon moves over
the field of dark cabbage and an
exchange fills
all veins.

The cabbage is also a globe
of light, the two globes

now two eyes in
my saturated

head.

II. "One Must Try Behind the Hills"

Eight Great Dahlias stood
beyond the Mountains

they set fire to the Sun
in a black wood
beyond the Mountains,

in the Valley of Vision

the Fission of
Flowers

yields all Power
in the Valley of Vision

eight suns,
on eight stems,

aflame

3. *Beside the Fount above the Lark's nest in Golgonooza*

Golgonooza?
Georgia?

You think Great Blake didn't know Enigma,
Alapaha, Sappville, Ty Ty, and Glory
were on Route 82, across south Georgia?

You're right, there's a lot Great Blake didn't know about —
larks' nests for one thing. Sing,
Rara (English) *Avis*
                    ("me immense world of delight;
                        me unclosed by senses five"),

rave on!

Let's talk about cardinals — *Richmondena cardinalis*.
Let's, because in the midst of writing this poem, which
is to be very pedantic and mildly arcane and written very
quickly to get rid of worrying just for once whether it
is prose or its blessed contrary, here is my old friend
the cardinal pecking and pecking at his rival's red image
in the newly washed window. He sits in the dry vines. I
don't know the name of the damn vine, but it's there,
it's been there nineteen years since we dug a root from
my great-grandmother's farmhouse after her funeral and
planted it. Planted it *votively*. Great. I know that
now but I didn't have to know it then.

O Linnaeus (always some taxonomist bugging us): "this
is the great alphabet: to affix to every object its proper
name."
Ok. *Richmondena cardinalis,* get your ass
out of mine nameless vine, nine feet above
my *asarum canadense!*
(Kinda dense, huh? Just wild ginger.) Prose or

poetry? Where are we? With emblems and birds,
and no fount — not in Golgonooza
at all.

Capital b-i-r-d-s: *Birds,* how do these airy spirits
stand it, O Despond? — they have never heard of
Odilon Redon
or George MacDonald or Denis Saurat, and think *Blake* sounds
                                                    just
as good as *fount* in

Golgonooza.

4. *Blues for Lonnie Johnson*

> "If you don't like my peaches,
> baby, don't you shake my tree."
> —Orpheus

Woke up this mornin'
Cape Canaveral can't get it up . . .
Woke up this mornin',
Cape Canaveral can't get it up . . .

But sent a cable to Great Venus —
told her, better watch her ass.

"Unravished bride of quietness,"
blasts off in my head . . .
"Unravished bride of quietness,"
blasts off in my head . . .

Liable to be a whole lot more people
than just John Keats dead.

Got us a brand new play-toy,
and the Green Bay Packers too . . .
Got us a brand new play-toy,
and the Green Bay Packers too . . .

Same old incestuous, eschatological, lunatic football
Apollo's used to.

5. *The Electronic Lyre, Strung with Poets' Sinews*

(for Elizabeth Sewell)

> "Orph's awfully gay,
> despite Eurydice."
> —The Oracular Cave at Antissa:
>   Music, Every Hour on the Hour

Hey, Dead-Head,
Maenads got your tongue?

You go dead inside,
and think you could

con me, the Shade
of Sigmund Freud?

Be polymorphous perverse,
Orpheus!

All orifices,
Orpheus!

"It's all good."

(signed)

God.

Ps/ "Sappho died the other day . . .
    all ass is grass, so let's make hay!"

6. *A Collect Night-Letter for Mr Arthur Golding*

. . . "EXILED
    AWHILE

    TO ISLE
    OF CAPRI,

    PERFERVID,
    IVIED OVID —

    TOO TOO AVID —
    EVIDENTLY

    HAD HAD IT
    UP CUPID . . ."

    (U.P.I.:
    3 B.C.)

7. *Cobwebbery*

> *"The spirit and the will survived,
> but something in the soul perished."*
>   —D. H. Lawrence

the best spiders for soup
are the ones under
stones —

ask the man who is one:
plain white American

(not blue gentian red indian yellow sun black caribbean)

hard heart, cold
mind's found

a home
in the ground

"a rolling stone, *nolens volens*,
ladles no soup"

maw, rip them boards off
the side the house

and put the soup pot on

and plant us some petunias
in the carcass of the Chevrolet

and let's stay here
and rot in the fields

sit still

8. *A Mathom for J.R.R. Tolkien*

on the streams of Westernesse outside the Shire
the Pipe-Weed grows with the Golden-Seal . . .

do not forget this in your zeal:
the emperies of elves and men are flowers!

shun Ranunculus at Raven Knob,
and Black Cohosh and Columbine
and Rue-Anemone —

the human minions/
the eleven votaries!

beware the Hellebore
on Rabun Bald, or Barad-dur, or Erebor!

9. *The Flower-Hunter in the Fields*

(for Agnes Arber)

a flame azalea, mayapple, maple, thornapple
plantation

a white cloud in the eye
of a white horse

a field of bluets moving
below the black suit
of William Bartram

bluets; or "Quaker Ladies," or some say
"Innocence"

bluets and the blue of gentians and
Philadelphia blue laws . . .

high hills,

stone cold
sober

as October

10. *The Familiars*

(for Geoffrey Grigson)

in the Appalachians
we plant a campion,

a "Rattlesnake-Master."

Master Thomas Campion,
plant your garden in our face,
turn all our thoughts to eyes,

> Where we such pleasing change
> doth view
> In every living thing,
> As if the world were born anew
> To gratify the spring.

O Starry Campion, *silene
stellata,*

laudamus te, benedicimus te!
*

today is March twenty-first; the temperature sixty-one . . .

masses of rattlers as large as wash tubs,
as large as watermelons,
lying in the sun by their dens.

the Indian said:
deer and ginseng and snake are allies
avenging each other;

but it is another, Spring Rain, god of rattlesnakes, puts
their signature
on the plantains by the ledge.

laudamus,
Crotalus Horridus
horridus!

lead us
into the crevice into
the central den.

*

our insufflator, the warm sun,
warns us of the excrescences of language —

ecdysis, exuviation, desquamation —
it's the words that need to be shed.

so we coil on the stones with our blue eyes
calling for Mnemosyne to install
a new endothermal
control,

for the myth was: the shed skin was
immortal

(afflatus filling the skin
in the wind at night).

"the skinne that ye snake casts in ye spring tyme, being sod in
wine, is a remedie for ye paine in the eares"
                                        —Dioscorides

paeans in our ears!
Greek, Cherokee & United States of American paeans,

that a caduceus of Viper's Bugloss
may cleanse our ears to hear —

even to the language of the birds!

for the scripture is written:
"Plants at One End, Birds at the Other."

*

house-leek & garlic,
hyssop & mouse;

hawk & hepatica,
hyacinth, finch!

crawl, all
exits

from
hibernaculum!

JOHN WOODS

The Deaths at Paragon, Indiana

1. SANDRA, THE WAITRESS

Sun streaked the coffee urn
And wrote AL'S LUNCH across the cups.
I saw no harm in summer then,
And held against the scorching sun
A spring, touching the deepest earth,
That trickled in the bearded tub
Behind the store. But nothing holds
When fire levels on the frying concrete.
Thermometer said, "Go easy, girl.
Dodge trouble." And so I fed
The truckers, watching the tube of coffee
Twitch along the urn, the street
Repeat itself across the mirror.
I washed an egg beneath the tap.

Then, too sudden for the mind,
The car came rolling, spraying parts
And boys across the road outside.
He came, and comes forever, sliding
Headfirst into the curb, bursting.
The egg broke below my hand.
O this to say: his arm was bent
Behind his back; dust and leaves
Crawled downstream in the gutter.
O this to hope: someday his staring
Eyes will close upon my dream.

2. GOSS, THE AMBULANCE DRIVER

My head goes spinning in the siren,
But I hold the road. Muscles
Keep the old shapes. When oaks
Are ripped by lightning, tip to root,
Will sap spring out until the tree
Hangs wrinkled as an inner tube
From junkyard fences? Dr. Sweet,

This siren calls: "I am the cross
Your training binds you to." But hear,
One behind is crucified
Upon a steering wheel, and bleeds
His heart away. Sew on him
A year, and he will lie unbuckled.
But now to drive this ambulance
With all my riders emptying
Behind me.
          O this to say:
Lives are balloons; and when the moorings
Drop, the wind takes you sailing.
Like inner tubes, they round around
Their hold on air. O this to cry:
Someday the wind goes slack, and they
Go spinning like my passengers.

3. CHAUNCEY, THE JUNK MAN

Scatter me, wind. I am the king
Of bang and rattle, of fall apart
And rust in weeds. Here is where
Things wobble off to. My offerings
Come sailing from back doors: wires
Distracted into sparks, handles
That give you pains, and broken holders.
If I were mayor, every matron
Would come unglued and hit the spot
With all her joints aglow. But I
Can coax a shape in anything,
And make it stick, and tend and solder.

O this to say: today I dragged
A mash of wheels and sparking sides
Into my shed. First I cluttered
Ledges with all unwired cubes;
Then I festooned rafters with
The unlinked flexible. But when
I gathered shape into my brain,
I cowered under fenders, reeling.
The shape was fall and spin and blast.
The shape was death. I let it go.

4. DOCTOR SWEET

Yesterday I fished for bass,
But now I fish for breath in bones
Clasped as bottom roots. The pulse
Nibbled like a chub but got
Away. All five of you are dead.
Light beaks my eyes, and edges
My knives with fire. Though I link
You by my chart, you'll dangle empty.
Even Chauncey, with his shed of parts,
Can never make you run. I know
He'll tow your flattened car away
And hang its pieces from his roof
Like sausages and collarbones.
I fear he'd bandage you with earth.

I know those visitors below.
They come to lynch you with their pity.
You left them with their loves and debts,
Responsibility and guilt.
This mob of tears will not forgive.
O now I give you to their hands
For burial in summer's earth.
O this to hope: that you will never
Wake upon an empty world
And cry for love, and hear no answer.

When Senses Fled

I am custodian of close things.
Even winter trees have blurred
To leaf, and faces come upon me
Suddenly. I am a startled man
To half the town, and half my yard
Is blunderland. First, I lost
The violets, then the grass,
And now, the red and wren white fence.
Farewell, the bright decay of oak,
The crewcut water, the black assizes
Of the night. Farewell, the visual.

Today, the wind began to lag
And all its freight of season drained
Into the neighbor trees. And all
The smoking, sideburned streets
Dropped ashes on the muted playground.
Let lightning slam the screen, I cry,
Let neighbors war, a shop of cats
Tear metal. O stone me with shouting.
But the grating thunderhead suspends
Its buzzing nest beneath my bough.
Farewell, the audible.

              Touch,
Tell me what the world displays
For now I rain behind my eyes.
If you would hurt me, gather close,
For in the last deception, skin,
I must be broken by a kiss.
Love is a cave of scrolls, and I
Have thrown away all spectacles.
I roll horizons like a hoop
Among the mufflered trees, and see
Nerve ends crackling in the dark.
Farewell, the tangible.

              Inside,
I stand, a coalescent dust.
When I sing, my voices turn
To stone, and where I touch, veins
Stand out. When I am alone, the forest
Swarms with nakedness, and where
I point, pole stars waltz along
My finger. Look, the fence appears,
Then grass. And all my senses step
On naked feet into the garden
To ring, an anvil of the storm,
To name the kneeling animals.

Poem At Thirty

                                   for David

On the morning of noise
Our eyes kindled the hills.
Wind put the smallest leaves to our love.

With walnut hands we wrung the great coiled flight
From bitterns and other long birds
Of the long morning.
Windtips blurred on the cedar
In persuasions of tilt and glide, give way
And spring back, touch wood and run home.

If we cried cold, the streams rang like bells
Through tiers of oaks,
And a brown sun circled the horizon;
And weeping, trailing mufflers of coarse flame,
We chopped for fish and bombed the shelterhouse
With disappearing snow.
If we cried stop,
Bright occasions held their slide
From flaming oak to shale alley.
On tip and toe the fishing birds
Would weld upon their diving images.

On the morning of color,
On the morning of first-seen,
When every acorn rolled into place,
When every child seemed the final incident of poise,
When the great waters
Were one small stream carrying out to river
The reflective world,
We could not sing of love or loss,
Or count to thirty, holding our breath.

But now we say, God, sun,
Circumstance, whatever riddles us,
Send us one such morning to grow on.

Playwright

1

Suspecting hollow trees, the barn to be
Held together by the manes of hay,
The pickshank surrey with its sail of webs,
I poked around the yard, kicking weeds.
Manure reassured me, the voiding mare,
And rain that swept the picnic under elms,
That more than painted canvas stood around.

I cast my images to every wind.
Milkweeds, plantain, chickweed, mustard, buckhorn
Burst again from notched and drying furrows,
Again in wagon track, and once more swarmed
In wild and wooly sheep pen, boiling seeds
And bees into the air. *Order,* I cried,
Order, sitting by the dry stream bed,
And start again.
           Wondering if the trees
Were full of air, the barn was swept together
By brooms of hay, or held by atmospheric
Pressure to the surrey with its vacuum horse
A-prance . . .
           Order, winked the dry stream stones.
The world is reaffirmed by sweet compost.

Think in acts, the preacher and the teacher
Said; in scenes, my mother and another
Warned; in symbols, ironies and myth
Said all the seedless, seedy Criticals.
Which is the play? Look at the world until
It thins: the overthrust of meeting oaks
Refines into proscenium, the arcs
Of swallows are the moths of summer stock,
The backlog in the willow close becomes
The greenroom with an arty couch; and, crouched,
The hunter and his dog with nose alight
Become the critics from the New York *Times.*

Again: oppressed by paper trees, afraid
The barn was a cleverness of brushwork,
In short, afraid of art, I pinched myself.
The stream sprang back, the sparrows bobbed for apples,
The play lay neatly stacked beside my bed.

2

Look at the water. It tells the sky.
Look at the sky. It tells the way
That all the casuals of eye
Can richen to a voice, and say:
Shiftiness is absolute,
So be a prince of enterprise.
The banner falters from its root.
A little breeze destroys the skies.

Or so I wrote at twenty-five.
A lovely concept, honestly
Arrived at through experience.
If change is all, let every sense
Ring jubilance and gramercy!
Wide to the world and broad alive!

But this destroyed my poetry.
When Frost denied his glacial fence
He failed to see the strongest gyve
Is verse of place. One must connive
With rebel leaders in their tents.
Only at home must one be free.

The play is not the thing, but dense
Enough with life for Lear to shrive
Us with a family, the angry
Genes of Adam's curse; to die
With every surrogate, to wive
Our mothers, kill our innocence.

The villain, ingenue, and clown
Crackle at my finger tips.
The cave at night, the praising town
Swing in my orbit, and at your lips
You make a god of cold precision;
And heaven, a critic's indecision.
I cast my selves into the day.
Your faces flicker, well and ill.
I walk apart; and parallel,
You almost risk my life in play,
Until the final curtains spill.
Then, safe until the matinee.

LOUIS ZUKOFSKY

Poem Beginning "The"

First Movement: "And out of olde bokes, in good feith"

1 The
2 Voice of Jesus I. Rush singing
3   in the wilderness
4 A boy's best friend is his mother,
5 It's your mother all the time.
6 Residue of Oedipus-faced wrecks
7 Creating out of the dead, —
8 From the candle flames of the souls of
            dead mothers
9 Vide the legend of thin Christ sending her
            out of the temple, —
10 Books from the stony heart, flames rapping
            the stone,
11 Residue of self-exiled men
12 By the Tyrrhenian.
13   Paris.
14 But everywhere only the South Wind, the
            sirocco, the broken Earth-face.
15 The broken Earth-face, the age demands an
            image of its life and contacts,
16 Lord, lord, not that we pray, are sure of
            the question,
17 But why are our finest always dead?
18 And why, Lord, this time, is it Mauberly's
            Luini in porcelain, why is it Chelifer,
19 Why is it Lovat who killed Kangaroo,
20 Why Stephen Daedalus with the cane of
            ash,
21 But why les neiges?
22 And why, if all of Mary's Observations
            have been made
23 Have not the lambs become more sapient
            drinking of the spring;
24 Kerith is long dry, and the ravens that
            brought the prophet bread

25 Are dust in the waste-land of a raven-
         winged evening.
26 And why if the waste land has been explored,
         travelled over, circumscribed,
27 Are there only wrathless skeletons exhumed
         new planted in its sacred wood,
28 Why — heir, long dead, — Odysseus, wan-
         dering of ten years
29 Out-journeyed only by our Stephen, bibbing
         of a day,
30 O why is that to Hecuba as Hecuba to he!
31 You are cra-a-zee on the subject of babies,
         says she,
32 That is because somehow our authors have been
         given a woman's intuition.
33 Il y a un peu trop de femme in this South Wind.
34 And on the cobblestones, bang, bang, bang,
         myself like the wheels —
35 The tram passes singing
36 O do you take this life as your lawful wife,
37   I do!
38 O the Time is 5
39   I do!
40 O the Time is 5
41   I do!
42 O do you take these friends as your loves
         to wive,
43 O the Time is 5
44   I do!

45 For it's the hoo-doos, the somethin' voo-doos
46 And not Kings onelie, but the wisest men
47 Graue Socrates, what says Marlowe?
48 For it was myself seemed held
49 Beating — beating —
50 Body trembling as over an hors d'oeuvres —
51
52 And the dream ending — Dalloway! Dalloway —
53 The blind portals opening, and I awoke!

54 Let me be
55 Not by art have we lived,
56 Not by graven images forbidden to us
57 Not by letters I fancy,
58 Do we dare say

59 With Spinoza grinding lenses, Rabbaisi,
60 After living on Cathedral Parkway?

Second Movement: International Episode

61 This is the aftermath
62 When Peter Out and I discuss the theatre.
63 Evenings, our constitutional.
64 We both strike matches, both in unison,
65   to light one pipe, my own.
66 'Tis, 'tis love, that makes the world go
                round and love is what I dream.
67 Peter is polite and I to me am almost as
                polite as Peter.
68 Somehow, in Germany, the Jew goat-song
                is unconvincing —
69   How the brain forms its vision think-
                ing incessantly of the things,
70 Not the old Greeks anymore, —
71   the things themselves a shadow world
                scarce shifting the incessant
                thought —
72 Time, time the goat were an offering,
73 Eh, what show do we see tonight, Peter?
74 "Il Duce: I feel God deeply."
75   Black shirts — black shirts — some power
                is so funereal.

76 Lion-heart, frate mio, and so on in two
                languages
77 the thing itself a shadow world.
78 Goldenrod
79 Of which he is a part,
80 Sod
81 He hurried over
82 Underfoot,
83 Make now
84 His testament of sun and sky
85 With clod
86 To root what shoot
87 It sends to run the sun,
88 The sun-sky blood.
89 My loves there is his mystery beyond
                your loves.
90 Uncanny are the stars,

91 His slimness was as evasive
92 And his grimness was not yours,
93 Do you walk slowly the halls of the heavens,
94 Or saying that you do, lion-hearted not ours,
95 Hours, days months, past from us and gone,
96 Lion-heart not looked upon, walk with the
          stars.
97 Or have these like old men acknowledged
98 No kin but that grips of death,
99 Of being dying only to live on with them
100 Entirely theirs,
101 And so quickly grown old that we on earth like
          stems raised dark
102 Feel only the lull, heave, phosphor
          change, death, the
103 One follow, the other, the end?

104 Our candles have been buried beneath these
          waters,
105 Their lights are his,
106 Ship-houses on the waters he might have lived
          near.
107 Steady the red light and it makes no noise
          whatever.
108 Damn it! they have made capital of his flesh
          and bone.
109 What, in revenge, can dead flesh and bone
          make capital?
110 And his heart is dry
111 Like the teeth of a dead camel
112 But his eyes no longer blink
113 Not even as a blind dog's.

114 With the blue night shadows on the sand
115 May his kingdom return to him,
116 The Bedouin leap again on his *asilah*,
117 The expanse of heaven hang upon his shoulder
118 As an embroidered texture,
119 Behind him on his saddle sit the night
120 Sing into his ear:

121 Swifter than a tiger to his prey,
122 Lighter than the storm wind, dust or spray,
123 The Bedouin bears the Desert-Night,
124 Big his beard and young with life,

125 Younger yet his gay, wild wife
126   The Desert-Night.
127 Some new trappings for his steed,
128 All the stars in dowry his meed
129   From the Desert-Night.

130 I've changed my mind, Zukofsky,
131 How about some other show —
132 "The Queen of Roumania," "Tilbury,"
       "The West-Decline,"
133 "Hall's Mills," "The Happy Quetzal-
       coatl,"
134 "Near Ibsen," "Dancing with H.R.H.,"
       "Polly Wants a New Fur Coat,"
135 "The Post Office" —
136 Speaking of the post office, the following
       will handicap you for the position,
137   my dear Peter,
138 Your weight less than one hundred
       twenty-five pounds,
139 One half of a disabled veteran, and
       probably
140   the whole of an unknown soldier,
141 That's indomitaeque morti for you.

142 Is it true what you say, Zukofsky,
143 Sorry to say, My Peter Out.

144 "Tear the Codpiece Off, A Musical
       Comedy,"
145 Likewise, "Panting for Pants,"
146 "The Dream That Knows No Waking."

Third Movement: In Cat Minor

147 Hard, hard the cat-world.
148 On the stream Vicissitude
149 Our milk flows lewd.

150 We'll cry, we'll cry,
151 We'll cry the more
152 And wet the floor,
153 Megrow, megrow,
154 Around around,
155 The only sound

156 The prowl, our prowl,
157 Of gentlemen cats
158 With paws like spats

159 Who weep the nights
160 Till the nights are gone —
161 — And r-r-run — the Sun!

Fourth Movement: More "Renaissance"

162 Is it the sun you're looking for,
163 Drop in at Askforaclassic, Inc.,
164 Get yourself another century,
165 A little frost before sundown,
166 It's the times don'chewknow,
167 And if you're a Jewish boy, then be your
          Plato's Philo.

168 Engprof, thy lectures were to me
169   Like those roast flitches of red boar
170 That, smelling, one is like to see
171   Through windows where the steam's galore
172   Like our own "Cellar Door."

173 On weary bott'm long wont to sit,
174   Thy graying hair, thy beaming eyes,
175 Thy heavy jowl would make me fit
176   For the Pater that was Greece,
177   The siesta that was Rome.
178 Lo! from my present — say not — itch
179   How statue-like I see thee stand
180 Phi Beta Key within thy hand!
181   Professor — from the backseats which
182 Are no man's land!

183 Poe,
184 Gentlemen, don'chewknow,
185 But never wrote an epic.

Fifth Movement: Autobiography

186 Speaking about epics, mother,
187 How long ago is it since you gathered
          mushrooms,
188 Gathered mushrooms while you mayed.
189 It is your mate, my father, boating.
190 A stove burns like a full moon in a desert night.

191 Un in hoyze is kalt. You think of a new
            grave,
192 In the fields, flowers.
193 Night on the bladed grass, bayonets dewed.
194 It is your mate, my father, boating.
195 Speaking about epics, mother, —
196 Down here among the gastanks, ruts,
            cemetary-tenements —
197 It is your Russia that is free.
198 And I here, can I say only —
199   "So then an egoist can never embrace
            a party
200   Or take up with a party?
201   Oh, yes, only he cannot let himself
202   Be embraced or taken up by the party."
203 It is your Russia that is free, mother.
204 Tell me, mother.

205 Winged wild geese, where lies the passage.
206 In far away lands lies the passage.
207 Winged wild geese, who knows the pathway?
208 Of the winds, asking, we shall say:
209 Wind of the South and wind of the North
210 Where has our sun gone forth?
211 Naked, twisted, scraggly branches,
212 And dark, gray patches through the branches,
213 Ducks with puffed-up, fluttering feathers
214 On a cobalt stream.
215 And faded grass that's slowly swaying.
216 A barefoot shepherd boy
217 Striding in the mire:
218 Swishing indifferently a peeled branch
219 On jaded sheep.
220 An old horse strewn with yellow leaves
221 By the edge of the meadow
222 Draws weakly with humid nostrils
223 The moisture of the clouds.
224 Horses that pass through inappreciable
            woodland,
225 Leaves in their manes tangled, mist, au-
            tumn green,
226 Lord, why not give these bright brutes —
            your good land —
227 Turf for their feet always, years for their mien.

228 See how each peer lifts his head, others follow,
229 Mate paired with mate, flanks coming full
        they crowd,
230 Reared in your sun, Lord, escaping each hollow
231 Where lift-struck we stand, utter their praise
        aloud.
232 Very much Chance, Lord, as when you first
        made us,
233 You might forget them, Lord, preferring what
234 Being less lovely where sadly we fuss?
235 Weed out these horses as tho they were not?
236 Never alive in brute delicate trembling
237 Song to your sun, against autumn assembling.

238 If horses could but sing Bach, mother, —
239 Remember how I wished it once —
240 Now I kiss you who could never sing Bach,
        never read Shakespeare.

241 In Manhattan here the Chinamen are yellow
        in the face, mother,
242 Up and down, up and down our streets they
        go yellow in the face,
243 And why is it the representatives of your,
        my, race are always hankering for
        food, mother?
244 We, on the other hand, eat so little.
245 Dawn't you think Trawtsky rawthaw a
        darrling,
246 I ask our immigrant cousin querulously.
247 Naw! I think hay is awlmawst a Tchekoff.
248 But she has more color in her cheeks than
        the Angles — Angels — mother, —
249 They have enough, though. We should
        get some more color, mother.
250 If I am like them in the rest, I should
        resemble them in that, mother,
251 Assimilation is not hard,
252 And once the Faith's askew
253 I might as well look Shagetz just as much
        as Jew.
254 I'll read their Donne as mine,
255 And leopard in their spots
256 I'll do what says their Coleridge,
257 Twist red hot pokers into knots.

258 The villainy they teach me I will execute
259 And it shall go hard with them,
260 For I'll better the instruction,
261 Having learned, so to speak, in their
              colleges.
262   It is engendered in the eyes
263   With gazing fed, and fancy dies
264   In the cradle where it lies
265   In the cradle where it lies
266 I, Señora, am the Son of the Respected
              Rabbi,
267 Israel of Saragossa,
268 Not that the Rabbis give a damn,
269 Keine Kadish wird man sagen.

Half-Dozenth Movement: Finale, and After

270 Under the cradle the white goat stands, mother,
271 What will the goat be saddled with, mother?
272   Almonds, raisins
273 What will my heart be bartering, mother,
274   Wisdom, learning.
275 Lullaby, lullaby, lullaby, lullaby.
276 These are the words of the prophet, mother,
277 Likely to save me from Tophet, mother —
278 What will my heart be burning to, mother,
279   Wisdom, learning.
280 By the cat and the well, I swear, my
              Shulamite!
281 In my faith, in my hope, and in my love.
282 I will cradle thee, I will watch thee,
283 Sleep and dream thou, dear my boy!
284   (Presses his cheek against her mouth.)
285 I must try to fare forth from here.
286 I do not forget you,
287 I am just gone out for to-night,
288 The Royal Stag is abroad,
289 I am gone out hunting,
290 The leaves have lit by the moon.
291 Even in their dirt, the Angles like Angels
              are fair,
292 Brooks Nash, for instance, faisant un petit
              bruit, mais très net,
293 Saying, He who is afraid to do that should
              be denied the privilege,

294 And where the automobile roads with the
　　　　gasoline shine,
295 Appropriately the katydid —
296 Ka-ty did . . . . Ka-ty didn't. . . .

297 Helen Gentile,
298 And did one want me; no.
299 But wanted me to take one? yes.
300 And should I have kissed one? no.
301 That is, embraced one first
302 And holding closely one, then kissed one?
　　　　yes.
303 Angry against things' iron I ring
304 Recalcitrant prod and kick.
305 Oh, Baedekera Schönberg, you here
306 　　　　dreaming of the relentlessness of motion
307 As usual,
308 One or two dead in the process what does it
　　　　matter.

309 Our God immortal such Life as is our God,
310 Bei dein Zauber, by thy magic I embrace
　　　　thee,
311 Open Sesame, Ali Baba, I, thy firefly, little
　　　　errant star, call here,
312 By thy magic I embrace thee.

313 O my son Sun, my son, my son Sun!
　　　　would God
314 I had died for thee, O Sun, my son, my
　　　　son!

315 I have not forgotten you, mother, —
316 It is a lie — Aus meinen grossen leiden mach ich
　　　　die kleinen lieder,
317 Rather they are joy, against nothingness joy —
318 By the wrack we shall sing our Sun-song
319 Under our feet will crawl
320 The shadows of dead worlds
321 We shall open our arms wide,
322 Call out of pure might —
323 Sun, you great Sun, our Comrade,
324 From eternity to eternity we remain true to you,
325 A myriad years we have been,
326 Myriad upon myriad shall be.

327 How wide our arms are,
328 How strong,
329 A myriad years we have been,
330 Myriad upon myriad shall be.

So That Even A Lover

1

Little wrists,
Is your content
My sight or hold,
Or your small air
That lights and trysts?

Red alder berry
Will singly break;
But you — how slight — do:
So that even
A lover exists.

2

Hello, little leaves,
Said not St. Francis
But my son in the spring,
Doing at two
(Neither really begged)
What it took the other —
He'd agree and laugh —
44 years to do.

Chloride of Lime and Charcoal

I

1

    There when the water was not potable
    Because of too many microbes
    The health officer proposed
    Hanging a bag
    With a mixture of chloride of lime and charcoal
    Ten feet down in,
    To purify the well.

2

Zinnias you look so much like Gentiles
Born among butcher furniture
Who lived Easter and Christmas
Whose fathers died without wills
And left land to divide
        among they forget
Which spinsters and
The son a saint they must have called him
        soft in the head
To whose salt marsh — it happens I like
        cattails — Jewish I am mortgaged.

Almost prize flowers, large —
I am taken aback by a difference
As by his small wife's girth
While the rest of her sweetness suffers arthritis
Whom I greet in the way
My own wife hurried to arrange you in our coffee pot
The first vase at hand
A something to give
One whose cares should be
A velvet painting of zinnias
But not her sons running off
        she might think not to learn.

As your rose, pink, yellow, and orange
Are mixed in the melting pot
That the kindness of our mortgagers
Created with you at leaving you at our door
And tho your givers begin to shake hands with my kind
Do the snobs, salvagers of culture and religion dare suspect
We are saved, formally, by green?

So: these are your lancet leaves, tubular stems
Stopped in the lotus or artichoke of your sepals
Of Egypt.

3

How sweet is the sun, is the sun
How sweet is the sun
With the birds, with the summer months
                the notes of a run
How sweet, sweet is the sun.

You ask what I can do —
My name is Jackie
I am Jack-of-all-trades:
Homer — the carpenter —
Did you write that book?
Is your fir squared
             and its end true?

How sweet is the sun, is the sun
How sweet is the sun
With the birds, with the summer months
             the notes of a run
How sweet, sweet is the sun.

II

Homer's Argos hearing
Handel's Largo as
The car goes

       Or

The dog in the third story
Brownstone window looks
Down into the street
Left and right
Much like his master
Distracted,
To see
What is going
On in the world.
Is the skyline still there
Are the buildings
A new bridge
Or the new ramp?
Philosophy moves
Faster than sound
To what purpose?

Until lights hang —
As if — from the skyscrapers —
Down a mist?

Indian summer, november first,
Evening of cantilevers of finance
Death (is?) the common share
Of the loved.

Stone struck
By hanging jewels
And hung off iron.

Are they coming home, master?

III
W

Ah, my craft, it is as Homer says:
"A soothsayer, a doctor, a singer
and a craftsman is sure of welcome
where he goes." Never
have I seen anything like you,
man or woman.
          I wonder looking at you.
Well, in Delos
once I saw something like you,
a young palm sprung at Apollo's altar,
I've been even that far — along
with others and their raft of trouble.
Seeing that sapling I was stunned
for no other tree like it grows out of the earth.
And yet I wonder and am stunned —
you might be that girl —
at the thought of touching your knees.

The Guests

In the mountains
the finches

are
four chairs

arranged
catty-corner

before the window
on whose sill

tomatoes ripen

from above
on the
chimney
piece
the clock

ticks
down

at the door
the lawn
rolls
to the road

lined
one side by

rock wall
the space
in it
the gate to
the garden

a side post of
goldenglow
a side post of
apple tree

the garden
for what

came
to the table

as herb
or green

or vine

a mown
tract then rolled

to the two-hundred
year pines
the brambles
the woods
the sometime dry brook

brimming for once
with

wished-for
rains

and the range's
rim rose

five thousand feet

the view
from the window

two chairs
for the occupants

two chairs
standing
for the ever-returning
guests

This is after all vacation

This is after all vacation. All that
matters is, all that matters — neither am
I, intent on poems, desirous of hearing
all these violin and piano sonatas
every morning for over two weeks and —
tired you would rather not —
as for the young violinist who'ld gallivant
rather than work fingers for stops,
fingers for keys —
yet really not. He will say: *all that* matters.
The music comes from another time
and sings it is *so*,
by it *may we* be believed,
know fingers for keeps,
creditably conceive the changes of times
retained in different pieces of music
as a *matter* of us so *they* are believed:
Beethoven's second and fifth violin and piano
sonatas have come to the measure
of two different rooms,
two instruments affecting a third creature
so young he exists in all rooms;
from low string sounds hautboys, such
as treasure today mere oboes, and now

hunting horns, and again strings are themselves,
or flutes in the higher positions,
and from piano keys,
which some fiddlers scorn,
cellos, and from
the G string — airs, airs.
All who matter have come
without effacing *ever,*
so easily said, as unlacing
what is
from what was
those who have just got up
may lead or be led back to bed
having contemplated without template to
flower so.

You who were made for this music

You who were made for this music
or how else does it say you,
move thru your fingers, or your bow arm, lead
to this glory: God has — God's —
but one's deepest conviction —
your art, its use — you, happy,
by rote, by heart. Is thought?
What was broken was sense
but is happy again almost seen,
the first trembling of a string a worth
whose immortal ground drops so often
you plait viable strands for your use.
Or so pride loving itself looks
to more fortunate glory, with a power
apart from the trembling sense
only glory restores.

The green leaf

The green leaf that will outlast the winter
        because sheltered in the open:
the wall, transverse, and diagonal ribs
        of the privet that pocket air
            around the leaf inside them

and cover but with walls of wind:
it happens wind colors like glass shelter,
    as the light's aire from a vault
    which has a knob of sun.

Peri Poietikes

What about measure, I learnt:
Look in your own ear and read.
Nor wrest knowledge
        in no end of books.
Pyrrhic nor *Pirke* do.
Mind, don't run to mind
boys' Greeks' metres gnome,
rummage in tee tomes, tee-tums,
        tum-tees.
Forget terms.
No count is sure,
more safe, more stressed,
more heard, or herds peace more
in world where hearing
is a going out
or instance up or down;
from in, different instance out.
Trust: to lip words
briefs what great (?) discourse well.

A 11

for Celia and Paul

River that must turn full after I stop dying
Song, my song, raise grief to music
Light as my loves' thought, the few sick
So sick of wrangling: thus weeping,
Sounds of light, stay in her keeping
And my son's face — this much for honor.

Freed by their praises who make honor dearer
Whose losses show them rich and you no poorer
Take care, song, that what stars' imprint you mirror
Grazes their tears; draw speech from their nature or
Love in you — faced to your outer stars — purer

Gold than tongues make without feeling
Art new, hurt old: revealing
The slackened bow as the stinging
Animal dies, thread gold stringing
The fingerboard pressed in my honor.

Honor, song, sang the blest is delight knowing
We overcome ills by love. Hurt, song, nourish
Eyes, think most of whom you hurt. For the flowing
River's poison where what rod blossoms. Flourish
By love's sweet lights and sing *in them I flourish.*
No, song, not any one power
May recall or forget, our
Love to see your love flows into
Us. If Venus lights, your words spin, to
Live our desires lead us to honor.

Graced, your heart in nothing less than in death, go —
I, dust — raise the great hem of the extended
World that nothing can leave; having had breath go
Face my son, say: 'If your father offended
You with mute wisdom, my words have not ended
His second paradise where
His love was in her eyes where
They turn, quick for you two — sick
Or gone cannot make music
You set less than all. Honor

His voice in me, the river's turn that finds the
Grace in you, four notes first too full for talk, leaf
Lighting stem, stems bound to the branch that binds the
Tree, and then as from the same root we talk, leaf
After leaf of your mind's music, page, walk leaf
Over leaf of his thought, sounding
His happiness: song sounding
The grace that comes from knowing
Things, her love our own showing
Her love in all her honor.'

BIOGRAPHIES AND BIBLIOGRAPHY

The biographical and bibliographical information which follows is, for the most part, such as the poets have indicated they wished to be put before their readers. Each poet was asked to respond to questions like these:

What books of poems have you published?
What other books have you published?
What articles have you published which you think should concern an interested follower of your work?
What reviews of your work have you found to be useful or relevant?
Are there recordings of your work available?
What magazines do you find open to new poetry of significance?

Finally, each poet was invited to submit his biography in his own terms; and (with the exception of one poet whose material amounted to six pages and hence required condensation) the poets speak pretty much as they wish to be heard. The reader may learn something of the poet's feelings about the relation of his personal life to his published work in the biographical section. Many poets wish the details of their personal lives to remain radically distinct from their work; others find their work an intimate extension of their own lives, and welcome an opportunity to talk about it. Neither point of view is, of course, necessarily right.

JOHN ASHBERY

"Born July 28, 1927, in Rochester, New York. Grew up on my father's farm in Sodus, New York. Graduated from Harvard, 1949; M.A. in English, Columbia, 1951, after which I worked four years in publishing before coming to France on a Fulbright (1955). Except for ten months in New York in 1957–58 have lived mostly in Paris ever since. Since 1960 have worked as art critic on the Paris *Herald Tribune,* and starting this year am an editor of the quarterly *Art and Literature.*

"I originally wanted to be a painter, and did paint until I was eighteen years old, but I feel I could express myself best in music. What I like about music is its ability of being convincing, of carrying an argument through successfully to the finish, though the terms of this argument remain unknown quantities. What remains is the structure, the architecture of the argument, scene or story. I would like to do this in poetry. I would also like to reproduce the power dreams have of persuading you that a certain event has a meaning not logically connected with it, or that there is a hidden relation among disparate objects. But actually this is only a part of what I want to do, and I am not even sure I want to do it. I often change my mind about my poetry: I do not, for instance, think it has much relation to painting, though I have said I did in previous statements of this kind. I would prefer not to think I have any special aims in mind, as I might then be forced into a program for myself—statements such as I have just made can anyway only be made after the poetry has been written and are therefore not of much use to the writer, and, by extension, to the reader."

Books of Poetry

Turandot and Other Poems, Tibor de Nagy Gallery, New York, 1953.
Some Trees, Yale University Press, New Haven, Conn., 1956.
The Poems, Tiber Press, New York, 1960.
The Tennis Court Oath, Wesleyan University Press, Middletown, Conn., 1962.

Other Publications

The Heroes (prose play) in *New York Theatre,* Grove Press, New York.
The Compromise (prose play) in *The Hasty Papers,* New York, 1960.
Articles on Artaud and Roussel in *Portfolio,* New York.

Magazines Liked

Poetry, Big Table, Location, Partisan Review.

PAUL BLACKBURN

Born November 24, 1926, St. Albans, Vermont, died May 17, 1958, and February 11, 1959; rebirth May 9, 1963 (future deaths and rebirths should be noted in subsequent editions). Youth spent in Vermont, New Hampshire, South Carolina, New York State, New York City (this takes us to 1944 and age seventeen; after that it spreads out considerably by means of hitchhiking, the U. S. Army, etc.). Attended NYU and University of Wisconsin; B.A., University of Wisconsin, 1950. Fulbright 1954–55, University of Toulouse; Fulbright *lecteur americain,* 1955–56, University of Toulouse; of the four years 1953–57, almost half was spent in Spain. At present, I work as an editor in New York City.

Books of Poetry

Proensa (translations), Divers Press, Palma de Mallorca, Spain, 1953.
The Dissolving Fabric, Divers Press, Palma de Mallorca, Spain, 1955.
Brooklyn-Manhattan Transit, Totem Press, New York, 1960.
The Nets, Trobar Books, New York, 1961.

Other Publications

An article on Catharism and the Albigensian crusade in *Black Mountain Review* 5, Summer 1955.

Pertinent Reviews by the Poet

"The International Word," *The Nation,* April 21, 1962.
"The American Duende," *Kulchur* 7, Autumn 1962.

Recordings

WBAI tapes.

Magazines Liked

Yugen, Trobar, Black Mountain Review, Origin (both series), *Genesis West, Fuck You: A Magazine of the Arts, Matter, Sum, The Floating Bear, Wild Dog, El Corno Emplumado.*

ROBIN BLASER

Born in Denver, Colorado, 1925. Grew up in Idaho.
"Always resist the temptation to make biography important."

Books of Poetry

Boston Poems, 1956/1958, Open Space, San Francisco, 1964.

Other Publications

The introduction to *An Exhibition of Six California Painters,* Peacock Gallery, San Francisco, 1963.

Magazines Liked

Locus Solus, Nation, Open Space.

GRAY BURR

Born: March 20, 1919, Omaha, Nebraska.
Educated: Harvard College; Harvard University.
War Service: U. S. Navy 1943–1946 (Asiatic-Pacific Theatre Operations; Occupation of Japan).
Livelihood: teacher, Department of English and Philosophy, The State University College at New Paltz, New York.

Recordings

Collection of the Poetry Room, Lamont Library, Harvard University, LP and tape.

Magazines Liked

Accent, Beloit Poetry Journal, Diliman Review, The Massachusetts Review, New World Writing, The New Yorker, Poetry: A Magazine of Verse, Quarterly Review of Literature.

GREGORY CORSO

"I was born in New York's Greenwich Village in 1930 and left that neighborhood to live with five different foster parents all over the city. After twenty years of wild desperate hopeful hopeless jail and high-road adventures I returned to the Village to speak poetry amongst new friends, Kerouac, Ginsberg, being a few — I showed them my prison poems and they showed me their Columbia U. poems — somehow they (the poems) and we hit it off."

Books of Poetry

Vestal Lady On Brattle, Brukenfeld, Cambridge, Mass., 1955.
Gasoline, City Lights Books, San Francisco, 1958.
Happy Birthday of Death, New Directions, New York, 1960.
Long Live Man, New Directions, New York, 1962.

*There Is Yet Time to Run Back Through Life and Expiate All That's
    Been Sadly Done,* New Directions, New York, 1965.
Selected Poems, Eyre & Spottiswoode, London, England.

Other Published Work

American Express, a prose fantasy, Olympia Press, Paris, France.

Pertinent Reviews of the Poet

Times Literary Supplement review of *Selected Poems,* Eyre & Spottis-
    woode, London, England.

Recordings

Bomb in German Anthology. For copy and price of recording, write
    Carl Hansen Verlag, Munich, Germany.

Magazines Liked

*Evergreen Review, Partisan Review, Fuck You: A Magazine of the Arts,
Locus Solus.*

ROBERT CREELEY

"I was born May 21, 1926, in Arlington, Massachusetts. Educated at
Harvard, 1943–46; B.A. got from Black Mountain, N. C., middle fifties; M.A. from University of New Mexico, 1960. I'm presently a Lecturer in English at the same university. I have traveled a good deal:
France, Spain, Guatemala, and Canada—in all of which places I've lived
for a year or more. I was in the American Field Service during World
War II, in Burma. Presently (1964) I'm a Guggenheim Fellow in poetry,
and live with my wife and daughter in the small town of Placitas, New
Mexico.

"With respect to readers—I think it's relevant to emphasize that I
feel poems and prose equally are given me to write; I do not feel *I*
create them. I have no patience or sympathy with writing that dictates
its concerns as a *subject* proposed by 'choice.' 'Choice' for me, as Duncan says, is more accurately recognition. I want to live in the world—
not 'use' it as 'subject', etc."

Books of Poetry

Le Fou, Golden Goose, Columbus, Ohio, 1952.
The Immoral Proposition, Jargon, Highlands, N. C., 1953.
The Kind of Act of, Divers Press, Palma de Mallorca, Spain, 1953.
All That Is Lovely in Men, Jargon, Highlands, N. C., 1955.
If You, Porpoise, San Francisco, 1956.
The Whip, Migrant, Worcester, England, 1957.
A Form of Women, Jargon/Corinth, New York, 1959.
For Love, Charles Scribner's Sons, New York, 1962.

Other Publications

The Gold Diggers, Divers Press, Palma de Mallorca, Spain, 1954
    (brought out by John Calder Ltd., England, October 1964, with added
    material).
The Island (novel), Charles Scribner's Sons, New York, 1963.

Pertinent Reviews by the Poet

"To Define" and "Olson & Others: Some Orts for the Sports," *New American Poetry*, Grove Press, New York, 1960.

"Robert Creeley," an interview, *The Sullen Art* (David Ossman, ed.), Corinth, New York, 1963.

"Robert Creeley (in conversation with Charles Tomlinson)," an interview, Oxford, England, *The Review* 10, 1964.

Magazines Liked

Origin, The Nation, Evergreen Review, Big Table, Yugen, Poetry, Paris Review, New Directions Annual.

PETER DAVISON

Born June 27, 1928, New York City. A.B. *Magna Cum Laude,* Harvard College, 1949; Fulbright Scholar at St. John's College, Cambridge, 1949–50. Worked as page in the U. S. Senate, 1944; assistant editor Harcourt, Brace and Co., 1950–51, 1953–55; assistant to the director of Harvard University Press, 1955–56; at present Director of the Atlantic Monthly Press. Served with AUS 1951–53. Won the first prize in the Yale Series of Younger Poets contest, 1963. Married, one son. Lives in Boston.

Books of Poetry

The Breaking of the Day, Yale University Press, New Haven, Conn., 1964.

Pertinent Reviews by the Poet

Regular poetry critic for *The Atlantic Monthly.*

Recordings

Collection of the Poetry Room, Lamont Library, Harvard University, LP and tape.

Magazines Liked

Atlantic Monthly, Harper's, Hudson Review, American Scholar, Poetry.

JAMES DICKEY

Born in Atlanta, Georgia, in 1923. He has taught at Rice University and the University of Florida, and worked in the advertising business. He has received a Guggenheim Fellowship, the Union League and Vachel Lindsay prizes given by *Poetry,* and an award from the Longview Foundation.

Books of Poetry

Into the Stone, Charles Scribner's Sons, New York, 1960.

Drowning with Others, Wesleyan University Press, Middletown, Conn., 1962.

Helmets, Wesleyan University Press, Middletown, Conn., 1964.

Two Poems of the Air, Centicore Press, Portland, Ore., 1964. (300 copies)

EDWARD DORN

Born in Illinois, April 2, 1929. Graduate of Black Mountain College. Teaches at Idaho State University at Pocatello. Festival of Contemporary Art, Vancouver, 1963. First Conference on Modern Literature, University of Buffalo, 1964. A Western traveller. Editor of *Wild Dog* (Pocatello, Idaho).

Books of Poetry

Selection in *The New American Poetry* (Donald Allen, ed.), Grove Press, New York, 1960.
The Newly Fallen, Totem Press, New York, 1961.
From Gloucester Out, Matrix Press, London, 1964.
Hands Up!, Corinth, New York, 1964.
Idaho Out, Matter Books, New York, 1965.

Other Publications

What I See in the Maximus Poems, Migrant Pamphlet, Ventura, California, 1960. (Reprinted in *Kulchur*)
"New York, New York," in *The Floating Bear* 8, 1961.
"The New Frontier," in *Kulchur* 11, 1963.
"Beauty," "Rumination on 1st Avenue," and "C. B. & Q." (fiction) in *The Moderns* (LeRoi Jones, ed.), Corinth, New York, 1963.
Interview in *The Sullen Art* (David Ossman, ed.), Corinth, New York, 1963.

LARRY EIGNER

"Born August 1927, Swampscott, Massachusetts (out of nearby hospital in Lynn). Palsied from hard birth, never had a job but got through high school at home, then seven correspondence courses from University of Chicago, a toe-hold of application and hope.

"I'm cautious, and come onto things by under-statement. Wary of exaggeration. Sotto voce has resulted in the suppression of words. Don't like to begin with a big B, as if I was at the Beginning of all speech, or anything; which may also have something to do with why usually I've had an aversion more or less to going back to the left margin after beginning a poem, but otherwise than in hindsight I just tried to do the best I could, the simplest and most immediate thing being punctuation,* once words were forceful enough — a matter of getting the distances between words, and usage of marks to conform as well as might be to what there was to say, as spoken, then these typographical devices entering themselves into the discovery and the initiation of attention. As with any other detail, after dispensing with a routine duplication device — eg a period as well as a capital letter — a new thing immediately (neither period nor capital results in sentence splice, a poem without very explicit rests, if that's what seems good), then, the availability of the device for vital use in some other connection that may crop up, possibly. Oaks from small acorns. Forests of possibility. But they can't reach the stratosphere or leave the ground. In the stratosphere you get very stark claustrophobia. Now that I've met up with a good number of things and people I'm less able to keep open and give everyone the

---

* "From a confrontation, first, with work by E. E. Cummings, then by Williams and others."

benefit of the doubt, than I used to, which was the only way I found of getting along, just about, and it still is practically my only way — kind of a bootstrap affair.

"(A limitation is, that though I seem to do all right al fresco, later when my nose is out of it two inches away the stuff is more doubtful and apt to go flat. Many lines flush with one another can go more permanent flat, in the other hand and billboards seem heavy.)

"Parodying Socrates a little, you might say I know enough to feel naïve."

Books of Poetry

From the Sustaining Air, 1953, Divers Press, Palma de Mallorca, Spain.
Look at the Park, Lynn, Mass. (privately mimeo'd)
On My Eyes, 1960, Jargon, Highlands, N. C.

Magazines Liked

Wild Dog, Sum, Yu Gen, The Floating Bear, Poems from the Floating World, Migrant, Poetry, Origin, Magazine, Outsider, Mother, Mica, Chelsea Review, Delta, Combustion, Contact, Kulchur, University of Tampa Review, Nomad, Foot, Measure, Tish, Imago, and *Fiddlehead* in Canada; *Poor·Old·Tired·Horse* (Edinburgh); *Satis* (Newcastle, England).

THEODORE ENSLIN

"Born March 25, 1925, Chester, Pennsylvania. Grew up there. Lived on Cape Cod, 1946–1960. Raised cranberries. 'Retired' to northwestern Maine in 1961 to live a quiet uncluttered life in my work and to feel the pulse of life there. Studied music with Nadia Boulanger as a young man, but abandoned composition for poetry.

"I feel that my work is intimately connected with my life in that it is often a direct statement of my involvement in it. The work itself says far more about *me* than I would care to outside of it."

Books of Poetry

The Work Proposed, Origin Press, Kyoto, Japan, 1958.
New Sharon's Prospect, Origin (second series) 8, Kyoto, Japan, 1962.
The Place Where I Am Standing, Elizabeth Press, New Rochelle, N. Y., 1964.

Other Publications

Three Letters, *Crozer Quarterly*, 1958.
Newspaper column, *The Cape Codder*, 1952–1956.

Pertinent Reviews by the Poet

"Robert Kelly — A Response," *Northwest Review*, Summer 1964.

Magazines Liked

Origin 1st and 2d series, *El Corno Emplumado, Matter, Genesis West, Elizabeth, Migrant, Mica.*

LAWRENCE MONSANTO FERLINGHETTI

Born 1919 or 1920, Yonkers, New York, or Virgin Islands. Doctorat de l'Université de Paris, 1950. M.A., Columbia University, 1947. Principal owner and editor of City Lights Booksellers and Publishers, 261 Columbus Avenue, San Francisco 11. Married: wife, Kirby; daughter, Julie, aged 3½; son, Lorenzo, aged 2.

Books of Poetry

Pictures of the Gone World, City Lights Books, San Francisco, 1955.
A Coney Island of the Mind, New Directions, New York, 1958.
Starting from San Francisco, New Directions, New York, 1951.

Other Publications

Her (a novel), New Directions, New York, 1960.
Unfair Arguments with Existence (seven plays), New Directions, New York, 1963.
Routines (short plays), New Directions, New York, Fall 1964.

Recordings

Jazz and Poetry at the Cellar (with Kenneth Rexroth), Fantasy Records, San Francisco, 1959.
Tentative Description of a Dinner to Impeach President Eisenhower, and Other Poems, Fantasy Records, San Francisco, 1961.

Magazines Liked

Beatitude, City Lights Journal, Evergreen Review, Journal for the Protection of All Beings.

EDWARD FIELD

"Born 1924 in Brooklyn, New York. Grew up in Lynbrook, Long Island. New York University. Living in New York. Recently on Guggenheim Fellowship. Lamont Award, 1962. Narration for film *To Be Alive* at Johnson's Wax Pavilion at World's Fair.

"Favorite poets: Cavafy, Auden. Favorite American poets: Millen Brand, Robert Friend."

Books of Poetry

Stand Up, Friend, With Me, Grove Press, New York, 1963.

Pertinent Reviews of the Poet

Grandin Conover, *The Nation*, November 9, 1963.
Alfred Chester, New York *Herald Tribune* Book Section, June 23, 1963.
Peter Davison, *Atlantic Monthly*, December 1963.
Robert Friend, Jerusalem *Post*, June 28, 1963.
Winfield Townley Scott, *Saturday Review*, October 26, 1963.
James Dickey, New York *Times* Book Review, September 1, 1963.
Thomas Lask, New York *Times*, June 21, 1963.
Webster Schott, *Christian Science Monitor*, July 3, 1963.
Robert W. Flint, *Commentary*, August 1963.
G. S. Fraser, New York *Review of Books*, November 28, 1963.
Herbert Burke, *Library Journal*, July 1963.
Martin Tucker, Louisville *Courier Journal*, July 7, 1963.
A.L.A., September 15, 1963.
Howell Pearce, Nashville *Banner*, August 23, 1963.
Philip Stafford, Oakland *Tribune*, July 14, 1963.
Dr. Louis Haselmayer, Burlington *Hawk-Eye*, May 6, 1963.
Henry Hough, Denver *Post*, July 7, 1963.

Magazines Liked

Outsider, Radix, Prairie Schooner, The Floating Bear, The New Yorker, Evergreen Review, Harper's, Poetry, Kenyon Review, Partisan Review, Paris Review, Botteghe Oscure, Poetry Quarterly (England), *Amigo* (Denmark), *Cartons* (Holland), *The Listener* (England), *Western Review, Beloit Poetry Journal.*

DONALD FINKEL

Born in New York in 1929. Has taught at Bard College, at present teaches at Washington University in St. Louis.

Books of Poetry

The Clothing's New Emperor, Charles Scribner's Sons, New York, 1959. At the time of this printing a second volume is in the presses at Atheneum Publishers, New York.

ALLEN GINSBERG

Born June 3, 1926, Newark, New Jersey. A.N., Columbia College, 1948. Worked as dishwasher in Bickford's, 1945; also on various cargo ships from 1945–1956; as spot-welder in the Brooklyn Navy Yards, 1945; night porter at the May Company, Denver; as book reviewer for *Newsweek*, 1950; acted in two films, *Pull My Daisy*, 1961, and *Guns of the Trees*, 1962. At present in New York City working with COP to prevent suppression of the *avant-garde* arts by state and municipal authorities.

Books of Poetry

Howl and Other Poems, City Lights Books, San Francisco, 1956.
Kaddish and Other Poems, City Lights Books, San Francisco, 1960.
Empty Mirror (early poems), Corinth/Totem Press, New York, 1960.
Reality Sandwiches (poems 1953–60), City Lights Books, San Francisco, 1963.
Yage Letters (with William Burroughs), City Lights Books, San Francisco, 1964.

Pertinent Reviews by the Poet

"Notes on Howl" (appendix by Don Allen), *The New American Poetry, 1945–1960,* Grove Press, New York, 1960.
"When the Mode of Music Changes the Walls of the City Shake" (on prosody), *The Second Coming,* 1962.

Recordings

Fantasy Record 7005.

Magazines Liked

Fuck You: A Magazine of the Arts, Yugen, Ark-Moby, Black Mountain Review, Evergreen Review.

ANTHONY HECHT

Born in New York in 1923. Fellow of the American Academy in Rome. Teaches at Bard College and is one of those three judges who gave the National Book Award for poetry in 1964 to John Crowe Ransom.

Books of Poetry

A Summoning of Stones, The Macmillan Co., New York, 1954.
Seven Deadly Sins, Gehenna Press, Northampton, Mass., 1958. Illustrations by Leonard Baskin. (333 copies)

DANIEL HOFFMAN

Born in New York City, 1923, lived in Larchmont and New Rochelle, New York; Army Air Force; Columbia B.A., 1947, Ph.D., 1956; taught in English departments at Columbia, Dijon, and since 1957, Swarthmore. Married; two children. Prizewinner in the Yale Series of Younger Poets Contest, 1954.

Books of Poetry

An Armada of Thirty Whales, Yale University Press, New Haven, Conn., 1954.
A Little Geste, Oxford University Press, New York, 1960.
The City of Satisfactions, Oxford University Press, New York, 1963.

Other Published Works

Paul Bunyan, Last of the Frontier Demigods, University of Pennsylvania Press, Philadelphia, 1952.
The Poetry of Stephen Crane, Columbia University Press, New York, 1957.
Form and Fable in American Fiction, Oxford University Press, New York, 1961.
American Poetry and Poetics, ed., Doubleday & Co. (Anchor Books), Garden City, N. Y., 1962.

Pertinent Reviews by the Poet

"The Unquiet Graves," *Sewanee Review* 67:305–16, 1959.
"Arrivals and Rebirths," *Sewanee Review* 68:118–37, 1960.

Pertinent Reviews of the Poet

W. H. Auden, "Foreword" to *An Armada of Thirty Whales.*

Recordings

Library of Congress PL38.

THEODORE HOLMES

Born Jersey City, New Jersey, 1928. Hackensack High School, Princeton University. Taught at University of Iowa, Oregon University and Harvard University. Fulbright to Oxford, 1963; Yaddo, 1964–65.

Books of Poetry

Poets of Today IV, Charles Scribner's Sons, New York, 1957.

Pertinent Reviews by the Poet

Reviews of translations of Dante, *Comparative Literature,* 1958.
Reviews of Warren's *The Cave* and Porter's *Ship of Fools* in *The Carleton Miscellany,* Winter 1963.

Pertinent Reviews of the Poet

Donald Hall, *Western Review*, 1958.
R. P. Blackmur, *Princeton Library Chronicle*, "Seven Princeton Poets," 1964.

Magazines Liked

Partisan Review, Poetry, Hudson Review, Paris Review, Perspectives, Genesis West, Approach, Chelsea, Voices, The Carleton Miscellany, Contact, Southwest Review, Literary Review, Massachusetts Review, Transatlantic Review, New World Writing, Kenyon Review, Beloit Poetry Journal, The Nation, Burning Deck.

LEROI JONES

"Born Newark, New Jersey . . . October 1934, went to local schools, many scholarships. Went to Rutgers a year, then Howard University, D. C. Exit 1954, into airforce, where a weather-gunner on B-36 in Puerto Rico. New York 1957, married 1958, now two girls Lisa 3, Kellie 5. Started *Yugen* magazine, 1958, then Totem Press, for printing of new poets. People published include Charles Olson, Robert Duncan, Edward Dorn, Joel Oppenheimer, Gary Snyder, Philip Whalen, Ron Loewinsohn, Allen Ginsberg, Gilbert Sorrentino, Jack Kerouac, Frank O'Hara, *et. al.* 1962 Whitney Fellow. Began teaching New School Social Research, 1963. University of Buffalo, Summer 1964, Columbia University, Fall 1964. One Act play, *Dutchman*, long run at Cherry Lane, won Obie Award Best American Play (off-broadway)."

Books of Poetry

Preface To A Twenty Volume Suicide Note, Totem/Corinth, New York, 1961.
The Dead Lecturer, Grove Press, New York, 1964.

Other Publications

Blues People: Negro Music In White America, William Morrow & Co., New York, 1963.
The Moderns: An anthology of new writing in America, Corinth, New York, 1963.
Dutchman and The Slave (plays), William Morrow & Co., New York, 1964.

Pertinent Reviews by the Poet

"A Dark Bag," *Poetry*, April 1964.
"Putdown Of the whore of babylon," *Yugen* 7.
"How You Sound??", *The New American Poetry, 1945–1960*, Grove Press, New York.

Pertinent Reviews of the Poet

"Black Writing," *Dialogue*.
"Myth Of A Negro Literature," *Saturday Review*.
"LeRoi Jones Talking," New York *Herald Tribune*.

Recordings

Library of Congress.

Magazines Liked

Yugen, The Floating Bear, Fuck You: A Magazine of the Arts, Wild Dog, Sum, Matter, Niagara Frontier Review, Imago (Canadian), *C, Yowl, Trobar, Signal.*

ROBERT KELLY

"Born September 24, 1935, Brooklyn. Graduated from CCNY in 1955. Visited France 1954. Married Joan 1955. Graduate work at Columbia 1955–1958, mediaeval studies. Started and co-edited *Chelsea Review,* 1957 to 1960. In 1960 founded *Trobar* with George Economou. Lately started *Matter,* a privately circulated newsletter. Have taught at Wagner College and University of Buffalo, presently live and teach at Bard College."

Books of Poetry

Armed Descent, Hawk's Well Press, New York, 1961.
"The Exchanges" and other poems in *Origin* 5, Kyoto, Japan, 1962.
Her Body against Time, Ediciones El Corno Emplumado, Mexico City, 1963.
Round Dances, Trobar Books, New York, 1964.
Lunes, Hawk's Well Press, New York, 1965.
Lectiones, Duende, Placitas, New Mexico, 1965.

Pertinent Reviews by the Poet

"Notes on Deep Image," *Trobar* 2, 1961.
"As a start," *Nomad* 11, 1962.
Interview in *The Sullen Art* (David Ossman, ed.), Corinth, 1963.
"Song?/After Bread": notes on Louis Zukofsky's *A 1–12, Kulchur* 12, 1964.

Recordings

WBAI tapes.
CBC tape.

Pertinent Reviews of the Poet

Paul Blackburn, "The American Duende," *Kulchur* 7, 1962.

Magazines Liked

Origin, Yugen, The Floating Bear, Poems from the Floating World, El Corno Emplumado, Burning Deck, Set, Fuck You: A Magazine of the Arts, Tish, Wild Dog, Coyote's Journal.

X. J. KENNEDY

Born 1929 in Dover, New Jersey. Schooled in Dover public schools, Seton Hall College, Columbia (M.A., 1951), Sorbonne (a year in 1955–56), University of Michigan (graduate student 1956–62, leaving without Ph.D). Has taught in University of Michigan (teaching fellow), (later instructor), Woman's College of the University of North Carolina (lecturer), Tufts University (assistant professor, current post), Wellesley College (lecturer, currently). Four years as an enlisted man in the Navy, 1951–55, during which time began writing verse. During the past two years, have read and sung poems and songs at forty or so American colleges. Poetry editor for the *Paris Review* for three years, 1961–64.

"I do not believe in conventional theories of English prosody but in the ear's ability to chop off a line when it has run out of time. Do believe in rhyme and off-rhyme, the possibilities of which have not yet been exhausted. Have been accused of being a wit, which charge these days is like that of Lesbianism. I am never after laughs for their own sake."

Books of Poetry

Nude Descending a Staircase, Doubleday & Co., Garden City, New York, 1961.

Other Publications

Mark Twain's Frontier (edited with James E. Camp), Holt, Rinehart & Winston, New York, 1963. (textbook)
"Who Killed King Kong?", *Dissent*, Spring 1960.

Pertinent Reviews by the Poet

"The New American Poetry," *Poetry*, July 1961.
"Marianne Moore," *The Minnesota Review*, Spring 1962.

Pertinent Reviews of the Poet

Theodore Holmes, "Wit, Nature and the Human Concern," *Poetry*, August 1962, pp. 319–322.
Glauco Cambon, review of *Nude Descending a Staircase* in *Wisconsin Studies in Contemporary Literature*, 1962, pp. 108–113.

Recordings

Library of Congress.

Magazines Liked

Poetry, Paris Review, Hudson Review, Chelsea, The New Yorker, Burning Deck.

GALWAY KINNELL

"Born 1927, Providence, Rhode Island. Raised in Pawtucket, Rhode Island. A.B., Princeton University, taught at Downtown Center of University of Chicago in the early fifties. Spent 1955–57 in France; 1957–59, New York; 1959–60 in Tehran teaching at University of Tehran; 1960— in U. S. and France. Guggenheim Fellowship in 1961, Award for the National Institute of Arts and Letters, 1961, readings on various "circuits" of colleges, spent six months in 1963 working for CORE in Hammond, Louisiana. Translations from French."

Books of Poetry

What a Kingdom It Was, Houghton Mifflin Co., Boston, 1960.
Flower Herding on Mount Monadnok, Houghton Mifflin Co., Boston, 1964.

Pertinent Reviews of the Poet

Contemporary American Poetry, Glauco Cambon, University of Minnesota pamphlet.

Other Publications

The Poetry of François Villon (translation), New American Library, New York, 1964.

MELVIN WALKER LA FOLLETTE

"Born Evansville, Indiana, September 7, 1930. Grew up in Ridgeville, a small Indiana village. Attended Purdue University, State University of Iowa and University of Washington, B.A. from Washington in 1953. Returned to State University of Iowa for M.A., 1954. Further graduate work at University of California, Berkeley, where I was James Phelan Scholar in Literature during 1956–57. Won New Poets of the Midwest Award, 1954. Taught in University of British Columbia, Oregon State University, San Jose State College. Studied poetry writing with Paul Engle, Richard Eberhart, Robert Lowell and John Berryman. Married Alice Louise Simpson on December 26, 1958. One child, a two year old son, and one expected."

Mr. La Follette is at present studying for the priesthood of the Episcopal Church at Berkeley Divinity School, New Haven, Connecticut.

Books of Poetry

The Clever Body, Spenserian Press, San Francisco, 1959.

Other Publications

"Blue Eyes" (story), *Ramparts,* January 1963.
Poems included in the following anthologies: *New Orlando Poetry Anthology,* 1963; *New Poets of England and America,* First Selection 1957, Second Selection, 1962; *Oregon Signatures,* 1959; Borestone Mountain Poetry Awards anthology, *Best Poems of 1963.*

Pertinent Reviews of the Poet

"Hepcats To Hipsters," William Raymond Smith, *The New Republic,*
    April 21, 1958.
Kenneth Rexroth, New York *Times Book Review,* December 27, 1959.
Ralph Pomeroy, *Poetry,* September 1960.
James Dickey, *Sewanee Review,* Autumn 1960.

Recordings

Library of Congress.
The United States in Literature, Scott, Foresman & Co., Chicago, 1960.
    (includes an oral interpretation of "The Ballad of Red Fox")

Magazines Liked

Anagogic and Paedeumic Review, Beloit Poetry Journal, Botteghe Oscure, Experiment, New Orleans *Poetry Journal, New World Writing, The New Yorker,* New York *Times, Northwest Review, Poetry, Prairie Schooner, Prism, Time and Tide* (London).

GERRIT LANSING

"Born Albany, New York, 1928, grew up on farm in Chagrin Falls, Ohio, public schools in Ohio, B.A., Harvard; M.A., Columbia, worked for publishers George W. Stewart, Inc. and Columbia University Press in New York City as well as varied temporary jobs. Now living in Gloucester, Massachusetts, editor of irregularly appearing poetry periodical *SET.* (For those interested in starry symbolism, of strongly Neptunian character, Sun in Pisces, Scorpio rising.)"

Other Publications

"Liberation and Rebirth," in *Tomorrow* magazine, reprinted in *Does Man Survive Death?* (Eileen J. Garrett, ed.), Helix Press, New York, n.d.

Pertinent Reviews by the Poet

"Psychic Elements in Poetic Creativity" in *International Journal of Parapsychology*.

Magazines Liked

Semicolon, Folder, A New Folder, Trobar, Measure, Signal, Set, Matter, Yugen, Nomad, Northwest Review, The Floating Bear, Fuck You: A Magazine of the Arts, Poetry, The Nation, Burning Deck.

PARIS LEARY

"Born in Shreveport, Louisiana, in 1931, educated at St. John Berchman's, a Jesuit Preparatory school for boys in Louisiana, and at the Centenary College of Louisiana (*prix d'excellence* from the French Government for studies in French, B.A. *magna cum laude*). Went up to Oxford (college: St. Edmund Hall), taking the degree of D.Phil. in 1958. Nominated to a Fellowship at Yaddo by Saul Bellow in 1963 where, cheered and instructed by the company of Melvin Walker La Follette, Laurence Lieberman, Robert Sward, and Stephen Sandy, worked on a second novel. Fellow in Poetry at Bread Loaf 1963 where cheer and instruction continued in company of Robert Pack, Nancy Sullivan, William Wetmore and others. I teach in the Department of English and Philosophy at the State University College in New Paltz, New York. I live within hailing distance of Theodore Weiss, Anthony Hecht, Robert Kelly, Gray Burr, and Georgia Lee McElhaney, and our Hudson Valley has sometimes the feel of an eisteddfod. For 1964–65 I am Fulbright Lecturer in English Literature at the University of Leicester."

Books of Poetry

Views of the Oxford Colleges and Other Poems, Charles Scribner's Sons, New York, 1960.

Other Publications

The Innocent Curate (novel), Doubleday & Co., Garden City, New York, 1963.
A Rushing of Wings (three-act play), produced by the Laboratory Theatre, University of Kentucky, 1960.
Included in *Best Poems of 1957* and *Best Poems of 1963*, Stanford University Press, Stanford, Calif.
Included in *Oxford Poetry 1958*, Fantasy Press.
First Prize *Atlantic Contest* (poetry) 1950–51, Atlantic Papers, n.d.
Translations by Carlo Izzo, in *Poesia Americana del '900, a cura di Carlo Izzo,* Ugo Guanda editore, Parma, 1963.

Pertinent Reviews by the Poet

"Letter From Oxford," *Approach*, Winter 1959.
"Dinners And Nightmares" by Diane di Prima, review in *Village Voice*, September 21, 1961.

Pertinent Reviews of the Poet

"An Approach To Seven Poets," Sam Bradley, *Approach,* Summer 1960.

Recordings

Collection of the Poetry Room, Lamont Library, Harvard University, LP and tape available.

Magazines Liked

The New Yorker, Saturday Review, Antioch Review, The Humanist, Midstream, Ramparts, Poetry (Chicago), *Perspective, Approach, Southwest Review, Beloit Poetry Journal, National Review, Epoch, Arizona Quarterly, Compass* (defunct), *Compass Review* (defunct), *Outposts* (London), *Time and Tide* (London), *Spectator* (London), *Contemporary Review* (London), *Elegreba* (Wales), *Universities' Poetry* (Keele, Staffordshire), *Virginia Quarterly Review, Quarterly Review of Literature, Listen* (Hull, Yorkshire), *New Chapter* (London), *Shenandoah, Carolina Quarterly, The Bridge* (defunct), *Chelsea Review* (defunct), *Quixote.* The Third Programme of the BBC is also a friendly "publisher" of new poetry.

DENISE LEVERTOV

"Born in Ilford, Essex, England, October 1923. Educated privately. Grew up in England. Lived in other European countries. Came to United States in 1948 (citizen). Husband is Mitchell Goodman, novelist (*The End of It,* Horizon Press, 1960). Son born 1949, Nikolai. Spent two years in Mexico, 1956–1958. Guggenheim Fellow, 1961–1962. Associate Scholar Radcliffe Institute for Independent Study, 1964–1965. Poetry editor of *The Nation* for eight months in 1961 and now since fall of 1963."

Books of Poetry

The Double Image, Cresset Press, London, 1946.
Here and Now, City Lights Books, San Francisco, 1957.
Overland to the Islands, Jargon Books, Highlands, N. C., 1958.
With Eyes at the Back of Our Heads, New Directions, New York, 1959.
The Jacob's Ladder, New Directions, New York, 1962.
O Taste and See, New Directions, New York, 1964.

Pertinent Reviews by the Poet

Obituary note on William Carlos Williams, *The Nation,* March 1963.

Recordings

Collection of the Poetry Room, Lamont Library, Harvard University, LP and tape.
WBAI tapes.

Magazines Liked

Poetry, Quarterly Review of Literature, Sum, Matter, Rivoli Review, Origin, Black Mountain Review, Combustion, Migrant.

LAURENCE LIEBERMAN

"I was born in Detroit in February 1935. I received a B.A. and M.A. in English from University of Michigan ('56, '58) where I was awarded a Major Hopwood Award in poetry (1958). I have had fellowships to Yaddo (summer 1963) and Huntington-Hartford Foundation (summer

1964). I taught English in California for six years. I became Assistant Professor of English at the College of the Virgin Islands in September 1964.

"Poets talk too much about poetry. And about themselves. The subject of all my recent poetry is Orange County, where I have been a kind of inmate and spy for the past four years. I will be released from the County in three days, but will never go scot free: I will always be a spiritual parolee. There is no place more suited to disaster. Goldwater bumper stickers are only slightly less numerous than license plates. In this John Birch capital of the world, the roots of the grass stick up like nails. To go barefoot is to risk permanent impalement, crucifixion to the earth."

Magazines Liked

The New Yorker, Saturday Review, Atlantic Monthly, Harper's, Paris Review, The Nation, The New Republic, Poetry, San Francisco Review, New Campus Writing 4 (Grove), *Antioch Review, Beloit Poetry Journal, Agenda* (England), *Southwest Review.*

ROBERT LOWELL

"Born in Boston, March 1, 1917. Education: St. Mark's School, Harvard, Kenyon College, Louisiana State. I have taught at Iowa State, Boston University, the Indiana School of Criticism, and Harvard."

Books of Poetry

Land of Unlikeness, Cummington Press, Cummington, Mass., 1944.
Lord Weary's Castle, Harcourt, Brace & Co., New York, 1946.
The Mills of the Kavanaughs, Harcourt, Brace & Co., New York, 1951.
Life Studies, Farrar, Straus & Cudahy, New York, 1959.
Imitations, Farrar, Straus & Co., New York, 1961.
Phedre, Farrar, Straus & Co., New York, 1961.
For the Union Dead, Farrar, Straus & Giroux, New York, 1964.

Pertinent Reviews by the Poet

Interview with Frederick Seidel, Volume 2 of the *Paris Review* interviews.

Recordings

Yale Series of Poetry Readings.

Magazines Liked

Partisan Review, New York *Review of Books, Encounter, The London Observer, Poetry, Hudson Review, Kenyon Review, New Statesman.*

JACKSON MAC LOW

Born September 12, 1922. Grew up in Chicago and Kenilworth, Illinois. High School at New Trier (Winnetka). A.A., University of Chicago, 1941. Lived in New York City after 1943. B.A. *cum laude* (Greek major), Brooklyn College, 1958. Directed Dramatics at Camp Catawba for Boys, Blowing Rock, North Carolina, summers 1950 and 1951. Wrote the music for the Living Theatre production of W. H. Auden's *Age of Anxiety,* 1954. Musical compositions performed in America, France,

Italy, Germany, Denmark. Active in Pacifist and Anarchist movements since the 1940s.

"An 'anarchist' does not believe, as some wrongly have put it, in social chaos. He believes in a state of society wherein there is no frozen power structure, where all persons may make significant initiatory choices in regard to matters affecting their own lives. In such a society coercion is at a minimum & lethal violence practically non-existent. Certainly, there will still be situations where coercion may have to be exercised to prevent something worse, but, as Ammon Hennacy has demonstrated in life, even maniacs with knives may be sometimes pacified without violent coercion. A 'pacificist' believes that better methods than violence may almost always be found to solve social difficulties & resolve differences between individuals & groups. While not all anarchists are pacificists even now, & many pacificists are not anarchists, I think all agree in regarding the individual person as being infinitely precious & as being capable of cooperating with others for the good of all. Let us add to these attitudes that of the Taoist, Zen Buddhist or Kegon Buddhist wherein the elementary actions of the world itself & of 'all sentient beings' are regarded as being on a level with those of human beings in the narrower sense. One comes to a situation wherein 'even plants have rights' (one doesn't chop down a tree unless there's a damn good reason to). How better to embody such ideas in microcosm than to create works wherein both other human beings & their environments & the world 'in general' (as represented by such objectively hazardous means as random digits) are all able to act within the general framework & set of 'rules' given by the poet "the maker of plots or fables" as Aristotle insists—the poet is preeminently the maker of the plot, the framework—not necessarily of everything that takes place within that framework! The poet creates a *situation* wherein he invites other persons & the world in general to be co-creators with him! He does not wish to be a dictator but a loyal co-initiator of action within the free society of equals which he hopes his work will help to bring about.

"That such works themselves may lead to new discoveries about the nature of the world & of man I have no doubt. I have learned, for instance, that it is often very difficult to tell, in many cases, what is 'chance' & what is 'cause.' There are kinds of inner & hidden causation that are very difficult to distinguish, on the one hand, from 'chance' or 'coincidence,' & on the other, from 'synchronicity': 'meaningful acausal interconnection.' Also, absolutely unique situations may arise during performances of such works, & the experiences of those participating in them (whether as performers, audience or both) cannot help but be of new *aesthetic* (experiential) meanings. That is, not only do the works embody & express certain metaphysical, ethical & political meanings, but they also bring into being new aesthetic meanings."

Books of Poetry

The Marrying Maiden (play), The Living Theatre, New York City, 1961, mimeo., 100 copies, forthcoming in *Il Verri*, ed. Feltrinelli, (translation), 1965.

The Twin Plays: Port-Au-Prince and Adams County Illinois, JML & Jerry Bloedow, mimeo, 30 copies, May 1963.

Questions & Answers Incredible Statements The Litany Of Lies Action In Freedom Statements & Questions All Round Truth & Freedom In Action Or Why Is An Atom Bomb Like A Toothbrush? A Topical Play, JML & Jerry Bloedow, mimeo, 30 copies, May 1963.

In *An Anthology* (La Monte Young, ed.), JML & LMY, New York, 1963.

Other Publications

The Pronouns: A Collection of 40 Dances (poems as dance instruction) with Some Remarks To The Dancers, privately printed, April 1964.

Pertinent Reviews by the Poet

"A Poet Of Movement" (Gordon Bottomley and Denys Harding, eds.), Schocken Books, New York, 1961.

"Great Scots Poet," *Poetry* (Chicago), April 1955.

"Poetry, Chance, Silence, etc", *Nomad/New York:* nos. 10–11 of *Nomad*.

"Methods For Reading Asymmetries," *El Corno Emplumado*, Mexico, reprinted in *An Anthology* and *Nomad/New York*.

Recordings

Verdurous Sanguinaria, WBAI, November 1962, tape.

EDWARD MARSHALL

Born in Chichester, New Hampshire, in 1932. Went to school in Concord, New Hampshire, University of New Hampshire, New England College. Has lived in New York since 1956.

Books of Poetry

Hellan Hellan, Auerhahn Press, San Francisco.

MICHAEL McCLURE

"I was born in Marysville, Kansas, on October 20, 1932. Except for flights and trips I have lived in San Francisco for ten years. I have a wife and daughter.

"The INTERNALIZED MYTHOLOGY OF HEAVEN is where I am now! I am longing for my senses . . . I say *forget that.* Some days I am totally *with* my senses and everything is sharp and clear. Today I can barely recall. (The sheer real joy of a cherry blossom! The flaring of the intellect into the depth of the body where there is a one-ness with all of the dark figures of life — and without the sacrifice of each individual animal life.) Today I am not there. Today I am ME inside. It no longer matters whether *me* is EVERYTHING or *me* is the individual. Tomorrow I will be individual again. I will be better for *this* living. Today I cannot remember things, for I am filled with shapes so large they become ONE and vague. I am happier in that other burning state! I know the other state better. Comfort is not the end of life. BUT WE MUST ALL HAVE PLEASURE! Poetry is pleasure for it is the highest equation of our experiences. In its noblest shape poetry is experience. Experience is the cliche of our times! The experience of poetry is immortal. Perhaps this state I am in is poetry. I am devastated by the crushed silver of it! Yesterday I watched a friend of mine have a revelation. Everything he pictured became so beautiful he could not speak of it. My cares dropped away as I watched him. Perhaps this moment I have no cares — that is why I feel this strange way. I am the keeper of beauty. I am a man. My name is Michael. I love you if you are beautiful.

You must forgive me — I go away at times. I am difficult but I will return you to the loveliness of your senses."

Books of Poetry

Hymns to St. Geryon, Auerhahn Press, San Francisco, 1959.
Dark Brown, Auerhahn Press, San Francisco, 1961.
The New Book/A Book of Torture, Grove Press, New York, 1961.
Ghost Tantras, priv. printed, distributed by City Lights Books, San Francisco, 1964.

Other Publications

Meat Science Essays, City Lights Books, San Francisco, 1963.

Magazines Liked

Evergreen Review, Semina, Poetry, Yugen, Black Mountain Review, Chicago, Big Table, Origin, The Nation.

GEORGIA LEE McELHANEY

"Born 1934, Martinsburg, West Virginia, a suburb of Virginia; grew up in New York City. Variously indoctrinated: three and a half years at Shepherd College (history, literature, journalism) among the shades of the battle of Antietam (still in progress); American University; Joseph Grucci's Poetry Workshop at Penn State. Have lived in D. C., Maryland, enough of Pennsylvania. Moment among the Mandans, 1946. Married Jim McElhaney, writer and teacher; have seven year old daughter.

"Yearly practice is to burn all poems written previous year; these three, the first to be published, are among the few that have managed to survive. Dark gods are Kenneth Patchen and William Blackstone, he of the white bull."

THOMAS MERTON

"Born in Prades, France, 1915. Went to schools in New York, Bermuda, France, England, then to Cambridge (Clare College) and Columbia. Got an M.A. after studies on 'Nature and Art in William Blake.'

"Blake's ideas have always had a profound influence on me, also his poetry. Other influences, the metaphysical poets, Spanish modern poets especially Lorca, Altolaguirre, South American poets especially Vallejo, then also of course Dylan Thomas, Eliot. Was teaching English at a Franciscan college upstate, New York (St. Bonaventure) when it became evident to me that I should enter a Trappist monastery, 1941, and I have been here since, and have never questioned my vocation to the monastic life, but have needed more and more solitude. However in the last five years my writing has been very much concerned with the big issues of the day, war, race, peace, etc. I am a priest and am novice master at the monastery of Gethsemani, Kentucky, founded by a bunch of Bretons in 1848 in the knob country of Kentucky, right in the center of the biggest producing area for bourbon in the world."

Books of Poetry

Thirty Poems, New Directions, New York, 1944.
Man in the Divided Sea, New Directions, New York, 1946.
Figures for an Apocalypse, New Directions, New York, 1948.
Tears of the Blind Lions, New Directions, New York, 1950.

The Strange Island, New Directions, New York, 1958.
Selected Poems, New Directions, New York, 1960.
Emblems of a Season of Fury, New Directions, New York, 1964.

Other Publications

The Seven Storey Mountain (Autobiography), Harcourt, Brace & Co., New York, first published 1948, various editions.
Silence in Heaven, The Studio Publications, New York, 1956.
Silent Life, Farrar, Straus & Cudahy, New York, 1957.
Thoughts in Solitude, Farrar, Straus & Cudahy, New York, 1958.
Secular Journal, Farrar, Straus & Cudahy, New York, 1959.
Bread in the Wilderness, New Directions, New York, 1960.
Disputed Questions, Farrar, Straus & Cudahy, New York, 1960.
Behavior of Titans, New Directions, New York, 1961.
The New Man, Farrar, Straus & Co., New York, 1962.
New Seeds of Contemplation, New Directions, New York, 1962.
Original Child Bomb, New Directions, New York, 1962.
The Waters of Siloe, Doubleday & Co., Garden City, New York, 1962.
Thomas Merton Reader (Thomas McDonnell, ed.) Harcourt, Brace & World, New York, 1962.
Life and Holiness, Herder & Herder, New York, 1963.

Pertinent Reviews by the Poet

"Poetry and the Contemplative Life," *Selected Poems* and *Thomas Merton Reader* (see above).

Recordings

Collection of the Poetry Room, Lamont Library, Harvard University (recorded by Robert Speaight).

Magazines Liked

Sewanee Review, Texas Quarterly, El Corno Emplumado (Mexico), *Sur* (Buenos Aires), *Eco* (Buenos Aires), *New Directions Annual.*

W. S. MERWIN

Born in New York in 1927. Prizewinner in the Yale Series of Younger Poets Contest in 1952.

Books of Poetry

A Mask for Janus, Yale University Press, New Haven, Conn., 1952.
Dancing Bears, Yale University Press, New Haven, Conn., 1954.
Green with Beasts, Alfred A. Knopf, New York, 1956.
Drunk in the Furnace, The Macmillan Co., New York, 1960.
Moving Target, Atheneum Publishers, New York, 1964.

Other Books

Some Spanish Ballads (trans.), Doubleday & Co. (Anchor Books), Garden City, N. Y., 1961.
Song of Roland in *Medieval Epics,* Modern Library, New York, 1963.
Poem of the Cid (trans.), New American Library (Mentor Books), New York, 1962.

VASSAR MILLER

Born in Houston, Texas, in 1924.

Books of Poetry

Wage War on Silence, Wesleyan University Press, Middletown, Conn., 1960.

My Bones Being Wiser, Wesleyan University Press, Middletown, Conn., 1964.

FRANK O'HARA

Frank O'Hara first became associated with The Museum of Modern Art in 1951. An art critic, poet and playwright, he resigned in 1953 to devote himself to creative writing. In 1955 he rejoined The Museum and since that time has organized circulating exhibitions. In 1960 he was appointed Assistant Curator of the Department of Painting and Sculpture Exhibitions.

Among the exhibitions selected by Mr. O'Hara for showing abroad are the United States representations at the IV São Paulo Bienal, the IV International Art Exhibition of Japan in 1957, and Documenta II in Kassel, Germany, in 1959. A Jackson Pollock retrospective organized by Mr. O'Hara toured Europe in 1958. For the United States representation at the XXIX Biennale in Venice in 1958 he chose works by Seymour Lipton and Mark Tobey. He organized one-man shows of works by Robert Motherwell and Reuben Nakian which comprised part of the United States representation at the VI São Paulo Bienal in 1961.

Mr. O'Hara directed "New Spanish Painting and Sculpture" which was shown at the Museum in 1960.

Following service in the U. S. Navy, Mr. O'Hara attended Harvard University and was graduated in 1950. He studied English and creative writing at Michigan University and received a Master of Arts degree in 1951, and the Avery Hopwood Award for Poetry. In 1956 he had a one-semester fellowship at the Poet's Theatre in Cambridge, Massachusetts.

Mr. O'Hara has served as an apprentice in stagecraft at the Brattle Theatre in Cambridge and has had two verse plays performed—one at the Poets Theatre, and another at the Artists Theatre in New York.

Four volumes of his poems have been published, *A City Winter and Other Poems, Meditations in an Emergency, Second Avenue,* and *Odes.* He was formerly an Editorial Associate of *Art News* and has also published art criticism in *Folder, Evergreen Review* and other periodicals. He is the author of a monograph on Jackson Pollock published by Braziller, as well as the catalog published by The Museum of Modern Art for *New Spanish Painting and Sculpture.* In early 1965 City Lights Books published a new collection of his poems, *Lunch Poems.*

CHARLES OLSON

Born December 27, 1910, in Worcester, Massachusetts.

Books of Poetry

To Corrado Cagli, Knoedler Gallery, New York, 1947.

Y and X Poems, 1948.

Letter for Melville, 1951.

This, Black Mountain College Graphics Workshop, No. 1, 1952.
Anecdotes of the Late War, Jargon Broadside 1, n.d.
In Cold Hell in Thicket, in *Origin* 8, 1953.
Maximus 1–10, in *Jargon* 7, Highlands, N. C., 1953.
Maximus 11–22, in *Jargon* 9, Highlands, N. C., 1956.
O'Ryan 2, 4, 6, 8, 10. San Francisco, 1958.
The Maximus Poems, Jargon/Corinth, New York, 1960.
The Distances, Grove Press, New York, 1960.
Maximus from Dogtown I, Auerhahn Press, San Francisco, 1961.

Other Publications

Mayan Letters, Divers Press, Palma de Mallorca, Spain, 1953.
Call Me Ishmael, Grove Press, New York, reprinted 1958.
Projective Verse, Poetry, New York, 1950 (reprinted c. 1959 by Totem Press, New York, with Letter to E. B. Feinstein, and again in *The New American Poetry, 1945–1960*, Grove Press, New York, 1960).
Proprioception, in press. Essays reprinted largely from those which have appeared c. 1961–1962 in *The Floating Bear* and *Kulchur*.
Essays and reviews, especially in *Origin* 1 (1951), *Black Mountain Review* (passim), *The Floating Bear* (passim).

JOEL OPPENHEIMER

"Born Yonkers, New York, February 18, 1930, raised and schooled there till 1947, no degrees but some education at Cornell University, University of Chicago, and a good deal at Black Mountain College. Worked as a printer-typographer-advertising production man from 1953 on: Washington, D. C., Rochester, New Hampshire, Provincetown, Massachusetts, New York City. Believe with Williams that poetry is the most difficult of the arts, and, following his lead in another direction too, find it bugging but helpful to be working daily in another field; Olson once said I was the only man who had learned a trade I could live by at Black Mountain, and I'm only a little guilty about this fact. My verse seems concerned for the most part with the inter-personal relationship: man-to-woman, man-to-man, man-to-child; otherwise I drink, love, and play games."

Books of Poetry

The Dancer, Jargon Books, Highlands, N. C., 1952.
The Dutiful Son, Jargon Books, Highlands, N. C., 1957.
The Love Bit, Totem/Corinth, New York, 1962.
The Great American Desert (plays), Grove Press, New York, 1965.

Pertinent Reviews by the Poet

Statement, *Nomad* 5/6 (London, Villiers), Winter–Spring 1960.
Letter, *Yugen* 7, 1961.
"Not Even Important" (review of Sam Greenberg), *Kulchur* 3, 1961.
"Given Other Necessities" (review of Ed Dorn), *Kulchur* 4, 1961.

Pertinent Reviews of the Poet

Robert Creeley, *New Mexico Quarterly*, Spring–Summer, 1957.
Frederick Eckman, *Cobras and Cockle-Shells*, Vagrom Chapbook No. 5, 1958.
Gilbert Sorrentino, *Kulchur* 9, 1963.
Robert Sward, *Poetry*, August 1963.

Magazines Liked

Trobar, The Signal, Joglars, Wild Dog, Fuck You: A Magazine of the Arts, The Floating Bear, Black Mountain Review, Origin, Neon, Galley Sail, White Dove, Hearse, Chicago Review, Big Table, Nomad.

ROCHELLE OWENS

"Born Brooklyn, New York, 1936. Have resided in New York City ten years. Interested in archaeology, history, philosophy. Have written three plays, of which the first, *Futz,* is scheduled for off-Broadway production season of 1964–65 with Judith Malina and Julian Beck directing. Currently working on a novel, *Elga's Incantation.*"

Books of Poetry

Not Be Essence That Cannot Be, Trobar Books, New York, 1961.
Four Young Lady Poets, Totem/Corinth, New York, 1962.

Other Publications

Futz (a play), Hawk's Well Press, New York, 1962.
"The Girl on the Garage Wall" (story), *El Corno Emplumado* 3.
"The Obscenities of Reva Cigarnik" (story), *El Corno Emplumado* 11.

Pertinent Reviews by the Poet

Review of Armand Schwerner's *The Lightfall* in *Kulchur* 15, September 1964.

Pertinent Reviews of the Poet

Review of *Futz* in *Kulchur* 11, 1963, by Saul Gottlieb.

Magazines Liked

Trobar, El Corno Emplumado, Yugen, Fuck You: A Magazine of the Arts, Yowl, Poems from the Floating World, Matter, Hardware Poets Occasional.

ROBERT PACK

Born in New York in 1929, educated at Dartmouth College and Columbia University. He was poetry editor for *Discovery* magazine, and has lectured on modern poetry and Tennyson at the YMHA. He has taught a Writer's Workshop at the New School. He has received various awards and grants: a Fulbright Fellowship in Italy, a Grant in Literature from the National Institute of Arts and Letters, and has been several times a staff member at the Bread Loaf Writer's Conference. He has taught at Barnard College, and is at present on the faculty of Middlebury College.

Books of Poetry

The Irony of Joy in Poets of Today II, Charles Scribner's Sons, New York, 1955.
Stranger's Privilege, The Macmillan Co., New York, 1959.
Guarded by Women, Random House, New York, 1963.

Other Publications

Forgotten Secret, The Macmillan Co., New York, 1959.
Then What Did You Do? The Macmillan Co., New York, 1961.

Mozart's Librettos, with Marjorie Lelash, Meridian Books, New York, 1961.

New Poets of England and America, ed. (with Donald Hall), Meridian Books, New York, 1962.

Wallace Stevens: An Approach to His Poetry and Thought, Rutgers University Press, New Brunswick, N. J., 1958.

Anthology of Religious Poetry, ed. (with Tom Driver), The Macmillan Co., New York, 1963.

KENNETH PITCHFORD

"Born January 24, 1931. (NOTE: Flap of Scribner's book incorrectly lists 1930, which was repeated in Cole's anthology.) Birthplace, Moorhead, Minnesota. Colleges: Moorhead State Teachers College, University of Minnesota (B.A., *summa cum laude,* 1952), University of Washington, Oxford University (Fulbright to Magdalen College, 1956–57), New York University (M.A., 1959). Army: Supply sergeant in infantry rifle company; 1953–55. Taught four years at NYU, including freshman composition, sophomore world literature, contemporary poetry, and poetry workshops. Taught writing of poetry at the New School for Social Research. I am at present a free-lance editor, which I prefer to teaching. Besides poems, I write plays, stories, and am now working on a long novel. Married Robin Morgan, poet and actress, in 1962.

"Content, frankly, interests me. I dislike the solipsism of many contemporary artists. I like art that is "about" something other than itself. Inbreeding is unwise. All this is heresy. In general, abstractions bore me (including these abstract comments). I look forward to a greater range and feeling in contemporary American poetry. The surreal image, "craziness," direct accounts of revelatory experience (rather than a casebook of autobiographical facts), jagged and cutting edges, ellipses, unexpected juxtapositions of time, place, object, character, symbol and concern for shared problems and worlds rather than purely private ones —all of these things interest me.

"I am sad that while religious convictions often form the background for good poems, political convictions seldom do. The thirties was a test case. Nonetheless, I feel that a poet's work should somehow reflect the whole range of his perceptions, concerns, and responses to experience and consequently I keep trying to write the 'engaged' poem with the hope that one day I shall be successful at it."

Books of Poetry

The Blizzard Ape in Poets of Today V, Charles Scribner's Sons, New York, 1958.

Other Publications

The Brothers, a novella, in *New World Writing* 21.

Templates for a Family Group, winner of the Isis Short Story Contest 1956 (judge: V. S. Pritchett).

Magazines Liked

Accent, Beloit Poetry Journal, Blue Guitar, The Carleton Miscellany, Carolina Quarterly, Chelsea, Chicago Review, Departure, Epoch, Gemini, Isis, Kenyon Review, The Listener, The Nation, The New Statesman, The Massachusetts Review, The New Republic, The New Yorker, Oxford Opinion, Perspective, Poetry (Chicago), *Poetry Broadside, Prai-*

rie Schooner, Shenandoah, Transatlantic Review, Quixote, Western Review.

RALPH POMEROY

"Born in Illinois on Columbus Day 1926. Name derives from apple country of Normandy (twelfth century) and appears—in original spelling (de la Pommeraie)—in discussion of place names carried on by M. Brichot in *Remembrance of Things Past*. Have worked as magazine editor, art gallery director, assistant stage manager, candy salesman in Radio City Music Hall, bartender. Have spent long periods abroad since 1947; England, Scotland, France, Italy, Spain, Belgium, Holland, Germany, Denmark. In America, grew up in Winnetka, Illinois. Attended Art Institute of Chicago Saturday classes and Summer School; University of Illinois; University of Chicago. No degree. First poem published in *Poetry*, 1948. Awarded fellowship to Yaddo in 1955 at recommendation of Katherine Anne Porter. Read poems for station WBAI, New York, 1963. Interviewed and reading in Flemish translation and English on Belgium Third Program, 1963. Gave up painting (after considerable early success) in Paris in 1949. Returned to it in 1960. One man show in Denmark in 1963. Living in San Francisco."

Books of Poetry
Stills & Movies, Gesture Press, San Francisco, 1961.

Pertinent Reviews by the Poet
Review of seven poets, *Poetry*, September 1960.

Pertinent Reviews of the Poet
X. J. Kennedy, *Poetry*, February 1962.
Thom Gunn, *Yale Review*, June 1961.

Recordings
Library of Congress.

Magazines Liked
Poetry, The New Yorker, Harper's Bazaar, Quarterly Review of Literature, Prairie Schooner, San Francisco Review, Paris Review, Botteghe Oscure, The London Magazine, The Times Literary Supplement, The Listener, New Statesman, Transatlantic Review.

ADRIENNE RICH

Born Baltimore, Maryland, 1929. A.B., Radcliffe College, 1951. Winner of Yale Younger Poets award, 1951. Guggenheim Fellowships, 1952–53, 1961–62. National Institute of Arts and Letters award for poetry, 1961. Amy Lowell Travelling Scholarship, 1962–63. Married Alfred H. Conrad, 1953; three sons, born 1955, 1957, 1959.

Books of Poetry
A Change of World, Yale University Press, New Haven, Conn., 1951.
The Diamond Cutters, Harper & Row, New York, 1955.
Snapshots of a Daughter-in-Law, Harper & Row, New York, 1963.

Pertinent Reviews by the Poet

"The Lordly Hudson: Collected Poems, by Paul Goodman," New York
Review of Books, 1st issue, n.d.
"Mr. Bones, He Lives," review of John Berryman's 77 *Dream Songs*, in
The Nation, May 1964.

Recordings

Collection of the Poetry Room, Lamont Library, Harvard University,
LP and tape.

Magazines Liked

The Nation, New York *Review of Books, Poetry, Paris Review.*

JEROME ROTHENBERG

"Born December 11, 1931, New York City, grew up in Bronx, graduated
CCNY, University of Michigan through M.A., two years in Army
(mostly Germany), since then living in New York where I founded and
still publish Hawk's Well Press and Poems from the Floating World,
translate, travel, teach. Had married Diane Brodatz: 1952.

"About then (1952) too began to sense 'Image' as a power (among
several) by which the poem is sighted & brought close—a concern that
developed quickly after 1958 & later in close workings with Kelly, Antin,
Schwerner, Bly, others, readings in Blake, Rimbaud, Neruda, Whitman,
New American & German Poets, Ancient Texts of Lost Tribes, Aztecs,
Navahos, etc., leading (in a world cut-off from vision & thereby incomplete) to reconsideration of the poem's roots in, e.g., shamanism & to
a growing sense of powers, new & old, of word & song & image still here
as keys for any man who reaches for them to-his-limits & spite of cau-
tionary schools, etc. But I hope never to have locked that door."

Books of Poetry

White Sun Black Sun, Hawk's Well Press, New York, 1960.
New Young German Poets, City Lights Books, San Francisco, 1959.
The Seven Hells of the Jigoku Zoshi, Trobar Books, New York, 1962.
Sightings I–IX, Hawk's Well Press, New York, 1964.

Other Published Works

New York playing version of "The Deputy" (Der Stellvertreter) by Rolf
Hochhuth—produced 1964 but not in print.

Pertinent Reviews by the Poet

"Why Deep Image?", *Trobar* 3, 1961.
"The Deep Image is the Threatened Image," *Poems from the Floating
World* 4, 1962.
"An Exchange: Deep Image & Mode" (with Robert Creeley), *Kulchur*
6, 1962.

Pertinent Reviews of the Poet

Anselm Hollo, "Write the Poem," *Kulchur* 11, 1963.
Robert Kelly, "Notes on the Poetry of Deep Image," *Trobar* 2, 1961.

Recordings

"Primitive & Archaic Poetry," Folkways Records.

Magazines Liked

Trobar, Poems from the Floating World, El Corno Emplumado, Some/Thing, Poor·Old·Tired·Horse, Nomad, Evergreen Review, The Sixties, Poetry (Chicago), *The Nation, Yugen, Folio.*

STEPHEN SANDY

"Born August 2, 1934, in Minneapolis, Minnesota, where raised. Service: Army and Navy; education: Yale and Harvard. Employers: Armed Forces and Harvard."

Publications

Caroms, Groton, 1961.
Mary Baldwin, The Dolmen Press, Dublin, Ireland, 1962.
The Destruction of Bulfinch's House, Identity Poetry, Cambridge, Mass., 1963.

Magazines Liked

Chelsea, Chicago Review, Minnesota Review.

FREDERICK SEIDEL

"Born February 19, 1936, St. Louis, Missouri. St. Louis Country Day School; B.A., Harvard. Now living in New York City."

Books of Poetry

Final Solutions, Random House, New York, 1963.

Magazines Liked

Hudson Review, Partisan Review, Paris Review.

ANNE SEXTON

Born November 9, 1928, Newton, Massachusetts. Married in 1948, two children, ages ten and eight. No visible education.

Books of Poetry

To Bedlam & Part Way Back, Houghton Mifflin Co., Boston, 1960.
All My Pretty Ones, Houghton Mifflin Co., Boston, 1962.

Other Publications

"Dancing the Jig" (short story), *New World Writing* 16.

Magazines Liked

Hudson Review, Poetry (Chicago), *Harper's.*

W. D. SNODGRASS

Born in Wilkinsburg, Pennsylvania, in 1926. Pulitzer Prize winner. Teaches at Wayne State University in Detroit. Deeply influenced by the Texas poet S. S. Gardons.

Books of Poetry

Heart's Needle, Alfred A. Knopf, New York, 1959.

GARY SNYDER

"Born in San Francisco, 1930. Grew up, Washington-Oregon. B.A., Reed College, 1951; Japanese and Chinese studies, University of California at Berkeley, 1953–1956; 1956–1964 mostly in Japan. Occupational skills —logging, forestry, carpentry, seaman.

"America five hundred years ago was clouds of birds, miles of bison, endless forests and grass and clear water. Today it is the tired ground of the world's dominant culture. Only Americans and a few western Europeans have lived with industry and the modern mass so long—the Africans and Chinese are fascinated children.

"There is not much wilderness left to destroy, and the nature in the mind is being logged and burned off. Industrial-urban society is not 'evil' but there is no progress either. As poet I hold the most archaic values on earth. They go back to the Neolithic: the fertility of the soil, the magic of animals, the power-vision in solitude, the terrifying initiation and rebirth, the love and ecstasy of the dance, the common work of the tribe. A gas turbine or an electric motor is a finely-crafted flint knife in the hand. It is useful and full of wonder, but it is not our whole life.

"I try to hold both history and the wilderness in mind, that my poems may approach the true measure of things and stand against the unbalance and ignorance of our times. The soil and human sensibilities may erode away forever, even without a great war."

Books of Poetry

Riprap, Origin Press, Kyoto, Japan, 1959.
Myths & Texts, Totem/Corinth, New York, 1960.

Other Publications

"Buddhist Anarchism," *Journal for the Protection of All Beings,* City Lights, San Francisco.

Magazines Liked

Evergreen Review, Northwest Review, Poetry, Trobar, Yugen, Open Space, Origin.

JACK SPICER

"Born in Hollywood in 1925. Am by trade a research linguist. Member of the California Republican Army which hopes by violent means to reestablish an independent California which will ally itself with France and China."

Books of Poetry

After Lorca, White Rabbit Press, San Francisco, 1957.
Billy The Kid, Enkidu Surrogate, Stinson Beach, Calif., 1959.
The Heads of the Town Up to the Aether, Auerhahn Press, San Francisco, 1962.
Lament for the Makers, White Rabbit Press, San Francisco, 1963.
The Holy Grail, White Rabbit Press, San Francisco, 1964.

Recordings

Included in Evergreen's recording of *San Francisco Scene.*

Magazines Liked

J, Open Space.

NANCY SULLIVAN

"Born in Newport, Rhode Island, on July 3, 1929. Brought up in New York City. Education: B.A., Hunter College, 1951; M.A., University of Rhode Island, 1953; Ph.D., University of Connecticut, 1963. I've taught at University of Rhode Island and Brown University. Presently I'm assistant professor of English at Rhode Island College. The summer jobs I've had have also been connected with books: editorial department of Oxford University Press and the advertising department of The Macmillan Company. One summer I wrote articles for a children's encyclopedia.

"My poem, 'The History of the World as Pictures,' began after I had read Ortega's theory that if you placed all the pictures ever painted next to one another in order, you would have represented there the history of painting. I decided that the history of the world might be represented by certain pictures from certain centuries. The poem traces our history from the B.C. cave to Pollock's post-war 'Number I.' I've tried to include East and West, different schools, different countries, different theories as represented in the paintings, as well as the similarities in each that is the essential struggle to express its own time for all time."

Pertinent Reviews by the Poet

"Robert Lowell, An Impression," interview with Robert Lowell, Providence *Sunday Journal*, November 5, 1961.

Other Publications

"Lawrence Durrell's Epitaph for the Novel" (essay), *The Personalist*, XLIV (Winter 1962–63), 79–88.

Magazines Liked

Chelsea, Southwest Review, Beloit Poetry Journal, New Mexico Quarterly, Poetry (Chicago), *Perspective, Accent, Transatlantic Review, The Carleton Miscellany, Wormwood Review, The Massachusetts Review, Quarterly Review of Literature, Ramparts, Poetry Northwest, The Georgia Review, Saturday Review, Southern Review.*

ROBERT SWARD

"Born in Chicago, 1933. Grew up and went to public schools in Chicago. Enlisted in U. S. Navy during the Korean War and served in the Pacific, in Korea and Japan. B.A. degree from the University of Illinois (1956); M.A. degree from Iowa State University (1958). Fulbright grant for study in England, 1960–1961. Guggenheim Fellowship for Poetry, 1964–1965. Have worked as a gardener and taught at Cornell University in the Writing Program."

Books of Poetry

Uncle Dog, and Other Poems, Putnam & Co., Ltd., London, 1962.
Kissing the Dancer, and Other Poems, Cornell University Press, Ithaca, N. Y., 1964.

Other Publications

Review of Webster's Third International Dictionary, *Poetry*, June 1962.

Pertinent Reviews by the Poet

"Signatures," *Poetry*, August 1963.
Review of *Borestone Awards Anthology, Best Poems of 1961*, in *Epoch*, Winter 1962.

Pertinent Reviews of the Poet

William Meredith, Introduction to *Kissing the Dancer*, Cornell University Press, Ithaca, N. Y., 1964.

Recordings

Library of Congress.

Magazines Liked

Ambit (London), *The Carleton Miscellany, Chelsea, Hudson Review, Mt. Shasta Selections* (MSS), *Poetry Magazine, Poetry Northwest, Shenandoah*.

DIANE WAKOSKI

"Born August 3, 1937, Whittier, California; grew up in southern California; B.A., University of California at Berkeley; have worked as bookstore clerk; junior high school teacher. I feel that poetry is the completely personal expression of someone about his feelings and reactions to the world. I think it is *only interesting* in proportion to how interesting the person who writes it is."

Books of Poetry

Coins and Coffins, Hawk's Well Press, New York, 1961.

Magazines Liked

Trobar, El Corno Emplumado.

THEODORE WEISS

Born December 16, 1916, Reading, Pennsylvania; grew up mainly in Allentown. A.B., Muhlenberg College, 1938. M.A., Columbia University, 1940. Taught English at University of North Carolina, Yale University and the New School. Was visiting professor of poetry at MIT 1961–62. At present professor of literature at Bard College. Ford Fellow 1953–54, winner of Wallace Stevens Award in 1956. Ten lectures on Shakespeare at the YM-YWHA, New York, in 1965. Has lived and traveled widely abroad, including Russia. An honorary Fellow of Ezra Stiles College, Yale University, and a member of the PEN Club.

"I am concerned in a proudly snippety time with the sustained poem, one that is more than merely personal and lyrical and happily fragmented. It is easy to go with the time or to cry out against it; but to do something with it, to take it by surprise, to make more of it (as poets usually have) than it can do itself—might that not still occupy poets? And let it be poetry, rather than the poor poet and his predicaments."

Books of Poetry

The Catch, Twayne Library of Modern Poetry, New York, 1951.
Outlanders, The Macmillan Co., New York, 1960.
Gunsight, New York University Press, New York, 1962.

Other Publications

Selections from the Note-Books of Gerard Manley Hopkins, ed., New Directions, New York, 1945.

"Franz Kafka and the Economy of Chaos," *The Kafka Problem,* New Directions, New York, 1946.

"The Nonsense of Yvor Winters' Anatomy," *Quarterly Review of Literature,* Spring 1944 and Summer 1944.

"How to End the Renaissance," *Sewanee Review,* forthcoming.

Pertinent Reviews by the Poet

"Gerard Manley Hopkins: A Realist on Parnassus," *Accent Anthology,* Harcourt, Brace & Co., New York, 1946.

"Towards a Modern Classicism and a Classical Modernity," reprint of a broadcast on the Voice of America, 1964.

Pertinent Reviews of the Poet

John Holmes, New York *Times,* October 28, 1951.
Warren Carrier, *Western Review,* Spring 1952.
E. L. Mayo, *Poetry,* February 1953.
Harry Berger, *The Fat Abbot,* Summer–Fall, 1961 (a major essay).
James Dickey, *Sewanee Review,* Spring 1961.
R. W. Flint, *The New Republic,* November 16, 1963.
M. L. Rosenthal, *The Reporter,* September 12, 1963.
David Galler, *Minnesota Review,* Spring 1963.
David Hughes, *The Nation,* June 29, 1963.
Richard Howard, *Poetry,* July 1963.

Recordings

Yale Series of Recorded Poets (YP315).
Collection of the Poetry Room, Lamont Library, Harvard University, LP and tape.
Library of Congress.
The Voice of America.

Magazines Liked

Poetry, Sewanee Review, Kenyon Review, Partisan Review, The Nation, The New Republic, Saturday Review, Yale Review, The Fat Abbot, Accent, Johns Hopkins Review, Contemporary Poetry, Beloit Poetry Journal, MS.

JOHN WIENERS

"Born, Boston, 1934; grew up in Milton, Massachusetts. Educated in Boston, at Jesuit College, Boston College; and Black Mountain College, 1955 and '56. Received A.B. from Boston College in English, 1954. Attended Black Mountain College and studied under Robert Duncan and Charles Olson. Lived in New York, San Francisco, before returning to Boston, 1963. Founded magazine *Measure* with Robin Blaser and Steve Jonas in Boston, 1957. Am now living at home and working in Jordan Marsh Co. part-time, selling magazines for a livelihood, $1.25 an hour, plus $10.00 a month commission. Received award from Poets' Foundation in 1961 for $1500, and grant from New Hope Foundation through Stanley Kunitz, for $300 in 1964. Plan to have new book of poems published by Auerhahn Press this year, after four years of planning. No hope yet.

"Would like to write for the theatre, poems and songs to be set to music, but know no musicians, à la Noel Coward, who really was Franz Lehar. So have to be content with poetry, which is my main source of dreaming. Also would like to see my work set to music, for torch-singers."

Books of Poetry

The Hotel Wentley Poems, Auerhahn Press, San Francisco, 1958.
Ace of Pentacles, Phoenix Bookshop, New York, 1964.

Pertinent Reviews of the Poet

Allen Ginsberg, "Notes On Young American Poets," *Big Table* 4, 1960.
LeRoi Jones, "The Hotel Wentley Poems," *Kulchur* 2, 1960.
David Schaff, "Some Statements on Projective Verse," *The Yale Literary Magazine:* "New Poetry, 1963."
Irving Rosenthal, "Poetas en Caballeros," *Lunes de la Revolución,* Cuba, 1961.

Magazines Liked

Chicago Review, Evergreen Review, Semina, Measure, The Floating Bear, The Nation, Poetry (Chicago), *C, Sum, Matter, Desert Review, Theo, Joglars, Poems from the Floating World, Trobar, Damascus Road, Granta* (England), *Paris Review, Open Space, Art & Literature, The Rivoli Review, Blue Grass, Kulchur, Tish, Audit, Potpourri, City Lights Journal, Set.*

RICHARD WILBUR

"Born New York City, March 1, 1921. Raised on a farm in New Jersey. Amherst, 1942. Two years' service with 36th infantry in Italy, France and Germany, 1943–45. M.A., Harvard, 1947. Member Society of Fellows, Harvard, 1947–50. Taught at Harvard, 1950–54; at Wellesley, 1955–57; at Wesleyan since. Married, four children. Travels in France, Italy, Russia. Various prizes and fellowships."

Books of Poetry

The Beautiful Changes and Other Poems, Reynal & Hitchcock, New York, 1947.
Ceremony and Other Poems, Harcourt, Brace & Co., New York, 1950.
Things of This World, Harcourt, Brace & Co., New York, 1956.
Advice to a Prophet, Harcourt, Brace and World, New York, 1961.
The Poems of Richard Wilbur, Harcourt, Brace and World (Harvest Books), New York, 1963.

Other Publications

A Bestiary (ed.), Pantheon Books, New York, 1955.
The Misanthrope (trans.), Harcourt, Brace & Co., New York, 1955.
Tartuffe (trans.), Harcourt, Brace and World, New York, 1963.
Candide (with Lillian Hellman), Random House, New York, 1957.
The Poems of Poe (ed.), Dell Publishing Co., New York, 1959.

Pertinent Reviews by the Poet

"Round About a Poem of Housman's," *The Moment of Poetry*, (D. C. Allen, ed.), The Johns Hopkins Press, Baltimore, Md.

"Sumptuous Destitution," *Emily Dickinson: Three Views*, Amherst College.

"The House of Poe," *Anniversary Lectures*, Library of Congress.

"Poetry and the Landscape," *The New Landscape* (Gyorgy Kepes, ed.).

Pertinent Reviews of the Poet

Randall Jarrell, *National Poetry Festival*, Library of Congress, 1964.

Recordings

The Poems of Richard Wilbur, Spoken Arts.
Library of Congress.

Magazines Liked

Poetry, The New Yorker, New York *Review of Books*.

JONATHAN WILLIAMS

"Born, March 8, 1929, Asheville, North Carolina. Education: St. Albans School, Princeton, Atelier 17, Institute of Design (Chicago), Black Mountain College. Since 1951 the publisher and designer of *Jargon Books*, Highlands, North Carolina. Since 1954 over 300 readings of my own work and the poets espoused in *Jargon* in America and Britain. Guggenheim Fellowship, 1957–1958, for poetry; Longview Grant, 1960, for editing of *Jargon*. Poet-in-residence: Aspen Institute for Humanistic Studies, 1962. Projects under hand: MAHLER, with images by R. B. Kitaj; *NC 64*, with photographs by Lyle Bonge; *AT: A Journal of the Appalachians*, with photographs by Nicolas Dean; SLOW OWLS, anagram poems with Ronald Johnson; *Walks & Writers: a Poet's Britain; Poeticules Criticasters Kitschdiggers & Justfolks: Essays on Caitiffs*.

"The concerns of my work: (1) social justice, (2) the demand for an ecological conscience, (3) the wit and play of the expansive imagination —or, life against death."

Books of Poetry

The Empire Finals at Verona, Jargon 30, Highlands, N. C., 1959.
Amen/Huzza/Selah, Jargon 13a, Highlands, N. C., 1961.
In England's Green &, Auerhahn Press, San Francisco 1962.
Elegies and Celebrations, Jargon 13b, Highlands, N. C., 1963.
Lullabies Twisters Gibbers Drags, Jargon 61, Highlands, N. C., 1963.
Lines About Hills Above Lakes, Roman Books, Fort Lauderdale, Fla., 1964.
Jammin' the Greek Scene, Jargon 13c, Highlands, N. C., 1964.

Pertinent Reviews by the Poet

"Wedging Them Out," *Talisman* 10, 1956.
"Is Pamela McFram Gleese America's Greatest Poet?", *Contact* 10, 1962.
"Edward Dahlberg's Book of Lazarus," *The Texas Quarterly*, Summer 1963.
"My Time Will Yet Come Said Some German," *The De La Rue Journal* 46, 1963.

"Zoo-cough's Key's Nest of Poultry," *Kulchur* 14, 1964.
"Notes on Rainer Maria Gerhardt," *Outburst* 3, 1964.

Pertinent Reviews of the Poet

"More Than Pretty Music," Hugh Kenner, *National Review*, November 19, 1960.
"The Jester," Gilbert Sorrentino, *The Nation*, June 2, 1962.
"on 'In England's Green &,'" Gilbert Sorrentino, *Kulchur* 11, 1963.

Recordings

"Blues & Roots/Rue & Bluets" (Jonathan Williams Reads His Poems), *Folkways Records*, Summer 1964.

Magazines Liked

Black Mountain Review, Origin, Ark II Moby I, The Nation, New Directions 16 & 17, Evergreen Review, Poor·Old·Tired·Horse, Between Worlds, The Review, Beloit Poetry Journal, Books USA, The Spero, Joglars, Vou, Unfolders.

JOHN WOODS

"John Woods was born in 1926 in Martinsville, Indiana, a small farm community near Indianapolis. After service in the Air Force in World War II, he studied at Indiana University, preparing his M.A. collection of poems under the guidance of John Crowe Ransom.

"Mr. Woods is currently an Associate Professor of English at Western Michigan University. He has served as poetry editor for the Indiana University Press, was Robert Frost Fellow at Breadloaf, and has been a resident at Yaddo."

Books of Poetry

The Deaths at Paragon, Indiana, Indiana University Press, Bloomington, Ind., 1955.
On the Morning of Color, Indiana University Press, Bloomington, Ind., 1961.

Pertinent Reviews of the Poet

Robert Huff, "There's Nothing Wrong with Barney's Sister," *Prairie Schooner.*
Robert E. Stauffer, "University Wits and a Western Bard," *Voices, a Journal of Poetry,* December 1962.
Mona Van Duyn, "Ways to Meaning," *Poetry,* September 1962.

Recordings

The Deaths of Paragon, Western Michigan University Aural Press, 1964. LP.

Magazines Liked

Poetry, Fresco (University of Detroit), *Saturday Review, Paris Review, Prairie Schooner, Poetry Northwest, The Massachusetts Review.*

LOUIS ZUKOFSKY

Born January 23, 1904, lower East Side, Manhattan. Has lived in New York City most of his life, the last thirty-two years in Brooklyn overlooking the harbor and skyline, and almost around the corner from the printing shop where Walt Whitman's *Leaves of Grass* was first published. Has taught at the University of Wisconsin, Queen's College, Colgate University and San Francisco State College; now at Polytechnic Institute of Brooklyn.

Books of Poetry

An *"Objectivists" Anthology*, To Publishers, France, 1932.
First Half of "A"-9, privately printed, New York, 1934.
55 Poems, Decker Press, Prairie City, Ill., 1941.
Anew, Decker Press, Prairie City, Ill., 1946.
Some Time, Jargon Books, Highlands, N. C., 1956.
Barely and widely, privately printed, New York, 1958.
"A" 1–12, Origin Press, Kyoto, Japan, 1959.
16 once published, Wild Hawthorn Press, Edinburgh, Scotland, 1962.
I's (pronounced eyes), Trobar Books, New York, 1963.
Found Objects, Blue Grass Press, Georgetown, Ky., 1964.

Other Publications

Le Style Apollinaire (criticism), Paris, France, 1934.
A Test of Poetry (criticism), Objectivist Press, New York, 1948. British ed., Routledge & Kegan Paul, London, 1952. Reprint Jargon/Corinth Books, New York, 1964.
5 Statements for Poetry, San Francisco State College, San Francisco, 1958.
It was (fiction), Origin Press, Kyoto, Japan, 1959.
Bottom: on Shakespeare (criticism), University of Texas Press, Austin, Texas, 1963.

Pertinent Reviews by the Poet

5 Statements for Poetry (reprint), *Kulchur* 7, 8, 10, New York.

Pertinent Reviews of the Poet

Polite Essays, Ezra Pound, Faber & Faber, London, 1937.
Profile Anthology, Ezra Pound, ed., Milan, 1932.
"A New Line is a New Measure," W. C. Williams, *New Quarterly of Poetry*, Winter 1947–48.
"Song/After Bread," Robert Kelly, *Kulchur* 12, Winter 1963.
"A Note on Louis Zukofsky," Robert Creeley, *Kulchur* 14, Summer 1964.

Magazines Liked

Origin, Poetry (Chicago), *Black Mountain Review, Criterion, Contact, The Dial, Exile, Transition, Trobar.*

POSTSCRIPT I

The preface to this book directs the reader's attention to contemporary *poems* and suggests that it is less than useful to consider them chiefly in the light of school or coterie. However, once having read this selection, even that reader most amenable to editorial direction will find it impossible not to wonder at their variety—and to begin to make connections.

He will not discover exactly two or three or four groups of poets under this set of covers, but will surely find it provocative that the same America could produce in the same period such disparate voices as Melvin Walker La Follette and Michael McClure. Both these poets are Western, about the same age, but the worlds they write out of (and to, presumably) seem to have little or no relation to one another, and fashionable classifications will not help in identifying those worlds. It is not that Mr. La Follette pursues the metrical path and is thereby in a tradition of verse that has its source in English, pre-American speech; or that Mr. McClure skips along the open road of free verse in search of native American rhythms and diction. Mr. La Follette's poems are peculiarly American in cadence and diction and sensibility—as any Englishman could tell at first glance. And Mr. McClure's prosody is no freer than that of the nineteenth-century Adah Isaacs Menken and his freedoms from convention no more advanced or uniquely transatlantic than those of the British poets of the thirties, Philip O'Connor and Roger Roughton. No, their differences must be sought elsewhere. The interested reader is encouraged to search out these differences not only between Mr. La Follette and Mr. McClure but also between the other poets (or poems) in this book.

Never, not even in the early decades of this century, has American poetry presented to the public such a bewilderingly various aspect. W. H. Auden, who probably understands Americans better than most people, including Americans, has said that the reason for such variety is that America has no tradition, and that each artist struggles to create one—to which he can subsequently be faithful. The riches of modern American poetry (he avoids the implications of the phrase *nouveau riche*) he ascribes to the solitude and independence in which the creative American mind comes to its own consciousness of itself. A transatlantic master may have his transatlantic disciples (note how many poems, depending on what magazines you read, sound more and more like Charles Olson sounding like W. C. Williams or Frederick Seidel sounding like Anne Sexton sounding like Robert Lowell), but such dependence never flowers into a lasting tradition; it either fades away or degenerates into a poetic fad and so comes to an early end.

American poetry seems rather like New York architecture: it is constructed, admired, attacked or praised, used—and soon destroyed, its site swept clean and then occupied by a form of building that has nothing in common with it. There seems little or no sense of continuity in American poetry. We build a Robinson and tear him down for a Williams. That the best features of both might be united in an "architecture" genuinely new but integrally continuous with both seems rarely to occur to the American mind.

In short, the co-editors of this book are in cordial disagreement over the enduring value of some of these poets but are firmly agreed that this is the time now to present together, in juxtaposition, the different sorts of poets who constitute, in fact, the significant American poetic scene. This is an anthology in tension: it is designed to bring together poets who have heretofore sat at different tables, to see if there can be any conversation. It brings together the leaders of the literary *maquis,* poets like Louis Zukofsky and Charles Olson, seats them next to Theodore Weiss and Anthony Hecht who travel port side out starboard side home, and unashamedly waits to overhear them speak.

The reader should be compelled by this anthology to ask questions and to read further for his answers. Is there a "new" poetry in rebellion against a "traditional" poetry? If so, what is new about the rebels and of what tradition are the Establishment stewards? Happily we no longer use the words "beat" or "academic" to describe American poems, but we must go further. Is Daniel Hoffman a "traditionalist"? Is Robert Sward an antitraditionalist? What entrenched Academy does Theodore Holmes or John Woods represent? What rigid canons have been broken by Denise Levertov or Edward Field?

Curiously the roles are somewhat reversed in contemporary American poetry. The reader will notice that the really academic —the learnedly arcane, frequent references to mythology and non-western philosophies, to other literary productions, esoterica of one sort or another—occurs most frequently among those poets usually thought of as antitraditionalist or antiformalist. Who is more restricted by his own chosen form—Robert Creeley or Kenneth Pitchford? Whose poetry smells more of the lamp—Charles Olson's or Robert Pack's, Robert Duncan's* or Laurence Lieberman's? An investigation of the literary magazines inhabited by those poets popularly supposed to be in revolt evinces an almost overwhelming preoccupation with style, with diction, with admissible or inadmissible ways of composing poetry in twentieth-century America, and, in nearly every case, a rigid dogmatism about what may and

---

* We regret very much that we were unable to obtain Mr. Duncan's permission to reprint any of his poems.

may not be allowed. Not that the answers to the questions just posed make any kind of critical judgment—except upon those who think they do.

Rather, it is a fascinating phenomenon for speculation: a poetic collection (they are scarcely a group or movement) whose so-called "Establishment" are, by and large, in their poems politically *engagé*, and in whose work the passions of men, their follies and achievements, are treated with sympathy and commitment, but most of all, with *concern*, to whom content is as important as form; and a "bohemian" underground, which earns its living frequently by teaching in the university next door, which is as obsessed and preoccupied with matters of style as any Neo-Classicists, and whose doctrinaire rejection of the musical substance of their own language drives its members deeper and deeper into the library stacks in search of epigraphs, tags, and allusive subject-matter. It is as if a Keats were Editor of *The Edinburgh Review* and an Alexander Pope a doctor from Hampstead (Paterson). It is bizarre, and reflects, I suppose, the common madness and wonder of modern America.

Paris Leary

New Paltz, New York

POSTSCRIPT II

Because we cherish life, we cherish the poem as a life-sustaining force. Its strength is the strength of an object: a thing made, a thing present in the orders of our perception.

In our time, in America, there is a vast separation coming more and more to exist between two distinct classes of poets. While other observers have chosen to distinguish the two classes as "schools," "camps," and so on, it appears to me that the separation of which I have spoken, and in recognition of which an anthology such as the present finds its origin, has to do finally not with groups or social arrangements at all, but with a corresponding separation which has, since at least the middle of the nineteenth century, taken place in the nature of poetry itself.

The poem is a life-sustaining force. With rare exceptions in all times, it has traditionally exercised its function by means that are basically decorative. In its substance, in its verbal-musical substance itself, much Western poetry has been content to be beautiful at best, agreeable at average, mildly disturbing at its fiercest, like Hollywood's treatment of a social problem. Those who today drink the bland waters of genteel orthodoxy from such journals as *The New Yorker* may expect to find in those pages verse that aspires to decorate the reader's consciousness in much the same way, and for many of the same reasons, that the furniture displayed in the same pages would decorate the reader's home.

Because of the overwhelming human desire for the familiar, it is to be expected that the bulk of such composition will adhere to traditional "forms"—patterns is a truer word. The harmony of symmetry has often enough before been used to assuage all loss, to shield men from an asymmetrical universe. Within traditional patterns, many an American poet writes to the best of his often great ability, producing work that can be exciting, but often by its ingenuity rather than by its inspiration. The subject-matter will often seem to be daring; but the effect is frequently simply an effect, an affectation of timeliness: saying *condom* in a sonnet is a titillation, a source of that *frisson* a child may derive from saying *damn* in church.

Such work, even the best of it, is to me a kind of perversity: an antiquarianism, whereby a poet insists on reaching his destination via outworn or originally ineffectual instruments. This quality of ineffectuality impinges on the goal itself: poets will write to less and less purpose, whittling their concerns down to the size of their tools. That is innocent enough, sad around the edges, but innocent. Literally perverse to me is the presumption or fatuity of some poets who choose to hum in the measures of Donne or Herbert about important human issues to a generation that has experienced Auschwitz, Nagasaki, Algeria, and the Congo. That is pure escapism, and can catch only the saturated ears of an audience attuned to the reviews and the world of little-magazine infighting. Nor is the perversion or betrayal simply a lack of cogent responsibility to the social and political world of the poet. More deeply, it is a betrayal too of the very achievement of the masters they follow, those masters who, whatever else their businesses, sang in their own voices in their own time.

It is not by subject-matter that we can distinguish between the two classes of poets today. As has been pointed out often enough, the so-called academic poets know as much about politics, sex, money, the racial issue, and despair as the so-called non-academic. Conversely, the so-called non-academic are typically as scholarly, and more allusive, than the so-called academic. All of these matters are general. The difference does lie in this: the so-called academic poet, whatever the urgency of his own convictions, chooses to write in time-worn, pre-existent patterns, and often enough in outworn language, as if he himself did not take himself or the poem seriously enough to want to make it heard *now* by all those beings in the midst of whom he must spend his life. There is nothing sinister in this, no conspiracy of the *laudatores temporis acti;* in all likelihood it is ephemeral, too often it is dull. Social decorative verse, verse that serves to reinforce the typical attitudes of its presumed readers, aims at the topical, yet may, if it's well done, last *malgré lui* as long as Hesiod, or as long as Pope. Men like pretty things; what cat's averse to fish?

There are a great many such fish in these pages; delicate as flounder, rich as pompano, they will please a palate well, and then slip digestibly down.

For the past hundred years (as, again, with preliminary flickers of anticipation all through man's verbal history) there has been a better possibility: to sustain life by the creation of new forms, genuine new verbal structures arising out of our condition to sing to us of all times. The work of Whitman or Rimbaud in the nineteenth century—with awful slowness—has at last alerted us to the possibility of a poem that means something. I mean a poem that is not, like a tune we can choose to hear or to neglect, something for the sake of something else, like a print tacked up on the wall to hide the wall. I mean a poem that means something because it is no longer *about* something but *is* something: but, and this is all-important, a poem that, as a thing, does not come to exist aesthetically and in remoteness, as a thing would be in a museum, unthinged, but as a thing would exist, and possess meaning, in a world of living men. As a chair possesses meaning. Not as furniture, but as a place to sit down.

The poetry of which I speak, the poetry that concerns me and that I have tried to display in this anthology, is a poetry that makes extreme demands upon the reader. It is not content to be background music—taken as background music it is, like all else in that category, aesthetically trivial. On the contrary: it demands everything the reader has; it demands that the reader bring himself to the place of the poem. That sounds like the maxim of an older aesthetic; it is not. He who would sit down must present himself to the chair, bring himself to the place of the chair. Then the sensuous impress of the poem begins.

Much of the poetry in this anthology is of a radical newness. The reader may detect echoes of Eliot, or Stevens, or Yeats: the radical newness of which I speak has nothing to do with illiteracy. Further, the reader may hear, beyond the familiar moderns, music and voices from all earlier ages, spelled over into our time by the poet fully alert to history, time's movement in him, in us. It is the responsibility of the radical poet to apprehend as much of all that has gone before him as he can: to bring that into our age, reviving the past not as antique, bringing it to life transmuted into the present, "set to a new measure," as Duncan defines it in his version of Shelley's "Arethusa." Radical newness fulfils the traditions in the creation of new forms, from which perhaps a tradition of the immediate will arise, one that will not bore us, one that will talk to us of life and in life, one that will be awake in the morning and summon us from sleep.

The prime material of the poem is words. Let there be no doubt about that. In general, the new poetry is the product of those poets who believe in the word, who believe in the word's strength, who do not say: *words fail me,* but who may confess: *I failed the words.* The words do not fail us, and in the strength of that conviction a poetry has lately grown up in America that enlarges human experience and human relations by discovering, in the orders of music, the clarity and meaning of words, the wood of our world that grows from the roots of our consciousness. Modern linguistics hypothesizes a tyranny which language, as a system, exerts over its unconscious users. The radical poetry of the American language would liberate us from that tyranny, in clear consecution of that primal statement of the modern: *je est un autre.*

Utter reliance on the word necessitates as well utter responsibility to the word: the word, shaping itself through the breath or utterance of the poet, rises into form. The only form possible is the form the poem spells itself out in; the traditional metres and stanzas and "forms" are always available for *tours de force,* for training or chaining infant ears. But they do not, cannot, talk to us in our own speech, our own asymmetrical, nervous, alive, embattled, *present* hearing. The true craft, then, of the poet is total response to his materials, to the words, total openness to the powers of source energy—memory or imagination or inspiration, *Mnemosyne* or *Mousa,* we shall not argue that here—arising in him. In that sense, craft is now exactly what it has always deeply been: perfected attention.

I would hereby identify the true tradition of craft and form in our time as the tradition of Blake, Whitman, Pound, Williams, the tradition of the poet bold enough and vulnerable enough to elicit the form inherent in the marriage of himself with his material, the incestuous *hieros gamos,* in Jung's sense, that is the root gesture of all art.

It is plain, then, that my intent in choosing poets for this anthology has been to present those of our contemporaries whose concern has been with formal invention and discovery, whose technical attentions have been devoted ever to sharpening their own instrumentality, who have honored and taught us to honor the words, who have taught us to disdain decorative metaphor for the sake of genuine root metaphor, that transference of charge to the reader (like that "single image" Pound asserts the *Paradiso* to be), who have taught us to be sharp enough to hear the story the words utter, to hear the words' music, to be attentive to that heurism or process of discovery a poem is, to value the breath of life: that is, the breath of a man shaping, being shaped by, the words, who have brought poetry to a new level of being, one that would make us and remake us, the readers, and would make everything new. It is one *god spell,* from Blake's "There Is No Natural Religion" to William Carlos Williams' lines, late in his life, from the incredible "Asphodel, That Greeny Flower:"

> My heart rouses
>   thinking to bring you news
>   of something
> that concerns you
>   and concerns many men. Look at
>   what passes for the new.
> You will not find it there but in
>   despised poems.
>   It is difficult
> to get the news from poems
>   yet men die miserably every day
>   for lack
> of what is found there.

This is a great age of birth in the arts; we must not be seduced by the sheer bulk of fashionable verse into overlooking the plain fact that in the past twenty years poets like Charles Olson, Louis Zukofsky, Robert Duncan, have brought the poem to the new world Whitman had a foothold on, and have reinterpreted and given new worth to the ancient understanding of the poet as custodian of the words (the mythos, the story) of the tribe. At the same time, we must not mistake the great separation between the radical poets and the lapidary antiquarians as a mere *lutte poétique* time's ineluctable dialectic will resolve: schools and groups are not at issue. What is at stake is a radical breakthrough in the nature of human consciousness and the nature of human verbal understanding. Because we cherish life, we must cherish to the uttermost the utmost power of the poem to sustain us.

Robert Kelly

Annandale-on-Hudson, New York

Anthologies are finite. At the close of the present specimen, this editor is concerned to direct the attention of the reader to poets whose work, for one reason or circumstance or another, has not been included. Long active or newly heard from, these poets are currently producing distinct and original work. Enough to suggest that from the roster that follows, an anthology of comparable merit could have been derived.

HELEN ADAM
DAVID ANTIN
CAROL BERGE
RICHARD BRAUTIGAN
CID CORMAN
JUDSON CREWES
GUY DAVENPORT
DIANE DI PRIMA
RICHARD DUERDEN
ROBERT DUNCAN
GEORGE ECONOMOU
CLAYTON ESHLEMAN
SEYMOUR FAUST
VINCENT FERRINI
MAX FINSTEIN
KATHLEEN FRASER
JONATHAN GREENE
KENNETH IRBY
STEVE JONAS
JOHN KEYS

PHILIP LAMANTIA
RON LOEWINSOHN
DAVID MELTZER
BARBARA MORAFF
LORINE NIEDECKER
GEORGE OPPEN
PETER ORLOVSKY
MARGARET RANDALL
M. C. RICHARDS
FRANK SAMPERI
ED SANDERS
ARMAND SCHWERNER
SUSAN SHERMAN
GILBERT SORRENTINO
GEORGE STANLEY
CHARLES STEIN
JOHN THORPE
LEW WELCH
PHILIP WHALEN

R.K.

ANCHOR BOOKS

POETRY

THE AENEID OF VIRGIL—C. Day Lewis, trans., A20

AMERICAN POETRY AND POETICS: Poems and Critical Documents from the Puritans to Robert Frost—Daniel G. Hoffman, ed., A304

THE ANCHOR ANTHOLOGY OF SEVENTEENTH-CENTURY VERSE, Volume 1—Louis L. Martz, ed., ACO13a

THE ANCHOR ANTHOLOGY OF SEVENTEENTH-CENTURY VERSE, Volume 2—Richard S. Sylvester, ACO13b

AN ANTHOLOGY OF FRENCH POETRY from Nerval to Valery, in English Translation with French Originals—Angel Flores, ed., A134

AN ANTHOLOGY OF SPANISH POETRY from Garcilasco to Garcia Lorca, in English Translation with Spanish Originals—Angel Flores, ed., A268

ANTIWORLDS AND "THE FIFTH ACE"—Andrei Voznesensky; Patricia Blake, and Max Hayward, eds., a bilingual edition, A595

BRATSK STATION AND OTHER NEW POEMS—Yevgeny Yevtushenko; Tina Tupikina-Glaessner, Geoffrey Dutton, and Igor Nezhakoff-Koriakin, trans., intro. by Rosh Ireland, A558

THE CANTERBURY TALES OF GEOFFREY CHAUCER—Daniel Cook, ed., A265

COLLECTED POEMS—Robert Graves, A517

THE COMPLETE POETRY OF JOHN MILTON—John T. Shawcross, ed., revised edition, ACO15

THE COMPLETE POEMS AND SELECTED LETTERS AND PROSE OF HART CRANE—Brom Weber, ed., A537

THE COMPLETE POETRY OF JOHN DONNE—John T. Shawcross, ed., ACO11

THE COMPLETE POETRY OF RICHARD CRASHAW—George Walton Williams, ed., ACO14

A CONTROVERSY OF POETS: An Anthology of Contemporary American Poetry—Paris Leary and Robert Kelly, eds., A439

ENGLISH RENAISSANCE POETRY: A Collection of Shorter Poems from Skelton to Jonson—John Williams, ed., A359

ENGLISH ROMANTIC POETRY, Volume I: Blake, Wordsworth, Coleridge and Others—Harold Bloom, ed., A347a

ENGLISH ROMANTIC POETRY, Volume II: Byron, Shelley, Keats and Others—Harold Bloom, ed., A347b

THE FAR FIELD—Theodore Roethke, AO20

FORM AND VALUE IN MODERN POETRY—R. P. Blackmur, A96

GOETHE'S FAUST—Walter Kaufmann, trans., bilingual edition, A328

IN PRAISE OF KRISHNA: Songs from the Bengali—Denise Levertov and Edward C. Dimock, Jr., trans.; Anju Chaudhuri, illus., A545

INSIDE OUTER SPACE: New Poems of the Space Age—Robert Vas Dias, ed., A738

13Ab

ANCHOR BOOKS

FICTION

ARROW OF GOD—Chinua Achebe, intro. by K. W. J. Post, A698

THE COUNTRY OF THE POINTED FIRS AND OTHER STORIES—Sarah Orne Jewett, A26

A DIFFERENT DRUMMER—William Melvin Kelley, A678

DOWN SECOND AVENUE—Ezekiel Mphahlele, A792

DREAM OF THE RED CHAMBER—Tsao Hsueh-Chin; Chi-Chen Wang, trans., A159

ENVY AND OTHER WORKS—Yuri Olesha; Andrew R. MacAndrew, trans., A571

GOD'S BITS OF WOOD—Ousmane Sembene, A729

HALF-WAY TO THE MOON: New Writing From Russia—Patricia Blake and Max Hayward, eds., A483

A HERO OF OUR TIME—Mihail Lermontov; Vladimir Nabokov and Dmitri Nabokov, trans., A133

INFERNO, ALONE AND OTHER WRITINGS—August Strindberg; in new translations, Evert Sprinchorn, ed., A492c

A MAN OF THE PEOPLE—Chinua Achebe, A594

MOTHER EARTH AND OTHER STORIES—Boris Pilnyak; Vera T. Reck and Michael Green, trans. and eds., A625

19 NECROMANCERS FROM NOW: An Anthology of Original American Writing for the 70s—Ishmael Reed, A743

POCHO—José Antonio Villarreal, intro. by Dr. Ramon Ruiz, A744

POOR PEOPLE and A LITTLE HERO—Fyodor Dostoevsky; David Magarshack, trans., A619

REDBURN—Herman Melville, A118

RETURN TO LAUGHTER—Elenore Smith Bowen, Foreword by David Riesman, N36

THE SCARLET LETTER and YOUNG GOODMAN BROWN—Nathaniel Hawthorne, Alfred Kazin, ed., A732

THE SECRET AGENT—Joseph Conrad, A8

THE SHADOW-LINE AND TWO OTHER TALES—Joseph Conrad, intro. by Morton Dauwen Zabel, A178

SISSIE—John A. Williams, A710

THE TALE OF GENJI, I—Lady Murasaki; Arthur Waley, trans., A55

TEN GERMAN NOVELLAS—Harry Steinhauer, ed. and trans., A707

THREE SHORT NOVELS OF DOSTOEVSKY—Constance Garnett, trans.; Avraim Yarmolinsky, ed. and revised, A193

UNDER WESTERN EYES—Joseph Conrad, intro. by Morton Dauwen Zabel, A323

VICTORY—Joseph Conrad, A106

THE WANDERER (LE GRAND MEAULNES)—Henri Alain-Fournier; Françoise Delisle, trans., A14

WHAT MAISIE KNEW—Henry James, A43

ANCHOR BOOKS

CLASSICS AND MYTHOLOGY

ANCHOR BOOKS

FICTION

ARROW OF GOD—Chinua Achebe, intro. by K. W. J. Post, A698

THE COUNTRY OF THE POINTED FIRS AND OTHER STORIES—Sarah Orne Jewett, A26

A DIFFERENT DRUMMER—William Melvin Kelley, A678

DOWN SECOND AVENUE—Ezekiel Mphahlele, A792

DREAM OF THE RED CHAMBER—Tsao Hsueh-Chin; Chi-Chen Wang, trans., A159

ENVY AND OTHER WORKS—Yuri Olesha; Andrew R. MacAndrew, trans., A571

GOD'S BITS OF WOOD—Ousmane Sembene, A729

HALF-WAY TO THE MOON: New Writing From Russia—Patricia Blake and Max Hayward, eds., A483

A HERO OF OUR TIME—Mihail Lermontov; Vladimir Nabokov and Dmitri Nabokov, trans., A133

INFERNO, ALONE AND OTHER WRITINGS—August Strindberg; in new translations, Evert Sprinchorn, ed., A492c

A MAN OF THE PEOPLE—Chinua Achebe, A594

MOTHER EARTH AND OTHER STORIES—Boris Pilnyak; Vera T. Reck and Michael Green, trans. and eds., A625

19 NECROMANCERS FROM NOW: An Anthology of Original American Writing for the 70s—Ishmael Reed, A743

POCHO—José Antonio Villarreal, intro. by Dr. Ramon Ruiz, A744

POOR PEOPLE and A LITTLE HERO—Fyodor Dostoevsky; David Magarshack, trans., A619

REDBURN—Herman Melville, A118

RETURN TO LAUGHTER—Elenore Smith Bowen, Foreword by David Riesman, N36

THE SCARLET LETTER and YOUNG GOODMAN BROWN—Nathaniel Hawthorne, Alfred Kazin, ed., A732

THE SECRET AGENT—Joseph Conrad, A8

THE SHADOW-LINE AND TWO OTHER TALES—Joseph Conrad, intro. by Morton Dauwen Zabel, A178

SISSIE—John A. Williams, A710

THE TALE OF GENJI, I—Lady Murasaki; Arthur Waley, trans., A55

TEN GERMAN NOVELLAS—Harry Steinhauer, ed. and trans., A707

THREE SHORT NOVELS OF DOSTOEVSKY—Constance Garnett, trans.; Avraim Yarmolinsky, ed. and revised, A193

UNDER WESTERN EYES—Joseph Conrad, intro. by Morton Dauwen Zabel, A323

VICTORY—Joseph Conrad, A106

THE WANDERER (LE GRAND MEAULNES)—Henri Alain-Fournier; Françoise Delisle, trans., A14

WHAT MAISIE KNEW—Henry James, A43

ANCHOR BOOKS

CLASSICS AND MYTHOLOGY

LITERARY ESSAYS AND CRITICISM

DATE DUE